D0107047

The Memoirs of
Christopher Columbus

The Memoirs of Christopher Columbus

with
STEPHEN MARLOWE

BALLANTINE BOOKS • NEW YORK

Library of Congress Catalog Card Number: 89-90644

ISBN: 0-345-36333-7

This edition published by arrangement with Stephen Marlowe and
Campbell Thomson & McLaughlin Ltd.

Cover design by James R. Harris

Cover illustration by Steve Lee

Manufactured in the United States of America

First Ballantine Books Edition: October 1989

10 9 8 7 6 5 4 3 2 1

to Petenera
and
for Ann

Contents

CHAPTER I
In Which the Colón Family
Italianizes Its Name
1

CHAPTER II
His Protégé Protects
Roderigo Cardinal Borgia
and Vice Versa
17

CHAPTER III
I Sail North Long Before Sailing West
or
Tristram, Isolde and Sister Death
38

CHAPTER IV
Being the Shortest Chapter of This Book
In Which, However, the Most Time Passes
and the Great Venture Is Born
70

CHAPTER V
Concerning the Marriage of My Brother's Fiancée
or
The World as Seen by Pozzo Toscanelli
79

CHAPTER VI
In Which I Learn Much
About Spain and Spaniards
and Even More About Myself
112

CHAPTER VII
1492!
144

CHAPTER VIII
1492!
(Continued)
167

CHAPTER IX
1492!
(Concluded)
198

CHAPTER X
How I Return to Spain in Triumph
and Become the Guest of the
Supreme and General Council of the Inquisition
238

CHAPTER XI
How I Mediate a Dispute Between
the Pope and Their Most Catholic Majesties
But Fare More Ambiguously
In My First Fateful Encounter
With the Lovely Petenera
261

CHAPTER XII
The Strange Tale of
the Cannibal Who Would Not Die,
the Tragic Fate of Christmas Town,
and Other Matters
Contributing to an Understanding of the Indians
290

CHAPTER XIII
How After Various Disasters
I Arrive at a Reunion
As Unexpected As It Is Poignant
317

CHAPTER XIV
How an Administrative Misunderstanding
Sends Me Back to Spain in Sackcloth and Ashes
344

CHAPTER XV
The Channel-Marker Papers
Have Their Day in Court
369

CHAPTER XVI
The Almost Undeniable Supremacy
of the Suprema
390

CHAPTER XVII
How Yego Recovers from Smallpox
But Has No Time
to Enjoy His Good Fortune
421

CHAPTER XVIII
Happy New Century
442

CHAPTER XIX
The Almost Unexpected Return
of the Blue Pimpernel
481

CHAPTER XX
The Whole Sick Syndrome
Takes On God
510

CHAPTER XXI
In Which a Single Loose End
Is Left Untied
552

My main concern is with the Columbus of action,
the Discoverer who held the key to the future in
his hand. I am content to leave his 'psychology,'
his 'motivation' and all that to others.

Samuel Eliot Morison

History is lived forward but it is written in
retrospect. We know the end before we consider
the beginning and we can never wholly recapture
what it was to know the beginning only.

C. V. Wedgwood

The Voyages

BAHAMAS

CUBA

Santa Maria
de la Concepción

Fernandina

Sand
Islands

Island of the
Holy Saviour

Isabella

1492-93 FIRST VOYAGE

WINDWARD PASSAGE

JAMAICA

Navidad

HISPANIOLA

XARAGUA

Guanaja
Cape Honduras

HONDURAS

Escondido
Bay

CARIBBEAN

PANAMA

PACIFIC OCEAN

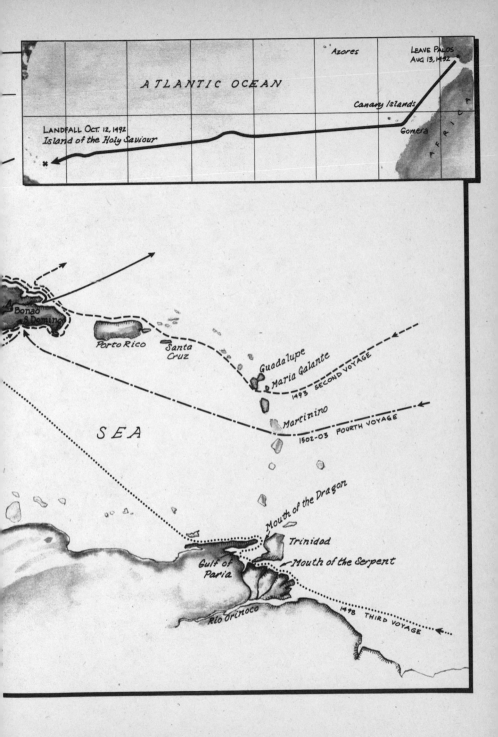

ATLANTIC OCEAN

Azores

Leave Palos
Aug 13, 1492

Canary Islands

Gomera

AFRICA

Landfall Oct. 12, 1492
Island of the Holy Saviour

Bonao
S. Domingo

Porto Rico

Santa Cruz

Guadalupe

Maria Galante

1493 SECOND VOYAGE

Martinino

1502-03 FOURTH VOYAGE

SEA

Mouth of the Dragon

Trinidad

Gulf of Paria

Mouth of the Serpent

Rio Orinoco

1498 THIRD VOYAGE

The Memoirs of
Christopher Columbus

❧ I ❧

In Which the Colón Family Italianizes Its Name

I F Holy Week and Passover hadn't fallen at the same time the year I was born, none of this would have happened. Someone else would have become the most famous man in the world, give or take a few. There's no telling what might have resulted. What if this other person, this surrogate me, didn't come along until a few years later, maybe giving the Indians time to develop the wheel, or to stop warring interminably among themselves, or to lose their awe of pale-skinned gods from across the sea? Could Cortés have conquered Mexico, or Pizarro Peru? Possibly there'd be an Indian capital on the Potomac, if you want to look that far down the road. History is, mostly, a toss of the dice, and that year the dice decreed that Passover and Easter should fall in the same week.

Mama and Papa skulked their way, the night this all began, through back alleys to Santiago Santangel's house, where the Seder would be. They couldn't skulk very fast. Mama was seven months pregnant with me. Not that Papa was in any hurry. He didn't want to go to the Seder at Santiago Santangel's house, or to any Seder anywhere.

Santiago Santangel — some name, isn't it? He was a Jew from Calatayud, now a New Christian, born Noah Chinillo. His son Luís, nine years old the night of the last secret Seder ever held in the Chinillo house, would eventually become the Keeper of Their Most Catholic Majesties' Household Budget, a sort of Chancellor of the Exchequer. Rich? Man! Much more about this later.

The alley Mama and Papa were skulking through opened on a wide thoroughfare. Torches streamed by. Robed penitents in pointed hoods chanted mournfully as they slow-marched, their chains clanking. Dust swirled in the torchlight. A great litter bearing the Virgin undulated perilously through the street. Mama and Papa waited.

'What a beauty, that Virgin,' Papa whispered reverently.

'Second-rate sculpture,' Mama sniffed. 'From a parish that can't even afford *that*.'

Papa told her, 'We shouldn't be going.'

'Why not?' This was not really a question. It was more an ominous warning. Papa knew he'd get no peace unless they went.

'It's dangerous.'

'To go to dinner at a friend's house is dangerous?'

'Maybe you better make new friends,' Papa suggested. 'If we're converts, we're converts. It's the warp and woof of our lives.'

Papa was a weaver. To him everything could be explained in terms of warp, woof, frame, shuttle. It was as good a paradigm as any I've heard, and better than most, and as you'll see I've been around a bit.

Gypsies carrying more torches followed the Virgin. Gypsies were pretty new in Spain. Thirty, forty years before, they just started trickling in through a hole in the Pyrenees from somewhere beyond all that France to the north – Egypt, Hungary, India, Cipango, somewhere out there. The trickle became a torrent. They kept spilling into Spain and there was no way out. Spain's the end of the line in Europe. They're illiterate, they live off the largesse of nature (meaning they rob anyone who isn't a gypsy), and they're even filthier and more lice-ridden than Old Christians. They never bathe. As for their underclothes, nobody ever got close enough to a gypsy (except other gypsies, who don't talk much to outsiders) to learn if they wear any, so I can't say whether they ever change them. The reason I mention this, Jews do. Change their linen. Once a week, for the Sabbath. It's one of the many ways the authorities have for ferreting out lapsed New Christians.

This is what Spain gets, gypsies. And what does Spain expel, not too many years later, as if to make room for them? Just the whole non-converted Jewish population of the country, a quarter of a million people, that's all – doctors, lawyers, savants, tax farmers, women, children, you name it.

2

A bad trade-off for Spain, you think? I won't argue.

Holy Mother Church seemed to suit the gypsies just fine. They took to it right away. Mama never really tried. That the Messiah had already come she found disappointing. There was nothing to look forward to. Idols realistically hewn from wood or stone with realistic blood running from their realistic wounds horrified her. Confession made her furious. Kneeling in a dark box, lying to a priest and asking God's forgiveness through him – because, being a backslider, Mama always had to lie for Papa's sake – that was the final cross Mama had to bear. Sometimes, without thinking, she even called it that.

Mama said, waiting for the gypsies to go by: 'The world isn't made up of warps and woofs. A weaver – I had to marry a weaver who thinks he's a philosopher.'

Papa almost made some observation or other about the loom of life, but he only shook his head and watched with yearning as the last of the gypsies disappeared. Gypsies were great ones for wandering. They just picked up and got going. Papa could appreciate that. When in doubt he moved. Anywhere. It was a trait I inherited.

'Hurry, we'll be late,' Mama said.

Papa stood there a moment undecided, history hanging on his hesitation, then sighed and followed Mama skulking across the thoroughfare to the alley on the other side.

He said suddenly, struck by inspiration, 'We'll call him Jesús.'

'*What?*'

Mama had red hair and a temper to go with it.

'I said, we'll call him Jesús.'

'Who,' said Mama in a soft and deadly voice, 'will we call Jesús?'

'The boy. When he's born. He'll be baptized Jesús.'

Whatever they named me, Mama had already decided she would rush right home from the baptistry with me in her arms to wash off the so-called holy water. Which will give you some idea of what she thought of calling me Jesús.

Two could play at that game. 'Moses,' Mama countered.

It was Papa's turn to say what.

'What?' Papa said.

'We'll call him Moses. Moses Maimonides Colón,' Mama said in a rapturous voice, warming to the mellifluous syllables of the name I would never have.

'In the first place, the warp,' said Papa patiently. 'Moses. An Old Testament name. A sure sign that we're backsliders. Every fanatic Old

Christian in Spain knows the list by heart. Clean underwear, no pork, a blessing without the sign of the cross, bathing too often, Old Testament names – '

'I know all that. I *am* a backslider, and proud of it.'

'Shh!' cautioned Papa.

Mama skulked resolutely forward into the alley.

'Moses Maimonides Colón.' The name rolled off her tongue stubbornly.

'Secondly,' said Papa in his Talmudic way, 'the woof. Every fanatic Old Christian knows that Maimonides, the famous doctor and philosopher from Córdoba, was a famous *Jewish* doctor and philosopher from Córdoba. What are you trying to do to us, Susanna?'

Mama laughed. 'My name's Maria del Pilar now. See? See, you New Christian who can't even remember his wife's New Christian name!'

They had converted ten years before at the synagogue there in Sevilla during Friday night services. A real fire and brimstone meeting it was, with a fat wild-eyed tub-thumper of a Dominican in dirty white robes carrying a Scroll of the Law in his left hand and a large crucifix in his right, and behind him a zealous mob of pyromaniacs with torches and pitch who soon set the synagogue ablaze. The Dominican stood in the doorway, his enormous body barring the way to literal salvation as he hurled the Scroll of the Law into the conflagration and held the crucifix high.

'Bow before this symbol and you will receive eternal salvation in Our Lord Jesus Christ!' he boomed over the crackle of flames and crash of roofbeams as worshippers stampeded for the doorway.

'Amen and line up!' shouted one of the pyromaniacs. 'Line up, everyone gets the chance to convert!'

Nobody could escape the falling roofbeams or the flames consuming the synagogue unless he passed through the doorway, where the Dominican stood like a tree, and kissed the crucifix in token of accepting the Faith.

It was a pretty realistic crucifix, over three feet tall, carved from olivewood and painted in living color; the poor Christ's eyes bugged upwards as if trying to see the blood oozing from His crown of thorns, and blood streamed down His side from the lance wound. Seven members of the congregation, on seeing that olivewood crucifix in all that living (especially blood-red) color, debated with their consciences too long and perished in the flames.

'Joseph,' Papa suggested. 'We can call him Joseph.'

4

Mama just gave him a look, but it was too dark in the alley to see.

'Joseph is a sort of neutral name,' he said hopefully. 'Like Bartolomé.'

Bartolomé was my brother, then just ten months old.

'I don't like it,' Mama said.

They crossed another thoroughfare. More torches, more penitents, more gypsies, another Virgin.

'What's wrong with it? Warp of the Old Testament, woof of the New.'

'I just don't like it, that's all.'

They were a hundred yards or so from the Santangel house when they heard screaming. Papa instantly grasped Mama's arm and drew her to his side in a providential dark doorway in the alley. Ahead, the door of the Santangel house burst open, spilling light and people. Soon the police came from the direction of the house, so intent on their prisoners that they never noticed Mama and Papa at all. Two bailiffs on spirited horses brought up the rear, hooves striking sparks inches from Mama's feet.

Years later, during the final siege of the Arabs in Granada, when I met Luís de Santangel, then an immense and immensely wealthy official of fifty or so, I asked him about that night.

'The last Seder? Oh sure,' Luís de Santangel would say. 'My father, my mother, the lot. What a shame! I remember it well, of course I do. I was the youngest. I was the one that had to memorize all the questions. You know — what's so special about this night, and all?'

What was so special about that night was that heresy-hunting fanatics had been informed of the secret Seder. Falling during Holy Week as it did, it was an especially heinous crime, because then it was said to make a mockery of Our Lord's Passion. All but one of the participants were burned at the stake.

Those were pre-Inquisition days. King Fernando wouldn't officially unleash Torquemada for another dozen years or so, and the Council of the Supreme and General Office of the Inquisition came later still, so the burning was a haphazard affair, not at all the orchestrated spectacle such events would become later.

'How did it happen?' I would ask Luís de Santangel while siege cannons hurled great iron balls at the earth-colored walls of Granada.

'How did what happen?'

'Who informed on your family and the others?'

A section of crenelated wall crumbled, disappearing in smoke.

And Luís de Santangel, second or third richest man in Spain, would look me straight in the eye and say: 'A fellow's got to start his career somewhere.'

Mama and Papa were still debating when, shaken and afraid, they returned home to little Bartolomé. Joseph and Jonah, Noah and Joshua, James and John, Timothy and Peter, all had been cast into limbo.

Papa said suddenly: 'What if he's a girl?'

But I was a boy, and I was born a month prematurely on a roundship sailing to Genoa, and by then terrified Mama was so convinced she would never see land again that she agreed to call me Cristóbal.

I hate the sort of biography that goes: At the age of eight the future Prime Minister (or Whoremonger, or Admiral of the Ocean Sea) had already turned his thoughts to the strife of nations (or sexual intercourse, or sea routes to the Indies). Because, at the age of eight, the future Prime Minister, etc., was only a boy with dirt on his face and snot running from his nose, and whatever thoughts he may have had are lost to posterity. Probably just as well, too.

I wrote elsewhere (not altogether accurately) that I went to sea at the age of fourteen, implying that it was all very sudden, that, perhaps, I was one good offshore breeze ahead of the police, leaving it to the reader to determine what dastardly crime I had committed.

My own son Fernando put it otherwise. Young Fernando, unwilling to spring from the loins of a semi-literate nobody who ran off to sea at fourteen, sent me in his biography (a book I don't recommend) to the University of Pavia to study mathematics, geography and astronomy, so I could become a suitable father for the illegitimate son of the Admiral of the Ocean Sea.

I was born at sea. This much could be attested to by Rodrigo Borja, a young Spaniard of the minor nobility traveling from Valencia to Genoa on the same roundship taking Domingo and Susanna (or Maria del Pilar) Colón and their son Bartolomé to their new home in Italy. Although the roundship was becalmed in fog, sails hanging slack, poor Mama was so seasick that giving birth to me seemed almost a welcome diversion.

The hidalgo Rodrigo Borja was on his way to Rome, where his family had connections. He had a retinue of fourteen, and fifty iron-banded oaken chests stocked with the impedimenta of an hidalgo's life. One chest, the lightest, held dozens of pairs of silken tights, no two precisely the same hue, for Rodrigo Borja's strong, shapely

6

legs. One chest was stuffed with redolent Spanish sausage. Rodrigo Borja was carrying garlic to Italy.

'Call him Cristóbal,' Borja suggested while Mama, screened by sailcloth, struggled with her seasickness and me. Papa was awkwardly holding my brother Bartolomé in his arms. Bartolomé started to cry.

'Why Cristóbal?' Papa asked, patting the red-faced little head. Mama gave a long loud wail and then began to curse in Ladino. To the roundship's Italian crew Ladino would sound enough like Spanish, but Rodrigo Borja would know the difference, would recognize the marketplace dialect of Spanish Jews when he heard it. Papa waited anxiously after asking his question. But Borja seemed to take no interest in Mama's colorful Ladino.

'Because you'll Italianize it as soon as you settle, and Cristoforo, that's a nice name.' Borja looked at the red-faced child in Papa's arms. 'Bartolomeo too,' he conceded.

'We'll Italianize our names?'

'Of course. We all will. What do you call yourself again?'

'Domingo. Domingo Colón.'

'So, Domenico. Domenico Colombo. Nothing could be simpler,' said Rodrigo Borja.

Mama hollered more imaginatively still in Ladino.

The fog lifted.

The late afternoon sun cast great sail-shadows across the water.

The sea swelled.

The roundship pitched.

Behind the sailcloth screen, one of Rodrigo Borja's maidservants or concubines gave me a sound whack on the rump.

I experimented with a tentative screech, then bawled.

Spaniards are the only people capable of forming easy friendships across class barriers, because each Spaniard is serenely secure in his own unique worth. So, when Rodrigo Borja said, a few hours before we docked in Genoa, 'If you ever get to Rome, look me up,' this was more than the farewell ploy of one bored ship's passenger to another at journey's end. He meant it. Papa's loom-philosophy appealed to the young hidalgo, and naturally Papa enjoyed basking in Borja's Renaissance Man glow. But it was more than that. The second morning out, they had sized each other up, and seemed satisfied with what they saw. This was at a time when, ironically, converted Jews stood in far greater danger than those still practicing the faith, and a lot of New Christians, or 'Marranos' (swine) as they were contemptuously called, left Spain in a hurry. That was Papa's situation. I don't know what Rodrigo

Borja's was. Papa didn't ask; it wasn't done. But they took to each other instinctively.

'Or, if you can't come, send Cristoforo when he's ready,' Borja said. 'And Bartolomeo too, of course.'

'Ready?' Papa asked. 'For what?'

Rodrigo Borja said, 'When the time comes, you'll know. Send him.'

Papa promised.

Some historians claim I've been guilty of certain exaggerations in recounting my early life. Maybe. What autobiographer isn't? Or even what biographer? One Bartolomé de las Casas, the next scribbler after my son Fernando to write about me, is a case in point. He alludes to 'noble ancestors', and to an imaginary course of university studies which paled Fernando's mathematics, geography and astronomy. In his pages, I served under an 'illustrious kinsman', admiral of France; I leaped from a burning pirate ship, which I commanded, off the coast of Portugal and swam 'while grievously wounded' to shore at Lisbon. Biographers? Why, some idiot even wrote somewhere that I believed the Orinoco was one of four rivers flowing from Paradise to Earth and that, Their Most Catholic Majesties willing, I would fit out 100,000 foot and 10,000 horse and slog upstream to find the Holy Sepulchre, the whole mad venture to be paid for with gold of the Indies.

Fool's gold.

Fool's words.

Domenico Colombo (formerly Domingo Colón) set himself up as a weaver near the Porta dell'Olivella in Genoa, and after a few years he indulged a secret fancy by opening a small tavern too. The clientele was rough – sailors and whores most days, whores and sailors the rest. Mama had her hands full with me and my brother Bartolomeo. That we were underfoot when Domenico Colombo plied his loom didn't bother her. But the tavern was off limits. 'Weaving sí, wine shop no,' she would say. Mama, who called herself Maria Susanna Colombo by then, was always slipping off to the synagogue. Domenico Colombo pretended not to notice. Things were freer in Italy. The Inquisition they had there was a joke, except to witches, who were burned regularly at the stake.

Six years after we landed in Italy, Mama gave light, as it's said in Spanish, to my brother Giacomo. It was a difficult delivery. Hardly had Bartolomeo and I seen our squealing, hairless little brother when a priest came to give Mama the last rites of Papa's church. A rabbi came too, but Papa became violent and wouldn't let him in. From that night until the day he died Domenico Colombo was a rabid Christian. He

8

seemed to blame the Jews for his wife's death, like some people blamed them for the Plague. He never married again.

He would, however, disappear upstairs every so often with one or another of the tavern's whores. Giacomo, when he began to talk, would call this whore or that one Mama. Auntie would have been more like it. They treated all three of us Colombo boys like favored nephews, even teaching us sums and how to read a few words. Giulia was our favorite. She was a big huge farm girl from the Abruzzi and noisy with her guests in the upstairs rooms Domenico Colombo rented for such purposes. Giulia could take a horseshoe in her two hands and, her face darkening to the color of red wine, straighten it. She was called The Amazon and she had a specialized clientele. Once when things didn't go according to plan up there she hurled her guest through the window, breaking both his legs and a few ribs. The police came, but Papa gave them each a couple of florins and a bottle of rare Five Earths wine, and Giulia's hapless victim had to face a charge of disturbing the peace when he got out of hospital. To my brothers and me, Giulia was gentle as a lamb. I think, in her own horseshoe-straightening way, she loved us.

Various biographers have, predictably, shown me mooning around the port and gazing out to sea as if I somehow knew from the age of nine or ten that it was my destiny. And it's true you could learn a thing or two mooning around the port and gazing out to sea. Such as, that the earth's not flat as a mariner's chart but round as a ball. At least, that was what Bartolomeo told me often enough, his homely face lighting up with excitement.

'The earth's round as a ball,' Bartolomeo said.

It hardly mattered to me one way or the other. 'Yeah? How do *you* know?'

Barefoot, he led me to the port where caravels and an occasional galleass and flotillas of smaller craft were moored. Bartolomeo mooned around for a while and gazed out to sea.

'There's one,' he said, pointing a long way out.

It was a clear day, and at the horizon could be seen a sail.

'The sail's visible,' Bartolomeo explained, 'but not the hull. That's called hull-down.'

'So?'

Bartolomeo mooned for a while longer and gazed at the hull-less sail on the horizon.

'*Now* look.'

You could see the ship then a long way off, toylike.

9

'It's round, I told you, I told you!' cried Bartolomeo.

'The boat? You mean she's a roundship? So what?'

'The world. It's curved. So when a ship comes in you see the sail first, then the hull. When she leaves, it's the other way around. See?'

'Sure,' I said, to humor him.

'You know what that means? You could sail west and sail and keep sailing,' said Bartolomeo, 'and keep on sailing and – '

'I get the idea.'

'And come back home from the east. That is, you could if India and Cathay and Cipango weren't in the way.'

'Nobody can sail west and come back from the east,' I said, ignoring India, Cathay and Cipango.

Bartolomeo sighed. 'If you were listening, you'd know I'm right.'

'You're crazy,' I said. 'West is west and east is – '

'Forget it.' Bartolomeo was exasperated. Can you blame him? 'I bet you never even heard of the Vivaldi brothers.'

'Musicians?' I guessed. The name had a nice musical ring to it.

'Explorers,' said Bartolomeo. 'From right here in Genoa. Lost on the west coast of Africa trying to find the east coast.'

'No wonder they were lost,' I offered.

So much for my biographers.

One autumn day when Bartolomeo was thirteen and I twelve, I found him in the shop of a mapmaker from Florence named Vongole. Bartolomeo was always hanging around mapmakers or ships' chandlers.

'Yes sir, Ultima Thule,' toothless old Vongole was saying, one yellow eye squinting nearsightedly at a mariner's chart drawn on parchment. 'Six days' sail north of Britain. A Greek named Pytheas, yes sirree bob. Sailed there four hundred years before the birth of Our Lord.'

'Gosh,' said Bartolomeo.

'Summer it was. No darkness, just your normal daylight all night long.'

'Wow,' said Bartolomeo.

'But mind you, they had no compasses then. As you see on the chart, I've placed Thule north*west* of Britain.'

'How come?' Bartolomeo asked.

'Pytheas', old Vongole said, 'got his directions a tad wrong.'

'How come?'

'Confused. Had his degrees of latitude and his meridians of

longitude all mixed up,' said old Vongole. 'It can happen. Especially to a Greek.' Vongole cackled and slapped his thigh.

He was rolling the chart carefully when a big huge shape filled the doorway of the tiny, windowless shop. It was The Amazon, breathing hard.

'You boys better get home.'

'How come?' said Bartolomeo, his mind still on Thule.

'Your papa's been hurt. Hurt bad.'

We tried to hurry, but the maze of streets around the port was crowded and the going slow until The Amazon scooped us up, one under each arm, and charged uphill past the customs building like a human battering ram. Every time her left boot hit the cobblestones, my teeth jarred. Every time her right boot did, Bartolomeo's teeth jarred. People went flying out of her way without The Amazon seeming to touch them. Maybe she didn't. She was that big, and she was dressed for work in leather and old-fashioned chainmail.

A crowd milled outside the tavern. Upstairs it smelled of incense. An angelic little acolyte in white was coming out of Papa's room carrying a censer. A doctor in wrinkled red robes emerged after him looking worried. The Amazon set us down.

'Is he dead?' she asked.

'No, sir. I mean, madonna,' said the doctor hastily after a second look. 'But I fear it's only a matter of time. And God's will, of course. Did all *I* could. Bled him twice and – '

'Bled him when he's been stabbed and already bleeding like a stuck pig?' shouted The Amazon.

Bartolomeo began to cry. I went inside. The priest was just corking his flagon of oil. Papa was stretched out on his bed, hands crossed moribundly on his chest. I never saw a face so white. His forehead gleamed with oil.

The Amazon and Bartolomeo came in behind me, and little Giacomo.

The priest said: 'Paradise. After some purification time in purgatory, of course. I'll gladly take care of the formalities, for a small consideration.'

But looking at us, he must have decided the small consideration was beyond our means, for he went outside to stand his vigil alongside the doctor.

'I blame myself,' The Amazon said.

'Papa,' little Giacomo said, and Domenico Colombo's white, white face turned toward the piping voice.

'It's all my fault,' The Amazon told us.

I went to one side of Papa's bed, Bartolomeo to the other. The white face rolled on the pillow in my direction. 'Rodrigo Borja,' said Papa faintly.

'Who?' I asked. It was a name I had never heard.

'Rome. Rodrigo Borja's got connections in Rome. Go to him. And take little Giacomo.' Papa's white face rolled in Bartolomeo's direction. He looked at his homely eldest son. 'And Bartolomeo too, of course,' he said.

'It's all my fault,' said The Amazon. 'If I hadn't thrown that fellow through the window because he wouldn't pay me *before*, like he's supposed to, his kin wouldn't have stabbed your papa.'

'Rome,' gasped Papa. 'The warp and woof of your destinies ... Rodrigo Borja.' Papa's blue lips frothed red, and with the unknown man's name on those bloody lips he died.

I saw his face through a film of tears. The cloying incense left by the acolyte made it hard to breathe. Papa kept looking at me and looking at me with eyes that saw nothing, and never would again.

The Amazon, with a gentle touch of one big huge hand, closed those sightless eyes.

'I'll take you to Rome,' she said.

'Is it a seaport?' Bartolomeo asked.

'Will Papa join us when he's better?' little Giacomo wanted to know.

Almost fifty years later, on my own so-called deathbed in 1506, I made my son Fernando swear to write nothing of my stay in Rome. Which is why Las Casas, primarily a local colorist and plagiarist, never mentions it either. Not that that pious old fraud would have. How could he have written of my strange service to the man who one day would mount the throne of St Peter? Still, it should be apparent to anyone who's read this far that the Roman years were crucial to my development. I was, until then, the semi-literate son of an indebted weaver and tavernkeeper, but in my maturity I could hobnob with the likes of Luís de Santangel, not to mention Their Most Catholic Majesties the Sovereigns of Spain, and I was entrusted with a royal letter to the Great Khan of Cathay himself. Obviously, I had to be prepared. Rome and Rodrigo Borja prepared me.

Little need be said of our overland journey from Genoa to the capital of the world. We had no money. Poor Papa's ancient loom was worthless, and when we went to the magnificent palace of the Bank of

St George in Piazza Caricamento, Bartolomeo and I learned that they, not Domenico Colombo, had always owned the tavern. In fact, the bank followed us home to foreclose. We three boys started south with nothing but the clothes on our backs and The Amazon.

Whenever we reached a city – Pistoia, Florence, Siena, Viterbo, Civitavecchia on the sea, where Bartolomeo tried to run away – The Amazon would find her way to the nearest smithy, ask the smith for a horseshoe, and show what she could do with it. They went into business, the smith charging admission and supplying light refreshment, the local bravoes trying, and failing, to straighten a regulation horseshoe. The Amazon, her face turning wine-dark, would straighten it, and little Giacomo would pass the hat. When we reached Rome four months after we set out, The Amazon carried a bag heavy with florins, ducats and lire.

We wondered how to find Rodrigo Borja, whoever he was. At the busy Porto del Popolo, The Amazon would grasp a sleeve and yank a man half off his feet to face her. 'Excuse me, sir, do you know where we can find Rodrigo Borja?'

Imitating poor Papa, she pronounced it the Spanish way, Bor-ha, and the passerby she accosted would manage to say, 'Begging your pardon, madonna, never heard of him.'

We had no better luck in Rome's great piazzas or at the new church of Santa Maria of the Peace, where we lit candles for the soul of Domenico Colombo. Finally, footsore and discouraged, we sat on the banks of the Tiber. Soon a barefoot friar came by leading a donkey carrying a load of faggots. It was a chill winter afternoon, the sun reflecting weakly off the sewage-brown water.

The Amazon politely asked her question.

'More Spanish cousins, are you?' said the friar without surprise.

'You know him?' The Amazon cried.

'Know him? Everybody knows him. But his name's Roderigo Borgia now, lady. Italianized, see? What's he got over there in Spain anyway, one of your regular medieval extended families? I mean, all those cousins he's given red hats and benefices, a person can't keep track.'

Actually the barefoot friar, to make his point, anticipated events. Roderigo Borgia didn't really pack the Vatican with Spaniards, many of them his cousins, until the conclave of cardinals elected him Pope, and that didn't happen until 1492. What a year that would be! The once indomitable Arabs thrown out of Granada, the always hapless Jews exiled from Spain. Me sailing from Palos with three small ships to discover a New World which the brand-new Pope, now bearing the name Alexander VI, promptly ceded to Spain forever. Not for nothing was he called the Spanish Pope, and sometimes even the Marrano Pope. 1492! Spain and Italy, one bobbing to the surface of history like a buoyant cork, the other sinking to the bottom like a lead weight. Not that it happened right away. But it often amuses me that Italians will draw blood for the right to call me *paisan'*, when I was the worst thing that happened to Italy until Mussolini. Because, after me, the way to the fabled East lay west across the Ocean Sea, not east from Italian ports and then overland in the footsteps of Marco Polo. Spain became the gateway to the riches of the Indies, Italy a backwater. Obviously, a great deal more about 1492 later.

I know what everyone says about Roderigo Borgia. That he was too proud to call his bastard children nephew and niece even after he became Pope, which is true. That he and his son Cesare fell out over which of them would be first to bed Cesare's virgin sister Lucrezia, which is false. That he was a world-class poisoner, which he may have been, though he was more poisoned-against than poisoning. That he sold churchly offices the way pedlars sell trinkets on the pilgrims' way to Santiago de Compostela, which is true. That he fornicated like a rabbit, which is false. He settled his mistress Vanozza, mother to Cesare and Lucrezia, in a good marriage when he became Pope, and remained reasonably faithful to his new mistress Giulia Farnese, called either The Beautiful or The Bride of Christ, depending on what you thought of Roderigo Borgia. There is no record of what Orsino Orsini, Giulia's husband, thought of him.

Like so many illustrious leaders, he had a bad press. But he always treated me well.

He loved power and money and women and Lucrezia (from her birth in 1480) and beauty and himself in that order. Which made him a sort of quintessential Renaissance Man, didn't it?

Well, the old barefoot friar led us to the Borgia Palace not far from the Vatican. The Amazon took one look and stuck her thumb in her mouth like the Abruzzi farm girl she was. There were columns and pilasters and fretted cornices, painted walls, gilded ceilings, sculptured chimney pieces. There were stucco carvings and arabesques, and floors of Lucca marble. There were carpets, curtains, chandeliers, lamps, fountains, silver plates to eat off and gold forks to use instead of fingers. There were rooms without end and servants without number.

One of them announced us, as the sons of Domenico Colombo.

Borgia, beginning to grow stout in purple robes, was a cardinal but not yet a priest, chief of the Papal Curia and thus, after the Pope, the biggest dispenser of jobs in Rome.

His mistress, Vanozza, then seventeen, came in. She wore a perky forester's hat like Robin Hood's and a gown that exposed her full breasts almost to the nipples. 'Who are these ragpickers?' she asked in her beautiful voice.

We didn't look like much after four months on the road.

'Cousins from Spain,' said Borgia.

'The east wing,' said Vanozza, 'is already full of "cousins" from Spain. Freeloaders every last one of them.'

'We're not looking for handouts,' I heard myself saying. 'We know how to work.' I wasn't sure at what, but somehow just being there in the Borgia Palace kindled my Spanish pride.

'He's cute,' Vanozza said.

'If we can't stay here, we'll go to sea,' Bartolomeo said hopefully.

'No, no, you'll stay,' said Roderigo Borgia. 'I need all the Spaniards I can get. With the Colonna clan and the Orsinis hiring bravoes to kill me, and the Sforzas and Cardinal della Rovere preferring poison — ' A speculative look touched Borgia's dark eyes. 'Taste this, one of you.'

A servant had appeared silently at Roderigo Borgia's elbow with a silver tray bearing a green flagon of wine and a golden goblet. He poured the goblet full.

It was another of those moments when history hesitated. But The Amazon had her thumb in her mouth, little Giacomo was too young, and Bartolomeo was asking, 'How come?'

So it was I who stepped forward, reached for the golden goblet and downed the wine. Cardinal Borgia watched me carefully.

'My last taster died suddenly the day before yesterday,' he said, possibly in answer to Bartolomeo's question. 'Tell me, Cristoforo, would you like the position?'

The Amazon's thumb popped out of her mouth and she demanded suspiciously: 'What'll he have to pay to get it? We're poor.'

'No, no. *I'll* pay *him*. Twenty gold ducats a year?' It was an unimaginable sum to the son of a poor weaver.

Vanozza said, 'And what about this one?' She indicated Bartolomeo's homely face.

'The Vatican Library,' Borgia decided promptly.

Bartolomeo stared glumly at the floor.

'Two thousand five hundred and twenty-seven volumes in Latin and Greek,' said Borgia.

Bartolomeo's eyes remained downcast.

'Seven hundred and forty-seven maps and mariners' charts of the whole known world,' Borgia tried.

Bartolomeo's head jerked up. 'When do I start?'

Little Giacomo, who was six, would have the schooling his elder brothers never had.

'And your large friend, what can we do for her?' Roderigo Cardinal Borgia asked.

But when we all turned to Giulia The Amazon, we saw that she had vanished.

⟅ II ⟆

His Protégé Protects
Roderigo Cardinal Borgia
and Vice Versa

As it was Bartolomeo's lot to be homely, so it was mine to be well-favored. I admit this with modesty instead of denying it. Roderigo Borgia taught me that.

And in those days in Rome a pleasing face and graceful figure were equally important to both sexes. (It was a time of women's liberation, the first since the fifth century B.C. in Athens. It would pass, unfortunately, with the Reformation and Counter-Reformation.) I wore my red hair to my shoulders, my eyes were a probing blue, a saddle of freckles bestrode my Roman eagle nose. I was tall for my age and my legs were long and shapely, as Vanozza soon remarked while she helped outfit me in the finery paid for by her lover Cardinal Borgia.

'You have long shapely legs, boy,' Vanozza remarked.

I was more concerned with the clothes. I didn't know what to do with them. Short boots, gartered stockings, skirted tunic had been my usual garb. But now I was confronted by a bewildering cornucopia of clothing. There was a choice of soft piked shoes and shoes with platform soles and high heels. The stockings, a dozen pairs of them, had no garters. But then, they weren't stockings really. The silken leg parts joined at the top and reached right up to the waist. The front had an odd arrangement called a codpiece, of which more in a moment. Above these came doublet and jerkin with hanging sleeves, and a forester's hat much like the one I'd first seen Vanozza wearing. I retired modestly behind a screen and drew a pair of joined stockings up my legs. I have never worn silk before; it was slithery to the touch. I pulled the doublet on over my head. Its bottom seemed fringed with ribbons. Then I realized these were ties but I couldn't figure out what to tie them to. The codpiece hung below, between my legs, exposing that part of me that distinguished my maleness. Flustered, I pulled the codpiece up and tucked its trailing edge, also fringed, into the waistband of the joined stockings. By then the stockings themselves had begun to wrinkle and slip down my legs.

'Boy!' Vanozza called from the other side of the screen. 'Are you having trouble trussing the points?'

I had no idea what she meant, but said, 'I never have trouble trussing the points.'

She laughed and joined me on my side of the screen. The fringe, as I'd surmised, was a row of fasteners. Vanozza's slim quick fingers felt cool as they touched my hips. 'Turn,' she said. I turned. 'Now the other way.' I turned the other way. 'How old are you anyway, boy?' she asked. She finished trussing the points of the codpiece to the doublet, her cool hands accidentally brushing me there.

'Twelve. Why?' I asked, flushing above and stirring strangely below.

'I just wondered,' said Vanozza.

'Be audacious,' Roderigo Borgia always advised me. Be audacious, he would say on greeting me in the morning before I tasted his breakfast, and audaciously I did. Audacity was the Borgia *sine qua non* (I was learning Latin in Rome) and I like to think it rubbed off on me. But he also had other advice, other theories. Like, to foresee the future, consult the past. Or, all men are by nature evil and the best path to civic order is religion. That is why Roderigo Borgia, who sought power, wore a cardinal's red hat and would become Pope. But Christianity with its otherworldliness could handicap the audacious man, who must therefore devote himself to all things carnal. He also said, humility serves only the defeated. And, occasional war is a healthful purge to the body politic. And, honor no treaty that becomes a burden. Win your enemies over or crush them. If you cannot be both feared and loved, give up love. Be subtle. But above all be audacious.

These words sound suspiciously Machiavellian, don't they? But when the Florentine philosopher wrote *The Prince* some years after these events, whom did he have in mind? Cesare Borgia, that's who. And at whose knee did Cesare Borgia learn? His father Roderigo's, that's whose.

Tasting for Roderigo Borgia gave me a certain fatalism, a *che sarà sarà* (or *que será será*; we had spoken both Italian and Spanish at home in Genoa, and both were used at the Borgia Palace). Tasters have to be fatalistic. Every time you lift a golden fork to your face you think: one taste and I could drop dead, zap, just like that, no more high life in Rome, no journey to England and the north, no Admiral of the Ocean Sea, no four voyages to the New World, no superstardom in Spain, maybe for all I knew no afterlife. In the taste of nutmeg or cinnamon, juniper or ginger, pepper or cloves, might lurk the taste of my own death. At first I sweated musket balls. But the food itself was superb and if death were to be the end result, why, death was the end result of everything, good and bad, including being born, *n'est-ce pas*? (During my years in Rome I picked up a smattering of French from the French cardinals, and English from the English.)

Bartolomeo emerged from the Vatican Library only on brief visits to the outside world, like a book from the reserve shelf. He spent most of his working hours studying the 747 mariners' charts in the library. Soon he began to draw his own. One year I got him a compass for Christmas. He got me a clock that chimed the hours but was small enough to hang around my neck on a silver chain. The next year Cardinal Borgia went on Vatican business to the protectorate of Ancona. I accompanied him to sample the cuisine. He picked up a minor venereal disease, which put him out of commission for a month, from a madonna with bleached blonde hair.

Back in Rome Roderigo Borgia was honest about his indisposition. This vexed Vanozza. Her first husband, the complacent cuckold Domenico d'Arignano, had forgotten how to bed her, if in fact he'd ever known. That was how Vanozza came to monitor my age again. 'How old are you this year, boy?' 'Fifteen. Why?' 'I just wondered.' To my quarters in the east wing of the Borgia Palace she had come bearing gifts. There were vermilion tights (as I learned the joined stockings were called), a variety of doublets and jerkins and a kind of unisex bonnet of some floppy napped cloth. We had maintained the tradition of Vanozza helping me dress and who was I to object? Her hand accidentally brushed my codpiece, as it had a habit of doing. I flushed above and stirred below. Vanozza always had an excuse for her visits and gifts; this time it was my birthday. 'Happy Birthday, boy,' she said. But it wasn't. My birthday, I mean. 'It's not my birthday,' I said as Vanozza removed her horned head-dress and the veil attached at the back. She took off her jeweled brass templets. Her natural blonde hair fell free to the high waist of her gown. She stared at me challengingly. I used a trick Roderigo Borgia had taught me. I stared back as hard, but at her plucked eyebrows, not her eyes. It was a contest I couldn't lose. Her gaze dropped. By this time I was fumbling with the points where my tights met my doublet, trying without success to untruss them. Vanozza laughed. 'You always have trouble with the points,' she said huskily. Clothing began to fly. Gown, kirtle, smock from her, piked shoes and tights from me. Conveniently nearby was my canopied bed. We fell across it diagonally, arranging arms and legs, she with practiced skill, I awkwardly. 'Lie to me,' she breathed in my ear. Not sure what she expected of me, I tried, 'You were right – it *is* my birthday.' She nibbled my ear. 'I mean tell me how you adore me.' Unfamiliar and ephemeral sentiments spilled from my tongue in three or four languages. Remembering the precepts of my master, I went at his mistress audaciously and devoted myself to things carnal. 'You're crushing me, boy,' Vanozza cried out. As she was hardly my enemy, I tried to make myself lighter by taking more weight on my elbows. But she said, 'Don't stop, I *love* it.' I rectified my mistake enthusiastically. Vanozza began to shudder. Startled, I thought I was doing something wrong again and started to withdraw. Her hands clamped me to her. She began to moan. I was desperate to learn what the trouble was. Just then my little clock went off. Her moaning had turned into the sort of soft sound a cat might make if a cat could laugh. It was obvious I had much to learn about women.

Vanozza, who could satisfy a demanding cardinal, proved an eager teacher, and this was only the first of many lessons.

But it was the beginning of the end of my stay in Rome.

Everything was wrong with Rome.

It had been ten times larger when the barbarians sacked it a thousand years before. Now Venice, Milan and Florence exceeded its population of 80,000. Those same barbarians had demolished the aqueducts. Most Romans drank the water of the Tiber, which also received their waste. In those flat parts of the city near the river, the air was bad. Such *mal aria*, as it's called in Italian, causes recurring chills, fever and eventual death. Vatican Town was a small suburb on the wrong side of the river, huddled as if for protection under the crumbling dome of St Peter's. Rome's so-called noble families fortified the ruins of antiquity, a tomb here, a theater or bath there. Hired bravoes would fight sudden deadly skirmishes for their possession.

Rome was an irreverent city. On the statue of Pasquino the tailor in Piazza Navona, in antiquity a statue of Hercules, people came by night to scratch, carve and paint their fiercely clever epigrams (called *graffiti*) ridiculing this or that noble family, this or that cardinal, this or that Pope. Some of it was pretty obscure. I did not know what 'Lorenzo Colonna sucks' meant until Vanozza enlightened me by demonstration.

Can you imagine my biographer Las Casas, a pious bishop of the meek-shall-inherit variety, mentioning any of this? No, Rome to Las Casas was the center of the world from which power flowed and to which gold flowed in return, and my friend and mentor Roderigo Borgia bred no bastards, sold no benefices, sequestered no dead cardinals' estates, and knew no more of poison than of acupuncture.

There is a philosophical point here. History flows not into but from the pen of the historian, so who can say that I am right and Las Casas wrong?

Rome, then, despite its defects, *was* the center of the world. And in the center of the world people in high places, or those who served people in high places, especially tasters, were poisoned.

I was poisoned – in the line of duty, it was thought at first.

It happened one hot summer evening when Cardinal Borgia and a few friends had gathered in the colonnaded garden of the Palace to celebrate the creation of twelve superfluous new Vatican positions awarded to deserving office-seekers who had shown gratitude to the amount of 10,000 gold ducats.

It was believed at the time that the man who tried to poison Cardinal Borgia was a disappointed office-seeker, the sort always assassinating cardinals, doges, kings and so forth. Had I died, it would have been the perfect murder. Taster as victim – surely an original idea worthy of a Lucrezia Borgia. But Lucrezia wasn't born yet. Besides, the reputation of that shy, misunderstood lady as the champion poisoner of all time is utterly undeserved.

But to resume. The sun was low in the west, the waxing moon rising in the east. Long shadows lay across the garden. The day was still hot. I stood three steps behind Roderigo Borgia's chair, flanked by the tasters of those guests important enough or suspicious enough to require their services. The way it worked, serving wenches would display the food to the guests at table, serve it up, then turn to the tasters with the very portions their masters would consume. I had my own fork and spoon, my own knife. But I sipped from Roderigo Borgia's golden goblet. By this time tasting was like any other job if you thought about it at all. Steeplejacking, for example.

The macaroni, the sole poached in white wine, the spit-roasted quails, the stuffed hare, the joint of beef, the various accompanying wines, the creamy custard pie — it being summer, the meal was light — all came my way, were tasted and approved. Another meal got through, the steeplejack's feet in thankful contact with the ground again. The tasters on either side of me began to relax. The wenches brought a platter of *dulcias romanas*, dates stuffed with ground almonds, rolled in salt and simmered in honey, for which Roderigo Cardinal Borgia had a particular weakness. He reached for the platter, in conversational midstream. I took three quick steps forward, touched his shoulder and stopped him, a *dulcia romana* inches from his face, with a waggling finger. He begged my pardon graciously. Vanozza, seated at his right, laughed her luscious laugh. He gave her the *dulcia*, and she half-turned and passed it to me. I bit into it delicately and tasted honey, salt, date, almond. Everything in order. I licked honey from my fingers. The conversation at the table continued. Vanozza laughed again, her head thrown back but her padded roll head-dress remaining in place when I was sure it would fall. Pins, I remember thinking, she does it with pins. I looked at the beautiful column of her throat and felt a sudden fire in my own. Someone coughed. I felt the blood drain from my face. Florence, someone said. But not without the Signoria of Venice, someone said. Try telling that to the doge, someone said. I couldn't breathe. I lurched along the table behind the diners. I heard shouts. Now the fire in my throat had reached my stomach. I was waving my arms frantically as the *dulcias romanas* were passed. I slapped a sticky date from feminine fingertips near the end of the table. The fire burned its way into my guts. Thumbs and forefingers everywhere around the table delicately held *dulcias romanas*. I had the satisfaction of seeing them drop before I pitched forward onto my face.

MEMORANDUM

TO: Roderigo Cardinal Borgia
FROM: Bartolomeo Colombo
SUBJECT: Poison

Poisons, whether derived from hemlock or bella donna, wolfsbane or hellebore, are divided into three types.

First, fast-acting poison. Its obvious advantage is speed. The victim often succumbs before help, or a physician, can be summoned. Its disadvantage is that symptoms manifest themselves promptly in the taster, *viz.* he is stricken immediately, and the intended victim can take the necessary precautions, *viz.* not eating or drinking in the poisoned food or drink. Galeazzo Maria Sforza, the Milanese expert, for this reason considers fast-acting poison more a tactical weapon than an actual assassin's tool, serving to terrify the intended victim through the death of his taster, and to coerce him into action counter to his own interests.

Second, medium-acting poison. Its advantage, according to the Genoese authority Grimaldi, is the lead-time, that is, the elapsed time between administration of the poison and death of the victim. This advantage is twofold. (1) A careless victim might assume all to be well with his taster when in reality the latter, already moribund, as yet manifests no symptoms. (2) If the poisoner is present at the scene of the poisoning, he may have time to absent himself before the victim's partisans can lay hands on him.

Third, slow-acting poison. This category is controversial, to the point that physicians dispute its very existence. Its advantage is most obvious of all, *viz.* if physicians dispute its very existence there can be no certainty that the victim was in fact poisoned and therefore no moral imperative to mount a vendetta. Physicians do, however, agree that if both taster and employer perish at roughly the same time, whether in a dramatic or an asymptomatic manner, slow-acting poison must be regarded as a possibility.

The poison administered in an apparently fatal dose to Your Eminence's taster, Cristoforo Colombo, was manifestly of the first type.

(This partial memorandum, only the first sheet of which found its way among my papers, is tear-stained.)

Rich beyond the dreams of all but cardinals and a Pope or two, the famous doctors of Rome and Florence, Venice and Milan, raced to the Borgia Palace in the weeks that followed, urging on their splendid Arabian steeds with golden spurs. All pronounced my case hopeless after cursory examination; perhaps they were just eager to dissect me to further the new science of pathological anatomy. But I persisted in breathing and my heart continued to beat, if feebly. Benivieni's *On Several Hidden and Wonderful Causes of Diseases and Cures* was consulted. Several doctors suggested surgery. Apothecaries compounded the medicines of Benivieni's wonderful cures. My feeble heartbeat became erratic. Benivieni was discarded, *Practica Medicinae* by the Florentine physician Savonarola (father of the controversial martyr-to-be) substituted. I lost weight. I remained feverish. Some suggested bleeding, others the new and promising but usually fatal art of transfusion. Roderigo Borgia prudently rejected both proposals. The physicians argued among themselves and prospered. Even the apothecaries added rooms to their houses or took concubines. The first crisp days of autumn arrived, and the doctors wore miniver-lined hoods against the cold wind. They force-fed me rich broth but even that tended to pass right through me. I dwindled.

And recalled nothing of that time but a single stark premonitory dream about a ship. In the lowest hold of that ship, right down in the foul bilge water, crouches a man, arms manacled, legs fettered. That man is me. A hatch creaks open and a ferocious ray of sunlight stabs the darkness. A bowl of some indescribable slop thumps down. A coarse peasanty voice mocks me: 'Admiral of the fucking Ocean Sea, are you? Fucking gold grows on fucking trees in Hispaniola, does it?' There is harsh laughter. Then heavy metal objects are brought, clanking, into the hold, whether weapons to crush me as I lie there or tools to strike off the irons I could not say, for there the dream ended.

The Apostolic See has a congregation for every purpose, even its own investigation agency. This is euphemistically called the Sacred Congregation of Rites, and what it typically investigates are your would-be saints. The Congregation can move like lightning or like molasses, there's no predicting which. For example, St Francis of Assisi (d. 1226) was canonized just two years later in 1228. But Joan of Arc (d. at the stake 30 May 1431 for blasphemous pride and transvestitism), officially declared innocent in 1456, was not sanctified, for God's sake, until 1920.

Even without the comforting knowledge that Joan eventually would achieve sanctification, Roderigo Borgia still called on the Sacred Congregation of Rites to discover who had tried to poison him. Their investigative machinery was already in place and their reach was long. Besides, Cardinal Piccolomini, chief of the Congregation, though he disliked Roderigo Borgia, owed him a favor. The investigation lasted three weeks.

'At this point in time,' reported Cardinal Piccolomini with a spiteful smile, 'no one anywhere in Europe wishes you dead.'

24

'No?' said Cardinal Borgia. The knowledge was somehow deflating.

'No,' said Piccolomini smugly, and suggested, 'The intended victim might have been one of your guests.'

The Sacred Congregation of Rites went over the guest list with a fine-tooth comb, which took another week. They drew a blank. And Piccolomini, drinking wine in Roderigo Borgia's study, gazed at the Spanish cardinal over the golden rim of his goblet and said, 'Tell me about your taster.'

The following Sunday two things happened which, like so much else in these pages, altered the course of history.

First, Vanozza's husband Domenico d'Arignano climbed Goat Hill (once Capitoline Hill) in search of wild honey, thrust his right arm into a hive, and was stung to death by a swarm of enraged bees.

Second, Roderigo Cardinal Borgia's own confessor, responding to an urgent summons from the physician on call, rushed to the east wing of the Borgia Palace to give me the last rites of the Church. The priest, called Salutati the Youngest (unlike most clergy, he had no children), was an extremely fat and unctuous man of sixty with pronounced B.O. This may be why Roderigo Borgia's own confessions were always so perfunctory.

A cold rain lashed the windows and in the gloom of midday Salutati the Youngest anointed and intoned.

'Stop that,' said Salutati the Youngest, interrupting himself.

His acolyte, swinging the censer, was crying bitterly.

Salutati the Youngest began again.

The acolyte bawled as if his heart would break.

'I said stop that, damn it!'

But the acolyte cried a gusher of tears.

'This man is dying,' said Salutati the Youngest.

'That's ... why ... !' cried the acolyte.

'Try to control yourself.'

The acolyte tried to control himself. Salutati the Youngest began at the beginning again. He reached '*In nomine Patri et Filii et Spiritu* — ' when the acolyte let out the most heartrending sob I have ever heard.

And I heard it. That's the point, I actually distinctly heard it. That sob, with all the world's pity and terror in it, somehow got through to me. Quite possibly it saved my life. I blinked my eyes open. I smelled Salutati the Youngest despite the incense, and turned my head in the other direction, facing the sobbing acolyte. The censer was forgotten. The acolyte approached my bedside, his tear-streaked face illumined, in the gloom of the rain-swept midday, by an angelic smile.

Salutati the Youngest began a third time.

I told him to keep quiet.

'Giacomo,' I said, reaching out my arms to my little brother, 'why are you dressed as an acolyte?'

'I *am* an acolyte. I'm studying for the priesthood.'

'That could change,' said Salutati the Youngest darkly.

'Cristoforo, you're alive!' shouted Giacomo. 'You're not going to die!'

I didn't know it yet, but that was the last time in my life anyone would ever call me Cristoforo.

Roderigo Cardinal Borgia came the next afternoon to see me. 'They say you are going to live, Cristóbal.'

I was propped up in bed eating three dozen coddled quail's eggs washed down with a large jug of white wine. 'Looks like it,' I mumbled around a mouthful.

'How soon will you be able to travel?'

Assuming he had learned of my affair with Vanozza, I bristled with defensive anger. 'What is this?' I said. 'Yesterday when you thought I was dying, you sent your own confessor Salutati the Youngest to give me extreme unction, and now you want to get rid of me.'

He said nothing. He smiled.

'Is it ... Vanozza?' I managed.

'Yes, but not in the way you think. Vanozza was part of your education. I bear you no malice.'

'Then what?'

But all he said was that we would talk again when I was stronger.

After receiving a report from Piccolomini on Saturday, Borgia had visited the Roman branch of Centurione's Bank. Usually to be closeted with a bank director for an hour is a real yawner, but this proved an exception. The director, one Amadeus Dinarius, a Venetian of Levantine extraction, spoke for ninety minutes without pause, Borgia hanging on every word. Dinarius concluded:

'But of course money talks, and if the Brotherhood contracted to assassinate your protégé, we need only exercise fiscal persuasion on the party of the first part to annul the commission. You understand?'

'Domenico d'Arignano,' Borgia marveled, shaking his head. 'Who ever would have thought it?'

'Psychology, my dear Borgia. To be cuckolded by a cardinal is, if anything, ennobling. To be cuckolded by the cardinal's no-account taster is degrading. But d'Arignano will have his price. I'll find out what it is and have my lawyers draw up the papers for his signature. Come back Monday morning.'

Sunday I took my turn for the worse but Giacomo saved me, and then Borgia got word of Domenico d'Arignano's unexpected death. He was waiting at the bank when it opened Monday morning.

'This *is* an unfortunate turn of events,' said Amadeus Dinarius.

'I'll pay the Brotherhood directly to call them off.'

'You can't.'

'I can't?'

'No one can but the party of the first part. And he's dead.'

'There must be something I can do?'

'I'm terribly sorry. I've been laundering Brotherhood money for years, and I know how they operate.'

I'd better say a word here about the secret Brotherhood of the Golden Stag (or Hind). It came into being among the Crusaders in the early twelfth century in response to Hassan-i-Sabbah's sect of Assassins who so terrified Europe and Asia for two centuries until their power was broken by the Tatar Prince Hulagu and the Egyptian Sultan Baybars. The Assassins, as their name suggests, were druggies and they killed people. The Brotherhood of the Golden Stag (or Hind), in turn, was chartered to assassinate Assassins. Then, when international trade developed international rivalries, when a Genoese caravel carrying British wool might turn up in Rhodes or Tyre, Rouen or Bruges, Tunis or Trebizond, the Brotherhood of the Golden Stag (or Hind) expanded operations. They became contract killers. If they accepted a job, the deed was done, without exception, unless the party of the first part cancelled. Their reputation was without parallel before or since, and I'm not excluding the Tongs of Cathay or a certain Sicilian organization of later date.

It is not outside the bounds of possibility to suggest that Sir Francis Drake, the British privateer who would ravage the Spanish Main more than a hundred years later, represented the final distant echo of Domenico d'Arignano's contract on my life. In a way, the Spanish Main was my turf; I'd discovered it, after all. And I don't have to remind you what name Sir Francis Drake chose for his piratical galleon.

'What are the terms of the contract?' Roderigo Borgia asked.

'To be hunted down like a wild animal until death or in perpetuity, whichever comes first.'

'In Italy?'

27

'Italy, certainly. As for elsewhere, who knows how long the Brotherhood's reach is? Let him change his name, his line of work, even his nationality, and hope for the best. What does he do?'

'He's my taster.'

Amadeus Dinarius allowed himself a fleeting smile. 'Well, then, changing his line of work could add decades to his life in *any* event.'

When I had recovered sufficiently to take long walks in the Borgia Palace gardens, Roderigo explained the situation to me.

A chill raced down my spine. 'And my brothers?' I asked.

'No, they're safe. This is a professional contract, not a vendetta. But you'd better understand this: they could strike anywhere, any time, without warning. Today, tomorrow. Or years from now when all your teeth have fallen out. The Golden Stag (or Hind) never gives up.'

I had a final meeting with my brothers. Giacomo, in angelic white, stood on tiptoe and placed his small hand on my head and blessed me. After some slight hesitation, he swiftly sketched the sign of the cross.

'How come you're going?' Bartolomeo asked.

'Because if I don't leave Italy I'll be killed.'

'But *how come*?'

'It's better you don't know.' I swallowed the lump in my throat. 'Take care of each other.'

'We will,' Giacomo promised with a stifled sob.

Bartolomeo told me, 'We'll meet again, I know we will. In some seaport somewhere, somehow.'

They gave me gifts – Giacomo a St Christopher medal and Bartolomeo an ancient map from the Vatican Library. He spread it on his knees to show me. The names were magic the way he spoke them. 'England,' he said. 'Iceland. Here's Greenland. Stepping stones to *terra incognita*.' His moving finger lighted on a large blank area at the left side of the map.

I had one last visit with Roderigo Cardinal Borgia. 'I've written to my bankers in Genoa,' he told me. 'They'll know what to do when you arrive. As for the future, you'd best have this.'

It was a letter on fine vellum, addressed to the Director, House of Centurione, Wherever Situate.

'The biggest merchant bankers in Italy,' he explained, 'with branches all over Europe. When there's a need, they're skilled at circumventing laws and formalities. *And* they owe me. If ever you're in trouble – well, read it.'

In a fine Latin hand, the initial R beautifully illuminated, it said:

Roderigo Cardinal Borgia, to all directors, sub-directors and associates of the House of Centurione throughout the world: Greetings in Christ. His Eminence requests the House of Centurione to extend on application all possible aid to the bearer, Cristóbal Colón, to assist him to pass without delay or hindrance into and out of city-states and nations, to protect him from the abuses of officialdom wheresoever they may occur, and within reason to place the pecuniary resources of the House of Centurione at the disposal of bearer's endeavors.

The proviso 'within reason' as much as Cardinal Borgia's own heavy seal authenticated the letter as coming from him.

'Colón?' I asked.

'Your original name. You were born at sea between Valencia and Genoa.'

'Then I'm really Spanish?'

The Cardinal shrugged. 'Your parents were, but the ship was Italian and you spent your boyhood in Genoa. You're whatever you want to be. Do something noteworthy and let the historians worry about your antecedents.'

After I rolled the vellum letter with Bartolomeo's map, Roderigo Borgia walked pensively with me as far as the river.

'In a year or two you'd have earned a cardinal's red hat and a taster of your own.'

'I wouldn't have made much of a cardinal.'

'Not many of us do.'

I turned to go.

'Be audacious,' Roderigo Borgia said.

Prospero Pighi-Zampini, one of the eight governors of the House of Centurione, Merchant Bankers, was expecting me in the magnificent palace in Piazza Caricamento when I reached Genoa.

'My poor boy,' Governor Pighi-Zampini said, 'forced into exile at the very height of the Italian Renaissance.'

He tossed a velvet drawstring pouch which I deftly caught.

'Our mutual friend in Rome thought these would be best,' he said. 'Florentine florins, accepted anywhere.'

The pouch was not heavy.

Governor Pighi-Zampini withdrew a gold chain from his jerkin and looked at his clock, while I looked at the tufts of hair sprouting from his ears and nostrils like small brushes and waited expectantly.

'You'll sail with tonight's tide,' Pighi-Zampini said. 'What's your preference?'

'Sir?'

'Depends what you want to pay. Some folks take small ships, boats really. Say, a two-masted Provençal felucca or a naviguela of thirty-five or forty tons. Can't recommend them myself. All that pitching, rolling and yawing about. Same's true of a caravel, a hundred tons max. A barque would get you up into the one-to-three-hundred-ton range, and they're fast. Sail close to the wind, they do. But if you want to go in jumbo comfort, there's nothing like a carrack. Thousand-tonner, say, sky-scraping masts, ten sails, five decks.'

Again Pighi-Zampini consulted his clock. 'If so, you're in luck. The carrack *Bechalla* sails with the tide tonight. Carrying alum from Phocaea and casks of Levantine wine to England.'

'England?' I remembered Bartolomeo's parting words and his map.

'Just wrote the insurance myself. Seven per cent of the cargo's value.' Pighi-Zampini opened a notebook and dipped his quill. 'Will you be aboard?'

I assured him that I would.

The pen scratched in the notebook. '*Fourteen* per cent of the cargo's value, in that case. Bon voyage.'

I was half out the door when he called me back. 'You forgot to sign for the pouch of florins. Count them.' And, when I had done so: 'Eleven, is that correct?'

It was.

Pighi-Zampini nodded. 'Precisely the cost of your passage to England on a carrack.' He snatched the velvet drawstring pouch and wrote my ticket of passage.

Penniless, hungry, I left Piazza Caricamento and walked in the cool of the afternoon along Via Balbi, my only possessions Giacomo's St Christopher medal and Bartolomeo's map. I went down the hill past the customs station toward the harbor, wondering if I should sell Bartolomeo's map to the old chartmaker Vongole so I could buy a meal at one of the many taverns along Via Balbi. The smells coming from them were driving me crazy. As I reached Vongole's shop and called his name, he rushed out into the narrow street.

'I remember you, young fellow. Never forget a voice, no sirree bob. You're Bartolomeo Colombo's brother,' he said, laughing and slapping his thigh.

I cast an anxious glance around, but none of the passing crowd seemed interested in the name.

'How is he?' old Vongole asked, squinting nearsightedly into the middle distance.

'Fine. He's fine. He's in Rome working in the Vatican.'

'Bartolomeo Colombo?' shouted old Vongole as loud as he could. I darted frantic looks in all directions. 'In that den of thieves? Ought to go to sea where the air's clean, that's what Bartolomeo Colombo ought to do.'

I hurried away as soon as I decently could and walked out along the breakwater still clutching the rolled map. A wind blew hard from the sea. Masts swayed giddily against the darkening sky. I saw a moored carrack the size of a palace with a dozen gunports on a side and masts as tall as cathedral spires, but her name was *Negrona*. Finding the harbormaster's shack, I inquired about *Bechalla*. 'Phocaean alum and casks of Levantine wine, isn't it?' he said grumpily, one blunt finger deftly exploring a nostril. 'She's not the ship for so heavy a cargo.'

'I've booked passage to England aboard her.'

'*Bechalla?*' He studied the substance on the blunt end of his finger. 'You mean she takes passengers these days? All the way to England? Jesus Christ!'

'Is she in yet?'

'No. Tonight. If you're unlucky.' He turned away and went to work on his other nostril.

Genoa is a city of hills climbing steeply from the harbor. Hoping to see *Bechalla* arrive, I climbed the highest hill of all, where a cemetery gave the dead as fine a view as any in Italy. With them at my back and the living city below, I gazed out to the horizon, remembering what Bartolomeo had taught me. From the hilltop the curvature of the earth was even more apparent as ships appeared and disappeared hull-down. The wind blew. I clutched Bartolomeo's map. High clouds roiled distantly out at sea and soon dusk settled below, but the late afternoon sun was still bright on my hilltop. More verification for Bartolomeo. I missed him, homely face, warts and all. And Giacomo, was he swinging his censer now to help prepare some poor soul for death? The wind was suddenly cold and I glanced behind me uneasily at the white wall of the cemetery and quickly descended the hill. Oil lamps already flickered on Via Balbi and in the main piazzas but gloom filled the sidestreets. The wind rose. I saw distant flashes of lightning, and thunder rolled in from the sea. Then the rain fell, great pelting sheets of it bouncing off the cobblestones. People scurried for shelter. 'There he is!' someone shouted, and bravoes of the Brotherhood of the Golden Stag (or Hind) rushed at me, brandishing daggers and swords.

I darted into the black mouth of an unpaved sidestreet and began to run, the street already muddy underfoot, the façades of buildings rising clifflike on either side, with here and there a faint spill of light from a high window. My footsteps instinctively led me toward the Porta dell'Olivella where my father's tavern had been, but though I ran as fast as I could, whenever I paused to gasp for breath I could hear the bravoes of the Brotherhood of the Golden Stag (or Hind) pounding and splashing after me. Still, I hoped to lose them in the warren of twisting lanes near the tavern. I plunged downhill toward the harbor and into the tiny piazza fronting the little church where the tavern's whores used to confess. But, dark and bolted for the night, it offered no sanctuary. I kept running. I heard shouts behind me. The bravoes entered the piazza at one side as I fled at the other. Then I stumbled, went careening out of control and fell before a doorway lit by two large red lamps, the wind knocked out of me. I had an instant to wonder if Giacomo would become a priest, if Bartolomeo would sail over the curving horizon to those distant lands he dreamed about. I wondered if they would ever learn I had met my end in the same street where we had been raised, between the church that could give me no sanctuary and the passage to far England that I would never make. Then, as I raggedly gulped air and tried to climb to my feet, the bravoes were upon me, two of them grabbing my arms. I fought free and stood an instant, chest on fire. Without hope but remembering Roderigo Borgia's advice, I sprang audaciously at my assailants. Just as one of them tripped me, tumbling me back down on the muddy street, the door flanked by the two red lamps burst open. I climbed to my knees. The tallest bravo began a sideways stroke with his sword, aiming to decapitate me. But a big huge silhouette suddenly intruded between us and the twin red lamps. Looking up I saw tall leather boots and old-fashioned chainmail. The bravo with the sword flew over my head to strike the wall across the street with a sickening *splat* like a ripe melon dropped on a marble floor. A second bravo swung through the air in three complete circles before sailing off headfirst through the rain back in the direction of the church, knocking two of his companions senseless en route. A fifth screamed in terror and fled. The sixth was hurled at him like a boulder from a catapult. The seventh alone escaped, running like a hell-bat.

The big huge silhouette helped me to my feet.

'Go with God and the tide, Cristóbal Colón,' said Giulia The Amazon.

The door between the red lamps slammed shut behind her. I raised the iron knocker and let it fall three, four, five times. No one came to open the door. 'Giulia,' I called. 'Giulia, just let me thank you.' As the door remained locked, I finally understood that The Amazon had returned to her old lifestyle and was ashamed.

'Giulia,' I said, 'Bartolomeo's going to be a famous cartographer.' The door remained mute. 'Giulia,' I said, 'little Giacomo's studying for the priesthood. Both of them think of you often.'

I let the knocker fall again. Did I hear a single sob of regret? It might have been the wind.

The rain had stopped and a full moon raced past the parting clouds when I reached the harbor. I saw eight carracks moored there, but none was *Bechalla*. Of feluccas and tartans, naviguelas and grippi, marani, marciliane and other small ships there were dozens. But only one was taking on cargo, so I went there to inquire. She was the smallest felucca of all, twenty tons with her rotting deck rain-soaked. I hailed the supercargo. 'You wouldn't happen to know where I can find *Bechalla*, bound for England?'

The man said nothing, only pointed to the stern of the little felucca. In the moonlight I saw: *Bechalla*, Genoa.

'But *Bechalla* is a carrack of a thousand tons,' I said, 'and she's already loaded with alum and Levantine wine for England.'

'You're looking at the only *Bechalla* afloat,' said the supercargo. 'As for the Levantine wine, we load it right here from the vineyards above Genoa. The English never know the difference.'

I studied the felucca in the moonlight. Twenty tons and not young. Ancient, if you got right down to it. A single not very stout mast. Hull barnacle-encrusted *above* the waterline, which meant she rode low in the water when loaded. Very low.

Still, I had no choice.

'I'm a passenger,' I said.

He seemed surprised. 'We don't take many. See your ticket?' He peered at it in the moonlight.

'This is no good,' he told me.

'Why not?'

'Says the "carrack" *Bechalla*, and this here's only an old felucca.'

'That's all right,' I said. 'I'll go anyway.'

'Not with me it isn't all right. This ticket's not valid and you'll have to work your passage.'

I sighed and debated thinking things over. But there was nothing to think over. I boarded with Bartolomeo's map and Giacomo's St Christopher medal. We sailed with the tide.

This is one of those places where my early biographers really go off the deep end.

Remember, this sea voyage was my first (excepting the one on which I was born). As yet I knew little about ships and less about the Mediterranean, let alone the vast uncharted Ocean Sea. But did this deter the scribbling hacks who tried to capitalize on my fame?

In fairness, the new invention of printing with separate and movable type compounded the problem. Note that Johann Gutenberg of Mainz, Germany, invented the printing press at the very time, give or take a few months, that I was born. Coincidence? Sure, but for the first time books were available to a mass market – paving the way for unscholarly hacks to whom the truth meant far less than a sensational story. Why, they even got the development of the printing press itself wrong. Gutenberg may have invented a crude press, but it was his typesetter Peter Schöffer who developed the punches of engraved steel for each letter, the metal matrix which held them, the mold which kept them from wandering all over the page. But that's another story.

So what do these sensationalist scribblers cast me as, on my first (other than natal) sea voyage? A pirate captain, for God's sake – commanding an armed-to-the-teeth caravel, lateen-rigged so that sailing close to the wind it could outrun anything afloat. And then these scribblers have that impressive ship, Captain Colombo commanding, sunk by a small flotilla of poorly armed merchantmen off Cape St Vincent, forcing me to swim for my life to the Portuguese coast.

Not that I can entirely blame them. Because, in one of those minor coincidences that abound in history, there *was* a pirate active then who called himself Colombo, a French corsair who preyed on shipping between Spanish Mediterranean ports and Lisbon.

But nobody sank this Colombo. Quite the other way around.

To tell the story briefly and factually:

Bechalla, in convoy with three other ships for mutual protection, sailed west from Genoa. It was a poor bargain for the others, all swift two-masters. Heavily laden, dangerously low in the water, her hull half caulking and half dry rot, *Bechalla* wallowed like a hippopotamus from the pages of Pliny. The others had to shorten sail from time to time so as not to outrun her.

I never learned the captain's name. Call him Captain Catastrophe.

The slightest sea and his scuppers were full to overflowing. A sudden gust of wind and his ancient brown foresail was in shreds. Having no replacement, he bought the spare carried by the felucca *Leghorn Lady*, which proved too large. As one of *Bechalla*'s three ordinary seamen, I had to help cut the heavy canvas and sew new grommets. A day lost. A day that made our encounter with my piratical namesake inevitable. Or take our anti-pirate equipment. A single gunport to a side, an ancient bronze cannon in each, their barrels cracked and held together by wire. One day as we neared Gibraltar, Captain Catastrophe told me to find the cannon balls. To find them! Which I did, in the hold, buried under tons of Phocaean alum. There were only four. Weight, said Captain Catastrophe, weight's the problem. Iron is heavy and no one pays us to carry cannon balls. And our rations! A sack of maggoty flour, a few ropes of garlic, a few dozen sprouting onions, a skin of oil, another of sour wine, a jar of honey, a sack of rock-hard biscuits, some salt. Water fit to drink only those nights we made port.

Ten days of this and we passed through the straits. Then on to Cape St Vincent, the extreme southwestern corner of Europe, where the Portuguese under Prince Henry had gathered world-class navigators to find safe passage around Africa to the Indies. One Vasco da Gama would finally succeed – a full six years after I first reached the Indies by sailing west across the uncharted Ocean Sea.

Captain Catastrophe was pissing off the rail to starboard, for once with the wind at his back, when *Bechalla*'s lookout shouted: 'Sail ho!'

'Where?' shouted Captain Catastrophe, trussing quickly.

'Ho!' shouted the lookout.

Those were not yet the days when pirates lurked in every cove and inlet, nor the days when Algiers and Malta grew rich on the resale of stolen goods, stolen ships, stolen people. The sail could have belonged to a merchantman like ourselves.

But it belonged to Guillaume de Casenove, the French pirate who called himself Colombo.

The caravel, long and sharp of prow, raced sharklike at the hapless convoy, firing her cannon as she came. The balls splashed perilously close but no felucca was hit. We scattered, *Leghorn Lady* and *Aguila* heading northward on a port tack, *Madre de Dios* returning south, *Bechalla* close-hauled and beating slowly for Cape St Vincent itself, where our lookout reported a fleet of small but heavily armed rescue ships leaving port. We cheered them on.

35

Just as Colombo's caravel bore down on us, we turned too close to the wind, our sails luffing. *Bechalla* swung broadside to the pirate vessel and lay dead in the water.

Captain Catastrophe shouted, 'Fire starboard cannon!' which was done, the ancient bronze gun exploding with a terrific roar, sending a sheet of flame across the deck to ignite the gunpowder of the port cannon too.

My namesake Colombo never touched *Bechalla*. The ill-fated ship sank as a result of self-inflicted wounds.

Captain Catastrophe and the crew dove overboard (except for the unfortunate gunners, who perished in the explosions) and floundered toward the fleet of rescue ships which was closing so fast that my namesake Colombo set all sail and sped away to the south.

I hadn't the faintest idea how to swim but I had seen dogs paddling in the water, and this I did, Bartolomeo's map between my clenched teeth. I gulped seawater, gagged and coughed, and kept paddling until I found a floating cask, which I clung to for dear life. The rescue ships approached and a felucca smaller than *Bechalla* made for me. Strong hands tugged me aboard, where I lay drenched and gasping. A couple of thickset sailors gave me brandy to drink and were friendly until one asked in Portuguese, which in those days differed very little from Spanish:

'Where you from?'

'Genoa.'

'Bound for?'

'England.'

This impressed them. They smiled at me and patted my back. I spat seawater.

One of them asked, 'What's your name, kid?'

I said, 'Colombo.'

They cursed me and lifted me over the gunwale to hurl me back into the sea.

I did not then know the pirate's name. What could I assume but that my rescuers belonged to the Brotherhood of the Golden Stag (or Hind)?

'*Plomo!*' I shouted. '*Como plomo!*' *Plomo* is the Spanish word for lead. 'What I started to say, I would have sunk to the bottom like a lead weight if you hadn't rescued me!'

The thickset Portuguese sailors looked at me dubiously. I was still poised over the water.

'What *is* your name then, kid?'

'Colón. Cristóbal Colón. I'm nobody special. Just a Spaniard named Colón,' I told them.

I felt the felucca's deck underfoot again.

'He ain't Colombo the pirate.'

'Nah. He's just some dumb Spanish kid.'

An hour later I stepped ashore in Portugal with Bartolomeo's map.

❧ III ❧

I Sail North Long Before Sailing West
or
Tristram, Isolde and Sister Death

THE conventional wisdom bungles the round-earth, flat-earth question. School kids are taught that only Columbus (they always put my name in Latin) knew the world was round. The truth is, those rare believers in a flat earth invariably made news. Nine centuries before my time, one Cosmas Indicopleustes sailed east from Byzantium for India to prove the world was flat by falling off en route. He failed. A few centuries after my time, one Wilbur G. Voliva of Zion City, Illinois, founded the Flat Earth Society, definitely a voice in the wilderness.

Anybody with a decent fifteenth-century education knew the world was round. They even had a pretty good notion of how big it was. (I myself would one day give a slightly inaccurate estimate, but that was a piece of deliberate salesmanship.)

Smart folks knew the world was round and 21,420 miles in circumference, only 3,500 or so off its true girth. Not bad for the fifteenth century, eh? And they had charts and maps divided into 360 degrees of latitude and meridians of longitude, so every place that God made could have its own distinctive coordinates. Sure, some maps depicted sea serpents rampaging in the Ocean Sea. Why shouldn't they? The Ocean's a dangerous place, and by my time the sea serpents were mostly symbolic.

Now, if you attribute all this knowledge, as some pop-historians do, to the observatory established by Prince Henry the Navigator at Cape St Vincent in Portugal, well, that's wrong too. Let me just drop a few names from antiquity – Hipparchus, Erasthenes, Ptolemy – and remind you that by 150 B.C. at Alexandria, Egypt, they were doing pretty much what Prince Henry and his adjutant Captain Perestrello would do at Cape St Vincent more than 1,500 years later. Of course, in between you did have your Dark Ages. So Prince Henry and Captain Perestello had to repeat almost every step – which only added to the excitement of their work. The world would see nothing quite like it until Cape Canaveral and the race for the moon.

Prince Henry's goal, given the available transportation, was about as remote. The Prince, who died ten years or so before I made my sodden appearance at Cape St Vincent, dreamed of sailing around Africa to India. Apparently sailing west to reach the fabled East never occurred to him, a surprising blind spot.

Perestrello, when he came down to the beach to greet us survivors, proved to be a disheveled-looking fellow, his long graying hair blowing in the sea breeze, his wide-sleeved gown flapping, his face wind-reddened.

'Why, if Prince Henry were alive today,' he said, 'pirates wouldn't dare come within a hundred miles of Cape St Vincent.'

'Papa,' said an exasperated child's voice. 'You *always* say that.'

With Perestrello was his nine-year-old daughter Felipa, named for Philippa, the British mother of Prince Henry the Navigator. Felipa was as winsome a little tomboy as I ever saw. Just visible hull-down at the horizon was Colombo the pirate's fleeing caravel. Little Felipa Perestrello skipped a few flat stones across the water in its direction.

'Fucking pirates!' she piped.

'Felipa!' cried her father.

But her face was so guilelessly pretty, I decided she didn't know what the word meant.

They fed and lodged us near the harbor. One day Perestrello asked me, 'What's that chart you're always carrying around? Are you a navigator? We need navigators here.'

I demurred modestly, 'Afraid not. It's just a keepsake from my brother who has an important post at the Vatican.'

We carefully opened the map in the chartroom and I had a shock. It wasn't the map Bartolomeo had given me at all!

Or, to be accurate, it was the same map and more. Europe and the Ocean Sea with Iceland and Greenland in the north and the Azores and Canary Islands central and south were as I remembered. But in the distant west beyond the Ocean Sea, where before a huge undifferentiated blob of land called *terra incognita* had taken up a full quarter of the map, I now saw a coastline with definite features, bays, coves, etc., and it even had a name.

'It's not the same map at all,' I said, mystified.

Perestrello was looking over my shoulder. 'Seawater will do it every time,' he explained. 'What you have there is a partial palimpsest.'

Now, as everyone knows, a palimpsest happens when a cheapskate scrivener who wants to save on parchment or paper bleaches out one manuscript to write another. Apparently mapmakers could be cheapskates too.

'Over there,' I pointed, 'used to be *terra incognita*.'

'Seawater dissolved the inks,' Perestrello told me, 'exposing the earlier map underneath.'

Near the new-old coastline with its bays, coves, etc., was written *Ireland the Great*.

'Ireland the *what*?' laughed Perestrello.

As the navigational heir to Prince Henry he knew Ireland to be a flea-ridden island west of far England, populated by religious zealots since the fifth century.

'But here's Ireland over here,' I said, pointing to the little island.

'True, true. And this "Ireland the Great" is where Wineland ought rightly to be.'

'Where where ought rightly to be?'

'I see you have a lot to learn,' said Captain Perestrello.

Precocious little Felipa came in and stood between us at the chart table, rubbing innocently against my thigh.

'Felipa, you're not allowed in the chartroom or anywhere in the Sprawling Navigational Complex during working hours,' her father scolded her. To me he explained, 'Her mother says I spoil her because I have no son. And it's true, I'm afraid, this is no place for a girl. Well, it's off to a convent before very long.'

'Your codpiece is bigger than Papa's,' Felipa told me.

Perestrello coughed.

I left quickly, rolling up Bartolomeo's map or palimpsest, and went outside into what Captain Perestrello had so accurately called the Sprawling Navigational Complex. Harbor, lighthouse, observatory, chartrooms, living quarters, shops, taverns, Old Sailors' Home, whorehouse – all together were known as Prince's Town in honor of dead Prince Henry.

Little more need be said about my first stay at Cape St Vincent. I learned navigation and chart-reading. I made a few short voyages to this or that Mediterranean port and one long one to the island of Madeira (rather promising wine). I became the confidant of Captain Perestrello and the dreamboat (to use her picturesque nautical locution) of precocious Felipa, the father frequently bemoaning the premature demise of Prince Henry the Navigator, who as far as I could tell had lived a normal life span (1394–1460), and the daughter becoming bolder with each passing month so that I did my best to avoid her.

Her twelfth birthday, three years after I'd settled in my own tiny fisherman's cottage in Prince's Town, happened to coincide with an eclipse of the moon. Astronomers and navigators from all over Europe had come to Cape St Vincent to view it and hear Captain Perestrello expatiate. An eclipse of the moon, as Captain Perestrello explained, paraphrasing the late Prince Henry, offers celestial proof of the earth's roundness.

'For mark you,' he observed as the earth's shadow began to bite into the face of the full moon, 'that the advancing shadow is a perfect arc of a circle.'

There was a polyglot hum of agreement there on the mobbed beach below the observatory.

Some spoilsport, speaking strangely inflected if melodious English, said, 'Sure and that needn't prove the global shape of the earth, Captain Perestrello. A *flat* disc would cast the same sort of shadow, wouldn't it, but?'

The crowd was searched but the unbeliever couldn't be identified, although he was roundly booed.

'Prince Henry himself couldn't have answered that doubting Thomas,' Perestrello grumbled. You could tell he was distracted. All day he'd been considering the merits of various convents, one of which Felipa was destined for. After the earth's shadow retreated, still a perfect arc of a circle, from the face of the moon, the crowd on the beach dispersed and I made my way home through the again-moonlit streets of Prince's Town, my unaided eyes (the telescope had yet to be invented) bleary from staring all that time at the eclipse.

Hardly had I unlocked the four locks and opened the door of my tiny fisherman's cottage when I heard a sound inside. In the darkness I drew the sword I'd worn day and night since my encounter in Genoa with the Brotherhood of the Golden Stag (or Hind).

'Who's there?'

Silence. Then I heard an ominous footfall in the darkness. I lunged with my sword and heard girlish laughter.

'Felipa,' I said, 'what are you doing here?'

'I had to go *somewhere*, what with the whole Sprawling Navigational Complex off limits, especially with all those strange men around.'

A spark was struck and a lamp lit, and there stood Felipa near the table, her back turned, naked from the waist up. She spun around. 'I bet you didn't notice. See how my boobs are growing? They're already as big as lemons, look,' she said, breathing deeply. 'Open your eyes, for God's sake.' She came closer. 'You can touch them if you want.'

I backed away.

'I said, you can touch them.' She stamped her little foot petulantly.

'Felipa, you'd better get dressed and go home,' I ordered sternly, and turned away. But she came up behind me and hugged herself against me, her slender arms around my chest, her budding breasts soft against my back.

'Don't you want to grope them even a tiny little bit?'

I declined.

She pirouetted in front of me. 'Hah! Liar! Just *look* at your codpiece now.'

'Felipa, if you don't leave this minute I'll have to spank you.'

She considered. 'You will? That might be *lots* of fun.'

I'd better mention in passing that Felipa's behavior, while undeniably forward, was no longer precocious. Girls frequently married at the age of eleven or twelve in Portugal and Spain in those days, with parental permission. At fourteen, no permission necessary. As for premarital sex, although frowned upon by the Church, it was the rule, not the exception, and would continue to be until my crew brought syphilis back from the Indies after my First Voyage, putting a damper on sexual freedom.

However. I regarded Felipa as a child, if a sexy one, and found myself fleeing my tiny cottage so aroused that I jogged along the beach to cool my ardor. I met Captain Perestrello lurching drunkenly from the direction of the whorehouse.

'Sometimes it's *so* difficult,' he cried lugubriously.

The way he was staggering, I thought it best to accompany him on his erratic way toward the harbor.

'What's difficult?'

'Everything. I've lived a lie for years. Why, if I didn't have

42

unswerving loyalty to the memory of Prince Henry, I couldn't go on.'
He stopped. 'I mean, damn it all, how can I keep preaching the
roundness of the earth when everything inside me insists it's really *as
flat as a pancake*?'

We stood near the breakwater and looked out to sea in the
moonlight. Perestrello began to giggle. 'Poor sad buggers on the other
side, any moment they're liable to fall off. But I keep the faith. It's all I
have.'

He gazed mournfully westward across the vast uncharted expanse
of sea. Abruptly he straightened. ''Member that map of yours? Ireland
the Great?'

'I have it right here,' I said, for, like my sword and Giacomo's St
Christopher medal and Roderigo Borgia's letter to the House of
Centurione, I was never without it.

'Well, I wrote some people. Just got an answer. Actually, an offer
to *buy* your map.'

'It's not for sale at any price.'

'On condition,' Perestrello went on with drunken doggedness, 'that
you deliver it in person. They'll pay a thousand pounds, and no
questions asked.'

'Questions?'

'About prov-provenance, dear boy. Provenance. One thousand
pounds, cash on the barrelhead.'

I said, in a less forceful voice, 'It's not for sale.'

Perestrello mumbled, 'It *looks* flat, it *feels* flat, it even *smells* flat. So
how can it be round?' He began to cry. With thumb and forefinger he
pinched his nose just below the bridge and blew it hard.

The conversation then moved in an unexpected direction. 'As you
know,' Captain Perestrello said, enunciating meticulously, 'the late
Queen Philippa, for whom my dear Felipa is named, was the daughter
of John of Gaunt, fourth son of Edward III and himself the ancestor of
several English kings, not to mention the royal family of Castile
through which ... '

Genealogies were never my strong point. Fortunately, his glazed
eyes couldn't see how my own eyes glazed over while he droned on.

' ... when you go to England ... ' I heard him say.

I began to listen again. He sounded half-way sober, and wholly
serious.

' ... bar sinister, unfortunately. But the fellow who wants your map
of Ireland the Great *is* a direct descendant of John of Gaunt. Calls
himself The O'Gaunt.'

Far England, at last. Almost the edge of the known world. I nodded. I couldn't trust myself to speak.

'You'll sail as supercargo aboard *Virgen Rampante*. And as Felipa will be entering a convent at St Malo in France, you can drop her along the way.'

From such stuff do legends grow.

Not that I really blame my earlier biographers for what they *didn't* say about my voyage to England. Oh, they knew I went. It's there in black and white in all their books. Landed at Bristol, such-and-such a year, carrying a cargo of Algarve olive oil and wine from Madeira and Porto. As if I were in common trade! I was carrying Bartolomeo's map (and Felipa); wine and oil were secondary. But, back to the stuff of legends. I have this awesome reputation for pacing the deck, day and night, fair weather and foul. That's in all the books too. But do my biographers even suggest the legend was born on my journey to England? They do not. They save it for my First Voyage across the Ocean Sea.

I can only conclude they didn't know that sailing aboard the carrack *Virgen Rampante*, bound for St Malo (where she would disembark) and Bristol, was Felipa Perestrello.

'Please, Cristóbal,' she begged me as soon as we were out of sight of land. 'It's my last chance for years and years. Holy Mary, don't make me enter the convent a virgin!'

But I thought of her father's parting words, and I was firm.

In his befuddled way, Perestrello had told me, 'She won't have much of a dowry after I'm through making my yearly donations to the convent. Her dowry, when she comes home a lady, will be, well, damn it all,' Perestrello struggled, his ruddy face darkening, 'in a manner of speaking, her dowry will be the fact that she *is* a lady, that she's still, er – '

I understood.

At first I paced the deck day and night, in fair weather and foul, because I knew Felipa was waiting in my cabin below decks. But when it became apparent that I wouldn't bed her, she continued to slip sleeping drops into her dueña's wine and began making eyes at the captain and selected members of his crew. Then I paced the deck day and night, in fair weather and foul, with a new worry, that Felipa might take any one (or more) of the thirty-five-man crew of *Virgen Rampante* as her ravager(s).

So instead of just pacing I would sometimes dart ferretlike below decks, scrupulously avoiding my own cabin of course. It is no short voyage from Cape St Vincent via Lisbon to St Malo in Brittany, and I never slept, not once. Soon the men were whispering.

'He paces the decks day and night, in fair weather and foul,' some whispered. 'Or darts ferretlike below decks.'

'He never sleeps,' whispered others.

Thus are legends born.

I began to hallucinate. Far out to sea I saw groves of lemon trees, each round perfect fruit dotted with a perky pink tip. The symbolism eluded me.

'Go to sleep, man, or you'll pass out and fall overboard,' the captain urged.

This made me suspicious of him. I assumed he had his eye on Felipa's virginity like everyone else. I spied on him. I took to popping up behind him at unexpected moments.

'*Will* you go to sleep, man?' he urged.

But I didn't. Never. Not once.

Felipa's dueña woke in time to see the breakwater at St Malo. The poor old auntie was disoriented. 'When are we leaving?' she asked.

'We're here,' Felipa told her, and glared at me malignly. 'I'll make you pay for this,' she promised.

On *Virgen Rampante*'s run across the Channel and along the south coast of England and around Land's End and then on up the Bristol Channel to Severn Mouth, no short voyage itself, I slept the whole time.

A warning about the pages to follow. The language may daunt even the stout of heart. But the English in those days, isolated on their island and unaware of the strides toward refinement and culture made by the Renaissance in Italy and elsewhere on the Continent, spoke as they lived — crudely.

They may to some degree be excused. Everyone knows what happens after a war, say your average four-or-five-year war — carpet-baggers, Lost Generations, Iron Curtains, etc., etc. But suppose a country fought a war *continuously for a hundred years and* LOST? This was England's predicament at the end of the Hundred Years War, as it's called, and I got there less than twenty years after the final battle at Castillon and the retreat from Bordeaux in 1453, which settled the conflict in France's favor. Following a century of casualties, privation, uncertainty, Joan of Arc, plague and finally defeat, the English wallowed in a kind of joyless carnality, and this was reflected in their speech.

To put it in terms Domenico Colombo the weaver might have used, the very fabric of society had come unraveled.

Now, on rereading my notes I see that I had better compromise after all between respect for the truth and respect for the squeamish in recounting my adventures in England. The compromise I have worked out is this: I'll report verbatim the conversation, if that is what it was, at the Plank & Anchor in Bristol the night I arrived to rendezvous with the bar-sinister descendant of John of Gaunt. Subsequently, I'll have only occasional recourse to the colorful vocabulary to remind you that we are still in England.

Well, then.

PLACE: The Plank & Anchor, a crowded public house of the sort Hogarth would later immortalize, hard by the Stone Bridge over the River Avon in Bristol.

TIME: Well past sundown.

CHARACTERS: Cristóbal Colón, Publican, Barmaid, various Masters and Mistresses (the title for all men and women in fifteenth-century England, whatever their station in life), and Tristram, a Student.

Enter left CRISTÓBAL COLÓN, *Bartolomeo's tightly rolled map in his hand, sheathed sword at his side.*

COLÓN: (*in fluent but accented English*) Begging your pardon, Master.

FIRST MASTER: That's all-fucking-right, Jack.

COLÓN: (*working his way through the crowd to the bar*) Excuse me, I'm looking for a man called The O'Gaunt.

BARMAID: That cocksucker!

PUBLICAN: That arsepronger!

SECOND MASTER: That cuntlapper!

ALL: (*muttering but restrained*) That layabout!

COLÓN: He's expecting me.

BARMAID: Is he? Better buy yourself a tankard then, dearie. *He* effing won't.

PUBLICAN: Where's that fucked-up accent of yours from anyway?

FIRST MISTRESS: You some kind of scummy Eye-tye, stranger?

COLÓN: (*eyes darting around*) NO!!!

ALL: (*muttering but restrained*) Effing foreigners.

COLÓN: Really, I'm nobody special. Just a Spanish sailor.

BARMAID: Sailor, eh? Stick it to cabin boys, do you, dearie?

SECOND MISTRESS: How's about giving the sailor lad some of that piss you call ale, you old arsehole?

PUBLICAN: The O'Gaunt, you said, Master Buggerer?

COLÓN: The O'Gaunt, yes.

FIRST MASTER: That mick prick!

THIRD MASTER: That grannybanger!

ALL: (*muttering but restrained*) That snatch-cradler!

BARMAID: Be 'alf a bob, Master Buggerer.

COLÓN: Pardon? My English isn't —

BARMAID: Half an effing bob, for shitsake.

COLÓN: I'm afraid I'm not familiar with your money. (*Holds out a handful of coins.*)

PUBLICAN: (*relieving him of all coins*) He ain't effing here, The O'Gaunt. And he ain't effing coming.
(ALL *laugh.*)

TRISTRAM, A STUDENT: Give the sailor his change.

PUBLICAN: What?

ALL: *What???*

TRISTRAM, A STUDENT: I said give the sailor his change.
(PUBLICAN *does so, grumbling.*)

COLÓN: (*to the* STUDENT) Thank you. (*Turns to the* PUBLICAN.) When do you expect him? (*Puts tankard down, grimacing as if the ale does taste like piss.*)

BARMAID: Who-the-fuck knows with that fartbag?

ALL: (*muttering but restrained*) Never'd be too swiving soon.

COLÓN: Er, swiving? I fear I don't know the word.

BARMAID: Just another way to say 'fucking', dearie.

FIRST MISTRESS: You sure you ain't no Eye-tye?

COLÓN: No!! I mean yes, I'm sure.

TRISTRAM, A STUDENT: (*thoughtfully*) Actually, 'swiving' is but a tame euphemism, a further indication of the decadence of society.

ALL: Huh??

TRISTRAM, A STUDENT: You see, *swive* refers only to sexual intercourse, whereas *fuck* actually connotes to strike, to hit most horribly, or even to place under a malevolent spell. The etymology of the word can be traced to *peig*, and thence to *poikos*, both of which mean unspeakably evil, and then to *gefah*, from which derives our rather more harmless word *foe*, and even to *faege*, a sad old word that means, uh, slated for death, and gives us the trivialization *fey*, and back also to

47

fehida, from which ancient word comes our *feud*. I could go on –

ALL: Don't.

SECOND MISTRESS: (*bemused*) And all the time I thought I was just swiving.

FIRST MISTRESS: (*to* COLÓN) Because, if you *are* an Eye-tye, there's a *paisan'* of yours – Jenny, what's that scummy Eye-tye's name again?

BARMAID: I don't remember.

FIRST MISTRESS: Sure you do. Giovanni.

BARMAID: That's it. Giovanni. Giovanni something.

FIRST MISTRESS: What I mean to say, Giovanni knows The O'Gaunt. They're friends – if anyone's a friend of that peat-bog puddle of pus.

SECOND MISTRESS: (*speculatively*) I've heard Eye-tyes are pretty swiving good if you're looking for good swiving.

TRISTRAM, A STUDENT: (*laughing*) That old Latin chestnut!

SECOND MISTRESS: (*grabbing* COLÓN's *codpiece and seeming to weigh it*) We-ell ...

(COLÓN *flees*.)

The student Tristram left the Plank & Anchor with me. We walked companionably throught the misty rain and stood a while on a small hill overlooking the confluence of the Avon and Frome rivers.

'Aethelred the Unready, in the tenth century, fortified this very spot,' Tristram told me. 'Bristol's been England's number-two port after London ever since.'

'What happened to the fortifications?' I asked. The hill was bare except for a few smashed blocks of stone we had tripped over while ascending.

'Aethelred was, as ever,' said Tristram with a shrug of his slender shoulders, 'unready.'

Tristram was a slim youth of sixteen or so with long legs, the left sheathed in black silk and the right in red, and a bulky jerkin to keep out the cold.

'Cold for summer, isn't it?' I said.

'We don't have a summer here,' Tristram explained. He had a pure tenor voice as attractive as the rest of him.

My reaction to him began to alarm me. The English have a reputation for inversion, and I wondered if it might be contagious.

He touched my arm. A shiver ran through me.

48

'Have you anywhere to go, Master Cristóbal? To spend the night?'

'Don't worry,' I said quickly, 'I'll be all right.'

'I've plenty of room.'

'Thanks, I'll find a place.'

'A foreign sailor? Innkeepers'll cheat you blind.'

The rain was coming down harder. It seemed to bring out a faint enticing fragrance from Tristram's skin. He said, 'I know Bristol. I could help you find The O'Gaunt.'

The rain, no longer misty, pelted us.

Tristram took my hand. 'Come, Master Cristóbal, you'll catch your death of cold.'

I drew back, but he tugged and began to run, and I ran with him.

He had rooms in an inn on the heights of Bristol Town known as Clifton. We arrived drenched to the skin. Once inside, Tristram twisted his long blond hair and wrung it out. He tossed me a cloth to dry myself while he lit a fire in the hearth and disappeared through an archway to return wearing a dry robe.

He handed its twin to me. 'Go get out of those wet clothes, Master Cristóbal.'

I went into the dark bedroom. The air was musky with Tristram's fragrance. It was driving me crazy. I stripped. Tristram's spare robe was too small for me, especially across the shoulders, but I put it on and returned to the sitting room.

Tristram wasn't sitting. He reclined, head propped on one elbow, on some sort of white animal skin in front of the blazing hearth.

I asked quickly. 'Where are you a student?'

'Oxford. The Queen's College.'

'Oh,' I said, determined to lose my unseemly lust in conversation.

'Bring the wine, would you? It's rather a good Madeira.'

I brought the wine and two goblets and knelt, careful to stay off the animal skin.

'Come sit here by the fire where it's warm,' Tristram suggested.

'What do you study there at The Queen's College?' I countered quickly. By then everything about Tristram was exciting. I wanted to touch him, to embrace him. Along with desire an intense self-loathing engulfed me.

'Metaphysics, with a side glance at Platonic philosophy. You *do* know Plato's theory of love?'

'No,' I said hurriedly. But I did know that Plato's Athens had been a hotbed of homosexuality. The struggle within me made it difficult to breathe.

'I like the part in *The Symposium*,' said Tristram in his fine high tenor voice, 'that says lovers were joined in a previous incarnation and must seek until they find each other and are joined again.'

I poured the wine, my fingers so unsteady that some spilled on the animal skin.

'Never mind, it's only ermine,' Tristram said, sipping the Madeira. When his beautiful lips parted I saw the gleam of white, even teeth.

I tossed my wine back and poured another gobletful and tossed that back too. He looked at me, a faint smile on those beautiful lips. I was ablaze with desire; it overwhelmed me. If this was my fate, I thought in a frenzy, so be it.

I dropped Bartolomeo's tightly rolled map, stripped off the too-small robe, tearing it across the shoulders in my haste, and leaped at Tristram. He had meanwhile slipped gracefully from his own robe, a Mona Lisa smile (Leonardo would paint the well-known portrait between 1503 and '06) on his mouth as his smooth arms rose up to receive me. I halted, astounded, in mid-leap. Tristram gently touched, then explored with the delicate tips of two fingers, my erection. Tristram's breasts were high and saucy, her waist so slender I could compass it with my two hands. Her hips flared over long lovely legs, setting off the magic triangle in splendid parentheses. The triangle itself was covered with a delicate down of fine blonde hair.

'Isolde,' she said. 'My name's really Isolde, but they don't take girl students at Oxford, so you see – '

'Mistress Isolde,' I said, breathing the fragrance of her damp hair and flawless skin and looking deep into her sea-green eyes.

We swived.

Tristram (I had better call her that, since she always appeared as Tristram, a Student, except when we were alone together, and one other time) was a foundling raised in a convent at Wainfleet All Saints near Skegness. Until the age of thirteen she never saw a man, except for priests, and her curiosity finally became too great. Tristram left the convent and, seeing what society had to offer each sex, masqueraded as a boy. A brilliant boy, I might add. At fourteen she entered Oxford, reading metaphysics and the entire Platonic *oeuvre*. She neglected to tell me how a penniless foundling could matriculate at The Queen's College, Oxford, but the customs of the country were still new to me and I did not inquire. She spent her summers in Bristol, where she was apprenticed to an alchemist.

For three days and nights we were too deliciously occupied for me even to think about The O'Gaunt or the mysterious Italian Giovanni, but on the fourth day I asked her: 'Do you really know where I can find this O'Gaunt or Giovanni the Italian?'

We were walking down from the heights toward Stone Bridge. A fine misty rain was falling and it was cold for August. It would have been cold for November.

'I might be able to find The O'Gaunt. He has this yen for me.'

'Finding him's no job for a lady,' I said quickly, jealous of my love.

'I thought you just asked me to.'

'I asked you how *I* could find him. There's a difference.'

'Silly. *I* don't have a yen for *him*. At least not anymore,' she admitted with a light squeeze of my arm. 'What's so important about finding him?'

Telling her about Bartolomeo's map, it occurred to me that I hadn't seen it since first we swived. I searched Tristram's rooms frantically, and soon she joined in. It was Tristram who found it. The map, its tight roll flattened now, had somehow worked its way under the ermine rug.

'We'd better find a safe place for this,' I said.

'Nothing could be simpler. Magister Norton.'

I looked at her blankly.

'Magister Tom Norton, the alchemist I work for. It will be safe with him. Which reminds me, if I want to keep my apprenticeship, I'd better report in tomorrow. But about the map – do you intend selling it to The O'Gaunt?'

I evaded the question. 'Do you believe in fate, Mistress Isolde?'

'That we were fated to meet, Master Cristóbal? Oh yes, I do believe that. Or do you mean the idea of *faege*, of one's doom? I think I believe that too, though it terrifies me.'

If only she had known then, if only *I* had known, that the time would soon come for us when fate and doom were one!

'And I believe that in some way I don't yet understand my destiny is bound with this map,' I told her.

She accepted that with a thoughtful nod of her beautiful head as we entered the Plank & Anchor to learn if The O'Gaunt had been there since my first visit. He had not. Nor had Giovanni the Italian. We left messages for both.

Our fruitless search took four days, or rather nights, Tristram joining me each evening after her work at Magister Tom Norton's laboratory. We visited public houses where everyone was roaring drunk, and public houses where the silence was broken only by the

51

click of checkers, chessmen and backgammon dice. Once we spent the night at an inn near the Church of St Mary Redcliffe where The O'Gaunt was reputed to have slept on occasion (without Tristram, I hoped). There we found roaches and rats and an army of fleas, but no trace of The O'Gaunt.

On the streets an olfactory disaster from tanneries and pigsties, impromptu latrines and discharged chamber pots assailed our noses. But there was another miasma more sinister in the air of Bristol Town, the miasma of fear. Bristol could afford no police force, and each man policed his own space as best he could. Death by violence left rotting corpses in random corners. Armed bands of demobbed soldiers looted, following the example set by the nobility, who had spent the time since the Hundred Years War busily killing one another off in a dynastic struggle between Lancastrian and Yorkist forces called the Wars of the Roses. It was hardly two years since the House of York had prevailed, with handsome Edward IV now on the throne. Tristram tried to explain it all to me but the only part I grasped was that the House of Lancaster, now the 'outs', were the descendants of John of Gaunt, which brought me back to The O'Gaunt, the object of our search.

On the fifth night, Tristram failed to join me at the Plank & Anchor to start our rounds. I asked Jenny the barmaid, 'Has Tristram left a message for me?'

'Who?'

'Tristram, a Student,' I said.

'Nope.'

'You sure?'

'Didn't I fucking well say so?'

Tristram did not return that night to her rooms on the heights of Clifton. The next day I searched the streets of Bristol. Remember that there were no police. If a loved one vanished, the only recourse was to find him/her yourself. But there might be some simple explanation for Tristram's absence and I didn't really begin to worry until the second night, when she was again a no-show both at the Plank & Anchor and at her lodgings.

'Didn't I fucking well say so?' said Jenny the barmaid in answer to my question.

'Rent was due day before yesterday,' glowered the innkeeper in Clifton, in answer to the same.

First thing the next morning I went to the laboratory of Magister Tom Norton the alchemist.

The one word to describe Tom Norton was ordinary. He was neither tall nor short, not noticeably fat or thin, nor did he have any identifying scars or marks. His nose was ordinary, his mouth just a mouth, his gaze neither commanding nor deferential. He was your average Englishman, a real get-lost-in-a-crowd type, who happened to be wearing a frayed laboratory smock.

'It's bad enough not to look the part,' he told me, apparently aware of my appraisal, 'but who'll take seriously an alchemist named Tom Norton? Now, if I were called Zosimos Rhazes or Melchior Tetragammaton, there's no telling how far I'd go. Can you start right away?'

'I'm looking for Tristram,' I said.

'Run off on me. College kids, summer jobs, what can you expect? It never works out. *You're* not one, are you?'

I said I was not.

'Well, think of our work as a sort of chemical mysticism or mystical chemistry, and we'll get on fine.'

Tom Norton bent over a crucible on a low table. In it a thick grayish liquid was boiling furiously but I saw no fire heating it. 'The basest of base metals, lead,' he told me. 'Molten, of course.'

The laboratory stank like rotten eggs, only worse, of putrefaction perhaps. From the crucible, tubes extended to a dome-shaped glass receptacle that would collect and, I assumed, condense the vapors being distilled.

'The aim being, of course,' said Tom Norton, 'to transmute base lead to gold. But forget your secret herbs, your mastic and other gums, forget mandrake, wax, honey, wine, arsenic, vitriol, urine, jism — these are added to the boil only by charlatans. No, my boy, all that is required is the philosopher's stone.' In his now trembling hand he held a disappointingly small something about the shape and size of a pigeon's egg. But it drew my eyes as a lodestone draws the iron needle of a compass. Saffron-colored, it gleamed like highly polished glass. It seemed to glow with an inner fire or life.

'Fire and life are one,' said ordinary-looking Tom Norton. 'Take the burning of wood. When you burn it, which is to say kill it, the corpse of wood is ash, and the smoke and flame which rise from the pyre are the living spirits of the wood. Every substance on God's earth, or off it for that matter, is composed in certain fixed proportions — '

'Tristram,' I began, but he overrode my concerned voice with his ordinary one.

' – of a few basic building blocks. These are, so the ancients told us, earth, air, fire, water. Right? Wrong. You have to keep up with the journals. Four's now three. Mercury or quicksilver, sulphur, salt. That's the lot of them, and never mind that Lucretian nonsense about atoms and so forth. Sulphur's soul, male, fire. Salt's body, female, earth. And mercury? Mercury's spirit, androgynous, and both air *and* water. Mercury, you see, has a doubly dual nature. So the basic three are actually four or possibly even five. It's not easy, keeping up with the journals, believe me.'

'Yes, but have you seen Tristram?'

Overriding my concern again, ordinary Tom Norton said, 'Now, it follows that, from understanding the basic elements, the adept can change anything into any other thing, simply by altering the proportions of those elements. Here, for example, the classic case of lead-into-gold. Well, I think we're ready.'

Tom Norton passed the philosopher's stone three times around the crucible, muttering, 'Eight ounces of lead to produce sixteen-hundredths of an ounce, which is to say two-thirds of a grain, of pure gold.'

As he spoke the crucible shattered, the molten matter therein, now congealed into a leaden lump, fell heavily to the table, and from the cracked dome-shaped glass receptacle he plucked with tweezers a tiny gleaming golden speck.

'The problem, of course,' he sighed, 'is quantity. What can you do with two-thirds of a grain of gold? Why, the equipment alone's worth more, and the transmutation destroys the crucible and damages the glass dome every time. Well, we'll solve the quantity problem, I know we will. Some day,' he said dispiritedly. 'Now clean up this mess, will you?'

'*I'm* WORRIED *about* TRISTRAM!' I shouted at the top of my voice, and just as Magister Tom Norton asked, 'Why didn't you say so?' there was a crashing sound, the door burst off its hinges and flew into the room, smashing what laboratory equipment was still intact, and three ruffians armed to the teeth crowded through the splintered doorframe.

'We're worried about her too, fellow,' their leader said, 'and we're paid to worry. You're coming with us.'

Each of them outweighed me twice, and among them they had more daggers and swords, lances and muskets, than a small army. At such times audacity simply doesn't pay. I went peacefully.

Outside the laboratory they hustled me into a waiting coach. A crowd had gathered, for coaches were still a novelty, having been invented only a decade or so earlier by a Hungarian in the village of Kokz, pronounced more or less 'coach', just as the sedan chair was invented in Sedan, France, and the limousine would be invented in the Limousin, that is, the region of Limoges, etc. Two horses stood in the traces, whip in hand the coachman sat above, and before we climbed into the vehicle a blanket was thrown over my head.

'Drawing and quartering's too good for him!' cried the crowd, possibly mistaking me for Magister Tom Norton the alchemist, whose laboratory added its decided stench to those others I have mentioned and on occasion, usually at night, produced loud explosions.

I was tumbled, blinded by the blanket, to the floor of the coach, the three seated ruffians using me for a foot rest. The coachman cracked his whip and we were off, the coach pitching and yawing like a small boat adrift on the Ocean Sea.

Who they were I never learned, nor precisely whom they served. When the coach stopped and they led me across a courtyard and down a flight of stone stairs, where the blanket was removed from my head, I found myself in a large dungeonlike room lit by torches in sconces, its walls seeping moisture and overgrown with thick green mold.

The three ruffians stationed themselves so that without turning my head I could see only one of them at a time. It was the fourth man in the room, however, who drew my attention. He was somewhere in his middle years, sepulchrally thin, with a face like parchment, a robe of unrelieved black, and a desiccated manner somehow more disturbing than the obvious menace of the three ruffians.

'The interests we represent,' he began in a parched voice, 'have charged us to see that no harm shall befall a certain party. What makes the problem awkward is that the party is no longer within reach of Royal justice but is now to be found among the most disputatious people that ever walked the face of the earth, the Irish.

'Our reasons are more sentimental than dynastic, for the party in question is a bastard, though I use the word in a progenitive, not a pejorative, sense.

'To fill you in dynastically:

'John of Gaunt, Duke of Lancaster and fourth son of King Edward III, had three wives, sequentially of course: Blanche who was his cousin, Constance who was heiress to the kingdoms of Castile and León in Spain, and finally Catherine the widow Swynford. These don't interest us.'

Oh God, I thought, not another genealogy!

'John of Gaunt also had a number of fecund overlapping mistresses. Of these we are only concerned with Margaret. Now Margaret bore Louisa, who married one Roger Brand with whom she produced two daughters, the elder of whom married an Irishman of Norse descent with whom she in turn ... '

The desiccated voice droned on and I had a strong sense of *déjà vu*. Of course: befuddled old Captain Perestrello with his genealogical imperative that had brought me to England in search of the The O'Gaunt and had deposited me in this very dungeon to listen to another genealogy.

' ... at The Queen's College, Oxford, calling herself Tristram, a Student,' said the dusty voice, and my eyes deglazed.

'Which brings us,' he said, 'to you.'

'Now, you have two options, and only two.'

'Here is the first.' He unrolled Bartolomeo's map, which the ruffians must have taken from Tom Norton's laboratory. 'You take this map personally to Galway where you present it to The O'Gaunt – '

'*Present* it to him? He offered to buy it. A thousand pounds, cash on the barrelhead.'

' – in exchange for the safe passage back to England of Mistress Isolde, a/k/a Tristram, a Student.'

'She's with The O'Gaunt?' I cried. 'In Ireland?'

'Kidnapped. Held to ransom for your map.'

'But why? I'd have sold it to him,' I said, and wondered if I would have.

'For a thousand pounds sterling, I believe you said?'

The three ruffians, two of them unseen, laughed raucously.

'The O'Gaunt,' said the dusty voice, 'never had his hands on as much as a hundred quid at once. He's a small-time crook, our principals believe, who outrageously employs as *nom de guerre* an illustrious name to which he has no right. Simply put, the offer was a come-on. You have been the victim of a swizz.' The skeletal figure leaned toward me and unrolled a sheet of vellum.

'Is this document from the Vatican authentic?'

It took a moment for me to remember what is was. 'Oh, sure. It's authentic.'

'Well, how you contrived to get it from Cardinal Borgia is no concern of ours, Cristóbal.'

Not Master Cristóbal, as form required. Just Cristóbal, the voice of authority speaking with the degrading familiarity they always use.

'We suggest you arrange your own passage through the merchant bank of Centurione, Bristol branch, so that our connection does not become known and jeopardize the rescue of Mistress Isolde.'

I thought a moment. 'You mentioned two options. What's the second?'

'The second is simpler put. If you refuse, we kill you here and now.'

Less than an hour later a flunky showed me into the office of the director of the House of Centurione, Merchant Bankers, Bristol branch. It was a small office, meagerly furnished. The bank itself shared with tooth pullers, astrologers and other questionable types a dilapidated building between Stone Bridge and the harbor.

The director sprang to his feet. 'I know you!' he cried.

I looked at the tufts of hair sprouting from his ears and nostrils like small brushes. 'Pighi-Zampini!' I said, as surprised as he.

After his first enthusiasm at seeing a familiar face, he became morose. 'No more Genoa, no more Governor of the House of Centurione, no more Italian Renaissance. They finally caught me with my hand in the till. I was lucky to be kept on at all, even in a backwater like England. But after I was so helpful to you in Genoa, Cardinal Borgia had to put in a word for me. What can I do for you this time?'

I told him of my need for swift passage to Galway, Ireland.

'No problem. Centurione's bankrolls a fleet of merchantmen sailing from Genoa as far as the Faroes and even Iceland. Galway's a regular port of call. Now, what's your preference? Depending on what they want to pay, some folks take small ships, boats really. Say, a two-masted Provençal felucca or a naviguela of thirty-five or forty tons. Can't recommend them myself. All that pitching, rolling and yawing about. Same's true of a caravel, a hundred tons max. A barque would – '

I interrupted this set speech, not quite shouting. 'I want the first available transportation and I won't pay a farthing. Plus, you owe me eleven gold ducats, which I'll take now in local currency.'

'You've changed, young man,' sighed Pighi-Zampini.

He hadn't, but I saw no need to tell him so.

I sailed on a galleass of close to a thousand tons that, four days later, dropped anchor in Galway Bay.

This was early August, and the herring fleet was just leaving Claddagh quay heading south, a hundred currachs or more, those strange small deep-water boats of warped laths covered with tarred canvas that look so unseaworthy yet can ride out the fiercest westerly better than many a merchantman ten times their size. Legend has it that St Brendan in the sixth century sailed in a currach across the Ocean Sea to the very Ireland the Great which magically appeared on Bartolomeo's map and brought me here to Galway. But I would learn that the legend of St Brendan was typical Irish mismanagement of fact.

Legend also has it — are you ready? — that I, Cristóbal Colón, before sailing west across the Ocean Sea from the southern coast of Spain in 1492 stepped ashore on Claddagh quay right here in Galway from my flagship *Santa Maria* to pray in the church of St Nicholas of Myra for a safe voyage to America. I don't have to tell you how many things are wrong with *that* legend!

But strange to say, when I did step ashore at Claddagh quay, after watching the priests bless the herring fleet and then climb aboard to sail with the currachs past the Aran Islands to where the herrings run, I sought a church and it was St Nicholas of Myra I found. Perhaps the priests sailing forth with the fleet inspired me. I was until that time not a notable churchgoer, Cardinal Borgia and the whole Roman curia having amply demonstrated that religion is more politics than faith. Whatever, I went inside and knelt in the dimness. An intense longing for Tristram shook me; it was suddenly inconceivable that I could live without her, and I prayed to the Christ and His Blessed Mother that I would find my love unharmed and take her with me wherever I might go.

Outside I blinked in the sunlight, a phenomenon rarer in the west of Ireland even than in Bristol Town. In my religious transport I credited it to the priests sailing with the herring fleet.

A considerable crowd had gathered in the square before St Nicholas of Myra, the men wearing belted tunics to their knees, hoods thrown back, or loose sacklike surcoats, the women simple kirtles and hairnets. I mention this because such garb hadn't been seen in more civilized parts of the world since my grandfather was a child.

At the center of their attention slumped a drunken beggar in filthy rags towered over by a friar wearing the brown robe of a Franciscan. The friar wore no tonsure; his blond hair hung long and free. His face, which would have been handsome in a sort of pretty way except for the gleam of madness in his aquamarine eyes, seemed hauntingly familiar, yet I knew I'd never seen him before.

'Take it,' he said in Latin, 'I don't need it.' Even his melodious voice sounded familiar.

The drunken beggar shook his head. Perhaps the Latin was incomprehensible to him, or perhaps he didn't want to take it, whatever it was.

'I'd like you to have it,' insisted the almost pretty friar with the wild eyes.

'Oh my, oh yes indeed,' wheezed a toothless old man near me, speaking not Gaelic but English for the benefit of the foreigners in the crowd, Galway being the most cosmopolitan town in Ireland. 'Oh my, he'll be after doing it again, Brother Brendan will. You women there, don't you be looking now!'

But the women certainly were looking.

'The clothing off his back, he'll do it every time,' predicted another man in the crowd.

'Oh, and I do hope so,' said a comely young woman eagerly.

At that moment the Franciscan friar tugged at the beggar's filthy rags, which came loose in his hands along with a quantity of fleas, and before the beggar could be shamed in his washboard-ribbed, pendulous-bellied, wizened-membered, scrawny-shanked nakedness, the friar with a swirling motion whipped off his own robe and with it covered the man. For a moment the obsoletely dressed crowd was silent, then the oohs and ahs of the women competed with the more forthright comments of the men. The friar called Brother Brendan, naked as his Lord made him, had a classically beautiful male body.

'Sure and he fancies himself St Francis,' said one man.

'That he's not,' laughed another. 'He's just the crazy hermit Brother Brendan.'

'But man, the dong on him,' said the first enviously.

St Francis of Assisi, you'll remember, was so obviously holy that the often laggard Sacred Congregation of Rites canonized him just two short years after his death in 1226. And it was equally obvious that poor demented Brother Brendan had taken it on himself to relive certain episodes in the hagiography of St Francis, for example giving his robe to a beggar and flashing in the process. In the beautiful stories of the saint, called *The Little Flowers*, his constant companion Brother Leo was always ready with a spare garment and, sure enough, a second Franciscan carrying a brown robe rushed through the crowd to cover Brother Brendan's nakedness. 'Some days,' said the second Franciscan, panting, 'when he comes down from his hermitage between the mountains of Slieve Aughty and the River Suck – how the birds do love him there! – some days it's impossible to keep him clothed for half an hour together. He's a saint, he is.'

'But in the body of a pagan god,' breathed the comely young woman who had hoped Brother Brendan would disrobe.

The two friars walked off, Brother Brendan less wild-eyed than before. 'Twice the size of your ordinary currach, and I'll give her three coats of tar,' he was telling the other Franciscan earnestly as they passed me, 'so what are you worrying about?'

'Dress warmly,' advised the other with a resigned sigh.

If there was much talk in Galway that summer about Brother Brendan, there was more about The O'Gaunt.

'The O'Gaunt's back,' men would say in tones of satisfaction tinged with fear.

'Where is he?' I would ask.

'Told you. Back.' And they would look at me suspiciously.

I persisted. 'Alone?'

'Back. He's back,' they informed me.

The Irish are the world's greatest talkers, unless it suits them better to keep their mouths shut.

Galway is no large town; you can circumambulate its stone walls in an hour. I took lodgings and searched every street and lane within those walls and, in the days that followed, explored the countryside from Lough Corrib north of town to the River Suck and the Slieve Aughty mountains in the east (where I stumbled on the abandoned hermitage of Brother Brendan and, at the time, thought nothing of it) and as far as the River Shannon in the south. But I could find no one who would admit to having seen The O'Gaunt or who would harbor any opinion except that he was back.

To the east across Galway Bay lay the Aran Islands: Inisheer, Inishmaan and Inishmore. Sometimes I would stand on the crown of Salt Hill outside the walls and gaze at those storied isles, as if somehow I sensed that the *faege* or doom Tristram so dreaded awaited us there.

Although I found no trace of The O'Gaunt, I heard enough about him to fill a good-sized book. He was the Robin Hood of Ireland, stealing the British blind in the Pale around Dublin Town and distributing the booty among the poor tenant farmers, absentee landlordism being Ireland's chief lament, as you could hear sung to the accompaniment of a thirty-stringed harp on any street in Galway. He also disappeared for months on end traveling to far places. And of course from time to time he was 'back'.

He was back now. And with him that half-fearful anticipation that I observed everywhere.

Why? In a word, or a name: Lynch.

The Lynch clan, largest in Galway and most powerful in all Connaught, controlled the town so completely that they regarded any challenge to their preeminence as lese-majesty, and even a Brother Brendan with his head in the clouds and his robe on a beggar would know that The O'Gaunt was the biggest challenge of all.

Padraic Lynch, the young hothead of the clan, lived for those times The O'Gaunt was back. Padraic Lynch had vowed to kill the Robin Hood of the British Pale, but not before desexing him with a razor-sharp knife he kept whetted just for that purpose. On a previous occasion when he was back, The O'Gaunt had seduced Deirdre Lynch, Padraic's wife. But so far Padraic Lynch had no better success at finding The O'Gaunt than I did.

This Lynch clan meant business. Whether a matter of law or the Irish equivalent of a vendetta, if they said a thing needed doing, they did it. In evidence I offer one James Lynch, son of Padraic, who would be elected mayor of Galway in 1493, the year of my Second Voyage. It was the fate of the Lynch clan, despite its power, to choose weak-willed women. James's son Walter, on seeing his fiancée in the embrace of a houseguest (who, strange to relate, was a Spanish captain off a Centurione ship), murdered the man with one swordthrust. Walter was condemned to death but, as he was a Lynch, the terrified hangman refused to perform his duty. Mayor Lynch, the condemned man's father, dismissing the hangman on the spot, executed his own son and six short months later married the girl who had caused all the trouble.

If you are reading the English-language edition of this book, I might point out that the term 'lynch law' derives from these happenings.

One afternoon toward the middle of September I was returning along the shore from my strange vigil on Salt Hill when a sudden westerly struck. Soon the bay was lashed to foaming froth, the daylight faded, currachs at what had seemed safe anchor were smashed to splinters on the rocks. I ran along the strand for the town gate, pelted by hailstones as big as hen's eggs and almost knocked flat by the wildly gusting wind. One small currach had been beached and weighted down with stones. As I approached I saw a man in an old-fashioned cloak, billowed out by the wind, struggling with a large bundle as he tried to reach the vessel. Thinking to persuade this maniac not to embark until the westerly let up, I ran toward the pounding surf. The fool had already reached the currach, removed the stones, deposited his bundle and dragged the light canvas boat half into the water.

'Are you crazy, you'll get yourself killed out there,' I shouted, and as he turned suddenly I recognized Tristram.

An agonized look on her dear drenched face, she leaped into the currach without a word. I waded in pursuit. Had this been a straight stretch of coastline, I might have stopped her. But the coast south of Galway is all bays and inlets and coves, and this one twisted back on itself, facing almost east, so that the howling westerly drove the currach swiftly out to sea.

Splashing to my chest in the furious surf, I cried Tristram's name. 'Isolde!' I cried.

But Tristram dipped an oar (at least she wasn't foolhardy enough to raise sail) and soon the currach was a small black dot on the face of the deep.

Shivering, I returned to the strand, where I saw a figure darting into the bracken. I was too exhausted to give chase, so I didn't learn then who he was – though to this day I'm not sure it would have made a difference.

The next morning the wind was down and Galway Bay glassy calm under a blue sky. On Claddagh quay I rented an old currach too small to sail with the herring fleet and somewhat battered by the storm, but sound enough to take me across thirty miles of bay to the Aran Islands. The tarred canvas boat rode high in the water and responded so easily to the tiller that I could almost believe St Brendan had sailed across the Ocean Sea 900 years earlier in a larger model.

I carried Bartolomeo's map with me, and high hopes. Inishmore, largest of the three Aran Islands, was scarcely fifteen miles long and never more than three wide, and Inisheer and Inishmaan were tiny by comparison. All were sparsely populated by fishermen and subsistence farmers. Here and there, often in crumbling prehistoric forts, lived a religious hermit or two. Surely I must find my Tristram soon. Strangers would attract attention on these changeless, rocky, inhospitable islands.

I tried Inishmore first (and, as it turned out, last), beaching the small currach near the wee village of Kilronan and weighting it with stones as I had seen Tristram undo. Three fishermen watching from the reeds at the head of the inlet disappeared with scarcely a rustle when I hailed them. I walked into Kilronan. Except for the blue haze of hearth smoke, it could have been deserted. I knocked at all ten locked doors of all ten rude cottages. Scurryings could be heard inside, like giant mice at play, but no door opened.

I walked up the hill of Kilronan's single street and into open country. There were large rocks everywhere and from behind one darted a hermit recognizable by his stout walking stick, his unkempt white hair and beard, his tattered robe and the huge wooden pectoral cross he wore. He circled me, head aslant and nostrils aquiver like a hound appraising a stranger.

'You wouldn't be looking for guidance of the spiritual variety?' he asked hopefully.

'No, I'm looking for Tristram.'

He at once raised his stout staff protectively to port-arms and shouted, 'I don't know anything about any Tristram or Isolde or none of them!' before running off.

I hurried after him as he mounted a steep goatpath to what had once been a watchtower on a headland but was now a tumbledown pile of rocks. I thought he would try to lose me there but instead he climbed the largest rock and gazed seaward.

'Thought so,' he said. 'Here they come.'

I joined him.

'And I don't know anything about any O'Gaunt, neither,' he said.

In the bay, half-way from the mainland to Inishmore and coming hard, I saw a fleet of currachs, black dots tipped with white sails on blue water.

'Who are they?' I asked.

'Lynches. Half the goddamn clan and you can bet your boots Padraic's got that knife he always keeps whetted. Not that I know anything about it,' he added quickly and asked me: 'Where you from, anyway?'

'Spain,' I said. 'I'm just a Spanish sailor.'

'Imagine that,' he said, trying to. 'They got Christians there?'

I assured him they did.

'You sure you don't need guidance of the spiritual variety? I'm a Seventh Day Inventist.'

'Inventist?'

'Take this staff, for example.' He grasped his stout walking stick near the top and unscrewed a six-inch length, from which a cork protruded. When he pulled it I smelled raw distilled spirits. 'Neat, ain't it? I got a cave full of similar inventions.' He tipped the six-inch length of staff to his lips, then wiped them with the back of one gnarled hand.

The fleet of currachs was noticeably closer.

He offered me the length of staff and I tilted it as he had. Liquid fire spilled down my throat. I coughed. My eyes streamed.

'A *man's* drink.' He laughed gleefully. 'You should have seen poor Tristram when she ... oh shit! If that ain't gone and done it.'

'Where is she?'

'They won't take kindly to intruders.'

I drew the sword I always wore at my side since my run-in with the Brotherhood of the Golden Stag (or Hind).

'All right, all right, keep your sword on,' he told me, and I girded it.

'Up there on Dun Aengus,' he said, pointing west. Silhouetted against the sky on the opposite side of the island I could see what looked like a circular stone fort.

I thanked him and swiftly set out in that direction.

'Wait,' he called after me. 'You better know she's with The O'Gaunt.'

That only made me run faster. I covered the two miles of rock-strewn terrain in a quarter of an hour, climbing steadily until I could see that the circular fort stood on the island's highest cliff at the very edge of the Ocean Sea. I had clambered through the first defense perimeter, a horse-trap of wickedly pointed, almost man-sized stones set close in the ground like giant teeth, then passed through an archway in the outer wall of unmortared stone and another in the inner wall, when I heard a scream.

'Master Cristóbal, no!'

Tristram stood thirty feet above me on a catwalk near the top of the wall. Calling my name she saved my life, for what I thought a round stone fort proved to be only a semi-circular one, its seaward half having weathered away leaving a sheer drop at my very feet.

In her billowing cloak, her long blonde hair hanging free, Tristram came running down from the catwalk.

'You've come,' she cried. 'You've come, Master Cristóbal. I prayed you would, and I prayed you wouldn't ever since – '

But she could say no more until I finished kissing her.

She withdrew from the circle of my arms, tears welling in her sea-green eyes. 'You mustn't stay,' she said.

'I know The O'Gaunt's holding you to ransom for Bartolomeo's map,' I said. 'Did you think for even a minute I'd refuse? Where is he?'

'You don't understand.'

A voice rose faintly from somewhere below: 'Did you call, darling?'

'No, it was only the wind,' Tristram shouted back. Tears were bright on her cheeks as she swiftly removed from her finger a gold ring in the shape of two hands clasping a heart. 'Take it and go,' she said. 'I'll always love you, Master Cristóbal. Take my Claddagh love-ring to remember me and go quickly now.'

Buffeted by the wind, I stepped to the edge of the cliff where Dun

Aengus's seaward defenses had once stood, and looked down. A steep path descended the cliff. In a cove at the bottom bobbed a currach of impressive size. A blond man in a brown robe was loading it with cases and jars.

'The O'Gaunt?' I asked when Tristram came up behind me.

'You don't understand how it is,' she said.

'I understand that Padraic Lynch is sailing here with twenty currachs full of armed men and they'll round the south end of the island within half an hour.'

'Oh God!' she cried. 'So soon?'

At her anguished words, the man far below looked up and his voice rose again. 'Did you call, darling?'

I stepped back quickly from the edge of the cliff and told Tristram, 'I've a currach on the other side of the island. We can still get away.'

She shouted into the teeth of the wind, 'It's only the gulls you hear!' and indeed gulls by the dozens soared overhead with wings motionless on the stiff wind.

She told me, 'Go quickly then. I can't. My *faege*, my doom, is here.'

'He didn't kidnap you – you came willingly, didn't you?' I accused her, my heart as heavy as the lead that had fallen from Magister Tom Norton's crucible.

'You don't understand,' she said.

Below us on the shingle beach as he loaded the currach the brown-robed man was singing in a pure tenor voice, half his words swept away by the wind.

> Be Thou praised, my Lord, with all Thy creatures,
>   above all Brother Sun, who gives the day ...
> Be Thou praised, my Lord, of Sister Moon and the stars ...
>   of Brother Wind ...
> Be Thou praised ... of Sister Water,
>   ... of Brother Fire,
>   beautiful and ... strong ...
>   of Sister Mother Earth
>   which sustains ...
> Be Thou praised, my Lord ...
>   endure ... tribulations ...

And finally that pure tenor voice sang, as if he already knew:

> Be praised, Lord, for our Sister Death,
>   from whom no man can escape.

Tristram was crying openly now. She came into my arms and I held her against me hard.

'Would you take him with us?' she asked.

'It's you I came for,' I told her, 'just as The O'Gaunt did. Choose.'

'But don't you see? I love you, I *do* love you. Can't you try to understand? He's not quite right in the head, the poor lad. I *have to* care for him.'

'Choose,' I said coldly.

'Don't ask me to do what I cannot, I beg you, Master Cristóbal.'

'And do you lie with him too?' I asked, my voice ice.

'Oh please – that's a question you mustn't ask.'

Then she withdrew a second and last time from my arms and I went again to the cliff edge and saw that The O'Gaunt had begun to mount the steep path. He must have seen me too, for he climbed faster.

I drew the sword I'd worn at my side ever since my run-in with the Brotherhood of the Golden Stag (or Hind).

'Don't! Oh, Master Cristóbal, for God's sake don't, for he won't defend himself.'

I felt drained as I sheathed the sword. She cared nothing for me, I thought, despite her words. She feared only for her lover, The O'Gaunt.

He reached the top of the cliff and stood an instant tall in his brown robe.

I staggered back in amazement. 'But – it's Brother Brendan!'

While we stared at each other, Tristram said tonelessly: 'Yes, today. Sometimes he fancies himself St Brendan. Sometimes St Francis of Assisi. John's helpless without me. It's my *faege* to care for him.'

It took me a moment to realize that by 'John' she meant The O'Gaunt.

'But why?'

The simple question seemed to confuse her. 'I don't know,' she admitted after a while. 'It just is.'

'He's *not* St Brendan and he's *not* St Francis,' I persisted, 'he's just plain Brother Brendan who lives in a cave between the mountains of Slieve Aughty and the River Suck, and there's a real Franciscan brother who takes care of him.'

'Brother Brendan is only his disguise,' Tristram explained.

'Wrong,' he corrected her petulantly, and for the first time I now saw the maniacal gleam I'd seen in Brother Brendan's aquamarine eyes that day outside St Nicholas of Myra when he gave his robe to a beggar. 'Wrong, wrong, wrong! *The O'Gaunt is my disguise!*'

'Dear God,' Tristram said softly.

I had no time to consider which of them was right, for suddenly I knew where I had heard his melodious voice before.

'You were the Doubting Thomas at the eclipse of the moon at the Sprawling Navigational Complex at Cape St Vincent in Portugal,' I accused him.

'True, true. But I've learned much since then thanks to Mistress Isolde.'

That raised another question. The voice I knew, but why did he *look* so familiar?

They stood side by side, ranged against me. So much for her deceitful words, her perfidious kisses, her artful swiving.

From the edge of the cliff I saw the first of Padraic Lynch's currachs rounding the point. Turning, I slapped Bartolomeo's tightly rolled map into the hand of Brother Brendan/The O'Gaunt. 'Try to outrun them. Hurry!'

He held the map. He looked at Tristram, bewildered that the moment had come so swiftly.

She spoke to me one last time. 'I have to go with him, Master Cristóbal. I wish it could have been otherwise.'

She raised one arm, as if she might reach out and touch me, but it dropped to her side.

Then hand in hand they went down the steep path together.

For a long moment I stood there dumbly watching the fleet of Padraic Lynch approach, and then all at once I knew.

I couldn't let her go with him, live with him, because *she didn't know*.

But what could I do?

Whatever I did would be the wrong thing.

I was trapped in a *faege* not my own.

Recklessly I plunged down the steep path, ignoring certain death if I fell. Swiftly I closed the gap between us, but when it was clear I would overtake them before the bottom, Brother Brendan/The O'Gaunt stopped, stooped, straightened, turned and made a hurling motion.

The stone crashed against the side of my head and I tumbled into limbo.

Tristram might have screamed, but it could have been the crying of the gulls.

I regained my senses in the golden light of the westing sun. Bright spots danced before my eyes as I struggled to my feet on the narrow path clinging to the face of the cliff. I touched the side of my head, felt blood-matted hair over a throbbing bump. I looked out to sea. Of Padraic Lynch's fleet of twenty currachs I saw nothing. Then I looked below.

What delayed them in their attempt to escape I never learned. I like to think that Tristram tried to climb back up to where I had fallen, but that he hadn't let her. Their currach still bobbed in the cove on a line made fast to a rock spire. I went down the rest of the way slowly.

Some supplies still remained on the shingle, waiting with inanimate patience to be loaded aboard. It was I who finished provisioning the currach for its long journey, Brother Brendan's journey to Ireland the Great. He lay draped face-down over a gunwale, brown robe stripped from his body, long blond hair streaming into the water. I turned him over gently and eased him into the boat. Once and quickly I looked at the lower part of him. The knife Padraic Lynch kept whetted for the purpose had been used. I went forward in the currach to Tristram. Unlike his staring aquamarine eyes, her own sea-green eyes were shut as if she were sleeping. Her long blonde hair fanned on a crate of provisions. The wood is hard, I thought, it will hurt her. I moved her head but could find no soft place to rest it. Then I saw her cloak crumpled in the bottom of the boat and I folded it and on the soft wool I pillowed her head. There was no wound I could see, but her body was already cold. I put the Claddagh love-ring on her finger.

I stood for a moment not knowing what I must do, the sea wind strong on my face as the sun touched the horizon. And then I did know. Near Brother Brendan's body I found Bartolomeo's map. I tore it across and across again, gathering the dry parchment in a pile. Then I searched among Brother Brendan's provisions for what I needed, and found the oil and the flint and steel. The currach with its sleeping passengers had to sail, and I knew that somehow it would, despite the wind that blew from the sea.

I raised the single sail and felt how the boat strained. I uncorked the flagon of oil and emptied it on what had been Bartolomeo's map. Then, about to strike flint against steel, I paused. The thing still wasn't right.

I went back to where I had tipped Brother Brendan into the boat, and lifted him and carried him to where Isolde lay waiting. I placed him close to her. But the setting sun turned his aquamarine eyes a baleful crimson and that wasn't right either. I shut his eyes and leaned over Isolde to kiss the half-smile on her lips. I stood back and the wind spoke. Not right, not right, not right, it said.

So I did one final thing and then I ignited what had been Bartolomeo's map and released the line that held the straining currach to the rock spire.

The currach swung to windward, miraculously the sail filled and the boat raced from the cove hard into the teeth of the wind toward the setting sun. I saw a tendril of smoke, then another. Tarred canvas would burn swiftly, yet I could see no flames against the great orange ball of the sun.

But when the sun was down, in the twilight the boat too had vanished.

And Brother Brendan and Isolde sailed west as I had placed them — lying side by side in one another's arms like sleeping children, the same long blond hair, the same sea-green eyes forever shut, the same, the same, like the brother and sister they were.

≈ IV ≈

*Being the Shortest Chapter of This Book
In Which, However, the Most Time Passes
and the Great Venture Is Born*

In those days we still went by the Julian calendar, its Gregorian successor not coming into use anywhere for a hundred years and more, not until Pope Gregory XIII's decree of 1582. The Julian calendar's year was 365¼ days long which, Gregory's calendar commission would determine, was 11 min. 10 sec. too much. Gregory lopped off ten days with one cut of his papal authority, subtracting them forever from time and advancing the spring equinox to 21 March. Previously, equinoxes and other key dates tended to wander all over the map of time, with periodic adjustments. For example, the spring equinox fell on 25 March when Julius Caesar crossed the Rubicon to rule Rome (and give us the Julian calendar) but would fall on 11 March when Pope Gregory did his papal hatchet job on time's map.

I can see the need for year-in, year-out precision in a more rigorously scientific age than mine. But I *like* the Julian calendar, for all its bumbling inaccuracies.

The Julian calendar, in its very waywardness, somehow captures the essence of time.

For, have you ever found two years to be of the same duration?

No, some years, while you live them, soar by on wings of eagles. And some limp painfully along like lame tortoises.

And the eagle years, when you look back on them, aren't they filled paradoxically with long, full, richly memorable days? While the tortoise years, aren't they a blur of days without meaning, unmemorable and unremembered?

Time lived and time remembered are not the same.

I'll always like the Julian calendar. It understands.

After Tristram's death I spent most of ten years in the far North trying to forget her, but looking back on those years they seem a single long night's dream in someone else's unlived life.

What I sought was impossible – that time move backwards, that Tristram be undead.

But if I could no more escape from the tyranny of time than any other man, I was a sailor and I could escape into the freedom of geography.

I have referred here to the 'map of time', and that's no accident. Days, months, years – these are time's coordinates that locate a moment as precisely as latitude and longitude locate a place. My escape was from one map into the other, and it saved my sanity. I struck the shackles of time with the limitless horizons of space. To replace Tristram, if anything ever could, I found the sea – the Ocean Sea.

And I found the Great Venture.

As mountains rise precipitously from a skilled mapmaker's two-dimensional chart, or a sudden hush in the voice of a gifted saga-teller signals the high point of his tale, so certain memories have etched themselves sharply in that blur of geographical time, that Julian decade I spent on the northern rim of the Ocean Sea.

How did I get there? Cardinal Borgia's letter to the House of Centurione obtained for me, through the good offices of Pighi-Zampini in Bristol Town, a rating in the Genoese fleet plying between the Mediterranean and Iceland. Not that I went the entire way. I stayed north. Many sailors in those days found England plenty north enough, and if some fool wanted to replace them for the run from Bristol to Galway, the Faroe Islands and far Iceland, why, he was welcome to it.

These were big galleases and roundships, and they carried rich cargo – Levantine silver, copper, spices, cotton, silk, the exotic (and scurvy-preventing, as would be understood later) oranges and lemons of the Mediterranean. From the north in return went English fabrics – linen, serge, kerseys – and those Icelandic specialities, whalebone and salt cod.

I wish I could say that the Great Venture came roaring into my mind like a fierce westerly. But it didn't. It came uncertainly and almost sneakily at first, like the early warning tendrils of fog before the fogbank moves at you like a cliff. It came with talk of stepping-stones one day in Thorshaven, capital of the Faroe Islands, while my Genoese roundship was careened to have her seams caulked. Picture the harbor on Stromo Island, midway between England and Iceland, rainclouds scudding low and emptying on drenched Thorshaven as they did most days of the year. Picture a rocky landscape, treeless and − well, northern. And feel the cold, although it was (if memory serves) a day in earliest autumn. The sailor, an Icelander of Irish ancestry like not a few of that hardy breed, was one Harald Flakehair, so nicknamed for his unfortunate dandruff. We met in a seamen's tavern. 'What brings you to the northern edge of the world?' he said to me in a strange variety of English. By then I could understand any accent if I put my mind to it. 'Oh, distance is nothing to a Spanish sailor,' I said. He motioned for two more tankards of strong Danish ale. 'Been here long?' We both knew that by 'here' he meant not Thorshaven but the far north of the Ocean Sea. I shrugged. 'At least you can go home when you want,' he said. 'Last I heard, Spain's still there. Not like Greenland.' He gestured vaguely westward. 'She's gone, you know. Clean gone, left not a wrack behind. Just like Wineland a few centuries back. Makes a fellow wonder what's going to go next.' I asked him what he meant by Greenland being gone, and he dipped a finger in his ale and drew on the plank table. 'Here's Europe. That itty-bitty part down there's Spain and Portugal and the other itty-bitty one's Italy. Here's England.' The further north his finger drew, the bigger things got. 'Here's the Faroes where we are, here's Iceland, and this is where Greenland ought to be.' His wet finger stabbed the plank table. 'Then from what I hear, if you keep following the sun west, there's another island or two and then you're in Asia.'

I let Asia go at the time. 'What do you mean, where Greenland *ought* to be?'

'What I said. Ought to. But she's not. And if we can't even find Greenland any more, how can we find out what's beyond? We've lost our stepping-stone, if you see what I mean.'

I saw what he meant, but I still wanted to know what had happened to Greenland.

'What happened to Greenland?' I asked, but he couldn't tell me.

The Great Venture also nudged me one night, I can't say how much later, since I had abandoned time for geography. It was late spring, some year, on the open sea between Thorshaven and Reykjavik, Iceland. No moon, no stars, the air thick with fog, both prow and roundtop manned by lookouts shouting their heads off while the watch officer (this was me, newly promoted to master or first officer) listened for the telltale echo from an iceberg.

The second joined me. 'Hell of a night, First,' he said. Off the map of time, I discouraged the use of my name.

I said, 'Seen worse.' I did not encourage conversation during that phase of my life either.

We listened to the hoarse voices of the lookouts shouting 'berg!' every few moments, into the night, possibly in the belief that to name a thing is to master it.

'Je-*sus!*' said the second. 'Fog like this and iceberg season, it makes a man think. All fifteen hundred tons of roundship, you and me included, could be smashed to splinters while we're standing here talking.'

'Umm-mm,' I contributed.

'And it's your *usual* weather up here on the northern rim of things,' the second went on. 'Only the worst weather on earth, that's all. Why, if they had the kind of stepping-stone islands down south they have up north here, a brave skipper on the right kind of ship just might ... ' He shook his head. 'But unfortunately they don't. Have them, I mean.'

'Berg!' shouted the roundtop lookout.

And 'Berg!' echoed an unseen iceberg.

'*Ice*berg?' shouted the lookout, louder.

'*Ice*berg!' echoed the iceberg, also louder.

In fog it is hard to tell what direction sound is coming from.

'Yes sir,' said the second calmly, 'smashed to splinters while we're standing here talking.'

I told him to shut up, and ordered the prow lookout to shout, hoping I could triangulate the sound.

'No iceberg?' he shouted hopefully.

'No iceberg!' echoed the iceberg.

'Iceberg!' shouted the roundtop lookout, his voice no longer rising, and I thought I had it. I rushed back to the steerage hatch and called to the helmsman, 'Put her all the way up!' But he heard 'iceberg' and 'no iceberg' and couldn't make out what I said.

'You say up or down, sir?' he shouted.

I dropped through the hatch and brought all my own weight to bear against the tiller and, when he joined in, the ship slowly came around, her prow swinging toward the eye of the wind.

And the mountain of ice loomed, terrifyingly visible despite the fog, despite the night, as it slid past to starboard, and we felt the cold of its passing like the hand of death.

Later in that Julian decade of my life I met Harald Flakehair again in Reykjavik and he persuaded me to join an expedition to find Greenland.

The situation was this. Shortly before A.D. 1000, a Norwegian called Eric the Red, blown off course en route to Iceland, discovered a huge island (or Asian peninsula, as the case might be), built a house there, misnamed the glacier-covered place Greenland in the first recorded real-estate scam, and so founded a colony. It prospered on the narrow habitable coastal strip for some generations, despite periodic raids by strange flat-faced people called Eskimos (a type of Indian, I believe) and years of isolation when the Ocean Sea was so stormy or icebergs so numerous that travel between Greenland and Iceland became impossible. Sad to relate, these bad times increased and soon filled most of that part of the map of time called the fifteenth century. All contact with Greenland was lost. Greenland, as Harald Flakehair had said, was gone. Later, when my friend Roderigo Borgia became Pope in 1492 (that year again!), Icelandic prelates sent him the gloomy tidings that no word had been received from any of Greenland's sixteen churches for eighty years. An expedition more successful than ours would find the ruins of Greenlander longhouses and passage-houses, but no clue to the fate of the settlers except that the Eskimos (or Indians) seemed sleek and well fed.

Three times we sailed west from the Bay of Smokes in Iceland. Twice unseasonable icebergs drove us back and the third time we were becalmed until our provisions all but ran out, and then a westerly blew us straight back to Iceland. Our furthest westing occurred on the second attempt, and one night I stood my watch thinking that no man of the civilized south had ever penetrated the Ocean Sea this far west. Thus the idea of the Great Venture came up behind me and whispered again. But I still wasn't ready to listen.

On our return to Reykjavik from the third expedition, a *sagafest* was held on the shore of the Bay of Smokes. It was summer, the final summer of my Julian decade on the northern rim of the Ocean Sea, and there would be no real darkness that night. Picture then the scene: the steam of hot springs drifting wraithlike from fissures in the ground, the dwarf willows and stunted birches and mountain ash casting faint shadows all night long, the cormorants and grebes and red-necked phalaropes and snow buntings calling in the twilit sky, the longhouses built of sod on frames of whalebone or driftwood where the women waited, and, in the changeless twilight, the saga-tellers singing the history of their race, off time's map as I was, as if it all were happening while we listened, as if all time were now.

They sang of the first Vikings to reach Iceland, and how they found already settled there wild and zealous men from Ireland who, bested in battle, fled, presumably back to Connemara. They sang of Eric the Red, discoverer of Greenland, and of Eric's son Leif, called the Lucky – Leif who sailed for Greenland but was blown off course and continued west for days that became weeks until he came to a land that was fair and truly green which he called Wineland the Good. They sang of Wineland's Indians (but called them *skrellings*) and of the Indians' strange tale of wild zealous white men who chanted loudly to their God as they slow-marched behind pennants marked with the sign of the cross. These were the descendants of the Irish zealots who had fled Iceland, blown off course as surely as Leif the Lucky had been.

Harald Flakehair translated for me as I sat on the beach under the midnight sun, filling my belly with mutton and ale and listening to the song of the saga-tellers. But in a way I wasn't there, for I wandered west with the saga-telling, and the Great Venture came on me then at last, and I knew it was my *faege*.

These were my thoughts: if the Irish in currachs no bigger than those I had seen, and the Norsemen in their merchantmen called *knörrs*, so different from the longships that sped them to battle, could cross the Ocean Sea to Wineland with neither mariner's compass nor any knowledge of geography, how much might be accomplished by seamen of the civilized south, armed with charts and compasses, in swift caravels that sailed close to the wind? Let a fleet of caravels sail from the Azores or, better yet, drop south to the Canary Islands and then head west at what I calculated the latitude of Cipango to be – with no icebergs, no fog, no killing cold. . .

Harald Flakehair shook me. I woke.

'What ails you?' he asked, alarmed, for I was trembling violently.

But instead of answering I walked alone down the beach, watching the sudden swoop of an Iceland falcon.

That night marked the end of my Julian decade on the northern rim of the known world. I was ready to return to the map of time, though I didn't know it yet. I sailed twice more from Reykjavik to Bristol with my own command, a Centurione galleass of near 2,000 tons, before an encounter long delayed, and a letter long lost, opened my eyes.

One day as I stepped ashore in Bristol Town, a new first came up the gangway, a man of about my age and almost my height, long-nosed, shark-jawed.

'Captain Colón?' he asked.

When I nodded, he broke into a smile. 'Lord, man — I've been looking for you for years!'

'Have you,' I said indifferently.

He pounded my back and shoulders as if we were long-lost brothers. And when he spoke his face came close to my own. Here in the north I had grown unaccustomed to this. Here, men stand a distance apart when they speak. The new first was no northerner, and when he next spoke I detected traces of an Italian, perhaps even a Genoese, accent. He said, 'I've been looking for you for three reasons — but here, let me buy you some good English ale.'

Jenny was still barmaid at the Plank & Anchor.

'I see you found your fucking mystery man at last, Giovanni,' she said.

'Captain of my own new ship,' said Giovanni, marveling.

We raised tankards.

'Years ago,' he told me, 'you left messages here and all over Bristol Town that you wanted to see me. Very well, here I am. What was it all about?'

I remembered then. An Italian sailor named Giovanni, a friend of The O'Gaunt.

'Nothing,' I said. 'It no longer matters.'

'Well,' he said, 'it so happens *I* want to see *you*. I'm Genoese,' he explained. 'Name's Gaboto, Giovanni Gaboto, but I'm settling with my family right here in Bristol Town to organize what I call my Great Enterprise.'

'Your what?'

'I'm prepared to devote the rest of my life to it, and my son's life too if necessary,' said Giovanni Gaboto.

'What is this Great Enterprise of yours?' I asked uneasily.

He lowered his voice and leaned close, his mouth an inch from my ear when he spoke. 'I'm going to cross the Ocean Sea and rediscover Wineland, if I can get the English king to sponsor me.'

'There's nothing out there,' I said quickly, waving vaguely west and overturning his mug of ale. 'Just a bunch of myths and things.'

'Clumsy Eye-tye,' muttered Jenny as she mopped up the spilled ale.

Gaboto ignored my lack of enthusiasm. 'I'm looking for a partner, an experienced mariner like yourself.'

'Sorry,' I said. 'I have more important business.'

I drank my two, and Gaboto his one and a half, tankards of ale. Just as Jenny brought more, a boy of eight or nine entered the Plank & Anchor. He found Gaboto right away. 'Papa!' he called, 'Mama says if you're late for supper one more – '

'Come here, son, and have a sip of Papa's ale,' Gaboto said.

Jenny the barmaid fussed over the child. 'You're a handsome little man. What's your name?'

'Sebastiano,' the boy said. 'No, I forgot – Papa says it's Sebastian, now that we're English.'

Jenny the barmaid seemed less than delighted with the slight alteration. 'Still sounds like a fucking Eye-tye name,' she muttered, turning to the boy's father. 'And Giovanni, I suppose, will be John?'

Gaboto nodded.

'You sure you can't be persuaded?' he asked me. 'There's a place in history for the men bold enough to cross the Ocean Sea and rediscover Wineland.'

'Sorry, Gaboto. I have more important business,' I said. I was trembling, like the night of the *sagafest*.

'Gaboto, that's no proper English name either,' Jenny the barmaid said.

'No, no, it's to be Cabot,' said Giovanni impatiently.

'Hey, not too fucking bad,' Jenny the barmaid allowed. 'John Cabot, that has a good English ring to it.'

'The third reason I was looking for you', said Giovanni Gaboto or John Cabot, 'is this letter.'

The paper was old, faded yellow, creased, stained, spindled, mutilated. I broke the seal.

Young Sebastiano or Sebastian looked up at me and said, 'Your friend has funny hair, Papa.'

My long red hair, in the Julian decade I'd spent off time's map, had become streaked with white.

The letter was from Bartolomeo, written in Portugal. My brother called himself Bartolomé Colón now, I saw. His letter was dated 7 August 1476.

'What month is this?' I said.

The Cabots father and son looked at me. Jenny the barmaid said, 'Why, it's March, you nerd.'

'And the year?'

That almost broke Jenny up. 'I swear, he's barmy.'

'The year, what year is it?' I shouted.

77

'Why, it's 1479,' she said.

And so at last my feet were planted firmly back on the map of time, where I learned that I was now twenty-eight years old.

Almost three years ago Bartolomé had written from Lisbon:

Dear Brother Cristóbal,

I have heard that you are sailing in the pay of the House of Centurione in northern waters. I have done some sailing myself for Captain Perestrello and the Sprawling Navigational Complex, south along the African coast to the island of Fernando Po, just 3° 30′ north of the equator. Between voyages, I am a mapmaker here in Lisbon, where I have made my home, and where I like to think I make some small contribution to the Great Attempt – the Portuguese endeavor to reach the Indies by sailing south around Africa. Nothing would please me more than to have you join me here both in my cartography business and in the Great Attempt, a project to which His Most Serene Majesty John II is deeply committed.

Felipa de Perestrello, to whom I have the honor to be affianced, sends warm regards.

Your loving brother
Bartolomé Colón

My head swam with it all – John Cabot and his Great Enterprise, my brother and the Portuguese king's Great Attempt – and me with my own Great Venture not even fledged yet.

Even the news about Bartolomé and Felipa paled before that.

I had to hurry.

'You're quite certain I can't persuade you?' John Cabot persisted.

Without replying, I hurried from the tavern and to Pighi-Zampini's office to find passage south.

V

Concerning the Marriage of My Brother's Fiancée
or
The World as Seen by Pozzo Toscanelli

IF this were a more orderly narrative, or if I had led a more orderly life, I would have reached Lisbon to find Bartolomé and Felipa already married with one toddler underfoot and another on the way. In a more orderly narrative, or a more orderly life, I would have taken up John Cabot's proposal to join forces. Who knows what might have happened had the discoverer of the New World (I admitted it was that during my Third Voyage, as you'll see) teamed up with the discoverer of North America?

But no, this narrative is full of perverse twists because it mirrors life. Take John Cabot's place in history. Here's a *real* Italian, born in Genoa but a citizen of Venice even though he would be sailing under charter to England's King Henry VII when he made landfall in North America on Midsummer Day of 1497. And here am I, born at sea of recently converted Spanish Jewish parents, an accidental Italian who went almost everywhere but sailed exclusively for Spain. And how do the historians write it? They make me out as the authentic *paisan'* and call him plain John Cabot. Maybe one man in a hundred knows Giovanni Gaboto's the real *paisan'*, not me, and all he did was discover *North* America where an Italian population almost as large as Italy's would eventually hold annual parades in my honor.

79

In a more orderly life, I would have taken one look at glorious Lisbon rising on its hills above the Tagus estuary, where ten times twenty ships from as many ports strained at their cables as if longing to be at sea again, and I would have swiftly thrown in my lot with Portugal's Great Attempt, as my brother Bartolomé had done. Then mightn't it have been I, not one Vasco da Gama, who rounded the bottom of Africa at Cape Storm, by then already renamed Cape of Good Hope with touching marine optimism, to sail to Calicut and all the riches of the fabled East? But da Gama wouldn't reach Calicut until the year after John Cabot made that Midsummer's Day landfall on the North American shore, and I had an earlier date with destiny.

I might as well admit it, why not? During my Julian decade on the northern rim of the Ocean Sea I was bitten by the glory bug.

It's tempting to imagine this da Gama himself the year I returned to Portugal. He would have been a boy in his early teens. Was he down at the Tagus docks looking dreamily to sea, a second Bartolomé? Had he already apprenticed himself to a shipmaster? Did he feel a preternatural sense of dread the moment I stepped ashore?

Eat your heart out, Vasco da Gama.

Being first is not the important thing, it's the *only* thing. Or so I believed then. Time and circumstance would humble me.

Bartolomé had no idea I was coming, or even that his three-year-old letter had found me. And here I was on a bright morning in May, seabag slung over one shoulder as I walked with a sailor's swagger across that great waterfront plaza called Palace Terrace. To locate you: Lisbon was three towns in one — the Lower Town on flat ground between Palace Terrace and the even bigger plaza called the Rossio; the Upper Town climbing a steep hill to the northwest; and the Alfama, the old Arab quarter, an even steeper hill to the northeast. Between Palace Terrace and the Rossio ran the Street of Gold. From Lower Town to the two hillside districts climbed Lisbon's steep and endless staircase streets.

In Palace Terrace I asked directions to the shop of mapmaker Bartolomé Colón. It was a simple matter of following the Street of Gold to St Nicholas Street, and there turning left. But everywhere I looked I was distracted. That teeming polyglot waterfront! Just to rub shoulders with the crowds of Danes, Norwegians, Flemings, Genoese, Venetians, Berbers, plus a few gawking, bewildered-looking English sailors, not to mention mariners from lands I couldn't even name, who mingled with the native Iberians — just to cross Palace Terrace rubbernecking at the open-air shops, sniffing the smells, touching the merchandise –

'Don't touch the merchandise, sailor.'

'Sorry.'

– God, after England and the rest, just to be back in the civilized world!

I entered the Street of Gold, well-named for the stalls of Italian moneychangers and Jewish moneylenders. I must admit here that, witnessing their frenzied activity, I felt superior to both. The only Italian banker of my acquaintance, after all, was Pighi-Zampini. As for the Jews, they were said to be a clannish, stiff-necked people, and at that time in my life I had no idea I'd all but been born one. The blow when it came would ... but my narrative is not *that* disorderly and I'll save those events for their proper place.

On a small plaza off the Street of Gold I saw human beings for sale – blackamoors, of course, but still it shocked me. A big gleaming black (skin oiled, I assumed) mounted the block naked, the auctioneer indicating his strong points with frequently coarse commentary. Then the bidding began, as if he were an Arabian stallion or some piece of furniture from a foreclosed house. I soon left the place, barely looking as two young girls mounted the block in tears, both of them but recently nubile if the budding softness around their nipples or the downy hair covering their pudenda were any indication.

Turning into St Nicholas Street I saw at last the sign:

B. Colón
FINE MAPS AND CHARTS

hanging over a shop next to a dealer in Malagueta peppers.

Bartolomé's shop, to my disappointment, was shuttered. On the door a sign instructed me, *Shout for Joy*.

Shout for Joy? I wondered.

I went next door to the Malagueta pepper shop. A grizzled blackamoor in a long-skirted jacket with a standing collar greeted me.

'Help you?'

'"Shout for Joy?"' I said, still puzzled.

The Malagueta man chuckled. 'You've got to be the fifth customer this morning to ask. That old Barto, he's one nervous groom. What he meant to write – '

'Groom? I thought he'd be married long since with one toddler underfoot and another on the way.'

'They're being married this morning at the Saints Chapel of St James convent school. What he meant to write, I guess, was *shut* for joy. Because he sure is a happy young fellow, even if he is a bit nervous.'

'When's the wedding?'

'Right around now I reckon.'

'Where?' I shouted.

'Told you.' He took in the seabag slung on my shoulder. 'Oh, you're new in town. You mean *where*.'

'I'm his brother,' I said, and he told me how to get there, and I ran.

Soon I was racing up stairs. And stairs. And more stairs. The original Lisbon, the Arab fortress of the Alfama, had been built on the highest point overlooking the estuary, and even those lofty Arab heights had heights of their own. The St James convent, once a retreat for the ladies of crusading knights of the Order of St James, now a fashionable boarding school, was on the highest height of all.

At last I reached an escarpment, saw a building surmounted by a cross and plunged inside, luckily – or so it seemed at first – hitting the Saints Chapel on the first try. It was a cozy if high-vaulted place, the pews occupied mostly by fashionable young ladies from the fashionable boarding school, all of whom now turned away from the altar to stare at the loutish, sweating, seabag-toting sailor who came charging in.

I learned later that the priest, one Father Jerónimo, had just reached that traditional place in the ceremony where he departs from the religious text to ask in the vernacular (which, incidentally, was Castilian Spanish in educated Lisbon circles) whether anyone knew any reason why this couple should not be joined in holy matrimony. But all I heard was the twittering of the fashionable young ladies, all I knew was that the ceremony seemed almost concluded and I wanted to stand up at his wedding with my brother Bartolomé, whose broad back I could see next to the slender bride in white gown and veil. So I shouted, still out of breath, 'Wait! Wait!' and, dropping the seabag, rushed to my happy brother's side.

There followed a moment of stunned silence, then in the babble of the chapel I heard snatches of speculation:

'Who is he?'

'What does he know?'

' ... a sailor ... '

'Well, Felipa being twenty-one and all ...'

'Still waters ...'

Bride and groom, she inscrutably veiled, he visibly shaken, were facing me. Father Jerónimo stared in patient canonical disbelief. 'If you have something to say,' he told me, 'say it.'

'I'm – ' I gasped, trying to get my breath.

'Well?'

' – his – '

Felipa then staggered back a step and raised her veil.

She cried: 'Cristóbal!'

Bartolomé asked: 'Cristóbal?'

Father Jerónimo demanded: 'Who in hell – sorry! – is Cristóbal?'

I was going to explain that I wanted to stand up with my brother at his wedding but, before I could, Felipa let fall her veil, lifted her gown high enough to show her ankles and, trailing two flower girls from her skirts like the tail of a comet, gave me one long anguished look and ran up the aisle and outside.

Later, while I waited in the flat above Bartolomé's shop, he went to see Felipa's mother, the widow Doña Isabel Moñiz de Perestrello (for Captain Perestrello, Director of the Sprawling Navigational Complex at Cape St Vincent, had died two years ago).

'She refused to see me,' a downcast Bartolomé said on his return.

'Doña Isabel?'

'No. Felipa. Not that Doña Isabel was what I'd call friendly,' Bartolomé told me. 'How come you stopped the wedding?'

I explained that I hadn't meant to stop the wedding, I'd only wanted to stand up with him.

Barto sank dispiritedly into a chair after pouring us each a cup of green wine, and I had my first good look at him since we were teenagers. My brother Barto was powerfully if squatly built, somewhat bowed in the leg, with a great frizzy head of almost African hair and that unfortunate face, warts and all – yet when he managed a wan smile, his generous personality shone through and made you forget all the rest, even the endearingly crooked teeth.

'Her mother says she never wants to see me again.' Barto downed his green wine in a single gulp.

'She'll get over it.'

'I got the impression it has something to do with you.'

'It's a long story,' I told him. 'It's probably because she hates me, but I'm sure she'll see the light. I won't be her husband, after all, just her brother-in-law.'

'Why would she hate you?'

I said the answer was too complicated unless we had a lot of time to go into it.

'The shop's shut and as it turns out this isn't my wedding day,' Barto said reasonably, 'so we have all the time in the world.'

'I thought,' I quickly changed the subject, 'that you'd be long since married, with a toddler underfoot and another on the way by the time I got here.'

'Well, we were going to, but I was at sea a lot and then poor old Perestrello died. After that, what with one thing and another, Felipa kept putting it off. And now this happened. But I'm glad we're back together, Cristóbal, despite everything,' Barto told me, and he meant it.

Every day my brother set out hopefully to visit Doña Isabel at the walled Perestrello mansion in Upper Town, and every day it got him nowhere. At first, as on the non-wedding day, Felipa's mother coolly said the girl refused to see him. Next, her manner even chillier, she informed him Felipa was gone. Then, with a real frost in the air, she revealed that Felipa had returned to teaching at the St James convent school, where she had taken limited vows. Barto went, ever hopeful, to the convent school, but the Sister Superior wouldn't let him in. And after that Doña Isabel refused to see him too.

'But she wants to see *you*,' he said.

I felt my face going pale as I wondered what lies Felipa might have told her mother about me. Hell hath no fury, and so forth.

'Maybe she wants you to act as a go-between,' Barto said with his usual optimism.

The walls of the Perestrello mansion in Upper Town were the sort so beloved of tourists, crumbling into picturesque ruin. Doña Isabel herself, dressed in the widow's black she would wear for the remainder of her days, let me in through the wrought iron gate that hung askew on a single squeaking hinge. The patio was so weed-grown I had to follow Doña Isabel through a natural maze to the front door. On its worm-eaten wood could be seen the outline of a heavy iron knocker, but it had long since fallen off and I would later see it in the parlor (from the French *parler*, to talk) where it served as a rusty paperweight. The interior of the house smelled of mold and damp rot. No servant was in evidence.

'Sit down, Don Cristóbal,' the widow Doña Isabel told me. She had a severe face with a small square mouth. 'I see my daughter was right. You don't resemble your brother in the slightest.'

The tile-floored room was almost devoid of furniture. I sat on one hard-backed chair facing Doña Isabel on another. A simple table, bare except for the rusty door-knocker, completed the decor.

84

'I also see that you're surprised by the unpretentiousness of the Perestrello mansion.'

'Well,' I said gallantly, 'it's obvious you're not *nouveau riche*.'

'We have fallen on hard times. Perestrello, God rest his soul, made some poor investments.'

I seized my chance. 'Barto's a good catch. Steady, reliable, kind. Generous to a fault.'

'Perestrello, however,' she said, ignoring my pitch, 'did leave a sea chest containing his charts and correspondence, which he willed to Felipa's husband-to-be.'

'Barto will make good use of it, I'm sure.'

Remembering what difficulty poor old Perestrello had in believing the world was round, I wondered what there could be in his sea chest of value to anyone.

'Among his papers are several letters, and I believe some maps and charts, from the hand of the Florentine Ser Paolo dal Pozzo Toscanelli.'

'The great Pozzo Toscanelli?' I couldn't help blurting.

Pozzo Toscanelli, physician, humanist, mathematician, astronomer, was just one of the world's two leading authorities, that's all — the other being Regiomontanus (born Johann Müller) the Nuremberger. With Leonardo da Vinci still trying his wings and Erasmus not out of his teens, they were the only absolutely world-class Renaissance Men around.

'The letters and charts of Pozzo Toscanelli are, you could say, Felipa's dowry,' the widow Doña Isabel said after a significant pause.

'Then Barto's even luckier than I thought.'

'Don Cristóbal, concerning women you really are at sea. *Auntie!*' she shouted, and in a few moments a sleepy-looking woman, also in black, appeared in the doorway. I recognized Felipa's dueña on the voyage aboard *Virgen Rampante* from Cape St Vincent to St Malo. I wondered if she had become addicted to sleeping drops.

As I went upstairs with her all I could think of was the well-known fact that Pozzo Toscanelli had measured the earth, the continents, the Ocean Sea, with incredible exactitude, but had thus far revealed his measurements to no one.

Auntie said, 'Felipa is a headstrong girl. Always was.'

I was thinking: I'd give my right arm to get my hands (or one remaining hand) on Pozzo Toscanelli's charts and letters.

Walking along a dim corridor, Auntie said, 'I know it's ancient history, but what exactly did you do to the poor defenseless little girl after you slipped me those sleeping drops aboard the Virgen Whatever-it-was?'

'I didn't slip you any sleeping drops,' I protested.

'No need to deny it. I'm very grateful to you. I'd suffered from insomnia for years, and you cured me.'

'I didn't do it.'

'Surely you're not suggesting the Captain did?'

How could I tell her little Felipa had been the culprit?

'All I know is, it wasn't me.'

But Auntie just laughed a knowing laugh and went with me into the upstairs parlor where Felipa Perestrello was seated on a large sea chest beside a desk, the only other furniture in the large, broken-windowed, missing-shuttered room. Felipa rose and offered me her hand. I bowed over it and kissed air.

'Don Cristóbal,' she said.

'Doña Felipa,' I said.

She wore a headcloth starched into giant butterfly wings that somehow didn't look convent style, and from the pearl-embroidered belt that cinched her green satin gown hung not only a rosary but a fan of ostrich plumes. Her eyebrows were arched and darkened, her cheeks tinted red, her deep décolletage powdered white. Little Felipa Perestrello had become an attractive woman.

But my eyes kept straying to the battered sea chest.

She saw what held my attention. 'That contains, among other things,' she informed me, 'the letters and maps of the Florentine Ser Paolo dal Pozzo Toscanelli.'

'I know. I know it does,' I said with an eager catch in my voice.

'Left in his will by my dear departed father to *whomever marries his daughter.*'

Her voice seethed with significance.

I said, 'Then Barto's doubly lucky.'

'That', Auntie said, 'was to have been a marriage of convenience.'

Noting the deliberately convoluted verb form, I still gamely essayed: 'Barto will make some lucky girl a wonderful husband.'

'I didn't stay long at St Malo,' Felipa said.

'No?'

'No. I had a nervous crisis. They had to send me home. I attended the St James convent school instead, and then went with my parents to the island of Porto Santo, where my father was appointed governor two years before he died. It was there that he concluded his correspondence with Pozzo Toscanelli. But it's all in the sea chest.'

86

'I'll tell Barto as soon as I get home.'

She said, 'I am not going to marry your brother Barto.'

If she had told me that he was repellent, too ugly to marry, I think I would have had the courage to flee that dilapidated place and never return — sea chest and letters and maps and Pozzo Toscanelli be damned. But she had the good sense not to say that.

What she did say was: 'I'm going to marry *you*.'

Of my courtship and marriage, my son Fernando has this to say in his nepotistic biography: 'Inasmuch as he behaved very honorably and was a man of such fine presence and withal so honest, Doña Felipa held such converse and friendship with him that she became his wife.' I will not comment on those lines, except to point out that Fernando was no closer to the facts than later biographers. Felipa was not his mother; she was long gone from the scene by the time he arrived. No, Fernando was once again busily inventing a suitable father for my second-born son.

Another, much later, biographer would write: 'My main concern is with the Columbus of action, the Discoverer who held the key to the future in his hand. I am content to leave his "psychology," his "motivation" and all that to others.' Thus this writer neatly sidesteps such questions as why I married Felipa, who had so cruelly rejected my brother Barto. But the 'motivation and all that' so cavalierly dismissed by the biographer is *me*, and I hope you'll agree that in this case it wasn't all bad.

My biographers seem to agree that we were married, as Barto almost was, at the Saints Chapel of St James convent school, although there is no shred of evidence to support this. In reality, Felipa and her mother not surprisingly couldn't face another large wedding. We posted the banns at an obscure little church on the western outskirts of Upper Town and were married there in a private ceremony three months after I set foot in Lisbon.

Until the day before the wedding, Barto and I were very correct with each other and took pains not to mention Felipa. He taught me to draw maps freehand. He taught me to carve and chisel them into woodcuts, so that with ink and paper I could soon produce editions of 500 maps or more. I cautiously told him about my Great Venture. He listened in silence and after a while said, 'King John's Great Attempt has a large head start, Cristóbal, and royal funding. If a way to the Indies is found around Africa, you can forget your dream of sailing west across the Ocean Sea.'

'That's why we so desperately need the letters and maps of Pozzo Toscanelli,' I told him.

This was the nearest either of us had come to mentioning his aborted and my pending marriage.

He admitted the truth of what I said and with his gouge attacked a block of wood.

The day before the wedding, I had Captain Perestrello's sea chest delivered to Barto's shop. We took it upstairs at once, and carried it past the door of my bedroom, Barto glancing at me in surprise. He must have assumed I would leave it locked in there until returning from my honeymoon. I continued instead to the back room, which was Barto's retreat. Inside was a jumble of old maps, books and native artifacts from Barto's voyages along the west coast of Africa.

Easing my end of the chest to the floor near a precarious stack of books, I said as offhandedly as I could, 'You'll be able to get Pozzo Toscanelli's papers all sorted by the time I'm back.'

'You mean you're going to let me do it?'

It was dim in there, but I think Barto's eyes misted over.

For a long time neither of us spoke. Then my brother said, 'Can I stand up with you at the church tomorrow?' and I felt my own eyes stinging as I nodded.

'I guess when you come right down to it,' Barto told me, 'I'm more a brother-in-law type than a husband type anyway.'

The island of Porto Santo, where Captain Perestrello spent the last two years of his life and Felipa and I our honeymoon, lies some 500 miles southwest of Lisbon off the coast of Africa. It is a barren, treeless place of strong sea winds, with a few rocky peaks and a fine golden beach on the south shore. Some people dismiss Porto Santo as a desert scarcely fit for human habitation and perhaps they're right. But we had our reasons for going there.

After her father's sudden death from apoplexy at the small governor's house in the island capital, Vila Baleira, Felipa had returned to Lisbon to teach at the St James convent school, and her grief-stricken mother, on following later, accidentally left most of her daughter's wardrobe behind. To retrieve these cedarwood chests was one reason we had come to Porto Santo.

Besides, I received a commission from Centurione's Merchant Bank, Lisbon branch, to supervise shipment of 200 tons of sugarcane from nearby Madeira, and my fee would pay for our honeymoon.

Of which, as you'll notice, I say little. It is unseemly to comment on intimate matters between husband and wife. But I can say this much without overstepping the bounds of good taste: Felipa assumed her wifely obligations in lusty high spirits, as my earlier adventures with her had promised.

Our days were spent outdoors in the fine weather walking on the southern beach and searching for driftwood – another reason for honeymooning on Porto Santo.

This wasn't your ordinary, bleached-bone-white, grow-anywhere, float-anywhere driftwood. Far from it. This was the mysterious wood that the currents and the westerly winds had brought across the Ocean Sea from God knew where, and my scalp prickled just to touch it. The driftwood came in three sorts. In addition there washed up on the beach strange chestnut-colored beans (eventually called colón beans in my honor) which grew nowhere on the Iberian mainland or in Africa. Later, in the Indies, I would see them on exotic trees with streamers of golden flowers. I would find two varieties of Porto Santo driftwood growing there also – the lightweight blue-black-striped trees and the canes so thick that wine to quench a dozen men's thirst could be poured into each joint. Surely this latter was the bamboo described by Ptolemy, the great Alexandrian geographer and mapmaker of antiquity.

The most intriguing of all was ordinary enough wood, but it had been worked with tools – by what unknown alien hands I knew I must someday learn or die in the attempt.

'Cristóbal, it's growing dark, the wind's up, come out of the water.'

I was wading hip-deep in the surf chasing a four-joint length of bamboo, the first I'd found. I made a fire that night on the shore and we watched fishermen in small boats row out to net sardines by flaming torchlight under a crescent moon. We lingered long after they had gone and that night I can honestly say I was in love with my wife. Bear in mind that most marriages were made for dynastic or commercial considerations, that love matches were rare, and that Doña Isabel, desperate to see her daughter married, let her choose one Colón brother over the other. So our start, at least, was better than most. But Felipa was an impetuous and very physical woman.

The final day of our honeymoon we rode mules to Calheta Point at the southwest tip of the island to see the famous rock horseman, my last reason for coming to Porto Santo. The beach there is spiked with black rock spires in weird shapes and the surf crashes among the black reefs offshore.

We arrived late, just as the sun was setting – and there he was, seated astride his warhorse, armored, visor down, hand resting on his sword as he gazed eternally out across the Ocean Sea. After I dismounted and helped Felipa to the ground I sank to my knees before him. I was moved by a profound sense of destiny, as if God were close. The huge black rock horseman faced directly west as if he would ride in pursuit of the setting sun, as one day I knew I must sail. And I think Felipa sensed this, for she remained silent at my side, her hand resting on my shoulder like the giant's on his black rock sword.*

Some biographers insist that I was God-driven. I'm not sure what they mean, but I have to protest if they are implying the Joan of Arc syndrome. Despite what you may have read elsewhere, I'm no mystic and, especially after I learned of my antecedents, I was no more pious than is necessary to get ahead in the world. But if to be God-driven is to recognize God in His glory, then I say a qualified yes. For if it is a short step from recognizing God in His glory to seeing God *as* glory, then it can fairly be said that I would do His work, after my fashion.

But enough. Such ruminations embarrass me.

Two days later we sailed across the strait to Madeira in a felucca loaded with Felipa's cedarwood chests and boarded the roundship with Centurione's 200 tons of sugarcane for the return trip to Lisbon, where the papers of Pozzo Toscanelli were waiting.

Not that I could devote as much time to them as I would have liked in the months that followed. Instead, I found myself confronted by a glut of money. This small fortune, the Julian decade of salary I'd earned while sailing northern waters, had finally reached Portugal.

On the Street of Gold at the Lisbon branch of the House of Centurione, I saw the new director. Pighi-Zampini had come up in the world. He sat behind a heavy walnut desk decorated with grotesque masks.

'Let me put your money to work for you, young man,' he advised, his ear and nostril bristles quivering. He suggested caravels and caravans.

'You'd be amazed,' Doña Isabel told me, 'how far I could stretch a few gold coins in restoring the Perestrello-Colón mansion.'

I told Barto, when I learned that the Malagueta pepper man was retiring, 'Why don't we buy his shop and expand our business?'

*This is the only footnote you will find, occasioned by the single inaccuracy in these pages. The famous rock horseman actually stands on a headland on the island of Corvo, westernmost of the nine Azores, not at Calheta Point on Porto Santo. But I claim poetic license for placing him there. I did in fact see the Corvo horseman on a different voyage, when nothing else of interest transpired.

Felipa said, with that special smile reserved for such occasions, 'In six months you'll be a father,' and pleaded to get the alterations to the house completed (except for interior decoration, of course) before the baby's arrival.

Barto suggested, 'Why don't we send for the great Pozzo Toscanelli? At our expense, naturally.'

But Pozzo Toscanelli was an old man and wrote to say that he was unable to travel, though he would send an emissary.

The great Florentine's letters to the late Captain Perestrello were a marvel of instructive clarity. In a few telling phrases he forever put to rest Perestrello's fears that he was living a lie on a world that in reality was flat. Pozzo Toscanelli took the trouble to do this as he had great hopes for the Sprawling Navigational Complex at Cape St Vincent, even though they had gone off in the wrong direction, which is to say south instead of west. 'Your interest,' he had written Perestrello, 'should be in a shorter sea route to the spice lands than the one you are seeking around Africa.' To sail west was the answer, he wrote in his succinct Latin. His most exciting passage was the assertion that Ptolemy, the geographer of antiquity almost deified by my contemporaries, was as prone to error as the rest of us, such as woefully underestimating the eastward extension of Asia.

'Read that!' I told Barto jubilantly, but he already had.

Pozzo Toscanelli believed the Venetian traveler Marco Polo, whom scientists of the Ptolemy school called a dilettante and a liar, was right regarding Asia. Pozzo Toscanelli demonstrated this on his most famous chart, and in his final letter to the Director of the Sprawling Navigational Complex *actually revealed his distances*.

'Pozzo Toscanelli says a course due west from Lisbon will take you to Quinsay, capital of the Chinese province of Mangi, a distance of five thousand miles,' I told Barto.

'Oh, wow!' he responded, although he had himself traced the route on Pozzo Toscanelli's chart a dozen times.

'And we can shorten that if we put our minds to it.' But I wasn't sure I was ready to discuss that yet, so it was perhaps as well that the workman knocking out the wall between our shop and the Malagueta pepper shop chose that moment to swing his sledgehammer.

'What?' Barto shouted over the din.

'The Great Khan, Emperor of China, resides in the next province, Cathay!' I shouted.

'Gosh,' said Barto.

'Though there's a lot to be said for the alternate route,' I went on, leafing through Pozzo Toscanelli's charts. 'You sail past the fabled islands of the Antilles and after only two thousand miles reach legendary Cipango, where the roofs of even the meanest hovels are tiled with gold — a thinner gold leaf than the palaces of the nobility, but still.'

'Jeepers,' said Barto.

I said, thinking out loud, 'Pozzo Toscanelli found no fault with Marco Polo's adding thirty degrees of longitude to Asia.'

Crash! went the sledgehammer.

'What?' said Barto.

'And if we had to convince someone, say His Most Serene Majesty King John II, just to pick a name, I think we might be able to stretch it a few degrees further.'

Brrr-oommmm! went the wall as it came down in a choking cloud of plaster dust.

'What?' said Barto, his frizzy hair powdered white.

'Besides, there's also the question of how large a degree of longitude actually is. And nobody knows for sure.'

A sweating, bare-chested man gestured with his sledgehammer. 'You want this other wall here up or down?'

'Up!' I shouted just in time.

Things were hardly quieter at the Perestrello-Colón mansion in Upper Town. I worried about Felipa in her delicate condition, but she seemed to thrive on walls being knocked down and ceilings replastered, on the smell of fresh whitewash everywhere, on new tiles for the floors and new tiles for the roof. Doña Isabel began on the interior decoration, having already seen to the boxwood maze, fruit trees and new plashing fountains in the patio enclosed by its new walls and guarded by its massive new bronze-studded oak gates. Every day cartloads of furniture would arrive. I marveled at what could be done with a few gold coins. There were canopied beds with embroidered hangings, walnut benches with wrought-iron bracings, credence tables to store the new silver flatware and Venetian glassware, heavy cupboards with wood tracery in imitation of thirty-two-point compass roses (especially designed, Felipa said, with me in mind), a great dining-room sideboard on whose oaken front, two by tiny two, beautifully carved ivory animals paraded into Noah's ark.

One day I received a message to see Pighi-Zampini at Centurione's.

'You've overdrawn your account,' he said.

I sat speechless.

'Merely your current account, not your deposit account,' Pighi-

Zampini lightened the blow. 'This represents forty per cent of your decade's salary sailing in the north for Centurione's.'

I was still dumbfounded. 'What can I do?'

'You have limited liquidity at present. Most of your deposit account has been invested in a twentieth share of a Genoese caravel and you also own a three-camel string in a caravan with our Damascus trading company. I suggest that you withdraw access to your funds from the women of your household.'

But how could I, with Felipa expecting and so happy commissioning what she and her mother called 'minor alterations' to the Perestrello-Colón mansion?

'They're almost finished,' I assured Pighi-Zampini.

'I'll have to transfer what little liquidity you have from your deposit account to your current account.'

I signed the necessary papers.

That April our son Diego was born and on the same day, almost at the same instant, Pozzo Toscanelli's emissary at last arrived in Lisbon.

I had been summoned home, of course, and Barto was in the double-sized shop alone, hacking away at a woodcut that would duplicate one of Pozzo Toscanelli's faded hand-drawn maps, when a horseman reined up outside. Barto was one of those kind and good-natured people who have no luck with animals, especially horses. As he related it to me later, he went outside on hearing the last thudding hoofbeats and the whinnying of the horse, and the instant he stepped out the door a great black stallion reared and kicked air inches from his face. When the horseman had calmed the beast, he demanded, still mounted:

'Are you one of the Colón brothers?'

'Bartolomé Colón, at your service.'

'I'd prefer Cristóbal.'

'He's home having a baby — that is, his wife is.'

The traveler's attire dazzled Barto. His green velvet jerkin had ballooning sleeves intentionally slashed in a dozen places to reveal gleaming gold silk beneath. Over short soft leather boots, his gold tights were festooned with patches of the same green velvet. Even his broad-brimmed hat, held at a rakish angle by a chin strap, was of an outlandish style. He wore a dark, pointed beard, the first Barto had seen on so young a man. Slowly and with stately grace he dismounted and, as most men and many women did, towered over Barto. But he did it condescendingly.

'My horse,' he said, holding out the reins.

93

When Barto approached cautiously, the horse shied.

So the man hitched his stallion to the post himself, his movements deliberate. 'I am Martin Behaim of Nuremberg, a student of Regiomontanus, the world's leading authority.'

'Gosh,' said Barto.

'I come as the emissary of the Florentine Ser Paolo dal Pozzo Toscanelli.'

'Oh, wow!' said Barto, and I can't help wondering what Behaim made of my brother's unique vocabulary. But he did present an itemized expense sheet for his long overland journey from Florence.

It was at that precise instant that Diego (named for my other brother who was still in Rome, Diego being the Castilian equivalent of Giacomo) uttered his first cry.

By the time he was speaking in complete sentences ('Look – Grandma's bought another new carpet for the parlor. It's even bigger than the other ones.') we were ready to start drawing up our presentation to His Most Serene Majesty John II's Maritime Commission of which, by then, Martin Behaim was sub-director.

But I received a sudden summons from Pighi-Zampini.

'They've overdrawn again?'

'Yes, but that isn't the bad news. You'll remember how your investments have grown, one-twentieth part of a Genoese caravel, a three-camel string in a caravan with our Damascus trading company, then one-tenth part of the caravel and six camels, and so on?'

'That doesn't sound like bad news.'

'Yes, well, the caravel was sunk by pirates off the west coast of Malta and the caravan is sixty days overdue at Damascus and presumed lost. I'm so sorry,' said Pighi-Zampini, 'but taking your former deposit account and former current account together, you are – in Genoese currency – one thousand gold ducats in debt.'

I waited until none of the servants was present before telling the family. They were incredulous, horrified, imitative and thoughtful.

'What?' said Doña Isabel, incredulous.

'What?' said Felipa, horrified.

'Wha'?' said Little Diego in smiling gap-toothed imitation.

'We could take a mortgage on the shop,' Barto suggested thoughtfully.

But the shop was the only source of income we had now and it was barely more than breaking even, what with the new presses I had bought and the special heavy-stock hammer-and-anvil-watermarked paper imported from Venice for our presentation to the Royal Maritime Commission.

'One of us,' Barto said, 'had better sign on with the Sprawling Navigational Complex. And, as you have a family ...' My brother shrugged, letting the thought dangle. In his mind he was already packing his seabag.

I knew that wouldn't be the answer. Barto's mapmaking skills far surpassed mine and although he wasn't much good with animals he did know how to deal with people. I explained all that, but Barto shook his head stubbornly.

We agreed to roll dice to determine who would go.

It was then that I became aware of Martin Behaim lounging in the doorway. 'I can keep the Perestrello-Colón mansion going while you get back on your feet, old boy,' he told me.

'Oh, Martin, would you?' Felipa said. 'You're wonderful.'

Martin Behaim, still in his mid-twenties, was one of those men known in later times as upwardly mobile. Of common background but with his impressive credentials (a self-styled student of Regiomontanus, an emissary from Pozzo Toscanelli), he had been immediately appointed to His Most Serene Majesty John II's Royal Maritime Commission, where he soon made his name setting the guidelines for determining degrees of latitude from meridian altitudes of the sun. He knew little enough about longitude, but then that was the difficult and sharply debated part of geography and Martin Behaim was always careful not to involve himself in anything controversial. The year before I went into debt, Behaim had been knighted by King John for his services to the Maritime Commission and promoted to subdirector. All this time he had been living in one of the many spare wings of the Perestrello-Colón mansion.

He was an impressive-looking man, always dressed in the latest fashion. His dark, pointed beard, rare in those days, enhanced his saturnine (some would have said vulpine) look; he walked with measured stride as if even his legs were thinking; when he sat he first moved the chair a few inches and then slid in gracefully, front to back, and placed an elbow, usually his left, on the chair arm, giving him an air of casual power. Men tended to defer to him. Women loved his dark, pointed beard and his consonantal German accent.

As his duties with the Royal Maritime Commission were less demanding than my work at the cartography shop, he had become Felipa's frequent companion, taking her for drives along the estuary road in his coach, the only one in Lisbon outside the royal stables, promenading with her along the Street of Gold or around Palace Terrace, and introducing her to such indoor sports as checkers, backgammon and that new fad, cards. They were close friends and I was grateful to Behaim for providing Felipa with these diversions.

Doña Isabel thought he was the greatest thing since lateen rigging.

When Barto and I rolled dice to determine who would sail south with a Sprawling Navigational Complex ship, I threw the lower number.

'Well, high goes,' said Barto, and began to whistle through his teeth.

'No, high stays.'

'Goes.'

'Stays.'

We tossed again, agreeing in advance that high would stay, and again I threw low.

Little Diego came to where I was sitting cross-legged on the floor, crawled into my lap and put his arms around my neck.

'Do you really have to go away, Papa?' he asked, and when I nodded he burst into tears.

'You'll have Uncle Barto to play with you,' I said.

'Yes, and Uncle Martin too,' he snuffled. 'But it's not the same.'

'I'll help you pack,' Felipa said. She was always a practical woman.

Some pages back I wrote about glory and destiny, but at times I can't help thinking these words mean only that the accidents of life happen in the right order.

If it was my destiny to cross the Ocean Sea, then even Centurione's loss of a caravel off Malta and a caravan somewhere east of Damascus helped by putting me deeply in debt. Was this fate, or just happenstance? Was it fate or happenstance that Doña Isabel (I couldn't yet bring myself to blame Felipa) had precipitated my financial difficulties by lavishly renovating the Perestrello-Colón mansion? Fate or happenstance that when I rolled the dice with Barto I lost not once but twice? Fate or happenstance that, it being late summer, a Portuguese fleet was even then assembling within sight of Palace Terrace for the annual journey south to reinforce and resupply St George of the Mine, the fortified trading center on Africa's Gold Coast? Fate or happenstance that for his own reasons Martin Behaim, as sub-director of the Royal Maritime Commission, could get me a last-minute appointment as captain of a caravel in that fleet? Fate or happenstance that dealing with the heathen Africans would prepare me to deal later with the heathen Indians?

We sailed at the end of August for the Gold Coast, four caravels and a roundship of 1,000 tons, holds crammed with hawk bells, colorful caps and bolts of fabric, Venetian beads and trinkets – all to be bartered for bags of Malagueta peppers, chests of gold dust, elephant tusks stacked like cordwood.

Deck-loaded aboard the roundship were two dozen horses. The going exchange rate was one sound horse for fifty young black slaves.

Of the journey south little need be said. I had sailed under more difficult circumstances during my Julian decade in the north, for en route to the Gold Coast our fleet hugged the land and every third or fourth night dropped anchor off one of the Sprawling Navigational Complex outposts strung along Africa's great western bulge. But I did become expert at clawing off a lee shore and I experienced again the exhilaration of sailing a lateen-rigged caravel into the teeth of a strong wind.

A stone castle as out of place on the Gold Coast as straw huts would have been in Lisbon, St George of the Mine stood at the head of an inlet. Turreted, walled, moated, it had a warehouse and vast market court to which the natives were admitted by day.

Some of these jungle tribes had titular kings who did nothing but look regal and 'fetish men' who did the real kingly work although, with their rattles and tattooed faces, their rolling eyes and weird grimaces, they all looked mad. Some tribes had witch doctors who captured souls that had strayed from people's bodies and held them for ransom, not out of malice but simply to earn a living. There was a tribe called Fan in which king, fetish man and blacksmith were one revered and almost deified personage, a sort of pagan Trinity. There was a tribe called Yoruba which sacrificed a fourteen-year-old virgin once a year to a god whose name I forget. She went happily to her own throat-slitting, having been bred for that purpose. The Fan chieftains traded Yoruba prisoners of war, fifty to one, for horses; the Yoruba chieftains did the same with captive Fan. The Fan king or fetish man or smith was blood brother to a leopard, which they kept in a cage. You may believe that leopard was well cared for, at least by the king/fetish man/smith. When the leopard died, the king would be immediately killed and replaced by a new monarch, blood brother to a huge black serpent or a wild boar or a vulture, the choice his to make. In another tribe that came to St George of the Mine, killing was the king's only function. Twice a year the sins of the people were laid on the shoulders of two human scapegoats. These innocents were well fed and all their desires met until the day of their sacrifice. Then they were dragged by the feet face-down through jeering crowds half a mile to the shore where the king, who had sharpened his skills on murderers, thieves, adulterous women, etc., awaited them with his axe.

Barbarous, you say? Darkest Africa, to coin a phrase?

Pass no judgment yet. The Inquisition had been flourishing in Spain ever since Pope Sixtus's decree six years earlier, and we will get there.

The fleet sailed back around the great western bulge of Africa when spring came, holds loaded with peppers, tusks, gold dust and slaves. I had now been as far north, as far west and as far south as any mariner of my time and I was as ready as I would ever be for the Great Venture.

But I was not, I would discover, ready for Martin Behaim.

We anchored off Palace Terrace in a cold May drizzle and I heard the brazen ringing of all Lisbon's church bells as I approached the landing stage in a longboat. I saw Barto at the front of the crowds surging across Palace Terrace. But unlike them, for whom the return of an African fleet was high excitement, my brother wasn't smiling.

I stepped ashore and we embraced.

'How's the family?' I shouted above the noise of the crowd.

'We're scheduled to make our presentation before the Royal Maritime Commission on Fifth Day,' Barto said somberly. The Portuguese, unlike all other Christian nations, don't name the days of the week except for Saturday and Sunday, but number them. Monday is Second Day, Tuesday Third, and so on. Fifth Day meant Thursday, the day after tomorrow.

'That's great,' I said.

'Yes,' said Barto. 'I suppose so.'

'How're Felipa and Little Diego?'

'I've prepared the map,' Barto said, still somberly, 'and written a draft of the argument.'

'There's time enough to change them,' I told him; my thoughts had crystalized in the nine long months I'd been gone from Lisbon. 'We'll stretch Asia even more than Marco Polo did and shorten a degree of longitude measured at the equator.'

Barto brightened as we approached the Street of Gold through the crowds still making their way to the waterfront. 'How many miles did you have in mind?'

'Asia or longitude?'

'Both. Tell me everything. Tell me about your trip south and your trip back north and St George of the Mine and all the native customs,' Barto said in a transport of eagerness. 'Go into lots and lots of detail.'

I smelled something decidedly fishy. 'Barto, what is it?'

We had stopped walking. The crowd surged around us like white water around a reef. I took Barto's arm and turned him to face me. 'What's the matter?' I said. 'Is it the family? The shop? What?'

'First of all, Little Diego's fine,' Barto said. 'He's home with his governess and dying to see you. He's lost some more milk teeth. She's new. The governess. So are all the servants up there at the mansion. We had to fire all the old ones.'

'Why, Barto?' I asked patiently. 'Why did you have to fire the servants?'

'Doña Isabel fired them before . . . ' Barto shook his head and lapsed into silence.

'Before what?'

Barto blew his nose hard while I stared down at his frizzy head. 'Remember,' he said slowly, 'remember the day before your wedding when I said I'd make a better brother-in-law than a husband?'

I said I remembered.

'Let me take your seabag,' Barto said, his mind plunging off in a new direction.

'No, that's all right.'

'Let me,' he almost shouted. I understood that he wanted to do something, anything, to help me. I slung the seabag off my shoulder and onto his.

All this time he kept looking down so he wouldn't have to meet my eyes. 'Well, I didn't make much of a brother-in-law after all. Even when I could see it coming I couldn't stop it. She was always so impetuous and physical.'

'Barto, what are you trying to say?'

He told me where to find her.

It was one of those instant slums that had sprung up on the outskirts of the city beyond the Rossio: narrow, crooked, unpaved streets, muddy now; hovels thrown together from bits of old packing crates, discarded furniture, any sort of debris; a hole in the roof for a chimney, no windows, and doorways sometimes closed only by a tattered curtain; poor country folk who had come to Lisbon to find work but had found only disillusion.

I asked the way to the home of Amalia Lopes, the name she was using. They spoke no Castilian here but the back-country dialect that in time would become a distinct Portuguese language. A shrug, a few muttered words, a retreating back, and I plunged deeper into the warren of muddy streets. If anyone had heard of Amalia Lopes they didn't say so, not to an obvious millionaire intruding on their misery. But finally a bent old woman said:

'Malia? Sure. Expecting.'

'Expecting me?' I wondered how that could be. But the answer was simple: the church bells.

I followed the crone's directions. The streets here were narrower, the hovels even smaller and flimsier.

I pushed aside the hanging in the doorway and went in without knocking. There was nothing to knock on that didn't look as if you might knock it down.

It was dark, the only light coming through the smoke hole in the roof. The place stank of rancid olive oil and unwashed body. Something small and furry scurried past my leg and outside.

When my eyes adjusted I saw that she was sitting, dressed in shapeless black, on a heap of filthy straw. I spoke her name but she said nothing, nor acknowledged in any way that I had come.

Her thick dark hair was matted. Her eyes stared out over dark unhealthy pouches. Lines of bitterness or fatigue bracketed her mouth. She looked old enough to be her own mother – older in fact, than Doña Isabel.

I spoke her name again and she gazed up at me blankly.

'Where's your mother?' I asked her, and her eyes seemed to come into focus.

'Porto Santo,' she said, her voice hoarse from lack of use. 'She went there to wait things out.'

'What will you do with it when it comes?'

'I don't know. Would you take me back?'

It was a question I couldn't answer. Nothing had prepared me for this. I moved a hand in a pointless indecisive gesture.

'A convent,' she said. 'They have convents for them.'

I looked down at her, she up at me.

'When?' I said.

'Three months,' she said.

'You can't live here all that time. I'll find a place for you.'

'I want to stay here. Penance.'

'You've seen a priest?'

'No.'

'Penance is not yours to impose,' I said. The words sounded pompous. I just wanted to leave that foul place.

'If I stay here I'll disgrace nobody.'

'What did you tell Little Diego?'

'That I was going to Porto Santo with his grandmother.'

'Why didn't you?'

'We're known there. She didn't want to face the shame.'

Then finally I closed the small distance between us and touched her shoulder, but she moved out of reach with heavy awkwardness across the filthy pile of straw.

'Why did he have to come to Lisbon? Why did you have to go away?'

'I'll always be going away. Somewhere,' I said.

'Yes. Yes, I know you will.' For a long minute she sat unmoving, fists clenched and face lifted to the light from the chimney hole, tears welling from her tight-shut eyes. Then she made a keening noise and turned her face to the wall.

I left her and found what passed for a shop in that awful slum, to arrange for eggs and cheese, bread and wine, to be sent daily to Amalia Lopes in her stinking hovel. But the balding shopkeeper told me, 'That's already been taken care of, Your Honor.'

'Who by?'

'Never left his name, Your Honor. Funny little fellow. Ugly as sin but you could tell he was kind.'

I found the milkman and his small herd of goats, their full udders swinging, and paid him to deliver fresh milk daily to Amalia Lopes — Amalia Lopes who wore black to mourn for the life she had thrown away and perhaps for the life that was coming. Then I went slowly across the Rossio and down the Street of Gold to the shop, where I knew Barto would be waiting.

He was cutting up a distorted-looking copy of a Pozzo Toscanelli map. On the table stood a large wooden ball mounted cleverly in a heavy-based bracket so it could swivel. Barto scowled in concentration. I looked more closely at his map segments. Long and tapering, they had the shape of slender leaf blades or Yoruba spearheads.

'What are you doing?' I asked.

Barto didn't look up. 'I'm not sure yet. But next time I think I can leave them attached at the middle.'

He put the scissors down and went for the paste pot and brush. He told me to hold the wooden ball still. Then, slowly at first but faster as his confidence grew, he pasted his map segments to the wooden globe. I didn't realize what he was doing until most of Asia, Europe and part of the Ocean Sea adhered to the ball of wood.

And there it was, Pozzo Toscanelli's map as God looking down from Heaven might see it. Although at that moment I believed more in Barto and his invention than I did in God.

'Well?' Barto said. 'Will this impress the Royal Maritime Commission?'

My speechless amazement was answer enough.

Thus — historians please note — it was Bartolomé Colón and not Martin Behaim who invented the terrestrial globe.

Barto twirled the globe idly and said, 'You saw her?'

'Yes.'

'And?'

But I shook my head and we did not speak of her again until it was too late — my fault more than his.

That night I took home with me Barto's draft of the proposal we would present to the Royal Maritime Commission on Fifth Day. Little Diego sat on the floor in the downstairs parlor listening with a bored expression on his freckled face while his dowdy new English governess read a fairytale in an atrocious accent.

' ... and then the pwince lipped up on his hawss ...'

'Papa! Papa!' Little Diego sprang to his feet and into my arms.

'Is *this* your papa?' The dowdy English governess looked down her nose skeptically, and I knew that firing the old servants had failed to quash speculation at the Perestrello-Colón mansion as Doña Isabel intended.

'Papa! You're home! You're home!'

I told the governess to leave us. After kissing Diego I held him at arm's length: my bright red hair (without the streaks of white) and freckles, Felipa's huge brown eyes, his own lovable gap-toothed grin.

'Are you home for good, Papa?'

'We'll spend a lot of time together.'

I hugged him tight. He asked about my journey and hung on my neck and on my every word about Darkest Africa. He never mentioned Felipa once, not until I had finished the tale.

'Is Mama coming home too?' he asked hesitantly. 'And Uncle Martin?'

'Where is your Uncle Martin?'

'Uncle Barto said he went to live in the Palace.'

'Do you miss your mother?'

Perhaps it was an unfair question to ask such a young child.

'Of course. I love Mama,' he said promptly. Then he frowned. 'Would Uncle Martin have to come back too?'

'I'm sure he's happy living in the Palace,' I said.

'Good. I didn't like it when they used to fight all the time.'

'Fight? You mean they'd shout at each other?'

'Not argue, Papa. Fight. They used to go to Mama's room. And when they got there they started right in fighting.'

'You shouldn't spy on people, Diego.'

'That's what keyholes are *for*. Even Miss Lake-Lake read me about it in a story. Uncle Martin's bigger, and he's a man. That's why he usually won.'

'You don't have to tell me about it, Diego.'

But it was obvious he did.

'Uncle Martin would throw her down on the bed and jump on top of her and hold her down by bouncing on her.'

'You don't have to − '

'But sometimes Mama would sit on him on the bed and bounce to hold *him* down. I liked it better when Mama won.'

'It wasn't light in the room, was it?'

'No-o. They always shut the drapes. But they lit candles like in church.'

'Then you really couldn't see. They were probably play-fighting. You know, the way puppies do.'

'Well, maybe,' precocious Diego said, doubtful.

'Sometimes grown-ups do one thing and little boys think they're doing something else entirely.'

Diego said, 'I don't like Uncle Martin any more.'

Then he said, 'Remember when Grandma got that really big new carpet? Do men who bring carpets play like puppies too?'

'Grandma played with one of the men?'

'No. Mama did. With both of them.'

I took Diego upstairs after his supper and tucked him into bed. Then I went to my own room and sat for a long time watching the darkness and trying to think of absolutely nothing.

I spent what remained of that night and most of the next day revising Barto's draft of the presentation to the Royal Maritime Commission.

None of my biographers knows what to make of my failure to convince His Most Serene Majesty John II and the commission of the soundness of the Great Venture. Some conjecture that I went too far in tampering with the world as seen by Pozzo Toscanelli. There were two ways to sell a shorter voyage to King and commission, and I used both.

First, since the size of a degree of longitude was in dispute, I simply whittled down the estimate even more than the great Florentine Renaissance Man had done. Using calculations based on Arabic instead of Roman linear measurement, I settled on an equatorial degree of just under forty-five miles, about three-quarters of the correct figure. When multiplied by 360, this gave me a correspondingly smaller planet.

Second, the speculation about what proportion of the world was actually known dated back to when Ptolemy made his educated guess in antiquity. Ptolemy thought that the known world, extending from Cape St Vincent in Portugal to a point in Asia he called Catigara (for no known reason), covered almost precisely 180° of longitude or half the circumference of the earth. But I could do better than that. I stretched the known world 28° for the discoveries of Marco Polo, whose book I'd read a hundred times, and 30° more for the distance from the Cathay coast to Cipango. Tack on the 45° already added to Asia by Pozzo Toscanelli, *et voilà*. I gave King and commission a known world of 283°. And, as I planned to sail west across the Ocean Sea from the Canary Islands, that left a scant 60° of uncharted water to cross, or some 2,500 miles.

Did I go too far in tampering with Pozzo Toscanelli's map? No, because I left the spirit of it intact. Men want to see their own world as larger and more important than it is. It's a matter of self-esteem. Witness the trouble poor Galileo would face in the seventeenth century when he insisted on putting the sun in the earth's place at the center of the universe. Mankind likes to be magnified, not diminished.

Besides, Barto and I had the commission eating off the palms of our hands the instant we undraped my brother's spectacular globe. How could it have missed? These philosophers, scientists and mariners (and one churchman, the Bishop of Ceuta) were seeing the earth from God's viewpoint for the first time. And Barto, in his final work on the globe, had done himself proud. Luminous with color – gold, silver and the deep aquamarine of the sea predominating – Barto's globe was girdled by the signs of the zodiac, each depicted in its own blue and gold medallion. Barto had even populated his globe: here in Darkest Africa a black primitive, there in distant Tartary a turbaned prince, and on the Ocean Sea ships and those stylized monsters to be found on your ordinary flat map but twice as realistic. Even Martin Behaim gazed at it in wonder. As for His Most Serene Majesty John II, in his excitement he was more twitchy than usual, the tic in his left cheek jumping violently as his eyes darted between the globe and my face.

After the presentation in the Hall of Cosmography overlooking

Palace Terrace and the waterfront, Martin Behaim as our sponsor escorted us outside to the long narrow waiting room, a palace corridor actually. By tradition he would say a few complimentary words about the proposal and then return to Cosmography to deliberate with his colleagues.

But he stroked his dark, pointed beard and what he said was, 'Have you seen Felipa?'

'Yes.'

'I deny everything.'

Just three words, but spoken with such drawling arrogance that the denial became an insolent admission.

With an effort of will I turned my back and stared out the window at the rain lashing Palace Terrace and the estuary beyond. I heard Martin Behaim's slow footsteps retreating as he made his stately way toward Cosmography. Then reflected in the window I glimpsed sudden movement – Barto leaping across the corridor, not at Martin Behaim but at me.

Living in civilized Lisbon I had thought it prudent to replace the sword I'd always worn at my side since my encounter with the Brotherhood of the Golden Stag (or Hind) with a poniard in an ornate scabbard that might pass for the minor eccentricity of a man of culture, and it was the hilt of this that Barto now grabbed. His intention was clear. Martin Behaim's three insolent words had been too much for my brother; Barto still loved Felipa, uncritically and from afar, with that special intensity lavished on one forever beyond reach. It was the way he had loved the sea when we were children in Genoa.

Martin Behaim was the corrupter of that object of pure love, and Barto intended to kill him.

We struggled silently for possession of the small dagger, locked chest to abdomen (he was that much shorter), while Martin Behaim, unaware, walked with his thinking man's stride toward Cosmography. Had he turned, he would have seen that most terrible of biblical tableaux, brother against brother. But the only sound was our labored breathing, and he did not turn. Barto's grip on the hilt of the poniard was steel; my grip on his wrist was steel. I watched the veins bulge on his forehead; he watched the veins bulge on my throat. Meanwhile, Martin Behaim's measured stride continued down the corridor. Barto's thick, powerful wrist grew slippery with sweat. I wouldn't, I knew, be able to hold it much longer. Then I heard the door to Cosmography open and shut slowly as Martin Behaim made his dignified, thoughtful exit, and I released Barto's wrist just as he released the poniard.

'Cuckold!' he whispered furiously. 'He practically admitted to your face what he did to Felipa. He deserved to die. Why'd you stop me?'

I knew I could never tell Barto that Martin Behaim only took what Felipa offered to many.

'Barto,' I said, 'they're deliberating our Great Venture inside Cosmography there. Would you jeopardize all we've worked for?'

'What about Felipa's honor? And your own?' His voice rose. 'What kind of man are you?'

'Stop shouting,' I cautioned. 'They'll hear you.'

My words were reflexive and I couldn't help wondering if, after all, Barto's accusation held a grain of truth. Did anything in this world or beyond mean more to me than the Great Venture? Could anything, ever?

A coolness would develop between my brother Barto and me after the events outside Cosmography, a rift far deeper than the one opened when Felipa fled her wedding at the Saints Chapel of St James convent school. Historians have often speculated why Barto, who had no nuclear family of his own, didn't join me when I left Portugal for Spain. I offer this in explanation. Nor can I find it in my heart to blame him.

His Most Serene Majesty John II and the Royal Maritime Commission deliberated two hours before the door slowly opened and Martin Behaim emerged with measured stride and in measured tones said, 'The Royal Maritime Commission, on which I have the honor to serve as sub-director, has come to a decision on the petition by Christophorus Columbus to sail in His Most Serene Majesty's service west across the Ocean Sea in an attempt to reach the storied East, otherwise known as the, ah, Great Venture.'

His face with its dark, pointed beard was inscrutable.

I might mention parenthetically that this was the first recorded mention of the Latin form of my name, for the proceedings of the Royal Maritime Commission were conducted in that language. Thus, for those reading the English language edition of this book, the name Christopher Columbus at last makes its appearance.

I followed Martin Behaim into Cosmography, his thinking man's stride making it difficult not to tread on his heels. Barto, encountering the same difficulty with regard to me, brought up the rear. We bowed low before King John while Martin Behaim took his place to the left of His Most Serene Majesty at the long table. The King finished nibbling on a torn cuticle and began to bite his left thumbnail. Barto's globe stood in its bracket at the far end of the table.

No one suggested that we sit.

King John nodded to his right. Admiral Dulmo de Terceira, a dazzlingly uniformed fellow not much older than I, rose to his feet, cleared his throat and spoke.

'In the matter of the petition of Christophorus Columbus to sail in His Most Serene Majesty's service west across the Ocean Sea, etc., etc., it is the decision of this commission that the petition be denied.'

There was a brief silence. Then my brother blurted: 'How come?'

This caused a stir. Papers were shuffled around the table. Paired heads turned to whisper. Tongues clucked. The King's left cheek went tic three times. Martin Behaim's beard almost succeeded in hiding his faint sneer of triumph.

It was a question, however curiously worded, that by protocol no one ever asked.

Admiral Dulmo de Terceira cleared his throat again and in a louder voice than before said, 'In the matter of the petition of the aforementioned Christophorus Columbus to sail in His Most Serene Majesty's service, etc., etc., etc., the petition is denied.'

I glanced slowly, in fact with the insolent slowness of Martin Behaim himself, from one face to another along the conference table. Every commissioner averted his eyes except the Bishop of Ceuta who served as the Royal Maritime Commission's spiritual advisor. It could have been sympathy I saw in the aged prelate's eyes but I took it for no more than reflexive Christian charity.

I bowed to the King and led Barto from Cosmography, stunned by my failure.

What happened during the two hours the Royal Maritime Commission considered my petition?

It would be years before I learned the truth, over a bottle of Valdepeñas wine with the Bishop of Ceuta, eighty years old and still going strong, who would then be serving as personal confessor to Luís de Santangel, the converted Jew who was Keeper of the Spanish Royal Household Budget.

The Bishop of Ceuta would say, 'Colón, of course! Castilian form of Columbus, am I right? I knew I knew you from somewhere. The Hall of Cosmography in Lisbon, 1487, I believe?'

I would say self-consciously, aware of the threadbare, much patched state of my clothing, 'Yes, Your Grace, that's right.'

Ceuta would say, 'Why did Martin Behaim hate you?'

I would say, startled, 'Behaim hate *me*? Good God, I was the one wearing the horns!'

Ceuta, wise in the ways of the world, would say, 'Indeed. But surely you realize, my dear Christophorus, that a man like Martin Behaim will naturally despise the man he has cuckolded?'

Eight scientists, philosophers and mariners had served on the commission, and one churchman, himself, Ceuta reminded me. The vote was four to four, with Behaim abstaining.

Ceuta would say, 'A tie meant that King John would cast the deciding vote. But then it was no tie, for Martin Behaim finally spoke up: "Columbus may have intentionally underestimated the distance to the Indies, but what man wouldn't, to sell his scheme? It doesn't detract from the basic soundness."

'Thus we all confidently expected Behaim would open his hand to reveal the small white marble signifying an affirmative vote. But he went on:

'"Still, if this parvenu Columbus knows a good idea when he sees one, it doesn't necessarily follow that he is the man to execute it."

'And with a measured opening of his palm Behaim let a black marble roll onto the long table.

'"For," he said, "there are other mariners, *native Portuguese mariners*, who are more able than the Columbus brothers to take up the challenge of this audacious enterprise."

'A look passed between him and Admiral Dulmo de Terceira, and the admiral retrieved his own white marble and displayed the black.

'"And foreigners of a different stripe whom we would be honored to have sail with us," said Dulmo de Terceira.

'So,' Ceuta would continue while we sat drinking the young Valdepeñas red in the sacristy of his church in the recently constructed siege city of Santa Fé a few miles from the last Arab stronghold, Granada, 'a caravel was fitted out, Dulmo de Terceira in command, Behaim his lieutenant, and with your brother's globe, which he had forgotten to take from Cosmography, aboard. They sailed southwest from Lisbon for the Azores, then west into the Ocean Sea.'

'What happened?' Not that I needed to ask. Westing at the latitude of the Azores, they'd sail directly into the prevailing winds.

Ceuta would chuckle a dry episcopal chuckle and put it differently. 'No *cojones*! Absolutely no *cojones*, Dulmo, Behaim, the lot of them! Four days out they hit their first bad storm, turned tail and let the wind blow them straight back to Lisbon. Behaim, discredited in Portugal, left for his native Nuremberg two months later. With, as you know, your brother's globe, which he palmed off as his own invention.'

So ended the little-known Portuguese attempt to reach the fabled East by sailing west prior to 1492.

To my biographers my wife Felipa was a shadowy figure, no more than a foil for me. As the daughter of a director of the Sprawling Navigational Complex, she was a good match for the aspiring discoverer of the New World. As a healthy young woman, she presented me with a son and heir, Little Diego. As a dead one, she provided me with the opportunity to give her the best funeral money could buy.

Her burial place, the obscure church of Carmo on the high outskirts of the city, was near the shantytown where Felipa spent her final days. Like most of Lisbon, Carmo church would be destroyed by the earthquake that struck at High Mass on the first day of November 1755, killing half the population and incinerating the city archives. These dated from the fourteenth century, so it is possible – had the earthquake not occurred – that some diligent researcher might have uncovered in the brittle, yellowed volumes an entry relating to the capture and summary execution of two gypsy murderers on the last Fourth Day in June 1487. Whether he would have connected these events with the death of one Amalia Lopes would have depended on the thoroughness of the archive entry. Would it have indicated the place of the fugitives' capture? Or the manner of the Lopes woman's death? Even if it had, to identify Amalia Lopes, pregnant unmarried nobody, with Doña Felipa Perestrello de Colón would have been difficult. Still, a diligent researcher might have noted that Amalia Lopes and Felipa Perestrello died on the same day, and the burial of only one was recorded.

But enough of conjecture. The sad events are simply told.

That final Fourth Day of June 1487 I was alone in the shop shortly before noon, Barto having business with a Maltese shipmaster, when a balding man entered breathless and red-faced. When he could speak he said, 'I'm looking for a funny little fellow, ugly as sin but you can tell he's kind.'

'That's my brother. He won't be in today.'

'Sure. Now I recognize you, Your Honor.' The balding man mopped his face, which I have to admit I couldn't place. 'Name's Isaac Levi, Your Honor. I'm the owner of what passes for a shop in the slum where Amalia Lopes lives. You wanted me to send her food every day, cheese and eggs, bread and wine, but the funny little fellow – begging your pardon, I mean to say Your Honor's brother – had already paid me to do just that. He also said to come here at once if she was in trouble. She is – and it's bad.'

Isaac Levi was forced to take two running steps for each of my long strides along the Street of Gold and across the Rossio and up the hill to the slum where Felipa lived.

As we crossed the Rossio he said breathlessly, 'This is where they did it. Gypsies. Knifed a gent to death and stole his portable clock and money. The hue and cry started here.'

The narrow streets of the shantytown were almost deserted until we neared Felipa's hovel. There the streets surged with raggedly-dressed inhabitants of the slum. People were running and shoving. There were shouts and oaths.

'They're hanging them!'

'They're drawing and quartering them!'

'Flaying them alive, I heard!'

All this was hyperbole.

Two mounted pursuers leading the hue and cry had overtaken the fleeing gypsies on the street where Felipa lived, holding them at swordpoint until those on foot arrived. The gypsies were beaten, stoned and kicked to death, and the crowd was now jeering their battered corpses at a crossroads just beyond Felipa's hovel. The two horses stood nervously nearby, eyes wide, nostrils flaring. One of the caballeros was talking to a skinny little man I remembered as the neighborhood milkman.

'Yes, certainly I'll pay you for them,' he said.

'Those goats are my livelihood, Your Honor.'

'I said I'd pay. It was just one of those unfortunate accidents.'

Two of the six goats were dead in the street a few yards from where the nervous horses stood. A small milk pail, one side crushed by a hoof, lay in a fading white stain right outside Felipa's hovel.

'Half an escudo for the pair of them, Your Honor.'

'Done,' said the caballero in a bored voice as he opened his purse.

I pushed aside the curtain in the doorway and went in, colliding in the dimness with a priest coming out. The filthy pile of straw on which Felipa lay was darkly wet. As my eyes grew accustomed to the faint light coming through the chimney hole, I could see that her bruised face gleamed with sacramental oil. Two old women knelt near her.

'There, dear, now there,' one of them said in a crooning voice. 'She's a fine baby girl.'

The women had already placed the tiny corpse on the floor in the furthest corner of the room.

'Can I see her?'

'In just a few minutes now, dear.'

The caballero came in. 'We're terribly sorry, you know,' he said in the same bored voice he had used with the milkman. 'Just one of those unfortunate accidents. She stepped into the road with her milk can as we galloped up. If there is some restitution we can make – '

'Get out of here,' I said.

'Now listen, fellow,' he began, but then saw I was dressed as well as he, while the woman he had run down was a nobody. This made him draw the wrong conclusion. 'Well, we seem to have simplified your problem for you, don't we?' he said, and laughed obscenely.

I shoved him out the doorway and knelt between the two old women and Felipa. 'Leave us,' I said.

Her torn lips tried to smile up at me and the eye that wasn't swollen shut filled with tears.

'You've come back.'

'Yes.'

'Are you going to take me home?'

'Yes, Felipa,' I said. 'You're going home.'

'I'll be a good wife, you'll see.'

A mangled hand reached up. I touched it. Blood welled from her lips and after that she couldn't speak.

I remained on my knees beside her until the end came.

Perhaps the dimness and the stale air had made me drowsy and that was why in the instant that she died I saw not the filthy hovel with a roof hole for a chimney, but a high cliff and single-masted boat silhouetted against the great crimson ball of the sun sinking into the sea.

❧ VI ❧

In Which I Learn Much
About Spain and Spaniards
and Even More About Myself

A QUICK glance at a map will show that sailing south from Lisbon and then east at Cape St Vincent you soon pass the Spanish frontier. The first port is Huelva, and next Palos. After a stretch of gloomy marshland comes the delta of the mighty Guadalquivir. Enter the river with the tide and you reach the great city of Sevilla. Continue along the coast and you raise Cádiz, Spain's other big Atlantic port.

Huelva and Palos on the delta of the unimpressive Río Tinto were, in 1487, backwaters. They had seen days of glory when Spain challenged Portugal for the West African gold, ivory and slave trade. But in 1481 King Fernando and Queen Isabel, mounting their Holy War against the Arabs in southern Spain, couldn't afford to risk war with Portugal and so relinquished all rights to the lucrative African trade. This confirmed Lisbon as a giant among cities. It turned little Huelva and Palos on the delta of the Río Tinto into depressed areas. Where once great fleets had sailed south almost to the equator, now only a few battered old fishing smacks slipped out at night to net their meager catch of hake or sardines, bream or mackerel.

I mention all this because no biographer ought to write as if his subject stands somehow outside the flow of history, yet this is what most of mine have done. They claim that I took ship from Lisbon (many of them getting the year wrong, by the way) with Little Diego and a seabag crammed with charts, maps, the four books I was never without, the letters of Pozzo Toscanelli and samples of Porto Santo driftwood, and landed at the first Spanish port of call, which happened to be Palos. But the ship on which we took passage went on from there to Sevilla and eventually Cádiz. Why did I disembark at Palos? Most biographers will tell you that I used my last handful of coppers to pay our passage and it only took us that far. But the ship was a Centurione felucca. Our passage cost me nothing. I could have sailed to the end of the line and, while I was at it, put more distance between myself and my creditors in Lisbon. (I had been unable to pay for Felipa's elaborate funeral and even Pighi-Zampini's patience wasn't endless.)

Dropping me and Little Diego in Palos, most biographers then go on to write how the very first Spaniards I encountered started a train of events that culminated in the success of the Great Venture, as if coincidence more than Columbus discovered the New World.

Ridiculous!

I knew exactly what I was doing by disembarking at has-been Palos. And to meet at once the very people whose help I needed for the Great Venture was hardly coincidence either. No: I was thirty-six years old, I had a motherless six-year-old son, my streaked hair was as much white as red by then, and I had felt the icy touch of mortality when Felipa died. In the great ports of Sevilla or Cádiz I would have been just another out-of-work ship's captain or a chartmaker without a shop, but the little port of Palos, bypassed by history, needed me. Or so I hoped.

As the Centurione felucca stood off the delta waiting for the flowing tide that would carry us upriver past the headland of La Rábida to Palos, I asked Little Diego, 'You see that handsome building way up there on the cliff?'

'Where?'

I took his hand and pointed it in the right direction, which was mostly up.

'It looks like a jail,' he said.

'No it doesn't. It's just sturdily built of good dark stone. It's a friendly place run by friendly Franciscan friars. They have a school there for boys your age.'

But Little Diego was right. Seen from the mouth of the river the Monastery of La Rábida high on its rock did have a certain gloomy penitentiary air.

'Is that where you're taking me?' he asked.

'To school, yes,' I told him brightly.

He began to cry. 'What did I do? I wasn't bad. I don't want to go there!'

I hugged him and said, 'It's really a very fine place, you'll see.'

We climbed the steep dusty road from Palos and reached the monastery in the heat of late afternoon, Diego astride my shoulders by then. We were received by the prior himself, Juan Pérez by name, who had served as Queen Isabel's confessor when she was just a teenaged princess in Castile, sister of King Enrique the Impotent. I had written ahead, knowing from scuttlebutt in Lisbon of Fray Juan Pérez's interest both in the sea and in the welfare of the unemployed citizens of Palos and Huelva.

'Well, so this is Little Diego,' he said.

Diego glowered at him. 'Don't want to stay here.'

Juan Pérez just smiled and gave him yeasty bread to eat and a cup of cool water. 'It is no bad thing, is it, to learn how to be a Christian gentleman?' he said.

Chewing, Little Diego said, 'Papa's always going away and leaving me.'

'Sometimes people have to do things they don't like to do. The little Christ Child was born in a manger and I'm sure His parents didn't like *that*,' said Juan Pérez.

'How old was Little Jesus?' precocious Diego asked.

'Why, He'd only just been born.'

'Then He didn't know He was born in a watchacallit. I know I don't want to stay here.'

'You'll change your mind, you'll see,' I predicted. But he never would, not in the five years he remained at La Rábida.

After we kissed goodbye, Little Diego tearful, me with a lump the size of a colón bean in my throat, Juan Pérez asked me, 'You'll stay the night?'

'Thanks, prior. But not if I'm expected in Palos.'

'You are. The man's name is Martín Alonzo Pinzón. You may find him somewhat – difficult, but he is the town's leading shipmaster.'

Just then Diego ran back into the room pursued by a puffing, corpulent Franciscan.

'Papa, give me one more kiss!'

I took him in my arms, the colón bean back in my throat, bigger.

'Bigger!' Diego urged.

I kissed his eyes and tear-stained cheeks.

When I put him down he went with the corpulent friar, but turned back hesitantly. 'Please don't die too, Papa.'

An hour later I was on the Palos waterfront looking at caravels, urcas and carracks, all veterans of the West African trade, hawsers slack, hulls turning listlessly with the current, as if they knew their sailing days were over. Barnacles encrusted them at the waterline and no doubt they were riddled with woodworm.

'Barnacles, woodworm, dry rot, rust – this ain't a shipyard, it's a graveyard!' a huge voice bellowed and I turned and got my first look at Martín Alonzo Pinzón, a man as tall as I with a big barrel of a belly over scrawny shanks.

At twilight we stood at the plank bar of a noisy men-only waterfront bodega, digging into a mound of succulent pink shrimp and drinking manzanilla, the desiccated white wine of Puerto Santa Maria across the bay from Cádiz.

'The law forbids you the African trade,' I was saying to Pinzón. 'Venice and Ragusa have a lock on the eastern Mediterranean, and Genoa and Lisbon can handle the north between them, with a little help from Cádiz and Sevilla – so what's left?'

'That says it all. Nothing's left,' boomed Martín Alonzo Pinzón in his bull bellow as he decapitated and shelled a plump shrimp and tossed it into his mouth. 'It looks like we clean ran out of directions.'

'Aren't you forgetting? The compass has four cardinal points.' I gestured out the open door, which faced west.

'Oh, sure. I was coming to that. The Azores and them,' Martín Alonzo Pinzón said confidently, while he tried to figure out what he was coming to. His face, its small features clustered compactly, the eyes close-set and small, the nose delicate (and delicately broken at the bridge), the lips tiny and pursed as if to ask a perpetual question, seemed far too small for his large head, which he now thrust at me on his thick column of a neck, waiting for me to point the way to what he would say next.

I said, 'No port on this coast can get back on its feet just by trading with the Azores.'

'Course not,' said Martín Alonzo Pinzón. 'That's part of the problem as I see it.'

'I meant further west,' I said slowly. 'Far enough west until west becomes East.'

Martín Alonzo Pinzón banged our empty wine jug on the planks and a man in a purple-stained apron took it to one of the huge casks behind the bar, unplugged the bung and filled it.

Pinzón looked at me. 'What'll you find — assuming you can get there?'

'Cipango,' I told him. 'The Indies, Cathay.' I spoke the names like a litany and he said, his eyes glowing like two lighthouse beams, 'Cipango, sure. I heard of Cipango. Gold! There's gold all over — '

'If I sailed from here,' I said, 'Palos and Huelva could have a monopoly on the trade for a hundred years. All the riches of the East.'

'That's it, man! We'd be wealthy again. It's the obvious conclusion I was about to point out.'

He was drinking manzanilla as fast as he could pour it. He called for another jug. His red face streamed sweat.

'Where do you figure to get backing?' he asked.

'Someone's going to cross the Ocean Sea,' I told him. 'If not me now, then others later. And if not flying Spanish colors, then French or English. I'll go to the Sovereigns. They'll have to back me.'

'The King and Queen are your answer,' Martín Alonzo Pinzón said, nodding sagely. 'Which I'd have told you if you were any slower to see it.'

He wiped his sweating face with a forearm as thick around as his scrawny thigh.

'What would you sail?' he asked me.

'Small ships. Fast, maneuverable.'

'Caravels,' he said. 'Not big ones — fifty-five tonners, say. Am I right?'

I admitted he was right.

'Nothing, man,' he said self-deprecatingly. 'Simple common sense.'

'And maybe a carrack of a hundred tons or so to carry more provisions,' I said.

'That's it!' he told me. 'That's exactly what I was thinking. You'll need plenty of hold space for food and water and them. A carrack's your answer there.' He looked at me. 'How many ships?'

'Two could do the job. I'd feel easier with three.'

'Three's definitely the number I had in mind. How would you rig them?'

'Square,' I said. 'I'd square-rig them.'

His small eyes widened and there was scorn in his voice as he told me, 'Man, you're loco! Lateen's the only rigging if you hope to cross the Ocean Sea. Those westerlies, they'd eat your square-rigged ships alive.'

This was the first time he hadn't turned my words into his words.

'They would,' I said, 'if I was dumb enough to sail directly west from here.'

'And what's wrong with Palos and Huelva that you'd have to be dumb to sail from them? Dumb enough!'

'I said dumb enough to sail directly west.'

But he was still enthralled by the novelty of disagreeing. 'Dumb enough! Shit!'

'Did you ever sail in the African trade?'

'Once.' He calmed down. He looked at me, waiting, but I did not speak. He said, 'All the way south to Fernando Po. What of it?'

'What happened when you crossed into the equatorial zone?'

'What the fuck do you think happened? We traded gewgaws for gold, and horses for people.'

'I meant the wind. It changes down there.'

'Wind's always changing. So?'

'The prevailing winds down there blow from the east.'

'And . . . and Cipango and them, they're west across the Ocean Sea.' He rubbed the four-day mat of whiskers on his jaw, waiting for me to inspire him.

'I'd drop down to the Canary Islands and head west from there with the wind at my back all the way,' I said.

'Then you'd have to re-rig, man,' he urged in an access of inspiration. 'Square rigging. Square rigging's the only thing if you're sailing before the wind. Your lateen-rigged caravels wouldn't be worth a damn.'

'I might carry lateens for the mizzen just to be on the safe side,' I conceded.

'To get back, you mean. You'd need lateens to get back, and not just on the mizzen.'

'No I wouldn't.'

'You wouldn't?'

'Not if I sail north from the Indies, pick up the westerlies and let them blow me back to Europe.'

'What amazes me,' he said, shaking his head, 'is how two men can be working on the same idea and they never even met before in their lives.'

He turned, graceful as a cat despite his barrel belly, and went to one of the simple plank tables in the bodega, where a man wearing a black velvet hat with a fluffy white ostrich plume sat over a jug of manzanilla. I saw Martín Alonzo Pinzón nod, and the man got up. He was tall and lean, his carriage erect. With Pinzón he joined me at the bar.

'I am Luís de Cerda,' he introduced himself, 'Duke of Medina-celi.'

I hadn't crossed paths with the likes of a duke since my boyhood in Rome, that nervous wreck of a Most Serene Majesty in Portugal excepted, and I stood for a moment awkwardly silent while Pinzón called to the barman to pay for the wine.

'Allow me, Don Martín Alonzo,' said the duke.

'I ain't so poor yet I can't pay for what I drink,' Pinzón said, and dropped a few copper maravedís on the plank. 'And fill a jug for the duke and my friend while you're at it,' he told the barman, then punched Medinaceli's arm hard enough to make him wince, said, 'See you around, duke,' and wandered outside.

Luís de Cerda, Duke of Medinaceli, saw my raised eyebrows. He smiled thinly and said, 'If treating me so offhandedly when he's down and out makes him feel more a man, does it make me feel any less a duke?' He turned sideways to me and rubbed his arm surreptitiously. 'What did you think of him?' When I hesitated, he said, 'You think he'll try to steal your thunder, don't you?'

'That's it exactly, man,' I boomed with Pinzónian heartiness. 'In fact, I was about to say he'll try to take the wind out of my sails to fill his own.'

The duke laughed and I knew it would be all right.

'Still, he's an experienced captain and there's not a seaman up and down this coast who'll ship with you unless Martín Alonzo Pinzón's for it. And to be for it, he has to believe the project's his own. By the time you're ready to sail he'll have convinced himself he planned the whole enterprise and the King and Queen just sent you here to put the royal imprimatur on it. He's bound to come up with some "improvements" of his own, too, by way of convincing himself. Can you live with that?'

Medinaceli's ducal seat lay northwest of Toledo, but I knew he also owned most of Palos and Huelva. I told him:

'I can live with anything if I get the Sovereigns' backing.'

'Write to them as convincingly as you wrote to my old friend the prior of La Rábida, and I'll deliver your letter in person. Don't forget that line about if not Spain today then France and England tomorrow. It's a nice rhetorical touch.'

I shrugged. 'It was nothing.'

He laughed. 'You're beginning to sound Spanish. Now try saying it with more self-deprecation – the ultimate metaphysical nothing, *nada.*' His face conveyed a sort of inner-directed scorn as he repeated: '*Nada.*'

'*Nada,*' I tried.

'Not bad. Where are you from anyway? You're not Portuguese.'

I had to answer something, so I said, 'Genoa,' which was in a way true. In later years his memory of my answer would help confuse my biographers, who are confused enough to begin with.

'The Sovereigns should pass through Córdoba in a month or so on their way to Málaga, where the Gran Capitán's besieging the Arabs. Can you be there?'

'Córdoba or Málaga, name it and I'll be there.'

'Málaga's still held by the enemy,' he pointed out gently.

'Then Córdoba if you prefer,' I said, implying that I could have got into Málaga if I had to.

'More Spanish all the time.' He chuckled appreciatively.

'*Nada,*' I said.

He let his eyes fall to my travel-worn jerkin and threadbare tights, then to my lumpy seabag on the floor.

'Your court clothes?' He smiled.

I said, 'The four books I'm never without and some driftwood.'

'Driftwood?'

'Driftwood.'

He didn't pursue the matter. 'Well, you'll have a month or so to wait, so if you – need anything, you have only to ask.'

But I remembered Martín Alonzo Pinzón's gesture of paying for his own wine and treating the duke. 'Thank you, Your Grace. I'll manage.'

'In that case, get your letter to me by this time tomorrow. And let me know how to reach you in Córdoba,' the duke said. He commended me to God and left the bodega.

Without a maravedí to my name, I walked the 160 miles to Córdoba in six days, sleeping where I could, begging food and wine along the way, wearing out two pairs of boots – one, I'm sorry to say, stolen. The begging I make no apology for. It was a respected profession in Spain, a holdover from the almost 800 years of Arab rule. Some of the proudest, most arrogant, and in their own way most socially demanding people I have ever met were Spanish beggars. The important thing, as in any other line of work, was to be a *good* beggar. In Spain it isn't so much what you do as how you do it.

After the invention of the printing press in Mainz by Peter Schöffer (or, if you insist, Johann Gutenberg, whose real name by the way was Gensfleisch, or Gooseflesh), Germany had been spewing Germans all over Europe to start publishing houses. Two German printers opened shop in Rome in 1464; by 1470 at the latest a pair were at work in Venice and three in Paris; Holland's turn came in 1471, Switzerland's in 1473 and Spain's in 1476, when three brothers named Waldseemüller set up a press in Córdoba.

There were the usual protests, predictions and warnings. Manuscript copyists complained bitterly that the printing press would put them out on the street; the nobility were up in arms over the vulgarization of books by mass production, which would deflate the value of their own libraries; politicians and clergymen saw any book but the Bible as a means of spreading subversive ideas, and some had their doubts about the Bible.

The youngest of the three Waldseemüller brothers, Martinus, was the only one I ever met. His older and more experienced brothers were always on the road selling, since it was soon established that salesmen, more than books, determine success or failure in publishing.

Martinus Waldseemüller stood precariously on a ladder outside the brothers' shop, second on the right from the Iron Gate, the day I arrived in Córdoba. He was an almost neckless man of thirty or so who shaved his head to flaunt rather than hide incipient baldness, an affliction rare in Spain, where much garlic and olive oil are consumed. Perched on the third rung of the ladder, he was whitewashing over the graffiti painted in blood red on the shopfront while a crowd heckled. Only parts of three lines remained:

> ugger goats and small boys
> uck Arab pussy
> üllers go home!

As he whitewashed out each word, the crowd chanted. He painted out 'uggers' and they chanted 'goats!', painted out 'uck' and they chanted 'Arab pussy!', painted out 'üllers' and they chanted 'go home!'

A nearsighted little Spaniard came out of the shop just as Martinus Waldseemüller finished the whitewashing.

'I quit,' said the squinting little Spaniard. 'I can't take any more.'

'If you can't take any more, you aren't working, so you can't quit, you're fired,' Martinus Waldseemüller told him with ponderous German logic.

When the German alighted from the ladder, his shaven skull speckled with whitewash, I asked, 'Are you in need of an experienced literary person?' As a sea captain and chartmaker I was unemployable in inland Córdoba, but like most chartmakers Barto and I had also occasionally dealt in books.

'Him, in editorial?' said Waldseemüller with a contemptuous head jerk at the departing little Spaniard, his consonantal German accent stronger than Martin Behaim's. 'My papermaker he was. If you're interested, sixteen hours a day, in the plant and in the town.'

'Why in town?'

'Acquisitions. Someone has to collect the old clothes to make the paper,' said Martinus Waldseemüller. 'I pay eight maravedís a day, take it or leave it.'

On eight maravedís a day a man could keep body and soul together and have a jug of wine on Saturday night. But I needed a new wardrobe for my audience with the Sovereigns.

Waldseemüller said, 'The usual fringe benefits – Sunday off and every other Thursday afternoon. So? *Ja* or *nein*?'

I hefted my seabag containing the hand-copied editions of the four books I was never without. I knew that books for setting into type were in short supply. 'What will you pay for the right to copy these four volumes?'

'Depends,' he said with a show of uninterest. 'We only do titles with strong sales potential.' But his eyes gleamed avariciously at the lumpy shape of my seabag. 'What do you have?'

'*The Book of Ser Marco Polo*, for one.'

'That old dog? Couldn't give it away nowadays.'

'Pliny's *Natural History*.'

'Hopelessly dated. It just wouldn't earn out.'

'Pierre d'Ailly's *World Picture*, and *The Story of Geography* by Aeneas Sylvius. That's the late Pope Innocent II's pen name,' I added quickly, for I could see he didn't think much of my properties.

'The d'Ailly's old hat, especially now that Ptolemy's been redis-covered. As for His Innocence, all *he* did was plagiarize Ptolemy and his pen name's the worst-kept secret in publishing. No,' said Martinus Waldseemüller, 'I'm afraid all of them are depressingly mid-list. However, as books are still a novelty in Spain, they'll sell a few copies anyway. Double your salary as long as it takes to set them in type? So? *Ja* or *nein*?'

I accepted philosophically his cavalier dismissal of the four volumes so central to the development of my Great Venture, and agreed on condition that I receive an advance payment for the books, possibly originating the tradition. Which was how I became a papermaker for Waldseemüller Brothers, Fine Books.

It was hard work. You beat the old clothes with a wooden paddle to break the fibers, you chopped them in a trough, you boiled them with bleach, you added a hundred parts of water to one part now-white linen pulp, and put in just the right amount of stinking animal glue to make the eventual paper water-resistant, you removed some of the water by a back-breaking screening process and the rest by pressing, you cut the wet paper like a baker cuts dough, and you hung the sheets out to dry.

Saturdays you made your rounds of Córdoba in a mule cart to buy old clothes.

This left me barely enough time for eating and sleeping at the inn just inside the Iron Gate, first on the left. I never would have met my son and biographer Fernando's mother, except that every few days at unpredictable intervals Martinus Waldseemüller would put on his Sunday best (black velvet beret, purple satin gown with black velvet collar and cuffs, red high-heeled shoes) and disappear for a few hours, probably to eat iron.

One afternoon when he had departed, leaving me in charge, a young woman entered the shop.

'I want to buy a book,' she must have said.

I didn't hear her because the press in the room next to the paperworks at the back was making more than its usual clatter and thump, as it did when Waldseemüller's nephew ran it.

'I didn't hear you,' I said.

'I want to buy a book,' she said, louder.

'What sort of book did you have in mind?'

This obvious question seemed to alarm her. 'Why, just your regular kind of usual book. I haven't really given the matter much thought.'

I helped out with: 'Is it a gift for someone?'

'No. No, it's just for myself.'

I continued helpfully: 'Well, what kind of books do you like?'

These innocent words made her bite her lip in what I took for indecision. 'I don't really know,' she said in a small voice.

There were no display shelves. Books were printed and bound in goatskin, then sold here in Córdoba by Martinus Waldseemüller immediately after a press run, or elsewhere in Spain by his traveling brothers. But sometimes a few might be left lying around, and some customers unwilling to risk the ire of nobles, priests or politicians came furtively in the back way through the paperworks, leaving with their purchases wrapped in plain, frequently brown, wrappers.

This young woman, though, had come in the front way with a proud, animated expression on her face. It was, in fact, an attractive face to look at. Her undeniably Iberian eyes, dark, mysterious, reflexively flirtatious (though shy now), her possibly Berber lips, full, red, sensuous (though shy now), her conceivably Semitic nose, haughtily high-bridged (though shy now), all clearly indicated the diversity of her Spanish ancestry. She was tall and well-proportioned in an hour-glass sort of way. With her rosy, perhaps Visigoth cheeks and large hands she looked like a farmgirl just come to the city.

'Actually,' she said, 'I'm a farmgirl just come to the city and I intend to buy a book.' She had conquered her shyness and now spoke firmly, almost belligerently.

'How about Plutarch's *Lives*?'

'Does it have a happy ending?'

Plutarch, as you know, takes his *Lives of the Noble Grecians and Romans*, to give the book its full name, to their very end, and the very end of no life can be said to be happy.

'Well, yes and no,' I informed her.

She made a chirpy little sound of delight. 'Oh, I hoped it would be like that – mysterious!'

'Some of them have unhappy love affairs.'

'And romantic too!'

'Several of his heroes die young.'

'So beautifully tragic! I'll take it.'

I found the damaged copy of Plutarch that Martinus Waldseemüller had put aside for just such an emergency.

She examined the crooked spine and said, 'Is it a good book to learn to read from?'

'You mean you can't? Read? Then what do you want a book for?'

'Why, to learn how, of course.'

'It isn't done that way,' I said, as gently as the Duke of Medinaceli had told me the Arabs still held Málaga.

'You mean I have to know how to read before I can buy a book? It isn't fair. How can I learn to read *unless* I buy a book?'

I tried to explain.

'Then *if* it's not against the law and *if* selling it doesn't put you out too much, I'll take this Pluto anyway,' she said icily.

'Plutarch,' I said, while she carefully counted out tarnished copper maravedís, sixty-eight in all, to total two silver reales. I returned a dozen coppers to her, explaining that the book was damaged. Wald-seemüller would have skinned me alive.

'Wrap it for you?'

'Not on your life. I want the whole world to see it.'

She turned to leave. On her jet black hair she wore a Turkish bonnet, and her pale blue kirtle was belted, emphasizing the slimness of her waist and curves like wind-filled sails above and below. Delighted with the book but not the salesman, she flounced away from me, a movement I found pleasantly disconcerting.

She was out the doorway and almost out of my life when I called after her. 'I'll teach you to read if you want.'

Beatriz and I would meet every Sunday after Mass and every other Thursday afternoon at her uncle's seasonally disused olive press inside the Iron Gate, fifth on the right. There she had gone prior to calling at Waldseemüller Brothers, Fine Books, to dig up the jar of tarnished maravedís she had buried under the floor in the furthest back of the three pressing rooms, and to that room we repaired for her lessons. Beatriz, whose farmer parents had died when she was young, had determined not to tell her uncle's family that she was studying until she could read directly from Pluto – that is, Plutarch.

There was, from the beginning, a certain physicality in my teaching methods. Bear in mind that I learned to read not at but *on* the knee of Giulia The Amazon. Beatriz misunderstood at first.

'Keep your hands to yourself.'

I had been holding her hand from behind as we leaned over the table while she attempted to trace her name with a charcoal stick on stained rejects from my less than perfect papermaking efforts.

'Sorry, but if I don't help you at first – look.'

Her writing had degenerated into a meaningless series of squiggles, like a physician's prescription.

'Then just teach me to read, not write.'

But I didn't know how to do one without the other.

We continued innocently enough. Soon we were passing little notes back and forth, the great black iron olive press our only witness.

Me: Write four words that are the names of things.

She: kirtle turkish bonnet buskins

(I hadn't gotten around to teaching her capital letters or punctu-ation.)

Me: I said four.

She (looking at me): blue eyes

(We progressed ambiguously.)

Me: Exactly what are you thinking now? Ten words or more.

She: leave that there so I can see how to spell the first word

Me (helping her write 'exactly' three times): Like that.

She: it is a difacult word

Me: Difficult. But never mind that for now. Are you happy?

She: learning to read and write oh yes

Me: I wonder how you can come here with no dueña. Is one hiding outside? Ha ha.

She (taking two of the small scraps of paper we used, to prepare for the longest sentence she had written so far): first i am a farmgirl from the tiny mountain village of santa maria trasiera where no dueñas are needed as everyone knows every

Me (interrupting with my charcoal): But Córdoba isn't Santa Maria Trasiera.

She: one else second you are an educated man and i trust you not to take advantage of the situation

Me: I suppose you mean that as a compliment but it sounds insulting somehow.

She: must you be so macho let me finish my real name scares men and if worst comes to worst i tell them and they keep their distance or even run away so i really have no need for a dueña

Me: Your *real* name?

She: what does it mean when you draw a line under a word

Me: I thought Beatriz was your real name.

She: i mean enríquez de harana is not my family name i am an orphan remember

Me: Then what is your family name?

She: never mind you are the last person i would tell go on with the lesson please

(We proceeded with a certain inevitability.)

She: you are sad today

Me: It's nothing.

She: why are you sad today

Me: The King and Queen passed right through Córdoba without stopping, and six months late at that.

She: that is just a line you were not really going to see them

Me: It's pointless discussing it now, but you're wrong.

She: i am sorry i did not mean to anger you

Me: Sometimes I feel like Don Quijote tilting at windmills – the futility of it all.

(Note that Cervantes wouldn't publish the first part of his master-

125

piece until 1605. So this couldn't have been precisely what I wrote on my scrap of paper in the olive press room. But it captures the flavor admirably.)

She: if you say you will cross ocean sea someday for royals i believe you

Me: Whether or not you believe me, I'm going to.

She: you are still angry

Me: Me?

She: i will do something to make you feel better if you do not think me too bold

Me: I do not think you too bold.

(Hiatus.)

She: is that better now

'Beatriz, oh God, I – '

She: write please remember you are teaching me

Me: I love your undeniably Iberian eyes.

She: i love your barberpole striped hair

Me: I love your possibly Berber lips.

She: then write about them less and kiss them more

(Longer hiatus.)

Me: This won't end with kissing unless we stop right now.

She: i never told you my real name did i? don't stop!!

(This was her first use of punctuation, and a good place to put a period to this scene.)

When the Gran Capitán took Málaga, the Sovereigns themselves planted the twin standards of Aragon and Castile high on the Arab fortress overlooking the harbor. This done, they left to continue their interminable rounds. Theirs was arguably the most peripatetic royal court of all time, King Fernando and Queen Isabel ever on the move, as if campaigning for the offices that were their birthright. They visited Valencia, Barcelona, Tarragona and Fernando's Aragonese capital of Zaragoza. They then visited Valladolid (near Medinaceli, but no word from the duke), Oviedo, León, Burgos and Isabel's Castilian capital of Toledo. All the while they were drumming up support among the nobility for the final siege of the Arab citadel of Granada.

No wonder they had no time for my Great Venture!

I tried to console myself with that thought, but it didn't help. My only real consolation was Beatriz, with whom I took rooms half-way between the Judería or ghetto and the square a short way north that eventually would be named Plaza de Colón in my honor. Thus I avoided your usual courtship in which the woman sits in comfort inside a grilled window while the man stands outside in all weather proclaiming his love – the old Spanish custom known as eating iron.

Martinus Waldseemüller had grown dependent on me and I was able to insist on Monday off as well as Sunday and every other Thursday afternoon. All this free time I spent with Beatriz. Having abandoned our little scraps of paper, we could converse more profoundly. The big topic of conversation those days in Córdoba, not counting the War of the Holy Faith against the infidel in Granada, was fornication. You couldn't remain neutral. Conservatives insisted, echoing the clergy's public pronouncements, that fornication was a mortal sin. Penance would be heavy, perhaps a difficult journey to some holy shrine. Liberals believed, in accord with the clergy's private feelings (for many churchmen either kept concubines or slept around), that fornication was a venial sin and merited only a few Hail Marys or Pater Nosters.

The church we attended had as pastor a particularly zealous hypocrite.

'Well, what did he say?' I asked Beatriz after confession.

'First, he wanted to hear all the sordid details.'

'Did you – '

'Of course not. Then he said I had to stop seeing you before he could absolve me.'

'Will you – '

'Silly man! I told him my real name instead and he absolved me on the spot.'

'What *is* your real name?'

But she shook her head.

By early November it was obvious even to the casual passerby that Beatriz was pregnant.

Her family asked her if we would wed before the baby came.

'What shall I tell them?' she asked me.

It was a good question, and it occasioned the usual divergence between my biographers and the facts. Take the fellow who flatly said he would leave my 'psychology, motivation and all that' to others. So what does he do, every chance he gets? Probes my innermost thoughts anyway, then presents his insulting speculations not as conjecture or psychohistory but as fact.

Simply put, he said I never married Beatriz because it wouldn't be an advantageous match for me, as marrying the daughter of poor old Perestrello had been.

I was preoccupied when Beatriz asked her question because I had just written my fourth letter to the Duke of Medinaceli. The first three had gone unanswered, as if poor old Perestrello's secret fears had been correct, the world was really flat, and Medinaceli somehow had fallen off the edge.

'Cristóbal, I have to tell them *something*.'

I was standing moodily at the window. Someone who might have been a royal courier came galloping down the street and I watched with sinking heart as he applied the spurs and charged on out of sight.

'Tell them whatever you like,' I said irritably.

One day in early December Beatriz asked me not to be late getting home from Waldseemüller Brothers, Fine Books, and I was in our small but cozy parlor by eight-thirty. Delectable cooking smells, heavy on the garlic, filled the apartment.

'They'll be here in half an hour.'

'Who will?'

'Emissaries,' she said mysteriously.

I wondered if I dared hope, but before I could she saw the flash of eagerness in my eyes and said quickly, 'From my family, I mean. My cousin Diego Enríquez de Harana is coming and the family's closest friend and advisor, Dr Juan Sánchez.' She came to me and held my hand. 'I am sorry, Cristóbal. You thought I meant emissaries from the royals, didn't you?'

'*Nada*,' I managed fatalistically, getting the face almost right.

Diego Enríquez de Harana was a tall, broad-shouldered, athletic-looking man of perhaps thirty. Dr Juan Sánchez, his hair developing a natural tonsure, his eye corners crinkled, his paunch ample, looked as if he would have a fine bedside manner.

'I'm going to be civilized about this,' Enríquez de Harana said in an ominous voice.

Juan Sánchez said, 'Now, Diego, you promised.'

'Her father,' Enríquez de Harana said, 'was – '

'No, Diego!' Beatriz screamed. 'No!'

The good doctor was shocked speechless.

'Her father was Pedro de Torquemada and there's only one Torquemada family in Spain, they're cousins, and if you don't do the right thing by her, guess who's coming to dinner next time?' said Diego Enríquez de Harana in his civilized manner.

Juan Sánchez shook his head in profound sadness.

Beatriz's right hand flew to her mouth in horror.

Strange to think of that night in retrospect. It seemed that I was being forced into what later would picturesquely be called a shotgun wedding, while as it turned out I was recruiting members of the Colón faction of my crew who would prove such valuable allies against the Pinzón faction and others.

'I can never marry,' I said.

I was tall but Enríquez de Harana taller. 'Why not?' he demanded, looming over me.

'It wouldn't be fair to my bride. I'll be leaving Spain soon and I might be gone for years.'

This was true enough. Either I would sail for the Spanish Sovereigns or go north and, despite John Cabot's head start, try my luck in England with King Henry VII, at whose royal court my brother Barto was even now a petitioner. Time and distance had taken care of the coolness between us, and a series of letters had resulted in Barto's journey to the English court. Things were easier for petitioners in England. King Henry VII was far less peripatetic than the restlessly wandering Fernando and Isabel.

'Why will you be leaving Spain?' demanded Enríquez de Harana. He had the manner — suspiciously thorough and thoroughly suspicious — of a policeman. This was something I would remember.

'Hasn't Beatriz told you about the Great Venture?'

Both men shook their heads, so there was nothing for it but to take out maps, charts and driftwood and begin at the beginning with my Julian decade in the north.

'Dinner,' said Beatriz at eleven.

'Then you never did reach Greenland?' Juan Sánchez asked, marveling at it all.

'No. No, it's still lost.'

'The fish is cold and the roast will be shoeleather,' said Beatriz at midnight.

Her cousin Enríquez de Harana, ever suspicious, pursued the matter of rigging. 'If lateen sails always worked on the West African route, why abandon them now?'

I began to explain, but was interrupted by the sound of hoofbeats outside. The horse whinnied to a stop. Boots thudded and spurs jingled in the patio and there came a great pounding at the door.

For an instant I thought of Beatriz's real name and her cousin Tomás de Torquemada, the Grand Inquisitor of Spain.

'Colomb!' a voice shouted. 'Don Cristóbal Colomb!'

'The name's Colón,' I said.

'Well, it says Colomb a Foreigner on this royal summons is all I know,' said the courier as I almost ripped the door from its hinges getting it open.

Thus as Colomb a Foreigner I received my first communication from the King and Queen who, a few years hence in appreciation of the War of the Holy Faith, would be given by no less a personage than my old friend Cardinal Borgia, then Pope Alexander VI, the official title of Los Reyes Católicos or The Catholic Sovereigns.

But in my excitement I'm getting ahead of myself.

The summons, gorgeously illuminated on fine vellum, was unrolled with a flourish by the courier, and I read:

Fernando and Isabel,
by the Grace of God King and Queen
of Castile, León, Aragon, Sicily, etc., etc.,
to Don Cristóbal Colomb, a Foreigner,
Greetings and Grace.

In the matter of the Enterprise of the Indies
or Great Venture
You are ordered into Our Presences
when the Royal Court sits in Salamanca,
that most beautiful city in Our Realm
and indeed all Christendom,
toward Christmastide.

(signed)   (signed)
I The King   I The Queen
Fernando   *Isabel*

Tremblingly I showed Beatriz the summons, Enríquez de Harana and Juan Sánchez listening in amazement as she read it aloud.

'You never told me you could read,' her cousin said.

The doctor beamed his bedside smile.

Enríquez de Harana frowned. 'How do we know it's authentic?'

The royal courier grasped the hilt of his sword.

'Say that again, fellow,' he suggested.

'Sorry. But the timing *is* so incredibly good for Colón here that it makes a man wonder.'

This was the last allusion to the question of matrimony made that night or any night by any of them, at least in my presence.

'Colomb,' said the courier. 'His name's Colomb. And right here's the official royal seal, fellow.'

Enríquez de Harana mumbled acknowledgment. He had a faraway look in his eye that I would come to recognize.

'I was wondering,' he said. He scuffed his buskins on the floor. 'I've done some sailing, you know. Nothing world-class, but I'm a fast learner. See how easily Beatriz learned to read? It runs in the family. So, I was wondering if there was any chance – ' His voice dropped, then rose suspiciously. 'Unless of course you're already overbooked.'

Juan Sánchez got the same faraway look in his eye and asked in his persuasive bedside voice: 'You wouldn't happen to need a ship's doctor?'

How I left Córdoba the following morning for the trek north, first assuring Beatriz of my love and my intention to provide for our child; how I struck off across open country to avoid the long highroad via Sevilla, getting lost in the endless wheatfields beyond Pueblonuevo del Terrible; how I covered the 300 miles to Salamanca in just under three weeks, on foot, on donkeyback and muleback, and in a variety of peasant carts; how I was set upon by highwaymen outside Cáceres but escaped with my seabag intact because in their illiterate rapacity they saw no value in books, maps or driftwood; how I almost froze when I tumbled into the appropriately named Río Frío and how in the curiously misnamed Montañas de Francía I strayed from the route over the pass during a blizzard, almost perishing of hunger and exposure; how I crossed the Roman bridge more dead than alive and through feverish eyes at last beheld Salamanca, that most beautiful city in Christendom (for the King and Queen were right), which had in turn been conquered by Carthaginians, Romans and Arabs; how a clash between the *bandos* or street gangs of Santo Tomé and San Benito resulted in my loss of the four books I was never without, not to mention the two or three remaining of those I had borrowed from Waldseemüller Brothers, Fine Books, to sell along the route; how I collapsed at nightfall Christmas Eve on the cobblestones of University Square, the brazen ringing of all the churchbells of Salamanca falling on my deaf ears; how members of the Holy Brotherhood, or Castilian secret police, cared for me when they saw my summons from the King and Queen – all this can be found in various sources, some obscure, but are not the proper stuff of an autobiography concerned with 'psychology, motivation and all that.'

I prefer to take this opportunity to excoriate one Washington Irving, a young New World diplomat who would spend a few months living in the Alhambra of Granada and write an amusing little book of tales about it some three and a half centuries after I personally marched in with the army of liberation, of which more in its chronological place. This same Washington Irving would write a not so amusing book grossly mistitled *The History of the Life and Voyages of Christopher Columbus*, and it is this egregious volume I wish now to condemn for the most glaring of its countless untruths.

Picture the scene at St Stephen's College, Salamanca U., when the Talavera Committee convened in a locked room to hear me propound the Great Venture. Picture the chairman Hernando de Talavera, the Queen's ascetic, burning-eyed confessor, and assorted other clergymen, astronomers, mathematicians and so on, gravely impressive in their priestly vestments and academic gowns. Then consider this fellow Irving's nonsense. To hear him tell it, all those learned types believed, as poor old Perestrello almost had, that they lived on a flat earth, and despite all my considerable rhetoric, not to mention Pozzo Toscanelli's maps as improved by my brother Barto, I could barely hold my own against them. In fact, this Irving would even portray me as concerned that the Inquisition, for my belief in a round earth, might condemn me for heresy.

What drivel!

The whole civilized world, the Talavera Committee and the Supreme and General Council of the Inquisition included, knew itself to be round and had known so since antiquity. As I've said before.

The actual events were these:

I arrived in the committee room promptly at ten. At eleven-thirty ascetic, burning-eyed Hernando de Talavera entered and explained that the Sovereigns' itinerary was as ever behind schedule and they would miss the hearings. As he spoke, his fellow committeemen filed in to look curiously at my seabag, no longer bulging with the four books I formerly was never without.

My presentation of the Great Venture, abridged by the lack of those books and hampered by the laryngitis I hadn't quite got over, seemed otherwise to go well enough. My driftwood samples, a novelty, were passed around the conference table with various apposite but sometimes disconcerting comments such as, if you've seen one piece of driftwood you've seen them all.

The world of Pozzo Toscanelli as altered by Barto was at last unrolled on a Spanish royal table before a Spanish royal committee, while in my faint laryngitic voice I lucidly explained its relationship to the Great Venture.

'The question and answer period, alas, went poorly. Ascetic, burning-eyed Hernando de Talavera was a skilled interrogator.

'And you've said the western Ocean is how wide?'

'Twenty-five hundred miles, prior.' When not with the royals he was prior of the monastery of El Prado near Valladolid.

'St Augustine would hardly have accepted such a figure,' said Talavera, 'would he?'

'With all respect to the saint, it was a subject he never touched on.'

Talavera changed tack like a fast caravel beating into the wind. 'But there are those who say the world is infinite, aren't there?'

'One cannot call "infinite" a sphere whose precise circumference can be calculated. There are three hundred and sixty degrees of longitude, each some forty-five miles at the equator.'

'St Augustine would never have accepted that figure.' A flat statement this time.

'With respect, St Augustine knew absolutely nothing about meridians of longitude.'

'You see? Then it would have been impossible for him to accept that figure,' said Talavera, his eyes burning brighter as he again changed tack. 'How long would this ... Great Venture of yours take?'

'That depends on how long I stay in the East. Time at sea, a month or six weeks to get there, the same to get back.'

'But if St Augustine is right and you are wrong, if the Ocean Sea is wider – how long would it take then?'

'Then it would take longer. But it isn't. So it won't. I'll get there in a month.'

My laryngitic voice was by then a faint croak.

'What? Speak up, man!'

'(squawk) month to get there.'

'And where, precisely, is *there*?'

'Either Cipango or the islands off the coast of India, that is, the Indies.'

'You mean you don't even know? St Augustine was never so imprecise.'

'St Augustine never had to deal with variables like a change in the wind or – '

'Have you considered that, for two reasons, it is decidedly possible no land whatever exists in the so-called antipodes on the other side of the globe from Europe?'

'Then where did the driftwood you've just seen come from?'

'The first reason is that the antipodes, according to various authorities from antiquity, may well be covered with water. The second is because St Augustine says so. Tell me, don't you believe in your heart that if there were other lands and God meant us to find them, they would already in all the centuries since the Creation have been discovered?'

'All I'm trying to discover,' I said patiently, 'is a sea route to lands we already know are there.'

'So you say. But St Augustine knew nothing of them.'

And so it went – St. Augustine, dead a millennium and more, always the ultimate arbiter, Talavera's voice becoming more righteously vehement as mine became more laryngitically faint.

How I wished for the four books I was formerly never without! How I could have quoted to refute the doubting cleric and his long-dead saintly ally! Seneca, for example, that great Roman of Spanish birth who in antiquity had prophesied: 'A time will come when the Ocean will surrender its mysteries to reveal a huge new land; when a great Navigator will discover New Worlds and Thule no longer be ultimate.'

But unfortunately I was able to quote no one that day.

Finally, toward sunset, the committee gathered at one end of the table. Heads huddled. Voices whispered. I sneezed. Darkness seeped into the room. Candles were lit. I sneezed again.

Talavera said: 'You will be lodged in the Students' Hospice, now under construction, and will await there the pleasure of the Sovereigns.'

Not a word one way or the other about the Great Venture. But they kept my maps, charts and driftwood.

'When will they arrive?'

'Soon.'

To say that the Students' Hospice, which would house no students until 1533 but only petitioners and beggars, was under construction was an exaggeration. Ground had been broken. Perhaps a floor-plan existed somewhere. A few sheds had been knocked together in the construction area, and it was in one of these that I was quartered with a half-dozen other petitioners awaiting the pleasure of the Sovereigns. We slept on the floor, ate in the large dining shed – fried bread crumbs and garlic sausage in the afternoon, watery soup at night, sometimes a little cheese from La Mancha, and La Mancha's rough but friendly red wine. My laryngitis and grippe ran their course, the winter showed signs of spring, and every day one question haunted the Students' Hospice:

'When are they coming?'

But no one knew.

I wrote to Barto and received an answer when spring was in full flower. My brother was fed up with England, King Henry VII was a ditherer who would never make up his mind, and Barto would shortly leave for the court of Charles VIII at Fontainebleau to try his luck in France.

I wrote to Beatriz and learned that our son had been born. Except for his bright, inquisitive blue eyes, Beatriz wrote (no capital letters, scant punctuation), he was more a Torquemada-Enríquez de Harana than a Colón. They had delayed the baptism, awaiting my return, but with a sad heart I wrote back that they should proceed without me because there was still no sign of Their Majesties. Preoccupied with thoughts of royalty, I added, 'Name the boy Fernando for luck.'

I wrote also to Fray Juan Pérez, prior of La Rábida, to inquire about Little Diego. To my proud amazement, the letter that came in return, all eleven words of it, was written in a simple, childish hand. But amazement gave way to sorrow and a profound sense of failure when I read the stark words so laboriously formed by Little Diego.

'Papa I am homesick. When can you take me home Papa?'

Homesick? I thought. For where? We had no home. Here I was thirty-seven going on thirty-eight and I could provide no home for my son, nor would I stand proud at the font when my other son was baptised. Was I any closer to realization of the Great Venture to which I had devoted my life? It scarcely seemed so. Was I any less mad than the wild-haired, wild-eyed petitioner with his elaborately drawn plans for an airship from which enormous stones or cast-iron cannon balls could be dropped on Granada?

'When are they coming?'

But who could say?

All the other petitioners at the so-called Students' Hospice had ideas for one sort of military invention or another. Many were taken from the Hospice and seen no more, but word filtered back that this or that artist (as artillerymen were called) had had a foundry placed at his disposal, or a laboratory equipped. One petitioner was a Frenchman who brought to Spain a new sort of cannon, mounted on its carriage by crosspieces at right angles to the firing tube or barrel, so that the tube could be aimed and the carriage would absorb the shock of discharge. I would see these cannon at the siege of Granada.

Another was a native Spaniard who had served in some Italian army and brought back that brilliant improvement on gunpowder, corning, in which 'powder' became grains of varying size so that the explosive substance, when transported, would no longer separate out, sulphur to the bottom, charcoal to the top, saltpeter between. Since re-mixing on the battlefield was perilous, what with lit matches of musketeers all around, grained powder was seen everywhere at the new siege city of Santa Fé and prolonged the lives of the artists who therefore had more time to kill larger numbers of the enemy.

In those days of the War of the Holy Faith the military sector had things pretty much its own way. I almost think that if you actually found the fountain of youth (which Ponce de León would seek in 1513 on the mainland peninsula he called Florida northwest of my first island landfall), you would have been told to come back later – after the fall of Granada.

'When are they coming?'

But how could anyone even try to guess?

Summer's heat gave way to cool autumn nights and soon hard frost glittered on the ground mornings and we shivered in the so-called Students' Hospice. The first snows of winter fell. Christmastide again approached, and at last came that glorious day when fashionably dressed courtiers and their dazzling ladies appeared among us. At least the royal advance party had reached Salamanca.

But still no King and Queen.

'When are they coming?'

They came on Christmas Eve, one year to the day since I crossed the Roman bridge and collapsed in University Square.

A royal page slogged through the snow to the Students' Hospice, where he beat his gloved hands together and stamped his feet against the cold.

'I'm looking for the Students' Hospice,' he said.

'You're in it,' he was told.

Disbelief touched his youthful features. 'You mean this place is *indoors*?' He stamped and clapped some more and, partially thawed, said: 'Colomb – the royals sent me to fetch a fellow named Colomb.'

They sat on identical thrones in the great hall of some nobleman's requisitioned house.

I made my balky legs carry me the length of the hall, I knelt before the dais, I heard my heart hammering in my ears and faintly through it the page's voice mispronouncing my name: 'Cristóbal Colomb, a Foreigner – five minutes.'

I opened my mouth to protest that my Great Venture involving half the earth surely merited far more than five minutes, but no words came.

I heard the King's voice say, 'Rise,' and I rose.

I heard the Queen's voice say, 'Approach,' and I approached.

They gazed down at me.

I gazed up at them.

It was common knowledge that Fernando and Isabel were first cousins who had needed papal dispensation for the dynastic marriage that united their kingdoms. That this was genetic folly would become apparent in their daughter Crazy Joan, who after a two-year reign withdrew into seclusion, refusing to dress or even wash, but visiting daily the grave of her husband Philip the Handsome of Burgundy (who had been grossly unfaithful to her), whether to grieve or to gloat history does not say.

As first cousins, I expected Fernando and Isabel to resemble each other, but in this I was mistaken.

King Fernando in his royal winter robes with his lightweight traveling crown on his large head was a swarthy man with dark, transfixing eyes, a long torso and disproportionately short legs. The toes of his royal fleece-lined slippers barely touched the dais.

Queen Isabel in her royal winter robes with her lightweight traveling crown on her normal-sized head looked hauntingly familiar.

She must have felt the same about me, for she couldn't stop staring. 'Come closer,' she said. 'Mount the dais.'

I climbed the two steps and bowed low.

We resumed staring at each other.

King Fernando cleared his throat impatiently.

The Queen was regally tall. Her auburn hair had coppery highlights. Her nose was a delicately feminine version of a hawk's beak, most becoming. She had bright blue eyes and her cheeks were rosy. Was there a faint sprinkling of freckles?

The red hair, the blue eyes, the suggestion of freckles on the rosy cheeks – all were much admired in Spain because rare.

We continued to stare at each other.

The Queen smiled.

Did comprehension dawn first for her or for me? I like to think it was simultaneous.

Queen Isabel did not resemble her cousin King Fernando, *she resembled me*. Or perhaps to state it that way is lese-majesty. Better to say I resembled her. We were as alike as first cousins, even brother and sister.

King Fernando, last to see the fortuitous resemblance, was least delighted. He blew a plume of breath down at me through the cold air. 'Where are you from, Colomb?' he demanded.

'Genoa, Sire.'

There I went again. But it was complicated to explain I'd been born at sea. And, for all I knew, my parents might have been fleeing this country now ruled by the King addressing me. It was true I was 'from' Genoa, and so I said it. I have no regrets.

'We gather,' said the King dryly, 'you have already tried Portugal, where His Most Serene Majesty John II has declined to back your Great Venture.'

I bowed my head, remembering my failure.

'It is our royal pleasure to affirm that we are not disposed at this time to back it either,' said the King.

'And likewise our pleasure,' said the Queen, 'to affirm that we are not altogether disposed to reject it.'

Did they glare regally at each other?

'Granada comes first,' said the King firmly.

With this the Queen agreed, her blue eyes radiating hatred as she spoke. 'All else must wait until the dark and sinister shadow of the infidel no longer falls across our realm.'

A poetic statement, and predictably zealous. For the Queen, otherwise so splendid and broad-visioned, was notably narrow on the subject of religion, as the sizeable Jewish population of Spain would learn to its dismay on 30 March 1492.

The King snapped his fingers and a footman produced a portfolio. In it I saw the maps of Pozzo Toscanelli as refined by my brother Barto. I wanted to ask the whereabouts of my driftwood, but prudently kept silent.

'You drew these?' demanded the King.

Again I bowed my head, this time modestly. The page, offstage somewhere, called: 'Two minutes!'

'They were drawn, carved and printed at the mapmaking establishment my brother and I ran in Lisbon,' I said as quickly as I could.

'And where is your brother now?' demanded the King.

'In France.'

'Why is he in France?' demanded the King.

'Visiting,' I said even more quickly. 'Just visiting friends. Barto's very popular, Your Majesties. He has friends all over.'

'He wouldn't by any chance be at the court of that jackass Charles trying to drum up French support for this Great Venture of yours, would he?' demanded the King.

There was anger in his small dark eyes, amusement in the Queen's bright blue ones.

'And why shouldn't he?' she said.

'Because we haven't yet exercised our royal prerogative to say no,' said the King.

'Nor our royal prerogative to say yes,' pointed out the Queen.

He glowered down at me; she smiled down at me. Then they bent over the maps and whispered together. I began cautiously to hope.

'One minute!' shouted the page.

Abruptly the King demanded, 'Can you draw closer scale maps of this quality?'

I managed a decisive if puzzled yes.

The Queen said, 'Would you lend us your talents — to help remove the dark and sinister shadow of the infidel that falls across our realm?'

He said, 'Can you draw them in secrecy, utterly on your own, in hostile territory?' The prospect seemed to appeal to him.

'Thirty seconds!' called the page.

She said, 'But with Santa Fé always as your safe haven.'

I thought at first, zealous woman that she was, that she meant my Holy Faith would sustain me. Then I realized she spoke literally and meant the siege city of Santa Fé under construction a few miles west of Granada.

'Can you start at once?' demanded the King.

'It's Christmas,' pointed out the Queen.

'Ten seconds!' called the unseen page urgently.

But I wanted to spend no second Christmas at the so-called Students' Hospice. 'I am at Your Majesties' disposal,' I said.

Thus I entered the service of the Spanish monarchs not as a sailor but as a spy.

For almost two years after I bowed out of their presences I disappeared from history. I mean that literally. There was no trace of me. In their speculations, historians made me everything from a houseguest of the Duke of Medinaceli to a tramp on the low roads of Spain, a failure even at the honorable but undemanding profession of beggar. Some have speculated I joined the army gathering at Santa Fé to besiege Granada, and these were as close to the truth as the proponents of mendicancy were. Some conjectured I spent that hole in history with Little Diego at the monastery of La Rábida. How I wish that had been so! *Ojalá*, as the Arabs say. For I learned something of their difficult language during my two perilous years among them.

Let me say a word here about the Arab mentality, which so often came to my rescue when all seemed lost. The chronic paranoia that afflicts Arabs in the best of times flared acutely in the decade prior to 1492. Nobody trusted anybody, fellow Arab, Christian, Jew, it didn't matter. A slave girl in the harem of Sultan Abu-al-Hasan was responsible, for when al-Hasan turned for his carnal needs exclusively to her, the Sultana Ayesha deposed him and crowned their son Abu-Abdallah sultan in his place. At the same time (for history never stands still for amorous dallying) the border warfare between Christians and Arabs intensified. The deposed sultan soon distinguished himself in battle in the mountain passes above Málaga. Jealous, Abu-Abdallah led an army out of Granada to the western edge of the fertile valley where the first low range of mountains demarked the Christian frontier. Taken prisoner, Abu-Abdallah was released only on paying a ransom and swearing to join the Christian forces against his deposed but formidable father. But meanwhile his uncle az-Zaghral, seeing his chance, had himself in turn crowned Sultan of Granada. Thus began a three-way civil war, an Arab specialty. The father al-Hasan was slain in battle, the son Abu-Abdallah took the fortress city of Granada, forswearing his oath to fight for the Christians, and the uncle az-Zaghral fled to the caves of Guadix where his guerrilleros preyed on fellow Arabs, Christians, Jews, it was all the same to him.

Since nobody trusted anybody, one beggar more or less scrabbling for a living in the fertile valley of Granada would not be a particular object of suspicion.

I was the filthiest, scruffiest beggar that ever walked an Andalucian low road seeking alms. I was speechless, an unusual state for me, but my tongue had been pulled out by the roots in accordance with Islamic law for uttering some blasphemy. At least this is what I explained, with much gesturing and various wordless sounds, to anyone who fell in with me on the road. I had a donkey, filthier, scruffier, mangier than I, and in his saddlebags I kept the paper and charcoal that were my real reason for leading the life of a mendicant. I went wherever a man could go in the valley of Granada as yet unoccupied by Spanish forces. I investigated every hill, every hillock, every stream, every rill and freshet, every village and hamlet, every grove of olives, of almonds, of pomegranates (from which Granada takes its name); I became intimate with the immediate environs of the city itself, which was perched on an ochre mountain crowned by a fortress and almost impossible to conquer. I entered the city at night with the other beggars, and the barbican gate was locked behind me. Then I would find an obscure corner somewhere between angles of ochre stone, the fortress towers brooding above me, and sketch by moonlight what I had seen during the day. Prowling the city, as I sometimes did, I found Cistern Plaza where the Arabs stored their water, and I knew that no diversion of streams could force their surrender.

One day I explored below the northern wall of the fortress, where a great fissure cleft the ochre rock, mute testimony to some ancient earthquake. This, I knew, was one way in, and quickly I began to sketch it for later incorporation in a map.

'You! Beggar! You there!'

A scar-faced soldier wearing the uniform of Abu-Abdallah's forces and armed to the teeth, that's all.

Holding out my alms cup, I made tongueless noises.

'What have you got there?'

By then I understood some Arabic but I shrugged mutely. He snatched the map-sketch from my hand and studied it. Upside down, rightside up, then sideways.

'What is this?'

I kept shrugging, mutely mendicant, mendaciously mute.

My donkey was sufficiently noisome, I hoped, so that the soldier would soon be on his way.

'Ah, you're one of those poor devils had his tongue pulled out by the roots for some blasphemy,' he said, the coin finally dropping. Literally. For he dropped a copper coin in my cup as he returned the map, of which he could make no sense.

I lived alone, except for the noisome donkey. I shunned human company, thus limiting my success as a beggar. But in solitude lay safety. I watched the hawks wheel and soar, and the swift darting flight of swallows, and nights I often heard the owl-call that meant someone would die the next day. And of course someone would. The armies were skirmishing between Santa Fé and Granada and clashing on the highroad to the arid mountains between Granada and the sea. I sketched elevations, depressions, clearings, copses; I suggested gun emplacements and lines of march. In the heat of summer I lingered in the shade of poplars on the banks of the Darro. In the cold of winter I huddled in my woollen burnous and froze along with everyone else.

Always the fortress loomed, and always beyond it the high snowy crests of the Sierra Nevada.

Once every eight days I would cross the ravine southeast of the fortress city and hike to the Vermilion Towers, a former Arab outpost where my control waited.

She was a woman of ninety or more, toothless, her face deeply furrowed; the grandmother, some said, of the Gran Capitán himself. She entertained soldiers on leave with mournful singing in her startlingly clear and youthful voice, repeating the same lines over and over in a minor key, a pure and terrible wail.

> When I think that one day
>   I must die,
> I cover my head
>   And try to sleep.

Such existential fatalism earned her tears from her audience; I gave her maps. She instructed me which sector of the broad mountain-ringed valley to map next.

When inclement weather made reaching the Vermilion Towers impossible, I resorted to cut-outs. These freelance agents might be Arab or Christian or Jew, owed allegiance to no one, worked for money, and knew neither my identity nor what I gave them in sealed leather bags to carry through the Christian lines to the stronghold of Santa Fé.

For in this Queen Isabel was wrong. Holy Faith was not my sanctuary. To approach the siege city itself would have been folly. I was sure most of the cut-outs were double agents.

So for two years I was a spy – soon weary of the world's most thankless profession and full of *angst*, as Martinus Waldseemüller might have said. My safe haven was movement. The words were engraved on my brain – when in doubt, move. And I did. Up into the foothills of the sierra, down into a ravine, along the steep trails in the parched southern mountains where I might hear the bells of a distant mule train or see a single shepherd with his staff standing lonely sentry over his flock.

'What are you doing here?'

A soldier wearing the uniform of Abu-Abdallah's forces and armed to the teeth, that's all.

'Just watching that shepherd with his staff standing lonely sentry over his flock.'

Too late I saw the scar on the soldier's face.

He scowled in ferocious recognition and exclaimed: 'You're talking now. Didn't you used to be one of those poor devils had his tongue pulled out by the roots for blasphemy?'

I faced him alone, my noisome donkey having succumbed to the cold during my second winter as a beggar.

While he drew his sword I thought frantically.

'Allah,' I explained, 'is most merciful.'

'He is,' the soldier agreed, raising his sword, 'and you'd better pray for some of that mercy right now.'

'I have already known it,' I said unhurriedly. 'Allah showed me His mercy by giving me back my tongue.'

'God! Really?' The scar-faced soldier fell to his knees and prostrated himself, facing east of course.

I edged away – west of course. I began to walk faster.

But something about my story didn't quite satisfy him, or possibly he wasn't a true believer. Whatever, he came storming in pursuit and I fled in the direction of the nearest Christian settlement, the Vermilion Towers.

There were no Christian soldiers on leave but old Granny was singing

> When I think that one day
> I must die,
> I cover my head
> And try to sleep

in her pure and terrible existential wail.

'Hide me! Quick! My cover's blown!'

But the scar-faced soldier was on us, running full tilt.

Old Granny, her lament still echoing from the surrounding hills, calmly extracted a poniard from her voluminous shawl and with a deft movement let him impale himself on it. A worn buskin against his ribcage and a surprisingly hard kick for so frail an old woman released the blade from the corpse.

'First one this week,' Granny said simply, and drove the blade into the ochre earth to clean it. 'I've got a message for you – they want you in Santa Fé. The final assault's about to begin.'

It was the end of November 1491.

❦ VII ❧

1492!

O N 2 January 1492, not yet at ease in the company of men after my two years of itinerant solitude, I stood apart from the crowd on the eastern ramparts of Santa Fé and watched a flash, a sudden puff of black smoke and, seconds later, a spurt of ochre dust as a section of Granada's battlements crumbled and fell.

Except for sporadic artillery fire during December and the occasional sally of a troop of Arab horsemen required by form (they were quickly chased back through the barbican gate with minimal casualties), the final assault announced by old Granny proved unnecessary. The secret way into Granada, that deep cleft in the rock I had discovered on the north side of the fortress, provided the key to an almost bloodless victory. Or rather, an almost bloodless defeat. For with Christian forces guarding the fissure below, the Arabs were unable to slip out at night to provision the beleaguered city, which was brought to its knees by the grim specter of starvation more than by cannon fire.

While I watched the final salvoes — the surrender was expected momentarily — a man in ornately etched armor of impressive girth detached himself from the courtiers surrounding the King and Queen not fifty yards from where I stood and clanked in my direction.

'You're Colomb, aren't you?' he said. 'Been wanting to meet the man who delivered Granada. That's what the royals call you now, you know that?'

'It was nothing,' I said, with a self-deprecating cast of features the Duke of Medinaceli would have applauded.

Seen close, the ornately armored fat man's face conveyed an air of controlled power except for his heavy, sensual lips. Those lips looked somehow empty; they champed as if impatient for the advent of cigars.

'Actually,' I said, 'the name's Colón.'

'Sure. Colomb. Everybody knows who you are. I'm Luís de Santangel, Keeper of Their Majesties' Household Budget and one of the two or three richest men in Spain.'

'It's Colón – c, o, l, o-accent, n.'

'Yes, exactly, just as I – *what* did you say?' Luís de Santangel struck himself an open-handed blow on the side of the head. Fortunately, he wasn't wearing his iron gauntlets. '*Colón*! I should have made the connection, of course – the red hair and all. It *was* red, all red that is, at one time? I mean, it isn't a wig or anything?'

I assured him my hair was my own.

'Your mother Susanna had red hair too. You look a lot like her. Your father's name was Domingo. And you had a brother – uh, Bartolomé.'

'Who are you?' I cried.

'Told you. I'm Luís de Santangel, Keeper of the Household Budget and one of the two or three richest men in Spain.'

But he knew that wasn't what I meant, and as we watched the bombardment he began to talk.

Cannon fire punctuated the tale, black smoke drifted across the years, red ochre spurted from the walls of Granada like blood, Jewish blood, from my arteries.

'Then – then I'm a Jew,' I blurted.

'Don't talk nonsense, of course you're not. No more than I am. You're a New Christian, far better than the other kind.'

I was forty years old and suddenly inhabiting the body of a stranger.

'My parents never told me,' I said.

'Nor should they have. Why complicate things? Mine didn't either, not that they had to, it was so obvious. They were both dead by the time I was nine – hopeless backsliders, the pair of them,' said Santangel, chewing his invisible cigar.

'You mean, the Seder the year I was born?'

'The Seder, all of it. They were living a lie. Until it killed them.'

I asked him what had gone wrong, already feeling defensive about his, as well as my, Jewish ancestry.

'The last Seder? Oh sure,' Luís de Santangel said. 'I remember it well, of course I do. I was the youngest. I was the one that had to memorize all the questions. You know – what's so special about this night, and all?'

But I didn't know. Trumpets blared and I watched horsemen in burnished armor, pennants flying, advance through the black smoke drifting across the battlefield.

'Who informed on your family and the others?' I asked Luís de Santangel. It was his past but mine too, and I thought I had a right to know.

A section of distant crenelated wall fell, disappearing in ochre dust.

And Luís de Santangel looked me straight in the eye and said: 'A fellow's got to start his career somewhere.' He chomped hard on the invisible cigar. 'They were out-and-out heretics, after all. Mark you, with the fall of the infidel and the Inquisition gearing up under Torquemada, the royals will finally have time to attend to even minor heresy. So it's going to be worse than ever before.' He looked around uneasily. 'I mean, better.'

'They ... in some ways they have more in common with the Arabs over there.'

'Who do you mean?'

'Jews. The Jews. And I'm one of them by birth.'

'No you aren't. Your parents had already converted.'

'Because,' I resumed my theological debate with myself, 'Arabs and Jews believe in one God, Allah, Jehovah, whatever they call Him. And they claim we believe in three – Father, Son, Holy Ghost.'

'All aspects of the One God, my friend,' said Luís de Santangel urbanely. He scowled. 'Still, the Virgin *is* a problem, isn't she?'

'What am I?' I asked rhetorically.

'Listen, I'm sorry I started this.'

'*Why* am I?' I asked. It was a question as existential as Granny's pure and terrible wail.

I would spend the rest of my life trying to answer it.

'Can't you forget I brought the whole thing up?' said Luís de Santangel just as a great shout rose from the battlefield, for a white flag had appeared on the battlements of Granada in the swirling ochre dust.

The armored knights on their armored horses closed ranks, wheeled, and faced back toward Holy Faith to hail the King and Queen.

'We're going in,' Santangel said in a hushed, theatrical voice, and we did, King and Queen leading the way, he astride a great warhorse, she on her palfrey, immense Luís de Santangel right behind in the second rank on an even larger warhorse than the King's, and I in the rear of the retinue among those riding mules.

At noon that day a huge silver crucifix rose atop the highest tower of the Alhambra while in the square below King and Queen, both still in armor, gave thanks to Christ and His mother that the last infidel stronghold in Spain had been delivered after eight centuries of Arab occupation.

Christ and His mother. Not just God. Ordinarily I would have thought nothing of it, but now, still numbed by Santangel's revelations, I felt like an impostor unsure whom he was impersonating.

Along with all the Court that could be accommodated, I was quartered in the fortress itself. This was a signal honor. But looking from within at the thick ochre walls and the embrasure slits of windows, I thought: how very like a prison.

They received me a few weeks later in an audience chamber of modest size, hardly a throne room. High along one side ran a gallery where blind musicians used to play for their sultan.

The King looked morose, as if something had gone out of his life with the fall of Granada.

The Queen, her face still aglow with the passion of victory, looked radiant, like a woman who has been well and thoroughly bedded – but there I go again. A flagrant case of lese-majesty.

The King said, 'To business,' but before we could proceed, a distant voice called, 'Two minute warning, Sires!'

'So soon?' said the Queen. Her passionate blue eyes restlessly searched my face. I blushed. The Queen, blushing too, settled back more deeply in her improvised throne, a chair which it was said had belonged to Sultan al-Hasan's sexy slave girl, the one that caused the three-way civil war.

The King perched further forward on his improvised throne so his regally slippered feet could touch the floor. 'The Talavera Committee has grave reservations about your Great Venture.'

'And even if they hadn't,' said the Queen, 'you must understand that other things of consequence to the realm — '

'*Real* consequence to the realm,' amended the King.

147

' – will occupy us for the foreseeable future. The civil administration of Granada, the Jewish problem, that sort of thing.'

She might as well have said the Colón problem, I thought, just as the page shouted, 'One minute, Sires!'

'The Talavera Committee,' the King said, 'has prepared a report on your Great Venture.' He tapped a meaningful foot. 'Which the page will give you on your way out.'

'Not,' the Queen assured me, 'that we are ungrateful for all you have done.'

'A suitable medal,' the King informed me, 'shall be struck. But naturally you must never wear it.'

'There is,' said the Queen, 'a small estate near the town of Rincón de la Victoria – most aptly named, don't you think? – which we should be pleased to settle on you.'

'Formerly the property,' said the King, 'of Judaizing Marranos who attracted the attention of the Inquisition.'

'A minor title, *prócer* of Rincón de la Victoria, goes with the estate,' said the Queen. 'Higher than an hidalgo.'

'Yet lower than a count,' said the King.

Land of my own, even if confiscated from backsliding New Christians, a noble title to pass to my son Little Diego, the end of a hopeless quest too long pursued – it was almost tempting.

But I bowed stiffly and said, 'I thank Your Majesties but I will take my Great Venture to the French court where my brother is even now a petitioner.'

Then I committed a real act of lese-majesty. Without waiting to be dismissed, I turned on my heel and strode from the audience chamber, under the empty gallery where blind musicians used to play for the sultan.

I heard Queen Isabel gasp, but no one stopped me.

What happened during the time it took me to pack my seabag and ride my mule through the barbican gate and west from Granada ten miles to the Pinos bridge across the Genil River (where Arab blood and Christian had flowed these past few years, but not Jewish) Luís de Santangel told me that very night.

He learned of the Great Venture only after our meeting on the battlements of Santa Fé, when King Fernando asked him for an estimate of the cost. Santangel had given it – 2,000,000 maravedís – still not knowing whose Great Venture it was. This he learned from the page who tried to hand me the official transcript of the Talavera Committee's objections, which I tore in two and flung at his feet.

Santangel called an emergency meeting of his Movers and Shakers, the most influential New Christians at Court. Chomping furiously on his invisible cigar, he outlined the situation and asked, 'What shall we do?'

While they mulled it over, he told them.

'I'll tell you,' he said. 'Now that Granada's fallen, the Inquisition's going to jump on any New Christian who so much as looks crosseyed at a crucifix, if you know what I mean.'

They knew what he meant.

'But suppose this fellow finds the Indies. He'd convert the heathen Indians to Christianity, wouldn't he? Isn't that one purpose of all those expeditions? Look at the Canary Islands or the blackamoors of West Africa.'

'More Christians we don't need,' said one of the Movers and Shakers.

'Oh, but you're wrong,' said Santangel. 'And I'll tell you why. *If* he finds the Indies or wherever, and *if* he converts all the Indians or whoever, he'll take the grand prize for Christian zeal. And *he* is one of *us*. Zeal by association, you see? The benefit to all New Christians would be incalculable.'

'We-ell,' they all said, giving the word an indecisive double beat.

'I'm not finished. You all have sons, grandsons. Some of them are hotheads, am I right?' Chomp went his mouth on the invisible cigar. 'How much can they take from a heresy-hunting monster like Torquemada before they explode? You see?'

To make sure they saw, he showed them.

'Suppose this Colón crosses this Ocean Sea and finds his mainlands, islands, whatever size lands. They'll need explorers and maybe even colonists, won't they? We colonized the Canary Islands already, right? Can you think of a better outlet to keep your hothead sons and grandsons out of trouble *and* prove their Christian zeal at the same time?'

The Movers and Shakers couldn't.

'Chinillo is right,' they said. Among themselves they always called Santangel by his old family name.

'We're missing the chance of a lifetime', he said, 'if we don't send a representative in there right now to the blind musicians' chamber to show the royals which end is up. Now, who's it to be?'

Elected unanimously, he feigned surprise and rushed to the audience chamber.

Later he told me, 'I hit them right in the old exchequer. But believe me, at first it wasn't easy.'

At first the morose King said, 'Colón? That insufferable foreigner? He committed a gross act of lese-majesty not four hours ago.'

The Queen, still radiant, said, 'Which we magnanimously forgave, of course.'

The King made an unpleasant sound but waved a hand to indicate that Luís de Santangel could proceed.

'Suppose we just sit here,' Santangel said, 'and let him go to France. And suppose – just suppose – King Charles decides to back him. What'll it cost that French dandy anyway, a couple of million maravedís? And what if this Colón really reaches India or Cipango or somewhere like that? Everybody knows the rooftops of Cipango are tiled with gold, and as for India, the poorest peasants wear emeralds and rubies, right? What if France gets there and we don't? I'll tell you – France will become the richest nation in Christendom, that's all. And Spain? Spain will go into a decline, Your Majesties. We'll end up a backwater, romantic and quaint, with nothing but gypsies and bull-fights and the picturesque ruins of castles. What have we got to lose, Your Majesties? Two million maravedís – nothing!'

'Well, you're too late, Colón's already on his way,' said the King.

'Send a courier after him,' said the Queen. 'It's a long way to France.'

It was a royal impasse, Santangel told me later. He had one last weapon, and he used it.

'In fact, I believe in this Colón fellow so strongly that if Your Majesties won't back him, I guess I'll just have to raise the money myself. Then of course he couldn't fly the royal ensign – it would be a strictly private undertaking, me and a few associates.'

Santangel puffed a cloud of invisible smoke from his invisible cigar. Private enterprise on so large a scale was unprecedented and not to be permitted; it would signal the end of absolute monarchy and the divine right of kings (and queens) almost 300 years ahead of schedule.

King Fernando gave Queen Isabel an uneasy glance.

More radiant than ever, she said, 'If Don Luís is so sure, I say let's back the Great Venture. Has he ever given us a bad tip financially?'

Apparently he hadn't. For the King, looking no less morose, nevertheless said, 'All right, all right, send for the fellow, but don't expect me to sit around and watch him gloat.'

Their messenger overtook me just as I urged my mule across the Pinos bridge, and Santangel was waiting on my return.

'They've changed their minds,' he said. 'You're going.'

I did the last thing he expected. Me too, for that matter. I dropped to one knee, crossed myself, and gave thanks to God.

Luís de Santangel watched this approvingly. 'You're a good New Christian,' he said. 'Much better than the old kind. Didn't I say so?'

I got up and headed for the chamber of the blind musicians.

'Wait! Agree to no specific terms. I'll represent you.'

'But all I want is royal backing for my Great Venture.'

'Ridiculous. You want a high-sounding title, a hereditary one, for starters. Admiral of — what's it called?'

'The Ocean Sea.'

'Right. Admiral of the Ocean Sea — the only such in all the world. And you want a percentage.'

'Of what?'

'Who knows what? Don't sell yourself cheap, it's bad for your image. Say, ten per cent. And you'll want to be appointed viceroy and governor.'

'I will?'

'You bet your ass you will. Over all islands and mainlands you find on the way to India or wherever you're going. There's lots of details to be ironed out. It'll take months. Where are you sailing from?'

'Palos.'

'Then I'll have to get in touch with Medinaceli. Listen, kid, I'll get you an advance of a couple hundred reales. Why don't you take a few weeks off, have a well-earned vacation? I'll take care of your interests. Are you going to Cathay?' he asked.

'If I can find it.'

'So you'll need a letter of introduction to the Great Khan.'

He began scribbling notes as I went inside.

I knelt before the Queen. She was dazzling in a gown of ermine-trimmed gold brocade that flared open from her slender waist to reveal a vivid slash of red velvet underdress. She wore ear-rings of pearl and a single rope of pearls at her beautiful throat. Her hair was caught in a gold net chignon. I was surprised to find us alone after the page left.

With the radiance of victory still lighting her face, she looked like another Joan of Arc. No, not that chaste maiden. If I've been reluctant to say it until now, these pages won't be published until we're all of us long dead, so where's the harm? The Queen looked erotically aroused.

How long we faced each other in charged silence, I don't know. At last she spoke.

'What do you hope to find out there?'

'All the wonders of the fabled East, Your Majesty.'

'Won't you be frightened, going where no man has gone before?' She reached out a hand but let it fall.

I stepped back, casting a glance up at the gallery where blind musicians once had played. 'Sometimes it's prudent to be frightened, Your Majesty.'

'Medinaceli says you're as daring a sailor as the world has seen. Can this be possible, Don Cristóbal, when you project such an air of innocence?'

'Innocence?' I said. 'No, I lost my innocence in Ireland – it seems a hundred years ago.'

The room was windowless. We talked in a torchlit dream where shadows flickered, at once timeless and insubstantial, like the stucco arabesques that circled the walls.

'Yet you look quite young, Don Cristóbal. How old are you?'

I told her.

'I would have guessed even less, despite the white in your hair.'

She herself had to be my age or close; she'd married her cousin King Fernando in '69, in her teens. Yet with her slender figure and clear blue eyes and soft smile and the way the torchlight flickered golden in her red hair, she might have been in the first flush of young womanhood. I told her so – circumspectly. After all, she was my Queen.

'It is not with your eyes that you see, Don Cristóbal. But it is kind of you to share your dream.' Her smile became wistful. 'Will you think of home often when you're on the other side of the world?'

'I have no home, Your Majesty.'

'No home? Then you've never married?'

'My wife died.'

'I'm so sorry.'

'It was a long time ago, in another country.'

'Sometimes I wonder what it would be like to be ... well, not a commoner exactly but ... free like yourself. But that's only a dream too, isn't it?'

For a while she was silent, conflicting emotions playing on her lovely face.

'So you have no one?'

'I have two sons.'

'And are they old enough to understand where you're going?'

'One is. Almost.'

'Then when you're far across the Ocean Sea, further than man has ever gone, Don Cristóbal, think of your Queen – for she will be thinking of you.'

The torch-cast shadows moved mysteriously like half-hidden watchers among the arabesques. I could almost hear the blind musicians playing.

The Queen rose. She wore no crown. She touched the chignon at the nape of her neck and her long red hair fell shimmering free to her waist. She reached out a steady hand to me.

But perhaps, as she said, I was dreaming.

Postal service being what it is, I could not be sure that any of the letters I wrote soon after my arrival at the Monastery of La Rábida ever reached their destinations. I wrote to Barto at the court of Charles VIII in Fontainebleau, telling him to drop everything and meet me in Palos. I started a letter to Roderigo Cardinal Borgia in Rome, asking if my younger brother Giacomo might join me too in an unspecified but important undertaking for the Spanish Sovereigns. Then I realized that the boy Giacomo would now be a man of thirty-four, so I wrote the letter to him instead, not even knowing if he had become a priest as planned. I wrote to the Duke of Medinaceli, further thoughts on provisioning for the voyage, a follow-up to an earlier letter I'd left for him in Granada with Luís de Santangel. I wrote to Beatriz at the small apartment just north of the Judería or ghetto in Córdoba, telling her we were coming.

We left La Rábida without stopping at Palos to see Martín Alonzo Pinzón. It was true I needed Pinzón if I wanted to recruit my crews from Palos and the nearby villages, as I'd promised, but it was better to let Medinaceli deal with him. The longer we delayed before bringing him in, the less time he would have to claim my Great Venture for his own.

As I directed our mule past the eastern gate of the Córdoba ghetto I heard a mournful wailing inside. Passover had come and gone, so I assumed it was some heavy holy day I knew nothing about. I even remember thinking then: the Jews are a doleful people, what can you expect? It was my way of dissociating myself.

Still, curious as the lamentations grew louder, I stopped the mule outside the gate.

'Are we home?' Little Diego asked, cocking an uneasy ear to the lugubrious racket inside the ghetto. He turned in his seat on the pommel, his face flushed with excitement. His bright red hair had been cut in a bowl-crop by the La Rábida monks but would soon grow out to a more becoming length. His freckles were now more pronounced than his father's, and he was tall for not-quite-eleven.

'Almost,' I said. 'It's only a few minutes from here.'

'Will I like my new mother?' he asked for the hundredth time.

'You'll love her. And she'll love you.'

He looked around. 'Is all this Córdoba?' he asked, meaning the dirgelike sounds coming from the ghetto.

'Part of Córdoba, yes. It's the Judería. Where the Jews live.'

'The Jews, huh?' Little Diego said thoughtfully. 'They did something evil that makes people hate them, didn't they?'

At that moment an old man passed through the gateway from shadow to sunlight. He wore the round red shoulder patch mandatory for Jews leaving the ghetto.

'Oh, sure!' Little Diego blurted. 'Now I remember. They're the Christ-killers!'

The old man looked up.

'You teach your kids lies like that,' he said, 'no wonder the King and Queen are throwing us out of Spain.'

This was the first I'd heard of it, and I was too astounded to speak.

The old man waved a feeble, yellowed hand back toward the ghetto. 'Go have a look, why don't you? Lots of Christians do these days. You can pick up a nice house with a patio for a song.'

'Queen Isabel is banishing the Jews?' I said.

'King, Queen, it makes a difference? All I know is – get baptized or get out of the country by the end of July. Leave most of your money, leave all your silver and gold. Leave your property or sell it at the going rate. But since the Edict of Expulsion the going rate's been going just one way – down.'

'She wouldn't do a thing like that,' I said.

'Him, her, who knows? It's superstition that's really running this country. You call it Christianity,' he said defiantly. 'Report me, why don't you, I'm an old man, I don't care.' He shook an angry, impotent fist. 'Jews slaughtering Christian babies – ' I felt Diego flinch ' – to drink their blood in a profanation of the Mass, that's the kind of lies your own men of God spread. Is it any wonder we're being thrown out?'

I just sat there on the mule listening. What could I say to him? What consolation could I offer?

'And I'll tell you something else, Christian, the real reason they're throwing us out. The Church is afraid unless they get rid of us, we'll contaminate your New Christian children with the ways of their ancestors, that's why. The Church has no faith in its own faith, so it's afraid of ours. So out we go.'

I clutched Little Diego more tightly about his slender waist.

When the old man saw I had no interest in entering the ghetto or continuing our one-sided conversation, he went muttering on his way.

'Why are the King and Queen taking his home away?' Little Diego asked.

'It's hard to explain,' I said.

'I hope they don't take *our* home away.'

'They won't.'

I flicked the reins and the mule plodded forward.

'What if I don't like it?'

'You will.'

'What if my new mother doesn't like me?'

'Diego, stop worrying about it.'

'What's my little brother like?'

'I don't really know.'

We had gone through these questions more than a few times already.

'How old is he?'

'Three.'

'He's just a baby. Fernando — is he named after the King?'

'That's right.'

'The King who took that old man's home away?'

'Here we are,' I said.

I directed the mule into the narrow cobbled street near the plaza that one day would be called Plaza de Colón, and to the hidden patio inside, where geraniums hung in pots on the dazzlingly whitewashed walls. The windows were grilled with wrought iron and canaries in cages sang up at the blue sky. The second door on the left stood open. It was ours.

Now that we'd arrived, Diego wanted to talk about other things. 'What'll we do with Toothsome?'

Toothsome was the mule.

'Sell him. We don't need him here.'

'Oh.'

I climbed off the mule and after Diego slid down I began to unstrap the saddlebags. Diego saw Beatriz first.

'Is that her?' he asked. 'Is that my new mother?'

I turned. Beatriz was hurrying out the door, a look of astonishment in her undeniably Iberian eyes.

'Cristóbal!' she shouted. More a scream.

She ran at me full tilt and flung herself into my arms. I kissed her full, red, possibly Berber lips.

Little Diego tugged at me.

'Why didn't you write and let me know you were coming?' Beatriz asked.

'I did.'

'It never came.'

Little Diego kept tugging me, but it was Beatriz with her woman's instinct who took the initiative. She turned with a motherly smile to the boy, who had backed up shyly against Toothsome.

'Why, you must be my son Diego,' she said. And, knowing a great smothering hug and kiss would have been intimidating, leaned down to touch his cheek with her lips. 'Did anybody ever tell you how much – ' here her voice caught ' – you look like your handsome father?'

Diego's face glowed with pride. 'When I grow up I'm going to be Admiral of the Ocean Sea too.'

Beatriz looked at me an instant wide-eyed, mouthing silently the words 'you're going?' When I nodded she turned back at once to Diego who was explaining:

'Papa says it's heri-tary.'

'It's what? Oh – hereditary. What is?'

'The title,' Diego explained patiently, 'Admiral of the Ocean Sea.'

'Have you ever been on the sea?' Beatriz asked. 'I haven't.'

'Oh, sure,' Diego said, very grown-up and offhand. 'I've lived on the seacoast my whole life.'

'I've only lived in the village of Santa Maria Trasiera and right here in Córdoba. Tell me what it's like, will you, Diego?'

'Well, from my window at La Rábida ... ' And he was off, giving her a Diego's-eye view of the sea, the changing winds, the surf, the occasional ship outward bound on the ebb tide, the gulls nailed to the sky and either shrieking or laughing depending on his, Diego's, mood.

I finished unstrapping the saddlebags. Beatriz and the boy were still at it, she questioning, he answering. His face became more and more animated.

I hefted the saddlebags and suggested, 'Why don't we all go inside and see Fernando?' But by then I was addressing Toothsome because mother and son, hand in hand, were already passing through the doorway between the pots of geraniums.

I became a legend in my own lifetime and, modesty aside, for all time in 1492. My every move from the moment I crossed the gunwale of the carrack *Santa Maria* in the port of Palos would belong to the ages. Before they did sums, small children in school would study the legend into which my life disappeared; for many I became their first undeniable hero.

And yet, until past the age of forty, until my barber-pole-striped hair was more white than red, I was unknown, and by inclination a very private sort of person. So the change – one moment Mr Nobody, the next the best known of mortal men – was more on an Olympian than a human scale.

I have often pondered what becomes of the man when the legend achieves its own life, when the myth becomes more enduring than mere flesh and blood. Must he become enslaved by that legend, trapped in that myth, forever denied a moment's privacy? This is the danger but, living legend or not, I intend to keep private those final few weeks with my united family in the hidden patio near the Plaza de Colón (sic), almost the last real privacy of my life, for the intervals I could steal later from that difficult taskmaster, history, were brief and rare.

I ask you then to see (or rather not see) this episode in my life as Lope de Vega, that prodigy of nature with his 1800 plays, might have written it some 130 years later. He would write of Rodrigo, the last Visigoth king of Spain, and of El Cid, so why not of me? Or if not Lope de Vega, then his English contemporary William Shakespeare who, if he mined Spain for the material he cheerfully lifted from just about everywhere else, might have written a drama called *Columbus*.

A play, then. The curtain falls on the hidden patio to rise on the same set several weeks later. It is a cool dawn, the dew still glistening on the cobblestones. Beatriz stands in the doorway between the pots of geraniums with plump Fernando on the crook of her arm and Little Diego at her side, gripping her hand tight. Three mules with stuffed saddlebags wait patiently, one of them Toothsome whom I haven't sold after all and won't until he carries me to Palos. On the second mule sits a middle-aged man whose hair has formed a natural tonsure. With his sympathetic bedside manner he watches the farewell scene in no hurry. Astride the third mule a tall man waits suspiciously, possibly wondering what will go wrong at the last minute.

As I step into the stirrup and swing aboard Toothsome, Little Diego comes running over. I lean down and tousle his hair. His eyes are shining. Lope and Shakespeare might both have him say, 'I wish I was old enough to go,' without the subjunctive.

'Take care of your mother and your little brother.'

'I promise.'

Fernando calls, 'Papa! Papa!' and I blow him a kiss. Beatriz sets him down and walks swiftly to me, Fernando toddling behind. I lean from the saddle, and then swing down when I see the tears in her eyes. She hugs me hard.

'Be the best admiral in the whole history of the world,' the playwrights might have her say, and that too isn't very far wrong. 'Do all those things an Admiral of the Ocean Sea's supposed to do, only better, but then come back. Come back to us.'

'I will,' I tell her, and mount again. Fernando sees the look on his mother's face and begins to cry.

Departure is ever the same, the traveler feeling the tug of the journey while the stay-at-home feels only the foretaste of loneliness. So almost impatiently, even though I love her, I turn away from the tears threatening to overflow Beatriz's eyes and lead my two companions out of the patio and onto the road south.

Again Lope's curtain falls, or Shakespeare's, and next rises to show the red-faced notary of Palos at center stage as five days later he reads to the entire population of the town gathered in St George Plaza the royal document that has preceded us there.

'Fernando and Isabel, by the Grace of God King and Queen of Castile, León, Aragon, Sicily, etc., etc., to the Lord Mayor of Palos and all other inhabitants, Greetings and Grace!'

Royal greetings are rare in back-country Spain, and Palos receives these with good-humored shouting and applause until the notary reads the part of the document relating to the port's failure to pay its taxes the past two years.

This is met with grumbling, and a few in the plaza even turn away in disgust from the momentous event.

'Wait!' shouts Martín Alonzo Pinzón in his bull bellow, his small eyes squinched almost shut. 'Wait, you fools, it gets better!'

It gets worse. Palos is directed, reads the notary, to furnish two fully equipped caravels to the Crown for one year in payment of said delinquent taxes.

The crowd erupts noisily. Angry faces turn to me, to Dr Juan Sánchez and to Enríquez de Harana, still on our mules. The Duke of Medinaceli, riding a white palfrey, trots in our direction and wheels to take his stand with us. He raises a landlordly hand, silencing the crowd so that Martín Alonzo Pinzón's bull bellow can be heard: 'I tell you, it gets better!'

This time it does, momentarily.

A third ship will be chartered for cash, crew rosters filled with priority going to experienced local seamen, the Crown guaranteeing their wages until completion of the western voyage of discovery –

'Western?'

'What's he saying, western?'

'What's out west?'

– under the command of Don Cristóbal Colón, a Foreigner, Admiral of the Ocean Sea.

'Admiral of the which?'

'He said Ocean Sea, I swear he did.'

'Jesus bloody Christ, which one's this son of Neptune?'

Barrel-bellied Pinzón points and there's nothing for it but to urge Toothsome forward a pace and raise a hand dramatically high. I feel strangely alone and vulnerable, possibly the first stirrings of the alchemy that will change me from man to legend. Then someone – it is Medinaceli – thrusts a flagstaff at me, unsheathing the flag as he does so. I lift it high, the breeze flutters it out, and over my head flies the royal standard of united Spain, gold tower and purple lion for Castile and León on a field of white above, and Aragon's red and yellow vertical stripes below.

This flag, so proudly whipping in the offshore breeze, silences them until a voice (stage left) asks: 'Jobs for how many?'

I stand in the stirrups, alarming Toothsome, and tell them: 'There's work and wages for the whole town getting the fleet ready to sail.'

The scene shifts to the river's edge, the crowd following Medinaceli, Pinzón and me as if we were a trio of pied pipers from Hamelin. Painted on a backdrop, the requisitioned caravels lie offshore at anchor. Their names are *Santa Clara* and *Santana*. At least these are their official-religious names. But Spanish ships always get nicknames, far more real to the men who sail them.

COLÓN: What are they called?

PINZÓN: *Santa Clara* on the left there, the slightly smaller one, she's called *Niña*. The other's *Pinta*.

COLÓN: (*angrily, seeing that* Niña's *foremast and mainmast lack the big spars to support square sails*) Niña's lateen-rigged.

PINZÓN: (*with a stubborn man's bluster*) Sure she's lateen-rigged. What in hell did you expect? Oh, I gave a lot of thought to your pretty theories about square rigging, but I *know* lateen, I've *sailed* lateen, and lateen *works*. So here's what we'll do. I'll command *Pinta* and my younger brother Vicente Yáñez here, he'll command *Niña*. As I'm the more experienced seaman I'm willing to suffer your square-rigged foolishness as far as the Canary Islands to prove my point. Vicente Yáñez'll sail lateen. Then when you see how much better he fares, I'll re-rig *Pinta* for lateen before we sail into uncharted waters.

(COLÓN *glances at* MEDINACELI *who nods almost imperceptibly.*)

COLÓN: (*aside, after a meaningful silence*) They're the leading seafaring family in Palos so the duke won't want me to antagonize them before we recruit our sailors. Besides, won't the shakedown cruise show Pinzón his error? But he's staking a claim to leadership right now and I can't ... (*turns to face others*) You're wrong, Pinzón. Your brother in *Niña* will get to the Canaries after you and in worse shape. But I agree to your test.

MEDINACELI: Fair enough. Now, for your other ship? (*points offshore where, beyond* Niña *and* Pinta, *lie two larger, broad-beamed vessels*) That nao's forty years old but she's still sound, built in Barcelona. The carrack *Santa Maria* was built in Galicia ten years ago. They're both about a hundred tons. The choice is yours, Admiral.

PINZÓN: (*dogmatically*) *Santa Maria*'s the better ship.

COLÓN: (*aside*) Ought to row out and look them over, especially since the one I pick will be my flagship. But I already challenged Pinzón on the first point so maybe it'd be politic to give him this one. (*to* PINZÓN) *Santa Maria* it is.

A word here about the naming of ships and the inconsistency in the legend even then being born. The ships of my fleet could have been called either *Santa Clara*, *Santana* and *Santa Maria*, their official-religious names, or *Niña*, *Pinta*, and *Gallega*, which was the carrack's nickname. Then why the world-famous muddled mix of *Niña*, *Pinta* and *Santa Maria*? This one time, don't blame the historians, blame me. I began the practice in my *Book of the First Navigation and Discovery of the Indies* (nicknamed *Columbus's Journal of His First Voyage*, unfortunately lost and available only in an inaccurate copy made by my biographer Las Casas). Why did I do it? Because the caravels *Niña* and *Pinta* were sweet ships to sail but if ever a slow, cantankerous, wallowing, too-tall-in-the-mainmast sea-pig of a ship was undeserving of a pet name, *Santa Maria* was that ship. So I spoke of her with rigid formality and the historians took their cue from me. Eventually, she would bear the third name Christmas, as will become tragically clear.

Now Lope or Shakespeare would have carpenters fitting fresh planks to cambered decks, coopers banding new barrels, sailmakers sewing canvas, caulkers mixing their brews of whale oil and pine tar or pitch and tallow. An ambitious producer might even show the stretch of beach called a boatyard, with teams of oxen dragging the three ships ashore on the flood tide, and men scurrying like insects to caulk the beached ships. All versions would have the workmen grumbling about the foolishness of readying two caravels and a carrack for a voyage to nowhere – for sailors are a conservative lot and, their age-old superstitions excepted, they must experience a thing for themselves before they believe it.

'West, for godsake!'

'Well, they're paying us.'

'But who'd be fool enough to sign on, tell me that?'

For answer the playwright shifts the setting again to St George Plaza on the morning after the ships are back in the water. The men of Palos, in their daily ritual, have gathered in small groups to wait for work. As I approach, trying for that look of eagles in the eyes so indispensable to history and legend, they avert their gaze or even turn their backs, except for the three Pinzón brothers and a few Pinzón relations who have already signed on.

Soon I feel isolated among Pinzóns, and not enough even of them.

I want to be at sea by early August, before the northerlies that will take us down to the Canaries break up in the squalls of autumn. But the last days of July are already upon us.

I tell Martín Alonzo Pinzón dispiritedly, 'There's no way we'll ever sail on schedule.'

'No, we'll be late,' he agrees, paraphrasing my words as he so often does when he hasn't a thought of his own.

'Why do sailors have to be such skeptics? They refuse to believe there's anything across the Ocean Sea but water.'

'In all directions,' agrees Pinzón helpfully.

'So how can we convince them?'

'I was asking myself that very question,' says Pinzón, and just then the Duke of Medinaceli like a *deus ex machina* from a drama by the Greek Euripides enters the plaza with an ancient peglegged fellow, his one foot bare, a black beret worn at a rakish angle above one eye, a black patch covering the other.

'Where is he? Where's Admiral what's-his-name?' cries this ancient mariner, and when I am identified does a sort of hopping, barefoot, peglegged dance in my direction, shouting, 'You sumbitch!' and shaking both his fists at me. 'You're the luckiest sumbitch that ever lived! Why, I was almost there, and now I'm too damn old to go back, but you're going.'

'It's Vásquez de la Frontera,' someone says.

'Him? I thought he died years ago,' says someone else.

'Hey, gramps,' shouts a third, 'got any of that Sargasso Sea seaweed left?'

There is much rib-nudging and laughter, but still their eyes are respectful.

'The Duke here,' shouts Vásquez de la Frontera, who has to be eighty if a day, 'says you're all too soft between the ears and too yellow in the region of the backbone to sign on with the Admiral. Why, you ignoramuses, you're missing the chance of a hundred lifetimes! I'd give my right arm and the only leg I got to be young enough to go. Because I was almost there once, and all of you know it.'

They do, if they believe old Vásquez's story, so well-known locally. Native to the nearby village of Moguer, he sailed as a pilot or second officer aboard one of Prince Henry the Navigator's caravels on a western voyage of discovery back in '52. 'Southwest from Fayal in the Azores we went,' he says now, doing his odd, hopping dance from group to group in St George Plaza, his one eye gazing backward in time, 'and you all know we reached the Sargasso Sea because I brought back the seaweed to prove it, and then we sailed north and discovered Corvo, furthest west of the Azore Islands, right smack in the middle of the Ocean Sea, and we went west and north from there to search for O'Brasil, that's what the Irish call the island of gold that disappears just after you see it on the horizon, and there was one morning I could smell the land, like all the perfumes of Araby. Land birds, speckled they were, came flying out to look us over, and I swear to Christ what they were speckled with was gold dust. A day's sail from O'Brasil – I'm as sure of that as I'm standing here among a bunch of pitiful landlubbers scared to get their delicate feet wet – and what happened? The telling pains me still. We turned back. Turned back because the crew got the edge-of-the-world shakes – which *you've* got before you ever step on board. But you've got to go. *You've got to.*

'Ain't this Spain? Ain't this Andalucía? Ain't this Palos, where women are so beautiful they stop your heart and men so brave they start it beating again?' perorates Vásquez de la Frontera in a frenzy of barefoot, peglegged dancing. 'You going to stand there and admit that Admiral what's-his-name, a foreigner's got more guts than our good old boys? You going to bring eternal shame on Palos?'

And old Vásquez, sweating in the heat, hippity-hops to St George Church where he leans panting against the wall in the shade. His one eye blazes challenge. No one moves. He spits a large contemptuous gob. Still no one moves.

Then in the sun-glare of the plaza three men from Vásquez's village of Moguer come forward scuffing their feet in the dust, like fighting bulls persuading themselves to charge. These are the Niño brothers, Juan, Peralonso and Francisco. Juan Niño, owner of the requisitioned caravel *Niña*, is as highly regarded locally as Pinzón, but until now the loss of his ship for a year has embittered him.

'I reckon I'd like to see them birds all speckled with gold dust,' he says. And he'll sail aboard his own caravel as master or first officer under Vicente Yáñez Pinzón.

'I'll miss all those women so beautiful they make your heart stop,' says twenty-four-year-old Peralonso Niño, 'but I've been on the beach too long and maybe mine needs some starting.' And Peralonso Niño, a skilled pilot or second officer, will serve me well aboard that cantankerous carrack *Santa Maria*.

Young Francisco Niño, not yet seventeen, just smiles his Billy Budd smile and ranges himself alongside his hulking brothers. He'll sail as a grommet or ordinary seaman aboard *Pinta*.

So the Niño brothers of Moguer, two of them looking like desperadoes and the third like a saint, break the ice.

By 1 August there are eighty-eight officers and crew to man the three vessels, and one passenger – Rodrigo de Segovia, the Crown comptroller, sent to watch the spending of every copper maravedí and to make sure the Crown gets its ninety per cent share of any gold or precious stones found. For ten per cent belongs to me, along with viceregency over any islands and mainlands discovered en route to the Indies or wherever. I have even been given credentials by the King and Queen to present to the Great Khan of Cathay, and three other unnamed monarchs I might chance upon along the way. My agent Luís de Santangel made no idle boasts.

Another Luís unexpectedly joins our company on the eve of our departure. It's Barto, I remember thinking as a man on a donkey plods down from St George Plaza to the port, it's my brother Barto come to join us at the last minute. But it isn't. This fellow is in his early twenties and slender as a girl. When he slips from the donkey to the ground, the poor beast at once collapses, as if its role in life has been accomplished. And maybe it has.

The young man is wearing a felt hat with a turned-up brim from which a sad feather droops. His eyes sparkle green in a weary, dust-covered face.

'These the ships?' he asks me. I'm alone at the water's edge, everyone else spending a final night on the town. Superstitiously I have been telling myself that if I stand this vigil Barto will come.

I say it depends on which ships he means.

'The Jewish ships. But there's supposed to be twelve of them. We paid every maravedí we had – a thousand people, Jews from Castile and Cataluña.'

I shake my head, not understanding.

'Isn't this place Huelva?'

'The other arm of the river, west of here,' I tell him.

His green eyes shut. 'Nice work, Luís,' he tells himself. 'You've done it again.'

'What's the trouble?'

'The royal extension only lasts until tomorrow. Any Jew still in Spain who hasn't converted, he'll be killed. Is it far to Huelva?'

'Not by boat.'

'What are these ships, anyway?'

'Voyage of discovery under royal charter,' I tell him. It is the first time I use those words. They make it all seem somehow more real.

'Bound where?'

He's not just making talk. You can see the eager interest in his youthful green eyes.

'West across the Ocean Sea.'

'Man!' he cries. Then he does a jig-step as a whole Vásquez de la Frontera might have done sixty years ago, and claps his hands. 'Does your fleet need an interpreter?'

I haven't thought of it until then.

'We hadn't thought of it,' I say.

'I speak Hebrew and Arabic and Aramaic – and, ha-ha, even some Spanish.'

It's tempting. Everyone acknowledges Arabic as the mother of languages. So this fellow could be an enormous help in the Indies, Cipango, Cathay, undiscovered but inhabited islands and mainlands, wherever. But I have to say no.

'Sorry, afraid not,' I tell him.

'Well, can I maybe see your captain?'

'I'm the Admiral.'

'Oh. The Admiral. Oh, I see,' he says glumly. But he persists. 'Why not, Admiral?'

'Couldn't take you even if we wanted to. This is a Christian expedition,' I say firmly. Still I feel sorry for him.

He looks down, then brightens. 'I'm sort of a free thinker. I mean, I just happened to be born a Jew, you know how it is?'

I admit I know how it is.

'I mean, I could have been born Christian, Moslem, whatever. It's only an accident, like *where* you're born. Like you being a Spaniard, for instance.'

'I'm not.'

'You're not?'

'Well, not officially. It's a long story.'

'Then you know what it's like − to be an outsider.'

We stare seaward together. I clear my throat. He skips a stone across the water.

'I guess you're set against converting?' I say tentatively.

'It's ... well ... I just don't like being pushed, you know?'

I clear my throat again. He skips another stone.

'Across the Ocean Sea, huh?'

I know when to remain silent.

'The Indies and like that?'

'Say something in Arabic,' I tell him, and he rattles off a swift speech in that guttural language.

'What's that mean?' My own meager Arabic is rusty.

'That if you can find a clerical gent to baptize me I think I'm kind of ready to convert.'

Fray Juan Perez has come down from La Rábida to give Holy Communion to my officers and men, and has stayed in town to see us off. We go in search of him together, and find the good prior − not as ascetic as he looks − in the tavern where I first met Pinzón and the duke. A half hour later Luís Torres is baptized in the tidewater.

We are all aboard at four the next morning. Barto hasn't come. Soon *Santa Maria*'s pilot Peralonso Niño of Moguer calls, 'Tide's turning,' and in a flat calm voice I tell *Santa Maria*'s Galician owner and master, Juan Cosa, to take her downriver. The anchors are weighed, the great ash sweeps manned to give us steerage way. The sails hang limp in the river's calm. It lacks half an hour of sunrise. I hear the creak and thump of rowports, I watch the long oar blades walking on water. The land retreats. No Barto. And then Palos is a disappearing blur. In the dawn light La Rábida looms on its cliff. The monks are saluting dawn with their devotions and the men on deck with me listen to the pure voices across the water and drop to their knees to pray. Luís Torres kneels abruptly beside me. He crosses himself. It is an unexpected and profound moment. Then the sails are less slack as we join the other arm of the river coming down from Huelva. Ahead appears a ragtag fleet of small vessels, many dangerously low in the water. Faintly from them, then louder as we approach, and then engulfing the last clear notes from La Rábida, can be heard the sound of tabor and pipes. A single high male voice sings a hauntingly sad melody.

Luís Torres rushes to the bulwark while our sweeps carry us through the strange fleet. I place a hand on his shoulder. He is trembling.

'They're hoping to reach Italy,' he says. 'Italy will take some of them. Won't it?' I say nothing. 'Won't it? he repeats softly.

Then the fleet of Jewish exiles falls behind and Luís Torres turns his face resolutely forward.

Sand dunes sparsely covered by wind-stunted pines pass slowly on either side. The new day is bright but overcast. Suddenly *Santa Maria*'s sails fill with a sea breeze.

It is 8 a.m. on Friday, 3 August 1492.

ॐ VIII ॐ

1492!
(Continued)

THE earliest written account of a voyage I'm aware of is *The Odyssey*, which tells of Odysseus's long journey through the world of Homer's imagination on his way back to Ithaca after the Trojan War. The next earliest is the biblical story of Noah's ark. In deciding how to relate my First Voyage of Discovery, I studied those earlier travel stories. I mean no sacrilege by calling Genesis 6, 7 and 8 a story, but what else is it? Note that whoever recorded God's word on the journey of Noah knew nothing of seamanship. Was the ark propelled by sails or sweeps? We're not told. He wasn't much of a geographer either. How far was it from East-of-Eden to Mount Ararat? Another blank. The ship's company we know: Noah and his three sons, and their wives; but whoever he was, God's amanuensis apparently wasn't interested in 'psychology, motivation and all that.' Noah and his family spent 150 days on the ark, not counting the forty days and forty nights of rain. Also along, as everyone knows, were seven of each clean beast of the earth, seven of each bird, two of each unclean beast. That's a lot of people and animals cooped up in a three-deck houseboat-zoo all that time. Was there dissension in the human or animal ranks, a mutiny maybe? Did they run out of food, perhaps slaughtering some hapless, now extinct, species to keep the others alive? Noah's journey is told pretty skimpily, if you ask me. But God was chiefly concerned with His wrath against the wickedness of man and His covenant with Noah, so it's possible He knew what He was doing.

Homer crams a decade's worth of incident and local color into *The Odyssey*, but he was no seaman either. The only time the reader gets the feel of the ship is when Odysseus has himself lashed to the mast after stuffing his crew's ears with wax, so he can listen to the irresistibly luring song of the Sirens. For the rest, Odysseus island-hops, encountering danger whenever he ventures ashore. Of the dangers at sea, except for Scylla and Charybdis (sort of a rock and a hard place) we are told nothing.

But Homer, like God's anonymous secretary, knew how to build a story around its high points, which is what I intend doing here. So you won't find anything like a day-by-day ship's log. For those nautical buffs who insist, I recommend (with reservations) the Las Casas copy of what would eventually be called *Columbus's Journal of His First Voyage*. But you'll have to search for it. Unlike the volume you're now reading, it's out of print.

The sea is well charted from Palos across the Gulf of Mares to the Canary Islands off the west coast of Africa. Barto and I printed many such charts ourselves on fine, large sheepskins. Eight days, nine, ten, and you raise Las Palmas. A good following wind takes *Santa Maria* there in six and we sail on to the smaller island of Gomera, with the most protected anchorage in the islands, where we are to rendezvous with the caravels.

It is my intention to let the fleet separate, ordinarily a very poor piece of seamanship. But Martín Alonzo Pinzón needs to be taught a lesson, and not merely that square rigging's better than lateen. He needs to learn who's Admiral.

Three nights out of Palos lateen-rigged *Niña*, Vicente Yáñez Pinzón in command, drops far astern. When we light the signal fire in the brazier hanging aft, only Martín Alonzo aboard *Pinta* responds. Just as I've anticipated.

But two nights later we lose *Pinta* too.

Now, our second morning anchored in Gomera harbor, I'm learning about cost overruns from Rodrigo de Segovia, the plump, fussy little royal comptroller. We stand on deck, his portable desk between us near newly-secured water butts filled at Gomera's sweet streams and newly-lashed-down piles of firewood from Gomera's forests.

'The artillery was far dearer than projected,' he says. 'Dear me, yes.

Why do you need *two* sorts of cannon?'

I explain that the breech-loading falconets fire shrapnel to repel boarders, while the larger carriage-mounted lombards fire iron cannon balls.

'And the small arms?' Segovia asks, writing something on the manifest. 'Muskets *and* crossbows?'

Patiently I explain that muskets, with their noise and smoke, are more a psychological weapon, while I'd rely on tried and true crossbows for accuracy every time.

Again he writes on the manifest in his crabbed hand, so indecipherable it might as well be code.

'Victuals,' he says, shaking a cost-conscious head. 'Salt beef *and* jerky, sardines *and* anchovies, not to mention the cheese from La Mancha. Olives. Beans, chickpeas *and* lentils. Oil, vinegar. Almonds, molasses *and* honey. God, man! And the bread stores – ship's biscuit, salted flour *and* all those bushels of wheat. There's not even a cook aboard, let alone a baker.'

'The wheat's to grind flour. The flour's to mix with water, and roll out, and bake in the ashes of the firebox. Anyone can do it. Presto, fresh bread.'

Luís Torres emerges from the sterncastle and comes forward into the waist of the ship in time to hear me.

'Matzoh!' he cries in surprise.

To bake fresh unleavened bread aboard ship is actually an Arab idea, but I have no wish to disabuse him. Besides, cost-conscious Segovia is far from finished.

'Three kinds of wine.' He frowns and asks, 'Does this say fishing tackle?' The hooks and lines we'll use to troll for fish are his bridge to hard goods. 'Timber, knock-down barrels ... pitch, tallow ... '

I stop listening until he leaves ship's stores for salaries. 'Ninety men including yourself – '

'And yourself,' I can't help saying.

' – and a monthly payroll of 250,180 maravedís. Two thousand a month for masters and pilots, it's outrageous. And twenty-two coppers a day for ordinary seamen? They're most of them mere boys, it can only spoil them.' He returns unhappily to stores. 'Seventy-three maravedís per bushel of wheat and *how* many are aboard *Santa Maria*?'

'To be on the safe side,' I explain, 'we've provisions for a full year's sail.'

'Sail!' comes a shout from the quarterdeck, where Peralonso Niño of Moguer is officer of the watch. Before I can join him, Segovia wags a hectoring finger and says, 'I must insist on fiscal prudence in future.'

'There's nothing more to spend,' I tell him impatiently, and swing up the ladder.

The caravel, hull-down at the horizon, is not *Pinta* but *Niña* with her huge triangular mainsail.

Enríquez de Harana comes up the ladder right behind me. 'I tell you Pinzón's up to no good,' he says. 'What's keeping *Pinta*?'

Peralonso Niño's face looks more sinister than ever with the dark stubble along his jaw. We have no razors aboard. My own beard itches and is growing in gingery-white. 'There's no way *Niña* could've got here first unless *Pinta* ran into trouble,' Peralonso says in a worried voice. The youngest of the three Niño brothers, that seventeen-year-old angelic Billy Budd prototype Francisco, sails as a grommet aboard the overdue *Pinta*.

Chachu, *Santa Maria*'s boatswain, stands on maindeck openly eavesdropping. He's a squatly built fellow with stunted legs but his arms are long and immensely powerful. His face, with its unblinking toadlike stare, is the sort that frightens young children, timid virgins and insecure housepets. Ringleader of the northern clique of nine Basques and Galicians who stayed aboard *Santa Maria* with her indebted owner, shipmaster Juan Cosa, his Spanish is spare and ungrammatical; he grew up speaking Basque.

'Dat Cap'n Pinzón he from sout', not much sailor, hey?' On Chachu's toadlike face is stamped the look of implacable hostility with which he confronts all of life. 'He get here 'ventual. Nex' mont' maybe, hey?'

Chachu isn't far off. It is two weeks before *Pinta* staggers into Gomera harbor, yawing erratically.

I order *Santa Maria*'s boat lowered. Half an hour later, accompanied by Constable of the Fleet Enríquez de Harana, I climb the Jacob's ladder to *Pinta*'s maindeck. The crew watches us silently. Martín Alonzo Pinzón is in no hurry to appear. When he does, it is with a swagger.

'What took you so long?' I demand.

Barrel-bellied Pinzón is unfazed. 'Come aft and I'll show you.'

As we follow him, I hear the squeak and clatter of *Pinta*'s wooden pump. Her bilges smell foul.

'Run before a heavy sea with a busted rudder and you'd ship water too,' Martín Alonzo says coolly as we climb up to the quarterdeck and then down into the steerage. 'Take a look out there.'

I lean out the wide port, head and shoulders alongside the huge oak tiller.

'First taste of foul weather and she jumps her socket,' Martín Alonzo says in disgust. I lean further out the tiller port. The oak rudder post has been secured with stout hemp rope. The topmost iron pin or pintle on which the rudder pivots, the only one above water, is bent half off the deadwood.

'How'd it happen?' I ask. I'm already thinking that we'll have to make for Las Palmas, the only port in the Canaries with a smithy capable of repairing the damage.

Martín Alonzo's head appears on the other side of the tiller. His beard grows high on his cheeks, making his close-set eyes look even smaller. 'We're running before a heavy sea when a sudden gust aft hits those square sails of yours and lifts the stern straight out of the water like a sounding whale.' His voice is condescending. 'No need to blame yourself too much. Better we find out on the shakedown cruise than half-way across the Ocean Sea.'

Harana has said nothing so far. As Pinzón and I straighten to face each other, he leans in turn out the tiller port until only his dangling legs, his backside, and his hands gripping the sill are visible. His voice is muffled. 'Grab my legs, will you?'

They are already rising, his backside disappearing. I grasp his ankles and hold him. After a while I feel his weight pushing up. His hands return to the sill, and I haul him in. He turns slowly. He says nothing, just stares at Martín Alonzo, the usual Harana suspicious glower giving way to contempt.

'You could have sunk your own command,' Harana says, his voice a deadly sort of soft. 'You could have lost all hands, not to mention your worthless self.'

The enormity of the accusation makes Martín Alonzo back against the steerage bulkhead. 'Get off my ship, you titty-sucking wimp of a landlubberly liar!'

Harana's voice remains soft. 'Maybe I'm no seaman, Captain, but I recognize the marks left by a crowbar when I see them.'

Martín Alonzo's close-set eyes are bulging. His hand closes on his sheath knife. I'm certain he's going to attack Harana. But instead he appeals to me.

'Are you going to stand there and let this fellow talk to one of your captains like that?'

'As Constable of the Fleet,' I say, more stuffily than I have intended, 'he speaks for me.'

And then I know the tone is right. Martín Alonzo's hand drops to his side and Harana, confident of my backing, goes on:

'We'll want to question everyone who came near the steerage the day of the — accident.'

'Suit yourself,' Pinzón says with admirable bluster. 'I'll have the boatswain whistle up the port watch right now, and you'll see how ridiculous — '

'We'll start with the starboard watch, Captain.'

'My brother's watch? What're you suggesting? You mean to slander the whole Pinzón family?' Paco Pinzón, as master of *Pinta*, is officer of the starboard watch.

'I'm suggesting, Captain, that someone on board here may have seen someone else, Captain, or heard someone else, Captain, lever the rudder post out of its socket. Or even helped him. Whoever he was. Captain.'

Harana abruptly climbs from the steerage and goes to the bulwark. *Santa Maria*'s boat has drifted several lengths from *Pinta*. 'Bring her in close, boys,' Harana calls. 'We're about finished here.' I follow Pinzón up the ladder. Harana tells him: 'We'll want to start interrogating your starboard watch aboard *Santa Maria* immediately. The first batch can follow the Admiral and me back now.'

'On the flagship? Not here, all open and above-board?'

'I thought you understood, Captain,' says Harana, sounding genuinely surprised. 'It's the truth we're after.'

I hear an oar fending the boat off *Pinta*'s hull, and the gentle slap of water. Gulls hang overhead, their wings unmoving. *Pinta*'s crew is studiously looking everywhere but at us.

Martín Alonzo mumbles something.

'What?' shouts Harana. 'Speak up, man!'

Martín Alonzo expels his breath slowly and seems to deflate to half his size. Even his barrel of a belly seems smaller. His voice is a low croak. It's obvious he doesn't want the crew to hear. 'I had to, don't you see? Otherwise, with *Niña* dropping behind, how could I convince you to convert to lateen rigging?'

'But that's the point,' I say. 'She *was* dropping behind. So you were wrong about *Niña*'s rigging.'

'No, I wasn't.'

Harana and I look at each other, speechless.

'I did what I had to do,' Martín Alonzo says. 'I know I ain't wrong. It was for the good of the expedition.'

'For the good ... ' I begin.

'Because square rigging's dangerous!' Martín Alonzo shouts, not caring now who hears him. 'I know it is. I know it!'

I come as close then to understanding him as I ever will. There is no motiveless malignity in the man, of the sort so often portrayed in later sea stories like *Moby Dick* or the works of Joseph Conrad. Nor is he trying, for some obscure reason, to wreck the expedition before it's fairly underway. No – Martín Alonzo Pinzón, like so many mariners, would dive into shark-infested waters to rescue a shipmate but dreads what he doesn't understand.

'If I had any sense, I'd cashier you when we get to Las Palmas,' I tell him.

'What's wrong with right here and right now?' suggests Harana.

Martín Alonzo pleads with me. The disgrace will kill him, he says, and I believe it. Such is Spanish pride.

What can I do? Of the fleet's six senior officers, myself included, half are Pinzóns – Martín Alonzo and his middle brother Paco are captain and master aboard *Pinta*. Vicente Yáñez is *Niña*'s captain. Obviously I can't put them all ashore.

And, pride and fear of the unknown aside, Martín Alonzo's a skilled mariner. Bringing *Pinta* in with a sprung rudder proves it.

'Can you make Las Palmas without a tow?'

Eyes downcast, he nods.

'We'll put spars on *Niña*'s fore and mainmasts and cut her lateen sails square while they forge your new rudder hardware,' I tell him.

'Square rigging for *Niña*, new pintles and gudgeon for *Pinta*,' he says, changing my words to his as he studies my face for a sign. When he sees none, he asks hesitantly, 'And?'

'And nothing. The incident's closed.'

His pursed lips open into a smile. 'You won't regret this, Admiral.' It's the first time he's called me that, but still I'm not so sure.

Half-way back to *Santa Maria*, I tell Harana, 'You've got good eyes. I didn't see any signs of a crowbar being used.'

Suspiciously he asks me, 'You didn't?'

'No.'

And he smiles. 'That's hardly surprising. Neither did I.'

The fleet rides at anchor between Gomera and the larger island of Tenerife. Las Palmas lies far astern, *Niña* is square-rigged, *Pinta* has her new rudder hardware. It is the night of 7–8 September.

The compass card glows in the light of the copper binnacle lamp. I unhook the lamp, handing it to Peralonso Niño, and crouch to peer across the card in the moonlight first at Gomera, then Tenerife, to take their bearings. With ruler and dividers I prick a single point – the fleet's exact location – on a Barto copy of a Pozzo Toscanelli chart of the Ocean Sea. Peralonso's watch, the port watch, is on duty. I'm pleased that I share this moment with one of the Niño brothers of Moguer, that ancient mariner Vásquez's hometown, instead of the glum Galician shipmaster Juan Cosa.

'Well?' I ask. But it isn't really a question.

Peralonso answers in a whisper. 'Why not? Wind's rising.'

'Tell Chachu we'll have fore and main courses, no bonnets. Signal the caravels.'

'Aye,' says Peralonso, and I can hear the awe in his hushed voice.

Soon there's the shrill of Chachu's whistle, the shout of orders, the thud of bare feet on *Santa Maria*'s deck, the rumble of anchor cable, and that most beautiful of all sounds to a sailor's ears, the sharp crack of canvas tautening before the wind. Timbers creak and groan and I hear a shriller note in the wind through the rigging.

Peralonso stares at the bow wave, silver in the moonlight, as if he still can't believe we're underway.

'Course southwest until we clear Gomera,' I tell him, and he acknowledges, an idiotic grin on his face that with its heavy beard looks more like a desperado's than ever.

Just before dawn the wind shifts to the northeast. I hear Peralonso call for the starboard tack to be brought aboard and, a moment later, the roar of rope through the blocks. *Santa Maria* reaches then, a horse straining at the bit as she enters her best point of sailing with the wind abaft the beam.

Gomera and then the little island of Ferro, westernmost of the Canaries, drop astern. By sunrise, the wind still steady on the starboard quarter, we are sailing directly west to where no ship since the beginning of time has gone.

I doubt words exist in any language to describe those first ten days on the uncharted Ocean Sea. With the northeast wind holding steady on the starboard quarter, *Santa Maria* buoyantly crests the swells of a following sea so that each of us almost feels he can spread invisible wings and fly. The color of the sea is so deep that I tell myself the poet Homer could not have been blind when he called it wine-dark. The air is soft and sweet as an April day in Andalucía. Fair-weather clouds rise billowing astern and pass lazily overhead in the direction we are heading, as if showing us the way. Like a pair of brackets, *Niña* and

Pinta flank our wake. Every morning the decks are sluiced with buckets of seawater, and every midday, as ceremoniously as an African fetish man working his magic, I stick a pin in the center of the compass card and, when its shadow falls on the *fleur-de-lis* of north, correct ship's time to the noon of our new, westing day, surely the most glorious day ever except for the one to follow and the one after that.

Every four hours, or eight upendings of the sandclock, a grommet calls the new watch. The weather is so fair, the nights so balmy, that everyone sleeps on deck. When the new watch wakes, even that gloomy Galician first officer Juan Cosa almost smiles and speaks an almost friendly word as he takes command of the ship from Peralonso Niño, while both watches gobble biscuits, some cold chickpeas and garlic and a sardine or two, washing the quick meal down with a cup of watered wine. At the tiller the port watch helmsman gives the heading to Peralonso, who repeats it ritually to Juan Cosa, who repeats it to the new, starboard watch helmsman, who repeats it yet again. The wind is so steady those ten days that the heading and destination remain one — that single glorious word, west.

I stand on deck midway between the towering mainmast and the raked mizzen barely a third its height and watch the men lace both bonnets below the main course, as Master Juan Cosa has called for more sail. When he gives me a wary look, as if expecting me to countermand his order, I wonder how a man can so miss the joy of life. I smile at him and wish him a fine, a splendid day.

On my rounds I see the good ship's doctor, Juan Sánchez of Córdoba, seated on the edge of a hatch peering sympathetically into a scared young grommet's mouth while probing with the lightest of touches the offending molar. And there, walking forward, his weather eye appraising the activities of even his old friend the doctor, is Constable of the Fleet Enríquez de Harana. I climb to the forecastle. That fellow at the firebox watching two grommets prepare the midday meal, the only hot meal of the day, is Chachu, the Basque boatswain. See how low to the deck he's built, his thick legs so short it almost seems his Maker fashioned him to stand easily on a rolling ship's cambered planking. Chachu's hostility, those first ten days, is limited to baleful stares and an occasional colorful expletive. But the young seamen are nervous while he hovers close.

'A very good morning to you, Boatswain,' I say cheerfully.

Chachu grunts something that sounds like 'Admiral' and for a moment returns his attention to the firebox, or pot island as it's called, then stalks aft to the ladder. I say a friendly word or two to the impromptu cooks and return to maindeck.

Around the mainmast a number of grommets have gathered, all of them young boys. The focus of their eager attention is Cristóbal Quintero, the thirty-year-old baby-faced former owner of *Pinta*, who has fallen on hard times and sails aboard *Santa Maria* as an ordinary seaman. He has quickly established himself in the eyes of his juniors as the flagship's resident expert on all matters sexual.

'Two of them,' he is saying now, his innocent baby-face giving credence to the words, which the boys take in with wide-eyed wonder.

'*Two?*'

'Sure. They have two breasts in the general run of the population, don't they? Two's normal, if you stop to consider it. Two arms, two legs, two hands, two feet, two ears, two nostrils. English anatomy of the female persuasion's more consistent, you might say. It's how you can tell an English girl from any other, every time. They always have two of them.'

'Where?' ask the eager young grommets in chorus.

'In England. Didn't I say? It's the English girls have two of them.'

'But where,' plead the grommets, 'on their persons?'

'The usual place, you nits,' says innocent-looking Cristóbal Quintero. 'Only, as they're side by side, the magic triangle's closer to being a square, if you see what I mean. Now, you take your Scottish lasses and there you're really in for a shock because ... ' And Quintero is off again.

So am I, having in mind a visit to the afterguard garden to attend to a necessary function. But the little seat built out over the quarterdeck port rail is already occupied by its semi-permanent inhabitant, Master Juan Cosa. His face red, he stares straight ahead with a look of bleak concentration as if he's trying to work out some difficult problem in navigation. Grommets on maindeck cast surreptitious glances in his direction. There are frequent wagers as to how long Cosa will remain in the garden and with what results. Because that glum man's glumness increases in inverse proportion to his success fertilizing the garden, the grommets have a stake in things.

They also wait to see if *Santa Maria* with her too tall mainmast might roll a few degrees more than usual to port while glum Cosa sits in the garden. This would give the Galician an unexpected bath of the nether regions. It doesn't happen today. Cosa is still there, still hard at work on navigational problems, when I enter the sterncastle.

Peralonso Niño is watching my steward Pedro Terreros set the table for the afterguard. Peralonso, true to his size, is *Santa Maria*'s trencherman and the only man aboard who seems to enjoy the stringy salt pork that's the mainstay of our table. 'It's a question of mind over matter,' he assures me. 'Why, today while you're all choking down sow's belly, I intend dining on plump well-hung partridge stewed in red wine with raisins and pine nuts. It's simple, if you apply your imagination.'

Every evening shortly after sunset when pot island is extinguished for the night, the youngest grommet of the new watch lights the binnacle lamp and comes aft with it, chanting, 'May God give us a fine night and a safe night's sail, yes sirs and amen!' The entire crew then solemnly recite the *Pater Noster*.

Sometimes I wake mornings at first light to a pure tenor voice singing

Be Thou praised, my Lord, with all Thy creatures,
 above all Brother Sun, who gives the day ...
Be Thou praised, my Lord, of Sister Moon and the stars ...
 of Brother Wind ...

and my heart jolts hard as for an instant I'm back in Galway a lifetime ago and see Tristram's dear and indescribably beautiful face. Then Pedro Terreros knocks at my cabin door, bringing my breakfast of sardines, an onion, ship's biscuit and wine, and I'm aboard *Santa Maria* again.

But the haunting memory, brought back by a pure tenor voice welcoming the dawn, makes me wonder. What of those others, forty men aboard *Santa Maria*, ninety in the fleet, do I really know any of them? Why are *they* here, and not forty or ninety others? What secret memories drive them, or torment them? Do thoughts like mine cross their minds? Can any man ever truly know another? Or even know himself?

Such Oceanic musings lead sometimes in a direction better not explored — that all is chance, that man's will is illusory, that God is not. But then perhaps a school of dolphins appears, to sport beside us and bear us company a while, or a pair of seabirds alight to rest in our rigging before they again take wing, circle and soar away, silvery flashes in a sky almost as blue as the sea, and I know not only that God is, but that He is everywhere.

Only with Luís Torres, the expedition's lately-added interpreter, do I sometimes share such thoughts at night over a last cup of wine.

According to Peralonso Niño, an uncanny judge of ship's speed solely by the look of the bow wave, we sail 1,165 nautical miles those first ten days. My own figures, I might as well admit now, are both greater and lesser. The lesser, as every schoolboy learns, are my necessary fiction for the crew. They will inevitably become fearful that we have sailed further than God meant man to go. Against that day, I chop twenty per cent or so off Peralonso's reckoning. My other set of figures is more difficult to explain. Have I put these exaggerated estimates in my journal, sometimes close to 200 miles noon to noon, to impress the royals, who will read what I have written? This is what Peralonso, who alone shares the secret of my double-entry reckoning, believes. But it isn't true. No, the truth is that I am in such a great hurry to reach the East that the bow wave moves faster for me than for Peralonso, and I convince myself that my private set of figures is correct.

A ship's crew, more perhaps than any other group, is prey to sudden swings of mood. Thus we can ride the glorious crest of ten days of perfect sailing weather only to be plunged in the space of one watch into the gloomy trough of the Sargasso Sea.

I wake on the morning of 16 September instinctively knowing something is wrong, but not knowing what, or even how I know. And then I realize it's the silence, the human silence – not a snatch of song, not a shout, not a footfall, as if I'm the only one left aboard *Santa Maria* and maybe (Oceanic thought, first thing on waking) in the world.

Pulling on my doublet, dealing my head a fierce blow on the low door lintel, I step barefoot from the sterncastle. The planking is still slippery with dew as I hurry forward to where a frightened grommet casts the sounding line under Juan Cosa's direction. The crew lines the bulwark, watching. Then I see what has caused the unnatural silence, the sudden fearful hush. Thick clumps of leathery weed float by, dark green or, less often, yellow.

'What reading?' Cosa breaks the laden silence. His hangdog expression, all sagging vertical lines and grooves that make his face look like a mask in danger of slipping off, is more pronounced than usual.

The boy hauls on the hemp line. It comes up with weed clinging to it. 'None, sir. She played all the way out and hit no bottom.'

'You've got two hundred-foot lines bent together there, boy,' scoffs Cosa, grabbing the lead line from the grommet and heaving it himself.

But he too fails to find bottom.

'Too much sail,' he says, dewlaps quivering as he shakes his head. 'We lost too much line to our headway. Chachu!' he calls.

Soon the boatswain orders grommets to shorten sail by unlacing both bonnets from the main course, drastically reducing our speed. I'm less than delighted with this. All around me are fear-pinched faces and I know that the sooner we put the Sargasso Sea behind us the better off we'll be. Because the weed, if old Vásquez de la Frontera was right, threatens only morale.

But command aboard ship is a subtle thing.

You've noticed that I'm officer of no watch; Juan Cosa, as master or first officer, and Peralonso Niño, as pilot or second, split the four-hour watches. As officer of the starboard watch, on duty now, it is Cosa's right to call for shortened sail. As captain I can, if I choose, countermand that or any order. But Cosa, part-owner of *Santa Maria*, ought to be sensitive to every balk and timber, every quirk of her, and the men know this. Besides, if I override his authority once, I diminish it for all time. Not only will he resent me, but the crew will be less sure of both of us.

So I hold my silence and watch while Cosa hurls the lead again. 'All that weed has to mean submerged rock,' he says, clutching stubbornly at his fear.

Peralonso Niño appears at my side. As Cosa's alternate watch officer, he can do what I cannot. He says, 'Sure, ordinarily, of course. But didn't old Vásquez sail right through the Sargasso Sea and out again?'

'I say there's rock down there,' shouts Cosa, 'rock that could cut our bottoms open!'

From Peralonso's fierce face comes the gentlest of remonstration. 'A little vegetable matter, Shipmaster. Harmless as a strawberry patch.'

Four days later Peralonso's 'little vegetable matter' has become a green and yellow meadow stretching to the horizon in all directions. The fleet barely moves. So negligible is our headway, so light the breeze, that we can shout from ship to ship. All three Pinzón brothers are for sailing a zigzag course to find open sea. Juan Cosa clings to the idea of continuing slowly west, constantly sounding. Peralonso Niño and his brother Juan, master aboard *Niña*, agree with me: the weed is a danger only to morale.

Knowing I've waited too long, I summon Chachu. 'Crack on all the sail you have — main course with both bonnets, fore course, spritsail, mizzen, topsail, the lot.'

Peralonso's smile is fierce. 'How about rigging the boat's sail on the poopdeck?' he suggests, and that's done too. *Santa Maria* begins to really move.

'A man can't cast the sounding line at this speed,' Juan Cosa complains.

'Stow the lead, Shipmaster,' I tell him. 'You won't need it.'

His gloomy eyes and downturned mouth accuse me of calamities about to happen. He can already see the ship, *his* ship, splitting open on hidden rock. But he's still seaman enough to ask, 'And the heading?'

'Why,' I tell him blandly, 'west as usual. Due west.'

'Dat damn fur'ner be deat' us all,' comes Chachu the boatswain's atrocious Spanish in what will eventually be called a stage whisper.

On the sixth day of our passage through the Sargasso Sea, the lookout cries, 'Blue water!' and sure enough, there it is glinting ahead like steel in the sunlight. The meadow gives way to clumps of weed, the clumps disperse, soon there is nothing but open sea.

I hear Chachu's stage whisper: 'Dat damn fur'ner he lucky dis time.'

But after the Sargasso Sea, every change in the weather means trouble. If the wind drops, the men grumble that we'll lie becalmed until we starve to death. If the breeze shifts to the west and, sailing close-hauled, we can hold our course no better than west-northwest, there are dire predictions we'll miss Cipango or the Indies entirely. Even if we pick up the prevailing winds again, there's muttering. A wind dead astern resurrects the memory of how *Pinta* allegedly lost her rudder. And a perfect starboard reach uncovers the lurking fear that we're sailing further than God intended and will never get back.

Mutiny!

What a sinister word – yet what a stirring one!

Admit it, doesn't sympathy lie most often with the mutineers – good men and true, while the captain against whom they rise is a despot?

I offer the case of Captain Bligh of H.M.S. *Bounty*, as cruel a commander as ever lashed an innocent at the mainmast, and his antagonist Fletcher Christian, that reasonable fellow whose very name so obviously signals his virtue.

Or Captain Queeg of U.S.S. *Caine* – is there ever any question? There the unfortunate crew is really afloat on perilous waters, because

Queeg is not only cowardly and incompetent but, it becomes harrowingly clear, insane.

So who can blame the mutineers?

One can only wonder, in fact, why the crew of *Pequod* fails to rise against the monomaniacal Captain Ahab, determined to glimpse behind the 'pasteboard masks' that hide reality, at no matter what cost – even the sacrifice of his ship, his crew and himself to the monstrous white whale Moby Dick, that most Oceanic of symbols. But here's the question. Is Moby Dick evil, or is Ahab?

And try this. Am I any less monomaniacal than Ahab? Isn't the fabled East my white whale? What wouldn't I sacrifice to get there?

But I'm no despot, I'm not cruel, certainly not sadistic.

All of which make me worse than Ahab, for misleading my crew with a ready smile and kind words. The most truly villainous wear their own pasteboard masks to camouflage evil.

I'm trying to be fair about all this.

It is Chachu, I'm sure, who first gets the notion that killing the Admiral of the Ocean Sea is the best way to rid the poor fellow of his fantastical delusion that sailing west will bring him to East, while at the same time ridding the rest of them of the foreigner leading them to watery graves. A quick rush of bare feet across planking, perhaps at night when the Admiral is checking Polaris against the compass (which occasionally deviates in response to some natural phenomenon I don't understand), a faint splash lost in the rush of the bow wave and – reach for home, lads, where all women are beautiful and all men brave!

A conversation one afternoon in early October on the quarterdeck:

JUAN COSA: There's talk among the crew ...
COLÓN: I know what they're saying.
COSA: That we've already sailed further than the Admiral's estimated distance to Cipango.
COLÓN: My figures were optimistic.
COSA: The men aren't. They want to turn back.
COLÓN: With or without the Admiral, I take it?
COSA: Well, aye. I've heard some of that.

We're sailing close-hauled to a northwest wind and barely holding west. Suddenly the mainsail begins to shiver and the helmsman instantly puts the tiller up. We heel steeply. Cosa stumbles. I grab him. The deck swoops underfoot. He clings to me and I feel the bulwark against the backs of my legs. His face, close to my own, is garden-fertilizing red. I shove him away. He is – or pretends to be – off balance, and drops to one knee.

Chachu watches us impassively from maindeck.

Close to four weeks without sight of land. The men are surly. Fights erupt over little things: a mislaid marlinspike, a place in the lee of a hatch on a windy night, a grommet a few seconds late turning the sandclock. Chachu's hostility increases and his northern clique huddles secretively. Conversations are chopped off as I pass on my rounds. I feel eyes on my back.

Harana advises: 'Keep to the quarterdeck, Admiral.'

Dr Sánchez smiles his best bedside smile and agrees. 'After all, that's where a ship's run, isn't it? From the quarterdeck?'

'A ship,' I tell them, 'is run by its crew,' and go down to main-deck.

From that moment on, Harana or Sánchez or my steward Pedro Terreros manages always to be near at hand, and Peralonso Niño finds excuses to come on deck during starboard watch.

One evening Martín Alonzo Pinzón aboard *Pinta* makes things worse by signaling he has sighted land. *Pinta*'s lombards belch smoke and flame as the cry of 'land! land!' is picked up on all three ships. In the fading light men jump and cavort and hug each other, convinced land lies to the southwest, a distant cone of a mountain crowned with snow. I see only clouds piled high on the horizon.

Still, there's nothing for it but to change our heading and chase the nonexistent mountain southwest all night.

In the morning there's no sight of land, mountainous, snow-capped or any other variety, but the sky is a hard flat yellow and that means wind.

It rises directly astern shortly after we change our heading back to west. A heavy following sea spills through the tiller port, drenching the helmsman. Water pours out the scuppers and the clattering pump raises the stink of the bilges.

Peralonso Niño, legs braced against the lurching of the deck, estimates our speed at over seven knots.

'A wind for the Indies!' he cries as the prow goes under and rises again spewing great wings of water. I'm exultant too – until I see the faces of the crew. It is as if Juan Cosa has stamped them all with his gloom. For them now the howl of wind through rigging, the rush of the bow wave, the pronounced arch to *Santa Maria*'s mainmast – all mean only that with every passing minute we are racing further from the possibility, already remote, of ever returning home.

The wind does not drop until dawn of 9 October. I'm on deck watching the new day come. The sea is flat and still night-dark, but the sails are already golden with the light of the unrisen sun. Then the deck too is touched with gold as the rim of the sun appears on the horizon. Hull-down, I think, the sun is hull-down, and I smile remembering Barto, when we were boys in Genoa, trying to convince me the world is round.

As night gives way to Homer's rosy-fingered dawn, a small bird flutters into view and alights on the taffrail to chirp at me. Its feathers are a pale iridescent green. Peralonso Niño, who has just extinguished the binnacle lamp, sees the bird too. 'A land bird,' he says softly, almost doubting his own words. 'It's a land bird.' His teeth flash in his beard; his voice wavers.

The bird flutters off with a burst of brilliant white underwings and soars high to join three others overhead. We watch them fly west. All iridescent green except for their underwings, they're like no bird we've ever seen.

My eyes sting, probably with salt spray.

Peralonso Niño stiffens suddenly. He is looking over my shoulder. Turning, I see activity aboard *Pinta*, which is matching our course perhaps a mile to starboard. On go the mainsail bonnets. Soon the spritsail is set and the mizzen boom gybes to port. At *Pinta*'s new speed she will close with *Santa Maria* inside of an hour.

With Peralonso I'm waiting on the foredeck as the faster caravel under full sail cuts across our bow.

'That fool,' Peralonso says. 'What's he up to?'

Pinta passes so close that I can see Martín Alonzo Pinzón's face clearly as he cups his hands to his mouth. Through the boiling of *Pinta*'s bow wave and ours comes his bellowing voice.

' ... want a captains' meeting!'

Pinta shows us her stern and races toward *Niña*, half a mile to port. We'll have both Pinzón captains aboard by noon. I can think of no reason for a captains' meeting but one.

Peralonso says, 'What'll you do?'

I remember my first meeting with Martín Alonzo in a Palos bodega, and the gross way he wolfed down shrimp and wine.

'I'll feed them,' I say, and call for my steward Pedro Terreros. 'What sort of feast can you lay on for three people?' I ask him.

'Salt pork, dried beef, sardines or anchovies,' Pedro singsongs with a grin.

'I'm in earnest, boy.'

'In that case I'll go fishing.'

And he does, trolling from the poopdeck. I return to my cramped quarters, the only private cabin aboard, and squint a jaundiced eye at the small looking glass nailed over my washstand. A wild-bearded apparition with a peeling sunburned forehead and a thatch of barber-pole straw hair squints back at me. I find a pair of scissors, deciding to look more an admiral, and trim my ginger-white beard to a sort of spade shape. I put on my other set of clothes, which have been washed often in seawater and itch as badly as those I have stripped off. What passes for a dress uniform I leave in my sea chest; I'm saving that for landfall.

I return on deck in time to see *Niña*'s and *Pinta*'s boats converging on us. Pedro Terreros is still trolling from the poopdeck. Suddenly he cries out and begins to haul on his line. Instead of waiting to see his catch, I enter the sterncastle again and knock at the door of the common cabin shared by master, pilot, comptroller, interpreter, doctor, constable. I rouse Harana.

'Pinzóns are coming aboard.'

'Oh?' A single syllable, suspiciously uttered.

'You have those reports?' I ask. Harana nods. 'I'm going to need them.'

There is shouting overhead. Back on deck, I see grommets in *Pinta*'s boat fending off with their oars while the Jacob's ladder goes tumbling down *Santa Maria*'s side. But the commotion is aft. Half the crew surrounds Pedro Terreros, who has boated a twenty-pound fish with scales, fins and tail of pale silver-red.

Martín Alonzo comes aboard. His hair is matted, his beard unkempt, his clothes a mess. I look at the excited faces around Pedro Terreros and his fish, then back to Martín Alonzo, who is striking an arrogant pose, fists on hips, barrel belly thrust out, as his small eyes fasten on me. I turn deliberately to Pedro Terreros and his fish, and pitch my voice to carry. 'A beauty, Pedro,' I tell him. 'For the forecastle's dinner, with my compliments.' A roar of delight greets these words. 'And please send wine, biscuit and sardines to my cabin.'

Twenty minutes later Vicente Yáñez Pinzón, a younger version of his brother, refills his wine cup as he tells me, 'That's it. It's non-fucking-negotiable.'

Martín Alonzo nods. Like his brother, he has left the sardines and

184

biscuit untouched, but is working steadily through my wine. He says, 'Vicente's right. It's nothing against you, man. We all made the same mistake.'

'It's no mistake.'

'Face it, why don't you?' urges Vicente Yáñez. '*We* have. Better to take it like a man.'

'It's no disgrace,' says his brother.

'There's no land ahead or we'd've fucking found it by now,' says Vicente Yáñez illogically, but his point is made.

'It got so bad I was seeing mirages,' his brother says. 'Like I was, uh – ' He searches for a word.

Vicente Yáñez supplies two. 'Fucking obsessed.'

They both stare at me. Obsessed. They honestly believe I am. And wouldn't they be fools to follow a man blinded by a dream? Are they so far wrong – even if I'm right?

'But not anymore,' says Martín Alonzo. 'Ain't no mainland, no islands. Ain't no Cathay or Cipango or none of them. Nothing but Ocean Sea out there. Stretching on forever.'

I'm going to argue, but what's the use? They'd just see it as another manifestation of the Ahab mania.

'We're turning back,' says Vicente Yáñez. 'Right now.'

'Today,' says Martín Alonzo.

And that's it as far as they're concerned.

I study their truculent faces. All during the meeting Martín Alonzo Pinzón has deferred to his brother, content to echo and embellish. This I know means he is unsure of himself – which will help when the time comes. But what's keeping the Constable of the Fleet?

'And your crews?' I ask them.

'Most of them sailed under me or him before,' says Vicente Yáñez. 'So if it comes to a showdown, you better understand our people will back us.'

'Back us, hell,' says Martín Alonzo. 'If I didn't call this captains' meeting today, my own crew – '

'That's enough,' Vicente Yáñez interrupts him, and in a more reasonable voice urges me, 'Man, we're only asking you to use the head God gave you. You could lead this fleet – your fleet – back into Palos harbor a hero. We'd all be heroes. Already wested beyond the Sargasso Sea, where no ship's ever sailed before, ain't we? Did ourselves proud, man. Only the theory's wrong – there ain't no way East by sailing west. We tried. Can men do more? Failure in a noble attempt ain't exactly the end of the world.'

I wonder if it is – for me.

'Not,' says Vicente Yáñez, 'that we got any intention of leaning on you.'

'You're free to sail on,' says Martín Alonzo magnanimously.

'And on and on,' Vicente Yáñez adds with a mocking laugh.

I want to set one thing straight right here. Note the words 'sail on'. This is the only time they're spoken, and Martín Alonzo Pinzón is the speaker. I never, despite anything you may have read, say 'sail on' – with or without an exclamation point. No, the word I use in the captains' meeting that October ninth and the next day with *Santa Maria*'s mutinous crew is '*adelante*', and I speak it calmly. '*Adelante*' means forward, and since it is forward, not backward, that I want to go, that is the word I use. There is a false note of melodrama in the words 'sail on' and of parody in Vicente Yáñez's mocking 'and on and on', and I'm certain a Lope or a Shakespeare would be guilty of neither. Nor am I.

'*Santa Maria*'s going forward,' I tell them.

'Then go with God,' says Vicente Yáñez, not piously.

'But without us.' Martín Alonzo rises, signaling that the meeting is over.

Such insolence is too much. 'Sit down!' I shout.

Startled, Martín Alonzo complies.

'There may be some confusion as to who commands aboard *Niña* and *Pinta*,' I say coldly, 'but there's none aboard *Santa Maria*.'

I hear footsteps outside and a soft knock at the door.

'Come!' I shout, still angry.

Harana looks into the cabin, which is too small for four large men, and remains stooped in the doorway. I tell Vicente Yáñez, 'Get out.'

His eyes widen.

'Out.' I jerk a thumb at the door. He glances at his brother, who shrugs. Vicente Yáñez squeezes past Harana. At a nod from me, the Constable of the Fleet shuts the door and, brandishing a few sheets of paper, sits on the just-vacated three-legged stool.

'Let Captain Pinzón have a look at the report, Constable,' I say.

Harana holds onto his papers. 'Which one, Admiral? Your message didn't say, so I brought both.'

Harana has written two totally different reports on the incident of *Pinta*'s sprung rudder. The first supports Martín Alonzo Pinzón's claim that a rogue wind put the rudder out of commission, and goes on to describe his skill in bringing *Pinta* to the Canaries under extremely difficult, if not downright impossible, conditions. The second condemns him as a captain who sabotaged his own ship. Both have already been signed by the Constable of the Fleet and await my counter-signature.

'In that case,' I suggest, 'why not let him read both?'

Martín Alonzo starts with the encomium. His pursed lips move as he reads. He nods and smiles. Then he begins the second, shorter report. I watch the color leach from his face.

Blandly I say, 'You seem to have a preference for the other one.'

'A preference? A *preference*? Shit, man!'

'Then your options are simple. First, you can turn back, against my orders. If you do, *Santa Maria* will sail for Spain with you – and I'll deliver that second report to Their Majesties.'

'You can never prove that's how it happened.'

'I wouldn't be so sure of that,' Harana says mysteriously. 'Besides, the suspicion would be enough to ruin you. You'd never get another command.'

Before Martín Alonzo can reply, Harana turns to me. 'I believe you said, "You can turn back, *against my orders*." Were those your words, Admiral?'

'Why, I believe they were.' Mildly.

Harana leans across the table at me, his face so grim it is hard to be certain whose side he's on. 'Just for the record, Admiral, would you mind making those orders explicit?'

So I say, 'Captain Pinzón, I've heard you and your brother out, and the answer is no. This fleet will continue forward, and you'll sail with it.'

Adelante. I want to drive this point home. The word frightens Martín Alonzo as much as the melodramatic 'sail on' embarrasses me.

Harana sits back and stares at Pinzón. 'Well?'

A stubborn shake of his head, a further pursing of his tiny mouth. 'We're going back.' But Martín Alonzo's voice is subdued.

'Against the Admiral's express command?'

'Got nothing to do with any command he gave me after.'

'Captain,' Harana purrs, 'there's a word for what you and your brother are doing. Would you care to supply it?'

Sweat like oily blisters has popped out on Martín Alonzo's face. He brushes at it with his sleeve. 'Disagreement,' he says. 'A minor disagreement with the Admiral here. Disagreement, now there's the word you're looking for.'

Harana's gaze is a study in incredulity.

'Insubordination?' Martín Alonzo suggests on a hopeful note. 'A small matter of a little insubordination, now that's certainly your word. But we're all reasonable men here, and in the heat of the dispute there's bound to be a tiny touch of the slightest suggestion of insubordination.'

Harana's voice almost knocks him off his stool. 'MUTINY!'

The single word hangs in the stale air of the cabin.

'Mutiny?' Martín Alonzo echoes, his tiny eyes round with disbelief. 'Oh, I can see how there's some might make the mistake of calling it that but – '

'They'd call it mutiny because it is mutiny,' says Harana.

Sweat blisters roll down Martín Alonzo's face. He sits silent, withdrawn. His crowded features seem to contract further, as if they'd barely cover a good-sized Valencia orange.

'Say it, Captain.'

But Martín Alonzo remains tight-lipped.

'Get used to the sound of it because you'll be hearing it the rest of your life if you run back to Spain. Surely if you can commit it you ought to be able to say it.'

Martín Alonzo merely slumps, one big hand hiding his reduced face.

Gambling on the morning's strange land bird, I tell him, 'As you said, we're all reasonable men here. I'm willing to let you tear up that second report on the rudder, in exchange for three more days.' I know I won't get more, no matter what Martín Alonzo's willing to promise now.

'Three?' he says. 'Just three days?'

'If after three days we haven't sighted land I'll order the fleet home. And we'll forget what happened today.'

'No disagreement or slight suggestion of insubordination or . . . like that?'

'We held a captains' meeting, we decided to give it three more days. That's all.'

Martín Alonzo reaches for the jug of wine and drains it. Then looking straight at Harana he carefully rips the condemning report in half and in half again, compressing the torn paper into a ball in his fist. This he studies, as if it holds some unexpected truth in its new shape. Then he tosses it contemptuously at the Constable. 'Three days,' he says, and a grin, tentative at first, spreads on his face. 'I'll be at *Pinta*'s tiller myself when we turn back – Admiral.'

Santa Maria leaps, lurches, comes smashing down. My cabin sways

188

and jounces like that Hungarian invention the coach. I try to rise. In the pre-dawn darkness I'm hurled from my berth and crash into the bulkhead near the door. The ship groans like a stricken animal as she pitches into the heaving swells. I make it to my feet. To the door. I crack it and the wind tears it from my hands. I stumble and am reduced to crawling out.

The mainmast curves like a drawn bow. The binnacle lamp has gone out but there is enough light to see that the quarterdeck is deserted. I peer into the steerage, then *Santa Maria* rolls sharply to port and I'm thrown against the bulwark. There's a loud ominous creaking, audible even over the howling gale, from the mainmast. I crawl back and shout down into the steerage:

'Can you hold her?'

The voice that answers me is no seaman's but young Pedro Terreros's. 'Not much longer, I'm afraid, sir!'

I lurch to my feet and let the forward pitching of the ship carry me to the ladder. I climb down when she pitches aft.

The too tall mainmast swings across the wrathful sky, arching further. In dread I await the thunderous cracking sound the spruce will make when it goes. *Santa Maria* seems to jump clear of the sea, then drops back down with a bone-jarring thud as if she's grounded herself on rock. Tons of green water spill across the deck. Like a log in a millrace I tumble to starboard, gasping, choking. I wonder if Pedro Terreros has drowned in the steerage, wonder if the tiller is untended. I see a figure struggling to reach the block that guides the sheet to the near clew of the main course. *Santa Maria* shakes herself like a drenched dog.

'Slash the sheets!' I bellow.

It's our only hope. Cut loose the mainsail and we can still save the mast. And the ship.

But the figure is no longer moving.

Half at a staggering run, half on hands and knees, I reach him and recognize Peralonso Niño. He tries to rise, sinks down again.

The deck, except for us, is deserted.

For one awful instant I see a towering wall of water directly aft. It comes crashing down and the poop and sterncastle vanish. I hold Peralonso until the prow explodes out of the water. On elbows and knees I pull myself along the bulwark to the waist of the ship. My sheath knife is in my hand. So tautly strung between the bulging mainsail and the block is the stout hempen sheet that a single stroke of my knife severs it. The hemp lashes past my face. The great sail flaps

189

and cracks like a volley of musket fire. Here to starboard the canvas flies free. Not so to port. *Santa Maria* begins to swing athwart the wind. Already she is heeling alarmingly. I drag myself across the deck and then in despair realize I have lost the knife. It's finished, I tell myself. You can do no more, just wait for the end. But then the port sheet goes and the mainsail blows free to billow wildly in the rigging, to slap the no longer straining mast, to rise over the huge main yard, to flutter, to rip. I see Peralonso at the port block, head bowed, knife in hand.

Somehow I get back to the steerage hatch. Even with nothing on her spars but useless tatters of sail, *Santa Maria* is driven mercilessly before the gale. I'm sure the tiller's too much for young Pedro Terreros by now. If he's alive.

I half-jump, half-fall into the steerage.

Pedro Terreros is slumped across the tiller. Barely conscious, he tries to fight me when I pry him loose from the stick. Water pours through the tiller port. It is thigh-deep where I stand. Hoping he has followed, I shout for Peralonso. Pedro Terreros will drown unless he's supported, for as soon as I release him and put my weight against the tiller he collapses in the flooded steerage. I let the stick go and lift him out of the water. Peralonso starts down the ladder and slides the rest of the way. The water pouring through the tiller port now reaches my waist.

'Take the wind abaft the beam!' I shout.

'We'll heel over!' Peralonso protests.

'And we'll be swamped if we keep the wind astern at this speed.'

I try to wrestle Pedro Terreros up the ladder but can't. Peralonso strains futilely at the tiller. Something in the relieving tackle has fouled. He slashes it and leans on the tiller once more. *Santa Maria* heels to port as Peralonso brings her slowly three, four points off the wind. He holds her heeled over so steeply she's in danger of going flat on her side, but the water in the steerage rises no higher. I lean Pedro Terreros against the ladder. Feverishly I warp lines to the sea anchor and stream it from the tiller port to check our speed. Then I join Peralonso at the tiller. He hacks away more rope. Against the weight of sea and wind we ease the helm up once more, and lash it fast with the remnants of the relieving tackle. *Santa Maria* shudders but we're running without canvas before the wind again.

A long time later I'm aware the wind has dropped.

· · ·

Niña and *Pinta* are sailing back and forth on short tacks (we call this jogging off and on) while aboard *Santa Maria* the main yard is lowered and the spare mainsail taken from its locker. It is early afternoon and those winds from the northeast that will one day bear the name Trade Winds have moderated from whole gale to strong breeze.

All hands have been turned up, for all will be needed when the main yard is raised again. The job is usually accomplished to the singing of a high-spirited, bawdy chantey. But the yard has come down only to the squeak of pulleys and the grunts of sweating men. Now braces, lifts, buntlines, bowlines, clewlines, tacks and sheets are attached to the new sail, all in an oppressive quiet, every pair of hands doing its job but every face bleak and gloomy as Master Juan Cosa's.

From the forward edge of the quarterdeck, the shipmaster surveys the scene below. The gleaming new white sail ripples in the fresh wind, a living thing eager to be aloft. Chachu the boatswain comes aft.

'Got da bastid all bent on,' he says.

The men have turned to stare silently at the quarterdeck.

Cosa nods. He tells the boatswain, 'Dismiss the port watch.'

I gape at him. 'Aren't you forgetting something?' The wind carries my words away, for I haven't raised my voice. The crew sees only a dumb show.

Juan Cosa's arms are crossed over his chest. Slowly he shakes his head, his lugubrious face set. 'No sir, I'm not.'

Softly I tell him, 'Let's have the main yard up, Shipmaster.'

He stares silently ahead. Below us Chachu grunts something in his native Basque.

Louder I say, 'The yard needs hoisting, Shipmaster, and you'll need all hands to do it.'

My voice has carried to maindeck. The men stir uneasily, looking everywhere but at the halyard lying like a thick snake on the planking.

Juan Cosa darts a nervous glance down at Chachu. After an almost imperceptible nod from the Basque boatswain, he turns to me. 'The men don't want any more,' he says.

I look past him down at Chachu's hostile face.

'I want you to tell Chachu to raise the main yard,' I say slowly.

'The men,' says Cosa, 'have had enough of west. They won't raise your main yard to sail west. They're all finished with west.'

It's a long speech for the shipmaster, the longest I've ever heard him make.

I haven't given an order, not quite. He hasn't refused one, not quite. Like so many men who must live with their own inadequacy, Juan

Cosa is a trimmer. He has still to commit himself openly to mutiny. The mutiny, if it develops, is Chachu's — Chachu and his clique of nine northerners who dominate the starboard watch.

'Chachu!' my voice lashes out.

The unblinking eyes lift to me.

I am about to give him, not the shipmaster, a direct order to raise the main yard. Then I have a better idea.

'We'll have a cask of wine up,' I say. 'There's hard work ahead.'

Chachu's eyes drop. That I have avoided, or at least postponed, the reckoning disappoints him. When the cask is brought on deck, Chachu himself yanks the bung and dispenses the wine. Beside the squat, powerfully built boatswain stands Peralonso Niño, who just happens to have a belaying pin in his hand.

Nonchalantly I look on for perhaps twenty minutes, letting the men drink until the sandclock is turned and Peralonso is due to replace Juan Cosa as watch officer.

'Pilot!' I call, and Peralonso springs to the foot of the quarterdeck ladder. 'We'll have the main course raised now.'

Except for one quirked eyebrow, his desperado's face remains impassive. His composure is admirable, for he knows as well as I the mood of the crew. But, 'Aye, sir,' he says casually, and gives the order.

The crew responds — every man of them — with a minute scrutiny of the deck planking, as if searching for the telltale piles of sawdust left by woodworm.

With sinking heart I realize it's not just Chachu and his northern clique, nor just starboard watch, which would be bad enough. No, the débâcle is complete. Chachu's got to the entire crew.

Will Captain Bligh ever have to face such total rebellion? Far from it — many of his people remain loyal. As for Captain Queeg of the *Caine*, he'll be too far round the bend for it to matter.

It matters mightily to me.

Here on my flagship, Admiral of the vast Ocean Sea which surrounds me, I stand alone.

And then, not quite alone.

The first man to reach the halyard is Luís Torres, the interpreter. Soon the ship's doctor and the Constable of the Fleet join him. Then I see what has to be an apparition. Rodrigo de Segovia, the comptroller, hasn't shown himself on deck — except to rush for the nearest rail — since our first hour on the Ocean Sea. Poor Segovia has died a hideous death from seasickness half a dozen times every day. His face is haggard now, his clothes hang slack on the skin and bones that remain of his recently plump figure. But he's here to take a stance behind Constable Harana and grasp the halyard in his two weak hands.

These non-nautical gentlemen of the afterguard are not expected to demean themselves with physical labor any more than ship's officers are.

Least of all the Admiral of the Ocean Sea.

There is something very Spanish about this. Gentlemen reserve their strength for such gentlemanly pursuits as bullfighting. If they earn their bread by the sweat of their brow, they cease being gentlemen.

After an instant's hesitation, I position myself behind Segovia.

I have no idea how the crew will react. For the first time it's driven home to me that I *am* a foreigner, as uncertain of their response as if I didn't speak the language.

'We'll hoist the main yard, Pilot,' I say calmly in the absolute silence.

Peralonso Niño nods. He plants his feet, grasping the thick hempen rope behind me. The gentlemen of the afterguard and we two officers bend to it.

All that happens is the halyard draws taut through the block at the masthead. The enormous double spar to which the new sail is attached doesn't budge from the deck.

'Heave!' shouts Peralonso, and we put our weight to it again.

Pedro Terreros comes up behind us to add his slight strength to our hopeless effort.

'Sing us a chantey instead,' I suggest, for it is Pedro's pure tenor voice that I sometimes hear mornings.

'Dirty as sin?' he asks. All sailors know more than a few like that, and Pedro is a master at improvisation.

'No, let's make it inspirational.'

At a nod from me, Peralonso shouts, 'Yo! Haul away!' and the young steward begins to sing.

The way this works, the chanteyman sings half a line alone while the crew bend their backs to the task at hand, then in chorus they echo the second half of the line while resuming their start position, then the chanteyman sings the next half line while they haul away again, and so on.

> O God (*sings Pedro*) help us
>   help us (*chant the gentlemen of the afterguard*)
> who are (*Pedro*) Thy servants.

> Thy servants. (*us*)
> We wish
>   well to serve,
> the faith
>   to preserve —

At this point, two or three members of the port watch join the line straining impotently at the halyard.

> the faith
>   of a Christian.
> Turn Thy wrath
>   on the pagan

A few more men are chanting, a few more step up to haul on the halyard, Luís Torres ready to take it onto the capstan as needed.

> mired in error,
>   and the saracen
> Arab and Moor
>   infidel dogs!
> The sons
>   of Abraham
> do not believe

Men silently file past Luís Torres. Two or three pat his hunched shoulder as they pick up the chant:

> — O! that they did! —
> do not believe
>   in the holy faith.
> In the holy
>   faith of Rome,
> of Rome,
>   is redemption.

'Is redemption!' chants the entire port watch, and all are hauling mightily at the halyard now. It begins to budge. The yard lifts a hand's breadth, then a foot off the deck.

> O Saint Peter,
>   man among men!

O Saint Paul,
His right hand!

From the cluster of men around the wine cask a grommet steps uncertainly forth. Soon three, then four members of the starboard watch join the line.

May you pray
to God for us,
pray for us
men of the sea!
In this world (*soars Pedro's pure tenor*)

And starboard watch is streaming to the halyard now.

so few are we.
O West wind,
no, I say East,

The main yard ascends with each chant.

O East
the sun rising.
In the West
a shining!

Up, up goes the double spar. The unfolding sail begins to catch the wind.

Westing we go (*Pedro improvises*)
with God's help!
Westing we go
with God's love ...

And finally Pedro Terreros's pure tenor voice holds 'westing we go' aloft a third time, and the main yard is aloft too, the sail filling and *Santa Maria* reaching for west, the groan of her timbers managing somehow to sound like a benediction.

Had we needed the full three days of grace I got from the Pinzón brothers, I actually believe the weeks at sea, the Ahabian challenge to the unknown (and possibly unknowable), the hubris of it all, might finally have gotten to me. For aren't even over-achievers – perhaps over-achievers most of all – spurred on by doubt? Isn't self-confidence just another pasteboard mask behind which lurk the terrible questions no one dares ask?

What if I'm wrong, what if all my life I've been wrong?

What if Barto was wrong, the great Pozzo Toscanelli wrong, the legendary Ptolemy himself wrong? What if Peralonso Niño's faith in me, and young Pedro Terreros's, is woefully unwarranted? What if, as some believe (and not all uneducated louts as I claim), the Ocean Sea really does go on forever? Or what if poor old Captain Perestrello's worst fears were no less than the awful truth – namely, that despite our brave talk (all mere conjecture) and the work of various valiant navigators beginning (possibly) with St Brendan, what if the earth really *is* flat, with an edge off which the ships of a foolhardy dreamer must fall – to what eternally gruesome fate I won't even try to imagine.

But fortunately there's time for none of this, and if a doubt or two cross my mind that final day they can be attributed to fatigue.

All day Thursday, 11 October, flocks of strange land birds soar overhead and signs of land are fished from the sea – a broken board, a cane like a shepherd's crook, a green branch to which a single pink flower still clings. The water even takes on a new smell, the salt-iodine-rotting-shellfish smell of shore which landsmen mistakenly believe is the smell of the sea.

At 5:30, give or take the twenty minutes our ship's time might be off, the sun goes down and the off-duty watch – Juan Cosa's starboard watch – line the forward bulwarks peering westward to catch a first glimpse of land. But only crimson sky and ocean can be seen. Peralonso Niño, as the light fades, is for heaving to until morning. Shoals, rocks – who knows what may lie ahead, unseen by moonlight?

But audaciously I tell him, 'We'll sail forward.'

'All night?'

'*Adelante*,' I say, and two lookouts are sent to the roundtop, two more forward.

Juan Cosa wants to cut our speed. 'We're carrying too much sail,' he says gloomily.

I answer with Peralonso's earlier inspiration, and the boat's sail is set on the poopdeck to give us still more.

I put my best hand at the helm, Cristóbal Quintero, that baby-faced teller of tall sexual tales.

'Dat spritsail drag da prow unner,' warns Chachu in his stage whisper, for the sea is running high.

The spritsail remains set.

Santa Maria reaches hard, the breeze freshens to near gale force. We're making nine knots, says Peralonso nervously.

Pinta and *Niña*, faster still, forge ahead.

Now it is two hours past midnight of what will be called in Spanish *El Día de la Raza* and in English 'Columbus Day', that is to say, 12 October. The moon, just past full, rides high off our port quarter, searchlighting the sea ahead. Deneb, among the brightest fixed stars, hangs on the western horizon. The moonlight turns *Pinta*'s and *Niña*'s straining sails into silver wings, and throws into sharp relief the great cross on *Santa Maria*'s mainsail. Our prow disappears in a cresting sea and bursts clear spewing silver spray, and at that moment there is a bright orange flash from *Pinta*, and the roar of cannon rolls back across the water.

Land!

Suddenly *Pinta* seems to stand still in the water. We rapidly come up on her, hove-to for the Admiral of the Ocean Sea.

Ahead in the moonlight lies a low line of silvery cliff.

'Well now, by God!' bellows Martín Alonzo Pinzón from *Pinta*, and a great surge of sound rises from every throat on *Santa Maria*. On *Niña* lombards roar.

Peralonso Niño shouts close to my ear: 'No more than six miles, I make it.'

I answer, or try to. At first no sound escapes my mouth. Then I tell him, 'Shorten sail, Pilot. We'll have the main course only. Tell the caravels.'

Now it is Peralonso who is all fiery eagerness, while I'm the cautious one.

'You mean we're not going in?'

It would be foolhardy to rush upon a lee shore at night, but Peralonso is beyond thinking now.

'We'll jog off and on until daylight,' I tell him.

'But Admiral! It's land! We've crossed the Ocean Sea! That's land there!'

I say nothing, just wait. Then he smiles, a boyish grin on his desperado's face, and shakes his head at his own foolishness. 'I'll brace the main yard.'

'Right you are, Pilot.'

I stare forward to where land awaits us silver in the moonlight.

❧ IX ❧

1492!
(Concluded)

WE pull steadily for the shore, ten men in each caravel's boat, a round dozen in *Santa Maria*'s. For once even the slovenly Pinzón brothers, who have trimmed their beards and slicked down their hair over their close-set eyes, look presentable. They have broken out new clothes that can almost pass for uniforms – clean white jerkins, black velvet doublets, black tights. Oarsmen, musketeers and crossbowmen wear clean, sun-bleached jerkins and hose. As we approach the shore I stand in the prow to unfurl the colors of Castile and León, the golden castle and the purple lion, and the red and yellow stripes of Aragon.

Behind us *Santa Maria*, *Niña* and *Pinta* ride at anchor in a bay sheltered by reefs of a porous pink coral the likes of which no European has ever seen. Ahead is a dazzling crescent of white sand beach, and beyond the beach a wall of green jungle. The surf here on the western side of the island (where we have sailed, seeking a safe passage through the reefs) is gentle.

As we sweep close to that dazzling beach, I experience an intense yet dreamlike feeling that I have stood in this boat's prow before, and yet, paradoxically, that this is the first day of Creation.

'Up oars!' shouts Peralonso Niño and in unison eighteen oars flash skyward. A wind ruffles the royal standard; I can feel it tug at the staff. A single large green and yellow bird darts close and raucously welcomes us with a voice eerily human. The three boats simultaneously scrape bottom. I raise one bare foot over the gunwale.

But wait – this is a historic moment.

Am I prepared for it? As I take that first step ashore, do I say something deathless and profoundly appropriate, casting my words like a challenge down the corridors of history to intrepid explorers as yet unborn? Do I perhaps say, as I plant the royal banner on the beach, 'One small step for a Christian, one giant step for Christendom,' thus beating Neil Armstrong by almost 500 years?

No, there are no half-billion T.V. viewers around the world to watch me, no periodical has purchased the serial rights to my adventures for a king's ransom, no publisher has advanced an even greater fortune for *Columbus's Journal* (so-called), no mission control exists to monitor my every move. Only the citizens of Palos, and a few score people at that Peripatetic Royal Court visiting God-knows-where in Spain right now, even suspect we have crossed the vastness of the Ocean Sea to this small and lovely tropical island, part of the Indian archipelago, I am convinced, with fabled gold-roofed Cipango just over the horizon.

So I do not utter wisdom for the ages.

What I do say, uneasily and with reason, as I nudge Peralonso Niño, is: 'There's someone in the woods over there.'

We all freeze, our eyes scanning the foliage (sun-dappled, secret, alien). Again there is a flash of movement, and suddenly there they are, no longer in the woods but coming out.

'Crossbowmen, front!' says Martín Alonzo, but I raise a hand and shake my head.

These natives of the Indian archipelago are but ten in number and not only unarmed, except for small harmless-looking spears with fish-tooth points, but naked. They are neither black-skinned (as might have been expected, according to Aristotle, since we are more or less on the same latitude as the west coast of Africa) nor white like Europeans. No, they are of an indeterminate shade between, a sort of bronzy color that, with imagination and in dim light, you could almost call red. Tan then, a sort of ruddy tan. Tall, well proportioned, their coarse (but not African-kinky) hair worn horse-tail long, their limbs straight and smooth-muscled. They peer at our tall-masted ships at anchor, our boats at the water's edge, ourselves taking our first steps across the dazzling (and hot underfoot) sand – their whole world, their whole conception of the nature of things altered at a stroke forever. And innocently and with a naive delight, they smile.

Inspired, I drop to my knees and thank God for sending us here safely, across that vastness of Ocean Sea, and on both sides of me the men are kneeling, and then I rise and draw my ceremonial sword, jewel-encrusted hilt catching the sunlight, and in fine theatrical style raise it skyward as I plant the royal standard and claim this island for the Kingdoms of Castile, León and Aragon, for Queen Isabel and King Fernando, for Spain, for Christianity. In thanksgiving I name it the Island of the Holy Saviour.

The Indians – for what else can I call natives of this Indies archipelago? – come closer to watch the arcane ceremony.

Some crewmen remain on their knees, praying. But Vicente Yáñez Pinzón, neither rising nor praying still, does an odd sort of a pivot on his knees to face me and in a humble voice speaks. I won't reproduce the precise, embarrassing words, but on behalf of the men of *Niña* he apologizes for not giving the Admiral of the Ocean Sea, not to mention the Viceroy of the Indies which I now am, his full trust.

One by one the landing party comes to me to ask forgiveness. Only Juan Cosa and Chachu stand silently by, watching.

'Command us, Viceroy!' passionately exclaims Constable Harana, even as he casts suspicious glances at the advancing Indians who, by this time, have ringed us close so that Martín Alonzo again turns to his crossbowmen and again I must signal him, no.

The boldest of the bronzy-skinned men approaches me and with a smile and a mouthing of gibberish (which anthropologists will later learn is the Arawak language) touches my left sleeve, gently rolling the soft velvet between his fingers. It is clear he has never seen a man clothed before.

I call Luís Torres the interpreter forward.

'Ask him the name of this place, and of himself,' I say.

Torres does so, with a show of confidence, in Latin.

The Indian responds incomprehensibly, if musically.

Torres, less confidently, tries Hebrew.

The Indian responds with equal incomprehensibility.

Torres, clearly worried, tries Ladino, Aramaic, Spanish.

Same lack of success.

We all wait for Arabic, that mother of languages.

Torres takes a deep breath and tries Arabic.

And the Indian, who I now realize is a boy of no more than fourteen, throws back his head and laughs.

We all assume this signifies comprehension. But his response is again incomprehensible, if musical.

Gentle, green-eyed, girlishly slim Luís Torres is now desperate. He has come with us, he must feel, under false pretenses.

He tries a sort of sign language, poking his chest and saying, 'Torres.'

The Indian, grinning, pokes his own chest. 'Torres.'

Luís Torres sighs and tries again. He spreads his arms broadly to include the beach, the jungle. He bends and scoops up a handful of sand, lets it trickle through his fingers, then spreads his arms again as his expressive face asks a silent question.

The Indian jumps with excitement. 'Guanahaní!' he cries. Then he pokes his own chest and makes the same sound: 'Guanahaní!' And, touching another of his kind, he says also, 'Guanahaní.'

Comprehension comes to Luís Torres. 'Their name for this island is Guanahaní and the people call themselves that too – Guanahaní. Get it?'

I get it. Torres and the Guanahaní spokesman continue to smile at each other in a kind of basic sub-linguistic communion.

'Ask him which way's Cipango,' says Martín Alonzo, 'ask him where's the gold.'

But, 'One thing at a time,' I tell him with a viceregal smile, and send two oarsmen back to *Santa Maria*'s boat for the sea chest full of trinkets, the sort that have proven so popular with the Fan people of West Africa. The chest is set on the sand and with a flourish Pedro Terreros opens it.

'Don't,' cautions Rodrigo de Segovia, 'give all your trinkets to the very first natives you encounter. Trinkets don't grow on trees.'

The royal comptroller fails to curb Pedro's munificence. Out of the sea chest, like a magician, he plucks red wool caps, brass rings, strings of bright glass beads and little round falconry bells.

Collective oohs and ahs come from the Guanahaní as Pedro distributes the trinkets. The bells are the clear favorite. Soon their tinkling fills the air, along with Indian laughter, very like our own.

I send to the boat again, this time for empty oak water casks. Luís Torres goes through a frenzy of sign language to indicate thirst and drinking. The Guanahaní spokesman claps his hands, grins, jumps up and down and jabbers to his cohorts, who lift the casks to their shoulders.

So laden, the Indians (or archipelagans, if you prefer) march off. Constable Harana gives them a suspicious look and I know that

Martín Alonzo will call for his crossbowmen again.

'We'll go with them,' I say to forestall him, and detail a guard to stay with the boats.

With us lumbering behind, the ten archipelagans slip silently with our casks through the deep shadows of the jungle (bird calls, strange small unidentifiable crunching sounds, cheeps and chirps and pips and squeaks, sudden slithery rushes, frail querulous cries, clicks and howls and mini-grunts, all slightly unnerving) to a spring, where we are not permitted to lift a finger. The Indians draw water, letting us sample its sweetness from a calabash; then we Spaniards sit against the broad reddish-brown trunks of unfamiliar trees, relaxing as the complexity of jungle noises assumes its proper place as natural background music, and watch the Indians, in high good spirits, *do our work for us*.

Thus the first step that will lead to their enslavement is taken.

'Snap your fingers and they'd be slaveys,' marvels Vicente Yáñez.

'Give 'em a handful of glass beads or hawk bells and you'd never have to lift a finger,' agrees his brother.

'Baptize them first, of course,' says Luís Torres.

'Not unless they lead us to the gold,' threatens Martín Alonzo.

Sounds pretty exploitive, doesn't it?

In defense, let me say this. The idea of a superior primitive humanity, uncorrupted by civilization, uncorrupted by *us*, has been around a long time. But how accurate is this myth of the Noble Savage? What's it based on? The earliest version I know of was by the Italian Pietro Martire (Peter Martyr), who claims to have learned about noble savagery from Vespucci, Magellan and me. Let that crass eponymous opportunist Vespucci speak for himself. But poor Magellan will die (at the hands of Noble Savages) before he can refute Peter Martyr. As for me, whatever he claims, I never met the man. Next comes the Englishman John Dryden, who coined the term Noble Savage in 1670 in his book *The Conquest of Granada*. But who's the Noble Savage there? The Arabs? We Christians? It's unclear to me. Then finally comes the Frenchman Jean-Jacques Rousseau, who really put the Noble Savage on the map in 1755 with his well-known *Discourse on Inequality*. But Rousseau spent his life in Italy, France and Switzerland. Where did he ever see a savage, noble or any other kind?

Let's be objective about this. Is there anything intrinsically noble about savagery? No, no more than there's anything intrinsically savage about nobility. It's just one of those pop-culture ideas that grow like weeds further down the road of history in the fertile soil of a latter-day decadence.

For myself, living in a far simpler time, I can only take the Indians as they seem. Which is: primitive, superstitious, heathen, curious, friendly and eager to please. A nice balance of traits, but they just don't add up to noble savagery. We ruined no earthly Paradise. How could we have? We never found one.

I intend no ethnic slur by these remarks.

Nor was I personally responsible, as Las Casas and some others insist, for starting the whole deplorable relationship between lordly white Christian and oppressed bronzy-skinned archipelagan. I did *not* take half a dozen Indians captive aboard *Santa Maria*. The Guanahaní spokesman and his five companions who came aboard to serve as guides and interpreters during our almost nine weeks of island-hopping were willing volunteers. And all would be rewarded with a trip to Spain, baptism, and exposure to the incalculable benefits of fifteenth-century Spanish culture. Does this sound like exploitation?

'Where's the gold? Ask him, will you? Where's the gold?' Martín Alonzo demands impatiently of Luís Torres as we return to the boats, the archipelagans sagging under the weight of our full water casks.

Second time around, my viceregal smile's a bit forced. 'All in good time,' I tell Pinzón, not wild about the look on his face – an apparent compression of the small features, a meanness especially around the eyes. Gold fever if ever I saw it.

The Guanahaní spokesman jabbers at his followers, who load the casks aboard the three boats. Then the spokesman, whose name shortly will be Yego Clone, gazes across the bay to where *Santa Maria* and the two caravels lie at anchor, and turns to Luís Torres with . . .

But hold on a minute here. Yego Clone? you ask. And how does he get this name, at once unplaceable (neither Guanahaní nor Spanish) and suspiciously familiar?

He calls himself Guanahaní. He calls his companions Guanahaní. He calls the Island of the Holy Saviour Guanahaní. He calls a species of large reptile (delicious when roasted, Peralonso Niño will tell us after shore leave) Guanahaní. Luís Torres believes that the archipelagans guard their names as alchemists do their secrets, fearing that to know a man's name is to gain control over him.

I've encountered this superstition before, in Africa.

Anyway, just as Yego Clone and Torres commence a kind of dumb show in lieu of speech, Martín Alonzo grasps the Indian youth's elbow, swings him around, and snarls at him, 'Where's the gold, you damned heathen?'

Gold fever, all right. He has it bad.

The other Guanahaní stand stock still, not making a sound. Even their hawk bells are silent.

'Let go of him,' I order Pinzón, but swiftly learn that mere words avail nothing against fulminating gold fever.

So I grab his arm, as he has grabbed the Guanahaní's.

For an instant nobody moves.

Then Pinzón releases the archipelagan and confronts me with a wordless gold-fever snarl and a drawn sheath knife. I see Constable Harana moving fast from my left side but I'm watching the Guanahaní (not to mention Pinzón and his knife) so I'm not certain of the sequence of events. But the next thing I know, Martín Alonzo is stretched out on the sand and Harana is standing over him with one foot on the knife.

Slowly Martín Alonzo drags himself upright. On his face is a bewildered look. Also a bloody nose.

The soon-to-be Yego Clone looks at him, at Harana, at Torres, at me.

There goes our chance for friendly, helpful Indians, I'm thinking. Martín Alonzo blew it.

With a long indrawn breath he sucks in his barrel belly, the most aggressive part of him, and in the smallest voice in his possession tells the assembled shore party, 'I don't know what came over me.'

There's an immediate chorus of: 'Gold fever!'

Even Martín Alonzo's brother looks at him pityingly. How can I do anything but forgive him?

I turn to the teenaged Guanahaní spokesman, wondering how to undo the damage.

The boy drops to one knee before me, stretches out a hand, bows his head. At once all the Guanahaní do likewise, their hawk bells tinkling.

Christ, I think, I don't want to play God to these people. Far from it – I want to bring them the One True God.

I tell Luís Torres, 'I don't want to play God to these people. Explain to them I'm only the Admiral of the Ocean Sea and viceroy and governor of all the islands and mainlands in it.'

When the Guanahaní all rise, there's a complicated dumb show between Torres and the spokesman, ending with the latter cradling and rocking his arms while he shakes his head sadly. 'I think he's telling us he's an orphan,' Luís says. Then the boy looks at me hopefully, cradling and rocking his arms again, this time in a decidedly positive way. All the while his hawk bells, fastened around his wrist, tinkle.

'I think,' says Luís, 'he wants to be your son.'

Adoption, realistic or not, is vastly preferable to adoration.

'Tell him,' I say cautiously, 'I have no objection to being a father-*figure* to him.'

Obviously my sentiments are too complex for dumb show to convey their entire meaning. Luís Torres signals a few things and the young archipelagan grins, claps his hands and jumps up and down, the characteristic indications that he's excited.

'What's your son's name?' Torres asks me with a wink.

'Well,' I consider the problem out loud, 'my older boy is Diego and – '

'Diego Colón,' Torres says, impatient to get on with it.

The young Guanahaní, after a frenzy of grinning, hand-clapping and leaping, taps his own chest and says: 'Yego Clone?'

'Diego Colón,' agrees Torres.

'Yego Clone!' says my new, and I think temporary, son.

An hour later he and five of his companions are aboard *Santa Maria*, volunteers all, after Luís Torres assures them of a virtually limitless supply of '*tin-que tin-que*', as they call the hawk bells.

There are the usual misunderstandings. Yego Clone immediately approaches the furled mainsail, examines it, then spreads his arms wide and makes a flapping motion (hawk bells tinkling madly) to indicate flying. With a questioning look on his young, eager face, he then points skyward. Have we come from there? I point east. Stubbornly Yego points skyward. Meanwhile, the five other archipelagan volunteers are busily flapping their arms (with a tintinnabulation of *tin-que tin-que*). Like it or not, we're from Heaven.

Heaven unfortunately produces some dangerous artifacts, notably the sword. For after Constable Harana, innocently if a bit enthusiastically, demonstrates the suppleness of good Toledo steel, one of the archipelagans grasps the sword – blade first. The Indian howls, blood wells from his hand, and Dr Sánchez has his first archipelagan patient.

His first Christian patient in the Bahamas (for this is the name history will bestow on the archipelago of which Holy Saviour is a part) is Cristóbal Quintero, that thirty-year-old baby-faced teller of tall sexual tales. His case is far more complex, not to mention fateful.

Quintero returns from forty-eight hours of shore leave and, though he's obviously exhausted, can't wait to talk. Soon his coterie of young grommets has gathered at the mainmast.

'Has anybody,' Quintero asks, 'ever done it in a hammock?'

'Done what?' one of the younger boys asks, but he's immediately shouted down. With Cristóbal Quintero, there's only one answer, ever.

'What on earth's a hammock?' someone asks.

'Well,' says Quintero, 'if you contrive to effect a cross between your ordinary bed and your ordinary fishnet, then string the result between two posts or trees or what-have-you, you begin to grasp the idea of a hammock.'

'What's it for?'

'Didn't I tell you? Also sleeping,' says Quintero.

They wait for him to continue. He doesn't disappoint them. 'It swings,' he says.

'Swings?'

'Swings. At the slightest motion of its occupant or occupants. And, like your ordinary inferior bed, it sags where the weight's most concentrated, only more so. This makes the sides rise and imprison you, if you follow, the way a pair of large copulating fish might be imprisoned in a fishnet. Doing it in a hammock,' says Quintero, 'takes considerable skill.'

'Do fishes copulate?' one young grommet asks.

This budding ichthyologist is also shouted down.

'I,' says Quintero with a grin, 'was trapped in a hammock for two nights and a day.'

'Trapped?'

'Well, it's possible I could have made my escape, but I wasn't particularly tempted. They all wanted to try it.'

'*Who* all wanted to try it?' asks an eager young voice.

'The nubile maidens of Guanahaní.'

'They wanted to try the hammock?'

'No,' says Quintero patiently. 'What the nubile maidens of Guanahaní all wanted to try, of course, was *me*.'

'And did they?'

'*Did* they!' says baby-faced Quintero, his eyes rolling as he goes into rapturous (if fanciful) detail.

Some three weeks later, when the fleet is sailing south through the dangerous shoals of what will eventually be called Columbus Bank, he goes into clinical (if embarrassed) detail. This part of the story I get from Dr Sánchez.

'I'm afraid we have a strange disease aboard,' he tells me, his customary bedside manner conspicuous by its absence. 'It's like nothing I ever encountered before.'

'Who's the patient?'

'Grommet Quintero.'

I admit it, my first thoughts are for the ship. Quintero is our best helmsman. 'How sick is he?'

'Well, there's no fever. But I don't like the look of it.' He describes the hard red swelling, called a papule, on poor Quintero's penis. 'Plus, there are further swellings which are resilient, discrete and non-tender on palpation. These are located in the unfortunate chap's groins.'

'Prognosis?'

But Dr Sánchez only shrugs.

A few days later, as we approach the huge island of Cuba (where we hope to meet the Great Khan of Cathay), Dr Sánchez tells me, again clinically rather than bedsidely, 'Grommet Quintero's papule has now eroded into a painless ulcer with an indurated base.'

'Then if it's painless, what's the problem?'

'When abraded it exudes a clear fluid. The patient has also begun to complain of a wide range of possibly psychosomatic symptoms including malaise, headache, nausea and stiff neck. But that fluid discharge disturbs me. We could well have a contagious disease on our hands.'

Later still, a few days before the calamitous events of Christmas Eve: 'That grommet Quintero? Remember when we left Cuba I told you he'd also developed a rash of pale pinkish round spots on the palms of his hands, the soles of his feet, and the flexor surfaces of arms and legs? With papules, macules, pustules and squamous lesions?'

I say I remember all too well.

'Thank God, these epidermal manifestations are disappearing and Quintero says he feels better. I have reason to hope the disease has finally run its course.'

What a futile hope, as anyone who knows the dreadful nature of syphilis will immediately realize!

'For all I know,' speculates Dr Sánchez, 'it could have been no more than an allergic reaction to some unfamiliar food − cassava bread, yams, maize, pumpkin. Still and all, Grommet Quintero is our most intrepid, uh, sexual adventurer, and has apparently had congress with the greatest number of archipelagan women, so I can't help suspecting the disease *is* contagious, and sexually transmitted. Well, no matter. He's better every day, so not to worry.'

Not to worry ...

Were we guilty of bringing syphilis back to Europe? The thought haunts me still.

If we were, Cristóbal Quintero, alas, was exactly the fellow to give it the widest possible dissemination.

I wish I could agree with those who attribute a European, probably French, origin to syphilis. It is documented that a prostitute in Dijon, brought to court in July 1463 by a spurned suitor, testified in her defense that she rejected him for his own good because she was suffering from *le gros mal*, which sounds pretty awful but is not otherwise described. Some thirty years later the authorities in Paris chased from that city anyone suffering from *la grosse vérole*, again not otherwise described. Around the same time a French army invaded Naples, retreated, and either left behind or carried away a poxy disease called *il morbo gallico* or *le mal de Naples*, depending on who did the calling. From 1500, 'French disease' (Latin: *malum francicum*) is the term in common use all over Europe, except in France, for syphilis.

But the French wouldn't invade Naples and *il morbo gallico* ravage the city until 1495 — more than enough time for baby-faced Quintero to have spread the poison through the seaports of southern Europe. One Ruy Díaz, a physician of Barcelona, mentions in his memoirs (1534) a patient *in the entourage of the famous explorer Admiral Colón* whom he treated in 1493 for what he, Dr Díaz, calls a relapse of hideous skin eruptions consisting of squamous lesions. I wish I could say that Cristóbal Quintero did not join my triumphal march across Spain to the Peripatetic Royal Court then visiting Barcelona, but in fact he did. And, in characteristic Quintero fashion, he was a favorite with the groupies who besieged us on our long overland journey from Palos.

Le gros mal, la grosse vérole, il morbo gallico (*malum francicum*), *le mal de Naples* — such a welter of linguistic confusion will always becloud the origin of syphilis. Similar linguistic confusion sends Luís Torres on a fool's errand to the mountainous interior of Cuba to deliver on my behalf to the Great Khan of Cathay the ambassadorial credentials entrusted to me by Their Most Catholic Majesties in Granada.

For eleven days the fleet lies at anchor riding out a storm in the mouth of a broad river on Cuba's northern coast. Soon from the largest village we have so far encountered, boats called canoes (similar to West African dugouts but more seaworthy and propelled by small oars resembling bakers' peels) swarm out to our ships. Yego Clone assures these Indian canoeists of our peaceful intentions, and before long we're trading red wool caps, glass beads and hawk bells for food and hammocks.

Luís Torres asks our standard question in his standard Latin, Hebrew, Ladino, Aramaic, Spanish, and Arabic. How far and in what direction lie (1) the island of Cipango where the roofs are tiled (and the streets paved, we've now convinced ourselves) with gold, and (2) the City of Heaven, called Quinsay, where the Great Khan (*El Gran Can* in Spanish) of Cathay holds court?

At mention of the alliterative if elusive *Gran Can*, the Indians grow enormously excited, stamping on the deck and tinkling their newly acquired hawk bells.

'Cubanacan!' they shout. 'Cubanacan! Cubanacan!'

'What's that they're shouting?' I ask Luís Torres.

'Cubanacan,' he informs me.

Try it yourself, especially with an optimistic ear.

Cubanacan.

El Gran Can.

El Gran Can. Cubanacan.

'A natural Indian corruption of the Chinese emperor's title,' I say emphatically, and send a delegation led by the resplendently attired Luís Torres, with twenty native guides and bearers, to the interior, to deliver my credentials (on fine vellum, gorgeously illuminated) to the Great Khan. Also a solid gold *excelente* minted in 1485, its head a stylized likeness of Fernando and Isabel in crowned profile.

The embassy's return is awaited tensely. Until now gold has always been just over the horizon on the next island – but Cuba is not exactly a speck lost in the enormity of ocean. England-sized is our estimate. Could it really be Cathay? After two days, doubts assail me. Marco Polo never wrote anywhere that Cathay was an island. After four days, optimism prevails. Perhaps, I tell myself, he crossed an un-noteworthy causeway.

'What's keeping Torres?' demands Martín Alonzo. 'What do we know about the fellow anyway? An eleventh-hour convert, after all. He's liable to sneak off with all the gold.'

'And paddle a canoe back to Spain?' says Constable Harana dryly.

After six days the Torres embassy returns, without gold but madly fumigating themselves.

Dr Sánchez exchanges a nervous glance with me. He clearly fears they have encountered some pestilential disease, worse perhaps than poor Quintero's pox, in the interior highlands. But the fumigating smoke has a decidedly pleasant aroma, and neither Torres nor any of his guides are visibly suffering in any way.

On closer inspection we see that two of the bearers carry fire-brands, while others are holding small greenish-brown cylinders that appear to be tightly wrapped leaves. When one end of such a cylinder is inserted into a nostril with a simultaneous intake of breath, the other end of the cylinder glows and smoke pours from the bearer's mouth.

Luís Torres himself exhales a plume of smoke at me, making my eyes sting.

"Tobacco,' says Luís, then adds a bit condescendingly, 'It's an acquired taste.'

'What about Quinsay?' I ask. 'Cathay? The Great Khan?'

But he shakes his head. 'Just another one of your usual Indian villages with palm-thatched huts and promiscuous maidens.' He stands there fumigating both of us, terribly blasé.

'What about the gold?' asks Martín Alonzo with a pathetic catch in his voice.

'Sorry. Just the usual tiny nose-plugs or ear-rings, that's all. But here's a fellow – ' Luís gestures with his smouldering tobacco at one of his native companions ' – sent by the cacique, or chief, to tell the Admiral about the big island east of here where gold is plentiful.'

Luís Torres calmly nose-puffs his tobacco.

'Where?' begs Martín Alonzo in a hoarse growl. 'Where's the gold?'

When Yego Clone questions the man from the interior, his bronzy face goes pale.

'What's the trouble?' I ask.

'Where's the gold?' pleads Martín Alonzo faintly.

Yego, definitely not happy with what he's heard, performs an agitated dumb show.

'Apparently Arawaks once occupied that big island,' Luís tells me. 'But something's wrong, I'm not sure what.'

The native from the interior seems to be making the sign for eating, and he looks scared. Yego nods, very subdued now.

'It's something about their cuisine,' Luís says.

'Oh?' Peralonso Niño's ears perk up.

More dumb show.

'This fellow believes the Arawaks no longer occupy the mother island in appreciable numbers. They were chased off by a warlike tribe known as Caribs whose cuisine is ... well, I'm not sure what he's trying to tell me.'

By now we're surrounded by a group of anxious Arawaks, all jabbering and dumb-showing at Luís Torres.

'Poisonous?' he wonders out loud, and makes eating and staggering motions.

Yego, exasperated, shouts, 'Carib!' at the top of his voice, reaches out, grabs Luís's arm, and bites it hard enough to leave tooth marks.

'Carib,' the Cuban Arawaks nod unhappily.

Torres rubs his arm. 'I believe', he says, 'that the preferred diet of these Carib Indians consists of other people. Especially Arawaks.'

Everyone is appropriately appalled – except gold-crazed Martín Alonzo. 'Exactly where is this island?' he wants to know.

At dawn I'm awakened by a muffled shout. Rushing from my cabin (clouting my head as usual on the low door lintel) I see Chachu the Basque boatswain planted on his short legs on the forecastle.

'Der go dat loco Pinzón,' he chortles.

Backlit splendidly (if rebelliously) by the rising sun is *Pinta*, already half a mile outside the mouth of the river and sailing close to the wind, heading east.

I order a lombard run out and fired.

Pinta continues east.

'What it dat loco Pinzón, he find gold 'fore you?' laughs unblinking Chachu.

Vicente Yáñez comes aboard, his face grave. He is followed by a soaking wet Francisco Niño, who has just been picked out of the sea by *Niña*'s boat. 'I don't know what to say,' says Vicente Yáñez. 'My brother just hasn't been himself.'

I pat his shoulder in sympathy; his own loyalty is touching. That our Billy Budd prototype has deserted the deserting ship is less surprising.

'I wonder what Martín Alonzo knows that we don't,' muses Constable Harana.

I shake my head. 'It's just gold fever.'

We spend several more days on the north coast of Cuba, collecting and pressing plant specimens, catching and salting down fish specimens.

Every time I come near Pedro Terreros's pet parrot (one of those large green and yellow birds, which he bought for a handful of lace points our first day in Cuban waters) it squawks, 'gold fever, gold fever, gold fever!'

Who can really blame Martín Alonzo? He knows as well as I that whatever else we find, gold is crucial to the Great Venture. Gold – gold in quantity – will alone persuade the royals to send out a second, larger expedition.

With me in command, naturally. I'm Admiral of the Ocean Sea, not to mention viceroy and governor for life.

Sometimes I dream of myself living the viceregal life in a vast, princely palace in a vast, princely realm. It could happen. In Cathay and Cipango, there's gold aplenty. Marco Polo said so, and he was there.

But where, exactly, are *we*?

How can I be viceroy and governor of anywhere if I can't even locate it on a map?

Earlier in these pages I wrote that I wouldn't refer to the Indies as a New World (actually, an Other World) until my Third Voyage. That's true enough. But believe me, my thoughts were leading me, however reluctantly, in that direction as early as the second week of December 1492.

I never wanted a New World. Why should I? I wanted Cipango with its golden roofs and Cathay with its Great Khan. But deep down I was beginning to suspect, anchored in the mouth of a Cuban river, our weeks of Bahamian exploration behind us, that some hitherto unknown islands, and possibly even a mainland or two, bestraddle the Ocean Sea between Europe and the fabled East, and that we have blundered on them. Surely these Arawak Indians, living a Stone Age existence, have had no contact with civilized Cipango or sophisticated Cathay. Surely Marco Polo could not have seen archipelagan canoes (even the sleek seventy-passenger models almost as long as *Niña*) and described them as Chinese junks top-heavy with sail. Surely even I know the earth's circumference to be larger than the figure I conveniently arrived at to make the Great Venture seem feasible.

What if this truly *is* a New World?

But as you may have noticed, I'm a stubborn person. The purpose of the Great Venture was to sail west to Cipango and Cathay, and by God that's what we've done. One or the other's just over the horizon, like Martín Alonzo's gold.

One week after his desertion we steer for the large island to the east, the original Arawak homeland, and I urge the Caribbean (as it later will be called) to be the China Sea, and beg the island rising mountainously into view to be golden Cipango.

Yego Clone and his companions remain below decks, scared stiff.

It is a few days later at dusk. From canoes surrounding *Niña* and the flagship, excited Indians swarm aboard whooping and hollering. More swim out to our anchorage to emerge with their gaily painted skins (red stripes and whorls and such, definitely holiday attire) hopelessly smeared and their green and yellow head-feathers limp. With huge proprietary smiles, all fear forgotten, Yego Clone and his companions show their Haitian Arawak cousins around *Santa Maria*. Not one comes aboard without bearing a gift. We receive and are soon stockpiling yams and pumpkins, ears (as they are picturesquely called) of maize, unglazed pottery in three inconvenient sizes, parrots, hammocks, skeins of cotton, crude fishing tackle, fresh-caught fish, large greenish-brown tobacco leaves and

NUGGETS OF GOLD!

to dazzle the eye and gladden the heart, oh yes, smiles are everywhere, eyes go teary, voices quaver, heads bob emphatically, oh yes, Yego Clone grins at our pleasure, Luís Torres's dumb-show questions reveal that there lies to the south a vast mainland (I'm dubious about its size: one man's mainland can be another man's island) called Caniba, where gold is mined but *oh no!* where Arawaks dare not venture because Caniba is home to the human-flesh-eating Caribs.

Vast mainland called *what*?

Caniba. *Ca*niba. As in Gran Can.

And if these primitive islanders live on the fringe of the Great Khan's empire, couldn't their fear of his soldiers' superior weaponry give rise to fanciful stories of people-eaters?

I'm sitting in my cabin in the sterncastle with Luís Torres and the great (self-styled, but there is a nobility about him) Guacanagarí, cacique of all northwestern Haiti. On deck his people can be heard shouting, laughing and jingling hawk bells. This Guacanagarí is an impressively large fellow, muscular, in the prime of his young manhood, who can manage to look dignified wearing nothing but a broad gold armlet, some daubs of ochre paint, and a feather in his hair. With diplomatically concealed distaste Guacanagarí samples the ripe salt pork Pedro Terreros sets before him. He watches Luís tap a biscuit on the edge of my small table to dispossess its family of maggots and, with a deft, hardly noticeable finger-flick, distances his own biscuit from his own self. Tomorrow, he insists, we must spend the night ashore as his guests.

Guacanagarí is the best dumb-shower we have run across, so expressive not only with hands but with body language that he almost seems to be speaking Spanish. And he's smart too. Not cultured in an Italian Renaissance or even a Spanish way, of course, but still. When I show him a map I've sketched of the northern coast of Cuba he studies it a while perplexed. Then you can see the light come on in his dark eyes as he traces the coastline and says, 'Cuba!' Quickly on the tabletop I sketch with charcoal a rough approximation of the coastline of Haiti as far as we've come. His long fingers pounce on this, unerringly homing in on the large and beautiful bay (wide sand beach, palm-thatched boathouses, brilliant green guinea grass, tall royal palms) where we have anchored. I don't tell him his Haiti has been renamed Hispaniola (Spanish Island in Latin), nor that I've taken possession for Their Most Catholic Majesties directly on arriving here at Mosquito Bay which, unfortunately, I've named all too well, for our conversation is regularly punctuated by the whine of those annoying insects and the slap of usually tardy hands.

Guacanagarí motions for the charcoal and sketches in the Haitian (or Hispaniolan) coast further east, pauses, then draws four small stylized suns. This puzzles me at first. Then I understand each sun represents a day's journey by canoe.

At the edge of the map and below the coastline (that is, four days east by water and a considerable trek inland to the south) Guacanagarí sketches another symbol, a bow and arrow. Since the only Arawak weapons we've seen are small fish-tooth-tipped spears, the bow and arrow symbol almost certainly represents a Carib stronghold. This immediately suggests two things. Yego's fears were not baseless. And my theory that the Caribs are a mythic representation of the Great Khan's soldiers (or slavers?) sounds more plausible all the time.

Guacanagarí begins a dumb show. He touches his golden armlet, then uses the charcoal to darken the line of coast from Mosquito Bay about a quarter of the way to the Carib stronghold. This brings him to another bay. Again he touches his golden armlet, then draws a line inland. In case we're dumber than we look, he touches his armlet and the map several more times, and draws a tiny circle representing the armlet. This has to signify gold, possibly a mine like St George in West Africa. Then, no part of the dumb show, he slaps his ear, studies the squashed mosquito on his hand (a tiny crimson stain, royal cacique blood). 'Cibao,' he says, touching the tiny circle on the map with the tip of a long cacique finger.

'What?' Luís Torres's eyebrows go up like a sail with all hands at the halyard.

Equally excited, I tell myself: all right, sure, Cubanacan and El Gran Can turned out to be unconnected, a linguistic coincidence. Maybe Caniba and Gran Can are another. But surely Cibao and Cipango have to be the same place.

When the rising sun touches the furled sails with gold, I escort the cacique from the sterncastle. Chachu the boatswain's whistle and Yego's voice clear a path for us through the crowds of naked Indians still aboard. At the ladder stands Juan Cosa, watching us approach. The golden dawn highlights the deeply etched vertical lines of defeats suffered and calamities impending that draw his long face down in an expression of gloom and bitterness.

Guacanagarí tenses at my side. 'Watch that one,' his hand and body language tell me. 'He means you no good.'

Standing tall at the gunwale he raises one arm and swings it in a wide arc from horizon to horizon, then he pats my shoulder: until tonight, my friend.

At a signal from Peralonso Niño, he's piped over the side and down the ladder to his royal canoe. At a second signal, as the long canoe draws away swiftly toward the beach, *Santa Maria*'s lombards roar and flames leap from her gunports. This startles but doesn't terrify our guests, indicating at once their awe of us and their confidence in our good intentions.

Since we come from the sky, why shouldn't we bring the thunder?

That night their confidence in our good intentions is put to a severe test.

Blame it on the climate, and the sensible Arawak accommodation to it. At the cacique's feast in our honor on the scimitar of white sand beach, not just the men but the comely young women of Guacanagarí's entourage wear nothing but gay patterns of red paint. As they walk among us, dine with us, smile at us, use sign language to communicate with us (a shapely breast lifting with an upraised arm or bobbing with head-thrown-back laughter), nature takes its inevitable course. Couple after couple disappear into the sylvan glades behind the scimitar of beach.

No problem here, not at first. There's no hint of force, nor any dangled reward of a hawk bell or a handful of lace points to mar the spontaneity of these liaisons. All is in the spirit of fiesta.

Now, it's true that the Arawak attitude toward sex is casual, but it would be harsh to call it promiscuous. Witness Chachu the boatswain. He is heard more than once that night to say with mingled hope and contempt, 'Jeez, dey fuck like rabbits,' but no Arawak maiden elects to tryst with the squat, unblinking, disappointed Basque in any jungle glade. They're more discriminating than that.

If sexual freedom – let's call it that to imply no moral judgement – is part of the Arawak lifestyle, then what was the problem that night?

Married women, to distinguish them from their unmarried sisters, wear tiny squares of cloth fore and aft on a slender string at the loins. These mini-aprons more or less cover their pudenda except when ruffled by breezes – which blow almost constantly on the northern coast of Haiti. The purpose is symbolic, not prudish. Sexual freedom ends in the marriage bed for Arawak women (not for Arawak men, definitely a double standard) and the mini-aprons signify monogamy.

I don't remember Guacanagarí or any of his associates explaining this to us at the time, a regrettable oversight when by chance seventeen-year-old Francisco Niño with his saintly Billy Budd face and pure sad smile and Greek god body is thrown together with a restless young Arawak beauty who happens to be wed to the ugliest sub-cacique in Guacanagarí's entourage.

The first I know of any trouble is when two stern-faced middle-aged Indians drag a lovely but weeping and mini-apron-disarrayed young woman before Guacanagarí, casting her on the sand between him and the great bonfire. There she huddles pitifully, as if aware of her nakedness for the first time. Soon four more Indians appear, armed with fish-tooth-tipped spears and looking grim. Walking among them, his head high, his Greek god body nude, is Francisco Niño. He is marched between cacique and bonfire and left standing there. The weeping woman looks up at him; he shyly smiles his pure sad smile down at her.

'What's going on here?' asks Francisco's brother Peralonso, reluctantly laying aside a half-eaten duck.

One of Francisco's escort is a triple-chinned fellow with a suety gut. This turns out to be the weeping woman's husband and also, as his golden armlet signifies, a man of rank. He jabbers at our host, managing to sound simultaneously respectful and furious, a nice trick.

Guacanagarí sign-languages the situation to me.

I sign back, 'What can we do?'

Here the dumb show becomes complicated and Luís Torres helps translate. 'To save face, the husband must publicly beat his woman.'

'And young Francisco?'

Luís assures me no punishment is planned – your double standard again, but a lucky break for our Billy Budd prototype.

Peralonso resumes his attack on the half-eaten duck.

By now all the Indians have formed a circle on the beach to watch the fat sub-cacique regain his face. I feel sorry for the woman but cheered by the concept of face-saving, suggestive as it is of Marco Polo's experiences in the fabled East.

There's a dead silence (except for the raucous squawk of an unseen jungle bird) as the young woman, no longer weeping, assumes before her husband the kneeling position apparently prescribed by law. Her eyes are shut, a half-smile quirks the corners of her mouth (recent secret jungle-glade memory?) and she seems oblivious to the fat man now poised over her with a supple wooden switch. Grunting, he rises on his toes and with all the strength of his fat arm brings the switch down. Her eyes remain shut, the half-smile doesn't leave her lips, the only indication of the blow is the long red welt on her back. The fat man grunts, rises, raises the switch again.

A battering ram in the form of Francisco Niño crashes into him, smashing him flat (or as flat as you can smash an obese sub-cacique) on the beach.

Another dead silence, no raucous bird. Bronzy-hued hands reach for fish-tooth-tipped spears, paler European hands for sheath knives.

Guacanagarí stands regally tall, raises a regal arm, speaks in a regal voice. Bronzy-hued hands freeze.

Considerable dumb show commences between the cacique and Luís Torres.

'It's bad,' Luís tells me.

'How bad?'

'Under Haitian law the injured party has the right to choose a fitting punishment for his assailant.'

On hearing this, our Billy Budd prototype speaks with his slight, charming stammer. 'I d-did what I had to, Admiral. I'd d-do it again. If I've earned a f-f-few strokes of the lash or whatever, I'm ready to f-face Indian justice for the g-good of the expedition.'

Meanwhile the sub-cacique has laboriously regained his feet. Wiping blood from his mouth and spitting out a couple of teeth, he circles Francisco Niño to study him from every angle. Then he speaks at some length, his moon face (supported by three chins) modulating from concentration to anticipation. The woman screams. Guacanagarí looks regally unhappy.

Much dumb show, faces tormented, between him and Luís.

Peralonso Niño stops crunching on the remains of a bright red lobster.

Luís says, 'He's going to put out his eyes, cut out his tongue, slice off his manhood, and then kill him.'

Peralonso sighs, tosses away the lobster and rises to one knee, ready to spring to Francisco's defense.

'Take some men and get your brother back aboard ship,' I tell him.

This is accomplished smartly, ten seamen at a word from Peralonso whirling into position, knives unsheathed, in one seemingly choreographed movement. Surrounded by this graceful escort, Francisco is hustled to the surf and *Niña*'s waiting boat while the fat cuckold raves, rants, and jiggles up and down in a frenzy of frustration.

The rest of us withdraw in a body to the water's edge. Behind us oars rise and dip as *Niña*'s boat races across the bay. Before us, lined up several hundred strong with their fish-tooth-tipped spears at the ready, stand Guacanagarí's warriors.

In seconds the situation will be out of hand, a regular race riot, the first ever in the Indies and, for all I know, anywhere.

But Guacanagarí calmly walks through the ranks of his warriors, spears lowering as he passes, and approaches us alone, his stride measured, his face somber but strong, a most regal figure. It occurs to me that this naked Indian is at least as kingly as Fernando of Spain and far more so than that Portuguese nervous wreck of a Most Serene Majesty.

'What my brother wanted was wrong,' signs the great cacique.

'Your brother?' I sign back. This takes far longer than just saying the two words.

Unfortunately the fat cuckold is indeed his brother.

'Still, it is our law. You should have permitted it. What is one life,' signs Guacanagarí, 'compared with what you have sacrificed to save that life?'

My own hand and body language are incapable of replying to the moral question posed.

'When trouble next flares between our peoples,' predicts the great cacique in a stunning *tour-de-force* of sign language, 'and after tonight it inevitably will, for I know my brother, you and I may not be here to stop it.'

What a prophetic dumb show, and what tragedy it anticipates . . . !

All day December twenty-fourth we beat slowly to windward along the coast. Every cape and inlet, every beach and bay conforms to Guacanagarí's tabletop map, an almost perfect maritime chart except that it lacks one vital dimension. Guacanagarí has neither knowledge of nor interest in the coastal shallows, the shoals, the barely submerged coral reefs that can rip the bottom out of a ship. His canoes, after all, skim the surface. But *Niña* draws six feet of water, *Santa Maria* more than seven. Zigzagging east in long tacks, we confront that third-dimensional threat the usual way — by sending *Niña*'s boat ahead to cast its sounding lead frequently. *Niña* steers next in line, all sails spread to the light breeze. *Santa Maria*, towing her own boat as she often does when coasting, lumbers behind.

The watches come and go, the sun sets, there's a quarter moon to steer by. I see waves breaking silver over unseen reefs, deadly but beautiful in the moonlight. Visibility's no problem. Mark that, please. *Visibility is no problem.*

Every man aboard the flagship, not excluding Pilot Niño whose watch is about to end, nor Admiral Colón who has paced the quarterdeck most of the day, is exhausted from two consecutive all-night parties.

I see fierce-faced, lamb-gentle Peralonso nudge the grommet nodding over the half-hour glass, which has run out. 'Better turn the glass, kid,' says Peralonso, 'before the Admiral catches you.' Sleepily the young grommet obeys. Now Peralonso reminds him, 'Time to change the watch too, isn't it?' and the boy blinks, bounces to his feet, bawls, 'You sluggish starboard sailors, topside! Move smart there, time-a-get-up, let's move it, hey!' Five or six sleepy figures rise from the steerage where they've been bunking. A few who have slung Indian hammocks on the maindeck make their bleary-eyed appearance. Peralonso comes over to me. 'You ought to grab some sleep yourself,' he urges as Juan Cosa joins us with a hippopotamal yawn.

Captain, master and pilot confer briefly.

'Speed?' I ask.

'Three knots if that,' says Peralonso.

Wind's down, there's no lee shore to worry about, ahead in the moonlight we can see *Niña*'s sagging sails. It will be a quiet watch.

Juan Cosa gives another hippopotomal yawn. 'Me, I could use some more sleep.'

'In four hours,' says Peralonso, only a bit testy, 'you'll have earned it. We're sailing for Cipango, man.'

'Won't get much closer in this light breeze,' glumps Juan Cosa.

Again I see the silver flash of ground swell breaking on unseen coral, perhaps a lombard-shot to starboard.

Suddenly I realize it's Christmas Eve.

'It's Christmas Eve!' blurts Peralonso.

We commune silently with the birth of the Saviour. That bright star Deneb, still high above the horizon, could almost be the Star of Bethlehem.

'We'll have us a feast tomorrow,' I say.

Peralonso grins. 'Just so happens I managed in the confusion on the beach last night to liberate a few of those lobsters.'

Juan Cosa gives an indifferent grunt, whether to the thought of lobsters or Christmas I don't know. Soon Peralonso says goodnight and is gone. I try making small talk with Cosa, but as usual it peters out in a few minutes. Juan Cosa's dewlappy face could squelch the enthusiasm of a manic Neapolitan. Besides, I'm sleepy.

It's still an hour until midnight, until our first Christmas this side of the Ocean Sea. 'I'm turning in,' I tell the shipmaster. 'Call me at midnight, would you?'

Later, far too much later to alter the terrible course of events, Constable Harana will piece together *Santa Maria*'s final agony.

Excerpts from the investigation conducted Christmas Day aboard flagship *Niña*:

(testimony of JUAN COSA, master, *Santa Maria*)

COSA: I'm dead on my feet too, but I can't sack out in no fancy private cabin like the Admiral. *I* have to stay on deck, but that don't mean I have to stay on my feet. So I go up to the poopdeck and sit with my back to the rail. From there I can see *Niña* real clear. And the grommet on the sandclock can read me the compass in the binnacle and relay orders to the helmsman.

HARANA: Did you remain there, seated on the poopdeck, continuously until the time of the accident?

COSA: I did, and nobody can say I shouldn't of. No way I can't command the ship from there. No way at all.

HARANA: How long was it before you fell asleep?

COSA: *That's a goddamn lie!* I never shut my eyes. Oh, for a minute maybe, to keep my night vision sharp, like. But I was NEVER asleep.

(testimony of JOSÉ MARIA DURÁN, helmsman, starboard watch, *Santa Maria*)

DURÁN: ... after Master Cosa went up for his nap.

HARANA: The shipmaster was asleep?

DURÁN: I guess. That's what the kid says — the grommet Ruíz who was tending the glass. All I know is, Cosa gave the kid one order and we didn't hear another squawk out of him.

HARANA: What was that order?

DURÁN: To keep me on course following *Niña*, and not to bother him unless the wind changed.

HARANA: And that's all you heard? Did you actually see Cosa asleep?

DURÁN: Man, how long you been at sea? I'm a helmsman, I don't see *nothing*! A patch of sky and a patch of sail up through the steerage hatch, a patch of sea aft out the tiller port. And that's it.

HARANA: So you were steering the ship solely on the verbal instructions of a raw fifteen-year-old boy?

DURÁN: (*shrugs*) Better an awake kid than a sleeping officer. Sir.

HARANA: Now, before the ship grounded, did you have any indication that anything was amiss?

DURÁN: Me?? I wasn't on the stick then, Constable. I had to go take a leak. So instead of waking anybody, I got the kid to take over for me. Not that it was his fault, what happened. But the poor kid — he must feel awful.

(testimony of RICARDO RUÍZ, grommet, starboard watch, *Santa Maria*)

RUÍZ: The master? Well, sir, he was sitting sort of scrunched over. And he didn't answer when I spoke to him.

HARANA: Then was anybody awake on the whole blasted ship?

RUÍZ: I really couldn't say, sir. The prow lookout was one of Chachu's northern clique. I didn't hear anything from him. I did hear the roundtop lookout — snoring away overhead. But to be fair, she *does* rock like a cradle up —

HARANA: Yes, yes. So there was just you to con the helm. Didn't you feel Cosa was putting a lot of responsibility on you?

RUÍZ: (*earnestly*) I could do it, sir, I was tops in navigation class. I wasn't scared, honest. (*pause*) Not then.

HARANA: No? Then when?

RUÍZ: After helmsman Durán gave me the tiller.

HARANA: Because you weren't used to handling it?

RUÍZ: No, sir. It wasn't that. I could handle it okay. I started getting scared when I realized he wasn't coming back.

HARANA: *What???*

RUÍZ: (*in a rush*) You'll protect me from him, sir, won't you? You see, he threatened me. Soon as I got hold of the tiller, he told me to stay right there. And he's *big*, all helmsmen are big. So I did. I thought he just wanted a break. Even when he asked about the star.

HARANA: The star?

RUÍZ: Polaris. The pole star. He wanted to know if I could see it. And I could. And he said to steer by it, hold steady till he got back. But then — then he didn't —

221

HARANA: How long was this before *Santa Maria* grounded?

RUÍZ: (*protracted pause*) Hours, it seemed. But I know it was only minutes because I was just starting to think about why he wasn't answering me and whether he'd gone off to sleep or what, when it happened.

HARANA: When we hit the reef?

RUÍZ: Hit? Oh no, sir, we didn't *hit* it. I only knew because the tiller suddenly wouldn't move. We just *slid* up on that reef. To stay.

(testimony of ESTEBAN BUENO, leadsman in *Niña*'s boat)

HARANA: So it was never less than eight feet?

BUENO: Closer to nine. We were throwing as fast as the lead came up, both sides of the boat. Even with the flagship's draught, she'd have had a good foot of clearance. *If* she crossed the reef where *Niña* did.

(further testimony of JUAN COSA, master, *Santa Maria*)

HARANA: Did you feel the ship run aground?

COSA: Nope. Nothing to feel. But I heard the swell breaking over the reef all around us – and knew it for what it was.

HARANA: What did you do?

COSA: I banged on the Admiral's door. He come out of his cabin all bleary-eyed. I told him we were grounded.

HARANA: He couldn't tell for himself?

COSA: Well, I don't want to bad-mouth him and I know he's got friends at Court, but Admiral Colón's no seaman, leastways not in my book.

HARANA: What makes you say that?

COSA: Things. Like, the way he was in such a hurry to write off the ship. Takes one quick look around, hears the swell breaking and says, 'That's it, Shipmaster, take the boat over to *Niña* and tell 'em to stand by to take off our crew.' When all we done was run up on a shelf of coral and not very hard! *I* could've got her off, I know that ship like a man knows his own wife. Ah, what's the use? She's finished now.

(testimony of VICENTE YÁÑEZ PINZÓN, captain, *Niña*)

PINZÓN: The first indication of trouble? Why, the lombard signal. The flagship fires three shots in quick succession. That's ship-in-danger, as you no doubt know.

HARANA: Was there any other indication of trouble?

PINZÓN: The boy in our roundtop. He calls down that *Santa Maria*'s sitting stock still with water breaking all around her. That's got to mean she's hung up on the reef we just passed over.

HARANA: Anything else?

PINZÓN: How many indications you figure a man needs?

HARANA: I want to have the complete picture, Captain.

PINZÓN: Yeah, well, there was something else, something – suspicious.

HARANA: *(leaning forward with a sudden smile)* Suspicious?

PINZÓN: Inconsistent, anyway. First they signal ship-in-danger, then they send their boat with an urgent message they're going to abandon ship.

HARANA: Couldn't the situation have deteriorated?

PINZÓN: Then why not fire another lombard signal? Not that they had to. I was already coming about to stand by and help. But even if they had to send their boat, wouldn't they send their most junior crew? I know there was bad blood there on *Santa Maria*, but in an emergency – I mean, how could the Admiral send away his first officer, his boatswain and the whole northern contingent? They were the ones who knew the ship best.

HARANA: But no captain in his right mind –

PINZÓN: Your words, Constable, not mine.

HARANA: Are you suggesting – ?

PINZÓN: Hey, not me! Sanest foreigner I ever met, the Admiral is. It was Juan Cosa suggested it – how only an incompetent landlubbing foreigner temporarily deranged by fear wouldn't realize that the proper and simple way to get the flagship off the reef was to kedge off astern.

HARANA: 'Kedge'? I'm no mariner. Is this standard procedure?

PINZÓN: Sure, anybody'd try it. That's why sending the boat over here to *Niña* made no sense. The flagship's being driven higher on the reef all the time, even with moderate seas. You don't get her off in the first half hour, she's spiked up there for good. Which she was.

HARANA: Perhaps the Admiral hoped to do both simultaneously – send you a message and try to 'kedge off'?

PINZÓN: Shit! I'll say you're no mariner. Kedging off's a straightforward operation, but it does take two pieces of equipment. You need an anchor and *you need a boat*.

(testimony of RAFAEL RELÁMPAGO, gunner, *Santa Maria*)

HARANA: How soon after the ship grounded did the Admiral order you to fire your lombards?

RELÁMPAGO: Amazing man, the Admiral. I mean, I'm sleeping — off duty, as you can see by the roster — and I wake and hear surf, and voices shouting, feet running, and before I can even ask what's going on, there's the Admiral telling me to fire three quick ones. That's ship-in-danger. The Admiral sized up the sit-ye-ation in the time it took me to climb out of me hammock and pry me eyes open. You ever try one of them hammocks? Comfortable, no question, but if . . .

(testimony of CRISTÓBAL COLÓN, Admiral of the Ocean Sea, captain-general of the fleet, captain of *Santa Maria*)

COLÓN: Please question me as you would any grommet serving aboard here. (*sighs*) I mean aboard the ex-flagship over there.

HARANA: (*sympathetically*) Tired, are you, Admiral?

COLÓN: Exhausted. Half an hour's sleep in three nights.

HARANA: And when the ship grounded, were you exhausted then?

COLÓN: That was the half hour's sleep I got. So to that extent I blame myself.

HARANA: After *Santa Maria* slid up on the reef, and Shipmaster Cosa came to your cabin —

COLÓN: He did?

HARANA: He didn't?

COLÓN: The feel of the ship woke me. That and the sound of the swell breaking. I rushed out — for once not banging my head on that damn lintel. Cosa was on the poop, just getting to his feet.

HARANA: You mean he was asleep on duty?

COLÓN: I didn't say that. I said he was just getting up.

HARANA: Did he say anything?

COLÓN: Not that I recall. I told him to come with me for a preliminary assessment. We took a quick turn around the ship. Men were shouting questions at each other, at us. The swells were foaming on all sides. *Santa Maria* was rising to every

224

crest, and every time she fell I could feel the deck planking jolt, through my bare feet.

HARANA: Yes, I felt that too.

COLÓN: That sharp coral had to be punching holes in her each time we hit. So I knew we had to hurry.

HARANA: What did you do?

COLÓN: Three things. First, wake the gunner to signal *Niña*. Second, see about damage control. But Peralonso Niño was right with me there, already getting the bilge pump manned and checking the hull for sprung seams. So I could give my attention to the main thing, which of course was kedging the ship off.

HARANA: Now, this process of 'kedging off'. Without jargon, how does it work?

COLÓN: No mystery. If a wagon was stuck in the mud, you'd tie a rope around the axle and pull it out. With a ship that's nosed onto a reef, you want to pull her off stern first. The difference is, at sea you have to solve the problem of traction. The answer's a kedge anchor, a sort of grappling hook with a long line attached. You put it in the ship's boat, pass the end of the line aboard, take the anchor out astern into deeper water, and drop it to act as your purchase point. Then when you winch up the line on board, if the anchor's fast, it'll pull you off backwards.

HARANA: Hmm. Is this a complicated maneuver?

COLÓN: Takes longer to tell than to do.

HARANA: I see. So you ordered Shipmaster Cosa to –

COLÓN: Try not to lead me, would you? I told Cosa to have the boat hauled in – we were towing it then, you remember – and put the kedge anchor aboard and warp it astern.

HARANA: Did you wait to see him do this?

COLÓN: Of course not. His was the easiest part. I went to tell Peralonso to be ready to receive the anchor cable and make it fast to the windlass.

HARANA: While Cosa was presumably warping the anchor astern?

COLÓN: That's right.

HARANA: And?

COLÓN: It's still aboard the wreck, isn't it?

(testimony of PERALONSO NIÑO, pilot, *Santa Maria*)

HARANA: What do you mean by remarkable?

225

NIÑO: The man was everywhere. I'm in the steerage waiting for the anchor cable, he's there beside me. And a minute earlier, I know he's in the hold ordering restowing of –

HARANA: Let's go back to the steerage, if you don't mind. You were waiting for the anchor cable, you say.

NIÑO: With Cristóbal Quintero and a couple of his young sidekicks, right. But after enough time passed, it was obvious no cable was coming through that tiller port.

HARANA: You didn't actually see Cosa leave without the kedge anchor, did you?

NIÑO: Constable, would I have been fool enough to wait for the cable if I had?

HARANA: What did you do then?

NIÑO: That's when the Admiral came back to ask what was keeping me with the anchor cable. We both rushed topside and looked for the boat. It wasn't astern, though. It was halfway to *Niña* with a dozen men in it. So it wasn't a total surprise to find the anchor and cable still secured at the bulwark.

HARANA: Cosa never intended taking the anchor off?

NIÑO: He didn't take it off. Better ask him about his intentions.

(further testimony of VICENTE YÁÑEZ PINZÓN, captain, *Niña*)

HARANA: So what did you do?

PINZÓN: My own boat was back by then. I sent my master, my boatswain, my best men over to the flagship. Then I brought *Niña* herself up as close as I could.

HARANA: What did you do about Cosa and his northern clique?

PINZÓN: I sent them back there too.

HARANA: You ordered them back aboard *Santa Maria*?

PINZÓN: Was that wrong?

HARANA: (*mildly*) I don't do answers. Just questions.

PINZÓN: Yeah. Well. Let's say something smelled decidedly fishy about Cosa's story. No matter what state the Admiral was in, the master had no business leaving the ship in an emergency.

HARANA: Even if the Admiral was – deranged?

PINZÓN: Especially then. You can relieve a superior of his command, if it comes to that, to save your ship.

HARANA: So you ordered Cosa and his northerners back to *Santa Maria*. Did you see if they actually went?

PINZÓN: Made no difference. Either way, it was too late to kedge

226

the flagship off. Pretty soon everyone was being ferried to *Niña*. By the time I went over, *Santa Maria* was abandoned except for the Admiral and that Indian who goes around pretending he's his son.

(testimony of CRISTÓBAL QUINTERO, grommet, *Santa Maria*)

HARANA: How long would you say you waited in the steerage?

QUINTERO: When things are happening so fast, it's hard to keep track of time. Same as when you're having sex, if you know what I mean.

HARANA: Mmn. Was the Admiral with you during this time?

QUINTERO: Off and on. He was up and down, back and forth, never two minutes in the same place. Then I guess him or Pilot Niño seen the anchor still on board, because he sends me instead down into the hold to find out how the pump's coping. It ain't. Water's already to my thighs. I go back up to tell the Admiral, but of course first I got to look for him.

HARANA: Where do you find him?

QUINTERO: At the mainmast with the carpenter, Old Serrín. Serrín's got a couple of axes and I'm a warm body. So he asks me to give a hand.

HARANA: Doing what?

QUINTERO: Cutting away the mainmast.

(testimony of PABLO GÓMEZ, a/k/a OLD SERRÍN, carpenter, *Santa Maria*)

HARANA: When did the Admiral order the mainmast cut away?

OLD SERRÍN: (*cupping a hand to his ear*) What?

HARANA: When did the Admiral order the mainmast cut away?

SERRÍN: When? How should I know when? It's late, people are running every which way like your headless chickens when their heads is cut off, we been on the reef more than an hour. When? What kind of dumb question's when?

HARANA: Then it was at least an hour after the ship grounded?

SERRÍN: Ain't that what I said? You deaf?

HARANA: What did the order signify to you?

SERRÍN: What did the order *what*?

HARANA: Mean. What did the order mean to you?

SERRÍN: If you mean mean, why don't you say mean?

HARANA: Please answer the question.

SERRÍN: Meant the Admiral wanted the mainmast cut away.

227

HARANA: Why?

SERRÍN: You ever been to sea before, sonny?

HARANA: Answer the question.

SERRÍN: You cut away the mainmast to make the ship lighter. She's the heaviest part of her 'cept the keel and (*laughs*) you wouldn't want to cut away the keel even if you could, now would you?

HARANA: To make the ship lighter, why?

SERRÍN: Why? *Why?* You're asking *why?* That mainmast, it's like a hammer banging the ship down on the reef every time the swell lifts and drops her. Why? Cut her away and we'll be in less danger of splitting apart at the seams, sonny. That enough of a 'why' to suit you?

HARANA: Was the danger imminent – uh, that means –

SERRÍN: You bet your ass it was imminent. Otherwise, would the Admiral've ordered the mainmast cut away?

HARANA: Why did the Admiral wait a full hour to order it?

SERRÍN: The ship don't really begin to take a pounding till she's swung athwart the reef and the seas hit her broadside – and that's an hour or so after she's hung up.

HARANA: Then we agree on the time?

SERRÍN: At least an hour. Which makes a feller wonder ... (*hesitates*)

HARANA: If you've something to say, let's hear it.

SERRÍN: Well, I don't mean to be disrespectful, but I been a sailor forty years. And I can't help wondering why that hour wasn't better spent. The Admiral could've kedged her off astern the first few minutes after we hit. Would have been nothing to it. Would have saved the ship.

HARANA: So you cut the mainmast away?

SERRÍN: Sure did, me and that teller of tall sexual tales Cristóbal Quintero. Hasn't been himself lately, Quintero hasn't, but let me tell you he swung a mean axe last night. Sure bamboozles the youngsters, though. Can you imagine? *Two* of them?! (*pauses, then whispers*) You don't think it's possible, do you?

HARANA: Don't ask me, I've never been to England. (*hides a smile*) You were telling me about the mainmast.

SERRÍN: Already told you. Admiral orders me to cut her away, that's what I do. Her own weight takes her over the side, and takes a chunk of the starboard bulwark too. Sends a sheet of water spang across the deck.

HARANA: Thank you. That's all.

SERRÍN: What?

(testimony of JUAN URTAÍN, a/k/a CHACHU, boatswain, *Santa Maria*)

HARANA: Is there anything you *would* care to comment on?

CHACHU: (*sullen unblinking stare*)

(further testimony of JUAN COSA, master, *Santa Maria*)

HARANA: (*looks up from writing*) Was there something else?

COSA: (*fidgets*) I just – I just wanted to say one thing.

HARANA: Yes?

COSA: She was my ship. You understand? *My* ship! Mine.

HARANA: (*nods sympathetically*)

COSA: I sailed on her before that upstart Admiral of yours ever set foot in Spain. Worked up from grommet, did every dirty job aboard. But I had this dream. I was going to own her. You got any notion how long I scrimped and saved? Then finally she was one-third mine and *I* was captain. Me, Juan Cosa! You think I'd try to wreck her after all we been through together? (*pauses, fingering his downward-dragging dewlaps*) But I guess some men are just born to bad luck. From the time *Santa Maria*'s mine, the shipping trade's dead. I can't go back to Galicia or the bank'll take my ship. I can't get a cargo. I'm stuck in an Andalucían backwater with no way out. So when this crazy venture comes along, I'm so hard up I sign on. With all I been through, how am I to know this'll be the worst? Worse than anything, because you got to keep it all inside you, choking you, corroding your guts. Five months now I been watching him make the decisions on my ship, lording it over my quarterdeck, living in my cabin. Always a kind word to my face, and always – I know it! – laughing behind my back. Because he's had the luck and I haven't. Because he's the Admiral of the Ocean Sea and I'm a failure. Because he'll be immortal, and when Juan Cosa dies, nobody'll care. That's what he's been thinking. I know. (*goes to door, then turns back*) And I know what he's thinking now too, what he's feeling in his guts, with his flagship spiked up on a reef and her hull in splinters.

HARANA: Is that why you disobeyed his orders?

COSA: (*smugly*) It's why I didn't advise him that the way to save

229

the flagship was to warp an anchor astern and kedge off. As any real seaman would have known. Not so high and mighty now, that Admiral of yours, is he?

'I don't need a confession from him,' Harana tells me. 'The case against him is solid.'

It is late afternoon Christmas Day. We are walking on a long sand beach. At one end is a small Indian village, at the other a high promontory rising over a mangrove swamp. *Niña* rides at anchor in the bay. Further out the wreck of *Santa Maria* can still be seen perched on the barrier reef. I watch our footprints forming in the hard wet sand.

'Let it go,' I say. 'It's done.'

'You mean just let him off? But he destroyed his own ship to get at you! He couldn't have done anything more monstrous – more treacherous and twisted. I never saw a man so eaten up by bitterness.'

I don't argue with that, but say, 'Drop it, will you? I pity him. He's so terrified of failure that he'll never outrun it.'

(A parenthetical flash-forward here. Juan Cosa now leaves these pages except for a brief mention, but he has one more appearance to make in the history of the New World. In November 1509 he sails as pilot with Captain Ojeda (a swashbuckling neurotic it will be your misfortune to meet presently) under royal charter to colonize the coast of what will one day be called, after me, Colombia. Whether Ojeda or Cosa is to blame for what happens, history doesn't say, but given their characters it could be either. Whichever, shortly after landing, Ojeda and his crew fall under attack by Carib Indians. Ojeda's bull-like stamina allows him to escape but, failing one final time, Juan Cosa takes a poison-tipped arrow in his back and dies a raving madman. Thus the colonization of Colombia is delayed for several years – not that this prevents the increasing use of the egregious misnomer South America for that whole vast mainland, thanks to the efforts of my erstwhile employer, the German publisher Martinus Waldseemüller, on behalf of that crass eponymous opportunist Amerigo Vespucci. But we'll get to all that in its proper place.)

Now as I pace the long Haitian beach with Harana, I can look back without flinching on what happened. I'm not the same man I was this morning. I see myself again standing alone at *Santa Maria*'s binnacle in the dirty gray dawn, thinking, so this is the way it ends. Shipwrecked on Christmas Day on a barrier reef at the entrance to some uncharted bay on some uncharted island somewhere in the immensity of the Ocean Sea. It's over. Oh, it's over. It's finished, done, concluded, ended, terminated.

I walk the length of the bulwark to the bowsprit. My mind rejects further thought, except for the sudden eerie conviction that if I turn quickly enough I'll catch a glimpse of someone behind me. But of course no one is there. It is only the ghost of my own failure stalking me. I return to the waist of the ship. *Niña*'s boat is back and Vicente Yáñez himself is climbing the ladder.

'Admiral, you'd better come off. Nothing more to be done here, now is there?' Speaking as if to a child.

And if I follow Vicente Yáñez down into *Niña*'s boat and let him take me to the caravel? Little *Niña*'s full complement is twenty-two men. *Santa María* carries forty. Can *Niña* sail back to Spain, stuffed with people like a barrel full of salted fish? And if she can't, then what?

'Admiral?'

I wave him away. Standing amidships I touch the stump of the mainmast. I can smell the fresh-cut wood, almost as if the great spruce was felled in its distant forest only yesterday. The dawn has grown brighter, but deepest night is in my soul.

'There's no telling how long she'll stay spiked on the coral,' Vicente Yáñez warns me. 'She could break up without warning, Admiral. You better come on off.'

But I wave him away a second time.

It isn't that I want to die. I just need to step outside the flow of things, watch them from a distance. From a place where it doesn't matter what I do, where I'm uninvolved.

Let someone else make the decisions. I've used up all of mine.

I wonder what it's like to drown. Some say it's a peaceful way to go. Not that I want to die, I repeat. I just want to manage to contrive to somehow go away and *not be*. For a while. For a little while only. And then come back and —

And what?

Again I have the eerie feeling someone is behind me. I whirl — and see Yego Clone uncertainly emerging from my cabin in the sterncastle. He looks half diffident, half determined as he comes forward dragging my seabag and an unwieldy bundle done up in a hammock. He must have packed everything in my cabin. Lord knows how long he's been there.

'What are you doing here, boy?' I demand angrily. 'Don't you realize you could have been left behind to drown?'

Yego understands some Spanish by now, though he's never spoken a word.

He signals something so complicated I'd need a Luís Torres to translate it. I don't try to answer. Yego's face takes on a look of intense, almost agonized concentration. His voice makes small experimental noises, odd little syllables that almost sound like speech. He tries again. Then for the first time he's speaking words, real words. Yego Clone is talking to me.

'Please ... yes,' he says.

'Please we ... go out ship,' he says. 'Yes please.'

'You, I please go out ship ... now ... father,' he says, and he grasps my hand so hard it hurts.

I find myself returning the pressure. All at once my numbness is gone. Yego is waiting for me, depending on me. So are sixty-odd men. What ever can I have been thinking of? To *not be*?

Then how would I learn what happens next?

With Yego at my side I walk to the bulwark and the ladder that will take us down to *Niña*'s boat.

Yego's hawk bells, silent until now, are tinkling jubilantly.

The long sand beach at Snail Bay – the name I have given it for its whorled shape – is no longer empty forty-eight hours after my Christmas walk there with Constable Harana. *Niña* is anchored close in. Poor *Santa Maria*'s still spiked on the reef and still looking a whole ship from a distance. But closer inspection shows that most of her deck has been cut away, the work obviously of a skilled carpenter, none other than Old Serrín. Now it's an easy matter to reach cargo stored anywhere aboard. Not that that's the only reason the deck has been carefully taken up.

On the shore ship's stores are piled in what seems total disorder. Rodrigo de Segovia, the royal comptroller, scuttles up and down the beach, logging in every canoe-load that comes from the wreck.

'Won't waste a plank or nail of her, will you?' he asks.

'We'll find a use for everything,' I promise him, and he smiles, a happy man until he inspects a wine cask.

'Water!' he bleats. 'Seawater's got in. Dear me, it's a loss, a total loss!'

The contents of other barrels and crates are set apart to dry, Segovia checking the angle of the sun and allowing for the shadow cast mornings by the high promontory with the exactitude of an astronomer at Cape St Vincent studying an eclipse.

You wouldn't think one carrack, and a smallish one at that, could hold so much meat and fish, smoked and dried and salted, so many yams and pumpkins from the islands, so much timber, so many kegs of nails, so much sailcloth, so much rope, etc., etc.

And the job's hardly begun. All day long Guacanagarí's canoes ply back and forth with more crates and barrels and bales, more jugs and bags to make a growing mountain of supplies under Rodrigo de Segovia's fussy direction.

Other canoes arrive with pumpkins and yams and maize as gifts for us shipwrecked gods. Or men from the sky.

Or just men. Because, without placing any great importance on it at the time, I sense a difference in the Arawak attitude toward us. This isn't surprising. Our great flying canoe is hung up on the reef, a gutted hulk, and we are on the beach, some of us with that pole-axed look that attends catastrophe, some merely frightened, others sunk in abysmal gloom – none with any noticeable godlike attributes.

When Guacanagarí appears on the beach with his royal entourage, it is even clearer that roles have been reversed. For no Spaniards magnanimously distribute Venetian glass beads or red caps or hawk bells to supplicating savages. Far from it. It is Guacanagarí's entourage that distributes ... but let my crew tell it:

'Nuggets of gold!'

'Golden bracelets!'

'Little gold animals!'

'Give me that! The golden iguana's mine!'

'Get your filthy mitts off ... !'

'A tortoise all of gold!'

'God, it's a knife – a golden knife!'

'It's mine, I tell you!'

'If you don't take your dirty paws off that ... '

The Admiral is asked frequently to arbitrate, which he does with some impatience, being busy admiring the large golden mask with its baleful eyes (a tribal god? something to frighten children?) that is Guacanagarí's personal gift to him.

This great chief feels sorry for us, and like a benevolent deity grants us now the very thing we have so long sought.

That our straits aren't so dire he has no way of knowing, because he wasn't on the beach the day before yesterday when I stopped in mid-stride, looked speculatively from the Indian village to the wreck on the reef and back, and suddenly smiled.

'Constable,' I told Harana, 'I want you to take Luís Torres and a few able bodies, and bring back Guacanagarí with all the canoes he can muster.' And Harana went, not even asking me why. He's like that sometimes, forgetting his own suspicious nature. Or maybe even from the first minute it was obvious – I'm riding the crest again.

Just look at all those supplies on the beach! Little *Niña*, already well provisioned, couldn't hold the tenth part of them.

Nor is she going to.

For how can I abandon my viceregal visions? A colony across the Ocean Sea, me as Governor of the Indies, men flowing out from Spain, gold flowing back, the precious metal eventually augmented by the proceeds of medicinal rhubarb, that Chinese cure-all, and various valuable spicery? (I have to admit I haven't appreciated the potential of tobacco yet. Luís de Santangel, indefatigable smoker of invisible cigars, will enlighten me.)

The viceregal colony, the way I planned it, was to be founded on my next voyage. More ships, more men, more supplies. Horses too. Next year, or the year after.

But since we now have only one tiny caravel to take us all back across the Ocean Sea ...

The solution's so obvious I wonder that I didn't think of it pages ago. Despair stifles the imagination, keeps those creative juices from flowing.

Start the colony *now*.

Only, who'd be fool enough to remain here on the wrong side of the Ocean Sea while the rest of us sail for home aboard *Niña*? What would guarantee we or anyone would ever come back?

Gold. G-o-l-d. GOLD.

Take Guacanagarí's gifts back with us to convince the royals of the vast wealth of these Indies, let the word spread, and every Spaniard with adventure in his soul (and/or gold fever in his heart) will beg to join the next voyage. I can picture a whole flotilla of ships, really large carracks, floating warehouses to bring across the Ocean Sea the building blocks of a city, and its citizens too. Women, even. When I put it to them, there's no question of forcing anyone to remain behind. Almost to the last man they want to stake their claims before all Spain clamors to colonize the Indies. The problem's finding a full crew to sail back to Europe. But there's incentive enough there too, once I point it out. Bringing home the news of the most important voyage in history can make a man famous overnight.

Still, some obviously have to stay, just as others obviously have to go.

I'll want sturdy, loyal Peralonso Niño aboard with me and, though convalescent, that superb helmsman Cristóbal Quintero. Pedro Terreros too, who won't remain a steward long. And of course Yego Clone and his five volunteers.

Yego wants to go to Spain. He talks of nothing else in his eager, halting voice. And I know that to witness the baptism of half a dozen naked savages will confirm Their Most Catholic Majesties in their Christian obligation to colonize the Indies and bring the pagan inhabitants into the One True Faith. Yego definitely goes.

Gold and zealotry, it's a hard combination to beat. The great golden mask with its baleful and mysterious eyes I intend presenting personally to King Fernando.

Now, who stays behind?

It's best, Harana and I agree, to separate Juan Cosa from Chachu and his northern clique. As Cosa is pleading to go home aboard *Niña* – this broken man mistakenly believes his adventuring days are over – I'll insist if necessary that Chachu & co. remain behind in Hispaniola. But of course there's no need to. When Chachu learns they're to stay, for the first and only time I see him blink. He actually thanks me.

'They'll need watching, that bunch,' Constable Harana says. 'We don't want to get off on the wrong foot with the Indians.'

'I could leave Cosa here and take them instead.'

Harana's face goes hard. 'I won't have Juan Cosa here with me.'

'You're volunteering to stay?'

'As constable, I'll be needed here, won't I?'

Hearing this, Dr Sánchez ignites his warm, bedside smile. 'And don't you think an untested group of colonists will need their medical advisor too? Mark me down to stay.'

Luís Torres shuffles his bare feet in the sand. 'I know I'm not much of an interpreter, but I guess I'm the best around. So I'd better stay too.' More barefoot shuffling. 'Can I see you a minute, Admiral? In private?'

I walk off a little way with him.

'My parents,' he says. 'Could you get a message to them? They don't even know if I'm still alive.'

'They're in Spain? I always assumed they went into exile with all the other Jews.'

'No, they're converts. New Christians. As far as they knew, I was leaving Spain with the last of the exiles from Huelva. They have no idea what happened to me. Could you let them know and tell them I'm happy?' He glances back at the mess on the beach. 'At least, I think I am.'

He tells me where to find them in the city of Tarragona.

'Why not write them a letter?' I suggest.

In due course he gives me the letter, written on the back of an old chart of the Canary Islands. I wonder, would I have delivered it, had I known that simple favor would cleave me in two, Columbus the legendary figure and Colón the all-too-human man, for the remainder of my days?

Based on Old Serrín's sketches, the settlement grows before our eyes. Timbers and planking from *Santa Maria* become a stockade and watchtower. Seeing these, Guacanagarí eyes a question at me. He eyes it again, more insistently, when the flagship's lombards and falconets are brought within the walls for mounting. And when a dozen crossbows and as many muskets follow them within the stockade, he's really concerned. I make the Carib sign, notching an invisible arrow and drawing an invisible bowstring. Guacanagarí nods, satisfied. Weapons for use against Carib raiders are a reasonable precaution.

We watch his men swarming over the settlement site, happy workers all. Inside the stockade, ignoring Old Serrín's sketch of three cabins, they quickly erect a quartet of large native-style huts, palm-thatched, open to the breezes. Gradually the crates and barrels on the beach disappear into the wood-plank storehouse, Old Serrín's design this time. *Santa Maria*'s mizzenmast becomes a flagpole, and her flag is raised with a brief ceremony.

'A name – the place needs a name,' says Dr Sánchez.

Various suggestions are made but each appeals only to its deviser until Luís Torres says, 'Why don't we call it Christmas, since what happened on Christmas made it possible?'

'Necessary, you mean,' says gloomy Juan Cosa, but the rest of us take to Luís's suggestion. Christmas Town it is.

The day *Niña* is to sail, hundreds of Indians gather on the beach with the forty Christmas Towners to see us off.

Guacanagarí's people have baked quantities of cassava bread, which has a longer shelf life than ship's biscuit and proves unpopular with maggots. Guacanagarí makes a speech in Arawak, which no one attempts to translate. I make one in Spanish, the Indians hanging on every incomprehensible word. It's the spirit that counts, the so obvious good will that exists between our peoples.

At my last meeting with Harana, the constable tells me, 'I'm worried about fraternization. You've noticed how many native women are in the settlement already?'

'So? It's perfectly normal.'

'It's the Basques that worry me. They're the only ones who aren't joining in, and it's unhealthy.'

'Why aren't they?'

'They dislike them. They say they're definitely uncouth, unfriendly and unlovable.'

'The Indian women?' I ask, surprised.

'The Basques. The women want no part of them. But you don't think the Basques will take no for an answer, do you?'

I say a few calming words. In my mind I've already crossed the Ocean Sea. I'm entering Palos harbor standing tall on the quarterdeck, one hand nonchalantly gripping a shroud, the other waving to the cheering crowds lining the river. Yego Clone is at my side, wearing scarlet tights and a feather in his hair, his hawk bells tinkling madly as he jumps up and down. The rest of my life's like that. In the Indies, I long for Spain. In Spain, I can't wait to return to the Indies. At sea I'm happiest because I'm *getting there*, wherever *there* happens to be.

All this may explain why I make light of the constable's misgivings.

We have a final surprise for Guacanagarí and his Indians. They've heard the thunder of our cannons but haven't seen their lightning. In the stockade Gunner Relámpago, one of our colonials, has already primed three lombards. At my signal there's a spurt of flame from the palisade, a roar, a rushing sound overhead that makes Guacanagarí uneasy and terrifies his people – and then the wreck of *Santa Maria* shudders on the reef. Relámpago sends two more iron cannon balls on their way, blasting the wreck of *Santa Maria* into driftwood. The Indians run about shouting and gesticulating. With our display of gunnery, some measure of awe has been restored.

Guacanagarí walks down with me to *Niña*'s boat and signals, 'Come back soon, my brother.'

He has never called me that before.

We all line the starboard bulwark watching Christmas Town become smaller, until it is toylike, until all that remains is the tiny needle of its watchtower against the sky, and then that too is gone.

We are alone at sea.

No, not quite. For a single canoe, its twenty paddlers bending their backs with prodigious effort, Guacanagarí standing in the prow and signaling urgently, races to overtake us.

❧ X ❧

How I Return to Spain in Triumph and Become the Guest of the Supreme and General Council of the Inquisition

As *Niña* moved slowly upriver toward Palos harbor, her long ash sweeps providing steerage way, I stood on the quarterdeck, one hand nonchalantly gripping a shroud, the other waving to the cheering crowds lining the river. I tousled Yego Clone's hair, almost knocking off his parrot feather because he chose that moment to start jumping up and down with excitement, his hawk bells tinkling madly.

'Spain!' he shouted.

His happiness would have been complete, I think, if he hadn't been forced in the interests of modesty to wear a pair of scarlet tights.

But hold on – what about that canoe racing to overtake *Niña*, Guacanagarí bearing some urgent message? What about our journey back across the Ocean Sea? What about the gale that separated the two caravels near the Azores, almost sinking both and driving *Pinta* to an unplanned landfall near Vigo on the northern coast of Spain and *Niña*, only slightly closer to her destination, into Lisbon harbor...?

Pinta? Did I write *Pinta*?

Surely there must be some mistake.

Not at all.

How Guacanagarí brought the news that some Arawak fishermen had spotted *Pinta* a scant two days' sail along the coast; how I was re-united with, and forgave, Martín Alonzo Pinzón; how we conferred frankly on the subject of gold ('You find any?' Pause. 'Yes. You?' Pause. 'Yes. Find much?' Pause. 'Some.' Pause. 'Me too.'); how we careened the caravels on a broad beach to scrape and caulk them, then sailed north to pick up the westerlies that would blow us back to Spain; how from the moment that gale separated us, Vicente Yáñez did everything he could to reduce our own speed in *Niña* so his brother would be first home with the news; how the storm drove us, sails in tatters, into Lisbon harbor, and lucky to make it; how His Most Serene Majesty King John received the news that I'd crossed the Ocean Sea in the service of his archrivals the King and Queen of Spain and how he tried to seduce me back into Portuguese service; how with new sails *Niña* left Lisbon on 13 March 1493 for Palos with a fresh N.N.W. wind – it's all there in Las Casas's occasionally accurate extracts from my journal, in Fernando's encomium-cum-biography, and in other secondary sources too numerous to mention. But I can't help thinking that my First Voyage ended with the destruction of *Santa Maria* and the founding of the first settlement in the New World, Christmas Town. The rest was anticlimax.

Nor can I help thinking that biography is an imperfect medium to convey the feel of those heady days when we returned to Spain as living proof that you could sail west to reach the fabled East – or at least the Indies or wherever it was we'd been. What an exercise of their skills our return to Spain would have provided print journalists! But print journalism was slow to develop in the first few decades after the invention of the Gutenberg-Schöffer printing press. Publishers had a lot of catching up to do on the classics.

Not that I regret the lack of daily newspapers with their hastily-filed columns of shallow and sloppy prose. But a newsmagazine might have served nicely. Such a publication – although hardly a weekly – did exist in 1493. This was the great *Chronicle of Nuremberg*. But even as late as its edition of 12 July it would carry no account of our voyage. Why this omission? I can only make an educated guess. The driving force behind the *Chronicle*, the world's leading authority Regiomontanus, was no young man and must have turned increasingly for guidance of his faltering steps, and possibly mind, to his number one disciple, and that was none other than Martin Behaim.

I myself, shortly after landing, wrote a long newsy letter to Luís de Santangel, which was rushed by royal post to the Peripatetic Royal Court, then at Barcelona, arriving by the end of March, four weeks before I did. This letter, translated into Latin and printed in Rome a month later as a pamphlet of eight pages under the by-line Cristoferi Colomb (sic), became an international bestseller, going through three printings in the Eternal City and half a dozen in Paris. My prosaic letter informing Santangel of our success was even put into sixty-eight stanzas of somewhat fanciful and florid verse by one Giuliani Dati of Florence, possibly giving another Florentine, that crass eponymous opportunist Amerigo Vespucci, his introduction to the half of the world eventually named after him.

But for years such reprints of letters were all there was, so we can only conjecture what print journalism might have made of my triumphal return to Spain.

Certainly a portrait of me would have graced the cover of our hypothetical newsmagazine. What would it have shown? A tall, broad-shouldered man, his once barber-pole-striped hair completely white and belying the youthfulness of his recently-shaven, freckled, long, mostly unlined face. Blue eyes that have seen far distances, a proud prow of a nose, a controlled mouth that can suddenly flash a smile of almost childlike joy.

Mightn't the cover-story have begun like this:

Into the harbor of the sleepy little southern port of Palos one afternoon last week limped *Niña*, a storm-battered caravel of some fifty tons, bringing to a successful conclusion the greatest voyage in the history of Spain and possibly of mankind. For *Niña*'s score of mariners have sailed the virgin waters of the Ocean Sea to the very ends of the earth (*see chart*) and returned.

On one level, the journey was the culmination of work begun in Portugal fifty years ago by the late, great Prince Henry the Navigator. But on a deeper level, it has tapped a longing in Spain for national pride that was deadened after the fall of Granada last year by the expulsion of the country's 200,000 Jews. Just how deep that feeling runs can be seen by the outpouring of emotion that greeted the intrepid band of voyagers as they began at week's end their triumphal march from Palos to the Peripatetic Royal Court, now visiting Barcelona.

First among this intrepid band is white-haired, youthful-looking Admiral of the Ocean Sea and Viceroy of the Indies Cristóbal Colón, 42, arguably the finest seaman the world has yet produced. To be sure, Colón, a man who invites controversy as a lodestone attracts iron, has his detractors. He is, according to prematurely aged, bedridden Martín Alonzo Pinzón, captain of *Niña*'s sister caravel *Pinta*, 'something of a showboat. A little humility's overdue,' Pinzón suggests. But Colón, aware that he has been singled out by destiny, disagrees. 'There's Colón the living legend and Colón the man. I can't help that. We're two different people.'

'Legends in their own lifetime,' elaborates Fray Juan Pérez, prior of the nearby monastery of La Rábida and one of the first to encourage Colón, 'live in a high-rent district, morally speaking. Humility's in short supply there.'

But the Admiral's steward Pedro Terreros, 17, squints into the sunlight at the caravel anchored offshore and remembers what it was like at the beginning. 'He came here to Palos with his hat in his hand. He couldn't get anybody to go. He practically had to beg us,' recalls Terreros. 'Don't tell me that's not humility.'

Perhaps most surprising on the first leg of the long overland march from Palos to Barcelona were the tears. Such as those that filled the eyes of a young girl on the outskirts of Sevilla when she was forbidden to touch one of the half dozen semi-naked savages brought back from the Indies by the expedition. Even Pablo Romero, a 15-year-old apprentice bullfighter who hardly seems the crying type, admitted that the sight of the smartly uniformed Admiral, his bearded crew and the Indians with their painted faces brought tears to his eyes. Said Romero, 'They made me cry for Spain.'

Less surprising was the excitement: the armed outriders leading the way; the crowds thronging apparently from nowhere to cheer as the Indians improvised unprovoked flurries of sign language; the mob at Córdoba's Iron Gate that kept the Admiral pinned against a wall, delaying for hours his reunion with his family.

What sort of man is he, this Admiral of the Ocean Sea and Viceroy of the Indies?

With characteristic energy, in one spurt of non-stop activity the explorer ranged far and wide to: visit his old friend and supporter the Prior of La Rábida; conduct a seminar on Oceanic discovery for the nautical community of Huelva; present a souvenir of Sargasso seaweed to Ancient Mariner Vásquez de la Frontera; relate his adventures in passable Latin and barely accented Spanish to a group of skeptical geographers and clerics at Córdoba University; and, in a closed-door meeting, exhort the House of Centurione, Italian Merchant Bankers, to invest with the Crown for later trans-Ocean voyages.

Said New Director Prospero Pighi-Zampini of the House of

Centurione's Sevilla branch: 'I've known Cristoforo, I mean Cristóbal, ever since he was a youngster in the employ of a member of the Papal Curia. I always knew he'd go far.'

Cristóbal Colón was born at sea 42 years ago to Spanish parents, said by usually reliable sources to have been New Christians, emigrating to Genoa. He has never since felt entirely at home on dry land . . .

The breathy, stylized prose goes on for three more pages, which may be invoked again. But now it's time I slipped away from that mob of admirers at Córdoba's Iron Gate for my long delayed family reunion.

It was nightfall before I could get away. I ran the whole distance to the hidden patio half-way between the former Judería and the square that would eventually be named Plaza de Colón. In the fading light, pots of geraniums could just be seen against the whitewashed walls. Lamps glowed and candles flickered welcomingly inside the iron-grilled windows.

'Here he comes!' a voice shouted, and a tall, gangling boy came hurtling across the cobblestones and into my arms, knocking my seabag off my shoulder. 'Papa! Papa! It *is* you!' he cried, picking up my seabag and hefting it with almost a man's strength.

'It *is* you it *is* you it *is* you!' squawked the parrot, a gift for Diego and Fernando, from its cage on my other shoulder.

Diego recoiled, the seabag falling again. 'Who's – I mean what's – *that*?'

'A parrot, son,' I said. 'That's a genuine parrot from the island of Cuba, or was it Hispaniola?'

My initial unease at resuming a fatherly role didn't last long. I stooped for the seabag. So did Diego. We bumped heads. Then one of us began to laugh and soon, embracing, we were both laughing so hard the tears flowed.

Perhaps that was why it took three or four feminine throat-clearings before I became aware of Beatriz, or of plump little Fernando at her side. 'Don't I get a kiss too?'

'Kiss two of them, two of them, two of them!' squawked the parrot, which had previously belonged to Cristóbal Quintero.

Soon we were all inside seated around the dining table with the door securely locked against the outside world (and my status as a legend in my own lifetime).

Everybody was a little awkward.

'You've really grown,' I told Diego.

So had Beatriz. Her hour-glass figure was fifteen or twenty minutes more ample. She said, 'You were later than we expected, dearest. The roast will be shoeleather.' This gave me my first sense of *déjà vu*, a strong but comparatively harmless one.

The roast, as promised, was like shoeleather.

'But never mind,' Beatriz said in her chirpy voice, a remembered glow of mystery in her dark, undeniably Iberian eyes. 'The dessert's the *pièce de résistance* anyway. It's all the rage these days, from an old Roman recipe.'

She went; she returned; she passed a platter. I stared in mounting horror at the sticky amber-colored things heaped on it. Soon everyone but me was eating. Fingers were licked, fingers reached for more, as I stared at the single glistening amber thing on my plate. Beatriz consumed her fourth – or was it her fifth? – blissfully. 'Aren't they simply for dying? You stuff dates with ground almonds, then roll them in salt and simmer them in honey. I'm really into sweets and desserts and ... but you're not eating.'

'I'm allergic to poison – I mean honey,' I said, averting my eyes from the single *dulcia romana* lurking evilly in the middle of my plate.

'Nobody's allergic to honey. Try it, you'll love it.'

'I mean rich food,' I managed. 'I'm not really used to rich food – real cooking – anymore.'

Beatriz's conceivably Semitic, haughtily high-bridged nose flared a trifle to show she was miffed. Her tongue darted out to lick honey from her full, red, possibly Berber lips.

'Is anything the matter? What's the matter? Why's something the matter?' Diego asked.

It was probably as close to a complex, perceptive and even rhetorical question as a twelve-year-old could get, but Beatriz chose to answer simply – 'He doesn't like my *dulcias romanas*' – with a shake of her head that made her now decidedly plump, rosy, perhaps Visigoth cheeks quiver. 'But never mind. Your father must be tired after his trip.'

There was a long silence.

'Well, here we all are, together again at last,' Beatriz said, a strain in her chirpy voice. She ate another *dulcia romana*. Unable to forget that night in the Borgia garden, I had all I could do to stop myself from knocking it out of her hand.

Just then there was a clap of thunder and a sudden torrential spring rain began to fall.

'My seabag!' I cried, and ran outside to where Diego and I had left it.

That was how my homecoming began.

It got worse.

There's a latter-day Spanish proverb that goes, 'All men secretly love fat women, sweet wine, and the music of Tchaikovsky.' I can't say about this Tchaikovsky, but I never cared for sweet wine. As for fat women – well, Beatriz wasn't really fat. But her new amplitude was in such marked contrast to the lithe-limbed high-breasted Indian maidens who had walked with such insouciant boldness among us that, when *dulcias romanas* were finally left behind that night for the private joys of the nuptial bed, I found myself picturing a parade of bronzy-skinned Arawak girls, each wearing only a single feather in her hair, while making love to pillowy Beatriz.

In the morning she said, 'I can't wait to see my cousin Enríquez de Harana. And that nice Dr Sánchez too. Shall we have them to lunch?'

'They're not here,' I said.

'Oh? They're not in Córdoba yet? Didn't they come with you from Palos?'

'In the parade,' said Diego with a significant glare at his young half-brother.

'I tried to take them,' Beatriz said.

'To the *parade*,' Diego said.

'But the crowds at the Iron Gate were too much for Fernando.'

'So we didn't *get* to *see* the *parade*,' Diego explained.

I searched for a way to tell her. 'Parade's too grand a word,' I stalled, addressing Diego. 'Just a company of the Holy Brotherhood militia, and a few of my men, a couple of my officers, three or four cartloads of golden masks and other archipelagan exotica, plus some flora and fauna never before seen in Christendom. Hardly a parade at all.'

I was hoping Diego might ask a question: what's archipelagan, for example. But he just nodded and continued to glare at his half-brother.

'If they're not here, where are they?' Beatriz asked in a decidedly suspicious tone reminiscent of her cousin Enríquez de Harana's.

This made me defensive. 'I was forced to leave them in the Indies,' I said.

Of course, putting it like that was a mistake. I should have said, 'They elected to stay in the Indies,' which was closer to the truth anyway. But unfortunately, 'I was forced, etc.' is a direct quote.

Those rosy, perhaps Visigoth cheeks went pale.

'They're dead.'

244

'No no, they're fine! They're both fine. It's just that I had to leave half the expedition behind.'

'You *had* to leave them on the other side of the Ocean Sea, how many thousands of miles from anywhere?'

I tried to explain.

'Among all those pagan savages?'

'The king of those pagan savages is as fine a human being as any Christian I ever met.'

'Oh? And would you say that to the Inquisition?'

We were now eyeball to eyeball. There was no forgetting that Beatriz's cousin was Tomás de Torquemada, the Grand Inquisitor of Spain. I felt the color draining from my own cheeks.

'I'm sorry,' she said. 'I didn't mean that the way it sounded. It wasn't a threat or anything, I hardly know him. Will they come back on a later ship?'

'There is no later ship. They're stuck there till our next voyage.'

'Then you *did* abandon them! How *could* you, Cristóbal? What am I going to tell my uncle?' By her uncle she meant Constable Harana's father, who had raised her as his own daughter.

'Hasn't it occurred to you,' I said, still trying to explain, 'that they might have wanted to stay? That they volunteered?'

'You mean they'd want to stay among all those naked savages and my poor cousin Enríquez de Harana in the prime of his manhood and not a decent Christian woman within a thousand miles for normal social congress instead of coming home?'

This syntactical disaster of a sentence made me long for Christmas Town, and it was followed by a *non sequitur*.

'It was foolish of me,' Beatriz said with a bosom-expanding sigh, 'to hope I wouldn't lose you to . . . all that.'

All that – how fraught with significance those two small words! They encompassed Beatriz's stricken awareness that we had lost our common ground, that she would never again understand the now-legendary figure who had fathered her son; they hinted, subconsciously perhaps, at a future in which I would seldom see her; they even expressed her visceral knowledge that one day soon I must recognize that provincial Córdoba and Beatriz the farmgirl from Santa Maria Trasiera were not the place and the person to raise my sons, when instead they could receive all the advantages of a Court education.

'It was their duty,' I persisted, 'to stay.'

As she could say nothing to advance her own argument or to end ours, she retreated to a level of reality where she felt secure.

'What would you like for breakfast?' she asked.

Breakfast was large.

I stayed two days at the apartment in the hidden patio half-way between the former Judería and the plaza not yet named in my honor. It rained constantly, a relentless downpour as confining as prison bars. The tiny apartment, which I had remembered as cosy, was a cell. Everybody bumped into everybody, except little Fernando who was too small to bump and was merely always underfoot. Most conversation consisted of 'Oh, excuse me,' 'Sorry,' 'Will you look at that rain?' and from Beatriz a single brave 'It's so good to have you home,' that emerged as an almost plaintive wail for help.

Make no mistake about this. We felt fondly toward each other. We shared happy memories. Sentiment, if not overindulged, is a powerful bond, though no aphrodisiac. Had I outgrown Beatriz? This happens.

Once she said with surprising wisdom, 'Now that you've crossed the Ocean Sea and discovered all those islands and all, I know I won't be able to share your life or even understand you – '

I began to make a *pro forma* demurrer, but she continued:

' – but sometimes I can't help wondering if you even understand yourself.'

She didn't use the words 'midlife crisis' which weren't in vogue then anyway, but her meaning was clear.

Rained in, I wrote to my brother Barto at Fontainebleau urging him to return to Spain in time to join my second expedition and get into the colonial administration early. I wrote more or less the same letter to my brother Little Giacomo in Rome, whom I hadn't seen since he was a small child, adding in a postscript that if he had taken Holy Orders, all the better, as men of the cloth would be in great demand in the Indies to convert the heathen natives.

Fernando, just four years old, was bored with the rain, bored with his toys, bored with the sullenly uncommunicative parrot. 'What are you doing, Papa?' he asked.

'Writing.'

I had just turned a persuasive phrase in my postscript to Giacomo that made me smile with satisfaction.

'Is writing lots of fun?'

'Sometimes,' I said.

'I think I'll be a writer when I grow up.'

On the third morning Peralonso Niño found his way to the hidden patio. A grin split his ferocious desperado's face. 'Letter for you, Admiral.'

The seal's castle and rampant lion told me where it came from, and I slit the wax swiftly. My eyes skimmed the gorgeous hand and flowery salutation of the royal scribe before alighting with joy on these words:

We take much pleasure in learning that God has guided you in your Great Venture and brought it to so happy a conclusion, which will serve Him and us also, and bring to our realms so much advantage. It will please God that, as earthly reward for serving Him, you receive from us all that it is in our power to grant you.

Therefore make the most haste you can in coming, for it is our wish that that which you began with the aid of God be continued and furthered, and we want to provide you speedily with everything you need to return with His help to the lands which you have discovered.

From Barcelona on the 30th day of March 1493.

I The King   I The Queen

By order of the King and Queen (F. Alvarez, scribe)

Manic is the word for how I felt. I kissed Beatriz, kissed Diego, lifted and kissed little Fernando, embraced Peralonso Niño.

In my excitement I entirely missed the letter's disquieting tone. On second reading the ominously excessive zeal came through – Gods and Hims sprinkled so liberally that it might have been God that brought the Great Venture off and Him that sponsored it. But the Queen's piety was well known, I reminded myself, and optimistically attributed the exact wording to F. Alvarez, scribe.

'Good news?' Peralonso asked.

'We're to leave for Barcelona at once.'

I handed Beatriz the letter. She began to cry.

'You knew I'd have to go sooner or later.'

'It isn't that.' Wiping her eyes. 'I was just thinking. Remember when you were teaching me to read and we used to give each other little slips of paper with messages written on them? Remember when you were so sad because you *didn't* hear from the King and Queen that I let you – '

'The children,' I cautioned, but I was really thinking, perhaps selfishly, that a wistful woman's 'remember when' informs a thoughtful man that it's time to leave.

So it was with relief that I packed my still-damp seabag and, after submitting to tearful goodbyes, went out into the rain with Peralonso.

Everybody loves a parade, especially if he's its stellar attraction.

First came half the company of Holy Brotherhood militiamen. These had been Fray Juan Pérez's idea and a good one, for the crowds that followed us from town to town so swelled the ranks of our little procession that it might have been mistaken for a Holy Year pilgrimage to Santiago de Compostela or a long-belated Crusade. These camp followers created an impromptu floating fairground with games of chance, fortune tellers, a magician or two, jugglers, gypsy singers of the mournful 'deep song' then beginning to capture the heart of Spain, acrobats, mimes, horse copers, fast-food vendors, groupies and pickpockets.

Following the militiamen, if you could find them in the often unruly crowd, came two trumpeters and the town crier of Palos, then those three or four cartloads of archipelagan exotica I'd mentioned to Diego – nuggets of gold as big as pigeon's eggs, golden masks and jewelry, wall hangings embroidered with fish bones, harmless-looking fish-toothed spears, a mean-looking Carib bow and quiver of arrows (daringly stolen by one of Guacanagarí's warriors), a small canoe, several hammocks, cages of parrots and some animals that partook of both simian and rodent characteristics, samples of archipelagan hardwoods, a specimen box of archipelagan butterflies with wingspans smaller than people afterwards claimed, numerous salted-down archipelagan fish which, unfortunately, had attained a certain ripeness, a good supply of tobacco leaves that Yego Clone assured me were ageing well, etc., etc.

Next in line, wearing golden necklaces and ear-rings and an occasional nose-plug, their faces extravagantly painted with red ochre, their legs and private parts chafed by unfamiliar tights and codpieces, came Yego Clone and his five Indian volunteers, who were encouraged to employ sign language, the more recondite the better.

Finally, riding splendid horses in the place of honor before the militia rearguard, came the three Niño brothers of Moguer and I.

During the two days I spent with Beatriz and the children, the Niños had a Córdoba tailor run up a sort of admiral's uniform for me. Picture then, astride a white Arabian, the Admiral of the Ocean Sea: black velvet beret with narrow brim and parrot feathers instead of ostrich plumes, cocked over one eye; black traveling cloak brocaded with gold; soft bone-white leather gloves, changed twice daily;

doublet of gold cloth; supple black leather boots; jewel-hilted dagger worn at my side, although by that time in my life I had little fear of the Brotherhood of the Golden Stag (or Hind).

It took three weeks for this cavalcade to cover the almost 600 miles from Córdoba to Barcelona, through mountain passes and across countryside where the new green of summer grain and the wind-blown silver-green shimmer of olive trees were set off strikingly by the russet Spanish earth. Towns and villages followed one another in confusing succession: Montoro, Andújar, Linares, Úbeda, Alcaraz, Ballestero the Garden, Seven Waters.

Part of the confusion was my name.

In Montoro I was Colomba.

In Andújar the people shouted in friendly greeting, 'Hey there, Collumba!' pronouncing the double-l more like 'zh'.

In Linares I was back to Colomb, the most common variation on my name.

In Ballestero the Garden they called me Colonus.

No one got it right anywhere.

They got a few other things wrong too.

'That Captain (sic) Collumba you see there on the white horse went all the way to the coast of India and back,' they said in Andújar.

I heard the town crier in Ballestero the Garden proclaim: 'Vice Admiral (sic) Colonus and his crew! Six native sons of the Golden Chersonese, or Malay Peninsula, just north of Cathay!'

In Seven Waters they assured one another that Admiral Colonna had crossed the Indian Ocean to a group of islands all of whose streams and rivers ran with gold.

On the road as we approached the sea at Valencia, I heard this: 'Founded a city called Corpus Christi, they did, and left eight hundred men behind to garrison it against attacks from the nearby well-known island of Amazon women warriors.'

This disheartening dialogue, so sadly Perestrellan, was heard regularly with regional variations:

NEWCOMER: What's all the fuss about anyway?
KNOW-IT-ALL: Fellow on the piebald horse there next to the one in the footman's uniform?
(*Peralonso Niño, at my right, rode a piebald mare.*)
NEWCOMER: What about him?
KNOW-IT-ALL: That's the famous Neapolitan, Captain-General Reggio Calambia.

NEWCOMER: What's so famous about him?

KNOW-IT-ALL: Proved the world was flat by sailing west to reach the fabled East and then having to sail back to Europe the same way he went out.

Groupies, most of them sturdy teenaged farmgirls, were always on hand to enliven those nights that found us camped in open country. They came in awe of me, the Admiral, and a touch of the hand or a hastily snatched scrap of clothing was all they aspired to. (Autographs were not in demand, as none of them could read.) The Indians, although they groused about it, were off limits. Most sought-after by the groupies was Francisco Niño, but our Billy Budd prototype, remembering his misadventure with Guacanagarí's sister-in-law, was girl-shy and did his best to hide in dark corners of the camp. Not so Cristóbal Quintero, that infected teller of tall sexual tales. There was no night he failed to delight a groupie or two. Or three.

One night when we camped not far from Ballestero the Garden, I heard for the first time an old gypsy sing the authentic 'deep song'. Until dawn, plied with good Valdepeñas wine, he wailed and lamented for our pleasure melodies of ineffable sadness and beauty while a pair of his colleagues skilfully picked our pockets.

The most haunting song told of Petenera, a lovely Jewess who disavowed her baptism as a New Christian, and the Old Christian who paid with his life for love of her. The gypsy insisted this song was based on events fifty years before somewhere to the north, but though I knew it was only a good fiction, the power of the music made it live.

See then the dying fire and the first faint light of dawn, and hear a single mournful chord on the guitar and the abrupt but prolonged wail of deepest despair that seemed to rise and fall with the chill night wind, and then the words so romantic in their content, so classic in their simplicity, culminating in the lines

> Who called you Petenera?
> Your lovely name's a lie.
> You should be called Perdition –
> Men love you but to die.

> When you hear funeral bells
> Ask not for whom they toll.
> Your own remorse must tell you,
> His death is on your soul.

Petenera! Why did the melody haunt me so, like the memory of events as yet unlived? Often on the road I would find myself singing the refrain

> Where are you going, lovely Jewess,
> Dressed to kill and so late the hour?

and imagining what she might look like, this most beautiful of seductresses, until I reminded myself it was only a song and for each man she would look like his heart's desire and his own private hell.

As we approached the Mediterranean coast at the great city of Valencia early one morning, we expected the crowds to be bigger than ever.

They were – but they ignored us. This mystified me.

'We didn't come all this way,' growled Juan Niño of Moguer, expressing his mystification better than I, 'to be ignored.'

I tried to question the peasants coming sleepily out of orange groves along the highroad and heading for the city, but they wouldn't stop to answer me, so anxious were they to be in time for – what?

There was no way, having come this far, for our cavalcade to skirt the city without doubling back against that human tide. So we flowed into Valencia's gray stone heart with the country folk. Here the narrow streets were so thronged we had to dismount and lead our horses.

All the churchbells of the city were tolling with that resonant cacophony so jarring to any but Spanish ears. Spanish churchbells don't clang, they clank.

'It's some local holy day,' guessed Peralonso.

In even the smallest of Valencia's plazas, refreshment stands under gaily striped awnings dispensed cool tigernut milk and grilled garlic sausage.

'Grilled over an open fire,' said a sausage seller sweating at his brazier. 'Appropriate, ain't it? That'll be three maravedís, service and amusement tax included.' He thrust a sausage on a wooden skewer at me.

'Is it some holy day today?' I asked. The sausage was delicious.

The sausage seller gave me a pitying look and turned to his next customer.

Propelled by the mob again, we entered a huge plaza. At the far end stood what looked like a pair of wooden platforms, one heaped with logs and faggots, the other canopied with yellow cloth. Before we could get our bearings, a stout Dominican brother in white robes came belly-shoving in our direction, waving and calling.

'Admiral! So glad we found you in time! Knew you'd be coming through Valencia around now, but we'd almost given you up. Thought we'd have to begin without you.'

At that moment a scruffy fellow pushed through the crowd hawking pamphlets printed on what I recognized from my Waldseemüller days as good linen stock. 'Programs!' he cried. 'Get your programs here! Can't tell the condemned without a program. Programs! Only half a sueldo, get 'em while they last.'

'We don't pay, peasant,' said the Dominican, and he didn't. A program was given to me too, and the scruffy fellow quickly disappeared into the crowd.

'Consider yourself and your party our guests,' said the stout Dominican. 'Only sorry you can't be the guest of honor. But the Duke of Chispa de Cienmaricones is in town.'

'Chispa de Cienmaricones?' repeated Juan Niño skeptically.

'One of the great old families of the Turia river valley despite, or perhaps because of, their odd name,' was all the explanation the Dominican gave (and all I ever learned about the duke).

'You understand, we have to let the duke light the torch, not you, Admiral,' the Dominican apologized, then brightened. 'But you've been given a choice front-row seat.'

By this time, leaving our horses, carts and Indians in the care of the militiamen, we were approaching the pair of facing platforms. Shaded by the yellow canopy over the smaller one was a rickety structure that held tiers of benches, mostly occupied. The larger one, I could then see, was no platform at all – just stacks of crisscrossed logs and kindling.

What follows isn't pretty but I won't mince words.

When we were ushered to our places on the grandstand I found myself jammed in the first row of benches between a plump young Benedictine with a seraphic smile and a scrawny old Dominican with the haunted eyes of an ascetic or a madman.

Both of them got my name right, which seemed a good beginning.

'You missed the grand parade, Admiral Colón,' said the scrawny old Dominican in his thin, reedy whisper.

'But you're in time for the Act of Faith itself,' said the seraphic Benedictine in his orotund voice. 'Buil's my name, and the good Dominican to your right is, I hardly need tell you, Grand Inquisitor Tomás de Torquemada.'

I turned with interest to my right. So this was Beatriz's famous cousin. 'I'm a good friend of Beatriz Enríquez de Harana,' I told him conversationally.

'Never heard of her,' he said in his reedy whisper.

'She's a cousin of yours.'

'Oh?' he responded indifferently and returned his attention to the fellow on his other side, whom I took to be the Duke of Chispa de Cienmaricones.

Brother Buil explained the program to me, or tried. 'But you see, it isn't actually possible to predict precisely the course of events, because all the condemned who profess repentance on their way to the brazier, that is, the Burning Place over there, will receive a last-minute commutation of sentence. I'm pleased to say that the usual commutation rate is better than ninety per cent.'

'What happens when their sentences are commuted?'

'They aren't burned alive at the stake.'

I nodded. His words made me feel better. In companionable silence we watched the multitude crushing its way into the great plaza.

Brother Buil's face was rosy, and his hands. Even his tonsure was pink. There was an oddly childlike quality about him, as if, going straight into Orders, he'd never needed to grow up. This happens with academics too.

Fourteen living men and eleven women, according to the program, were scheduled to be burned for various heresies. The most common was Judaizing.

'It lists here twenty others "in effigy",' I said.

'Those are heretics who fled. So their likenesses have to be burned. We've no choice,' smiled Brother Buil reasonably. 'Otherwise their property can't be legally confiscated.'

'This,' I said, glancing at the program again, 'has to be a misprint. It says not only twenty-five of the quick but twenty-five of the dead are to be burned at the stake.'

'That always confuses our foreign guests,' said Brother Buil with his unfailing good cheer. 'But dead heretics have to be burned too, don't they? Otherwise their property can't be legally confiscated.'

'How do they burn a dead heretic?' I said.

'Same way they burn a live one.'

'But what if they've been dead for, uh, some time?'

'That's often the case. Same way. You'll see.'

I saw.

But first came a procession of gorgeously robed officials of the local

253

Tribunal of the Supreme and General Council of the Inquisition, the Suprema for short, followed by the town dignitaries.

'Oh, *that* Beatriz Enríquez de Harana,' said Tomás de Torquemada suddenly, as he rose to take the salute of the procession.

I smiled hopefully.

'Fornicator, isn't she?' And, expecting no answer, he turned his ascetic or mad eyes back to the marchers.

Before us now came several score penitents, men and women alike bare from the waist up except for placards identifying their minor heresies.

'The shaming does them spiritual good,' said Brother Buil. 'Also it deadens their pain centers, I'm told, so that when they are whipped they scarcely feel it.'

The whipping, which drew much blood, was carried out between the grandstand and the Burning Place. As there were so many penitents and only one whipping post it took considerable time. Screams were plentiful, particularly from those still waiting. Two-thirds of the women and perhaps half the men collapsed before the prescribed number of strokes. Their whipping continued.

'They don't feel it at all now, you see,' said Brother Buil with his seraphic smile.

A third of the way through the whipping I was squirming uneasily on the bench. Brother Buil misunderstood this for mere physical discomfort. He laughed. 'We'll spend most of the day here. Sometimes a padded posterior like mine is a help,' he said.

After several hours the whipped were carried away, leaving a trail of blood, and a dais replaced the whipping post. A priest began a sermon. This was drowned out almost immediately by the roars of the crowd, for the first of those condemned to the flames were then carried into the plaza. These turned out to be the lifesize pasteboard likenesses of heretics who had fled the country. I can't comment personally on their accuracy, but as each was paraded in, the hometown crowd would chant a name. The effigies wore the garb of the condemned, the tall yellow miter and the yellow robes emblazoned with red lightning bolt and stylized pitchfork-carrying Devil.

'It took us a while to settle on that particular design,' said Brother Buil. 'To be quite candid, I find the Devil a bit vulgar, but it does appeal to the masses.'

These words were shouted in close proximity to my ear, for the crowd was roaring again.

The second group of condemned were now entering the plaza.

These came on mule-drawn carts in boxes like upright coffins, and they stank. Flies swarmed around them. They too wore the yellow miter on their mouldering heads, and yellow robes covered their partially worm-consumed bodies. Their eye sockets stared at us and the rictus of their frozen smiles was greeted by an occasional outburst of obscene laughter, but at the closer approach of the corpses the crowd in general quieted down and a few words of the sermon could be heard.

' ... burn in everlasting Hell for their profanation. To embrace the Holy Faith publicly while yet secretly practicing another...'

The dead were removed from their upright coffins and, like the pasteboard figures before them, tied to posts set among the kindling and logs opposite the grandstand.

'Most of these are New Christian Judaizers,' explained Brother Buil.

'Is it a common heresy among the dead?'

'Top on the list every time. Some believe our real mistake was allowing them or their fathers or grandfathers or whoever to convert in the first place. Did you say "among the dead"?'

I seemed to remember saying it.

'I seem to remember saying it,' I said.

'Certain types of humor,' said Brother Buil with his seraphic smile, 'are discouraged here.'

Just then a faint breeze blew from the direction of the Burning Place and the stink of the heretics was wafted in our direction.

Tomás de Torquemada squared his scrawny shoulders and expanded his pigeon chest, filling his lungs with the smell. He shut his eyes and sighed.

Brother Buil dabbed at his nose with a scented handkerchief. 'Sandalwood,' he told me, 'works best.'

' ... for if any among you know of persons who wash their hands before praying, or bathe Friday evenings or too frequently, or bless their children without making the sign of the cross...' continued the sermon.

The living condemned were now entering the plaza.

' ... or have said or done anything against the Holy Catholic Church, or prepare on Friday in stewing pots over small fires the food for Saturday, or who place fresh napkins on the table Friday nights or clean linen on the beds, or who deny the divinity of Our Lord Jesus Christ and call Him a false Messiah, or eat no pork or snails or rabbits or fish without scales, or whose dead die with their faces turned to the wall and are washed before burial...'

The living condemned had crossed half the distance to the Burning Place, each man and woman accompanied by a pair of confessors to encourage the last-minute abjuration, Brother Buil explained, that could save them from being burned alive at the stake.

' ... who in their houses of mourning eat nothing but fish and hard-boiled eggs at low tables, who deny the resurrection and ascension to Heaven of the Son of God, or profess that life is only that brief period between birth and death, denying hope of Heaven and horror of Hell, who name their children on the seventh night after their birth whether with Old or New Testament names, and circumcise the males among them, or anyone, man or woman, who has taken possession of any confiscated money, furniture, gold, silver, pearls and other precious stones, or who at that mockery of Our Lord's Passion called Passover eats unleavened bread, celery and bitter herbs – I say, if there are any among you who know persons guilty of these or countless other heresies including but not limited to fornication, witchcraft, bigamy, saying Mass or hearing confession without being a priest, disturbing and interfering with the righteous and free functioning of the Supreme and General Council of the Inquisition, etc., etc. – if there are those among you with knowledge of such heretics who do not yourselves come forward you shall be excommunicated, anathematized, segregated and led, after suitable delay for the giving of torture and the taking of testimony, to the Place of Burning...'

'Oh look, Heavens, yes, this will be one of our more successful days,' crowed the beaming Brother Buil. 'Observe that they are now being separated into two groups.'

By 'they' he meant the twenty-five living condemned. But 'two groups' was misleading. There was now a group of twenty-three ringed by their confessors, and just two individualists, one young man and one very old woman, who stood apart.

'Marvelous!' cried Brother Buil. 'Twenty-three of the condemned have abjured their heresies and won't be burned alive at the stake.'

I felt sorry for the young man and the old woman, but it was comforting to know that twenty-three of the condemned would be spared.

Thus I could watch the activity instead of surreptitiously avoiding it by pretending an inordinate interest in my program, as a few seated on the grandstand were doing. And there was plenty of it. Activity, I mean. For one thing, the sermon had ended and stagehands dragged away the dais. In its place they erected what I took to be another whipping post. Indeed, a burly fellow who might have been a flogger took his place next to it. The young man and very old woman who had not abjured their heresies were led, meanwhile, to the Burning Place and tied to two of its many stakes, their confessors remaining on hand in case of any last-minute change in the program.

Those whose sentences would be commuted lined up.

Brother Buil cautiously removed the sandalwood-drenched handkerchief from his nose. 'Better,' he said. 'Ever so much better. The wind has shifted.'

The crowd screamed in a frenzy, possibly religious, as the new flogger withdrew from the folds of his robe not the hempen rope I had expected but a length of wire attached to two short handles.

'That looks like a garotte,' I said.

'That,' smiled pink, boyish Brother Buil, 'is because it *is* a garotte.'

The first whose sentence would be commuted was now made fast to the post. The burly man with the garotte took a stance behind her.

I was definitely getting bad vibrations.

'You said their sentences would be commuted.'

'They already have been, my friend. Those who have abjured will not be burned alive at the stake.'

The woman tied to the post suddenly jerked as the garotte was looped around her throat. The handles were crossed at the back of the post, and the executioner took a twist in the wire, a second, a third. With each the woman twitched convulsively, her eyes bulging, her tongue protruding. A man I took to be a physician trotted up, listened intently at the breast of the woman's yellow robe, and nodded. Her body was cut down and hustled by two stagehands to the Burning Place where she was bound again, this time to a stake for burning, the most recently dead among the many long-dead and the two living.

'They will,' explained Brother Buil earnestly as a second abjurer was made fast to the garotting post, 'be burned *dead* at the stake.'

Some of the abjurers were slow to die and the afternoon wore on. Through it all the two living condemned stared stonily ahead from their stakes. Their patient, loyal confessors remained nearby, sweating in their heavy robes in the sun.

A dozen abjurers were garotted by five in the afternoon.

It was the thirteenth that caused all the trouble.

This was a girl in her early teens, a pretty little thing with reddish blonde hair. I checked the program. She was one Susanna Olivares, fourteen, daughter of Julio Olivares, deceased, of the Parish of Nuestra Señora de los Desamparados. She had been, the program explained, 'pardoned twice before for the sin of blasphemy, and is again guilty of that sin.'

'Why, of course,' said Brother Buil while the girl was bound to the post. 'It's the Olivares child come back. I remember her case. She blasphemed against the priest who heard her late father's confession and, as was his duty, informed the authorities that the man was a Judaizer. How happy it makes me to see she has abjured!'

When the wire snaked around Susanna Olivares's neck, her sagging body jerked bolt upright. Off to one side, the two confessors who had accompanied her into the plaza could be seen arguing, one shaking his fist, the other looking skyward as if calling on Heaven for help. The fist-shaker must have prevailed, for he ran over to the garotter and spoke excitedly. By this time the garotter was taking a second turn with the handles. Three were usually sufficient to kill, but one skinny grandmotherly type had needed six. The executioner, with a look of disgust, withdrew the garotte from around Susanna Olivares's neck. She slumped against her ropes again. Two stagehands unbound her and laid her limp body on the ground, where the physician listened at her breast. He nodded and held a phial under her nose. Her eyelids fluttered. The crowd roared like surf breaking on a rockbound coast.

'Thank God they got her down in time,' I said.

Brother Buil gave me an odd, speculative look. 'Are you then so unforgiving?'

'Me? Why no, I just – '

'It seems,' Brother Buil said with no smile, 'that Susanna Olivares failed to abjure satisfactorily and will be burned alive at the stake after all.'

The girl was now on her feet, supported on either side by stagehands. Again the surf broke.

'Fourteen,' muttered Tomás de Torquemada, 'is too young to be burned dead.'

This observation, I had to assume, contained some philosophical nuance I had yet to grasp.

Teenaged Susanna Olivares, with help from the stagehands, mounted the Burning Place. They began roping her to a stake. This was never done by clerics. The condemned were, in the euphemism then in vogue, 'relaxed' over to the secular authorities, who carried out all sentences. Clerics don't kill.

A familiar voice a few tiers behind us shouted: 'Stop!'

'Well now,' said Tomás de Torquemada.

'Stop! You've g-got to stop!' shouted the familiar voice.

'Caught one,' said Torquemada.

He almost smiled.

The voice cried: 'The p-poor girl's tasted one d-death already. Are you g-going to make her die twice?'

The voice, the slight, charming stammer, belonged to our Billy Budd prototype, Francisco Niño.

'It always works. Every time,' said Tomás de Torquemada. He added, 'It never fails.'

I looked at him.

'To expose a closet heretic,' he explained. 'Especially if the victim, or rather culprit, is young and not unattractive.'

A dozen Holy Brotherhood militiamen came swarming onto the grandstand. I saw Peralonso Niño, seated beyond Brother Buil, getting to his feet. I began to rise too. There was a commotion above us, scuffling, a drumming of feet, a thud.

The whole rickety structure began to shake.

People screamed.

The canopy came down first, enclosing us all in a world of blinding yellow. Then the tiers of benches, spectators and all, collapsed.

In the confusion attendant on the cutting away of the heavy yellow canopy, Francisco Niño and the Holy Brotherhood militiamen disappeared.

The burning itself was delayed until sunset, when after a colorful ceremony the Duke of Chispa de Cienmaricones ignited the faggots with the torch of honor.

Earlier fifteen assorted broken bones including one fractured skull (prognosis: negative) had to be treated, and an area of the plaza cleared and roped off for the special guests of the Suprema, who now had to stand like everyone else. Then of course the garotting of the final ten, delayed by the collapse of the grandstand and these ancillary activities, had to be resumed.

The flames from the Burning Place competed with the beauty of the sunset, while the reliable surfsound of the crowd almost drowned out the screams of the very old woman, who proved to have a surprisingly penetrating voice.

'Look at those flames,' said Brother Buil, doing so himself with a professional eye and a smile.

There was no denying that the fire was exceptional.

Shortly after dusk the Burning Place, quick, dead, effigy heretics and all, fell into smoldering ashes.

'Which,' said Brother Buil, 'will be spread impartially over land and sea.'

As soon as decency permitted after the ceremonies were concluded, I asked him about Francisco Niño.

'Oh dear, was he a member of your party?'

'One of the three Niño brothers from Moguer who played such a crucial role in crossing the Ocean Sea and discovering the Indies for the Greater Glory of God, that's who,' I enlightened him.

'Oh, bad luck,' he replied. 'You see, it's considered rather a serious heresy to disturb and interfere with the righteous and free functioning of the Supreme and General Council of the Inquisition. Some consider it the most serious heresy of all.'

'I, to name one,' said Tomás de Torquemada in his reedy whisper.

'Life,' said Brother Buil with a sad smile, 'is full of these little unforeseen developments.'

Peralonso's face struggled for a reasonable expression but looked ferocious as ever when he asked in his gentle voice, 'Will he be tortured?'

'I don't like your attitude,' said Tomás de Torquemada.

In short, we could look for no help from the Grand Inquisitor. I did not think it politic, after his initial reaction to the subject, to mention the Beatriz connection again.

'What'll we do?' Peralonso asked me.

His brother Juan came over. 'I'm as anti-heretical as the next guy, but that's my baby brother they've got in a dungeon somewhere.'

I assured them we'd set out for Barcelona that very night and ask the King and Queen to intercede.

With those words I made an enemy for life of the Supreme and General Council of the Inquisition.

ᏋᏋ XI ᏋᏋ

How I Mediate a Dispute Between
the Pope and Their Most Catholic Majesties
But Fare More Ambiguously
In My First Fateful Encounter
With the Lovely Petenera

'No,' said the Queen. 'Absolutely not.'

I had just told her of poor Francisco Niño's plight.

'We never,' she elaborated, 'intercede with the Suprema. In their own field they are ... supreme.'

I persisted, explaining Francisco Niño's considerable contribution to our understanding of Indian ways.

Fernando leaned forward on his throne, dark eyes agleam. 'Well, did he have his way with the cacique's brother's beautiful young wife or didn't he?'

I had been circumspect in the telling.

'That,' sniffed the Queen, 'is hardly the issue here.'

I looked in vain for the Isabel I had known in Granada in a brief and intimate dream. In memory I saw torchlight shadows moving like half-hidden watchers among the arabesques in the room where once blind musicians had played for the sultan. Snatches of half-recalled dialogue mocked me. *It is not with your eyes that you see, Don Cristóbal ... it is far better just to dream ...* I recalled how her face had glowed with the radiance of victory (or was it passion?), how her beautiful red hair shimmered, falling free to her waist, how she reached out a hand to me.

That lovely royal lady was no more. In her place sat a starched, somewhat prissy middle-aged woman.

Such a drastic change was inconceivable – and inevitable. In Granada I had seen this zealous monarch incandescent with victory. Now the Holy War that had consumed her passionate nature was won. With no Infidel Arab to conquer she was bereft of external enemies. Wasn't it perfectly consistent, if lamentable, for her next to expel the hapless Jews? And then to turn her pent-up energies against heresy in an internal crusade, the theological equivalent of war – in a word, the Inquisition?

I mean neither to excuse her, nor to condemn. Only my interest in 'psychology, motivation and all that' has led me to these observations.

None of which was going to help Francisco Niño. But it did signal a reversal of roles between King and Queen. Where before I could count on Isabel to champion me, I sensed that Fernando was more my natural ally now. There he was, on the edge of his throne, regal toes touching the dais as he asked me, 'Are they any ... different?'

'Who, Sire?'

'The Indian maidens. Did you find them very different in your, um, social intercourse with them?'

History will tell you what a womanizer King Fernando was.

The Queen glared.

Just then there was a commotion in the antechamber. A door slammed. Voices rose in anger.

'Who are those ruffians in the antechamber?' the Queen demanded.

I seized my chance. 'Those are two – ' I held the number an extra sad beat ' – of the three Niño brothers of Moguer who played such a crucial role in crossing the Ocean Sea and discovering the Indies for the Greater Glory of God, My Lady.'

'We will henceforth,' replied the Queen, 'discuss your voyage without reference to the Moguer brothers of Niño.'

'The Niño brothers of Moguer, My Lady.'

The Queen's eyes blazed regal anger but the King wisely moved the conversation in another direction. 'When you vanished from sight for several weeks in Portugal, did that royal nincompoop John try to seduce you into his service?'

'That, Sire, is putting it mildly,' I said, seizing my second chance and making a better job of it.

As our hypothetical newsmagazine might have put it:

In the end, the Monarchs' hands were probably forced by, more than anything else, the fear that King John in Lisbon would yet persuade the Admiral to sail under Portuguese colors on his next expedition...

Colón's specific demands, palace sources say, can apparently be accommodated if the resulting compromise is couched in terms that give the Grand Inquisitor a face-saving reason to accept them...

An hour and a half later, we arrived at such a reason.

'We can tell the Grand Inquisitor,' said King Fernando, 'that while we recognize the guilt of this Francisco Moguer, he in turn must recognize the crucial role of the Moguer brothers of Niño, the *three* Moguer brothers of Niño, in crossing the Ocean Sea and discovering the Indies for the Greater Glory of God.'

'But only on condition', said Queen Isabel, 'that the primary purpose of your second expedition – '

'Primary after finding gold, of course,' interjected King Fernando.

' – is the baptism of the heathen Indians,' she continued. 'For believe you us, we know Tomás de Torquemada.'

I believed them – or, that is, her. The Queen, in keeping with her peripatetic lifestyle, had run through a score of confessors, ranging from humanist Fray Juan Pérez to pedant Hernando de Talavera to ascetic- or mad-eyed Torquemada.

'You must understand,' said the Queen, 'how eager Brother Tomás is to convert the Indians – because how can he examine them for heresy unless they become good Christians first?'

My heart plummeted. Must I also understand that Torquemada would return with me to the Indies?

'This youngest Moguer brother of Niño,' said the King, 'in recognition of his outstanding contribution to our understanding of the Indian way of life – '

'Said contribution facilitating their conversion to the Holy Faith,' amplified the Queen.

' – will have his sentence commuted.'

'Sire, did you say "commuted"?'

We agreed on a royal pardon.

'Brother Buil will be happy,' said the King.

'He'll smile,' said the Queen.

This seemed a safe bet. Brother Buil was always smiling.

The Queen went on: 'He'd have so hated to take up his new duties in an atmosphere of ill feeling.'

'When he sails with you as Chief Missionary, he'll have a clear conscience, an easy heart and an open mind,' the King assured me.

Then the Queen, leaning forward to reveal a tantalizing glimpse of royal cleavage, abruptly changed her demeanor and the subject. 'That is,' she said in a confidential voice, 'provided you ever sail at all.'

'Trouble, My Lady?' I guessed.

'We are experiencing,' said the King, 'some difficulty with the new Pope.'

'I didn't even know there *was* a new Pope.'

'Poor old Innocent died shortly after you sailed on your Great Venture,' said the Queen. 'They say the new Pope, who was still a cardinal then, of course, engaged in a fight, actual fisticuffs, with Cardinal della Rovere alongside poor old Innocent's deathbed. Can you imagine! Fighting for the Papal throne – or in this case, I suppose, bed – before Innocent had even breathed his last?'

'Typical of a new Pope,' said the King, 'who won't grant us in the Indies the very rights that that otherwise fine man Innocent so readily granted John of Portugal in West Africa – namely, a monopoly on colonies, gold and so forth.'

'It was that otherwise saintly Pope Sixtus, Innocent's predecessor, who granted King John the African monopoly, dear,' corrected the Queen.

'Whoever. This new fellow refuses to give us a *quid pro quo*.'

'That isn't quite what a *quid pro quo* means, dear,' corrected the Queen.

'Whatever. The ungrateful fellow won't give us it.'

I couldn't help contrasting their royal behavior with the cacique Guacanagarí's. But perhaps he wasn't married.

'Let's face it,' said the King, 'now that he's Pope, he considers himself more Roman than Spanish.'

My ears perked up. 'He's Spanish?'

They were too busy bickering to pay any attention to me. 'Now be fair – he did organize a genuine Spanish bullfight in Rome when he heard we'd conquered Granada. That showed class,' said the Queen.

'He was only a cardinal then. Being Pope's turned his head.'

I tried again. 'Did you say this new Pope's a Spaniard, Sire?'

'Yes, yes, Alexander VI's a Spaniard by birth,' said the King impatiently.

'He wouldn't happen,' I crowed, 'to be the former Cardinal Borgia?'

'None other,' sighed the Queen.

'We used to know each other.'

'Oh?' responded the King without really listening.

'In fact, I was his protégé for years.'

'Really?' said the Queen.

Neither of them seemed terribly interested.

'He once saved my life.'

'Oh?' and 'Really?' were repeated with more vigor.

'And *I* once saved *his* life.' Smug but cool.

They conferred in eager whispers.

An upholstered bench was sent for and placed on the dais in front of the twin thrones.

'Come sit by us, Admiral,' said the Queen, plumping the upholstery.

'You may wear your hat, Viceroy,' said the King. This was an even more signal honor than being seated in their presence.

Please note, my biographers to the contrary, that I wasn't invited to sit, head casually covered like a Grandee of Spain, merely because I'd made that round trip across the Ocean Sea.

My old friendship with the new Pope is one of those happy coincidences that abound in history. Which is just another way of saying that the old-boy network pretty much makes history happen, give or take a few factors like climate, mineral resources, natural catastrophes, population explosions, famines and wars. A simple exchange of informal letters between Roderigo Borgia and me would get the royals exactly what they wanted, a virtual Ocean Sea monopoly. Not until the next century would Papal geopolitical clout and Spain's New World dominance go down the tube together, thanks to Martin Luther with his ninety-five theses and Henry the Eighth with his six wives.

My letter was dispatched, but a Papal reply would take at least two weeks and I became restless.

One morning not long after my essay into diplomacy, I remembered that in my haste to reach Barcelona after that regrettable Auto-de-Fé, I'd passed through Tarragona without delivering Luís Torres's letter to his parents. There was time to do so now, it being an easy two-day ride.

To glance at our hypothetical newsmagazine one last time:

The measure of the man is that he left in the midst of these delicate negotiations, just when the monarchs had zeroed in on the issues and themes they would stress to the Vatican, in order to keep a promise made to a shipmate on the other side of the Ocean Sea...

I stabled my horse at Miracle Beach Inn outside the walls and, after a fair night's sleep (Tarragona is neither exempt from, nor noteworthy for, its bedbugs), entered the city on foot, passing through the gate near the ruins of the Roman arena and marveling at the Cyclopean stone blocks that made up the ancient walls.

The shell of the house stood on Augusta Street. It had been stripped of doors, shutters, windows, chimneys, roof tiles. Even the little privy at the back had been broken into. Two brawny men bare to the waist and sweating in the warm sunshine came through the gaping front doorway carrying a large credence chest. The usual THESE PREMISES SEQUESTERED BY ORDER OF THE SUPREMA sign had been pasted to one side of the doorway. The usual curious crowd looked on.

'Is this the Torres house?'

'Was,' said one of the men carrying the credence chest.

'Used to be,' said the other.

They set the chest carefully in a large, two-mule wagon already heaped with furniture.

'You wouldn't happen to know where they went?'

'We just have the Suprema's moving concession, pal,' said one.

'Which we'd like to keep,' said the other.

'So our interest in heresy is nil,' explained the first.

They went inside, and I followed. Soon they were banging their way out of what had been the dining room with an oak refectory table that could have seated ten on a side.

I heard the mule cart driving off and the crowd dispersing – and, from a nearby room, a clinking sound which I could not identify. There followed a tentative scraping, more clinking, then persistent scraping.

She was crouched with her back to the doorway, just putting a knife down near a pile of mortar. With both hands she lifted a floor tile and placed it beside the knife. A sound of triumph escaped her lips and she stood. She wore black to her ankles, and a black shawl covered her head. I approached to see what treasure she had found.

She whirled.

'Who the hell are you? What do you want here?'

In a dust-moted shaft of sunlight streaming through the hole in the wall that had been a window I could see the dull silver gleam of the tarnished seven-branched candelabra in her hand.

I couldn't speak, not at once, and it wasn't the illegal menorah that struck me dumb.

Her hair escaping from the shawl was dark and lustrous, like the darkest black on the underside of a raven's wing. Her eyes, flashing anger now, were the emerald green of a deep coral-girt Indies lagoon when the water is unruffled by wind and the sun directly overhead. Her lips were the precise off-carmine color of an exotic blossom highly prized by the Arawaks that only grows, I would learn, in the highlands between the sea and Cibao.

I finally said, 'Don't be alarmed. I'm a friend of Luís Torres.'

Her answering smile revealed teeth as white as the pearls I would find some years later at the pearl fisheries of Paria on the coast of South America, a place I named Earthly Paradise, possibly in unconscious memory of that smile.

'You're a friend of Luís? Really? Do you know where he is? Did he get away all right?'

Her voice, no longer angry, was silver, gold and precious stones.

In short, I looked at her and heard her speak, and I fell in love.

'That can get you into trouble, that thing you've got there,' I said.

'Mind your own business,' she said coldly.

'Tell me about Luís,' she said warmly.

'He gave me a letter for his parents.'

'They're dead.'

This was said matter-of-factly, as if they had died a long time ago. But Luís had thought them still alive.

'I'm sorry,' I said. 'I didn't know.'

'Did you know them?'

'No.'

'Then why say you're sorry? Nobody asked for your sympathy.'

'It's Luís I'm sorry for,' I said. 'He thinks they're still alive.'

'Of course he does. They weren't burned dead at the stake until last week in Valencia.'

'Valencia? I was there,' I blurted.

'Were you then? Tell me, how is it that normal people – at least you *look* normal – can actually get pleasure from seeing other people flogged and strangled and – '

'Me?' I said. 'I was only there as a guest of the Suprema.'

Her eyes looked like emerald-green glacial ice then. 'The Suprema's guest? You wouldn't happen to be this Duke of Chispa de Cienmaricones who lighted the fire that burned my parents and my grandmother and my little cousin?'

267

'God, no,' I said. 'I wasn't that kind of guest.'

'What other kind is there?'

'I was just passing through on my triumphal tour of Spain on my way to a royal audience in Barcelona and the Suprema invited me to sit on the grandstand that collapsed – '

'Are you this Colomb, then?'

'That's Colón, actually – l, o-accent, n.'

'You wouldn't win any popularity contests in Tarragona these days. They had all sorts of ceremonies planned in your honor but it turned out you passed through town in the middle of the night or something.'

That seemed to amuse her. She almost smiled again.

Then she bit her lip. 'Give me the letter and go. I don't want anyone to see me like this, damn it.'

'Grief's nothing to be ashamed of.'

She stared out the hole that had been a window.

'They're all dead, the whole family except Luís and me. And he's only alive because he had the sense to get out of the country instead of converting. As for me ... how come you're friends anyway? Where did you meet him? Hasn't he left Spain?'

'He left,' I said, and gave her the letter Luís had written on the back of an old chart of the Canary Islands.

Looking at the chart, she said, 'He went to the Canary Islands? They're out in the middle of nowhere on the edge of the Ocean Sea. There'd be no books for Luís there, no one to share his intellectual interests. That's no place for my little brother.'

That she was older than Luís surprised me. But then, he was probably no more than twenty or so. She certainly wasn't much more.

She broke the seal and read. It must have been a short letter. She crumpled it and flung it at me.

'He converted. He's a Marrano like the rest of the family was. You talked him into converting.'

'It was the only way he could come with us.'

'He was going to be a Talmudic scholar. And now you've stranded him on the other side of the Ocean Sea in an intellectual desert. That's the worst thing that can happen to someone with a mind like Luís's. You ... you're worse than the Inquisition!'

After Beatriz's outburst when she learned her cousin Harana and Dr Sánchez had been left behind in Christmas Town, I should have been prepared.

'In a place called Christmas Town!' she scathed.

'He suggested the name himself.'

'That's even worse. You obviously brainwashed him.'

'What's wrong with Christmas Town? I thought you were a New Christian yourself.'

'Would I be standing here if I weren't?'

'He wanted me to tell his parents he was happy,' I tried.

'Then why didn't he say so in the letter? He just said he was doing important work.'

'He's the community's official translator.'

'Oh? Of what?' The information seemed to mollify her.

'Between the colonists and the natives.'

'The natives? From what I've heard, they can't read, can't write, fornicate all the time, eat each other, have no clothes, no culture, no God, not that – '

'We're going to bring them into the Faith. A missionary's coming out on my next voyage, a Brother Buil, to – '

'Buil!' she cried. 'Brother Bernardo Buil?'

I told her I didn't know his Christian name.

'Smiles all the time?'

'That's the fellow,' I agreed.

She had, somewhere in the exchange of dialogue, picked up and smoothed the Canary Island chart on which Luís had written his letter. She now crumpled it into a ball again and threw it at my face.

'And when this Buil goes out to Christmas Town with you to convert the natives, he'll need a translator, I suppose? And Luís will be that translator?'

'Well, yes.'

'And how would *you* like to be translator for the man who sent every member of your family to his death except your sister, and the only reason I'm alive is ... get out of here! Just get out and leave me alone! Go die somewhere!'

Knowing when I wasn't wanted, I went slowly to the gaping front doorway and out. The day was bright, the air balmy. It was a nice neighborhood. I trudged back toward the gate that led out to the ruins of the Roman arena built into the outside of the city walls overlooking Miracle Beach. I scuffed my boots in the dust. I shut my eyes and saw her face. I opened them and still saw it, superimposed on reality and twice as real. I could still hear her voice, angry, accusatory. I didn't even know her name. I turned away from the city gate, then back, then away again. Such indecision wasn't like me, not since I'd become a legend in my own lifetime. But that's the point. Right now I wasn't. Right now I was living in time stolen from that legend and I was only a man like other men and newly, recklessly in love.

I ran back to Augusta Street. The empty house was quiet. She wasn't in any of the ground-floor rooms. I went upstairs. Nothing in the wide hall, nothing in the first two rooms. I tried a third. The large drawstring bag containing the menorah was on the bare floor. At first I didn't see her. She was kneeling at the hearth, leaning in. I heard a tapping sound, then the scrape of brick against brick. She backed, still on her knees, out of the hearth. She rose.

'I don't even know your name,' I said.

She dropped a little pouch and let out a little sound of fright. She dove for the floor. I could hear little objects rolling across the tiles. Notice my repetition of the word 'little'; it's no accident. All of this seemed somehow trivial compared with the fact that I was seeing her again.

I joined her on the floor to help find the little rolling objects. I found three of them – three large and perfectly matched pearls.

Words came to me from the Inquisition sermon in Valencia: *Anyone, man or woman, who has taken possession of any confiscated money, furniture, gold, silver, pearls or other precious stones...*

First the menorah, not only silver but illegal, and now these pearls.

'Give them to me!' she cried.

As part of a distraught and rather confused sentence I said the words 'sequestered,' 'confiscated' and 'heresy.' But I gave her the pearls. We got up together. 'You're inviting the same trouble that sent your family to the Burning Place,' I warned her, and it sounded callous and uncaring, quite the opposite of what I intended. My eyes were suddenly stinging. She had hit me in the face as hard as she could, and was ready to swing both hands again. I grabbed her wrists and we struggled, breast to breast. She was tall for a woman, and lithe, and by no means weak. The knife she'd used to pry the downstairs tile loose (and, I assumed, the brick from the fireplace here) appeared in her left hand. She's probably left-handed, I found myself thinking idiotically; I'd never known a left-handed woman before. We fought for possession of the knife. This echoed something from the distant past, but I couldn't remember what. I wrenched the knife from her and let it clatter to the floor, but I was still holding her. Our faces came close, mine above hers. Our lips touched. Hers were nectar, honey and ambrosia. She stiffened in my arms an instant, then her arms slid around my neck and her mouth opened under my insistent kiss – or did I imagine that? I couldn't be sure because a man's voice called:

'Petenera? Are you in here?'

Perhaps her mouth just opened in surprise.

Mine did. 'Your name's Petenera?'

But what else could it have been?

'Hurry,' she said, thrusting the small pouch into the large drawstring bag. 'Take these to Luís de Santangel in Barcelona. He's Keeper – '

'I know who he is.'

'Petenera?' called the man's voice. 'You upstairs?'

'The back way, along the hall and down,' she whispered. 'Santangel, Barcelona. Can I trust you?'

'Always.'

'I still hate you for what you did to my brother. I would have killed you if I'd been able. You know that?'

'Then why trust me with – '

'Luís wrote that you are a man of honor. Go now, quickly.'

'Petenera,' I said.

'What?'

'I just wanted to say it.'

'I'll hate you as long as I live.'

I went. The drawstring bag was heavy.

Luís de Santangel, in his private office in the wing of the Royal Palace, formerly the Palace of the Counts of Barcelona, reserved for the Keeper of the Royal Household Budget, stood at a table carefully rolling lengths of tobacco leaf into a cylinder. He licked the wrapper-leaf and said:

'I don't see why this shouldn't work.'

Gray-haired and obese, but still with the undeniable presence of a man of power, Luís de Santangel studied his invention. 'It look right to you?'

The fleshy, sensuous Santangel lips were at the moment chomping no invisible cigar. The dark Santangel eyes gleamed with anticipation as he sensed his invisible-cigar days were over.

'I only saw them once or twice,' I said.

'The nose, eh? Took it in through the nose, did they?'

'As I remember, yes.'

'Savages. Seems wrong to me somehow.'

The afternoon was bright but he had lit a candle. First biting one end delicately off the cylinder of tobacco, he held the other end above the candle flame. He rolled the cylinder, scowling, then held the bitten-off end to his nose, scowled some more, took it between his lips and breathed in. The opposite end of the tobacco cylinder began to glow. A smile built with sybaritic slowness on Luís de Santangel's round, many-chinned face. He exhaled smoke through his nostrils.

'Your Indian friends had it backwards, kid.' He breathed tobacco smoke in through his mouth again and sighed with contentment.

'What can you tell me about Petenera Torres?' I asked.

Luís de Santangel coughed. Smoke issued in a great cloud from his mouth and jetted from his nose. He coughed again and pounded his chest, spewing more smoke. He put the tobacco cylinder on the wide flange of the candlestick and went to the room's six windows, closing each in turn. Then he went to the door and bolted that. Then he unbolted and opened it to peer both ways outside before he shut and bolted it again. Then he returned to each window in turn, opened it, drew the shutters, hooked them and closed the windows again. He returned swiftly, despite his girth, to the door to make certain it was locked. By then the room was dark and he used the one lit candle to light half a dozen others. His tobacco cylinder had gone out. He rolled it again with thoughtful deliberation above the candle flame.

He turned to me, smoke issuing from his nostrils as he worried the cylinder of tobacco between his lips.

'Petenera Torres?' he said nonchalantly. 'I've heard the name. Why?'

I told him about our meeting while he smoked the first cigar ever smoked in Spain or anywhere in Europe.

'I see,' he said. 'And you have the ... items she took from the sequestered Torres property?'

I showed him the menorah, the pouch of pearls and the half dozen other pouches crammed with gold ducats I'd also found in the bag.

'You never saw these,' he cautioned me.

'No. I understand.'

But I didn't. What was Santangel's involvement with her?

'She's quite a girl, isn't she?' he said.

'If,' I said indifferently, 'you like hair as dark as the darkest black on the underside of a raven's wing and eyes the emerald green of a deep coral-girt lagoon on a windless day with the sun directly overhead, and lips like – '

'You better come back and see me tomorrow morning,' Luís de Santangel said firmly.

'Will she be all right? I mean, who was that fellow – '

'Tomorrow morning, my friend.'

That night Luís de Santangel (as he later told me) called an emergency meeting of his Movers and Shakers, the most influential New Christians at the Peripatetic Royal Court.

'The Admiral of the Ocean Sea,' he told them, 'is in love with our Blue Pimpernel.'

'What?' they cried. 'How can this be?'

Perhaps you're asking the same question. A Blue Pimpernel, in late fifteenth-century Spain? But wasn't the Pimpernel scarlet, and didn't he (it was a he, wasn't it?) rescue eighteenth-century noblemen from the French Revolution – at least according to the 1905 Baroness Orczy novel? This later usage of the Pimpernel has to be more than coincidence. All I can conclude is that the secret network at whose head stood that reckless beauty Petenera Torres was not entirely forgotten through the centuries, and that the bestselling baroness recognized a good subject when she saw it. She simply changed the Blue Pimpernel to Scarlet. Fair enough. For that matter, some pimpernels have white blossoms. Anyway, that was all after my time though before yours. But your before is frequently my after, and we shouldn't let it cause confusion.

Santangel told them how it could be.

The most cold-blooded Mover or Shaker suggested my premature demise. He was also, fortunately, the dumbest, and was immediately hooted down. All of them started talking at once.

'Shut up and let me figure this out,' said Luís de Santangel.

As usual, they shut up and let him figure it out.

'Sooner or later we intended bringing this Admiral of the Ocean Sea in on our plans, right?' he said.

'Chinillo's right,' they all agreed, using his original family name as they always did in their secret meetings.

'Actually, he's a pretty nice fellow,' said Santangel. 'And when it comes to religion, not to worry. He's all mixed up.'

'How can this be?' they asked, their rhetorical device for letting Santangel know they were listening.

'He didn't even know he was a New Christian until last year.'

'He grew up thinking he was an Old Christian?'

'Yes.'

'Then we can never trust him,' several of them said.

'You're wrong and I'll tell you why,' he said. 'It's not just that he's in love with the Blue Pimpernel. More important – and this you don't know – he was raised in the household of our churchly compatriot R. Borgia, now His Holiness Alexander VI.'

'Like I said,' suggested the dumb one, 'demise him prematurely.'

Again he was hooted down so the others could all ask: 'How can this be?'

'Pope or not, Borgia is a free-thinker, as you all know. So when it comes to religion the Admiral will probably remain all mixed up for the rest of his life. Besides, I have ways of getting him inextricably involved in our little project without bothering him with the details.'

'How much will you tell him?'

'For now? Only what I have to.'

'Chinillo's absolutely right,' they said, their usual formula to move adjournment of a meeting.

When I saw him the next day, Santangel was lighting a new cigar, more tapered, more slimly elegant.

'Listen, kid,' he said, 'remember when I got the royals to give you ten per cent of the profits from all gold and spicery found in the Indies? Well, they're so appreciative of your accomplishments to date, I think I can get them to up that to twelve and a half per cent. How's that for looking after your interests?'

I told him that ten per cent was a munificent figure, and it would never have entered my mind to ask for a raise.

'Good. In that case, you won't mind if the additional two and a half per cent goes into a fund for needy adventurers, will you?'

'Needy adventurers?' I repeated.

'Well, the fund is mainly used to find them before they're *too* needy. As I hardly have to tell you – ' a delicate but unmistakable emphasis here on the second-person pronoun ' – there have been *old* New Christians in Spain for several generations now and there are *new* New Christians, some of them baptized just before the exodus last year. And, while some families adjust splendidly to the Faith, others, even old New Christians, occasionally produce ... misfits. We try to ferret out these trouble-prone young hotheads before they fall afoul of the Inquisition.'

'We? Who's "we"?' I asked in an almost-Harana voice.

'Petenera Torres is one of the driving forces behind the network. You could even say she's its leader.'

'Where is she?' I cried. 'How can I find her? Who was that fellow who – '

'She doesn't want to see you,' Santangel said sadly, and puffed on his cigar. (I might say in retrospect that the only way he knew this was because I told him, but at the time I wasn't thinking straight.)

'She doesn't?'

'Sorry. How can you expect her to forget you were a guest of the

274

Suprema when her whole family except Luís and herself was burned dead *and* alive at the stake?'

'Alive? Oh, God. You mean that little old lady and the young man who – '

'Worse. Didn't you read the program?'

I admitted I'd no more than glanced at it a few times.

He found one in a stack on his desk. 'Here, right here on this page. The old woman burned alive at the stake was Petenera Torres, the grandmother whose namesake she is. And the teenaged girl partially garotted and then revived to be burned alive was her cousin, Susanna Olivares. Was that not your own dear mother's name, Susanna?'

His cigar smoke made my eyes water. 'Why were they all killed?'

'Who knows? Bathed too often, wouldn't eat pigs, swayed when they prayed, planned on turning their faces to the wall when they died. There are dozens of reasons but they generally boil down to this: informers receive a bounty, a percentage of the confiscated property of Judaizers – and the Torres family was far from poor. The Suprema itself is rich beyond the dreams of mere kings. Why, even though I'm one of the two or three richest men in Spain, compared to Tomás de Torquemada I'm a pauper.'

He had more to say about his needy adventurers, but I hardly required persuasion. If Petenera championed the cause, could I do less?

'How do you find them?' I asked.

'Hotheads get talked about. We hear. So does the Suprema. It's a matter of who hears first.'

'And when you do?'

'We try to find a wholesome outlet for their excess energies. I'll bet,' said Luís de Santangel through a cloud of blue cigar smoke, 'you've been besieged by volunteers clamoring to return with you to the Indies?'

I admitted that was so.

'So prepare to be besieged by a few more. We'll let you know who they are.' He stood. 'We can count on you then?'

When I nodded, he thumped me on the back and showed me to the door. A man-to-man embrace, and I was outside.

It wasn't until later that I realized he hadn't answered a single one of my questions about Petenera.

Yego Clone's big day came on a Sunday morning early in June a few weeks before we were to start south for our return voyage to the Indies.

He was resplendent in a gleaming white satin jerkin decorated at cuffs and V-neck with the fine gold and black embroidery known as Spanish blackwork. His doublet and tights were white Italian silk, and he wore gold-embroidered white kid shoes. His codpiece was a seemly, subdued off-white for the occasion, almost lost in all that dazzle. The King's own barber had trimmed his thick mane of black hair so that it fell becomingly just below his ears.

'How I look?' he asked me for the tenth time that morning. He spoke a simple but melodious Spanish, as the Arawak tongue is rich in vowels and musical sounds.

'Like a bride,' I told him.

'Don't joke me. How I look?'

'Ready for anything,' I said.

Anything, to begin with, was the episcopal residence across St James Plaza from the town hall of Barcelona.

'You're early,' said the bishop.

'The boy was impatient, Your Grace.'

His Grace beamed at Yego. 'And what is the young fellow's name going to be?'

Yego blurted it happily: 'Yego Clone!'

His Grace scowled. 'Perhaps you'd better spell that for me.'

'I no can spell yet,' admitted Yego. 'Maybe next year.'

I spelled it for him.

'There must be some mistake,' said His Grace. 'Yego is certainly no saint's name and the young man can hardly be baptized into the Holy Faith with a heathen name. It simply isn't done.'

'It's a slight modification of Diego,' I explained.

'No saint ever had his name slightly modified,' said His Grace.

'Then call me Yego,' said Yego with a cheerful nod.

'But I just now told you why we can't do that.'

'He means Diego,' I said. 'It's how he pronounces Diego.'

His Grace ruminated and understood.

'You're the father, I understand, Admiral?'

'I'm legally adopting him, yes.'

'And the mother?'

'His natural parents are dead.'

His Grace said the usual line about God moving in mysterious ways.

'How I look?' Yego asked His Grace, doing a flashy white-gold-black pirouette.

'Why, I suppose you are appropriately attired, young man. Yes, indeed.'

'King give suit to me.'

The King and Queen would stand as Yego's godparents.

'Your Grace like suit?'

'Yes, I already pronounced it a most handsomely suitable suit.'

'I swap Your Grace after for big crucifix with bleeding Jesus maybe?'

His Grace looked shocked.

Yego plucked at his sleeves, gathered tightly at the wrists, then unselfconsciously at his subdued but even tighter codpiece. 'Suit beautiful. Suit also uncomfortable.'

'Barter,' I explained hastily, 'is used instead of currency in the Indies. He means no disrespect.'

His Grace promised Yego a crucifix as a gift.

Half an hour later, Yego knelt at the baptismal font in the cathedral, the King and Queen flanking him on one side and I on the other, and all the notables of the Peripatetic Royal Court looking on from the pews. Brother Buil was there too, seraphically beaming from his stall in the chancel.

Every man and woman in that vast cathedral, I think, could feel the awesome responsibility of history as yet unwritten. For Yego, the first Indian received into the Faith, symbolized all his people, and it was as if generations of unborn Indians knelt at his side awaiting the touch of holy water.

In the intricately carved and painted chancel stall beside Brother Buil I saw Tomás de Torquemada. No less a symbol at that fraught moment than Yego, he sat in deep shadow while all else was brilliantly lighted in the sun-filled nave. Only his ascetic or mad eyes burned with a preternatural glow. A slight if unmistakable shudder of apprehension for those unborn multitudes went through me just before His Grace dipped a hand in the holy water.

Yego whispered with a quick uneasy glance up at me, 'I feel cold, Admiral Father.'

I silenced him with a look.

But he persisted. 'Why I feel cold?'

'Silk's cool on your body and it's always cold in a cathedral,' I whispered, and then Yego became the first Indian to be baptized.

It is possible that from the deep shadow of his chancel stall, Tomás de Torquemada almost smiled.

If ever history played a cruel joke on a city, it was Cádiz.

Ancient, dazzling, white-walled, it sat on its wave-girt rock and waited patiently as it had waited for twenty-five centuries, since first a Phoenician merchant outpost had risen here, for the inevitable day when the Ocean Sea would supplant the Mediterranean as the world's waterway.

Did Cádiz see itself, the moment I crossed the isthmus that bound it to the mainland, as the new Genoa, the new Venice, the new Ragusa?

Did Cádiz dream of all the wealth of the Indies flowing through its warehouses?

Poor, patient city on its rock!

I would make but one voyage from there, and Peralonso Niño another later, before upstart Sevilla, the sole southern port that boasted swift courier service to the Peripatetic Royal Court, would supplant it. Cádiz's twenty-five centuries of patience would be rewarded by just three years of glory.

The ironies of history notwithstanding, that summer of 1493 Cádiz belonged to me.

Less than a year before, I had set sail from backwater Palos with ninety men, three small ships and a dream – an Admiral still to conquer his Ocean Sea and with rights and privileges not yet worth the parchment they were written on. Now my lofty title was vindicated by my First Voyage and my rights and privileges confirmed by the King and Queen. Now Luís de Santangel had increased my take, as promised, to one-eighth of net profits. Now the Pope, thanks to me, had issued his famous bull granting King Fernando and Queen Isabel the monopoly they coveted. Now I would sail once more for the Indies, this time as Captain-General commanding seventeen vessels, my Admiralcy undisputed and inclusive from the end of the Canary Islands to Cuba and Hispaniola and as far beyond as I might carry the royal banner. As for my Viceregal dream, it would become reality when this mighty seventeen-ship flotilla delivered to Christmas Town almost 1,000 colonists, all eager volunteers and a good 200 of them caballeros, to transform the tiny fort constructed from ill-fated *Santa Maria*'s timbers into a real colony – town hall, court of justice, streets, a plaza or two, church, Viceregal Palace (or at least a governor's mansion), horses, dogs, swine, sheep, seed grain, sugarcane, grape vines – everything, in short, to make Christmas Town part of Spain, except Spanish women, who would have to wait until the settlement proved out.

In an office appropriated from the harbormaster near the lighthouse on Cádiz bay, wearing a summer uniform designed by the King's own tailor, white as Yego Clone's baptismal suit and heavy with gold braid,

I was seated at a table before the window making the final selection of colonists and crew. Upon these choices the success of the second phase of the Great Venture would depend. Still I went about the task with a certain relaxed air.

Niño, Francisco. b. 1475, Moguer. Grommet, First Voyage.

'Well, Francisco. Good to have you back.'

'G-good to be back, sir.' With his slight, charming stammer.

'Good to see you anywhere, in fact, but on the brazier.'

'They tell me I have you to thank for that, Admiral.'

'Nothing, boy, nothing.'

'There wouldn't happen to be a p-place for me on the flagship this time?'

'Where're your brothers?'

'Juan's coming.' Very shy now. 'Peralonso c-can't.'

I pushed back from the table. No Peralonso? 'Why not?' I thundered.

'He got married, Admiral. He's busy starting a family.'

I digested that, then said without inflection, 'I have no place for a grommet of your qualifications aboard the flagship.'

'Oh well, sure, that's all right, I was just hoping...'

'But *Niña* needs a master.'

'Me? A shipmaster?'

I nodded. Our Billy Budd prototype was rising in the world.

So was an even younger veteran of the First Voyage.

Terreros, Pedro. b. 1476, Palos. Steward, First Voyage.

'Nice to see you, Pedro. Don't tell me you haven't had enough of us yet?'

'It gets in a man's blood.' With a broad grin. 'I hear I'll have a real Admiral's suite to keep shipshape this time.'

The new flagship, familiarly called *Mariagalante*, was almost three times the size of poor *Santa Maria* but ironically bore the same official-religious name. Spanish seas are well sprinkled with *Santa Marias*. This one, as Pedro Terreros seemed to know, had a large Captain-General's suite befitting my rank.

'You hear wrong,' I told him with a straight face.

'You mean it's not so big?'

'I mean it's so big it needs a staff of five. They've already been hired.'

He stared at me, hurt. Pedro was no shy smiler like Francisco Niño.

I can't say what thoughts passed through his mind while I prolonged my little joke, but I was remembering a fierce storm and *Santa*

Maria's helm deserted and an inexperienced steward who leaped into the steerage to take the stick and save all our lives.

'Got a place for you aboard *Niña*, if you want it.'

Plucky little *Niña* was every veteran's favorite in the fleet, but, 'Don't tell me Juan Niño's getting airs and thinks he needs a steward on that little tub?' said Pedro Terreros, not trying to hide his disappointment.

'No. He needs a boatswain.'

Pedro Terreros's hurt expression gave way to a cocky grin. 'I'm his man, then.'

Ojeda, Alonzo. b. 1465, Sevilla. Royal recommendation to command a caravel.

Before me stood a bouncy bantam rooster decked out in a stunning crimson jerkin with sleeve slashings that revealed the white and gold splendor of his intricately embroidered silk doublet with its *dernier-cri* square neck. His muscular legs were sheathed in parti-colored tights, the left in a close cross-hatched red and white pattern, the right whimsically striped red and gold in no pattern at all. His bulging codpiece, of gold embroidered silk, was obviously stuffed with more than Alonzo Ojeda's sex. Surely, I thought, even that woman- and globe-stealing popinjay Martin Behaim would have hesitated before donning a costume like this.

'You dazzle the eyes, Ojeda,' I said.

His own eyes were hard and reckless. 'I'm not tall like yourself, Admiral. I won't stand out in a crowd unless I bedizen myself.'

'What else can you do?'

'Sail ships, fight wars, hold my own against any man and satisfy any woman. I'm an extroverted sort. Once when I was a boy I did a little tightrope stunt more than two hundred feet up on the Giralda tower in Sevilla, but that was because it'd been weeks since anyone paid attention to me. Besides, the Queen happened to be there.'

'You're to have command of a caravel,' I told him in a less than delighted voice that glanced harmlessly off the armor of his self-esteem.

'Are there no subdivisions of the fleet?' he asked. 'Say, a squadron of half a dozen ships or so?'

I assigned him his caravel, made a note to put an experienced master aboard, and wished him good luck.

Crew and colonists totaled close to 1,400 people, and I tried to have a word with each – when I wasn't busy fitting and provisioning seventeen ships and assembling farm animals and implements to equip the largest colonial enterprise in the history of the world. Names and faces began to blur before my eyes. There were Basques and Galicians, but thank God no Juan Cosa. There were men of Palos and Huelva but no member of the extended Pinzón family. I'm not the sort to bear grudges, but somehow word got around and no Pinzóns applied. There were men of the coast and inland men who'd never set eyes on the sea. There were even a score or so Genoese seamen. Two of Brother Buil's missionary assistants were Franciscans from distant Burgundy. There was Ponce de León who signed aboard *Mariagalante* as a grommet, and Captain of Lancers Mosén Pedro Margarit, the Queen's favorite cavalry officer, who would lead our troop of twenty lancers and command our armed forces. There was Pedro de las Casas whose son would later take such liberties with my life. There was Melchior Maldonado, he of the reverberating name.

Many who applied had rushed so impulsively to Cádiz that we had no form sheet on them.

'Name and place of birth?' I asked, bleary-eyed at the end of the final day of interviewing.

His voice, though deep, was so soft that a shout from the dockers loading *Mariagalante*, moored not twenty yards outside the window, drowned out the name. But I heard him say he was Genoese, and I looked up with interest. Wherever ships sail, Genoese seamen are in demand.

I saw a gigantic fellow in brown monkish robes. But he wore no tonsure. From his long-nosed face peered the eyes of a wonder-struck child.

'Age?'

'Thirty-six,' he answered in accented Spanish.

Thirty-six was old for a grommet, I thought. Maybe he held a master's rating or a pilot's. Certainly he was big enough to command respect.

'Experience?' I asked.

'Zero,' he said cheerfully.

I began to wonder how he'd got this far. The obvious rejects were usually screened out.

'None at all?'

'Coming here was my first sea voyage ever,' he said in that deep, soft voice, speaking Italian now.

'Then,' I asked with more than a touch of impatience, 'what makes you think we can use you?'

'The men in my family are splendid sailors,' he informed me with the same hearty cheer.

Hot, tired, irritable, I was ready to send him packing when he asked, 'You still have that St Christopher's medal?'

I gave him a blank look. 'St Christopher's medal?' But I'd worn one on a slim chain around my neck, it seemed, forever.

'The one I gave you when you left Rome.'

I sat for perhaps ten seconds, then shouted: *'Giacomo! Little Giacomo!'* and kicked over my stool and almost the table too as I rushed to embrace my baby brother who, in his gentle way, returned the embrace and came close to crushing all my ribs.

A brief word here about names. Giacomo is Diego in Spanish and from now on I'll be calling my younger brother Big Diego. But these pages are plagued with Diegos — my son Little Diego, my adopted son Yego, Diego Enríquez de Harana whose Christian name I dropped after introducing him, aware as I was of a surfeit of Diegos. There's also, I fear, a surfeit of Martins. Martin Behaim, Martinus Waldseemüller, Martín Alonzo Pinzón. Alonzos, too, come to think of it. Who is newly married Peralonso Niño but Pedro Alonzo Niño? And we've just met that reckless (I hope not feckless) popinjay Alonzo Ojeda. Then there are two Fernandos, two Isabels, two Rodrigos, and at last count five Johns or Juans. There's also a trio of Luíses — my ducal friend of Medinaceli, my immense and immensely wealthy friend-at-Court Santangel, and my scholarly young friend Torres, to whose sister I have irrevocably surrendered my heart.

I didn't name these people, so bear with me. I'll try to avoid confusion as best I can.

Juan Niño of Moguer happened to be in the building and I asked him to see the final few applicants while Big Diego and I repaired to a bodega. Had we really been apart a quarter of a century? That was most of our lives. Mine was so full I didn't know where to begin and didn't try. It would come out in bits and snatches on the voyage to the Indies. But Big Diego's didn't take long to tell.

'Oh no, no. I never did take Holy Orders. I'm not sure why. Didn't feel a real calling, I guess.

'For a while I wanted to be a chartmaker like you and Bartolomeo, but Rome's full of chartmakers.

'Leave Rome? Sure, I gave the matter some thought, but it seemed an awful lot of bother until I got your letter.

'No, never did marry. A family's an awful responsibility, I always believed.

'Oh, this and that. Odd jobs for His Holiness mostly. I keep busy.'

Big Diego, I told myself, just needed some direction, a push or two from his older brother. I would give him no specific duties but let him be the unofficial apprentice to the Admiral of the Ocean Sea and Viceroy of the Indies, and learn what stuff he was made of.

By the beginning of autumn ships' complements and colonial positions were filled — carpenters and stonemasons, wainwrights, shipwrights, coopers and blacksmiths, weavers, tailors, cobblers, bakers, a pair of veterinary doctors (one an experienced tooth-puller), several physicians, clerks, goldwashers and hundreds of simple honest farmers. Soon the air over Cádiz was hazy with wood smoke as every oven in the city worked overtime to stock seventeen ships with biscuit. My crews drilled daily on the rigging of their new ships and daily our cavalry paraded smartly along the waterfront, drawing crowds.

The day before we sailed, the parade was a travesty. Overnight spirited Arabian warhorses seemed to have become swaybacked nags overdue at the glue factory, so unsound of limb and wind that, to the beat of drums and shrill of pipes, they slipped and stumbled and farted their way along the quays.

Furious, I sent for Lance Captain Mosén Pedro Margarit.

'The Admiral wanted to see me?'

This lantern-jawed officer, secure in the Queen's favor, spoke in a loud bray of spurious *bonhomie*.

'What the hell happened to your horses?'

'We sold them, old boy.' Flashing his square, horsy teeth.

'You *what*?'

'Sold them. Those Arabians, they're delicate. Give them a mean look and they go into a decline. We figure these old hacks'll have a better chance of surviving the voyage.'

'Of course the fact that you turned a pretty profit had nothing to do with it.'

'Our only consideration was to guarantee we'd have serviceable horses in the Indies. Admiral.'

'Get out of here.'

Which he did, with a braying 'Serviceable horses, old boy, serviceable horses.'

His place was taken by a buck-toothed boy of thirteen.

'Admiral Colón?'

I nodded, still angry.

'I'm from the House of Centurione. Director wants to see you, Admiral sir. It's crucially vital and important.'

'To him or to me?' I snarled.

'I wouldn't know about that, Admiral Your Excellency.'

'Since when's there a Centurione's branch in Cádiz anyway?'

'We're just moving in, Admiral Your Lordship, which is one reason the Director didn't come in person.' The boy, encouraged when I had nothing further to snarl at him, grinned. 'Besides, he's an old fossil. Doesn't get about much these days.'

'He wouldn't by any chance be a fellow named Pighi-Zampini?'

'He would.'

'Why didn't you say so?'

My biographers all agree that I was sick on sailing day with some minor but incapacitating complaint, but there's no agreement as to whether I was on the quarterdeck or in the Captain-General's suite when we weighed anchor. Let me settle that right now. I was on the quarterdeck, gripping a shroud and staring eagle-eyed to the west in a typical pose. But closer inspection would have revealed how white my knuckles were and how my eagle eyes had an undeniable glassy look. The reason will become clear.

At the House of Centurione's brand-new Cádiz branch, Pighi-Zampini sat in a large office so full of crates and chests that at first I didn't see him. But there he was at his shiny new banker's bench. The boy was right; he had aged. His hair was wispy white, his eyes rheumy, the tufts sprouting from his ears and nostrils coarser than ever.

'Well, young man,' he said, taking in my gold-braided uniform, 'for someone forced to leave Rome as a boy at the height of the Italian Renaissance, you seem to have done all right for yourself.'

He withdrew the gold chain from his jerkin and looked at his portable clock. 'Speeding up on me,' he complained. 'Gains half an hour a day, sometimes more. Time flies for an old man. Well, I won't keep you long.' He sighed. 'Just when I get things set up in Sevilla, Centurione's transfers me here. What's this about Cádiz going to be the richest port in the world?'

'It's inevitable,' I assured him.

'Figures. Centurione's never misses a trick.' He consulted his little clock again dubiously and half-rose. 'Well, thanks for coming in, Admiral. Good to see you again.'

'You mean that's all?' I asked, startled.

He sat back down. 'Sorry. Getting too old for this sort of work. Almost forgot. Clock says it's six. That's probably half an hour fast. You're expected at number 17 Sacramento Street at a quarter before the hour.'

'Who by?'

An old man's shrug, an old man's querulous tone: 'Don't ask me, they never tell me anything anymore. Message came from the head office in Barcelona. Do an old friend a favor?'

'If I can.'

'You're an important sort of legendary person now, maybe they'll listen to you. Tell them I don't want to be transferred again. Please? I'm too old. Where does a man's life go, anyway? How does it all slip by? Once I was a House of Centurione governor, right there in Piazza Caricamento in Genoa, banking capital of the world, but somehow it all went wrong and ... where was I?'

'You didn't want to be transferred again.'

'Unless it's back to Genoa. I have grandchildren I've never even seen. One's engaged to be married. Well, that's 17 Sacramento Street and good luck to you, old friend,' said Pighi-Zampini. 'I doubt we'll ever meet again.'

At first I thought he'd given me the wrong address. Seventeen Sacramento Street was a sagging, derelict building that presented a blank wall (badly in need of whitewash) to the street, Arab style. When I banged at the deeply recessed door, nobody answered.

'Anybody home?' I called.

Still no answer.

I turned to go. Black clouds had rolled in from the Atlantic and the afternoon was dark. The first chill wind of autumn blew along the narrow, deserted street. Behind me I heard the door creak open. I hesitated a moment, then boldly went inside.

Still nobody. But who had opened the door?

Beyond the vestibule was a large unfurnished room, its single heavily draped window facing onto the interior patio. In the light of a pair of wall sconces I could see that the floor was covered with knee-high stacks of Persian carpets, the nearest, I thought, a Kirman.

'You're late,' she said.

Outside, the first rain squall hit. The wind was blowing fiercely.

We met at arm's length alongside the stacked Persian carpets.

In the lamplight her long lustrous hair was black as the space between the stars on a clear night at sea.

'A mutual friend tells me,' she said, 'that you have accepted certain ... resources for your colony. I'm very grateful.'

'It was noth – '

'But don't get the wrong idea. I still hate you. After what you did to my brother, I wouldn't even speak to you, except I want you to take something to him in Christmas Town.'

The oak chest was small but heavy. 'Books?'

'He has to keep up his intellectual interests.'

'I understand.' I hefted the oak chest to one shoulder and paused. 'Well,' I said provisionally, and when she made no reply I retraced my steps to the door.

When I opened it, wind came howling in and rain lashed me. The wall sconces flickered.

'Wait, I have a message for Luís,' she called and I put the chest down near the door.

We met once more at arm's length alongside the stacked Persian carpets.

'Luís your brother,' I asked, 'or Luís the – '

'My brother. Tell him he has to keep up his intellectual interests.'

I pointed out that she'd already said that.

There was a silence, except for the storm outside.

Then she told me, 'This part of the message is not for my brother,' and with a single lithe stride closed that arm's-length gap that separated us and kissed me savagely.

No woman had ever kissed me like that before.

At last she stepped back so that we stood once more at arm's length alongside those stacked Persian carpets.

'As I thought,' she said. 'You're a very sexy man, Colón.'

No woman had ever called me by just my surname before.

'But don't get the wrong idea. I still hate you. Anyway, it's not really you that's sexy. Fame's an incredible aphrodisiac.'

In the lamplight her eyes were that deep emerald green that John Cabot would see when his ships crossed the Gulf Stream in June 1497.

'As I'm sure you already know,' she said.

The rain had stopped. The very air we breathed crackled with challenge. My voice was thick when I spoke.

'It's stopped raining,' I said.

In the lamplight her lips were one sensuous half-shade deeper than incarnadine.

'Because,' she said caustically, ignoring my observation, 'you must have had lots and lots of groupies during your triumphal tour of Spain on your way to that royal audience in Barcelona.'

'Well, no. Not really. I – '

'I never made love with a legend in his own lifetime,' she purred and

286

with another of her lithe strides closed that arm's-length gap that separated us.

Again I experienced the savagery of her kiss.

In the lamplight her teeth were sharp as they nibbled at my lips.

At last she stepped back so that we stood one final time at arm's length alongside those stacked Persian carpets. On top was a Kirman, I was almost certain.

By now I was as randy as any seed-bull or stallion, but since I knew she hated me I hesitated, not wanting to come on too strong and be rebuffed. Finally I told her, 'Well, I've got a really long day ahead of me tomorrow so I – '

She swiftly changed her tack. 'It *has* stopped raining.'

'Yes, hasn't it?'

This exchange was laden with significance, as if both of us had always known we were fated to speak these words, or had spoken them before in the distant unremembered long ago of some previous incarnation.

'And, as you suggest,' she suggested, 'you've got to get back to being a legend again.' She added, 'In your own lifetime.'

Had I made such a suggestion? I doubted it. She was playing hard to get.

'There's no hurry,' I told her, more aggressively.

'Don't you have to sail with the morning tide?'

Hard to get, no doubt about it. Until now her behaviour had been bafflingly unconventional. But playing hard to get was something I could relate to.

I warmed to my task.

'It's a long time till morning,' I said.

With the tip of her tongue she subtly wet her lips.

I went to the attack. 'You're notorious, you know,' I said.

'Me?' Self-denigratingly. 'Oh, that Blue Pimpernel business.'

'Notoriety in a woman excites a man,' I said.

'But it's the best kept secret in Spain. Virtually nobody knows I'm the Blue Pimpernel.'

'I know,' I said ambiguously. 'That's what makes you so exciting.'

We each took a half stride to close that arm's-length gap that separated us. I was never sure which of us overbalanced, making us fall across the stack of Persian carpets. After a while I disengaged and got up to extinguish the lamps. When she saw what I intended, she said, 'I draw the line at darkness.'

I returned to her, uncertain in the lamplight.

'Whatever happens,' she said, 'you mustn't get the wrong idea. I still hate you. It's only your fame that – '

'Petenera,' I said, 'will you kindly sort of try to drop that for the time being? A man likes to be appreciated for himself.'

I kissed her savagely.

She lay back on the stack of Persian carpets. The top one was definitely a Kirman.

Some time later I awoke with goose-bumps. It was cold in there. I touched her into wakefulness and did a few of the things that had excited her earlier.

'I still hate you,' she growled against my mouth.

By then I was looming over her. But she said, 'Oh no you don't. There are other ways of doing this.'

I asked her what she meant.

She kissed me savagely. 'Don't pretend you don't know. That's just your hypocritical double standard.'

'My what?'

She was definitely back to being bafflingly unconventional.

'Oh, not you personally. The whole male half of the human race.'

By then she was looming over me.

Some time later her goose-bumps must have awakened her. It was even colder in there. She touched me into wakefulness and did a few of the things that had excited me earlier.

'I'm forty-two years old,' I said.

'That doesn't change anything,' she told me. 'I still hate you.'

'I mean, I can't keep this up all night.'

But we kissed savagely and I decided I was wrong.

Some time later we both awoke with goose-bumps. By then it was icy cold in there and I really hadn't been asleep anyway. I was thinking.

'I was thinking,' I said thoughtfully. 'Do you think fornication's a cardinal or just a venial sin?'

She considered this as we turned into each other's arms. 'Whatever,' she said. 'Enjoy.'

Some time later . . .

Here I had better resort to the ellipsis or three-dot school of writing, which I try to avoid except for special effects. But I had a ship to catch.

. . .

She was gone when I woke to find myself covered with a sheepskin rug. Throwing it back, I dressed quickly and lurched to the door, almost tripping over the oak chest. I took it and hurried outside and toward the harbor through a bloodshot dawn.

✑ XII ✑

The Strange Tale of
the Cannibal Who Would Not Die,
the Tragic Fate of Christmas Town,
and Other Matters
Contributing to an Understanding of the Indians

ONCE you are a bona fide legend in your own lifetime, there is no escape. Infrequent departures from the mythic persona only increase the aura of heroic mystery.

Even props like a small, heavy oak chest fortify it.

'The old man's gear's on board, ain't it? So what's he got there?'

'Where was he last night, anyway?'

Legends don't do normal things. An amorous dalliance is out of the question.

I almost wish I could tell them, but legends can't do that either. Legends don't tell stories about themselves. This is for lesser people to do. And, of course, historians and biographers.

Who, at an uncharacteristic loss for words, cannot recount the events of a single day (except for one four-hour thunderstorm) during the entire westbound voyage of the great fleet that left Cádiz for the Indies the morning of 25 September 1493. That one storm aside, they assume it was an absolutely uneventful crossing. Perhaps they're right. I don't remember. My thoughts were elsewhere.

Sailing day, however, I remember vividly.

Not the pageantry in the harbor — the guns of Cádiz fort and of every warship in the bay booming in salute as all sails were spread in

the light breeze to display great green crosses vivid against spanking new canvas, while from every mainstaff flew the proud banner of Spain, and below, rainbowing the bulwarks of every ship of the fleet, fluttered the coats-of-arms of our gentlemen volunteers – I remember nothing of this.

Not even my own coat-of-arms, so recently granted by King and Queen, a magnificent blazon at the waist of every ship, so glowing with color that it paled all 200 other escutcheons – a shield displaying in its four quarters the gold castle of Castile on a field of green, the purple lion rampant of León (green tongue, white field), silver islands agleam on an azure sea, five gold anchors adazzle on a field of royal blue – no, why should I remember any of this?

What I do recall, as *Mariagalante* seemed to stand still in the water and white-walled Cádiz slowly slid away, is a final glimpse in the surging quayside crowd of Beatriz and the two boys, brought down from Córdoba by her Uncle Harana to see me off – and where was I the night before when they reached Cádiz to surprise me?

But that pang of guilt vanishes when I spy, on the edge of the crowd on a pair of chestnut palfeys, a man and woman. He sits tall in the saddle with the arrogant ease of the Castilian nobility, somehow familiar despite the plumed hat that shades his face. She is bareheaded – and so breathtaking even at this distance that one look makes time reverse and brings the night with her hurtling back.

Who is the arrogant, tauntingly familiar Castilian at her side? Why is he there, leg to leg with her as they watch the fleet depart? And she, does she half-wave a hand in farewell as she leans forward to quiet her frisky mount?

This is when I grasp that shroud and turn my eyes resolutely westward – thereby nurturing the legend.

'Look at the Admiral, will you? His own coat-of-arms on every ship, twenty-one gun salute, blaring trumpets by the hundreds, Venetian galleys escorting us to the mouth of the harbor – but he's already on that Ocean Sea of his.'

'Heading back to those Indies of his.'

As if the Ocean Sea and the Indies are my personal property. That's part of the legend too.

'What's he got in that oak chest?' they ask again as I take it into the sterncastle. My personal staff of five is waiting at the door of the Captain-General's suite.

'Go topside and have yourselves a last look at land,' I urge them, and later one will say:

'The Admiral wanted to get rid of us. So it's got to be secret charts showing a shorter route to the Indies. He spent all morning locked in his suite studying them.'

I stow the chest of books and go to bed, or intend to.

But there on my berth I see, in a ray of sunlight streaming through the porthole, a single small flower. Almost, I don't want to touch it for fear of shortening its fragile life. The blossom – don't ask me how she put it there – is one perfect blue pimpernel.

The westbound crossing is as insubstantial as a half-forgotten dream. I try to keep a daily log as on my First Voyage, but it doesn't work. The night is Petenera's hair, the sea her eyes, sunset the Oceanic kiss of her lips. She smiles at me from the flashing white of the bow wave.

'What's that the Admiral's always humming anyway?'

'Sounds like some gypsy tune, don't it?'

'You think *he's* part gypsy?'

The legend again, no matter what I do.

Historians must settle for the bare facts. The grand fleet raised Gomera in the Canaries on 7 October, dropped the westernmost island of Ferro astern on the thirteenth, and crossed the Ocean Sea with the Trade Winds behind us all the way in an incredibly fast twenty-one days to make landfall at an island I called Dominica, the day being Sunday, on 3 November.

Embellishments, if any, will have to be supplied by others.

I find Yego Clone hiding in the Captain-General's suite, naked except for the large wooden crucifix given him by the Bishop of Barcelona.

'You're a Christian now and therefore a rational human being,' I try to reason with him, 'not a superstitious savage.'

His usually bronzy face pale, his arms crossed stubbornly over his bare bronzy chest, Yego says, 'I not go that island. You no make I go that island. They eat people.'

The fleet lies anchored in a cove at the southern tip of the large island I've just named Santa Maria de Guadalupe in honor of the famous shrine in western Spain. I'm sending a party ashore to find fresh water.

'Yego,' I say patiently, 'that's just an old wives' tale.'

'Old wives? Old wives no eat people. Caribs eat people.'

'An old wives' tale is a story containing little or no truth told by ignorant, frightened women,' I elucidate. 'These so-called cannibals of yours are in reality soldiers of some more advanced civilization, such as the army of the Great Khan of Cathay, aren't they?'

Yego shakes his head, bewildered.

I mean him to be. I want to overwhelm him with words, to shame him with rhetoric. The shore party will need him along as translator.

'Island is Kekeria,' he tells me. 'Farm on island.'

'What's so awful about a farm?'

For answer he unexpectedly makes the sign for sexual intercourse. Yego is prudish in this regard. He never speaks those words in his own language and, although he has heard them often enough, won't use them in Spanish either.

'What's that supposed to mean?'

'Fat farm for boys. For girls, they – ' His thoughts overwhelm him; his mouth clamps shut.

'I've ordered you to go ashore,' I tell him. 'Do you know what happens if you refuse to obey my order?'

I'm not sure I know myself, for Yego's status as my adopted son is a special one, but he nods a mournful nod.

'Well?'

'I stay here.'

'Look,' I tell him, suddenly inspired. 'I'll go ashore with the landing party. You trust me, don't you?'

'They eat people,' says Yego one-track-mindedly.

'You'll be at my side every minute.'

Yego, right or wrong, has tremendous confidence in me. 'You promise, Admiral Father?'

An hour later *Mariagalante*'s boat is beached on white coral sand, half a dozen other ships' boats waiting offshore while we reconnoitre. A high mountain looms inland, its top lost in clouds. Down the face of the mountain plunges a waterfall.

'Kekeria,' Yego repeats, gesturing at that marvelous cascade. Clearly visible far out to sea, it is the island's landmark. The sight of it has sent Yego's four baptized companions (the fifth, a minor cacique's son, remains behind by choice at the Peripatetic Royal Court) scurrying for the bilges.

Every man in the shore party wears a sword and carries either musket, lance or crossbow. I assign four, two veterans of the First Voyage and two newcomers, to remain with the boat.

'I stay too?' Yego says brightly, still seated on a thwart and nervously fingering his crucifix.

'Yego,' I say, 'everybody's waiting,' and he climbs from the boat unhappily.

One last time he mutters, 'They eat people.'

We march past a mangrove swamp and inland on a man-made trail through the deep jungle shadows. The usual bird calls, strange small unidentifiable crunching sounds, cheeps and chirps and pips and squeaks, sudden slithery rushes, frail querulous cries, clicks and howls and mini-grunts all slightly unnerve the newcomers but make us veterans of the First Voyage feel right at home. The feeling proves deceptive.

The trail opens on a large clearing at the foot of the mountain, a short distance east of the waterfall.

The place at first looks like your ordinary Indian village – thatched huts, the cacique's bigger house, gardens of yams and maize. But beyond is a palisade, its closely set pointed sticks as tall as a man, and from within can be heard shouts and crying.

'Farm,' Yego says. Do I see a look of anguish in his dark, expressive eyes?

We reach a gate in the palisade, secured by a simple wooden bolt. With lancers flanking me, I draw the bolt and pull the gate open.

Instantly naked children retreat from the fence in terror. Some of the girls, hardly in their teens, are in various stages of pregnancy. A few protectively hold nursing infants. The boys are all fat, soft jiggly fat, suety, breasty, with big bouncy hams and pendulous bellies that overhang their private parts so that it isn't until later we learn they all have been gelded. Yego speaks to them but they are so terrified that their answers at first are incoherent. Yego repeats the same question-sounds, louder.

'Caribs see ships, hide in swamp,' he informs me.

We penetrate deeper into what Yego has called a farm. A thatched structure opposite the gate holds pens full of babies.

The look of anguish in Yego's eyes is unmistakable now. He wants to communicate it and gropes for words. Finally he come up with, 'Veals. Caribs like veals.'

The chilling import of these words makes me think for the first time that Yego just might possibly know what he's talking about.

Two of the fat boys speak to him excitedly.

'They want please go on ships to Haiti,' he translates.

Geldings, girls, babies – there are scores of them.

'If they stay on farm, boys die.'

'What happens to the girls?'

Bronzy skin or no, Yego blushes. 'Caribs make more veals with them.'

At that moment Captain of Lancers Mosén Pedro Margarit comes running into the palisade. His lantern jaw hangs open. It's a while before this favorite of the Queen can speak, and when he does, it is to utter a bray of astonishment.

'Jesus Christ, Admiral, you've got to see this yourself.'

I go with him, Yego trailing along. Upwind of the cacique's house we can smell woodsmoke and the unmistakable aroma of roasting meat. Behind the house, over a pit of embers, forked sticks support skewered joints of meat, apparently left by the fleeing Caribs.

At such times I think the human mind protects itself by sorting impressions, cataloguing details, making comparisons, fending off the unfaceable with metaphor — anything to lock the emotions away and buy time to adjust.

So, feeling nothing yet, I find myself thinking: how like a ham is a neatly butchered human haunch, how like a leg of lamb a crisply roasted human arm oozing juices, how like a suckling pig, its tiny limbs trussed, a human infant —

Lean, lantern-jawed cavalry captain Mosén Pedro Margarit's bray breaks the silence.

'They ... eat ... EACH OTHER!'

He's trying to find some way to fit it into the ordered world he knows. The rest of us (for half a dozen men now stand around the ghastly barbecue) can't even begin.

'Of course, they're animals,' Mosén Pedro says, testing the words as he speaks them, as if they are unfamiliar food, 'and since they're animals...'

Still the rest of us remain mute.

Mosén Pedro seems to debate this point of his. 'It's obvious they're animals, isn't it?' he asks. Then he says more firmly: 'Animals. They just happen to resemble people. They don't think like us, or feel like us. They probably don't even feel pain or ... or anything.'

With a violent shake of his head he looks at Yego.

'Do you *feel*, boy? If I hit you, would you *hurt*?' The worst part of this is that he's smiling now. A sick sort of smile, but still.

Yego hasn't heard him. He can't take his eyes off the roasting joints of human flesh.

'If I cut you,' asks Mosén Pedro, 'if I cut you, would you feel the bite of the blade?'

No answer from Yego.

'Did you ever eat another Indian?' Mosén Pedro's voice is as reasonable as when he explained why he'd sold thoroughbreds and bought nags. But his eyes are wild.

For the first time Yego looks at him, and Mosén Pedro calmly draws his sword and takes a cut at my son calculated to decapitate him. I push the crazed Spaniard off balance. He stumbles and goes down, sword flying from his hand, and then my own control is gone. I kick the fallen Mosén Pedro Margarit once, twice, a third time. He huddles on his side, legs drawn up, arms protectively over head, and suddenly I turn to stagger a dozen steps around the corner of the cacique's house, where in a choking struggle with dignity I vomit up my breakfast.

Two men are helping the dazed Mosén Pedro to his feet when I come back. Someone finds water. Mosén Pedro drinks from a calabash. An ugly bruise covers the right side of his face.

We look at each other.

I want to apologize, but how can I? Hysterical or not, he tried to kill Yego.

His eyes are a glassy brown glitter.

'Are you all right?' I ask.

'Yes sir. Of course, sir.'

'Have all the children brought to the beach.' Deputizing him, I hope, will let him know I still have faith in him. Anything less would be unjust: haven't I behaved like an Icelandic berserker myself?

'Yes sir, at once, sir.' In a monotone.

'Then burn down that abominable human-cattle pen.'

'Yes sir. I understand, sir. Consider it done.' And Mosén Pedro Margarit marches off stiffly.

Head bowed, Yego drops to his knees before me.

'Get up, boy. Get up,' I say gruffly. 'Tell those children we'll take them to Haiti.'

Back at the beach the six other ships' boats have landed their shore parties to make room for the former Carib prisoners. Soon under Yego's encouragement the children are climbing or being carried aboard the boats to be ferried to *Mariagalante*.

I catch movement at the edge of my vision from the mangrove swamp, but when I turn I see only the dense tangle of air-roots.

Our boats are gone for an unnerving hour.

Alonzo Ojeda, that bedizened bouncy bantam rooster who commands the caravel *Colina*, is first back to the beach. 'Where are they?' he says. 'Haven't they shown themselves?' He means the Caribs and he's spoiling for a fight. But it seems he's to be disappointed, for soon the other boats return for us.

We're perhaps a hundred yards offshore when around a headland beyond the mangrove swamp comes a single large canoe. It is obvious from the sudden break in their rhythm that not only our boats but the great ships beyond come as a total surprise to the paddlers.

The Caribs can avoid a confrontation either by returning the way they came or by beaching their canoe.

They choose to head for the beach.

So does Alonzo Ojeda. Soon I see spurts of flame and puffs of black smoke, followed by the crack of muskets.

The Caribs, far from fleeing this terrifying volley, send a flight of arrows winging toward Ojeda and then swerve sharply seaward to meet him. Shields are raised at the boat's gunwale — but not before a single yowl of pain knifes across the water.

Standing in the prow, disdaining the wall of shields, bedizened Alonzo Ojeda raises one arm theatrically, brandishing a sword. He turns to shout to his crew, his eyes hard and reckless as ever, his teeth flashing a smile. Then he jumps back as oars are shipped and his heavy boat smashes into the side of the canoe.

The dugout splits in two, Indians flying in all directions. Most swim for shore. But some, and at these we all gawk in wonder, make for Ojeda's boat, yelping blood-curdlingly as they come. The few not dispatched by crossbow quarrels or musket balls cling so tenaciously to the gunwales that Ojeda's men have to hack off fingers before the Indians drift away, trailing threads of blood through the blue water.

'There's one trying to board us here!' shouts Mosén Pedro.

Yego, on seeing two bronzed hands gripping our gunwale, roars an Arawak oath, grabs the nearest sword and wields it wildly, endangering us more than the Carib.

It takes three men to restrain Yego. Then we haul the Carib aboard. He flops about like a fish in the bottom of the boat, the shaft of a crossbow bolt jutting from his belly.

Ojeda calls across to us. 'We've got a casualty.'

The wounded man is a Basque grommet named Echeverría, barely nicked by an arrow. But his face has ballooned, his tongue is so swollen it protrudes from his mouth, and his hands have puffed to twice their size. We take him aboard, for *Mariagalante*'s physician, Maestro Álvarez Chanca, sailed once to Fernando Po and has experience with African poisons.

While the transfer is made, the mortally wounded Carib, who has been all but forgotten, grabs with both hands the shaft of the crossbow quarrel and rips it from his belly. Blood spurts from the wound, which his efforts have enlarged, and an obscene coil of steaming tripes spills out. This the Carib tries unsuccessfully to stuff back in. He clamps a hand over the lot – gaping wound, blood, tripes – and snarls at anyone who approaches him.

It's the same aboard *Mariagalante* after he's winched up in a cargo net. He flops about the cambered deck, again like a boated fish. When anyone comes near, his teeth snap in quick head-darting bites that could remove a finger.

As for the wounded Basque Echeverría, Dr Chanca opens the gash and lets it bleed freely. Chanca is a no-nonsense fellow of forty or so to whom a bedside manner is as superfluous as a physician's red robes.

'You can never get all the poison out,' he tells me.

'What'll happen to him?'

'He'll die. Slowly.'

This is said within hearing of Echeverría.

The Basque's puffy eyes stare at Dr Chanca. 'I want a priest,' he says with difficulty around his swollen tongue.

Chanca shrugs. 'Plenty of time. I'll let you know when.'

And off he goes, turning his clinical interest on the Carib, who by this time has been bound hand and foot. Instead of examining the wound, Chanca spends a few minutes exploring the Indian, prodding here, poking there, running fingers along an arm, prying the mouth open with a stick to look at the teeth. The Carib immediately bites the stick in two.

'Healthy specimen,' Chanca says. 'Quite remarkable, actually.'

'He'll live?'

'Good Lord, no. With that wound he ought already to be dead.'

The Carib, bound or not, begins again to flop about the deck near the horse pens amidships. A deep rolling moan escapes his lips, his eyes bug wide, and suddenly the rope binding his thick-muscled arms parts with a twang like a plucked lute string. Just as suddenly, and more incredibly, he springs to his feet, which are still bound, looks Chanca straight in the eye, spits at him, clamps one hand to his loops of hanging tripes, hops to the starboard bulwark and vaults into the sea.

When his head bobs to the surface, he begins to swim for the beach, using just one arm, for his legs are still bound and with his other hand he's holding his tripes in. Yet the gap between him and *Mariagalante* widens.

My crew crowds the bulwark, and all around the slowly swimming

Indian musket balls and crossbow bolts raise little waterspouts. He continues swimming. Volley after volley foams the water around him. He has to be hit a dozen times, twenty. He continues swimming. Muskets are reloaded faster than in any drill. It becomes a contest, to see whose shot will stop him. There are cheers and jeers. He continues swimming. Soon he is out of musket range. Crossbowmen climb the rigging to gain distance with height. One of the starboard falconets is fired with a roar and a billow of smoke. By then he is almost at the beach. He veers, still swimming with agonizing slowness, for the mangrove swamp. There he drags himself ashore, a second falconet roaring and blasting away a section of air-roots. Hopping on his bound legs, he disappears into the swamp, bent over, hands clasped to his belly.

I report here only what I saw. He should have died a hundred times over. Perhaps he did die, huddled somewhere among those twisted roots. But I think not.

I feel a premonitory dread. If we make enemies of the Indians – and if these Caribs (or Mosén Pedro) are any indication, we inevitably will – we are going to need more than weapons to deal with them.

A conversation overheard at the bulwark, with the smell of gunpowder still in the air:

CAPTAIN MOSÉN PEDRO MARGARIT: I tell you, they aren't human. It's that simple.

DR CHANCA: That was a human being I examined.

MOSÉN PEDRO: But my dear doctor, you *saw* the creature keep swimming. It didn't even know it was dead. They say animals are like that – can't feel the death of their own bodies.

BROTHER BUIL: Exactly. Because animals have no souls.

CHANCA (*ignoring this interruption*): Do you want to die, Captain?

MOSÉN PEDRO: Of course not. Why should I?

CHANCA: Neither did that Indian, and he was trying his damnedest not to.

BROTHER BUIL: Damnedest they'll be – until we convert them.

MOSÉN PEDRO: Waste of time, fishing for souls among these barbarians.

And the Queen's favorite cavalry officer turns his dogmatic gaze on my adopted son.

Yego, now, is coaxing the rescued Arawak children out of the forecastle, where they have cowered ever since we brought the wounded Carib aboard. One by one they emerge from the hatch and come aft. Doing so, they must pass the horse pens amidships, and a strange thing happens. They walk right by those manure-smelling pens as if they aren't there, totally rejecting the existence of the huge impossible quadruped beasts. Almost, they succeed. But one of Mosén Pedro's nags chooses that moment to rear and whinny, asserting its reality, and the Arawaks disappear back down the hatch like a puff of smoke.

While it lasts, though, the Indians' negation of these equine monsters somehow ominously reminds me of Mosén Pedro's dogmatic dismissal of Indian humanness.

Yego stands on the pitching quarterdeck, and on the watch officer's slate chalks a rough chart. The dreaded island of Kekeria (or Santa Maria de Guadalupe) provides his reference point, and the chalk moves swiftly northwest and then west, sketching small islands and a single large one along the way, until he draws the outline of Hispaniola and an X on the north coast for Christmas Town.

'How far?' I ask. Now that we know where we are, I'm impatient to return to Christmas Town and see how our little settlement has fared.

Yego considers and says, 'Eight days.'

This figure, it should be understood, is characteristically Spanish. Eight days is a week (counting both ends), to be exactly, but Spaniards aren't, and Yego thinks more like a Spaniard all the time. 'Eight days' is a variable temporal commodity, like the words 'soon' and 'tomorrow'. Not only the present mood but the entire personality of the speaker must be taken into account. Since Yego is basically a can-do sort of person, and has learned a certain geographical optimism from me, I conclude: ten days, possibly twelve.

It seems a good time to apprentice my brother Big Diego as a watch officer, for the sea is moderate and the wind holds steady on our starboard quarter. Under such perfect conditions the great fleet can almost sail as a single ship with a single helmsman conned by a single officer.

Here then is Big Diego, this large, pale, soft man in his monkish robes with his kindly (not vapid, I assure myself) smile, standing before the binnacle on *Mariagalante*'s quarterdeck, squinting in the sunlight at the compass and shouting down the hatch to the helmsman in the steerage:

'Half a point left!'

'Left?' calls back the steersman.

'Port,' I prompt Big Diego. 'Half a point to port. Or, if you want, larboard.'

'Half a point to larboard!' shouts Big Diego, very professionally.

'We change our heading?' comes the puzzled question from the steerage.

Big Diego looks at me. I look at the binnacle.

'He means,' I call down, 'half a point to *star*board.'

'Oh, sure, starboard, that's it,' says Big Diego.

An hour or so later there's a minor problem with the spritsail, and I go forward to settle a difference of opinion between the boatswain and the sailmaker. It doesn't take long, but when I emerge from the sail locker into sun-glare I see what looks like two battle fleets engaged – seventeen ships on as many different tacks, signal braziers puffing frantic smoke, *Mariagalante* herself heeling sharply, helm all the way down, to avoid *Colina*, which is luffing into the wind as an alternative to crossing *San Juan*'s bow. I rush aft, past the pens where Mosén Pedro's horses stomp and whinny nervously on the wildly rolling deck.

Big Diego is calling down into the steerage, gentle-voiced as ever: 'No, I'm afraid what I meant was helm *up* after all. Sorry about that.'

A pair of brawny arms appear at the sides of the steerage hatch, a grizzled head in the middle. The helmsman has secured the tiller long enough to show his face and ask Big Diego: 'You trying to make me look bad?'

Then he sees the chaos in the water all around us. 'Gawd!' he bellows, and disappears below.

'I'll take over,' I tell my brother, trying not to shout.

At twilight on 27 November the great fleet drops anchor outside the bay where, on Christmas Eve just four weeks short of one year ago, *Santa Maria* ran aground on a reef. Nothing remains of the wreck, so effectively did Gunner Relámpago demolish it to impress Guacanagarí's Indians.

Thinking of Relámpago, I smile and tell *Mariagalante*'s chief gunner, 'Fire a lombard to let them know we're here.'

I tell Big Diego, 'You'll like Luís Torres, he has an open way of looking at the world.'

I tell Dr Chanca, 'You'll learn a lot from Dr Sánchez. He's had almost a year to deal with medical problems out here.'

I tell Mosén Pedro Margarit, hopefully, 'Wait till you meet the cacique Guacanagarí. If you're still wondering about the Indians' humanity, he'll settle your doubts.'

I tell Brother Buil, 'Wait till you see how gentle and unwarlike the Arawaks are — as if Original Sin bypassed them.'

Buil smilingly contradicts this. 'Original Sin has bypassed no one since Adam and Eve. To suggest otherwise is heresy. As for the Indians' unwarlike nature, I need only remind you of the sad ceremony in which we both played our parts three days ago.'

This was the burial at sea of the grommet Echeverría, who finally succumbed to the venom-tipped Carib arrow. Buil commended his soul to God and I commended him to history as the first Spaniard to die in the Indies. If only that had been true!

'The Arawaks and Caribs are different as day and night,' I explain to Buil. 'They're traditional enemies.'

'But if they have enemies,' Buil offers a reasonable smile, 'how can you maintain they are not warlike?'

'Well, anyway,' I keep trying, 'you'll see how eager they are to accept conversion. Look at Yego.'

'I'd feel better about your "son" and *his* conversion if he dressed in a Christian manner instead of running around with nothing on but a crucifix.'

'It's the custom of his people to wear nothing. You see, the climate — '

'Do their women also wear nothing?'

'Yes, but when you see how almost childlike — '

'How very interesting,' smiles Brother Buil.

By this time I'm surprised and a bit concerned that no answering cannon fire has come from Christmas Town. Night falls like a curtain in the tropics, and I have no intention of risking the fleet, or any part of it, by sailing through the shoals before morning.

Mariagalante's bulwarks are lined with crew and colonists, all awaiting some response from the settlement. But in the gathering darkness not so much as a spark of light can be seen.

'Give them another round,' I tell the gunner.

Hardly has the black smoke drifted away when the roundtop lookout cries: 'A boat's coming out!'

Soon we can see from the deck a single large canoe heading for the fleet. But it is racing the night, and by the time it nears us only the flash of dipping paddles can be seen. Down the line of ships those flashing paddles move, and a cry is heard across the water.

'Admiral! Admiral!'

302

This is one of the few Spanish words Guacanagarí's people know.

We light *Mariagalante*'s signal brazier to direct them to the flagship and watch the flashing paddles approach.

'Admiral! Admiral!'

A ladder is dropped down the side. Yego joins me there.

'Tell them to come aboard.'

He does, but the Indians just shout: 'Admiral! Admiral!'

A torch is brought. I stand at the bulwark in its light so they can see my face.

Minutes later, six naked Indians are on the deck, led unfortunately by Guacanagarí's fat brother, the one cuckolded by Francisco Niño. At least I can be thankful that our Billy Budd prototype is not aboard *Mariagalante*.

Two Indians step forward with a pair of golden masks.

'Big one from Guacanagarí,' Yego tells me. 'Smaller much beautifuller one – ' he is, of course, translating ' – from Guarionex.' This is the name of Guacanagarí's fat brother.

I thank him for the gifts, and a box of hawk bells is opened. Soon they are tinkling all around us. Wine is brought. The Indians, unaccustomed to alcohol, become garrulous.

'Ask Guarionex about the settlement,' I tell Yego. 'What's wrong there?'

A rapid exchange in Árawak follows. Guarionex puts down his wine cup and does not drink again.

'Fighting,' Yego says. 'Much badness of fighting.'

'Who? Who were they fighting? Have they suffered any casualties? Why isn't there any light at the fort?'

More Árawak talk. Then Yego says, 'Many men sick. Guacanagarí hurt when try – ' here Yego gropes for a word ' – protect.'

'From what?' I shout.

Guarionex's answer sounds something like 'Caniba'.

'Ask him how many casualties,' I say, really alarmed now.

The translated answer: 'None.'

'But he just now said – '

Considerably more Árawak talk. 'But many die from Yellow Sickness.'

'How many?' I shout.

Fat Guarionex is uncertain.

Half an hour later he is more uncertain. An hour later he won't answer any more questions.

Word has of course spread on the ship of fighting, and perhaps the outbreak of some fatal disease, ashore.

'Can't you get the truth out of that fat freak?' I hear a familiar voice demand. Mosén Pedro Margarit has pushed to the front of the crowd. 'Surely you ought to be able to wring a few facts out of a naked savage.'

I order everyone to withdraw, so as to remove Mosén Pedro from the scene. The last thing I want is a confrontation between the Queen's favorite cavalry officer and Guacanagarí's brother.

'Tell Guarionex we're going ashore at sunrise, Yego,' I say when we're alone with the sub-cacique and his men. 'Whatever the truth of the matter is, we'll learn it then. So he'd be better off telling us now.'

Yego explains this.

There is a long silence, the Guarionex speaks.

There is an even longer silence, then Yego speaks. 'They all dead,' he tells me, his voice choked. 'He say they all dead.'

'He's lying!' I shout. 'He's got to be lying!'

But Yego shakes a sad head. 'Caonabó,' he says. 'Very strong cacique. Guacanagarí and he, they are – ' Yego can't find his word.

'Enemies? Rivals?'

Yego nods. 'Yes, rivals.'

I look at Guarionex. 'They can't all have died,' I say.

But Yego repeats his words: 'All dead.'

At first light while the boat is lowered I debate the make-up of my shore party. I want no Mosén Pedro so certain of Indian subhumanity, and no Brother Buil so eager to condemn what he doesn't understand. But I'll need armed men, and an officer I can count on in a fight. So I signal *Colina*. If I can control his recklessness, that cocky bantam rooster Alonzo Ojeda's just the man.

I'll need a non-nonsense sort of fellow too, intelligent and not apt to jump to conclusions, whatever we find. I look at Big Diego and wish for Barto, then settle on Dr Chanca.

As *Mariagalante*'s boat and Guarionex's canoe approach shore, Christmas Town remains as silent as the mangrove swamp, as apparently deserted as the Indian village at the far end of the beach. The stockade seems intact, and I can see *Santa Maria*'s mizzenmast against the brightening sky, although no flag flies from it. But where the watchtower should be there is only a jagged stump.

I don't wait for the boat to be beached but lead my armed men through the surf to the coral sand. The stockade gates hang open. I run, Ojeda at my shoulder and then plunging ahead.

Within the stockade, Christmas Town has been burned almost to the ground. The native-built huts are totally destroyed. The jagged stump of watchtower is fire-blackened. We poke in the ashes and rubble where the storehouse stood. Here a few charred timbers remain. Here are smashed wine casks and what looks like part of a crude wooden plow. Something glitters off to one side. This proves to be a sorry handful of glass beads used for trading with the Indians. Alonzo Ojeda finds a small keg of nails, one of my men a besooted crucifix and chain. Watching us, Guarionex hangs back.

Dr Chanca finds the bodies.

There are two of them, at the base of the watchtower, partially hidden by the fallen timbers. The bones have been picked almost clean. Maggots swarm on clinging tatters of clothing. Hempen rope, almost burned through, still binds the arms of one behind his back. I see a shiny brown sluglike something crawl obscenely from an empty eyesocket. This body lies curled up. The other kneels prostrate, arms outflung.

Dr Chanca touches a boot to one charred skull. 'You can see,' he says clinically, 'where the skull has been smashed.' He prods the other head, to which a pitiful remnant of scalp clings. 'Same thing here. Clubbed to death.'

I feel none of the mind-numbing horror I experienced ten days before on the island of Guadalupe. I have no time for that. I see the dead men, but I also see Guacanagarí almost as if he stands beside me, and I see again his sign language, the day I sailed from the bay on *Niña*, clear as spoken words: *Come back soon, my brother*.

Coldly I tell Yego, 'Ask Guarionex if there are more bodies.'

But my adopted son is crying, and it is a while before he can speak. When he does, Guarionex leads us outside and behind the stockade. Nine more bodies are there, some with hands still bound behind backs, all with skulls smashed.

We walk along the beach to the abandoned Arawak village, Guarionex unafraid as he hurries, puffing, to keep up. In the headman's hut we find some jerkins and red caps, a bright Moorish silk scarf. *Santa Maria*'s kedge anchor lies on the ground next to the headman's carrying chair. How it got there, or why, I will never learn.

Suddenly Guarionex begins to jabber.

'He say,' Yego translates, 'Caonabó kill village men, friends of Spaniards.'

Encouraged by my somber nod, Guarionex goes on.

'He say Guacanagarí cannot come in time.'

Within the stockade, Christmas Town has been burned almost to the ground. The native-built huts are totally destroyed. The jagged stump of watchtower is fire-blackened. We poke in the ashes and rubble where the storehouse stood. Here a few charred timbers remain. Here are smashed wine casks and what looks like part of a crude wooden plow. Something glitters off to one side. This proves to be a sorry handful of glass beads used for trading with the Indians. Alonzo Ojeda finds a small keg of nails, one of my men a besooted crucifix and chain. Watching us, Guarionex hangs back.

Dr Chanca finds the bodies.

There are two of them, at the base of the watchtower, partially hidden by the fallen timbers. The bones have been picked almost clean. Maggots swarm on clinging tatters of clothing. Hempen rope, almost burned through, still binds the arms of one behind his back. I see a shiny brown sluglike something crawl obscenely from an empty eyesocket. This body lies curled up. The other kneels prostrate, arms outflung.

Dr Chanca touches a boot to one charred skull. 'You can see,' he says clinically, 'where the skull has been smashed.' He prods the other head, to which a pitiful remnant of scalp clings. 'Same thing here. Clubbed to death.'

I feel none of the mind-numbing horror I experienced ten days before on the island of Guadalupe. I have no time for that. I see the dead men, but I also see Guacanagarí almost as if he stands beside me, and I see again his sign language, the day I sailed from the bay on *Niña*, clear as spoken words: *Come back soon, my brother*.

Coldly I tell Yego, 'Ask Guarionex if there are more bodies.'

But my adopted son is crying, and it is a while before he can speak. When he does, Guarionex leads us outside and behind the stockade. Nine more bodies are there, some with hands still bound behind backs, all with skulls smashed.

We walk along the beach to the abandoned Arawak village, Guarionex unafraid as he hurries, puffing, to keep up. In the headman's hut we find some jerkins and red caps, a bright Moorish silk scarf. *Santa Maria*'s kedge anchor lies on the ground next to the headman's carrying chair. How it got there, or why, I will never learn.

Suddenly Guarionex begins to jabber.

'He say,' Yego translates, 'Caonabó kill village men, friends of Spaniards.'

Encouraged by my somber nod, Guarionex goes on.

'He say Guacanagarí cannot come in time.'

sun fills the cacique's hut. The extravagant bandage, wrapped so bulkily around Guacanagarí's leg, gleams whitely in the sun's last slanting rays.

'Did he say when our men died?' Dr Chanca asks me.

'No. Why?'

'It's been weeks, I know that much. But that bandage he's wearing isn't a day old, it's so clean. Are his Arawak medicine men so big on hygiene?'

I don't answer, but nudge Dr Chanca a step closer to the hammock and tell Guacanagarí, 'This man is the most famous doctor in all of Christendom.'

'I have many, many doctors,' signs Guacanagarí quickly.

'He has offered to examine your wound and heal it with powerful Spanish medicine.'

'I trust my many, many doctors.'

Dr Chanca sniffs. 'And I smell many, many rats.'

Yego begins to translate this, but I stop him with a glance.

Dr Chanca approaches the hammock. It swings a bit as the cacique shifts his weight away.

'Bend your knee.'

Guacanagarí can't.

'Move your toes.'

Guacanagarí does so.

'Just as I feared,' says Dr Chanca with a shake of his head.

'My medical advisors are top-hole,' signs Guacanagarí.

But, at a nod from me: 'We'd better have a look under that bandage,' persists Dr Chanca, and the cacique can find no way to refuse.

Off, winding after winding, comes the crisp white bandage, to reveal Guacanagarí's bare, muscular leg.

Dr Chanca examines it minutely. 'Not a mark on him.'

Guacanagarí grimaces. 'The knee bone is broken,' he signs.

Dr Chanca looks at me. Again I nod. With both hands Chanca grabs the bulging calf below the knee and quickly flexes Guacanagarí's leg.

Too proud to carry the farce any further, the cacique tilts his hammock and rises gracefully from it. 'It would appear,' he signs with rueful skill, 'that I am gifted with awesome recuperative powers.'

Nobody says or signs anything for a while.

'It seemed simplest to feign an injury,' Guacanagarí signs finally.

'Tell me what really happened,' I say, my voice hard.

307

With the sun down, a breeze has stirred. Torches are brought and set into the ground. Guacanagarí stands impassive.

'For every ship we had last year,' I tell him, 'now there are six. For every man last year, twenty. We bring terrible animals that go into battle with us, great four-footed creatures many times the size of a man.' I think of Mosén Pedro's nags and go on quickly, 'We have killer hounds and a hundred guns like the one that blew my flagship off the reef and a thousand muskets. I want the truth and I want it now.'

In the torchlight Guacanagarí's face is a study in bronzy sadness. 'And will you believe what I tell you, my brother?'

'You'd better hope I do. Because if I don't, there are captains outside who'll have your life.'

Guacanagarí ignores this threat. 'If you don't believe me – '

'Why should I? Your fat brother Guarionex lied every time he opened his fat mouth, and you were wounded in a battle you never fought.'

' – would you believe your own interpreter?'

The question surprises me. 'Yego Clone? I don't understand.'

'The interpreter who died at Christmas Town. The young one with eyes the color of a sunlit lagoon.'

He means Luís Torres, and for the first time the awful truth of Christmas Town really hits me. Petenera's brother is dead. They're all dead.

At a signal from Guacanagarí, a flat wooden box is brought by one of his entourage. In it is a charred something, once rectangular, what's left of a book maybe.

'Christian fingermark speech,' signs Guacanagarí. Fingermark speech is his sign for writing. 'Found with the body of the green-eyed interpreter.'

I pick up the charred book. The leather binding flakes and crumbles in my hands. The pages begin to crumble too, though I handle them gingerly. The paper is yellowed, the edges blackened to char, the ink brown as old bloodstains. Here and there words and whole sections of Luís Torres's diary have been obliterated.

I go outside with a torch. Men crowd around me, but I push through, answering no questions, to the edge of the squalid little village. The barkless native dogs sidle timidly from my path. A parrot screams in the encroaching darkness.

A wind flutters the pages of the little book as I sit and hunch over it protectively in almost the same position as the skeleton we found at the foot of the watchtower in Christmas Town.

Was that Petenera's brother?

From the diary of Luís Torres
... lief to learn, finally, there are no cannibals here on Hispaniola (or
Haiti as the Indians call this huge island). Looking back on our
mistake, it's almost funny. Seems a cacique called Caonabó holds
sway over the central highlands. It's said he has Carib (that is,
Canib-al) ancestry, hence the name. But though ... and poison-
tipped arrows, unlike Guacanagarí's less warlike folk, they're still
Arawaks, so there's little chance we'll wind up in the stewpot. Still,
this chief's name gives a man food for thought. If such arcane
writings as the *Sepher Yezirah* are right – and I'm less skeptical
than Petenera – then the name of a thing or person contains its
essence. Thus the cacique named Caonabó partakes of the fierceness
of cannibals (if not, thank God, their eating habits). The *Sepher
Yezirah* goes further, claiming a thing or person and its name are
one and the same. Even God. In the Bible, isn't God's name God
Himself? Otherwise how explain a line like 'He shall build a house
for my name'?

Here in the wilderness I find myself, like Petenera, fascinated by
the undeniable parallels between the forbidden lore – black magic,
The Key of Solomon, the cabbala, the teaching of Gnostics like
Simon Magus – on the one hand, and approved Judaic and
Christian doctrine on the other. So I jot down these somewhat
fuzzy ruminations to share with her someday even if they don't
belong in what purports to be a record of daily events in Christmas
Town. I can see I'll have to prepare an edited version for publication
– unless I want to face the Inquisition instead of the Indians.
Anyway, we don't really know that this cacique Caonabó...

(*Here the entry ends in a crumble of scorched paper and remains
indecipherable until:*)

... bound to happen, I suppose, but it still comes as a shock.
Harana's unsure what to do about it, but from now on he'll be
suspi ... Chachu makes, for whatever good that...

... ossible to forget the first time (how long ago it seems!) one of
us diddled fat Guarionex's willing wife ... to blame. But since
Chachu's hardly a benign deity's gift to women, the likelihood here
... in fact raped, but still Guarionex beat his wife to death, while
Chachu only...

...

4 May. I believe Chachu is insane ... he were the only one, we

could cope. But hard as it is to accept, he's now got fully half our people, twenty supposedly civilized Christians, running amok between here and the central highlands. They steal crops, rape women and, if resisted, raze whole villages. Harana suspects that something in cassava bread turns these men into vicious monsters, but Dr Sánchez says that's not possible. The bread *is* weird, though. How it's made, I mean. You grate the root (called manioc: interesting: see my earlier speculations on the names of things) on a board imbedded with flint chips. The liquid thus extracted is the deadly poison into which Caonabó's warriors dip their arrows. But the fibrous residue is pounded ... staple of the Arawak diet.

... showdown. I agree with the constable that it was inevitable. Only it's too bad that while we were throwing Chachu and his bullies out of the settlement, we couldn't have rid the whole island of them ... west to where Guacanagarí reigns and running so wild that even our loyal ally ...

... first direct contact. Caonabó might as well be a Carib! (No, belay that. Petenera's always inveighed against overstatement, and this Caonabó's no eater of human flesh. But he is one tough customer.) The first real trouble ...

...

16 July. Today the ... gging to be allowed back inside the fort. As only four are left, I think Harana will relent even though Chachu ... or else Caonabó's warriors will either kill them or drive them permanently into Guacanagarí's territory. The great cacique visited us here today and warned ...

As if that weren't enough, we have a strange disease to worry about. Dr Sánchez doesn't know what to make of it. Fever, hemorrhage, black vomit – ugh! Four have already died including poor Relámpago, and there's not another experienced gunner among us. Dr Sánchez is encouraged by something he calls the survival rate. Two out of three, he says. But they're left terribly weak, and their skin and the whites of their eyes are a sickly yellow.

... ner or later. Dr Sánchez and I are the only ones who haven't. Even Harana succumbed last month to the temptation (and it *is* a temptation), for he suspected that by not taking a personal harem he was losing face as our leader. So even the constable has five Indian women dancing attendance on him and sharing his hammock ... celibate, far from it, but my own pride extends to my sense of every other human being's worth, even a woman's. This is Petenera's influence, I'm sure, for if she ever drummed anything into my head (aside from an agnosticism that apparently has suffered a sea change: as Dr Sánchez says, there are no agnostics in Christmas Town) it is that the choice ought to be the woman's as well as ...

(From this point poor Luís's diary is so scorched that only isolated fragments are readable.)

... stantly encountering patrols of not just Caonabó's but Guacanagarí's warriors, who have begun to use bows and arrows too ... sadly inevitable ... called progress.

... Indian woman ventures outside her village. Guarionex threatens to ...

... good intentions of Guacanagarí. But sometimes I think part of the problem is that we're in disputed territory between the two caciques and Guacanagarí can't afford to show weakness before his ...

... think it's gone too far even for that. How I wish the Admiral were here!

3 September. Chachu is dead! He ...

... teen of us left and it isn't fat blustering Guarionex we have to worry about but Caonabó. Because Chachu, it appears ... ambush on his way back from a highland village with several women captives. In the battle ... of Caonabó's best warriors but half a dozen of our ... all the women ...

... up to his name. I fear for our lives.

12 October. Landfall a year ago this day. Probably, unless a miracle happens, the last entry I will make in these pages. And I expect no miracle. But surely the Godhead under whatever name — or the contending forces of good and evil, as the Gnostics maintain and Petenera half-accepts ... blame even more than Caonabó. There are six of us left as I write these words, and how many hundreds of Caonabó's warriors outside the stockade thirsting for our blood?

... late afternoon but the ...

If you ever see these words, Admiral, believe me that some of us remained loyal to the end to your vision of a colony that would be Spain's pride, but ... ested in gold and women, not in settlement. The very qualities that make a good seaman ...

Petenera (how unlikely, beloved sister, that you will ever read these pages!), I wish you could know that I await death, which can be only moments away, more with curiosity than with terror. For if the two religious traditions that nourished me are right, then life is no more than a preparation for something we can but vaguely comprehend, as we can but vaguely comprehend the evil in the world that exists despite God's love; whereas if you are right, dear sister, then all will soon be no more than an eternal sleep. I'll know in moments. But of course, if I am wrong and you are right, then I *won't* know, will I?

... Harana ...

... commend my soul to ...

I sit a long time without moving, except for my hands. These are trembling. Luís Torres's words have made it all so real I can see it.

Not that anyone else will. For the diary, while obviously a valuable historical document, is also as lethal as a poisoned Carib arrow. Luís's own admitted heresies no longer matter – he is beyond the Inquisition's reach – but his casual catalogue of Petenera's, however parenthetical and unmalicious, can send his sister to the Burning Place.

So, valuing my beloved's life more than my obligation to history, I feed the diary to the nearest cookfire.

It is at this point that Dr Chanca and his good friend Bernal de Pisa, the Crown comptroller with the fleet, come looking for me.

'Are you all right, Admiral?' asks Dr Chanca. 'We were getting worried.'

'What's that you're burning?' asks Bernal, who has the prim voice and bad posture of your average deskbound accountant.

'Surely,' Dr Chanca drops into the ensuing silence, 'it isn't the writings of the colony's interpreter?'

'It was his dying wish,' I say lamely.

'What was whose dying wish?' This is Bernal the Crown comptroller. As their fiscal agent with the expedition, he is accountable to the royals, not to me.

'Poor Luís Torres. It was a diary of his private thoughts. He didn't intend it to survive him.'

'Then why,' asks Bernal, 'didn't he destroy it himself?'

'He must have tried,' I say. 'It was badly charred.'

'But then why did he write it if he wanted it destroyed?' asks Bernal tenaciously.

'To get it off his chest,' I suggest. 'Ask the doctor to explain catharsis and the therapeutic effect of – '

'And what was so private,' demands Bernal, not at all waylaid by psychology, 'that he wanted it destroyed?'

Dr Chanca intervenes at this point. 'If the Admiral carried out the dead diarist's wishes, then obviously he can't answer that question.'

Bernal de Pisa adds this all up like a column of figures. 'I see,' he says in a voice that indicates the figures don't tally.

'I can say this much,' I try. 'The reputations of some brave men who died tragically at Christmas Town would have been grievously damaged by the diary.'

'There you are, Bernal,' says Dr Chanca in his no-nonsense voice. 'You see how simple it is?'

But Bernal adds his column of figures again. 'Well, Admiral, if this chief Guaca-whozits is your friend, which you said he is, how can we be sure, with all due respect, that you haven't destroyed the diary because it incriminates him?'

This becomes a refrain I have to live with, as I discover the next day. But first I call on Guacanagarí.

'Has the fingermark speech allayed your suspicions of me?' he signs.

I now realize he could not know it would, since he can't read. He's simply confident in his own innocence. But then I drift into some pre-Machiavellian thinking – possibly thanks to Bernal, or to my years with Roderigo Borgia. Guacanagarí might have hoped only for a certain ambiguity in the diary, which I would then interpret in his favor *because* he didn't destroy it when he could have.

'Yes and no,' I say in as decisive a tone as circumstances permit.

Guacanagarí makes the sign for 'Could you be a little more specific?'

And, finally, I am. 'There's no doubt that Caonabó and his warriors killed the settlers,' I say. 'But only you know whether you tried to prevent the slaughter, as Guarionex suggested, or were perfectly content to let Caonabó do your dirty work.'

Guacanagarí turns away from me and speaks softly to Yego, then bows his head. The incomprehensible words – or perhaps it is the cacique's body language – are simple, eloquent and sad.

In a shocked voice Yego tells me: 'Great cacique want you take knife you always wear at side and kill him.'

I am too dismayed to say anything.

'He want you kill him now unless you believe him same innocent of act of no as act of yes.'

After a while I interpret my son and interpreter to mean sins of omission as well as of commission.

Guacanagarí says he wants me to be his judge and, possibly, executioner. Is this a pre-Machiavellian ploy too?

Whatever, I can't do it. Which he probably knows.

Here, for the first time, I learn that being Viceroy and Governor is a lot more complicated than being Admiral of the Ocean Sea.

The lesson is reinforced the next day in the Captain-General's suite aboard *Mariagalante* where, at noon, I have assembled my senior captains, plus Big Diego and a smilingly insistent Brother Buil.

Not half an hour into the meeting Mosén Pedro Margarit, fingering his now-bearded lantern jaw, repeats the refrain I have to live with: 'Then how do we know, with all due respect, Admiral, that you haven't burnt the diary just to whitewash this Guacanagarí?'

There is a murmur of agreement around the table.

Only Melchior Maldonado, he of the reverberating name, booms out: 'The Admiral of the Ocean Sea's word is good enough for me.'

But, 'You miss the point, friend Melchior,' says Mosén Pedro smoothly. 'I wouldn't doubt the Admiral either. But I might be less sure about a viceroy who feels he has to make accommodations to live in peace with the Indians.'

There is more murmuring around the table. They are already taking for granted the conflict inherent in my dual commands.

Bland Big Diego says, brightly for him, 'Well, I think we've heard everybody. Let's vote on it, shall we?'

I gape at my brother.

Where did that idea come from? Who said we were going to vote?

But it's too late. He is my unofficial Number One, after all.

Fortunately, the vote is hopelessly split.

Captain Torres (no relation): 'Put this Guacanagarí in irons until we can get at the truth.'

Captain Maldonado: 'I'd be inclined to go along with whatever the Admiral counsels.'

Captain of Lancers Margarit: 'Clip the cacique's nose and ears like a common thief; as an example to the other wogs.'

The clipping of noses and ears is a fortunately moribund Spanish custom adopted from Arab law.

'After all,' elaborates Mosén Pedro, 'since it's well known that they can't feel pain, it would merely be a cosmetic punishment.'

Pink and smiling, his eyes atwinkle in his seraphic face, Brother Buil says: 'Then, if merely cosmetic, it won't do. The most edifying course, if we really intend making an example of him — ' here a little trill of eager laughter escapes Brother Buil's lips ' — is to burn him at the stake. And I might point out that such an exercise would be exemplary not just to the heathens.'

There are several other suggestions for dealing with Guacanagarí, ranging from extremely painful to life-threatening.

Then it is Big Diego's turn to speak again. 'I cast my vote with Captain Maldonado.'

So much of this voting has been going on that it's hard for me to remember Maldonado's position. Big Diego helps out with, 'Well, that's two votes for letting the cacique off and one each for a variety of other alternatives. So I guess we let him off.'

'Letting him off,' reverberates Maldonado, 'was not exactly what I said.'

'That's funny,' Diego tells him. 'I cast my vote with you, after all, and that's practically the same as saying you cast your vote with me, isn't it? And I know how I voted.'

Maldonado reverberates a doubtful 'I suppose so.'

Here I push back from the table and rise. Everyone looks at me. Justice, European style, is to be dispensed for the first time in our nascent colony. Perhaps I should have accepted Diego's sophistic attempt at democracy, thus taking no direct part in the exoneration of Guacanagarí. But our enterprise is hardly ready for the anachronistic political process urged on it by Diego.

'All votes,' I adjudicate, 'are merely advisory because, gentlemen, this is no fraternal organization or guild, one man one vote and all that, it is (or will shortly be) a Crown Colony of which I am Viceroy. My judgment – mine, gentlemen, and therefore my responsibility – is that the cacique Guacanagarí has done no wrong and will remain a trusted neighbor.'

At which I curtly dismiss the senior captains and Brother Buil.

Overweening arrogance, you think? The hubris of Greek tragedy transported to a Caribbean isle? The pride that everywhere goeth before a fall? Perhaps. But what other choice is open to me?

Being a legend in your own lifetime carries certain responsibilities, not least to that difficult mistress, history. And I've played fast and loose with the muse Clio once in this episode, which is enough.

'They didn't like that,' Big Diego sighs.

'Only because you brought up this hare-brained idea of voting. Are you a Freemason or something?'

'Good God, no!' cries Big Diego, shocked. 'But I did spend some time on Borgia business in the Swiss Confederation. I learned a bit about democracy there.'

'Forget whatever you learned.'

'All of it?'

'All of it.'

My brother, as will become apparent, takes me at my word.

⇛ XIII ⇚

How After Various Disasters
I Arrive at a Reunion
As Unexpected As It Is Poignant

M Y many biographers, so often disputatious, all agree on one
point: while I may have been a world-class Admiral of the
Ocean Sea, as Viceroy or Governor I just didn't hack it.

But ask them why, and they are at loggerheads as usual.

Sometimes I wish I could turn the tables, me holding *them* up to the
light. In fact, for just a page or two, I think I will.

Look at my most prominent twentieth-century Old World biographer, a Spanish man of letters who fled his country at a time of
troubles and wound up an Hon. Fellow of Exeter College, Oxford.
(That's in England, as you'll remember from my northern adventures.) How does this Hon. Oxford Fellow explain my shortcomings
as Viceroy and Governor?

Ready? He blames it on my Jewish ancestry.

Which, having no Luís de Santangel to tell him, he then tries to
prove.

His main argument is, if you leave your homeland to wander from
country to country, feeling at home wherever you go, you're probably
Jewish. *Ergo*, Colón had Jewish blood. Now, I'm not saying that I
didn't. But what about this self-exiled Hon. Fellow himself? I mean,
he left his Spanish homeland, and spoke a bunch of languages, and felt

317

right at home in England. This hardly proves *he* had Jewish ancestry, does it? Anyway, isn't the Hon. Fellow confusing Jews with gypsies? Sure I wandered. Could I change the *faege* that had driven me ever since my Julian decade on the northern rim of the Ocean Sea? But I didn't feel at home everywhere I went, I felt at home *nowhere* I went. I'm your perennial outsider. Maybe this, not my Jewish ancestry, explains why (as will be seen) I was death on colonies. Is a discoverer meant to stay put? Then how can he discover? You see the problem.

Not that I'm trying to avoid this Jewish business. Sooner or later I know I'll have to confront it head on.

However, my most prominent twentieth-century New World biographer (an Admiral in his own right, by the way) rejects it flatly — as far as I can see because the Hon. Fellow makes so much of it. Instead, this Admiral blames my undeniable inadequacies as Viceroy and Governor on the fact that I was a sailor, same as him, more fitted to handle a ship on stormy seas than a colony on the rocks. This tells us something about the Admiral In His Own Right, perhaps, but not much about me, which isn't surprising since we've met him before and know he's not interested in 'psychology, motivation and all that.'

It's somehow distasteful to watch my biographers squabble over my triumphs — yes, and my disasters — like heirs over a contested will. But this is a good time to get it over with, because right now my seventeen-ship fleet is beating slowly eastward along Haiti's northern coast into the teeth of the Trades, lucky to change tack only fifty times a day and make maybe two or three miles headway.

Heredity, claims the Hon. Fellow. Jewish ancestry.

Environment, insists the Admiral In His Own Right. The nautical life.

Do they try to resolve this Darwinian difference of opinion? Never. They are too busy excoriating each other.

The Admiral, who is a professor of history at Harvard University, dismisses the Jewish Experience approach of the Hon. Fellow as 'unsupported by anything so vulgar as fact.'

The Hon. Fellow in his turn damns with faint praise, calling the Admiral's biography 'interesting ... from a yachtsman's point of view.'

Why all the backbiting? Can't Oxford and Harvard get along? I'll never understand these things.

No, I'd better just write about myself. I'm what I know best. And if I occasionally depart from the traditions of autobiography, it's just to set the record straight.

While I've been doing that, the great fleet finally drops anchor off what I hope will be our permanent settlement. It's not your ideal site, with a deep-water anchorage close to shore and headlands protecting the bay, but it is due north of Cibao (which could well be Cipango with its roofs, streets, walls and culverts of gold). The harbor, unfortunately, is open to the north and northwest, so winter storms will come roaring in to menace shipping. One threatens, in fact, the day we arrive. But after an hour's downpour the skies clear, a good omen I think.

It is 2 January 1494, and I wish I could say we go ashore at the new site with all the hope a new year brings.

But the people are exhausted from a month of shifting sail, a few have already come down with the Yellow Sickness (which the Hon. Fellow dismisses as influenza!), our livestock are suffering (a prize Extremadura sow has expired at sea and Mosén Pedro's nags look worse than ever) and on all sides I hear voices begging me to drop anchor permanently somewhere, anywhere.

Once ashore, a few of us are enthusiastic. 'I'll build the first church on this side of the Ocean Sea right here,' Brother Buil smiles, staking his and God's claim to a slight rise a quarter of a mile inland.

I have a surprise for him. Aboard *Gallega*, broken down into its many components, is a small church, gift of Queen Isabel. This prefab structure will be the first to rise in Isabela — our settlement is named for the Queen — and its only substantial building.

Dr Chanca picks his spot. 'A good place for my clinic,' he says. 'Plenty of sun and it's on high ground so that river over there won't flood it out in the rainy season.'

In fact 'that river over there' — hardly more than a channel through swampy ground — proves too stagnant to provide safe drinking water, which can only be found a mile to the southwest in a stream rushing down from the central highlands. But what's a mile, with golden Cibao just three or four days' march inland?

I begin to imagine tidy little whitewashed Andalucían cottages, a cobbled plaza in front of the prefab church, a street of shops, a few small farms at the edge of town where Spanish livestock graze and Spanish wheat, cucumbers, grape vines and the like poke tender green shoots inquisitively into the Indies sunlight while gold from the mines of Cibao pours into the stronghouse.

And what's the reality?

Join me early on a February morning, scratching mosquito bites as I slip furtively from my wattled hut (assuring myself as I do every day

319

that we'll quarry stone for a proper governor's mansion once we're better organized and Dr Chanca gets the Yellow Sickness under control) to reach a muddy patch of desolation between the prefab church on its knoll and Dr Chanca's double-sized wattled hut of a clinic. I start across the plaza-to-be, skulking somewhat as my parents did in Chapter I, scene one, because I'd as soon reach the clinic unnoticed. A man with a bad toothache hardly needs to face, as well, the probing questions of his resident spiritual advisor.

But smiling Brother Buil appears at the prefab church door.

'Good morning, Viceroy,' the seraphic Benedictine greets me. 'What a splendid day God has given us for doing His work. Each according to his station, of course, as God intended. You *will* be relieving the caballeros of their brute labor today, won't you?'

Smiling Buil's complaint (and not just Buil's) is that I've assigned our gentlemen volunteers to such onerous tasks as plowing the soil, draining the marshes and digging a canal to the river for drinking water.

'Brother,' I mumble indistinctly through my swollen jaw, 'I just don't see how I can. Too many of our common settlers are down with the Yellow Sickness.'

'If the Lord meant caballeros to work like beasts of burden, He wouldn't have made them caballeros, now would He?'

For answer I hold a hand to my jaw and squinch my eyes shut in pain. This is no act.

'Well, think it over while the vet's yanking that tooth of yours,' Brother Buil advises me.

But I'm not headed for one of Isabela's veterinarians. Both are putting in twenty-hour days to care for the livestock, now mostly skin, bones and a growing mortality rate. Anyway, I have more faith in Dr Chanca as a tooth-puller. Plus, I want to consult with him about the emergency shopping list that will leave today for Spain.

Out in the harbor, past a line of wooden buoys that marks the channel for our smaller caravels (carracks have to anchor a mile offshore), twelve ships are preparing to sail under Captain Antonio Torres for Cádiz. These ships and their crews are now superfluous to our purpose, which is to find gold. Sending them back will show my frugality, so necessary now because the first expedition to Cibao, led by that daredevil Alonzo Ojeda, brought back no more than a few gold nuggets, gift of the cacique Mayrení. I am beginning to have large doubts that Cibao is Cipango. But at least Mayrení's Indians, Caonabó's allies, received Ojeda in peace, and now he's back in the highlands constructing a fort.

Inside the clinic Dr Chanca says, 'Sit on the stool here in front of the windowhole where it's light.' We have no glass, except in the church. I sit and await the worst.

'Open.'

I open.

'Gum's not just swollen, it's fiery red.' He touches my cheek. 'And you have a fever, you know.'

'Will I lose the tooth?'

'Of course you will. When a tooth's rotten, you yank it. Open wider.' His finger pokes. I stifle a yelp. Something seems to squirt in my mouth. 'Got some pus in there,' he comments in his no-nonsense way and pokes again. This shoots me bolt upright off the stool.

'Spit and sit down,' he says.

I spit on the floor and sit on the stool.

'About our shopping list,' I say quickly if thickly while he rummages among instruments that look, at least this morning, as if they belong in an Inquisition dungeon.

'No problem *if* the Crown complies.'

'And if they don't?' I sound, to my surprise, contentious.

'No problem either,' says Chanca. 'If they don't, in six months or so we'll all be dead, and dead men have no problems, do they? Open wide.'

But, 'Are you sure we've left nothing out?' I ask instead.

Dr Chanca waves his tooth- or thumbnail-extractor. 'I can't think what. We're asking them to send three or four caravels straight back loaded with (a) wine, oil, sugar, molasses, vinegar, grain and salt meat for the general population; (b) honey, rice, raisins, cheese and almonds for the convalescent; and (c) medicaments for the sick, including every herb I know to regulate the bodily humors and quicksilver to combat that pestilential sexual pox which surpasses what the gods of antiquity inflicted on the irreverent shepherd Syphilis (if you remember your mythology) or the God of the Old Testament on Job (if you read your Bible, and even if you don't). How much gold is Antonio Torres carrying back to Spain?'

'I make it barely thirty thousand ducats' worth, and to get that much we had to threaten every man who even knew an Indian and tear apart a few suspicious-looking wattled huts.'

'Hardly cover a tenth of our needs.'

'That's why I'm sending most of our sailors home. It gets them off the royal payroll.'

'True. Also it just could avert a mutiny,' says Dr Chanca. He looks reflectively wattled-ceilingwards and intones, 'Ah to be in Andalucía now that spring is there.'

Spring comes early to southern Spain and that wistful lament, predating Robert Browning by almost 400 years and sounding somehow like a threat, is heard everywhere in our struggling little colony. Or maybe it's the mood I've been in.

'Now open. I said *open*. This isn't going to hurt as much as you think it will.'

Surrendering to the inevitable, I open my mouth wide and shut my eyes tight.

There are several moments of outrageous pain that I feel clear down to, and for some reason especially in, my groin. I leap off the stool. Blood pours from my mouth.

'That didn't hurt as much as you thought it would, now did it?' asks no-nonsense Chanca. 'No, certainly not,' he answers for me. 'It hurt *more* than you thought it would.'

I stand against the wall gasping and swallowing blood. After stuffing a wad of cotton into the gaping hole in my mouth, he shows me an object pitted like worm-eaten furniture and streaked with a tracery of brown like crazed pottery.

Gingerly I touch the long, bloody, pincerlike roots. 'That thing came out of my mouth?'

'A rotting tooth,' says Dr Chanca, 'can cause a dangerous imbalance in the bodily humors, usually producing too much bile at the expense of phlegm. This leads to chills, fever and the like. Have you been feeling bilious lately?'

'I don't know what feeling bilious feels like.'

'Short-tempered, ready to fly off the handle at the drop of a hat, if you'll excuse the mixed metaphor.'

'Short-tempered? Me?'

'Take the day off, why don't you?'

'Day off? What's the matter with you? I don't have time for that kind of thing,' I say in a stiff-mouthed way, for my jaw is more swollen than ever.

'Bile,' nods Dr Chanca.

'Balls!' I retort.

'Well, if you won't take the day off, at least let up a little.'

'Impossible and you know it,' I accuse him.

Just as I say this a chill grabs me and shakes hard.

'Don't say you weren't warned.'

More reasonably I tell him, 'I have a million things to do.'

'It's your funeral.'

Chanca's a good doctor but somehow those of us who knew him long for the bedside manner of poor Dr Sánchez.

Still, Chanca may have a point about biliousness. So on parting I try for a conversational 'How goes the fishing?'

'Wouldn't know. Bernal goes out too early these days for me. I'd rather have the extra hour of sleep.'

Bernal de Pisa, the comptroller, is a Spaniard of Italian ancestry like a lot of officials at the Peripatetic Royal Court, and by inclination a real Izaak Walton. Out in his tiny (cost: two hawk bells) dugout canoe every day right after dawn, he used to have a regular cheering section as he cast his line for snapper, pompano or grouper. A large grouper can feed a lot of hungry mouths. But Bernal, claiming the racket from his fans drove the fish away, has taken to going out in the wee hours of the morning, hanging a lantern at the stern of his two-hawk-bell canoe to attract his finny prey.

When I emerge from the clinic into the sunlight of Isabela's plaza-to-be, I see men lounging about, leaning against the wall of the church, talking, smoking cigars (of inferior shape and aroma to Luís de Santangel's), making priapic comments on an Indian woman crossing with swift oblivious grace toward the waterfront, and in general doing nothing in that busy way that will in a later era typify street life in Latin America.

'These men ought to be working,' I say to the first person I encounter. This happens to be Juan Niño of Moguer. Hulking Juan Niño is the constable of Isabela, and since he looks like a one-man Inquisition, his mere presence usually suffices to head off trouble. But he doesn't know what to do about this wildcat strike of Isabela's 200 caballeros. He just stands there watching. Stick a smouldering roll of tobacco in his face and he could be one of them.

I find Mosén Pedro Margarit standing outside the prefab church door with Brother Buil. The tall, lantern-jawed cavalry officer crosses his arms over his chest.

'This is it,' he informs me ominously.

'Oh?' I counter, determined to control my biliousness.

'We have two demands. First, we do no work from now on but gentlemen's work. That's marching in parades and fighting on horseback.'

'You agreed to throw in an occasional joust,' Brother Buil smilingly reminds him.

323

'On special occasions,' says Mosén Pedro. 'And second, we caballeros demand some real Spanish food.'

The subtropical climate has putrefied all our salt pork, and biscuit maggots thrive in Haitian warmth. Even our reserve sacks of chickpeas and lentils have gone moldy. A diet of cassava bread and yams baptized with the thin, sour plonk sold to the fleet in Cádiz by profiteering wine merchants is hardly enough to keep body and soul together. Also, Dr Chanca maintains, it lowers the body's resistance to an imbalance of humors like the Yellow Sickness. Yet these alien rations are everyone's lot.

Mosén Pedro scratches his mosquito bites; mosquitoes afflict caballeros and commoners alike.

'That wouldn't be fair,' I tell him. 'We haven't enough even for the convalescents.'

'What,' he asks, surprised, 'does fairness have to do with it?'

I suggest a compromise. 'I'll relieve you caballeros of plowing, canal digging and marsh drainage on alternate days provided you spend those days fishing.'

An organized fishing industry would go a long way toward solving our hunger problem.

'Fishing,' says Mosén Pedro, 'is not gentlemen's work.'

'What is?' I ask.

'Anything to do with horses.'

'You won't even groom your own nags,' I point out.

'Groom them? That's different. Gentlemen don't groom horses.'

Indians won't because the beasts terrify them (the honeymoon period in which Indians pretended horses did not exist is over) and commoner colonists can't because they're too busy clearing jungle, building wattled huts, careening and scraping barnacles off our five remaining ships, and plowing, digging the canal and draining the marshes.

In these endeavors they get much encouragement but not a great deal of help from the scores of Guacanagarí's people who have settled on the outskirts of Isabela, mostly out of curiosity. Work as a lifestyle has not caught on big with the Arawaks, and it is a while yet before we will resort to force.

Still determined to control my biliousness, I suggest another compromise. 'Take the morning off. You probably just need a break. We'll work out a rotating schedule of free days.'

Mosén Pedro brays laughter. 'Of course we're taking the morning off, old boy. Not to mention the afternoon and tomorrow morning and – '

That does it. 'Arrest this man,' I say biliously, and Juan Niño of Moguer advances on the Queen's favorite cavalry officer in the sudden sunstruck silence of the plaza. There is the briefest of tussles as Mosén Pedro reaches for his sword, but Juan Niño gets a come-along grip on the soft flesh below the cavalry officer's nose and leads him at a bent-over lurch from the plaza to our still virgin jail.

'The rest of you get back to work!' I order.

No one moves. Cigar smoke wafts lazily skyward. I hear a few 'damn foreigners' drawled in high-born tones.

'No rations for any of you until you're back on the job,' I warn them.

For three days the caballeros shape up first thing each morning between Brother Buil's church and Dr Chanca's clinic, and loiter there all day long.

Before dawn on the fourth day I enter the dim prefab church to seek spiritual guidance, pretty much a last resort for me these days. I kneel and start asking God a few tough questions when Brother Buil enters from the side, back-lighted by votive candles.

'What are you doing in here, Viceroy?' he demands, *without smiling*.

'Praying for guidance,' I say simply.

'Well, I suppose that's between you and God. But personally I think what you are doing is heinous. I am therefore placing you under an interdict. From this moment, your divine offices are suspended until the caballeros are fed.'

'But,' I say.

It isn't necessarily that I'll miss Mass or crave confession, but a viceroy rules by the grace of his sovereigns who rule by the grace of God, and where Buil's interdict leaves me in this scheme of things I'm not sure.

'I'll lift the interdict the moment you restore their rations.'

'I'll restore their rations the moment they get back to work.'

Impasse.

'You can't expect a man of God to stand by while you use your control of our food supplies to exact complete obedience from all settlers, no matter what their station in life,' says Brother Buil.

'Maybe not,' I say, shifting to a possibly inspired attack, 'but how is it that in the two months we've been here this same man of God hasn't converted a single solitary Indian?' I stare accusingly at the prefab baptismal font, more virgin than the jail.

'Merciful Heavens!' cries Brother Buil with a huge, troubled smile. 'They're still lascivious, that's why. Sex is the problem, Viceroy. If only their maidens would accept a seemly position, but no – you'd be amazed at the acrobatic variations on the simple act of procreation of which those teenaged Indian girls are capable. And it's not just their impatience with the missionary position, Heavens no. They insist on fornicating in the nude.'

'That's not surprising,' I point out. 'They never wear anything.'

Brother Buil ponders this. 'I mean,' he says, 'the other fellow. Why do these Indian maidens always insist that their partner take his robes off?'

There is a gravid silence.

'Did you say "robes"?' I ask.

Brother Buil smiles and smiles. Then he says, 'It could have been Brother Ramón Pane or those two Burgundians.' But we both know Pane is practically a hermit and the two Burgundians are lovers. 'It could have been your almost clerically garbed brother,' Brother Buil suggests. But I'm convinced Big D is a virgin.

'I will remove the interdict,' smiles Brother Buil, 'if you will maintain silence with regard to the ... necessary research conducted by the Mission here.'

I agree. Church and State can live with such a compromise.

On the fifth morning at the opposite side of the plaza Dr Chanca predicts, 'If you don't restore their rations they'll all come down with the Yellow Sickness.'

But I stand my stubborn ground and personally unlock the storehouse every morning for the daily rations that are doled out to the colony.

Meanwhile, I'm not favored with the best of health myself. I'm losing weight, my joints ache at the slightest meteorological provocation, even a warm breeze is enough to send a chill through me, and my bloodshot eyes are constantly irritated because I seem to have completely run out of tears. I haven't told any of this to Dr Chanca for fear he'll yank another tooth. Yanking the first one, as far as I can tell, caused all the trouble.

'You look like hell, Viceroy,' he tells me in his unbedside manner.

'It must have been something I ate.'

'You look like hell, Viceroy,' I hear again, this time from young, clean-cut Pedro Terreros, my steward aboard *Santa Maria* and now

326

Niña's boatswain. Pedro, unlike our idle hidalgos, not only works by day but is a volunteer watchman by night.

'It's nothing,' I assure him.

'Could I talk to you privately, sir?'

We walk off toward my wattled hut of a governor's mansion.

'You really do look peaked, sir,' Pedro says sympathetically.

'I told you it's nothing!'

Inside, I snap, 'Well, what is it?' I go to the bucket in the corner and scoop up handfuls of water to soothe my burning eyes.

'A night watchman notices things,' Pedro begins, staring at me.

'Didn't you ever see a man wash his eyes before?'

'Sorry, sir. I wasn't staring or anything,' Pedro lies.

'Then what did you come here for?'

He looks at me, disappointment on his all-Spanish face. This is not the Admiral he knew and maybe even loved.

'No, I'm sorry, boy,' I tell him gruffly. 'I *have* been feeling a bit under the weather lately. Now sit down and tell me what's on your mind.'

'This,' says Pedro, taking from under his arm a leather slipcase of the sort used by pilots to protect their maritime charts. 'Here's how I found it,' he explains. 'Every time I pull the pre-dawn watch, I see the same thing – that light on Bernal de Pisa's two-hawk-bell canoe. And whenever I see it, sooner or later it drifts out to the third buoy in the channel.'

'Maybe it's a good place to fish.' I can't see that wimp Bernal de Pisa involved in anything of a skulduggerish nature.

'Then you'd think he'd park for a while, wouldn't you? But he just sort of calls there and moves on. So last night after he beached that two-hawk-bell canoe I swam out to have a look. The buoy had a kind of recess in it with a tight-fitting hatch. That's where I found this chart case.'

I open it. Inside are a few sheets of paper covered by what is probably handwriting. I give them a quick glance and slip them back into the case.

Pedro gets the wrong idea. 'I understand, sir. You'll want to read those in private.'

'Haven't you read them?'

Pedro says he figured that wasn't part of a night watchman's duties.

I rub my eyes, and give him the sheets of paper. 'Read it out loud, will you?'

'Me?'

'So you'll be able to testify if necessary that you read this before I had a chance to alter anything,' I improvise. I go to the bucket to slosh water at my burning eyes again. By this time even Pedro is blurry.

As Pedro reads, his voice grows increasingly indignant.

The papers are, in the dry colorless language an accountant would use, a bill of particulars against me.

Item. During an altercation between a heathen and Captain Margarit, the Viceroy not only sided with the former but struck the latter and kicked him while he was down.

Item. Although it was proven beyond reasonable doubt that the Indian cacique Guacanagarí acquiesced in the slaughter of the Christmas Town settlers, the Viceroy refused to punish him.

Item. When Isabela's 200 overworked caballeros requested some small redistribution of workloads of benefit to the entire community, the Viceroy withheld their rations.

Item. The Viceroy, in his searches for alleged impropriated gold, has violated all civilized standards of privacy and personal honor –

But I've heard enough, and storm outside looking for Bernal.

Fifteen minutes later we're at the Hall of Justice or Juzgado (loosely pronounced, especially by southerners, hoosegow), a triple-sized wattled hut with the jail at the back, where Juan Niño of Moguer meets us.

'Read this,' I tell him, and he quickly skims the channel-marker papers.

On his face appears a truly ferocious scowl as he grabs Bernal by the jerkin, jerks him close, and shouts, 'Who put you up to this, you wimp?'

Bernal just stands there, suspended from a big Niño fist while Juan fires a series of journalistic questions at him: who? what? when? where? how? why?

From the jail at the back comes Mosén Pedro's insolent voice: 'You don't have to answer any of that.'

And Bernal doesn't.

Whether Juan Niño would have resorted to certain interrogational techniques then in vogue in Spain is moot, for just then Yego Clone hurries into the Juzgado, his eyes big with excitement, a sheen of sweat on his bronzy skin, his breath coming hard.

When he can talk: 'Admiral Father, I run all way from Hidalgo Pass for to warn – '

'Over here,' I tell him and soon we're standing at the north

328

windowhole. 'Keep it down, Yego,' I say. 'There are enemies every-where.'

Hidalgo Pass is a high col in the mountains south of Isabela, a quarter of the way to Fort Santo Tomás, the strongpoint on the edge of Cibao that has been garrisoned by Alonzo Ojeda and eighteen men.

'Now what is it?'

'I keep ear to ground, Admiral Father.'

Yego's services as interpreter are less necessary now that Spaniards are beginning to pick up a few words of Arawak and vice versa. But as one of their own who can tell them about Spain or Heaven, Yego is much in demand among Guacanagarí's people and moves freely among them.

'Cacique Caonabó plan big surprise attack on fort.'

'When?'

'Soon.'

'How soon?'

'Eight days,' suggests Yego. I don't like the sound of that. Eight days (you'll remember) is a variable temporal commodity, and on rare occasions can vary on the short side.

'Put Bernal in the cell back there,' I tell Juan Niño.

'With that Margarit?'

'No. Release Margarit. We're going to need him.'

From the cell at the back the Queen's favorite cavalry officer brays an infuriating 'That's obvious, old boy, isn't it?'

That evening I confer with Dr Chanca. 'Well, are they fit for military service?'

'Healthy as horses, the lot of them.'

'But they've been on a hunger strike for almost a week.'

'You mean you cut off their rations.'

'Whatever.'

'Apparently they are not without their sympathizers. It's been a sort of Ramadan situation.'

This allusion to Islam I don't get. 'A what?'

'They fasted by day and gorged themselves by night.'

'Then we can march at once?'

Dr Chanca elevates his eyebrows. 'You mean you're going?'

'You don't think I can trust Captain Margarit in a position of command after this, do you?'

Looking back, this is not only a rhetorical question but a dumb one. Since Mosén Pedro will be getting exactly what he wants, a gentlemanly military command, the feel of a warhorse (or at least a nag) between his knees, the prospect of a nice bloody battle, why shouldn't I trust him?

Because I'm not used to being sick, that's why. I need an excuse to test my own powers.

Dr Chanca, in those pre-psychoanalytic days, doesn't understand this. He says, 'If you can't trust Margarit, send your brother.'

'Big D? He doesn't even know how to ride. I'm going, Doctor. I have no choice.'

'You've been losing weight, you know. What else is the matter with you?'

Since he is a doctor, I dole out a few symptoms – aching joints, chills, no tears.

'Listen, my friend. Yellow Sickness I can more or less understand, even if rest and wholesome foods are my only weapons against it. Even with syphilis we sometimes get encouraging results with topical application of quicksilver. But this syndrome of yours has me completely baffled. Chills, arthritic aches and pains, a bilious temperament, sore eyes – '

'Dry eyes,' I correct him. 'I have no tears.'

'Anything else?'

'Well, a sore back.'

'Where?'

'Here. Down low here.'

'I see. Anything else?'

There are a couple of other excruciatingly embarrassing aspects of my strange malady, hardly the sort you reveal in the fifteenth century even to your medical advisor, not if you want to be taken seriously as Viceroy.

'Nothing else at all!' I shout. 'What gave you the wild idea there's anything else the matter with me?'

'I think,' says Dr Chanca, 'you need a complete rest.'

'I think,' I say, 'you need your head examined.' I haven't intended saying that. It just came out. This is happening a lot these days, I don't know why. In a more reasonable voice I tell him, 'I've got a military campaign to conduct. And it can't wait while I take a vacation.'

'It's your funeral,' says no-nonsense Dr Chanca.

While Mosén Pedro Margarit assembles his 400-man army (half of them the no-longer-striking caballeros) and while the trumpets and drums of our martial marching band tune up in competition with a thunderstorm building to the south, I confer with Big D.

330

'You're in charge here,' I tell him. 'But I've named a council to advise you. They're reliable men, so take their advice.'

Large, soft, pale Big D in his brown monkish robes nods soberly. 'I'll do a good job, you'll see if I don't.'

'I know you will, bro.' I pat his plump shoulder.

Some readers may wonder why I place in the hands of someone so lacking in leadership qualities the fate of the troubled colony. I mean, the least astute observer must know by now that Big D is definitely not officer material. All I can say is this. In various ways, my antecedents are Spanish, Italian and Jewish. Family solidarity's as big in Spain as in Italy, and among Jews – so often faced with the alternatives of all-out exile or all-out death – it's even bigger. Despite his shortcomings, Big D is my own flesh and blood. I can trust him. Not necessarily to do exactly the right thing, but at least not to stab me in the back.

So I outline a few of our more pressing problems and how I think he ought to handle them.

He takes notes, then looks up, alarmed. 'Say, how long will you be gone, anyway?'

'I *am* going into battle,' I remind him.

I also remind him: 'And don't forget my plan for the cannibals.'

'Huh? What plan?'

There's a flash of lightning far off. Thunder rolls in the mountains south of Isabela.

'I've given Antonio Torres a letter to the royals about it. Here's the gist,' I tell my brother. 'People who eat people aren't normal. It has to be an acquired taste, and like any perversion it can be unlearned. So – '

The next lightning flash lights the whole sky.

'So here's my plan – or dream, maybe. We must try and save them all.' As I say these words, there's a really huge crash of thunder, very close. Big D looks up from taking notes as if to ask a question, then apparently changes his mind and resumes scribbling at a furious rate.

'In time,' I say, 'we can catch us a few shiploads of Carib prisoners, including a sprinkling of caciques and sub-caciques, I hope, and send them to Spain for re-education and conversion. Then they'll come back here and teach their people to be loyal, dietarily straight subjects of the Crown. In the process we probably can save a lot of Arawaks too,' I say, my words interrupted so often by thunder that an animist might conclude the rude and rudimentary gods do not smile on my plan. Again Big D looks up to ask a question, again he changes his mind.

331

Outside, there's the blare of trumpets.

'Well,' I say gruffly. I hate farewells.

Still, we embrace, very brotherly.

'I guess you must know what you're doing,' says Big D as he follows me outside.

My parting words are: 'Be audacious.'

Before my own role in this expeditionary force is abruptly terminated, I have the satisfaction of seeing the reaction of Caonabó's men to mounted warriors, and never mind the quality of our mounts.

This happens after we cross Hidalgo Pass and descend on the verdant interior of Hispaniola, great ebony and mahogany trees shadowing the way and flocks of parrots screeching at us (for all I know, calling down imprecations in Arawak). The first village we reach, a straggle of palm-thatched huts along a river, appears deserted. But suddenly from the high reeds lining the riverbank we hear yowls, yips, yaps, yipes and yelps, all meant to curdle the blood. We even glimpse them momentarily, these Arawak warriors of Caonabó, so like the Caribs in appearance. Angry slashes of charcoal mar their faces, their long hair is drawn back into nets of parrot feathers, and they are armed with bows and arrows, the latter presumably dipped in essence of manioc.

Only a few of these arrows are released, fortunately hitting no one. For at exactly the right moment, as if part of our game plan, Mosén Pedro's nag − hearing those blood-curdlingly onomatopoeic battle cries − whinnies and ramps. This prime candidate for the glue factory, eyes wide, nostrils flaring, long-in-the-tooth mouth agape, lets go a second whinny to the accompaniment of a final toot from our trumpets while, fighting desperately to stay aboard the now bucking nag and slashing his sword overhead, Mosén Pedro forces the beast into a sort of sideways canter toward the reed-lined bank.

It is all too much for Caonabó's warriors, who go splashing for their lives across the river.

Don't mistake this for cowardice. I mean, if you didn't even know horses existed, how would you like to be cantered at sideways by a sword-wielding, two-headed, six-limbed centaur?

When Mosén Pedro steadies his nag and trots back in triumph to the head of the column, it is noticed that I sit slumped in the saddle, face deadly pale, breath stertorous. At first a poisoned arrow is assumed. But when I'm eased to the ground I continue breathing, and no wound can be found.

'It's the Yellow Sickness,' Mosén Pedro misdiagnoses.

Someone else suggests a new, more virulent syphilis.

Understandable. How can they know that even in disease I'm an outsider? My weird syndrome will mystify not only my biographers but, in a broader context, medical science for the next half millennium or so.

Anyway, the immediate upshot is the fashioning of a litter and the detailing of eight men to take me back to Isabela, where I arrive, unconscious and burning with fever, forty-eight hours after we set out.

Dr Chanca shakes his head and relegates me to the lowest level of his triage scale. Big D, in the weeks that follow, never leaves my side. Had I been conscious both times, all this might have reminded me of when I was poisoned in Rome and given up for dead.

Big D won't let Brother Buil near me, possibly identifying him unconsciously with the priest Salutati the Youngest in Rome. But isn't this also reminiscent of Domenico Colombo and the rabbi, when my mother died giving birth to Big D? There are echoes in life, as in history.

Big D, until now a man of simple devotion to God and family, gives up on the former − at least as represented by smiling Brother Buil. Buil accuses him of apostasy.

In a coma, I keep my distance from this squabbling.

So it's a good opportunity to rebut my biographers on my disease. They're about equally divided between gout and arthritis, but that's just a problem in semantics because in Spanish *gota* is the word for both. The Hon. Oxford Fellow, for example, comes down squarely on the side of foot-gout; arthritis, says the Admiral In His Own Right. It's true foot-gout can be murder. One victim, the greatest humanist of all time, Desiderius Erasmus (a friend or at least correspondent of my son and biographer Fernando, as the latter is quick to point out), dosed himself, misguidedly, with large drafts of red wine to widen his arteries, so that after a life almost as peripatetic as mine, poor Erasmus spent his last days howling in pain in his celibate chambers in Flanders. Arthritis can also be hell on earth, though in my day (and Torquemada's) few dared to phrase it that way.

But my own hellish affliction was neither gout nor arthritis. Did you ever hear of gout or arthritis giving any one stigmata? Real Christlike stigmata?

These come later, though. Right now I am having this dream about ordinary, get-lost-in-a-crowd Tom Norton of Bristol Town, if you remember him (and even if you don't, as Dr Chanca might say).

'It's bad enough not to look the part,' Tom Norton's telling me in my dream in his ordinary voice, 'but who'll take seriously an alchemist named Tom Norton? Now, if I were called Zosimos Rhazes or Melchior Tetragammaton...'

At this point I call out for Melchior Maldonado, him of the reverberating name, as Big D tells me later. But nobody knows why, and when Maldonado arrives at the run, I'm in a coma again.

Where I see ordinary Tom Norton bent over a crucible in which a thick grayish liquid boils furiously without aid of fire. 'The basest of base metals, lead,' he tells me. From the crucible in that foul-smelling dream of a laboratory, tubes extend to a dome-shaped glass receptacle that will collect and condense distilled vapors. 'The aim being, of course,' says Tom Norton, 'to transmute base lead to gold.'

At this point I shout the word *gold!* and, as Big D tells me afterwards, a nugget is brought for the dying Viceroy to touch.

'All that is required,' says Tom Norton, 'is the philosopher's stone.' In his now trembling hand he holds a disappointingly small something about the shape and size of a pigeon's egg. This may be the nugget they brought me, the biggest they could find. So it's a case of reality and dream feeding each other.

'Every object on God's earth, or off it for that matter,' says ordinary Tom Norton, his speech patterns oddly like Dr Chanca's, as he moves the philosopher's stone, 'is composed in certain fixed proportions of a few building blocks. These are, so the ancients told us, earth, air, fire, water. Right? Wrong. Four's now three. Mercury or quicksilver, sulphur, salt.'

The word *syphilis* escapes my lips, a clear indication that even in delirium I'm concerned about the fate of the colony.

'Now it follows,' says Tom Norton, 'that the adept can change anything into any other thing, simply by altering the proportions. Well, I think we're ready.' He passes the philosopher's stone three times around the crucible. It shatters, the molten matter therein, now congealed into a leaden lump, falls heavily to the table, and from the cracked dome-shaped glass receptacle he plucks with tweezers a tiny gleaming golden speck. 'The problem, of course,' he sighs, 'is quantity. What can you do with two-thirds of a grain of gold? Well, we'll solve the quantity problem, I know we will. Some day.'

Two-thirds of a grain of gold – I start right in working on the problem (very clever for a dreamer) and soon transmute it into 30,000 ducats, which would have made ordinary Tom Norton of Bristol

Town ecstatic but won't even pay for a tenth of the emergency supplies we've requested from Spain, as Dr Chanca pointed out.

Since 30,000 ducats of gold can't be contained in Tom Norton's cluttered little laboratory, there's a crashing sound, the door bursts off its hinges and flies into the room, smashing what lab equipment is still intact, and hands shake me roughly.

'The problem of course is quantity,' I say, quite distinctly I think.

'He's trying to say something!'

Hands keep shaking me roughly.

'We're worried,' a dream voice says.

'You've got to come with us,' a real voice says.

I flutter one eye partially open. Big D and Yego Clone are hovering.

'We've got to find more gold,' I counter.

'They're killing them!' Big D says. Close to a wail.

'In plaza,' says Yego Clone.

'More gold,' I insist.

They spout more words. They sit me up. Big D is bawling.

They stand me on my bare feet. They dress me. Tentatively they release me. I sway.

'I've got to find more gold, I tell you,' I tell them.

'They're killing them for *nothing*,' Big D cries. 'For hawk bells!'

A cup of wine is held to my lips. This helps.

'Who's killing who?' I manage.

They walk me. I stumble when they try letting go again. We are at the door of my wattled hut. I insist on opening it myself and see by my white, gold-braided sleeve that they have dressed me in my Viceroy's uniform, which I have been saving for a special occasion, such as my presentation to the Great Khan of Cathay. Hat and all.

Outside the sun is too bright but the breeze blows no chills through me. This is encouraging. I hear shouts from the plaza, an ugly sound that for some reason I associate with Valencia. 'Let go,' I tell them. They hover cautiously on either side. I march. Not exactly quick-time.

'Hurry, Admiral Father,' urges Yego.

The plaza is mobbed. The whole colony must be there, I think. Fortunately, viceregal perks have placed my wattled hut of a governor's mansion on a slight rise, so we're approaching the plaza downhill and I can see over the mob to where an Indian, hands bound behind his back, kneels with his head on a tree stump. Above him looms a powerful-looking fellow bare to the waist holding an axe, its blade gleaming in the sunlight. Two other Indians wait, also bound. They have been given a last cigar and a Good Samaritan holds it to their noses for an occasional puff.

Except for Mosén Pedro's voice, the decibel level in the crowd drops instantly to zero when they see me. The Queen's favorite cavalry officer is reading a sentence of execution. I notice that the noses and ears of all three bound Indians have been cropped in that ugly manner learned from the former Arab masters of Spain.

' ... guilty of stealing two shirts, four red wool caps and six hawk bells. The punishment for such a second offense is death by decapitation. Headsman, do your duty!'

'Stop!'

This is me, and a pretty good shout, all things considered.

Viceregal in attire, shaky in gait, I advance into the crowd of gaunt, sallow faces. These Yellow Sickness survivors look so disheartened, so gloomy about their prospects, if any, that perhaps Mosén Pedro believes a good bloody execution's just the tonic they need.

But I have little time for such ruminations, for the headsman has raised the axe as high as his anatomy will permit, and is poised to execute the command.

'Drop that axe,' I tell him in a soft voice so as not to alarm him, and set all his coiled nerves and muscles into irretrievable motion.

Big D provides a thoughtful amendment: 'Over there to one side.'

When the headsman obeys both of us, I proclaim, 'These men are pardoned by Viceregal order.'

I won't attempt to describe the implacable hatred the Queen's favorite cavalry officer projects as he approaches.

'Out there in the boonies', he says, 'I am the law.'

Instead of disputing this dubious contention, I remind him, 'You're not out there in the boonies,' while I think: but you soon will be.

'That is where the crime was committed,' says Mosén Pedro.

'You think petty larceny rates a death sentence?'

'As an example, yes. I do. Besides, it's well known that they don't feel anything. Probably, like three-toed sloths or caterpillars, they aren't even aware of their own existence.'

'Heavens, no,' chimes in smiling Brother Buil, who has joined us, 'that would imply that three-toed sloths or caterpillars or Indians have souls.'

'How,' I ask him, 'can you expect to bring the Indians into Holy Mother Church if they don't have souls?'

'I have often prayed to God for guidance on this point,' Brother

Buil admits. 'Perhaps souls will be vouchsafed them upon their conversion.'

The three condemned Indians, still bound, have meanwhile been assured by Yego that their heads won't be lopped off.

'Untie them,' I tell him. I want Yego to get some of the credit for this.

But it is before me that the three Indians bow, almost prostrating themselves. Embarrassed, I touch each dark, glossy head in turn. This act quite inadvertently resembles a benediction without the sign of the cross, a strong indication of Judaizing according to Suprema guidelines.

Brother Buil smiles a note-for-future-reference smile, which I'm in no condition to notice.

Back in my sickbed, I tell Melchior Maldonado what I want done. It takes forty-eight hours.

'You've polled everyone?'

'Except Alonzo Ojeda and his garrison at Fort Santo Tomás,' booms Maldonado. 'But that's only nineteen men.'

'And?'

'Four hundred and two agree with Captain Margarit that a second offense of petty larceny's sufficient reason to execute an Indian. Three hundred disagree. The rest have no opinion. Of the four hundred and two Margaritites, half are caballeros. This is our entire caballero population.'

I put on my Viceroy's uniform and, with Melchior Maldonado as witness, send for Mosén Pedro Margarit.

'I'm giving you command of an army of four hundred and two men,' I tell the Queen's favorite cavalry officer.

'Viceroy, I don't know what to say,' he says.

'I want you to relieve Captain Ojeda at Fort Santo Tomás.'

'Viceroy, I really am quite speechless.'

'Your orders are to remain at the fort until further notice.'

Mosén Pedro's crest falls. 'It's a pretty small fort to hold a garrison of four hundred and two men. Almost like a prison, you might say.'

'The experience will temper you and your men for what's to come.'

After some reflection, 'You're planning something big, aren't you, Viceroy?' brays Mosén Pedro. 'A top secret campaign against the cacique Caonabó, am I right?'

'Whatever, it's going to take time. Meanwhile, the less contact you have with the Indians, the better.'

'I understand. I'm a patient man.'

I'm not. Three days later, pale and still weak, I stand on the quarterdeck of plucky little *Niña*, gripping a shroud in my familiar stance. I've had enough of Mosén Pedro and Brother Buil and Yellow Sickness and my own strange malady and even enough of well-meaning Big D. What did God put me on earth (or at sea) for, anyway? To coddle discontented colonials, or to discover?

Of course, I get the usual chaff from my biographers. This time they accuse me, as with one pen, of deserting my post, of abandoning a colony beset by troubles – to go off on some Caribbean pleasure cruise!

Never mind the misreading of my character. The misreading of the situation is bad enough. I mean, what can a convalescent Admiral (even a Viceroy) do that Big D and his council can't? Loving the sea, should I not try to get back my strength in the cool blue of its embrace, as Antaeus got his back from the earth? No, I have to go. Unknown islands, even mainlands, await me.

So up, up soars the mainsail as all hands heave on the halyard, and up, up soar my spirits with the glad cries of my youthful crew. Why, with the exception of hulking Juan Niño of Moguer, I could be the father of them all, of his brother Francisco, our Billy Budd prototype, of Pedro Terreros who once single-handed saved *Santa Maria*, of Yego Clone, my adopted son who counts as godparents the King and Queen who sent us here, of all sixty of these youngsters.

'Now, heave!' shouts boatswain Terreros.

'For we're going to Cathay!' thunder the others as higher still soars the mainsail.

'Now, heave!'

'We're bound away for the Golden Chersonese!'

And *Niña* and the two smaller caravels *San Juan* and *Cardera* ride the Trades west to Cuba.

But Cathay and the Golden Chersonese, you ask? Well, that was what I told the lads, so those were the names they sang. Did I suspect, even then, that my geography was a little bit off? Does it matter? Is there not, inside each man, the touch of the alchemist that can transmute the internal Cuba, the Cuba of the soul, into Asia, with Cathay and the Great Khan lurking forever just out of reach?

Here's a dream to ponder. Why couldn't I lead my little fleet, three caravels, a pair of salty veterans and sixty fearless boys, around the Golden Chersonese (or Malay Peninsula) and across the Indian Ocean with a fair wind, and around the Cape of Good Hope and up the African coast past Fernando Po to Spain, circumnavigating the globe almost thirty years before Magellan's lone surviving ship *Victoria*? But I didn't try, no; history said it was not to be, even if my own internal geography continued to insist that Cuba was part of the Asian mainland.

We drop south to the mountainous island of Jamaica and circle it before returning to Cuba, and the wind is a seaman's dream and the cynical schemers of Isabela are forgotten. Was I ever sick unto death, or was it no more than a sickness of the spirit?

Other questions trouble my biographers. Why, they ask, don't I also circumnavigate Cuba to learn what they know in retrospect, that it is no part of Asia but only the largest island in the Caribbean? Only!

Here's an 'only' for you. An island looms ahead, any new island, *terra incognita*. In the hour before dawn it is only a darker darkness against the sky, a ridge of unknown mountain blotting out the timeless stars. Then the first light gives form to the unknown land and the form takes on depth as the rim of the sun appears where sea and sky meet, and finally the first real light of day brings the birth of color to this land until now unknown, until now no part of the world, until now for all I know *not even existing*. Only!

Crabbily my biographers carp, wagging accusatory fingers and dust-dry volumes of geography. He didn't even try to circumnavigate Cuba, they repeat, as if that were the purpose of my existence. And then, to buttress their point, they fabricate. How they must grudge me my five-month idyll!

The fabrication strains credulity: I force my crew, my sixty innocent youngsters, to take a sacred oath (on pain of an unsurvivable hundred lashes or an unpayable 10,000 maravedís) that they all believe Cuba is part of the mainland of Asia.

Does this sound like me?

Before turning back we follow a coastline longer than Britain's, and we all agree that Cuba is too inordinately large in the geographical scheme of things to be an island. And if it isn't, we all agree, then it has to be part of Asia, doesn't it?

The truth is, I do make all of my sixty boys (and crusty, honest Juan Niño of Moguer, first to sign) swear an oath — an oath so secret that perhaps my earliest biographers invented their own oath about Cuba as a way of fishing for the real one. For though many of my shipmates will be questioned, none will jeopardize his sacred honor by revealing it.

Here are the facts. One morning as I rise from my hammock (it is late September and we are bound back for Isabela), without warning my joints groan like an old man's, I feel pain knife through what isn't yet known as the sacroiliac, and a racking chill grips me despite the sun's warmth. My tearless eyes burn so mercilessly that, instead of going below to splash them with water surreptitiously, I head directly for an open butt on deck.

The water dribbles through my fingers, for as I bring my cupped hands close to my eyes I see on my palms the angry sores.

I remember standing there and thinking, these look like stigmata on my hands.

'Those l-look like stigmata on your hands,' says the shy, wondering voice of our Billy Budd prototype Francisco Niño.

I clench my fists to hide the ulcerous sores. I hope vainly that in moments they will be gone.

'What are you talking about, you idiot?' I demand, as biliously as Dr Chanca could have predicted.

'I'm sorry, sir,' says Francisco Niño, 'but those look like stigmata on your hands, and if they're r-real, why ... then ... ' His voice trails off in confusion.

I open one hand quickly. Stigmata, all right. Very Christlike. I close the fist again.

By this time I have applied the so-called razor of Dr Invincibilis (real name: Bishop William of Occam or Ockham) which I encountered in England. This philosophical cutting edge slashes away complicated solutions to expose simple ones. And the simple explanation of my stigmata is that, since the Whole Sick Syndrome came back to smite me today, they are probably part of it. Who needs miracles?

But our Billy Budd prototype, himself so saintlike in his simple goodness, blurts, 'You – you're holy, sir!'

I ought to point out that holy and saint are the same word in Spanish, so Spaniards don't make quite the fuss over sanctity that some folks do. It's not altogether clear whether Francisco Niño means just holy or really a saint. I don't feel much like either.

'You saw nothing,' I say.

'I d-did not. I saw stigmata,' says Francisco Niño, hurt.

'Listen, boy,' I snarl.

By this time a small crowd of grommets has gathered.

'So you must be a saint, sir,' says our Billy Budd prototype.

'I'm warning you, boy,' I snarl, very mean.

'If you have stigmata, you have stigmata. I'm *sorry*.'

I also, by this time, have a fever.

'I didn't *do* it,' Francisco Niño tries, 'I only *saw* it.'

About twenty young voices shout, 'Let us see too, let us see too!'

Making matters worse, the wind today is light and fitful and *Cardera* and *San Juan* are drifting close, their sails slack. Some of the boys are in swimming. On such occasions visits are common and, wouldn't you know, we soon have grommets from the two smaller caravels aboard *Niña*.

'The Admiral has st-stigmata on his hands,' Francisco Niño is earnestly – almost with the pride of ownership – telling our dripping wet, naked visitors.

'They're just your ordinary open wounds!' I shout.

Juan Niño comes down from the quarterdeck. 'What the hell are you up to?' he asks Francisco.

'The Admiral's a saint,' says our Billy Budd prototype.

'He's *what*?' gasps Juan Niño in forgivable disbelief.

'Let us see too, let us see too!' everybody else keeps shouting.

My own morbid curiosity gets the better of me and again I open one hand for a quick look.

'Holy man! Holy Christ! Holy shit! Stigmata!' bellows Juan Niño of Moguer, instantly if temporarily a true believer.

Three days later the stigmata begin to heal, and in a week they're completely gone.

This is when the oath suggests itself to me. That it must be taken by every last man is obvious. I can't be a saint, even a rumored one, and still be Governor or Viceroy, not to mention Admiral. None of these offices goes with sanctity, and I have my career to think of.

The men of all three caravels are assembled. Crusty, honest Juan Niño of Moguer presides.

The only one who balks is Francisco Niño. 'I saw what I saw.'

'Forget it,' his brother Juan threatens.

'I can never forget it.'

'Then just keep your mouth shut about it. Besides, they went away, didn't they?'

'That's the way it sometimes is with stigmata,' says our Billy Budd prototype stubbornly.

'Forget it.'

'I can't.'

Etc., etc.

Juan Niño takes drastic measures. Secretly with a knife he gouges stigmata-like wounds on his own palms and shows them to Francisco. 'Is sainthood contagious?' he asks scornfully.

341

None but our Billy Budd prototype, himself not so very far from saintly, would ever swallow this refutation. But fortunately Francisco, very much in character, does.

Meanwhile, in semi-delirium, I'm beginning to have second thoughts about my sanctity (or holiness). I mean, they *were* stigmata, weren't they? But I let certain episodes in my life run through my mind, which quickly and permanently cures me of the delusion.

Meanwhile also, my Whole Sick Syndrome is getting worse. Nobody knows what to do. The fault of rudimentary fifteenth-century medicine? No – even half a millennium later, they can still do no better than pump in the wonder drugs and hope for the best. It's not even a regular sickness, dignified by a sick name and a lot of sick sufferers. Just a relatively obscure syndrome that will be named after the Dr R—— who first identifies it in a lucky patient. It does eventually get its own laboratory verification (a high incidence of the histocompatibility antigen HLA-B27 (W27) in the blood). I mention this only to emphasize that R——'s Syndrome isn't psychosomatic, despite its occasional neuropsychiatric manifestations (e.g. my wondering if I am holy (or even a saint)).

As we return to Isabela, all sails cracked on, I am one sick Admiral. Acute R——'s Syndrome is trying its best to kill me. I believe that if he were aboard, Brother Buil would have administered, with a smile, the last rites of the Church.

Dr Chanca, everybody says; we've got to get him to Dr Chanca in time.

But what can Dr Chanca do that even Dr R—— won't be able to, centuries later? Not bloody much.

Soon Dr Chanca is forgotten.

'He's a goner,' crusty, honest Juan Niño of Moguer says.

'D-don't even think it,' his brother Francisco whispers. Francisco blames himself, probably because he was the first (after me) to see the stigmata.

'He's a goner,' can be heard all over little *Niña*, and aboard *Cardera* and *San Juan*.

But how's this for transfiguration or at least one of history's best-timed *dei ex machina*?

I'm dimly aware, in a fever dream, that *Niña* has tied up at Isabela's makeshift dock. I hear soft crying nearby. This is Yego Clone. 'Please don't die, Admiral Father,' he pleads, as Pedro Terreros bravely tries to console him.

I hear no nautical sounds – no wind through the rigging, no creak of spars and timbers, no slosh of water in the scuppers. I hear shore sounds – the clatter of hooves on dock planking, the tolling (for me? I wonder) of our prefab churchbell, the barking of the Irish wolfhounds that are being trained (though I don't know this yet) to tear Indians to pieces. I feel myself being carried across the deck.

Juan Niño of Moguer shouts: 'Gangway, gangway there! It's the Admiral on this litter here and he's in a bad way.'

There's the sound of bare feet retreating, then the louder thud of boots approaching.

'Gangway, I said,' shouts Juan Niño. 'It's the Admiral on this litter here, I tell you.'

And a voice from out of the past, a voice I somehow thought I would never hear again, asks: 'The Admiral's on that litter there? How come?'

'Just move out of the way, fellow.'

'But how come?'

So finally, here at my side as he was always meant to be, making me blink my dry eyes open and in fact shed tears of joy as life comes surging back into me, is my beloved brother Barto.

~❧ XIV ❧~

How an Administrative Misunderstanding Sends Me Back to Spain in Sackcloth and Ashes

I WISH I could write, as a novelist would, that Barto made all the difference. A novelist can get away with anything if it's a good story. But unforgiving history looks over my shoulder as I pen these words.

I wish I could write, as a novelist would, that Barto got to the bottom of the Bernal de Pisa channel-marker papers, or put Brother Buil on the right track as a missionary, or taught Mosén Pedro Margarit to behave like a gentleman instead of merely being one, or curbed the swashbuckling neuroticism of Alonzo Ojeda, or maybe even talked some sense into well-meaning Big D.

I wish I could write, with a novelist's literary license, that Barto brought from Spain along with the provisions on his three caravels a cure for the Yellow Sickness, a sovereign remedy for syphilis, even a mosquito repellent that worked.

I wish I could write that we learned to live in harmony with the Indians.

But none of this happened.

In fact, in the eighteen months until I sailed for Spain, my heart so heavy with guilt that I hardly cared whether Mosén Pedro, Brother Buil, Bernal de Pisa and those others would succeed in destroying the last of my credibility at the Peripatetic Royal Court –

But I get ahead of myself.

Barto first, then.

Here is a man in his forty-fifth year, broad of shoulder, not tall but yet commanding in stature, well if not flashily dressed, voice deep, vocabulary still uniquely his own, confident and, as to physiognomy, utterly changed.

Because suddenly one sunny November day when my vision is almost back to normal and Dr Chanca has allowed how I can get out for a couple of hours daily without killing myself, I blurt: 'The warts and all, they're gone!'

My brother Barto is a handsome man. Even his head of formerly frizzy wild hair, now salt-and-pepper, is subdued.

'I was wondering when you'd notice,' he says. Shy but pleased.

'How'd it happen?'

'Oh wow, this is embarrassing,' he says after a short silence.

'I'm your brother,' I point out.

'Well,' he says, 'they just sort of fell off early one morning.'

That morning, like many before it and a great many after, found Barto in his own small suite of rooms at the French royal palace at Fontainebleau. By then (it was early in 1492 and might have been the day Granada fell) he knew King Charles would never back our Great Venture, but he had his reasons for staying on at Fontainebleau.

'She was really gorgeous,' he tells me.

'She' was Anne de Beaujeu, eldest daughter of King Louis XI and until shortly before Barto's arrival Princess Regent for her brother Charles VIII.

That morning, gorgeous Anne de Beaujeu rose before Barto did, climbed out of his big canopied bed, lit the fire, returned to the big canopied bed, quite splendidly nude, woke Barto with a kiss, started to say, 'Let's do it again,' but looked at his sleepy face in the firelight and gasped instead, 'The warts and all are gone!'

Which they definitely were.

'That was the first time I ever did it,' Barto says.

'With anyone, or with the princess?'

'The first ever. And the warts and all just fell off.'

'Then what happened?'

'I stayed at Fontainebleau for almost two more years, while she made a fool of me.'

'With other men?'

'No. She wanted me to stay, so she didn't give me your first letter –

or your second. I was living a sort of fairytale existence, you know? Early to bed, late to rise, a beautiful princess for company.' Barto sighs. 'I'd probably still be there except that her brother, who isn't very bright for a king, needed her advice on a few pressing matters of state. So *he* gave me your letters and a purse of gold (plus a retinue of servants and one of those Hungarian coach-things) and I set out for Spain.'

He arrived at the Peripatetic Royal Court brimming with confidence – for the interlude with the gorgeous Anne de Beaujeu, as you've seen, worked wonders.

'I caught up with the King and Queen at Valladolid and must have made a pretty good impression on them (actually, I think it was more the Queen) because they had just received Antonio Torres with your shopping list, and they, or she, immediately gave me command of three caravels full of provisions. *Et voilà tout*, as the French say. Here I am.'

'Where are the caravels?'

'That's another story.' Which he seems in no hurry to relate, probably because Dr Chanca told him not to get me excited. 'Oh, by the way, I managed to arrange what you wanted for your boys,' he says disarmingly. 'They're both at the Peripatetic Royal Court, pages to Crown Prince Juan.'

'Where are the caravels?'

'We had a super trip over.'

'Where are they?'

'Captain Torres is probably en route by now with four more. I was only bringing the emergency supplies.'

'What happened to them?'

'We unloaded most of our cargo.'

'What happened to the rest of it?'

'Maybe you better have a siesta. I'm not supposed to tire you.'

'I'm not tired. What happened to your caravels?'

'Go easy on Big D, okay? It really wasn't his fault.'

'I'm listening.'

I listened.

Barto and his small fleet arrived at Isabela on Midsummer Day, just when the conflict between Mosén Pedro and Big D reached flashpoint. Barto walked (or sailed) into the whole thing innocently. Until then he had no idea that our younger brother had even left Italy, or that I wasn't Viceroying on the island but off discovering somewhere. It took him a few days to get the lay of the land.

'How come some colonists are calling us "dirty foreigners"?' he asked Big D on Midsummer Day plus one.

'Smear campaign by a loudmouth named Mosén Pedro Margarit and his crony Brother Buil. Don't worry about it,' said Big D.

Mosén Pedro, as in my haste to go discovering I failed to foresee, wouldn't remain inside Fort Santo Tomás indefinitely with his 402 malcontents. Four hundred and two malcontented mouths are a lot to feed, and Mosén Pedro cleverly took along minimal stores. Pretty soon they were living off the countryside. The half dozen Indian villages in the immediate vicinity of the fort were hit in the first week, their meager food supplies carted off, their women raped, a complaining sub-cacique or two murdered. Soon Mosén Pedro's malcontents were ranging further afield, south into Cibao itself. This was no disputed border territory, it was Caonabó country. Before long Indian women could leave their villages only under escort – but equally, Mosén Pedro's malcontents could venture into Cibao only in large numbers, heavily armed. Small parties were ambushed, picked off, their severed heads hung prominently from trees where jungle footpaths intersected.

When word of all this filtered back to Isabela, the colonists blamed the Indians for everything. Caonabó's name, after all, is not one you routinely trust. Besides, asked Brother Buil with a sad philosophical smile at his daily sermons, what can you expect from soulless heathens?

The war intensified. When it spilled over the border into Guacanagarí's territory, the noble cacique sent a delegation to Isabela to apprise Big D and the Council of what was happening in the back country. The delegation was received with suspicion and dismissed with scorn. Mosén Pedro by then had lost twenty-four men, and half that many Indian villages had been either destroyed or abandoned. Big D sent a committee to investigate. They returned with three decaying Spanish heads found dangling from crossroad mahogany trees, arousing public outrage. Big D, summarily rejecting the Council's advice to send reinforcements, instead sent a deputy to Fort Santo Tomás to censure Mosén Pedro for stirring up the Indians. Mosén Pedro was predictably furious. With his remaining 378 malcontents, he marched on Isabela. The community, which Big D hoped would shun Mosén Pedro as an outlaw, received him as a hero. At a rancorous meeting of the Council he slapped Big D's face – whereupon Big D, much to everyone's amazement, knocked him down and kicked him (as I had done earlier). This indignity at the hands (or feet) of two Colón brothers, both dirty foreigners, was more than Mosén Pedro Margarit, officer and Spanish gentleman, could take. That night he broke into the Juzgado, freed Bernal de Pisa, rallied his most ardent malcontents (joined by a grimly smiling Brother Buil), seized Barto's three partially unloaded caravels and sailed with the tide for Spain.

'Where they'll try to discredit you with the royals,' Barto now warns me.

'Never mind them. What's the situation right here?'

'Better. We've got Guacanagarí back on our side and he's trying to convince the other caciques that Mosén Pedro wasn't your normal Spaniard or Christian.'

The situation does seem to improve for the next few weeks. With Brother Buil gone, shy Brother Ramón Pane the Jeronymite finally baptizes our first Indian on location – of all people that fat, wife-killing cuckold Guarionex, who is frequently in Isabela on his brother Guacanagarí's business. But as Big D says, you have to start somewhere.

My health has also improved and by mid-December when Captain Torres's fleet of four caravels appears off Cape Isabela, I'm down at the waterfront with the entire colony to greet it.

The four caravels are dressed to the masthead with flags and coats-of-arms, and the colony flies its proud colors too. But once Torres's fit, sturdy men spring ashore, the contrast with the gaunt-faced, bleak-eyed, half-starved, thirty-per-cent-syphilitic survivors of the Yellow Sickness and Indian trouble is dispiriting to veterans and greenhorns alike.

'Are these some of your Indians or what are these?' I hear one of Torres's sailors asking his shipmate.

'Hey, you! Are you an Indian or what are you?' the shipmate asks the man at my side, who happens to be Big D.

'I'm Don Diego Colón, one of the Admiral's brothers,' says Big D, who is nothing if not literal. His Spanish is only slightly accented. Big D, whatever else his shortcomings, is pretty good at languages.

The sailors exchange significant glances.

'Heard of you,' says the second, accusing.

'All three of you,' says the first, condemning.

Later, after the parade, Antonio Torres takes me aside and explains. 'Buil, Bernal and Margarit are at the Peripatetic Royal Court, which was in Burgos last I knew, spreading all kinds of malicious slander against you, Viceroy. If I were you, I'd take a couple of these caravels right back to Spain and defend myself.'

Dr Chanca concurs. 'Spanish climate, best in the world, and good wholesome Spanish food. Probably just what you need.'

Barto tells me, 'I can hold the fort, Cristóbal.'

'Fort Santo Tomás?' I ask.

'No, it's just an expression I picked up somewhere. I mean, I can take care of things.'

I have in fact already appointed Barto my adelantado or executive officer, and he's done a good job. The colonists like Barto. The same cannot be said of Big D, but at least the epithet 'dirty foreigner' is no longer heard. Instead there's a lot of: 'You'll never *believe* what they're accusing the Viceroy and his brothers of, back there at the Peripatetic Royal Court.'

Maybe it is a good idea to sail for Spain, but I don't, at least not right away. Feeling strong enough, I lead an embassy to Guacanagarí's latest squalid capital village to see how we're coming along in the mutual trust department.

The answer, to my surprise, is not so hot. For Guacanagarí signs with his usual eloquence: 'It's said you have taken five hundred prisoners – not just men but helpless women and children too – from Caonabó's and Mayrení's people. How can I be sure you won't raid my villages as well for slaves?'

'Prisoners? Slaves?' I repeat, startled, and Yego translates. 'What is this?'

'Don't play the innocent with me,' signs Guacanagarí caustically. This is the only time I have ever seen him angry.

I ask Melchior Maldonado, military commander of the embassy, if he knows anything about these charges. 'First I heard of it, Viceroy,' he reverberates reassuringly. Such a loud disclaimer mollifies Guacanagarí somewhat, and after he agrees to check his sources, we return with all possible speed to Isabela.

I can't find either Barto or Big D, not even down on the waterfront where Barto hangs out a lot. But Captain Torres joins me there.

'Well, the refitting's finished right on schedule,' he tells me, pleased with himself.

I give him a blank look. 'What refitting would that be?'

'All four caravels, exactly according to specification.'

'Specification?' My look is growing blanker all the time.

'Straight from your own office, Viceroy,' says this loyal but confused officer.

I board the nearest caravel with him. Except for the steerage, all

349

available space below decks is filled by three tiers of sturdy shelves with narrow aisles between.

'Done with a day to spare, Viceroy. Tomorrow's the twenty-fourth,' he reminds me, 'which was the latest you wanted me to sail to get my crews off the royal payroll.'

I just nod. The purpose of all that sturdy shelving eludes me.

Before Torres can explain, I hear outside that sound I'll always associate with Valencia, a sound like angry surf. Hurrying topside, I can't believe my eyes. Men are jostling one another to line the dock in that festive-cruel mood of a crowd gathering to witness something that, as individuals, most of them would reject as unpleasant, even horrible. But a crowd is, unfortunately, always more than the sum of its parts.

'Here they come!'

'Three cheers for Don Diego!'

For Big D? Yes, and the cheering is heartfelt as he advances, mounted uncertainly on one of the colony's few mules, at the head of a double column of manacled Indians flanked by armed guards that stretches all the way upslope to the plaza and beyond.

'Give 'em room!' shouts someone. 'Let 'em through!'

This appears scarcely possible until Alonzo Ojeda gallops one of Mosén Pedro's nags through the crowd on the dock. Half a dozen men tumble into the water, to be hooted and jeered by their fellows. But a way is cleared for the captive Indians.

Of whom, as Guacanagarí informed me correctly, there are 500.

Big D spots me standing with Captain Torres, grins and flashes a thumbs-up sign. The now-dismounted Alonzo Ojeda, barely restraining a huge Irish wolfhound on a short lead, encourages a few straggling Indians with some flank-nipping. But there aren't many stragglers. Smoothly, as if it has been rehearsed, 500 prisoners are split into four sections, which file onto the four caravel gangways and almost seem to fall, like rows of dominoes, into the four hatches. Soon there isn't an Indian in sight.

The crowd, disappointed by the spectacle's brevity and the Indians' domino-like docility, disperses muttering. Big D joins us. But it is Captain Torres he wants to see, not me. At least officially. To me he gives another big grin. To Torres he hands some official-looking document. Big D's a great one for papers and documents. 'The manifest, Captain,' he says. 'If you'll sign acknowledging receipt?'

Torres signs.

'Smoothest operation I ever saw,' he says admiringly.

350

'That's the Swiss influence,' says Big D. 'I learned a lot there.'

He grins a third big one at me.

Obviously I can't have this out with him in public. 'The mansion,' I tell him. 'Ten minutes.'

I find Barto in troubled conversation outside the church with Brother Ramón Pane. The latter, a very retiring chief of mission, at once disappears through the prefab door.

'What's going on?' I ask Barto.

'If you mean,' he says, a shade frostily, 'am I going to the spiritual authority behind the secular authority's back, no, I'm not. In fact, I was trying to assure Pane that you know what you're doing. It wasn't easy.'

'What *I'm* doing?'

'I'm not wild about the slaves and neither is Fray Pane. Apparently,' says Barto, uncharacteristically acerb, 'that makes two of us in the whole colony.'

'I never knew about the slaves until fifteen minutes ago.'

'Come on, bro — Diego said he was carrying out your orders. He said he wanted to surprise you with the Swisslike efficiency of the whole operation.'

'He,' I gasp, 'what?'

Five minutes later in the wattled hut of a governor's mansion, a bewildered Big D is saying, 'What are you so mad about, Cristóbal? I was only carrying out your orders.'

'I gave orders to send Indians in chains to Spain?'

'Sure you did. The day you led the army inland to Fort Santo Tomás.'

I mutter the Lord's name, definitely in vain.

Big D goes into his own small room in the mansion and comes out brandishing some papers.

'I have it right here, all down in black and white.'

But it's clear I've rattled him, and he shuffles through the papers nervously a while before finally sighing his relief. 'Here it is, in your own words ... Blah, blah, blah ... *Cristóbal's* PLAN FOR THE CANNIBALS.'

'Cannibals? We're not talking about — .'

'Just listen, please, for a minute, all right? Uh, here we are: *People who eat people aren't normal, it has to be an acquired taste and like any perversion can be unlearned.*' He looks up from the papers. 'Didn't you tell me that, the day you went inland?'

I don't remember, actually, but it sounds like something I could have said. I nod, and he continues: 'Uh, blah, blah, blah ... *So here's my plan – or dream, maybe.* Your own words, word for word as you spoke them, Cristóbal. I got pretty good at taking dictation when I was Cardinal Borgia's substitute private amanuensis. Well, to continue, and I quote: *We must try to enslave them all.*'

'I never said that,' I protest.

'Cristóbal, it's right here in my notes. *A few shiploads of Carib prisoners ...* blah, blah, blah ... *send them to Spain –* '

'Look,' I tell him, 'I never said that, but as long as it's Caribs you're talking about, I won't argue. Sending Caribs to Spain to teach them new dietary habits isn't a bad idea if we should happen to run across any. But what on earth made you think I wanted to send five hundred Arawak Indians to Spain in chains?'

'You said so, that's what. I've got your exact words right here.' Again he consults his notes. 'Uh, blah, blah, blah, uh-huh! *in the process*, blah, blah, *enslave a lot of Arawaks too.* That's what you said you wanted. So that's what I did. What are you so mad about?' he says again, plaintively.

'Big D,' I ask, 'what are all those blah, blah, blahs you keep inserting in there?'

'Well, if you'll remember, there was a thunderstorm that day, and I might have missed an occasional word or two.'

(The reader may wish to refer to pages 331–2 before going on.)

'I even,' says Big D, offended, 'can tell you our parting words. I said, "I guess you know what you're doing," and you said, "Be audacious." Which I was. You were down with that Whole Sick Syndrome of yours, don't forget. So I figured, why trouble you with details? I wanted to surprise you.'

I don't say anything, just stare at him.

Soon I become aware that he's gone. Have I dismissed him? It's probable. Curtly? That's probable too. I have to do some heavy thinking.

The question sounds simple – when Antonio Torres's four caravels sail for Spain with the morning tide, will it be with or without their cargo of 500 slaves? – but I find it is one of the most difficult decisions I'll ever have to make.

Big D's sudden popularity, however transient, is an eye-opener. Do our colonists so implacably hate bronzy-skinned heathens? Or is it just comforting to see 500 anybodies worse off than their own disillusioned, sick, half-starved selves? Or just a relief finally to be doing something other than barely existing?

Whatever, I won't find my answer there. A leader who bases his decisions on public opinion inevitably becomes a follower, as Roderigo Borgia often told me.

What about Big D then? While the road to hell may not be paved with Cipango gold, still he meant well. Wasn't I the one who told him to forget all he ever learned about democracy? What can be more antithetical to democracy than slavery? No, Big D was only obeying me in his own way. To march those 500 Indians off Antonio Torres's caravels would make him the laughing-stock of Isabela, and probably crush his spirit forever. Big D's sensitive.

Besides, what about those notes of his? Can I be absolutely sure he got the conversation wrong? Wasn't I coming down with the Whole Sick Syndrome? For all I know, I was already half-delirious. Maybe I said exactly what Big D wrote. The substitute private amanuensis of Roderigo Cardinal Borgia, now the Pope, ought to know how to take notes.

In fact, why shouldn't I have said what Big D wrote?

Here I am, well into my Second Voyage (as history will call it), still far from convinced I've discovered a New World and with very little gold in my coffers from the part of the Old I think I *have* reached. Is this any way to show my gratitude to the King and Queen? Won't they expect a profit by now? Do I want them to think the Ocean Sea is full of red ink?

Besides, isn't gold merely a matter of alchemy? Did my dream about ordinary Tom Norton of Bristol Town mean nothing? Alchemists work to change baser metals to gold. And colonists? What base substance can be found all over Haiti that, in the marketplaces of Spain and Portugal, can be transmuted to gold? What but warm Indian bodies?

And you better face this too, I tell myself. By now Mosén Pedro Margarit, Brother Buil, Bernal de Pisa and God knows who all else are carving up your credibility at the Peripatetic Royal Court. Won't four shiploads of slaves earning hard currency at the Sevilla slave market make you look better?

Barto breaks in on these ruminations to say flatly, 'Big D made a mistake. We're not slavers like the Portuguese, except for prisoners of war, which these poor Indians aren't. Set them free, Cristóbal. It's time our baby brother learned to face the consequences of his own acts. He's thirty-seven years old, for God's sake.'

This sounds harsh, coming from Barto, but is it? I'm so mixed up at the time I fail to see he's trying to protect us all from the final

353

reckoning of history, from which there is no appeal.

After Barto leaves, Yego comes into the wattled hut of a governor's mansion with a hangdog look on his bronzy face. 'Admiral Father,' he says, and shifts his weight some, and plays nervously with his wooden crucifix. 'Admiral Father, this I once believe – you, same God. Then I see you man like all peoples, only more greater. When you sick I pray Christian God you better. Now I ...' Yego coughs and clears his throat.

'You what?' I say irritably.

'Wish almost ...' Again he clears his throat. He changes tack. 'This five hundreds Haiti Indians, same peoples my little island. Speaking same language. Many between marriages. They, I, brothers, Admiral Father. I beg you by Christ Godson let Indians free.'

This is a long and passionate speech for Yego.

I tell him, brusquely I'm afraid, that the very kinship he cites prevents him from being objective.

So of course does mine.

Big D is my own flesh and blood, and things have gone too far to do anything but back him up. Despite various rationalizations, it is ultimately on this so Spanish, so Italian, so Jewish scaffold that, in the eyes of history, I hang us all.

In the morning before the fleet sails, I tell Big D, 'Pack your seabag.'

'How come?' Barto's words, but from him they're more a wail.

'You're going to Spain.'

He looks as if a mountain fell on him. 'You're mad at me, I knew it.'

'Not at all.' I explain about Mosén Pedro, Buil, Bernal de Pisa and God knows who all else. 'Somebody I can trust has to be at the Peripatetic Royal Court to protect my interests. If you have any trouble, our man at Court is the Keeper of the Household Budget, Luís de Santangel.'

'I won't let you down, Cristóbal, you'll see if I don't.'

This prediction, so ambiguously worded, is not comforting, but Big D is family and I need Barto here at my side to face the Indian troubles sure to come.

When Antonio Torres's four caravels sail with the tide and their dreadful cargo, almost the entire population of Isabela celebrates the great occasion.

But Brother Pane prays alone in the prefab church.

And Barto stares stonily out to sea.

And Yego cries softly behind bars in the Juzgado, where Juan Niño of Moguer finds him later that day.

354

And I, watching the caravels sink over the horizon, feel an Oceanic tidal wave of guilt.

War!

That swashbuckling neurotic Alonzo Ojeda greets it like a sunflower turning to the sun.

Eagerly he girds his sword, this carefree *condottiere*, this bedizened bantam rooster; eagerly he assembles his dog handlers with their slavering Irish wolfhounds and his brevet caballeros, replacements for those who fled with the Queen's favorite cavalry officer; eagerly he peers into the purple shadows of the foothills behind Isabela for a glimpse of an Indian war party slinking through a defile; eagerly he mounts his nag, which rears almost creditably and whinnies almost bravely.

'You need only point me, Admiral,' he says in a tremulous voice, 'and I'll ride.'

He is actually panting, for his battle-lust rises from the unplumbed depths of his – but it's a long way from Regiomontanus and Erasmus to Freud and Adler, so let's pass over the psychoanalytic subtleties.

'Here they come!' shouts one Francisco Roldán, our brevet cavalry commander, a pike-lean fellow with a face longer than Mosén Pedro's and palest blue, opaque, conquistador eyes, who sits his nag as if man and beast are the single awesome creature the Indians believe. And there, slipping swiftly through a shadowy purple defile just where Ojeda was peering, can be seen an Indian army.

The rest is history, and like a lot of history it's brutal.

Let me say this first. We were grossly outnumbered, some 4,000 Indians vs twenty inexperienced cavalrymen, twenty dog handlers with their Irish wolfhounds, fifty musketeers. Then how explain the one-sided carnage?

First, the centaurs. Our twenty (including Barto and me) outrageously improbable man-beasts, two-headed and six-limbed, were horribly intimidating.

Second, the wolfhounds. Until then, the only dogs known to Haitian Indians were timid little barkless creatures domesticated for their high protein content. So our slavering Irish wolfhounds were almost as improbable and intimidating as the centaurs.

Third, the musketeers. Muskets are no more accurate than Caonabó's poisoned arrows, which were in short supply that day anyhow, but they make a hideous racket.

Finally, that swashbuckling neurotic Alonzo Ojeda.

His joy of combat beggars comprehension. Marshalling our order-of-battle and leading our attack, he is always in the van, charging on his warhorse (for, alchemically, he seems to have transmuted his nag) with laughter not quite maniacal, slashing to left and right with his soon gory sword, ignoring the flights of poisoned arrows, finally standing among the windrows of enemy dead, right arm red to the shoulder with blood, enemy blood, as he raises his hand to the smudge of gunpowder through which gleams his bloodlusty grin.

Enemy dead? Enemy blood? Have I written those words?

How did it all happen?

I had a dream once in a Julian decade off time's map, long ago when I was young and full of grief, and this dream sent us to these islands where the natives raised no hand against us but revered us as gods from their very Heaven, and now we have brought them death.

Enemy? *We are the enemy*.

I wander in a daze past bloody-armed Ojeda among the corpses and into the woods.

Barto comes running after me.

'You're in charge,' I tell him, and wonder if it really matters to me if anyone is.

'Where are you going?'

'I don't know. But I want no more of this.'

'We have to fight now. If we don't, we'll be safe nowhere on the island. Can't you see that?'

'Yes.'

'At least take some men with you.'

'No.'

'You'll get yourself killed.'

'No.'

Somehow I'm sure of this. When a man doesn't care if he lives or dies, the fates let him live. Is this perverse? How would I know? I understand the fates no more than I understand God. If any.

Barto says, 'You think I like war?'

I shrug.

'I hate it. But we have no choice.' He sounds hard. 'Not anymore,' he says.

It is later, how much later I cannot say. For as in my Julian decade, I have walked deliberately off time's map, this time not into geography but into a profound metaphysical gloom, brother to a guilt so strong it nullifies normal space-time. I wander. I'm good at that, I tell myself, wandering through glades with mossy-soft earth underfoot, clambering over rocks, drinking at streams, eating alien berries and fruits. Am I fleeing from myself or toward something I don't as yet understand?

Almost, I don't reach it.

It is twilight, some night, somewhere in the purple-shadowed mountains, and I am in mortal danger. I can sense it, as a seaman can sense before it quite reaches him the first stirring of the wind that will fill his sails, or the fog that will leave him blind on a shrouded sea. I walk to meet it, caring not. Above is a rustle and I look up with indifference to see leaping from a tree a savage bent on my immediate demise. I am hammered to the ground, a club is raised, I am an instant from discovering whether poor Luís Torres or his sister Petenera had the final answer, when a musket roars and I roll out from under a dead Indian.

At first I believe my saviour has to be Alonzo Ojeda because in war Ojeda, like some stand-in for a strangely absent deity, is everywhere. But it is not Ojeda. It is the long-faced cavalry commander with palest blue, opaque, conquistador eyes, Francisco Roldán. Almost jerked back onto time's map against my will, I manage a cool, 'I owe you one, Captain.'

He inclines his head a moment, then those strangely opaque eyes search my face. 'Not my idea, Viceroy. Your brother sent me to look after you.'

We study each other with curiosity, one appraising the man who saved his life, the other the man he saved. The object of the rescue is filthy, with matted hair, a scraggly beard, clothing in rags. He probably smells. The rescuer somehow manages to be clean-shaven and crisply turned out in a bush-jerkin of Indian cotton.

His strangely opaque eyes crinkle with what I take for amusement when I say: 'Then report to my brother that you did. I'll be going on alone.'

He says in his deep, rich baritone, 'You value your life so lightly, Viceroy, you ought to make a splendid field officer. Why aren't you, I wonder?'

What I at first took for amusement in those palest blue eyes is scorn.

'But then,' he says, 'martial daring and a death wish are seldom the same thing.'

Can I resent his scorn? No, rather I admire his frankness.

But he's not finished. 'You'd better know what you're looking for out here. Because you're losing everything you left behind – position, power, prestige, authority. If you stop leading people, they pretty soon get out of the habit of following. Spaniards have to see the cut of a man's spritsail. But perhaps you Genoese are different.'

He searches my face. 'You won't come back with me?'

'I can't. Not yet.'

He sees that it is useless to argue.

'But I won't forget this,' I tell him. 'Neither that you saved my life nor that you're going back now.'

He goes, and I won't forget — and thus are the seeds of a bitter harvest sown.

I wander. Somewhere. Anywhere. Nowhere. Once or twice I hear the din of battle not far off, screams, musket fire, the deep bark of a wolfhound. Once or twice I come incuriously upon the bloated bodies of the dead. They are nothing. Nor am I. Only guilt.

How much later I cannot say, two withered Indian crones are helping me along a trail into a squalid little village.

They give me cool water to drink and feed me.

They strip the torn rags from my body and bathe me.

They lead me to a hammock, and time and no-time merge.

When I wake I am seated near the embers of a fire, and facing me, the fire turning his eyes to crimson glass, is Guacanagarí.

'You lied to me,' he signs, without anger.

'I didn't know the truth at the time.'

Time? Can I be back on its map?

'I believe you, my brother,' Guacanagarí signs. Then he asks me: 'Why did you come here to our islands?'

I dredge a word out of long ago. 'It was my *faege*.' I make no sign. I am talking. But he seems to understand.

And I too understand. This latest squalid little capital village of Guacanagarí is the place I had to go.

'My brother Guarionex is the first Christian among us,' he signs. I hear his ironic laughter, surprised. Prophets have little to laugh about. 'There will not be time for many others. A generation, two, and my people will lose the will to live. Once the old gods were good enough for us. If any gods are good. Are you a god? A tired and confused and defeated god? An inferior god? Or worse, a false god?'

I am on my knees before him. 'I'm no god, not even false. I never was. Tell me what I must do.'

'If your Father God and Son God and Ghost God came down from Heaven to kill you, would you defend yourself?'

'No.'

'Why did you wander in the jungle? Did you wish to die?'

358

'I wished to *not be*.'

'Shall I kill you, then, my brother Cristóbal Colón, or are there things you must yet accomplish?'

'I don't know.'

'The war is over.'

I am still on my knees before him. I raise my head.

'The small captain who smiles at death went into the highlands and brought out Caonabó in chains.'

There is silence. The embers sigh behind me. I look at his red glass eyes.

'My people won't pay the tribute.'

'What tribute?'

'So much gold a month, a head tax. Or in a region where gold cannot be panned, so much cotton, so much tobacco or hemp. They will not pay what is demanded, nor will they tend their fields, but flee instead into the high barren mountains where cold winds blow. They will have no congress with their women, no. Their spirits will wither. Many will take poison. For the rest, hopelessness can kill as surely as manioc or your thundersticks. Two generations, no more. Why did you come here?'

Again I say, 'It was my *faege*.'

'And will you go back ... where you came from?'

'Yes.'

'But you must return?'

I am silent a long time. The embers have died. But his eyes are still red glass.

'Yes.'

'When you returned this time, you saw an Indian who refused to die. A cannibal.'

I don't know how he knows this.

'Soon you will see Indians who refuse to live. These are no cannibals.'

'What does this mean?'

'That since you have come here, the evil refuse to die. And the good refuse to live. Do you understand?'

'No.' But, almost, I do.

'A storm will come such as no storm you have ever seen before. *Huracán*, we call it.' This single word *huracán* he speaks. His voice sounds like my own, but resonant with echoes beyond mere reality.

'When?'

'Soon. Soon. It will destroy your winged ships, all but one.'

'God!' I cry, dismayed.

'Perhaps,' he signs. He laughs, but there is no mirth in his laughter. 'It is not safe, is it, to go with a single winged ship, alone in the vast sea you must cross?'

'No.'

'You will build a new winged ship and leave for your distant home that is not Heaven, and then come back as you yourself have said. To wander is your — what word did you use?'

'*Faege.*'

'Yes.'

'And then?'

'Is the wandering not enough?'

'No.'

I wait to hear my fate, but, 'It is not fit that a man know too much of his destiny,' Guacanagarí signs, and when I look at his eyes they are no longer red glass but dark Indian brown, almost black.

'Go now,' he signs. 'The way back to the Spanish settlement will be safe, unless you tarry long in the mountains, for if *huracán* finds you there . . .'

He sees the prospect of my death, and shrugs.

One final thing he tells me. '*Huracán* comes, and seems to go, then returns with no warning from the opposite direction. Forget this at the peril of your life.'

I leave the squalid little village the way I came, in rags, guided by two crones. Then alone I hurry along jungle trails and over mountain passes where cold winds blow and down through purple foothills to Isabela.

Of course, it is possible I imagined all this.

In my day there was no clear demarcation between objective reality and the subjective experiences variously called metaphysical, mystical, delusional. Events slipped through, as often in one direction as the other.

But I know *huracán* was real.

I'm on *Niña*'s quarterdeck, facing seaward into a howling gale. The afternoon is dark, the sky overhead like black smoke. *Mariagalante* and the caravels *San Juan* and *Cardera*, anchored far enough apart to allow sea room, are just visible ahead. We have good holding ground out here, half a mile from shore, but no protection from that ever-strengthening norther. Still, this is the right place to ride it out. If any place is.

I avoid looking eastward to where our other carrack wallows on her side. Poor doomed *Gallega* has snapped a bow anchor cable and immediately broached. Her boat, carrying her storm crew, now labors toward where shore ought to be, if we could see that far. But I don't look there either.

I'm too abstracted by Guacanagarí's prediction – *It will destroy your winged ships, all but one.*

Is this why I am here? Some irrational certainty that only my presence can save beloved *Niña*?

When I boarded unannounced as she was casting off, it was not her captain Juan Niño who protested but Barto.

'Where do you think you're going?'

'It's obvious, isn't it? Out with *Niña* where I belong.'

Barto looked at me measuringly, then shrugged and walked off. Could I blame him for mistrusting me, after my weeks of disappearance into the wilderness?

Juan Niño said only, 'Glad to have you back, Admiral.'

His handpicked storm crew has lost no time getting *Niña* under optimal sail to claw offshore to the holding ground before the full onset of the gale.

Now she heaves there between her three straining anchor cables. The rain hammers down to slide off the deck in solid sheets. First *Mariagalante*, then *Cardera*, finally *San Juan* are lost to view. Green water swallows *Niña* to the quarterdeck, where Juan Niño and I cling to the rail. Water funnels down the steerage hatch. I look down at Francisco Roldán on the tiller, paradoxically relieving the relieving tackle in this wildly thrashing sea. *Niña* now crests high, her bower cables taut. The wind is like no wind I ever felt.

Did you wish to die?

I wished to NOT BE.

If I let go the rail, the devil wind will sweep me overboard.

I cling to it, struggling back to Juan Niño. He points suddenly. *Cardera* is, incredibly, riding the seas stern first in our direction.

'She's dragging her anchors!' Juan Niño shouts as the caravel hurtles past not a boat's length to starboard and, baresticked and backwards, careers toward shore.

'Sweet Jesus, she's going to beach!' cries Juan Niño.

Before she does, though, *Cardera* passes out of sight 200 yards astern, the limit of visibility.

The *huracán* wind rises, the *huracán* darkness gives way to the darkness of true night. Juan Niño and I have roped ourselves to the quarterdeck rail. Each of us stares grimly forward, willing himself not

361

to see through the darkness, at the last moment, the hulk of *Maria-galante* or *San Juan* bearing down on us, not to hear the death agony of her timbers as *Niña* comes apart at the seams, not to feel the sudden buoyancy that will mean her cables have snapped and she is anchored to nothing.

The wind seems to drop at dawn – if that murky, feeble lesser darkness can be called dawn – but looming close to starboard is *San Juan*, headed helplessly for the beach like *Cardera* before her. She bobs high on the water, all her anchors gone. Tiny figures on her quarterdeck, just visible through the pelting rain, wave frantically. Then *San Juan* is gone.

Perhaps two hours later that sky of black smoke gives way to a strange, surreal silver glow. The wind is down.

'The wind is down!' Juan Niño exults, and claps me on the back. Up from the steerage climbs Francisco Roldán, if possible more sodden than we. From the hold, where for sixteen hours straight they have been manning the pump, comes a small band including Pedro Terreros and that other Francisco, Juan Niño's brother.

'B-break out the wine,' says our Billy Budd prototype with his slight, charming stammer. 'We've b-beaten it.'

Gently his older brother tells him about *Gallega* and the two beached caravels. But at least *Mariagalante* is still there to seaward, riding easy at her anchors now.

We wash down chunks of cassava bread with wine under that radiant dome of silver sky. Fitful little bursts of wind blow spume from the crests of the still-heavy sea, but the rain has stopped and the great wind has passed with the smoke-black sky that spawned it.

By late morning we have *Niña*'s boat in the water and one by one the storm crew scramble down the ladder. That fitful wind has steadied, blowing at us from the land, but it is hardly more than a breeze. We'll have no trouble rowing to shore. With a full complement we could even raise sail and bring *Niña* herself in.

I'm at the bulwark, one foot already on the ladder, that off-shore breeze ruffling my hair, when I remember Guacanagarí's final sign.

Huracán comes, and seems to go, then returns with no warning from the opposite direction. Forget this at the peril of your life.

And if that devil wind rises again, blowing straight at *Niña*'s broad stern? Even loaded with extra weight, every spare piece of metal aboard frapped to their cables, how long can her anchors hold?

The breeze is freshening now. Nothing dangerous, not yet, but blowing stronger every minute from the hills that ring Isabela.

I call down to the storm crew, and they all look up at me as if I am crazy.

'Bring her about?' Juan Niño calls back. 'The boat? What for?'

'The *ship*. Hurry.'

But they stare up at me, at the Governor who has twice lain senseless in a coma or delirium, at the Viceroy who has disappeared for weeks into the jungle, and Juan Niño says, 'You better come down into the boat, Admiral.' Juan Niño of Moguer, my old friend. Pityingly.

It has begun to rain again, and that silver dome of a sky shades to a flat gray. Ignoring the men in the boat for the time being, I rush to the quarterdeck to signal *Mariagalante*'s storm crew. But the flagship's boat is already abreast, rowing for shore. I rip off my jerkin and wave it. 'Go back!' I cry. 'You've got to turn her into the wind!'

They can't hear me. Cheerily, they wave in return.

And that sky of black smoke creeps back to smother the purple hills behind Isabela.

I bow my head and wait for what must happen.

Then Francisco Roldán is at my side. 'Captain Niño's getting the rest of 'em back up, Admiral,' he says. 'What can I do meanwhile?'

I look at those palest blue, opaque, conquistador eyes, and remind myself that but for Roldán I would be dead.

Why did you come here to our islands?

It was my faege.

And where does Roldán fit into it? Why am I so sure he does? I am no prophet like Guacanagarí, but somehow I know that it was Roldán, first back aboard, who brought Juan Niño around. So now I owe him twice. Will that not surely prove too much?

Soon the storm crew races that blackening sky, that rising wind. The stern anchor and one of the great bowers, their cables doubly weighted by the extra metal frapped to them, must be winched up so that *Niña*, towed by her boat, can pivot around the cable of her other bower.

Even with every back bent to it, we can barely turn the windlass amidships. Faces are pinched white with fatigue before the second anchor has cleared the sea floor. One man drops away, falls gasping to hands and knees, then rises to come lurching back. Another drops away, and another, for a time. Only Juan Niño of Moguer remains unfaltering at the windlass. Then into the boat they tumble, everyone but Francisco Roldán in the steerage to put the helm all the way down, and myself on the quarterdeck to con the operation. The men bend now to the oars, but *Niña* might as well still be nailed to the sea bottom by her three anchors. By the time the stern comes around just one reluctant point, the wind has risen to a howl and the sky overhead is black. But then her momentum builds and *Niña* is moving better. A couple of points further, and the wind catches her abeam and takes her the rest of the way in a great slewing rush. Now the men in the boat must battle back to us and cast the other two dangling anchors before *Niña*'s driven out beyond the holding ground altogether. Finally, ground tackle deployed, boat streamed aft, the exhausted crew let the wind blow them into the shelter of the sterncastle. And again we wait out *huracán* through a blind night vigil.

Sometime in the pre-dawn hours the father of winds drops and, when daylight comes, the downpour has slackened to a steady vertical rain. Astern rides *Niña*'s boat, swamped but still there.

Of *Mariagalante* there is no trace.

As we bail out the boat and pull for shore, no one in our storm crew looks at me. It almost seems they are afraid.

How could I have known? How?

Half an hour later we land on a beach heaped with the debris of *huracán* – the splintered remains of our dock, the broken hulks of *San Juan* and *Cardera*. Further above the high-tide line, dazed colonists wander in the great clearing littered with wattle and thatch that yesterday was Isabela.

Of our whole hard-won settlement, only the prefab church survives.

Huracán demolishes our settlement on 28 June 1495, to give you the coordinates on time's map. For after the storm I am back, fully back, and in daily consultation with our two shipwrights.

'Just like *Niña*,' I insist.

'She's small, Admiral. She ain't young. We can do better than *Niña*.'

'She's a survivor.'

So month by month in her cradle on the beach, *Holy Cross* comes into being. For that is her official-religious name, as if I am trying to placate the God I cannot quite deny. But as she is the first ship built here, this twin to plucky *Niña* will be known as *India*.

From the wreckage of the other caravels every conceivable bit of material and gear is salvaged. We strip those pitiful hulks thoroughly enough to satisfy even a Crown comptroller.

Through the summer, building on *Cardera*'s keel and keelson, *India* acquires her ribcage of scavenged and rewarped timbers.

By November the work slows, for all our Indian laborers, Guacanagarí's people, have slipped away into the mountains. Francisco Roldán, whom I have named tax farmer (and will, when I leave, name chief magistrate) tells me, 'The tribute isn't coming in. No gold, not even cotton.'

I don't care about any tribute. I'm not even certain whose idea it was. The Council's perhaps, while I was off time's map. 'We've got to have cotton. Lots of cotton. We're so short now, we can barely give *India* one suit of sails.'

Roldán's palest blue, opaque, conquistador eyes look at me, and he nods. Cotton we get, I never ask how.

At the turn of the year Barto tells me, 'The Indians aren't tending their fields anymore.'

But I have no thought for that. Isabela is rising again, and on the beach right before our eyes a ship comes to life. By mid-January planks sheathe her timbers. The masts are up, three stately sprucelike trees felled in the Haitian highlands – native masts for the first Indies-built vessel.

In early February Barto reports, 'Every village within a two-day march of Isabela's abandoned.'

But what does this matter, when a ship is being born?

Soon the rudder is fixed to the deadwood, its hardware forged from an iron lombard long abandoned at Christmas Town. Toward the end of February the last of the cambered deck planking is in place, and running rigging is added to the stout hempen shrouds that guy the masts.

Holy Cross is now a ship – and at high tide one day early in March we give Yego the honor of raising her flags. Watching him run his Most Catholic godparents' royal colors up the mainmast, I think: he is more man now than boy. But sullen, moodily silent and – where is the large wooden crucifix the good Bishop of Barcelona gave him?

Then I have eyes only for *India*'s baptism.

Mirroring my eagerness, *India* herself is all confidence as she breasts the surf, and seems to shake herself awake, and points her bowsprit east toward Spain.

Barto says, 'We're leaving Isabela.'

'Of course,' I agree, looking at my beauty being moored now next to *Niña*. 'And high time. Buil and Mosén Pedro and those others have already been slandering us too long at Court.'

Barto says, 'That's not what I mean. You're going to Spain, but not me. One of us has to stay here.'

That's true enough. We'll be leaving a colony of almost 500 men, a far cry from Christmas Town's forty poor doomed souls.

'But not exactly *here*,' Barto goes on. 'While you were midwifing that *India* of yours, I found us a new home, a real home.' He describes the natural harbor on the south coast of the island and tells me, 'The Indians there have given us the least trouble with the tribute.'

Dr Chanca says, 'I'm convinced the air is not pestilential there.'

'And,' says shy Brother Ramón Pane the Jeronymite, 'since the native population seems more disposed to accept us there, perhaps we can make a fresh start bringing them into Holy Mother Church.'

'Then it's settled,' I say.

But who'll sail for Spain with me, and who remain behind?

It is the Christmas Town situation in reverse. Then, everyone was eager to stay, to be first to find the gold. Now the cry on all sides is, 'Take us back to Spain!'

'Soon there will be Spanish towns and villages all over Hispaniola,' I tell them. 'Those who stay now will be the first great landowners of the Indies.'

'We've had enough of your fucking Indies!'

Barto is on that man in an instant, pulling him out of the crowd, bunching his jerkin with one hand and slapping his face from side to side with the other.

'That's the Viceroy you're talking to. Show some respect, you son of a whore,' rages Barto.

Is this my brother? How come? What's happened to him?

Later when I see Dr Chanca, I ask him about Barto.

He spreads his hands. 'War makes pacifists of some men. Others it turns hard. Perhaps he'll get over it.'

Unsatisfied, I ask Brother Pane. 'Oh, he's very zealous about his religious offices, your brother is. Could he be zealous too about what he sees as his civic duties? The tribute makes me uneasy. I have prayed for guidance on the subject.'

'The tribute was my brother's idea?'

But Pane is reticent, so I see Barto.

'Sure,' he tells me. 'Why not? We defeated the Indians in battle, didn't we? So in a way the whole population of the island are prisoners of war. To be used as we wish.'

'But – '

'That's the way things are. Always have been,' says Barto.

366

'In Europe, but – '

'We're bringing Europe to the Indies, aren't we?'

I want to tell him that some things are better left behind, but all I say is, 'Go easy on them.'

'Are you planning to bring more colonists back with you?'

I nod. 'Women even, if the royals consent.'

'Then tell them they'll have fieldworkers. Tell them they'll have laborers and house servants, and you'll get more colonists than you'll know what to do with.'

All I can offer, again, is a dangling, 'But – '

'Listen,' says Barto reasonably. 'You'll be returning to Spain with two ships overloaded with misfits fed up with the Indies. And God knows what calumnies Buil and Mosén Pedro Margarit have been spreading about the colony. You need ammunition.'

I look at *India* moored alongside her twin. She lacks only sails and provisions and I am eager, eager to be away. Last night again I dreamed of Petenera.

'Do what you think best,' I tell my brother.

I ask my oldest friend on the island, hulking Juan Niño of Moguer, if he knows what's happened to Barto.

'Well, since you ask. You're a dreamer, you know.'

'Me? I'm the most practical man you'll ever meet!'

His eyes widen. He says nothing.

'It's Barto's the dreamer.'

'The Exec? Not anymore he ain't. See, sometimes a dream goes bad. Then, the way I see it, a fellow like the Exec resents it, and first he broods, then he attacks. Whereas you – ' here my old friend's desperado face softens into a fond smile ' – you just go looking for another dream.'

'Juan,' I tell him, 'you don't understand a thing about people.'

'Never said I did.'

Alonzo Ojeda, in peacetime again the preening popinjay in slashed-sleeved jerkin and particolored tights, tells me, 'I want to go back with you, Admiral. Things'll be slow around here for a while. A new settlement means *settling*, if you see my point.'

I intend loading both caravels to capacity, overloading them in fact, to get most of our malcontents off the island. And whatever else he is, Alonzo Ojeda's no malcontent. But, 'You've earned your passage if you want it,' I tell him.

'Someday when you least expect it, you'll see me back in the Indies.'

Roldán claims the right to stay. 'It's a chance to get in on the new start of things,' he says, his opaque conquistador eyes so pale in the sunlight they almost seem colorless. 'Big things, unless I miss my guess.'

'What things?' I ask the man who saved my life.

'Well, as I see it, the top priority has to be improving Indian relations. We can't go on extracting tribute forever, because then we'll need more soldiers than farmers or miners in the colony. There's got to be another way to make these lazy heathens work.'

Which is when, on an impulse born not entirely of gratitude, I make Roldán the chief magistrate of the colony, a post second only to Barto's.

Just then Francisco Niño comes running, breathless. 'Viceroy! Viceroy! Hurry! He's d-dying!'

And off rushes our Billy Budd prototype, me right behind, to where a crowd has gathered outside the new, if temporary, Juzgado. In irons inside is a single prisoner, Caonabó. Shortly he'll board *India* for the journey to Spain and the sort of enlightenment that on his return to Haiti, I hope, will make his people, fiercest on the island, our allies.

But it's not to be. I find Dr Chanca kneeling beside the body of the great warrior cacique.

'Manioc poison,' Chanca grunts.

'How'd he get it?'

But Chanca just shakes his head.

The next morning I find Yego, still minus his baptismal crucifix, at the docks watching grommets bend sails to *India*'s yards.

I've been avoiding this conversation. I know how Yego loves Spain.

'She's a beauty, isn't she?' I say as an opening gambit.

'Like *Niña*, Viceroy,' shrugs Yego.

'What did you say?'

'Like *Niña*, Viceroy.' Same flat voice, no shrug.

'Oh. Yes, well, Yego – Yego, my brother's going to need you here while I'm gone,' I finally get out. 'I know it's asking a lot, but will you stay?'

'Yes, Viceroy.'

'What?'

'Yes, Viceroy,' he repeats, and will not meet my eyes.

Twenty-four hours later the twin caravels, carrying more than 250 men including thirty Indians, when they're built for no more than fifty, sail for Spain.

⟫ XV ⟪

The Channel-Marker Papers
Have Their Day in Court

WHAT bilge historians write about this voyage!
That it took me three months to cross the Ocean Sea from Hispaniola to Cádiz, which is true. But was I a captain in some scheduled packet service, or a discoverer? Future generations of seamen would thank me for reporting the fitful winds of the Horse Latitudes, not ridicule me for the time I spent becalmed there.

That we ran out of food, which is pure hyperbole. If we had, would I be writing this? Of course I could not possibly fill the bellies of more than 250 people on a ninety-day voyage that should have taken no more than five or six weeks. But our reduced rations, six ounces of cassava bread and a cup of water per day, were not entirely exhausted when we made landfall on 11 June 1496.

That I was crazy to cram my twin caravels with the most vociferous of the colony's malcontents, thereby giving Mosén Pedro, Brother Buil & co. new allies with fresh grievances. Maybe. But didn't bringing them back with me make things easier for my brother Barto in Hispaniola?

That, as our rations grew short, there was a groundswell for eating the dozen plump cannibals we captured during a skirmish at our last provisioning stop, the island of Guadalupe. 'Biter bit' and all that. But no, the so-called groundswell was restricted to Ojeda and a few followers, and I like to think they meant it as a joke. Certainly they knew I hoped the cannibals would learn our dietary habits, not the other way around.

That, when I nixed cannibaling the cannibals, I was next urged to throw *all* Indians overboard to save food. This suggestion, unfortunately widespread and accurately reported, was overruled by firearms.

That, as our twin caravels limped into Cádiz harbor (weed-festooned, low in the water, downright scuzzy), three proud ships under Peralonso Niño, outward bound with supplies for the colony, passed close enough to see how cadaverously thin, yellow, ragged we were — giving Peralonso's trig crews second thoughts about the wisdom of sailing for the Indies. This is false. Peralonso's three gleaming ships intentionally cast anchor beside us so their captain-general and I could confer aboard his flagship.

It's true Peralonso didn't grant his crews shore leave during our two-day reunion, but it's a calumny on us both to suggest he was afraid to let his men listen to mine. Like any captain, he was simply on guard against desertion.

A hearty embrace told me that hulking, food-loving Peralonso had put on weight.

'How's the family man?'

'Oh, we've got two daughters. But I'm ready to go back. You know how it is. By the way, you look like hell, Cristóbal.'

'Never felt better.'

'If you say so.' Doubtfully. 'How're my brothers?'

'Fine. Neither one's caught the Yellow Sickness yet.'

'Yellow Sickness? Does that account for the complexion of your men?'

'What's been going on in Spain?' I answered.

Peralonso looked uneasy. 'They're saying that the whole glorious Indies venture is nothing but one big con job.'

This not unexpected statement made me think of Eric the Red's first-ever real estate scam on Greenland, and how Greenland had disappeared. I said casually: 'Oh well, Brother Buil and Mosén Pedro Margarit — '

'They've got friends in high places. Why haven't you done anything to defend your position?'

'I did. I sent my brother Diego.'

After a pause: 'Well, you must know what you're doing, I guess. Have much trouble with the archipelagans?'

'We mostly call them Indians these days,' I replied.

'Who'd you leave in charge out there?'

'My brother Barto.'

'Was that wise?'

'He's a strong leader.'

'What I meant, that just gives them something else to accuse you of, doesn't it? Nepotism.'

'Barto,' I said, stiff-backed, 'is the best man for the job. It has absolutely nothing to do with the fact that we happen to be brothers.'

'Well, if I were you, I'd get to Court in a hurry.'

'Where is it these days anyway?'

'Valladolid, but they're moving to Burgos. Or maybe it's Soria or León. How's the search for gold coming?'

'You'd be surprised how much prospecting we've still got to do,' I responded.

After Peralonso sailed, somewhat subdued, I bought a mule and went straight to the monastery at La Rábida.

Why?

As usual, my biographers are ready with theories.

To leave Spain with a grand flotilla of seventeen ships and return in a pair of overloaded caravels suggests something less than complete success. So one historian claimed that I hid at La Rábida for months in humiliation. Now, that's ridiculous. After Peralonso, whom I trusted like a brother, confirmed what Margarit, Buil & co. were up to, wouldn't I have rushed north right away if I could have?

A more inventive biographer suggested I merely pretended humiliation – monk's habit, right down to a hair shirt – so that when I did see the royals they'd feel sorry for me. Such a complicated stratagem is out of character for me; wily Odysseus I'm not.

A third explanation was that I retreated to La Rábida to search for God. If true, La Rábida was a good place to look. But with the Inquisition wielding as much power in Spain as the King and Queen – who anyway were busy arranging a dynastic marriage with Austria and fighting a war with France – no Converso so much as hinted he might have lost God, not even a Converso of generally unknown origins. So scratch my searching for God.

What does that leave?

No one mentioned Oceanic guilt feelings, and neither will I.

The simplest explanation is, I came down with a relapse of the Whole Sick Syndrome. Since chronic illness is death on the image of a public figure, let alone a legend in his own lifetime, I holed up at La Rábida until I felt better.

Fray Juan Pérez had aged, but comfortably, and he welcomed me as an old friend.

'I'll write telling the Sovereigns you're here,' he said.

But I wasn't ready for the King and Queen yet.

'No need. I already wrote to Luís de Santangel, my agent at the Peripatetic Royal Court.'

A nod. 'You look like hell, you know,' said the good prior of La Rábida with blithely unecclesiastic vocabulary.

'I need a good rest, is all.'

'What's wrong with your eyes?'

How could I explain, even to Fray Juan Pérez, that I had no tears? So I mumbled something about a bumpy crossing from the Azores that had kept me on the quarterdeck five nights running.

Then I asked, 'Could I have a room for a while?' I thought of my parched eyes. 'With its own washstand?'

'The biggest room in the house, old friend. Reserved for the Archbishop of Toledo when he visits.'

But I said I preferred a small room.

It was a windowless cell from which I had the straw mattress removed. I'm not sure why exactly; I just felt it was right to sleep on the hard, cold stone floor. To balance that, fresh yeasty bread and robust country wine seemed a sybarite's diet after stale cassava and brackish water. And the enveloping brown robe, mantle and cowl of a Franciscan monk – my idea, not Pérez's – were welcome in that dank cell. As for the hair shirt, after a while except for all the itching you hardly noticed it.

When Luís de Santangel came down in late summer from the Peripatetic Royal Court at Burgos I was feeling better except for some joint aches and my arid eyes.

I recognized him by his bulk as it passed between me and the cell's single candle. I also smelled his cigar.

'You look like hell, kid,' he told me.

I splashed my eyes at the washstand. Now I could see him as an overweight blur in a pall of cigar smoke.

'How's Petenera?' I asked. I should have played it more laid back, but I couldn't wait.

There was only the one small, stout door. Santangel went to it, listened, pulled it open suddenly, peered both ways in the corridor, then shut it and shot the bolt home with that echoing thud reserved for monasteries and dungeons.

'She's okay,' he said.

'Two and a half years and all you can tell me's okay?'

'Okay's not good enough? We live in dangerous times.'

He checked the door. It was still bolted.

'Where is she?'

'Up north. Anybody who's anybody's in Burgos these days. You ought to be there too, kid. I'm telling you for your own benefit.' My vision was clearing; I could see his troubled frown. 'Listen, is this Diego Colón really your brother?'

'Big D? Sure. Why'd you ask?'

'You have a good family relationship? No sibling rivalry?'

'None at all. Why?'

'I was just wondering.'

'Big D's the best advocate a man can have. Plus,' I said, stiff-backed, 'he's my brother.'

A thoughtful puff of smoke filled the small cell. 'Listen, kid, if I were you I'd shave off the patriarchal beard, get back into civvies and come to Burgos with me. That's if you're feeling strong enough.'

'There is absolutely nothing wrong with me.'

'Maybe it's the beard. It adds ten years.'

'It's traditional for sailors to wear beards.'

'You don't look like a sailor, you look like an Old Testament prophet, and that's not such a hot idea these days. How soon will you be ready to leave? We'll go by coach, one of those Hungarian coach things,' he said offhandedly. 'Brand new, the latest model, second one in Spain.' He couldn't help smiling with the pride of ownership. 'As a status symbol they're almost as good as an Indian slave.'

'You mean they're catching on?' I asked eagerly.

'I mean they're dying off. If smallpox doesn't do it, then measles. They've got no resistance. None. Zero. But when it comes to status symbols, the rarer the better. Coaches, Indian slaves. You're a rich man,' he said suddenly. 'I've been investing your percentage from the sale of those five hundred Indians. You own three caravels outright and half of five oth – you paying attention, kid?'

But all I could hear was the cries of 500 Indians dying of exotic diseases half a world from home.

'Come on, kid. Take an interest. There's enough over to buy yourself an estate or two.'

'I move around too much to own an estate,' I managed.

'That never stopped the royals.'

'I've got to keep moving.' I spoke with more urgency than I'd intended, the words welling from some secret depth of my soul.

'Then it's settled. Get rid of the beard, get some real clothes, and we'll get moving in my brand new, latest model Hungarian coach.'

When I hesitated, he said: 'Listen, kid. Don't you want to see those boys of yours?'

But I wasn't ready to see anyone, not in public. Not even my own sons.

'How are they? Do they like being pages? Is Crown Prince Juan pleased with – ?'

'They've been promoted. They're pages to the Queen herself.'

'Great!' I said. This was the first good news I'd heard since my return. 'Do they know I'm back? Does Little Diego still wear his heart on his sleeve and ask questions all the time? Is Fernando still more a Harana-Torquemada than – '

'Bite your tongue! Don't even mention that fellow's name.' Santangel crossed himself. I'd never seen him do this before. Perhaps he regarded it as a sign to ward off evil. Perhaps it was.

His cigar had gone out, and in his distraught state he didn't bother relighting it, another first. 'You don't know what it's been like these past two years,' he told me. 'It's open season on everyone with Converso blood in their veins, and the richer they are, the more likely they'll be hauled in.'

'Why's that?'

'The finder's fee. After the victim's found guilty, the Suprema auctions off the estate, and ten per cent goes to the denouncer. Now, this kind of a setup's got to encourage going after big game, am I right?'

'After they're found guilty of what?'

'Of what, he asks. Of not being able to withstand torture, that's what. I could see this from a business viewpoint if the Holy Office were in the business of making money, but it's not. Is it?'

I realized an answer was expected of me. 'I've been gone a long time. I don't really know,' I said.

'But from the human standpoint,' Santangel resumed, 'it's a whole new game of pelota. It's downright degrading. I mean, it's one thing for an ambitious young fellow to turn in his family for, say, Judaizing when they're bound to be caught sooner or later anyway. But when these ten-per-centers go around denouncing casual acquaintances on the flimsiest of evidence or no evidence at all – like, how sleazy can you get?'

After this diatribe Santangel again urged me to return with him by Hungarian coach to Burgos, but I declined.

'Even if I were ready,' I pointed out, 'I'd be expected to march north ostentatiously with my captured cannibals and gold and all.'

This, finally, made sense to Santangel. 'I'll look after your interests until you get there, kid,' he promised – and he would have, too, if he could have.

I went outside, the first time in weeks, and saw him off. His coach raised a cloud of dust that hung in the air a long time after it rolled, pitched and yawed out of view.

Then I returned to my gloomy cell and scratched furiously at my hair shirt.

And might have stared at four claustrophobic walls by the light of a single candle the rest of my days, except for the arrival of the one man who, after Luís de Santangel himself, had done most to turn my Great Venture from a dream into two round-trip voyages and a colony – prospering, I hoped – across the Ocean Sea.

He had to stoop to enter my cell, and even by the light of a single candle he looked every inch the aristocrat – lean, erect, with the refined features of generations of breeding, his dark hair silvered at the temples precisely the right amount, his eyes penetrating but not piercing (piercing would have been somehow *nouveau*), his smile fleeting but sincere, his embrace without condescension.

'Your Grace,' I said, for here inside my cell was Luís de Cerda, Fifth Count and First Duke of Medinaceli.

'Viceroy,' he said, 'it's good to have you back. I must say, though, you look like hell.'

He explored my monkish quarters, which didn't take long. 'Tell me, do you intend to sulk in this cell for the rest of your days? Why don't you at least take orders and have done with it? You wouldn't be the first man of action to get religion.'

'It isn't that, Your Grace. I – '

'Come, come, man, you've known me long enough to call me by name. So then, Don Cristóbal, tell me about the Indies.'

I told him. At first reluctantly and only as his due, but then unable to stop myself. It took most of the day.

'I see,' he said slowly. 'You feel guilty about what happened to the Indians.'

'I didn't say that. You mean because I'm here? I'm recuperating from the Whole Sick Syndrome, that's all.'

'And because you feel guilty,' he went on as if I hadn't spoken, 'you hide from the world. Man – don't throw your life away! Spain has too few men like you.'

I laughed self-mockingly and tugged at my beard. This was getting to be a gesture even I didn't like.

'Shave that thing off. Get rid of your guilty habit, put on a suit that suits the Viceroy of the Indies. Give the public their parade, and then see the King and Queen. Make plans for a real colony, the sort that will take permanent root on the other side of the Ocean Sea. Don't fight your destiny, man.'

I asked him why he was so interested.

'Palos and Moguer. Thanks to you, Don Cristóbal, they're back on the map. Their sailors are in demand everywhere, and their ship-builders have so much work they have to farm some to Huelva. These are my towns, my people. If you throw your life away, I'll feel guilty.'

'My life? It's already behind me.'

'What are you,' he scoffed, 'forty-five? I'm past fifty and I'm just hitting my stride. Come on, man. Where are your Indians and things?'

'Sevilla.'

He held a hand in front of my face and squinted. 'Without that beard, you know, you still look a young man. Well, what do you say?'

Such enthusiasm charged his voice that the very walls of the cell seemed to expand.

But, 'No, Don Luís,' I said. 'I need more time.'

'Then don't spend it here, man. This is a hell of a place to recuperate, no offense to the Franciscans. Come hunting with me at Medinaceli and in a matter of weeks I'll have you wanting to swim that Ocean Sea of yours.'

We worked out a compromise. I kept my guilty habit and white beard, and on the two-week parade north to Medinaceli rode a mule. The contrast with the duke, tall in the saddle on a mettlesome warhorse, was possibly more spectacular than our jabbering monkeys and screaming parrots, or even the manacled cannibals in their collars and crowns and girdles and masks of gold, and as we entered a town this sort of conversation was frequently heard:

'That's the Viceroy of Indiana.'

'Which one?'

'Which one? Which one you think? Tall in the saddle on the warhorse there. Lookit him. I'd follow a man like that to the ends of the earth, never mind just Indiana.'

'Pious too. Travels with his own Franciscan monk. See him there, the graybeard on the mule?'

Sometimes I almost think the duke arranged these conversations to make me get rid of the beard and the guilty habit. If so, it almost worked. But I didn't. At least not right away.

Medinaceli turned out to be one of those province-sized estates with its own park, trout streams, flocks of Merino sheep, herds of cattle and fighting bulls (too far north to be world-class, confided the duke), olive groves, wheatfields, vineyards, a few hundred outbuildings, a staff of thousands and a ducal palace so large that as we entered the duke said: 'Don't ask me how many rooms there are, because I just don't know. Once when I was a child I tried to explore them all and I was missing for two days.'

He looked at me. 'The trek's done you good. There's color in your cheeks. If you took off that beard you'd look as young as *I* feel.'

But I still said no.

'Then at least the guilty habit?' he urged, and another voice, a woman's voice, spoke.

'Hello, darling. How lovely to have you back.'

She was hurrying down a long, curving staircase in a long curvaceous gown. My heart jumped. I felt giddy and young and happy and hopeless.

'My dear,' said the Duke of Medinaceli, 'let me present Don Cristóbal Colón, Admiral of the Ocean Sea and Viceroy and Governor of the Indies. Don Cristóbal, this is my protégée, Doña – '

But she kissed him lingeringly, giving me a moment more to compose myself.

I should not have been surprised. It was not uncommon for a young and beautiful woman, with no husband or male relatives and no capital resources of her own, to take a wealthy, titled protector. No stigma was attached to the arrangement, especially as my friend the Duke of Medinaceli was a widower.

'Don Cristóbal,' he said, holding her at arm's length and smiling his love into her eyes, 'I'd like you to meet my protégée, Doña Petenera Torres.'

Sooner or later some well-meaning critic is bound to ask, 'Are you writing an autobiography, a historical novel, a romance or what?'

To which I'll answer promptly, 'Or what.'

He'll say, 'But why all the anachronisms? Can't you at least stick to your own century?'

I'll try to explain that my anachronisms are intentional. For isn't capturing the essence of a bygone day something like translating

377

poetry? Doesn't the spirit of the original matter more than mere vocabulary?

But the critic will miss the point entirely. 'If you want to capture the spirit of the era,' he'll ask, 'why don't you throw in a few appropriate wimples or dulcimers or bombards?'

'I call them lombards,' I'll say, glad we can agree on something, 'and I use a lot of them.'

'And the dialogue!' the critic will persist. 'Where are the nice old comfortable words like "prithee" or "zounds" or at least a "methinks" or two?'

'They're just not my style,' I'll try to explain.

'But you're flouting all the rules.'

'My voyages of discovery didn't exactly follow the rules. So why should my memoirs?'

'Please. If you just read a few blockbuster historical romances, you're sure to catch on.'

'I'm not sure what a historical romance is,' I'll admit. 'This book is certainly historical, and I hope even historic. I like to think it's romantic sometimes, too.'

'At least give it a try,' he'll urge.

And so, against my better judgment, I will:

She complained of headache the next morning.

'But you never get headache,' the duke said.

'It will pass in a few hours. Why do you not go to hunt for partridge without me?' she suggested guilelessly.

'Zounds, but it is odd,' he mused. 'Sir Christopher claimed he was indisposed as well.'

'Methinks 'twas something we ate.'

'Mayhap.'

'Prithee, do take care hunting for partridge.'

'I'faith, m'lady, I am always careful when I hunt for partridge.'

One perfunctory kiss and he went.

She did not bother to wave goodbye.

She luxuriated in a long, languid, scented bath, stroking the secret places of her love-starved body that longed to feel the touch of Christopher's voyage-hardened hands. Dressing, she rejected the modest wimple for something a bit more seductive and decided on a gold fillet to echo the gold brocaded velvet petticoat under her embroidered moiré gown of deepest burgundy. Both décolleté to the navel. She drenched herself in a complex, musky scent which would make him giddy with desire.

But would he be able to find the room she had indicated last night on the secret floor plan of the labyrinthine ducal palace? He often, she remembered with an anxious lurch of her heart, mistook west for east.

But he was there, waiting, with a lazy virile smile on his lips.

'My dear,' he said, rising at once from the couch.

'Oh, love! Love!' she cried in a transport of urgency. 'At last!'

Soon those voyage-hardened hands were roving freely over her many torrid erogenous zones. His own need was great, as the mounting fervor of his masterful kisses told her, yet with touching empathy he sensed her desire to prolong the exquisite agony of that need, for soon he stood back. Panting.

'Let me,' she breathed.

'My dear,' he acquiesced in that remembered voice which, at certain moments, could drive her wild. Such as now.

Slowly, tantalizingly, she undressed him. As each garment flew with abandon to one compass point or another, he murmured, 'My dear, my dear,' against the complex, musky scent of her hair, while her fevered hands caressed what they revealed. His manhood was overwhelming.

'My dear?' he breathed his question, as ever considerate, and at her eager whimper carried her to the couch where, as he lingeringly disrobed her, she lay on her back to feel first the gentlest probe of fingertips at the downy mound of her secret clefted crucible, and then, yes! oh God, then the rasp of his beard there between her silky white thighs as his tongue darted like a flame at the throbbing but tender tinder of her being, making her moan in her need as, with almost-forgotten skill, she cupped his face in her hands and drew the whole strong, lean, hard length of him slowly up, until his pulsating plutonic urgency plunged itself within her calescent very core to fuse its rhythmic thrusting with her own pelvic pitch and roll, sweeping them both away in that turbulent frenzy of indescribable ecstasy where but few –

No, no, no, that's all wrong, stop! This isn't my style, and beside it's not what happened in any style.

Let's do it my way, okay?

The truth's important to me.

The duke would spend the morning in the rough, he said, hunting pheasant, so I walked with Petenera in the dappled shadows of a dead-straight *allée* of plane trees under a hard blue birdless sky. (The duke was a thorough hunter.)

In consideration of his claim on her, or perhaps as another facet of my Oceanic guilt, I did my best to avert my eyes from Petenera's

379

beauty. But how could I forget hair like the darkest black on the underside of a raven's wing, or eyes the emerald green of a deep coral-girt lagoon when the water is unruffled by wind and the sun directly overhead, or lips that precise off-carmine color of an exotic blossom prized by the Arawak Indians that I'd seen growing only in the highlands between the sea and Cibao, or a smile that revealed teeth as white as the Paria pearls I would find when I first landed on the northern coast of South America and named the place Earthly Paradise, possibly in memory of that smile?

Thus, averting my eyes, I still remembered. And could I avert my ears from that voice of silver, gold and precious stones? For she spoke.

'Why don't you shave off that ridiculous beard? It makes you look like some crazy New Testament Talmudic scholar.'

Far off could be heard a single tentative birdcall, then contrapuntal musket fire, then silence.

'How did my brother die?'

I thought I would spare her the truth; sometimes it's best. 'Peacefully. In his sleep.'

Abruptly my head rocked back, my face stung and, for the first time in I don't remember how long, tears sprang to my eyes. She had slapped my face, hard. With her left hand. She was left-handed, I recalled.

'You're lying,' she said. 'I hate liars.'

'What do you expect me to say?'

'Tell me the truth.'

Which, unwillingly, I did.

I had never seen her cry before. I wanted to console her, to pull her close and feel her tears like hot wax on my throat, but how could I? The duke was my friend.

'Thank you for telling me,' she managed. 'But I can never forgive you for leaving my brother stranded to face his horrible fate. I hate you more than ever. You understand that, don't you?'

I said with a certain philosophical sadness that I did.

A bench materialized along the *allée* and we sat.

'Then as long as that's understood,' she said, 'you may kiss me.'

'The duke's my friend,' I said.

This got a surprised: 'He's my friend too. So?'

'Don't you understand?'

'All I understand is, I haven't slept with a legend in his own lifetime in more than two years.'

'The duke,' I repeated firmly, 'is my friend.'

'You – you lubber!' she said, and swung that sneaky left again. I grabbed both her wrists and, rising from the bench, we struggled breast to breast. She was tall for a woman, and lithe, and by no means weak. Our faces came close, mine above hers. Our lips touched. Hers were remembered nectar, honey and ambrosia. Her arms slid around my neck and her mouth opened. We kissed savagely, then hurried back along the dead-straight *allée* under the birdless sky toward the ducal palace to find a bed.

Medinaceli was just swinging off his horse with a brace of pheasant or partridge, or maybe they were guinea hens.

He must have noticed something. Possibly our bruised lips. After that he spent all his waking hours with both of us and all his sleeping ones with Petenera.

Within a few days I shaved off the white beard and accepted the gift of a ducal wardrobe from my friend Medinaceli. A fourteen-year-old stallion too, a little long in the tooth but plenty mettlesome for me.

'Off to Burgos?' the duke suggested.

Petenera at my side, I walked the stallion to the gate. I sensed that the duke was watching from a tower window, and climbed into the saddle without touching her.

She did not bother to wave goodbye.

Our next encounter would be at the dynastic wedding of Crown Prince Juan to Princess Margaret of Austria, when without warning everything changed for us. But that wasn't until springtime in Toledo.

Meanwhile, winter in Burgos.

This former capital of Castile stands exposed to the winds on a high plateau, and though the native-son contention that summer begins on Santiago's Day, 25 July, and ends on Santa Ana's, 26 July, is only an early example of reverse boosterism, still the nights were already cold by the time I got there in October and icy drafts whistled through the corridors of Cord House, the constabulary palace occupied, however transiently, by the Peripatetic Royal Court.

Along with meteorological cold, Burgos was then in the grip of that climate of icy fear which the Supreme and General Council of the Inquisition had bestowed on all Spain.

This fear remained unspoken, but everyone lived in terror of being greenlanded. (You'll remember how Harald Flakehair had put it: 'Greenland's gone, you know. Clean gone, left not a wrack behind.') People disappeared these days in Spain much as Greenland had done up there on the northern rim of the world during my Julian decade.

A man (or woman: fully fifty per cent of the Inquisition's victims

381

were women, no double standard there) could go for years leading a normal life, minding his or own business, prospering even (or especially), taking life one day at a time or trying their best to see the big picture, if any, when zap! they were greenlanded. As if they'd never been. Friends and relatives dared not ask questions, fearing guilt by association. Two or three years after the greenlanding, the name would appear in an Auto-de-Fé program somewhere, and the victim would be marched (or borne in a coffin) to the Burning Place.

The greenlanding that struck hardest that winter in Burgos was of Santiago Santangel, named for his grandfather (né Noah Chinillo) to whose last Seder my parents were on their way in the opening pages of this book. Santí was by now twenty-one or -two and the apple of his father's eye.

'He'll be one of the two or three richest men in Spain when he inherits,' Luís de Santangel told me one frigid morning with a proud chomp on his well-made cigar.

I had come to give Santangel a report on the thirty-seven hot-headed young New Christians who had joined my Second Voyage. There wasn't much to tell him.

'Six died of the Yellow Sickness and two contracted syphilis – well within the norms. But quick or dead, healthy or sick, they all kept a low profile.'

'I'd better warn you, kid. It's liable to change next time. We got a fellow named Cristóbal Rodríguez, for example, that's called the Tongue, who – '

Just then an aide came in and whispered in Santangel's ear. Santangel let his cigar go out, definitely a bad sign, as you've seen.

He said, 'My cousin. Also named Luís. He's gone.'

'Greenlanded?'

This euphemism for 'taken into custody by the Suprema' was, at my suggestion, already part of the professional jargon of Santangel and his Movers and Shakers.

'Looks like it,' he said. 'We weren't close, but Luís knows an awful lot about our network, so this ain't exactly good news.'

A week later Santangel called me in to say he'd finally set up a royal audience that very day.

'Don't think it was easy. No other man in Spain could have done it for you, kid. They're up to their crowns in that dynastic marriage, not to mention the war with France.'

Again an aide came in and whispered in his ear.

'Santí!' Santangel cried, and broke his cigar in half.

I didn't need to ask. The look on my friend's face told me his son had been greenlanded.

Then *he* told me, 'Santí knows even more about our network than my cousin Luís does. Or did.'

I was amazed that Santangel could think of that now.

He shook his head despondently. 'A couple of years ago I could have pulled strings, and not just for my son, even for my cousin Luís. But those days are finished. No one intercedes for anyone. Not even the royals intercede. The royals may reign in Spain, but the Suprema is supreme. Times are tough, kid.' Pulling himself together, he called in his executive secretary, a self-effacing sort of fellow named Espina de Chopito, and told him:

'Cancel all my appointments until further notice.'

'But you're to see the King and Queen shortly with – '

'What's the matter, you don't hear so good? I said *all* my appointments. And let Pighi-Z know I may have to tap the contingency fund.'

'Would that be Pighi-Zampini, Director of the Cádiz branch of Centurione's bank?' I couldn't help asking.

'Peripatetic branch. He travels with the Court these days. Where was I? Yeah. Have my latest model Hungarian coach ready to roll at a moment's notice.' Santangel lit a new cigar, without ceremony. 'Call an emergency meeting of the Blue Pimpernel's top people.' Espina de Chopito, all this while, was furiously scribbling notes.

'Will that include Petenera To – ' I began, but Santangel cut me off with a chopping motion of his hand.

'Don't bother me with your love life at a time like this, kid. Just keep your nose clean. We need you as Viceroy over there more than ever.' He returned to Espina de Chopito: 'Tell the usual hotheads to go into hiding, and get our moles inside the Suprema working on this right away.'

When Espina de Chopito scuttled out, Santangel told me: 'You're on your own. I won't be here if you need me.'

'I understand.'

'Knock 'em dead, kid.' He meant the royals. I watched him leave, moving fast for a fat man, trailing cigar smoke. Then I went, more than slightly unnerved, to my royal audience.

When it was over, a miniature page in gold and purple livery, not quite seven years old, told me: 'They must have liked you, Papa. You know why I think so?'

'No. Why?' I wanted to ruffle his dark hair but, not knowing if you could take such liberties with royal pages, I held back.

'More than an hour. The audience lasted more than an hour. That's really long. And with no time signals from me or Diego. Some people, five minutes is a long audience. But of course they get a lot of riffraff. We're basically a country of peasants.'

For a boy his age, Fernando had quite a vocabulary. He was also a bit of a snob. The pomp and ceremony of the Court thrilled him. But his fifteen-year-old half-brother, at least today, would rather have been spared the honor. The royals had given Little Diego an almost impossible job in there.

Because Cord House was normally the constabulary palace, the audience chamber, with its slitlike window embrasures and its make-shift throne that looked more like a judge's bench, suspiciously resembled the Juzgado in some unruly provincial capital newly liberated from the Arabs.

Stiff, formal, elegant in gold and purple, my son Fernando led me in. Just before I made my obeisances at that courtroom bench of a throne, I spotted Little Diego off to my left holding a rolled parchment and looking like he wished he were anywhere else. I flashed him a quick smile. He stared bleakly ahead. His Adam's apple bobbed. He was tall and gangly, his brilliant thatch of red hair and freckled face clashing with his gold and purple livery.

Neither King nor Queen asked me to sit.

Behind that judge's bench of a throne, I couldn't see much more than head and shoulders of either of them. She had aged; her hair was gray now and without luster, and her eyes looked tired. Her husband looked impatient.

'Welcome back and all that,' he said, fidgeting. From previous experience I assumed he was trying to reach the floor with his regally slippered toes.

'You must tell us all about your adventures,' said the Queen.

'When we all have more time,' said the King.

I sensed that their roles were reversed again, that if I could count on either of them today it would be My Lady.

'A most disquieting bill of particulars,' she said, 'has been lodged against you, Admiral.'

'The page,' said the King, 'will commence.' He snapped his fingers to get Little D's attention, for my older son was staring wide-eyed at me.

Was ever a fifteen-year-old lad who wore his heart on his sleeve given a more difficult task? There was something worse than Machiavellian in having my own son read the charges against me.

Torquemadan, perhaps.

Yet Little D unrolled the parchment with steady hands. He had one of those teenaged voices reaching hard for manhood and losing its hold every third sentence or so. But once he started he never faltered, much as this sick exercise in royal one-upmanship must have wrenched him.

Punctuate Little D's delivery with an occasional involuntary gulp and sporadic high notes in what would one day soon be a reliable baritone, and it went basically like this:

'Deposition . . . to Their Most Catholic Majesties . . . concerning the misconduct and malfeasance . . . of Admiral of the Ocean Sea and Viceroy and Governor of the Indies Cristóbal Colón, a Foreigner:

'The undersigned, most humble and faithful subjects and servants, desiring only . . . to defend the interests of Their Most Catholic Majesties . . . do on their sacred honor depose that:

'Item. During an altercation between a heathen savage and a gentleman officer in Royal service, the Admiral of the Ocean Sea and Viceroy and Governor of the Indies, hereinafter referred to as the said Viceroy, did not only take the part of the heathen savage, but did deliberately and with harmful intent strike the gentleman officer and fell him and kick him while he was down, and

'Item. Whereas testimony taken in the Indies and evidence there gathered established beyond reasonable doubt that the Arawak chieftain Guacanagarí acquiesced in the slaughter of Their Most Catholic Majesties' subjects, the forty colonists of Christmas Town, the said Viceroy refused not only to execute the chieftain Guacanagarí but to punish him in any way, and

'Item. On pardoning three vicious Indian criminals, the said Viceroy gave each in turn a benediction without the sign of the cross, and

'Item. When, after much hardship and disease, the two hundred overworked caballeros of the colony requested some minor redistribution of workloads that would benefit the entire community, the said Viceroy not only refused their reasonable requests but entirely withheld their rations, and

'Item. The colony's spiritual advisor, a friar of one of the Holiest Orders in Christendom, having prayed to God for guidance and pronounced such redistribution of workloads to be God's will, the said Viceroy withheld the friar's rations as well, wherefrom he might have died but for timely recourse to his stocks of sacramental cassava bread and wine, and

'Item. When an uprising of the savages was clearly imminent, the said Viceroy

    (a) Exiled to the wilderness his best troops and

    (b) Sailed away himself on a voyage of discovery, deserting his post for near six months, and

'Item. Without royal charter, the said Viceroy exported from Hispaniola to the slave market at Sevilla five hundred of Their Most Catholic Majesties' new subjects to be sold into bondage, and

'Item. The said Viceroy, or in his absence his brother(s), levied upon Their Most Catholic Majesties' new subjects a tribute in gold so exigent that the said Viceroy's returning caravels should have been unequal to the transport thereof, whereas in fact Their Most Catholic Majesties have received from the said Viceroy only a few token masks, artifacts and gold nuggets, and

'Item. When forced to return in all haste to Spain to defend himself against these and other charges, the said Viceroy, with more than four hundred good and loyal subjects of the Crown from whom to choose, did with malice bypass them all and appoint as his Executive Officer an inexperienced foreigner, one Bartolomé Colón, his brother.

'In consideration whereof, the undersigned do respectfully petition that the said Viceroy, so flagrantly in breach not only of the law of Our Lord and Lady the King and Queen but of the higher law of God, be stripped of his titles, ranks, honors, perquisites, etc., etc., and retired with a modest pension to a minor estate of land on the island of Hispaniola.'

In the silence following the last break in Little D's voice, which came on the penultimate syllable of Hispaniola, I thought: bravo, son, bravo! For his poise had been amazing.

And then I realized this was precisely what the King and Queen, or at least the King, hoped I would let distract me. So, not even looking at Little D, I said in as disdainful a tone as I could muster, 'Well, Your Majesties, at least they didn't suggest I be tried as a common criminal. A surprising lack of imagination, considering their otherwise phenomenal display of that commodity.'

'Bravo, Papa!' cried Little D, and clapped a hand to his mouth.

Fernando stared straight ahead, pretending he didn't know his half-brother – or me.

The Queen gave Little D a severe look, then bit her lip, possibly to keep from smiling.

This business of using my son Diego, I began to suspect, just might cut both ways.

'How,' asked the King, 'do you plead?'

'Sire, did you say "plead"? Am I being tried?'

My Lady whispered to her consort. I thought I heard, '. . . told you . . . wrong approach . . . let me . . .'

To me she said, 'If you care to defend yourself against these informal charges, Don Cristóbal, it will please us to listen.'

But I said, possibly showboating before my sons (this did cut both ways, I was sure now): 'Your Majesties are busy enough waging a war and, I believe, arranging a dynastic marriage. As for me, I have a fleet to assemble, crews, more colonists, women even – '

'Women?' said the King, perking up.

'Why not? Men need women.'

The King said a single heartfelt 'Amen,' at which, unfortunately, the Queen felt it necessary to remind me:

'But what about the charges?'

'My Lady,' I said with a bow, and then swiftly:

'Item one, the hysterical gentleman officer, far from being attacked by a heathen, assaulted with a deadly weapon my adopted son and Your Majesties' godson Yego Clone; I stopped him. Item two, the cacique Guacanagarí, far from murdering the Christmas Town colonists, did his best to save them.' I glanced at Little D, and his rapt expression made me tell the absolute truth, so I amended that. 'Or, all he thought possible under the circumstances as he saw them. Item three, the so-called vicious criminals were only petty thieves, and I have never in my life given a benediction to anyone – with or without the sign of the cross. Item four, the caballeros were so lazy they refused any work whatsoever. Item five, the friar is a liar. Item six, (a) my so-called best troops were all the colony's malingerers and malcontents and (b) discovering is my line of work. Item seven, nothing would please me more than to abolish the slave trade immediately and forever.' This I said fervently. 'Item', I continued, 'eight, I delivered to Your Majesties all the gold received, and may I expect my twelve-and-a-half per cent share when convenient? Item nine, my brother was the best man for the job or I wouldn't have appointed him.' I took a breath, possibly my first since itemizing. 'So those are all your items, Sires. Now can we get down to the business of colonizing and discovering?'

Little D just managed not to applaud. Even Fernando, that youngest of royal pages, looked impressed.

The King recovered first. 'What you seem to be saying, Don Cristóbal, is that once we have delegated authority to you, you should be free to wield it any way you see fit.'

'I have to be, Your Majesty,' I said simply. 'The Indies are a long way from Burgos or wherever, so how could I run the colony otherwise?'

Little D's face was suffused with a glow of filial pride.

The youngest of the royal pages looked at me as if he'd never seen me before. Which he hardly had. Then he looked at the royals. Then back at me. I winked.

These subtle little signs of victory were premature, for the King said: 'The question is not *how* you could run the Crown's colony but *whether* you should. Or rather, whether *you* should.'

'Or in fact,' said the Queen, dismaying me (and probably my sons) by a rare display of regal unanimity, 'whether there should even *be* a colony.'

Against these well-coordinated italicized attacks I could do nothing but hold my silence and try not to look churlish.

'Downcast, discouraged, diseased ex-colonials,' said the King, 'are as common as fleas in the audience chambers of Burgos or wherever.'

The Queen pressed this new sally. 'Even if the charges against you are as baseless as you have branded them, Don Cristóbal, the fact remains that you have still failed to recover from the Indies enough gold even to defray the cost of your voyaging, let alone the cost of colonial maintenance. God knows why.'

'God,' said the King, 'is as interested as we are in the bottom line.'

Hearing this premature Calvinism (the Protestant theologian wouldn't be born until 1509) the Queen looked a wordless but incredulous 'oh?' at her husband. To My Lady, God was obviously no Bernal de Pisa entering profits and losses in a dusty ledger or secretly compiling His own channel-marker papers.

The King sighed. The brief reign of regal unanimity was over. And wisely, before I could delivery my famous line, 'God is no tradesman, Sire,' he declared the audience at an end.

That unuttered line typifies the problems I faced in the ensuing months. Five more audiences were to follow right there in Burgos, and still I could secure no royal support for my Third Voyage.

I sometimes wonder what might have happened if Luís de Santangel had been available. Wouldn't he have wrapped up negotiations after just two or three audiences? And wouldn't I then have returned that much sooner to Hispaniola – possibly in time to forestall my brother Barto's ill-conceived liaison with the warrior-widow Anacaoná and its grave consequences both for the colony and for me?

But Santangel wasn't available, and I had to do my solitary best.

Perhaps, I told myself, I would fare better when we moved south. For it was March 1497 and the Peripatetic Royal Court was beginning its trek to Toledo, where wan, consumptive, ill-fated Crown Prince Juan and lusty Princess Margaret of Austria would be married.

Spain would never be the same – and neither would I.

❧ XVI ❧

The Almost Undeniable Supremacy
of the Suprema

THE fine art of poisoning – you'll remember the memorandum
written for Cardinal Borgia by my brother Barto as I lay dying
in Rome – had gone into a decline, at least in Spain, by the final years
of the century. To be awarded the services of a taster at a royal banquet
was now tantamount to heading the Queen's honors list in a latter-day
England or being made an officer of the Légion d'honneur.

It was the ceremonial procession of the tasters at the wedding
banquet, two files of young men in purple and gold livery flanking the
U-shaped table that ran the length of the great hall of the run-down
Alcázar or fortress of Toledo, that made me miss the beginning of
what would end in the humiliation of the Queen's favorite cavalry
officer – for one taster halted, pivoted a quarter turn, and took his
stance behind my chair.

I have to confess a certain smug pleasure in the way hundreds of
pairs of eyes swung in my direction while I affected an impassivity that
would have earned approval from the Duke of Medinaceli. It's
nothing, said my face. But my head was full of Rome and long-ago
banquets when I stood in attendance. It was almost like reincarnation
on a higher plane, this metamorphosis from taster to tastee.

I even stopped, for a minute or two, staring gauchely down and across the table to where Petenera sat between my equal in rank, the Admiral of Castile (whose fleet had brought the bride from Flanders but who was honored with no taster), and, as fate would have it, the Queen's favorite cavalry officer, Mosén Pedro Margarit.

After the final tasters mounted the royal dais, there was one of those unaccountable lulls in conversation. Though fully 400 people sat at that table, the proverbial dropped pin could have been heard. Even the royal wolfhounds, pacing the stone floor in expectation of scraps, were quiet. Any moment now the doors at the end of the great hall would swing wide and the serving wenches begin their steady red-faced parade from the kitchens with soups and savories and *salpicóns*, ragouts and rich spicy hashes, puddings of fish and pies of game, fowl in every guise, spit-roasted suckling pigs and kids and lambs, great bloody joints of beef, jellies and custards and fruits and sweetmeats – accompanied by the tuns of wine already broached.

Smugly aware of the taster at rigid attention behind me, I was thinking: I have arrived.

'*Arriviste*,' said a braying voice in that unaccountable conversational lull. 'Nothing but a vulgar *arriviste*.'

Only his immediate neighbors could have known who Mosén Pedro meant, for he hadn't raised his voice until that fateful conversational hiatus. To his left sat the Countess del Palo, eighty years old and deaf as a post, and to his right, as already noted, Petenera Torres.

'I must have misheard you,' she said, not loud.

'I said, my dear Doña Petenera, the fellow's more suited to be a taster than to have one. He's not only an *arriviste* but a slaver. Everyone knows how he made his money.'

Still not loud, but with some heat: 'He made his money as an explorer.' Then louder: 'Besides, you can talk? You who bought a major interest in the Sevilla slave market the moment you landed back in Spain with a fleet of stolen ships?'

'Merely a prudent investment. I don't make policy.'

'Hypocrite!'

'Come now, I'm hardly what you could call a slave-owner, am I? True, I do own a dozen head of women, but they were a gift from the Benedictine Order.'

'Benedictine Order? Brother Buil, you mean, and if that gleeful sadist is ... did you say *head* of women? Are women cattle to you, then?'

At that point in the increasingly hostile exchange one of them did something under the not-yet-groaning board that the now avidly attentive guests could not see. Whatever and by whomever, it brought Mosén Pedro and Petenera both springing to their feet. He, a split-second slower, had just reached that awkward not-quite-standing position when she swung her sneaky left, fetching Mosén Pedro an estimable clout on his lantern jaw that tumbled the off-balance cavalry officer over his chair onto the floor, whereupon, more symbolically than to hurt him, Petenera kicked him thrice, rather daintily, with one silver-slippered foot.

This, as an attentive reader will recall, was not the first time Mosén Pedro had been downed and kicked. It was not even the second time. He seemed to bring that out in a person.

What surprised me more than her decking him with that sneaky left hand, was Petenera's defending me against his slurs. As if she loved me, or something.

So I sat a moment longer with a bemused smile on my face while Mosén Pedro scrambled to his feet and, apparently forgetting his assailant was a woman, drew his poniard and assumed the classic crouch. He was instantly disarmed by the Admiral of Castile while a dozen men, some of us vaulting the table (fortunately not yet laden with the wedding feast), converged on him. Medinaceli was not among us.

There was, it seemed, no love lost between navy and cavalry, for with a flourish the Admiral of Castile presented Mosén Pedro's knife to Petenera and said in the penetrating voice of a boatswain, which he had been, 'Perhaps the lady would like this souvenir of her coquettish little conquest?'

This brought the house down. The laughter, echoing thunderously from the brick walls and vaulted ceiling of the great hall of the Alcázar, turned Mosén Pedro's cheeks pomegranate-red as, looking straight ahead, he stalked the length of that enormous table and out.

Petenera became the toast of the banquet, upstaging even Crown Prince Juan and his bride Princess Margaret. So besieged by gallants was she that it was impossible to approach her and learn if the winds of love, as I could now hope, were blowing in my direction. Worse, for an entire hour before she and Medinaceli left (together, but – did I imagine it? – unspeaking) I was cornered by the Admiral of Castile in a somnific discussion of the shoal-water capabilities of caravels the size of *Niña*.

The next morning, on a horse borrowed from the Alcázar stables, I raced as early as social custom permitted across St Martin's bridge to the estate of the Countess del Palo, where Medinaceli stayed when in Toledo.

For some reason the duke seemed to be expecting me. On his face was a smile at once self-mocking and sad.

'Treat her well, Don Cristóbal,' he said simply.

'What?'

'We're both men of the world, after all. A woman's love is as unpredictable as . . .' He sought a simile and didn't find one. 'Well, you know. I'll miss her, of course. But,' he added quickly, 'my feelings are nothing compared with her happiness.'

'What are you talking about, Don Luís?' I asked.

We looked at each other.

'You mean you didn't send a Peripatetic Royal Court courier with a message for her to meet you early this morning outside the Tránsito church, formerly the Ha-Levi synagogue in the old Judería, prepared to travel?'

'God, no,' I said.

'She was so excited.'

We were standing before the hearth and at this point the duke kicked the gnarled, smoldering olivewood roots back into flame and, turning, gave me a despondent look.

'It's one of their two standard procedures,' he said bitterly. 'Luring victims quietly to their arrest by making them believe they are going to an assignation. The other, of course, is the knock at the door in the middle of the night.'

Notice he hadn't mentioned the Suprema by name. One didn't.

'But why her?' I asked.

'Why anybody? Don't forget that her parents and grandmother were – '

'I know,' I said. 'What will you do?'

Again he kicked at the fire, a gesture at once fierce and futile that nevertheless reminded me of the dainty way Petenera had kicked Mosén Pedro.

He turned again, stood aristocratically straight and drew a significant few inches away from me. 'Nothing,' he said.

'Nothing?'

'Nothing.'

'But – '

'My dear Don Cristóbal, when I return to Medinaceli it will be to learn that her meager possessions have been sequestered. And of course for the next God knows how long she will be . . . interrogated.

She has,' he said not quite pompously, 'not exactly led a blameless existence.'

'But you love her.'

'Am I then in the name of a love she never really returned to risk everything in a doomed attempt to rescue her? I hardly need point out that no one can bear the scrutiny of their investigations. No one, Don Cristóbal.'

'Then you'll simply abandon her to – '

'What else can I do but cut my losses, try to forget her? The real question is, what will *you* do? I'd advise you, my friend, to do the same.'

I galloped back across the bridge to the Alcázar and hurried to Santangel's office in the vain hope that he would be in. I saw his executive secretary, Espina de Chopito.

'As he warned you,' Espina said, 'the Keeper of the Household Budget wouldn't be here if you needed him.'

'Then I want to call an urgent meeting of those Movers and Shakers he's always calling.'

'You can't. He's the only one who can.'

'But it's about the Blue Pimpernel.'

'Never heard of her.'

I turned to go. 'Did you say "her"?'

But he had insolently buried his nose in a ledger and I went to see if I could get an emergency audience with the Queen.

'We try,' she said, after I told her my problem concerned the Suprema, 'to make no waves with the Holy Office and they none with us, but if it's a *small* problem perhaps the Grand Inquisitor will look with favor on my intercession. He doesn't ordinarily, you know. Not these days. Render unto Caesar the things which are Caesar's and – well, you know how it goes. But tell me, it isn't that nice young man Francisco Moguer of Niño again? Is he in another trivial scrape with the Holy Office? I might be able to do something if that's all it is. Such a nice boy.'

This was not the time to straighten out Francisco Niño's name. So I just said, 'They've taken the Duke of Medinaceli's protégée, my lady.'

The Queen's face became less animated, her voice cooler. 'The Torres woman? Why in the world should I intercede for that hussy when all she's done for me is humiliate my favorite cavalry officer and disrupt the wedding banquet of my son? No. No, I regret, Don Cristóbal, I cannot help you. But I will offer a word of advice. You would be less than wise to risk your neck on her behalf, for not only is she a witch — '

'A witch?' I repeated, stunned. But at least I knew what the initial charges were.

'According to my favorite cavalry officer, she's definitely a witch. And, from what I hear, she has not exactly led a blameless existence. Drop her, Don Cristóbal.'

There was only one hope left, and it took me two weeks to arrange the meeting.

'We don't get many voluntary visitors,' said Tomás de Torquemada in his reedy whisper. His ascetic or mad eyes were more deeply recessed than I remembered and his skin had the glossy transparence of the terminal stage of a wasting disease. 'Indeed, I'm amazed that you of all people would show your face here, after the way you withheld rations from your chief missionary Brother Bernardo Buil so that only sacramental cassava bread and wine kept him alive.'

'Buil lies to you too, does he? Does he lie to God, I wonder?'

'You deny that you tried to starve him in those Indies of yours?'

'I do, but for the sake of argument let's say I did take him off rations. And then perhaps he came down with some tropical disease and I refused him medical care. Or say he went on a missionary trip upcountry — not that Buil ever would — and his guides deserted him a hundred miles from nowhere. Or he met with a fatal accident in some Indian village.'

'What are you trying to say?'

'You already said it for me — those Indies *of mine*. It's all Buil's imagination so far, but the next Bernardo Buils you send out there — '

'Will be in your power? Is that what you're threatening? That unless I cooperate with you, you will hound and molest any of my harvesters of souls who are foolish enough to venture to those Indies of yours?'

The last thing I'd intended was threatening the Grand Inquisitor the moment the interview began. I was simply following the Buil opening where it led.

Now more than ever I wished for Luís de Santangel. A smooth-talking agent would know how to exploit the situation, how to broker a deal. I tried to think what he would say now.

I tried: 'A threat? Surely not, Grand Inquisitor. But you have certain powers here, and I there. In serving our own interests, can't we — '

Again he interrupted me. 'Do business together? Immunity here in

Spain for certain persons, in exchange for your guarantee that my subordinates can perform their duties unmolested?'

'And count on all possible protection and assistance.'

'How very diverting you are, Admiral. But then, as I mentioned, we have very few guests. As you have very few converts – in your Indies. So what really are you offering me? Not to intervene between my heresy hunters and perhaps a dozen heathen converts? No, Admiral. The Holy Office is interested in numbers and it is patient. Come back and threaten us when we can examine a thousand, five thousand converted heathen souls for heresy. But you won't. Because before that time we'll both be long dead. Meanwhile, however, you may divert me further with your precise reason for coming here, as if I didn't know.'

My last hope I now knew was a forlorn one, but I saw it through to the end.

'Two weeks ago, a woman named Petenera Torres was taken into custody by the Suprema.'

'So you say.'

'She wasn't?'

'She was. We average two acquittals per year. She will not be one of them. However, while she has undergone her initial interview, her actual interrogation won't begin until tomorrow. Time, properly used, is a most effective persuader.'

'It would hardly redound to your merit,' I said formally, 'to let Spain's greatest beauty rot in an Inquisition dungeon merely because she humiliated the Queen's favorite cavalry officer.'

From Tomás de Torquemada's mouth issued the faintest of rustling sounds, like a bat's wings rubbing together – a vampire bat. I realized he was laughing. 'Surely you don't believe that is the charge against her? Although it is true that this Margarit person denounced her.'

'As a witch?'

'I see you have your own sources. But witchcraft is only the tip of the iceberg. She has not exactly led a blameless existence, as you, Admiral, ought to know.'

'On what grounds could anyone possibly accuse her of being a witch?'

'On any grounds, of course. But this Margarit person's denunciation – ' here the Grand Inquisitor reached for a dossier ' – says, and I quote, "since no mere woman could have knocked down a royal cavalry officer with a single blow, she must perforce be a witch." That's sophistry, we know. But the woman likes to air her beliefs,

Admiral, and she has made some damaging admissions, it pleases me to say, in her initial interview.'

Here Torquemada read from the dossier.

Q: Do you believe in God?

A: It stands to reason there's a God.

Q: We are talking about the conventional model – Father, Son, Holy Ghost.

A: Oh.

Q: Would you care to amplify that?

A: (*pause*) Describing God as an actual father and an actual son sounds like He's cast in man's image, and that's insulting to the Deity. If He is all-powerful, all-wise, all-good, how can He possibly resemble man? Anyway, what man? Your average Spaniard? Or an Englishman with a magenta face or maybe an Indian from across the Ocean Sea with a feather in his hair? Or come to think of it, perhaps even a woman?

Q: That's blasphemy.

A: Is it? It's just as sensible as saying God looks like *you*, Brother Buil.

(*For the first time I knew who her interlocutor was.*)

Q: Then you don't believe man is made in God's image?

A: That's not what I said. I said I didn't believe God was made in man's image. Although, logically, I suppose the end result would be the same.

Q: 'Logically – sensible – stands to reason – ' You humanists all think that reason can substitute for faith. Do you *believe* in anything?

A: I believe in Nature's God.

Q: (*laughs*) Nature's God?

A: Omniscient and beautiful and good and inexplicable ...

'This,' the Grand Inquisitor reedily whispered, 'we don't have to tell you is a terrible heresy. But notice how frankly the poor sinner answered. Do you know why?'

I said that I didn't.

'The brightest of our involuntary visitors know they are doomed and so they feel free to air the heresies they have kept bottled up so long. It's almost a relief to them. You will see this subtle psychological point again when the interviewer asks his second set question.'

He found the place in the dossier.

Q: We live in an age when secular humanists are demanding that our nation divest itself of religion. A cacophony of voices – the printing press, the universities, scientists snooping into God's secrets, explorers going where God never meant them to go – undermine the very moral and spiritual bedrock from which Spain became a great nation. True or false.

A: Jesus!

Q: You're being blasphemous again.

A: Then, true *and* false. Such voices certainly are raised. But this moral and spiritual bedrock you're talking about, humanists don't disparage it, they only want to view it as one of many alternative –

'Whoever,' explained Torquemada, closing the dossier, 'incorrectly answers those two questions at the initial interview is held over for interrogation – along with whoever correctly answers the questions. One cannot be too thorough these days. But mind you, there is in certain quarters a lamentable misunderstanding of our function. It is no intention of the Holy Office of the Inquisition to hurt a sinner like Petenera Torres. We are, in reality, dedicated to saving her immortal soul. And if, while she is being ... urged to confess, she inevitably names others ...' This thought ended in an eloquent shrug of bony shoulders. 'Ripples, my dear Admiral. You drop a pebble into the still waters of a lake and there are ripples. Well,' he said, and rose, 'this has proven most instructive. Perhaps – who knows? – if you are an assiduous reader of Tribunal programs you may eventually see the name Petenera Torres again.'

I returned to my quarters in the Alcázar gloomily contemplating failure. I had tried everything, but even a legend in his own lifetime couldn't rescue the woman he loved from the clutches of the Inquisition.

A scrofulous-looking beggar of indeterminate years was waiting in the corridor outside my rooms.

'Admiral, Viceroy or Governor Colón?'

I nodded bleakly.

'About time. Let's get a move on.'

'Where to?' Wherever, the notion had strong appeal.

'All I know, this fellow paid me fifty unclipped coppers to fetch you. A senior citizen he was, with pig bristles sticking out of his ears and nose.'

The scrofulous beggar led me to a small stone house between the marketplace and the ruins of the old Arab fortifications north of the cathedral. Where, of course, Pighi-Zampini was waiting behind a makeshift banker's bench, impatiently watching time go by on his gold portable clock.

'Come in, come in, young man! You're a sight for sore eyes, you are. But forgive me, it's you who have the sore eyes, isn't it?'

'How do you know that?'

'I know everything these days.'

Pighi-Zampini, who had to be over eighty, looked twenty years younger than he had in Cádiz. Even his ear and nostril bristles had a new springiness to them.

'Best thing that ever happened to me, opening the Peripatetic branch of Centurione's. Two years now I've been taking in all their dirty money and laundering it. I know everything about everyone of any importance anywhere. Never had so much fun in my life.' He put away the portable clock with a toothless smile and offered me a chair. 'I see you're doubtful. Name a name. Go on – anyone.'

'Uh, Brother Buil.'

'Buil? That's easy. You think Buil hates you because of that class-war hunger strike in the Indies, coming on top of your getting the King and Queen to intercede with the Suprema – the last time they did – in the affair of that young Moguer boy of Niño.'

'Niño of Moguer, actually,' I said, but I was impressed.

'Anyway, that's what you think, isn't it? But you're wrong. The reason Brother Buil hates you is, he blames you for the sexual pox he picked up in the Indies before he commandeered your brother's caravels and came crying back to Spain.'

'Buil? Buil's got syphilis?'

'Yes, but I can't divulge which Arawak maiden was responsible. Sorry. She's under age. Want to try another name?'

But I said he'd made a believer of me.

'You're also the only man of any importance in any way connected with the Peripatetic Royal Court who isn't terrified of me. Know why?'

'Why I'm not or why everybody else is?'

'Everybody else, that's simple. I have secret files on all of 'em. And I mean all. Just name me a name.'

'No, that's all right.'

'These files are well hidden, and in the event of my death from suspicious or natural causes will be turned over to the appropriate people.'

'What appropriate people?'

'Well, the Suprema gets the King and Queen's file, and the King and Queen get the Suprema's, just to give you a pair of matched examples.'

'But – natural causes? Everybody dies, and if you don't mind my saying so, you're no young man.'

'That's everybody's problem, not mine. They better just hope I keep peripatting around. Natural causes could be a slow-acting poison, after all. I'm taking no chances.' He laughed. His bristles bristled. 'Oh, but there'll be hell to pay when I die. Well, that's why everyone else's terrified of me. Now, why aren't you? Or, to ask the obverse: why do I do whatever I can to help you?'

'Because I still have this old letter from Cardinal Borgia to all directors, sub-directors and associates of the House of Centurione throughout the world requesting all possible assistance to the bearer?' I guessed.

'You mean,' chuckled Pighi-Zampini, 'now that he's Pope it carries even more weight? Not with me it doesn't. Popes come and go, like kings and queens and grand inquisitors. Money too, if you want to know the truth. No, I'll tell you why you can count on me. I'm an old sentimentalist, that's why. Borgia's was the first dirty money I ever laundered. Now, I gather you want to rescue a certain person from the clutches of the Inquisition, despite the fact that she has not exactly led a blameless existence, and before they can deface her incomparable beauty with certain of their interrogatory instrumentation.'

'Yes, please,' I said. Heartfelt.

Here my old friend waxed philosophical. 'Odd, isn't it, how they got so powerful? Your agent at Court, Luís de Santangel, asked me not long ago, "Prospero, why can't the nation that can send men across the Ocean Sea find a cure for the Inquisition?" Now how do you answer a question like that?' Pighi-Zampini rose and leaned both hands on his makeshift banker's bench, a board supported by two barrels. 'Well, come on back about the same time tomorrow and we'll see what I can do for you.'

'But tomorrow they're beginning her interrogation.'

'Been to Rome, haven't you?'

'You know I – '

'Then I needn't tell you it wasn't built in a day. And I'm trying to do this in a day. Maybe I know everything about everybody, but I'm no magician. Come back tomorrow.'

I was waiting there when he arrived, which wasn't until shortly before noon.

'Ever read Dante's *Inferno*, young man?' he asked as he unlocked the door.

'In the original Italian, when I was a boy.'

'Well, in a way that's where you're going. But it's right here in Toledo.' Sliding behind his makeshift banker's bench, he said, 'It's all arranged. You can get her out — provided you go *in*.'

'In exchange for her?' My mouth was suddenly dry, the palms of my hands wet. But I had misunderstood.

'Nope. They want you to see everything in there.'

'Me? Why me?'

'Why not you?'

The Book of Job, in two lines.

'Maybe,' Pighi-Zampini went on, 'they figure you need an object lesson. But that's only a guess. I said I know everything about everybody. But I never claimed I knew *what was behind* everything. Well, good luck to you, young man. His name's Brother Virgilio and he's expecting you.'

So it was that, in the middle of the journey of my life, I entered Hell, right there in Toledo.

The building enclosed a central garden where fountains plashed and nightingales sang. When the Supreme and General Council of the Inquisition was abolished forever in July 1834, it would become the Inn of the Holy Brotherhood. There was some talk of turning it into a parador open to the general public, but it came to nothing. There were too many ghosts.

My editors have urged me to omit the next few pages, and while in conscience I cannot, we have arrived at this compromise. First, I have tried to understate the horrors I saw. Second, the pages bearing a large check (√) prominently displayed are not recommended to the squeamish reader. But if, as Pighi-Zampini said, I was meant 'to see everything in there,' then my visit to the Palace of the Inquisition (the Grand Inquisitor's own offices in Toledo were located in an unprepossessing block closer to the cathedral) is part of my life story, and the curious and not easily daunted reader may want some idea of what I saw.

Brother Virgilio received me in the central garden, and we entered a vaulted gallery. The only light came through high embrasures in the courtyard walls so that we almost seemed to be groping our way through a subterranean tunnel. It smelled of damp, decay, doom and death.

'All prisoners must meet the expenses of their room and board,' explained Brother Virgilio. 'These on the three lower levels have been incarcerated in second class. First-class prisoners, who can pay more, are kept in cells off the topmost gallery.'

'Where's Petenera Torres?'

'Ah,' he said. 'Where indeed?'

We climbed steep stairs to the topmost gallery. The place was so cold and damp, and the atmosphere so without hope, the stone walls wept.

I saw a row of doors, each with a tiny Judas hole.

'You may look,' said Brother Virgilio.

'If I'd rather not?'

'Then you wouldn't learn if this Petenera Torres is in one of these cells, would you?'

There were thirty-two cells on this level. Each was occupied by a solitary prisoner. I shall describe what I saw in just three. Three is enough. A picture will emerge.

On the stone floor of the first cell a girl of ten or twelve sat naked in a pool of urine, huddled knees to chin, slender arms wrapped around slender legs. A rat crawled over her feet. She seemed not to notice. Her lips were moving, possibly in prayer.

'Judas holes are also for listening,' Brother Virgilio suggested.

I pressed my ear to the hole and heard, in a singsong voice that will haunt me for the rest of my life:

'What did I do? I wish I knew what I did, for I would confess if only I knew. But they won't tell me. If only they told me I would confess. I did it. I would say I did it, I would say I did anything, if only someone would tell me what I did. They ask me and ask me to tell the truth but I don't know what the truth is. Dear God, won't anyone tell me? I don't want to go down there anymore. No. No, please, no, just tell me and I will confess that I did it, whatever it is.'

When I looked again I saw that the puddle she sat in was not urine but blood.

'What crime is she guilty of?' I asked.

'We'll know when she confesses,' said Brother Virgilio.

I almost didn't ask my other question. 'And the blood?'

'She's young. She's small and tight. Sometimes they're hasty and unintentionally brutal with the young ones.'

I stood speechless.

'You're surprised? But they're trying to save her immortal soul, after all. And with young virgins of a certain class rape often works better than the strappado, or even the water torture. But come.'

In another cell I saw a burly wild-haired man coming. That is, he was masturbating furiously and just reaching climax. I turned swiftly away.

'Onanism again?' asked Brother Virgilio, clucking his tongue.

I nodded.

'Whenever they rape the young ones, he is taken to watch.'

'But why – '

'Because after two years here in solitary confinement he was seen abusing himself. This activity, once begun, is always encouraged. It seems to have the opposite effect from mortification of the flesh, that is, it lowers a certain sort of individual's threshold of resistance to the strappado, the rack, the water torture.'

'What's he guilty of?'

'We'll know when he confesses.'

In the final cell off the upper gallery, a large nine-foot-square model, light streamed down through a bigger than average ceiling hole.

'Our de luxe accommodation, for those that can afford it,' said Brother Virgilio.

The man was old and emaciated, his eyes so deep-socketed they were invisible, his sharp ribs threatening to burst the skin of his scarred, sunken chest. His elbows, knees and ankles were bulbous. He was grinning.

'Why is he grinning?' I asked.

'Because he's been here long enough – eleven years, I believe – to know he won't confess no matter what. And he knows we know it too.'

'Then, if he isn't going to confess to a sin which he and you are ignorant of – '

'I never said we were ignorant of their sins. I merely said we would know when they confessed. This is not to say we don't know before they confess or won't know if they don't confess.'

' – why isn't he released?'

'Our release quota is only two per year, as you know. Is he dead yet?' Brother Virgilio asked me.

'No.' Not even that question surprised me now. 'No, I don't think so.' For the poor unfortunate, sitting under the shaft of light, moved one sticklike arm, the bulbous elbow flexing with a stridulant sound.

'The reason I ask, we are starving him to death. This takes longer in some cases than others.'

'But why – '

'Overcrowding. We need his cell. If he won't confess, he's of no use to us in ferreting out other sinners and no use to himself in the salvation of his soul. And until he dies, his property stays in the hands of the bailiff instead of passing to the Suprema where it will defray our very considerable expenses. And, despite all our efforts to save his soul, our staff physicians tell us this fellow could go on living for years. Hence, starvation.'

'But what if he's innocent?'

'No one is innocent. Well, shall we go down below?'

At this point I was given a nondescript gray robe to cover my layman's clothing so as not to distract the busy attendants and the objects of their attention.

At the bottom of the stairs I hung back. As a Brother Virgilio, confronted with a caravel under full sail, might be bewildered by the nautical jumble of standing rigging, running rigging, cables and canvas and hardware, so I was bewildered by the chthonic chaos of those Inquisitorial dungeons. Attendants in robes of white, black and brown rushed about in a vast cavernlike hall from which corridors branched into nether darkness. The air reeked with smoke (suggestive of brimstone) and rang with the sound of machinery – the turning of cranks, the creak of pulleys, the sudden crash of iron against stone. From the darkness two ruddy, sweating attendants carried a stretcher bearing an inert object, while alongside hurried a physician in medical crimson, shaking his head either sadly or irritably. Into another corridor two brown robes dragged between them another object already working its vocal cords up to a pitch of undeniable complaint. Doors slammed, machines whined, harried voices called out:

'Let's have a consultant, we need a second opinion in here!'

'The pulley's still stuck, we're ready to drop him, where's that damn mechanic, they're never around when you need them!'

'No, no, no, now look what you've done, how many times must I tell you apprentices we're not supposed to kill them?'

'We go in here,' said Brother Virgilio.

I had steeled myself, but in that first corridor's first chamber there was neither strappado, rack nor water torture.

'The warm-up area,' explained Brother Virgilio. Here through sulphurous smoke I saw flames dancing in a great open hearth, a cheerful sight, almost, until I saw the three tables and the three objects lashed to them, fully swathed in gray except for their bare feet, to which an apprentice or acolyte applied oil liberally as the tables were moved in stages, feet-first, closer to the dancing flames. Soon the oil began to sizzle, then the flesh, but as the objects were gagged, their voices did not rise much above the fluttering roar of the fire, and when the physician present was satisfied with the amount of char and said, 'Suspend,' he could clearly make himself heard.

About this word 'suspend'. According to Inquisition regulations, an object could only be tortured once. That is, a torture discontinued could not, by law, be recommenced. For this reason, torture sessions were not stopped, but only suspended. Suspended, they might be resumed at any time, even over a period of years.

The pulley or strappado, which I saw next, is the noisiest device, not because the pulley itself (from which the object dangles by its wrists fettered behind its back) is in bad repair, but because increasingly heavy iron weights dangle from the ankles of the dangling object and when the pulley drops it from a considerable height these hit the stone floor before the object, and they are noisy.

The rack is a sort of table on which the object is strapped over a ladderlike arrangement of sharp supports. Two methods of persuasion are possible. First, the many head, arm, torso and leg straps can be tightened, causing discomfort. Second, the raised sides of the table, which often come with small blunted spikes, can be brought together, again causing the object discomfort.

The water torture is frequently applied while the object is on the rack. In this case, the foot of the table is elevated, the object's mouth is forced open and a long strip of linen is fed down the gullet. Over this, large jars of water are slowly poured. Some objects have been known to accept eight or even nine jars before manifesting symptoms of drowning – whereupon the physician present would suspend the proceedings to examine the object for a willingness to confess. Malingering was uncommon.

Objects, on their initial visits to the dungeons, were frequently given an introductory sample of the three (four, if you count the warm-up area) principal means of persuasion, and this, I learned to my horror, had been the case with Petenera Torres.

My guide Brother Virgilio stopped with me before a plain door at the end of the last corridor.

'That's where you'll find her.'

He made no move to open the door.

'You're not coming with me?' I found this, after all I'd witnessed, most alarming of all.

'I'm sorry, but I can't. It's considered bad for my morale to see the release of an object. But you just wait here. The examining physician will let you know when she is free to go.'

And Brother Virgilio was gone.

I waited, but no physician opened the door to admit me. After a while I heard familiar laughter. I smashed the door in and saw a man's broad back in robes not of medical crimson but of rumpled brown. These were just being hiked up over plump hairless legs and broad pink buttocks which almost hid the object stretched supine on the examining table. Only two blistered feet were visible. A moan came from the object, and a laugh from Brother Buil. He began to mount the table, with the clear intention of mounting the object as well. He almost succeeded, for I was struck for a split-second by an immobilizing horror in which I heard Pighi-Zampini say again *the reason Brother Buil hates you is, he blames you for the sexual pox he picked up in the Indies*, before I could launch myself at Buil, grab him around his doughy middle and hurl him across the room. Then I covered the object with my gray robe and gently lifted it in my arms and kissed its grime-streaked face, and carried it from that room and up from those sulphurous, chthonic regions and out to where, in the gathering dusk, Pighi-Zampini waited at the open door of what was, possibly, only the third privately owned Hungarian coach in Spain. On the driver's box, holding the reins in readiness, I could just make out my brother Diego.

Late one afternoon shortly before Christmas that year, my mule plodded patiently up the hillside of La Rábida through a pelting rain to the tiny stone cottage in a pine wood half a mile beyond the monastery. Smoke was rising from the chimney and, suddenly, welcoming light spilling from the open door. I dismounted before the mule stopped and gave him a slap and a shove in the direction of the stable behind the cottage.

Petenera flung herself wordlessly into my arms, oblivious of the rain. I had been gone three weeks, not my first absence since our arrival in April at La Rábida, but the longest.

Arms around each other, we went inside. The fire on the hearth made my sodden cloak steam. Petenera fussed over me. 'You're drenched, darling,' she said, and got my robe and slippers. Soon I was

406

drinking hot spiced wine. Outside, wind moaned and icy rain clattered against the window.

Petenera's poor burned feet had long since healed and her shoulders, so grievously dislocated by the strappado, only ached in weather like this. Her spine, which the Converso doctor in Toledo believed permanently twisted by the rack, had straightened.

Her hair, lustrous and black as the space between the stars with now a single vivid comet of white streaking one side, hung almost to her hips. Her eyes, that deep emerald green that John Cabot had seen when his ships crossed the Gulf Stream this past June – though word of his exploit would not reach Spain for some time – looked up into mine.

'It's as if I'm not alive when you go away,' she said. 'I'm like a bear hibernating for the winter.'

I kissed that white streak in her hair. I caressed her cheek. 'Some bear,' I said lightly.

But her dependence worried me, for she hadn't recovered her familiar feisty spirits along with her health. Even good Fray Juan Pérez, not a worldly man, had noticed. 'It hits the strong ones hardest,' he said as we strolled in the cloister of La Rábida after I returned from Sevilla the first time. 'She never believed she could be broken. When she was, it was you who gathered up the pieces and put them back together. So now she fears that when you go away the pieces will fall apart again.'

Once I told her, 'I'll have to go back across the Ocean Sea someday soon. Then what?'

'I'll be all right,' she said with a brittle smile. 'I love you very much, Cristóbal, but I want to be my old self again. And when I am, you'll love me more.' The smile crumbled then. 'But you don't have to go *that* soon, do you?'

This was after my second trip to Sevilla, where Big D was working with Juan Fonseca, archdeacon of the diocese and newly appointed president of the House of Trade which had its headquarters – was headquartered, as this Fonseca would have put it – in the gloomy old Alcázar. 'He's the wave of the future,' Big D assured me, but I didn't know what that meant. 'I've already learned a lot from him. Best of all,' said Big D, 'he's a great admirer of yours, Cristóbal – until I was certain of that, I didn't commit us to anything. You can bet I was leery when the royals fobbed him off on me. But they knew what they were doing.' When I asked exactly what he *had* committed us to, Big D was vague. 'Well, we can't be here in Spain and in the Indies at the same time, can we? Besides, he's well-placed to find us venture capital if the royals are ever short of funds, and I don't have to tell you war always takes precedence over discovery, so that could happen.' 'Venture capital?' I asked, but Big D in his enthusiasm went right on. '*And* he's an expert on such matters as agronomy and biotechnology, not to – ' 'Bio what?' 'Biotechnology – you know, that's the short way of saying breadmaking and fermentation and so on. Anyway, Cristóbal, you didn't hear from me till now because I wanted to make sure Fonseca was everything he said he was, which he is.' I asked, 'What if he wasn't?' but Big D just said, 'You're going to like him.'

But I didn't. Juan Fonseca, archdeacon of Sevilla, later a bishop, was not an easy person for someone as independent as me to like.

And now, having written that, I'd better put it on record that this book is no antireligious tract – for Fonseca, coming so soon after Tomás de Torquemada, Brother Buil and the whole horrible Inquisition scene, could give you that idea. But to get ahead in my day a man had to be a titled landowner like Medinaceli, or have connections at Court like Luís de Santangel, or join one of Spain's five great military orders, or go into the Church. My dislike was of Fonseca the man, and it was reciprocated. I found officialdom tedious, he found individualism odious. He was a gifted amateur who knew a great deal about how the world was run – from the viewpoint of his library. A thing was real to him if he read about it. Second best was if he wrote about it – and before long that became first best. Eventually the indispensable volume of universal research for Juan Fonseca was his own *Handbook of Regulations and Right Conduct for Colonial Administrators* (Waldseemüller Press, Córdoba, 1497).

Still, since he and Big D were close, I didn't mention my misgivings. They shared an office there in the Alcázar of Sevilla in what would be called (erroneously, as you will see) the Admiral's Apartments, where they 'bounced ideas off each other'. For Big D even picked up Juan Fonseca's colonial administration jargon, though whether or not this was part of the 'wave of the future' I couldn't say.

'You'll learn, Cristóbal,' Big D had predicted. 'Times are changing, and a man content with yesterday's way will be a has-been tomorrow.'

I wondered what was wrong with doing things today's way, but this wasn't the sort of remark you made to the new, idea-bouncing, cost-effective, infrastructure-planning Big D. Besides, everything he was doing at the House of Trade in Sevilla, as he was the first to tell me, he was doing for my benefit. Which I'm sure he believed.

Now in the La Rábida cottage I told Petenera, for she had begun to tremble, 'I'll always love you.'

She kissed me. 'Don't ever stop. I'd die if you stopped.'

Two perfect tears hung suspended from her long eyelashes before rolling down her flawless cheeks.

'How long will you stay in the Indies this time? Six months? A year?'

It would, of course, be far longer. But I did not say that. I held her close and said:

'You know, Pet, there are almost sure to be women colonists this time.'

'Then if I don't die of loneliness I'll die of jealousy.'

I said softly into the fragrant black hair with its single streak of white, 'Why don't you come with me instead?'

I touched the creamy skin of her throat. I kissed the hollow above her collarbone.

'Oh Cristóbal, do you mean it?'

'I never meant anything so much in my life.'

'I'll make a good colonist, you'll see.'

A few days after Christmas I left for Soria, where the Peripatetic Royal Court was mourning Crown Prince Juan who, it was said, had died of love during his extended honeymoon with lusty Princess Margaret of Austria.

The official period of mourning had just ended, but Soria still could have been a city of the dead. Snow shrouded streets and rooftops, snow muffled sounds, snow blew a fresh blizzard every day from a clear sky, the wind was that strong. Fingers and toes froze, and the frozen bodies of beggars were carted away every morning. A funereal atmosphere stifled the audience chamber in the old castle whose grounds fronted on the Duero River.

I had a few minutes with Little D in the anteroom before he ushered me in. 'I miss the Prince,' my son said. 'He was one of my best friends. Why'd he have to die so young like that?'

I might have said, just to say something, that it was God's will. But I valued Little D's respect, and I knew he was as much a questioner as I.

'I don't know,' I admitted. 'If there really is a grand design, I've never been able to find it.'

Fernando came by then on some nameless royal errand. 'It's God's will,' he said.

Little D and I exchanged glances. His eyes were almost on a level with my own.

'He's very sure of his ground for a kid,' my older son said as the youngest of the royal pages marched off. 'Papa, listen, they're gloomy in there,' with a toss of his red head toward the audience chamber. 'You can probably get what you want if you're brief and to the point, but be prepared for some dire predictions, even a threat or two. They're striking out at everybody.'

This was grown-up advice and it made me feel proud of my son. It also made me feel old.

They were gloomy, all right, and I was brief, and I did get what I wanted. Which was: money enough for eight ships, and for crews, colonists (women to men in a ratio of one to ten, but it was a start), farm animals, etc., etc.

My charter contained two unusual provisions. First, since Mosén Pedro, Brother Buil & co. had so thoroughly badmouthed the Indies, volunteers were not exactly fighting for places on my Third Voyage, so a pardon was offered to convicts willing to become colonists. Second – but hear this in the words of King Fernando, who read me the appropriate paragraph of the draft charter:

'Cosmographers and geographers since Aristotle, whether Europeans, Arabs, Indians or whoever, have agreed that precious things are most often found in very hot places whose inhabitants are either black or brown. Therefore the aforementioned Admiral of the Ocean Sea is ordered, before proceeding to his duties in possibly overrated Hispaniola, to sail further south on the western side of the Ocean Sea to the longitude of Fernando Po in Africa – '

'Latitude, dear,' corrected the Queen.

'That's what I said. To the latitude of Fernando Po in Africa in order to search out those great and precious things, such as gold, pearls and other gemstones, spicery and medicinal herbs, which must exist in abundance in those uncharted equinoctial regions.'

Wording aside, the prospect excited me. I was, after all, a discoverer, and as far as I knew Barto had things under control in Hispaniola. Peralonso Niño, returning late in '96 (his holds crowded with what should have been the last slaves ever brought from the New World to the Old by a Spanish fleet), reported that the new settlement of Santo Domingo was flourishing, Barto having somehow achieved a *modus vivendi* with the fierce Indians once ruled by Caonabó and now by his widow Anacaoná.

But the Queen, her face aged by grief, turned this provision of my charter into a veiled threat.

'The last thing we wish to do, Admiral, is abandon our overseas possessions after all your work and all our money that have gone into them. But unless something of value, *real* value, is discovered, it is not inconceivable that a time will come when these possessions will interest us no longer. Life, even royal life, is all too short.'

A grieving mother feeling her own mortality through the death of her son? Perhaps. But while this would have been the first, it would not have been the only instance of a queen abandoning a colony that lost her interest. I offer Queen Elizabeth of England and the cruel fate of Roanoke Island, 117 men, women and children abandoned off the coast of John Cabot's part of the New World in the ninth decade of the next century. Admittedly, Elizabeth could afford no resupply fleet at the time, for it was in 1588 that King Felipe II sent the Spanish Armada to conquer England (a doomed enterprise if ever there was one, but the Spanish king who decreed Madrid his capital could, I suppose, be guilty of any excess). It took two years for the Virgin (alleged) Queen's interest to be rekindled by her favorite courtier, one Raleigh, a sort of Old Christian Luís de Santangel, and by then it was far too late, for the Indians had killed every inhabitant of the island.

When the youngest of the royal pages came back from wherever he had gone after explaining God's will to his brother and me, I said, 'Fernando, do you think you might be able to get some time off?'

This was perhaps an odd question to ask a boy not yet nine, however precocious. But he was more steadily employed than I.

'Maybe it's possible,' said the youngest of the royal pages cautiously.

'I could ask the Queen.'

'No. Please don't, Papa. It's bad for my repution if you ask.'

'Your reputation?'

'That's what I said.'

'Well, if you can get away, how would you like to come with me to Córdoba and visit your mother?'

Purple and gold silk sagged at the little shoulders of the youngest of the royal pages. 'Do I have to?'

'It's over three years since you left home. Don't you miss her?'

Fernando hadn't learned to dissimulate yet. 'No. Why should I? She'd be the first to tell you she's just a farmgirl from Santa Maria Trasiera. And she's really fat.' He made an unpleasant face. 'A fat peasant.'

'Fernando,' I said, 'this is your mother we're talking about.'

'I didn't choose her, you did, Papa.'

For the first time I had an impulse to strike one of my sons.

He made it still more tempting. 'She's not even married.'

'Fernando,' I warned.

'Do I have to go?'

While I thought that over, he said:

'She really grosses me out.'

I left Soria without him and took the Mérida road south, bypassing Córdoba and delaying my own surprise visit to Beatriz. If I came to see her straight from La Rábida, she wouldn't expect to find Fernando with me.

At the stone cottage behind the monastery Petenera met me with fire in her emerald-green eyes.

'Oh that bastard! Wait till you hear!' she cried, not even giving me a welcome-home kiss, though I'd been gone almost six weeks. 'The nerve of him! The utter, unmitigated, arrogant, aristocratic, conceited, cock-sure gall!'

'Who?'

'Who do you think who? Rides up here brazen as you please, reminds me that someone in his position can't create a disturbance at a royal banquet just because some lout pulls a knife on me — I mean, how attenuated can you get? — then claims he had no idea I was in a Suprema dungeon or he would have written — *written!* — to the royals on my behalf. And finally says — are you ready? oh that bastard! you're not going to *believe* this — says since everything turned out for the best, he'll overlook my past crimes, let bygones be bygones even where you're concerned, and take me back. *He's* willing to take *me* back. The total, irredeemable, insolent, overbred effrontery of that pedigreed peacock!'

'Medinaceli?' I said mildly, trying not to smile.

'Men!' she raged, and turned her lips away from my kiss. Then she turned them back. 'Well, just a little one.'

It was barely a peck. For she wasn't finished. 'You'll have to tell Fray Juan Pérez that I broke a few dishes and things.' She giggled. 'You should have seen him try to beat a dignified retreat — that inbred, imperious, insufferable fifth count and first duke of a pompous patrician poltroon! My only regret is that my aim wasn't so good.'

'I gather this was a recent visit?'

'Day before yesterday, but I'm still fuming. He came in one of those Hungarian coach things. Expected me to drive right off with him.' A small pause for breath. 'Now tell me about your trip.'

'It was all right. A bit on the cold side.'

'It's always cold in Soria in — oh, you mean Their Most Close-

Fisted Majesties. Sorry, darling. Did you get anything like what you went for?'

'Near enough.'

'You can tell me about it over dinner. Meanwhile – any plans for this afternoon?'

'Well, no. I'd like to wash and – '

'Good thinking. I like you freshly scrubbed when I ravish you.'

Soon I was, and she did, and I began to think Petenera was her old self again.

I told her I'd be leaving in a few days for Córdoba, before going on to Sevilla, from where the fleet would sail.

'Why Córdoba?' she demanded.

'To see Beatriz.'

'That's what I thought.'

'Pet, believe me, there hasn't been a thing between us in years. It's just the decent thing to do, to see her before we sail.'

'Well, I suppose. When are you sailing?'

'As soon as we can get things organized in Sevilla. End of May, early June at the latest.'

'Oh.'

'What's with the "oh?"? Have you forgotten you're coming too?'

'I could easily forget my name. It's only . . . '

But though I pressed her, she would say no more.

We arranged for her to travel with Fray Juan Pérez to Sevilla in May, when he would be attending a convocation of his Order.

I reached Córdoba early in March and went straight to the hidden patio not far from the plaza that one day would be named in my honor. It was a warm day, spring already in the air, geraniums in pots hanging on either side of the door as I remembered, canaries singing like mad in their cages.

The door was opened for me by a ghost.

'Hi,' he said. 'I'm Pedro.'

'Harana!' I blurted. For there he was, standing right before me, tall, broad-shouldered, athletic-looking, and despite the smile of welcome a wariness on his face that could blossom into open suspicion.

'Right you are,' he said. 'Pedro Enríquez de Harana, at your service. I don't have to be told who you are, Admiral.'

As I continued gaping at him, he asked, 'What's the matter?'

'Nothing's the matter. It's just that you're the image of your cousin Diego. You even sound like him.'

'I want to take his place,' he said simply. 'He was like a big brother to Beatriz and me. It's – well, it's like he left something unfinished in the Indies and I want to finish it for him. That's why I became a sailor.'

'What kind of experience have you?'

'Three voyages with the Portuguese down to Fernando Po, the last one as constable.'

'Constable Harana,' I said. I couldn't get over it.

'Does that mean I can sign on or what?' he asked.

I assured him he could sign on.

'Well, then what are we standing here for, man? Let's go inside and tell Beatriz.' And, when I didn't move, 'Don't you want to see her?' he demanded. More like his cousin all the time.

'You're standing in the way,' I pointed out.

She had a new way of wrinkling her haughtily high-bridged, conceivably Semitic nose when she smiled. A lot of ample women do that.

'Cristóbal!'

She rose, graceful for so large a woman, licking a dab of honey from her full, red, sensuous, possibly Berber lips. We hugged. Her hour-glass figure had lost its nipped-in waist to the passing years. Her rosy, perhaps Visigoth cheeks dimpled deeply with a second smile.

'You ought to warn a person.'

'I was just passing through,' I said.

Those dark, undeniably Iberian eyes probed my own. 'You've been to Court? How are they?'

They, not he. I could have kissed her. In fact, I did.

Then I said quickly, 'Diego's almost my height and Fernando looks like a little man in his livery. He was really disappointed. For a while there we thought he'd be able to get away and he was telling all the other pages that he was going with me to see his mother who lived in Córdoba, but at the last minute all the pages were needed to do something important, a state visit I think, and he couldn't come with me after all.'

About half-way through this speech her brother Pedro, who was standing behind her, began to shake his head at me.

Beatriz said, subdued, 'Well, I knew he'd be busy.'

'Yes,' I said. 'But he was a little man about it. You'd have been proud of him. He never even cried. At least not in front of the other pages.'

Pedro kept shaking his head.

Beatriz ran, lightly for so big a woman, from the room.

414

Pedro asked me, 'Where did you ever learn how to lie? Don't use a trowel, man. You didn't fool her at all.'

When Beatriz returned, her eyes were red but she could smile. 'Now tell me all about everything. When are you – '

'I'm going with him,' said Pedro offhandedly.

'You think I didn't know?' Beatriz said to her younger brother. 'I knew the minute you came in.'

I expected her to be reproachful, but she wasn't. 'It's a long time since our cousin and those others were killed. And the Indies are all he's been dreaming about for years. Now let's have something to eat. I don't know about you men, but personally I'm starving.'

Three days and some ninety miles later, young Pedro Enríquez de Harana and I stabled our mules in the Alcázar of Sevilla and crossed the Montería Court to what in later years would be called the Admiral's Apartments, in the mistaken belief that when in Sevilla I occupied those cold, drafty rooms built in poor imitation of a section of the Alhambra of Granada by King Pedro the Cruel back in the fourteenth century. George Washington would appreciate how I felt about those so-called Admiral's Apartments; they were like all those houses he never really slept in.

The receptionist – a new concept in Spain – asked if we had an appointment.

'Colón needs an appointment?' asked Harana II.

'Colón,' he was told, 'never needs an appointment. He's inside with the President of the House of Trade bouncing ideas around.'

'I'm his brother,' I said.

'The President of the House of Trade has no brother.'

I explained.

We were each handed a copy of the *Handbook of Regulations and Right Conduct for Colonial Administrators* and invited to wait. I glanced through it. At least this was no compendious tome. It was aphoristic, actually, if you could understand the vocabulary.

'What's an innovative product concept?' Harana II asked me.

But I shook my head.

'How about incremental costs?'

'Search me.'

'Arising from the introduction of a second gender into the Indies – does that help?'

But it didn't.

Archdeacon Fonseca, though no monk, wore monastic garb like Big

415

D. It was practical. In its voluminous folds a great deal of paper could be carried, and paperwork was always necessary in this nascent bureaucracy of theirs. In fact, when we finally were ushered into their presence, both were scribbling on pads while bouncing ideas back and forth.

' ... definitely upscale,' Big D was saying.

'But for a big-ticket item it has no proven track record,' disagreed Archdeacon Fonseca.

'We-ell,' said Big D comprehensibly if doubtfully.

Harana II said, 'Code. I know code when I hear it.'

A brief aside here. In preparing the English edition of these memoirs, considerable thought has been lavished upon translating their bureaucratic jargon, but the actual words in the Spanish of my day would have been different. As usual in such cases, I opt for the spirit of the thing.

Harana II was introduced and given a chit entitling him to quarters in the Court of the Maidens, a name which delighted him in prospect but proved misleading, as it turned out to be the House of Trade's Bachelor Officers' Quarters. Then Fonseca, Big D and I got down to work.

'The sluggish economic performance of the colony, of course,' said Fonseca, 'leaves us with an unfortunate bottom line.'

'The Crown's losing megamaravedís,' agreed Big D.

'Of which,' said Fonseca, 'the higher echelons of the Peripatetic Royal Court hierarchy are fully cognizant even though you, Admiral, have claimed all along that it would be one of the fastest growing economic sectors of the realm.'

'I have?'

Both nodded, Big D with some sympathy.

'But women are a nice bravura touch,' said Fonseca, 'indicative of a colonial vision not evidenced prior to the present time. Though how they will interface with the male population remains to be seen.'

This went on all day, and then all week, and then all month.

To prevent what Fonseca called a cost overrun, my fleet was cut from eight to six ships, and the number of colonists (including women) reduced from 500 to 330, a quarter of the men pardoned convicts. Economy was also invoked in purchasing. Fonseca seemed to have a lot of cousins scattered around Andalucía (though the word cousin in Spanish often means no more than close friend), and it was with these cousins that he contracted for various items – crossbows and muskets from a cousin in Málaga, lances from one in Granada, gunpowder and cannon balls from a cousin right there in Sevilla.

Meanwhile, information processed in Sevilla was rushed to the Peripatetic Royal Court, still in Soria, by regular express courier service, and the courier service brought back almost daily letters from Soria urging me to provision my six (formerly eight) ships and sail for the Indies at once. 'Time is money,' Fonseca told me, as if somehow the delay was my fault. All I did was check things. For example, the wine barrels supplied by Fonseca's cooper cousin in Cádiz were beautiful to look upon but they leaked. Such troubles stemming from what a later age would call not wine- but pork-barreling invariably brought me up against Fonseca. When I canceled our contract with his Cádiz cousin, I had the barrels made in Sanlúcar at the mouth of the mighty Guadalquivir, where the fleet was assembling anyway. 'They don't have the right product concept in Sanlúcar,' Fonseca told me testily. 'But they make good wine barrels,' I pointed out.

So it went. I resented Fonseca's salary of 200,000 maravadís, which could have paid the upkeep and wages of the scratched 170 colonists for a couple of years. Fonseca resented my various titles, which he didn't believe applied in Sevilla anyway, as Sevilla was neither the Ocean Sea nor the Indies. This personality clash carried us into May, the fleet still far from ready to sail. I got a letter from the royals reminding me that Fonseca was their official representative and he got one reminding him that he was no Admiral, Viceroy or Governor, and I was all three. Big D, caught in the middle, resorted to aphoristic if incomprehensible quotes from the *Handbook*, which flattered Fonseca but set my teeth on edge. Fonseca's belief that conquistadores were difficult to deal with probably started with me, though I never thought of myself as one. By the time the years rolled around to Balboa (misnamed) and Cortés, Fonseca was seeing red at the very word conquistador. History will attest what a thorn he was in the sides of these bold, simple, visionary men. So I think you may regard my account of our clash as objective.

Ship chandlery, livestock, women, tools, farm implements, seeds and cuttings, etc., etc. finally began to flow into Sevilla for transhipment to Sanlúcar in ferryboats owned by a cousin of Fonseca's, and it actually looked as if we might just weigh anchor by the end of May. So I went with Big D and Harana II downriver on one of the cousin's ferries, leaving a message with the Franciscans in Sevilla for Fray Juan Pérez. We arrived at the mouth of the Guadalquivir on the twenty-ninth of the month.

I was on the docks the next afternoon confirming what Harana II already suspected, that out of the Sevilla pork barrel and into our ships' holds had spilled not iron cannon balls, which we'd paid for, but cheaper ones of stone, when I saw Fray Juan Pérez urging an exhausted donkey in my direction.

'Is she here?' he asked as he slipped to the ground.

My heart lurched. 'No.'

'I prayed all the way that she would be here. You've had no word?'

I shook my head and sent a grommet aboard the flagship for some strong red wine. After the prior drank:

'Has Luís de Santangel been in touch with you then?'

'Prior,' I said, indicating some barrels on the dock, 'you better sit down.' I refilled his wine cup. 'Now tell me what happened.'

'But I don't know what happened.'

Petenera, I kept thinking, Petenera's not coming. Worse: she's gone. Greenlanded again.

And we were sailing before dawn.

Gradually color returned to the prior's face. He said, 'About a week ago Santangel came to La Rábida in that Hungarian coach of his. You wouldn't have recognized him. He was all skin and bones.'

'The last time I saw him, over a year ago, he'd just learned his son had been taken by the Suprema,' I said, trying to picture a skin-and-bones Luís de Santangel. No, make that skin, bones and a big cigar.

Fray Juan Pérez sighed. 'The functionaries of the Holy Office worship the same God as I do,' he said in a barely audible voice, 'and I know He is a God of universal love. But surely His universality cannot include love of deceit, love of treachery and bigotry, love of torture? How can such atrocities be committed in the name of the God I worship?'

'Prior,' I said firmly, for I wanted him to get on with his story, 'there are no easy answers to the Big Questions. That is why they are Big Questions.'

He said nothing, merely seemed to ruminate.

'Did she leave with Santangel?' I prodded.

'No, no. He left alone in that Hungarian coach of his. Then, I think it was three days later, when I visited the little cottage at midday, as I did most days, she was gone.'

'No note, no message of any kind?'

'I'm sorry,' said the good prior of La Rábida. Then he looked up defiantly. 'But I'm not sorry I eavesdropped. Even if I seem to have misunderstood.'

'Tell me.'

'Well, I'm no botanist, after all. But isn't there a wildflower called a pimpernel that grows in ditches and things? And isn't it sometimes blue?'

I said yes, twice.

'Well, I'm certain I heard Santangel say, "Unless we reach Santiago soon," – did he mean the pilgrim city of Santiago de Compostela, do you suppose? – "everything the blue pimpernel has worked for will be endangered. Everything." There was also something about an island. There *is* an island near England somewhere called Greenland? But why would all the young hotheads in Spain be sent there? But perhaps I misunderstood that too.'

I found the royal comptroller logging supplies aboard plucky little *Niña*, and borrowed writing materials.

While I wrote, the gulls soaring overhead in the brilliant May sun seemed to scream her name – Petenera, Petenera, Petenera.

But what choice did I have? Hundreds of men ready to sail – women too – depended on me.

I gave the letter to Fray Juan Pérez. 'See that this is delivered to Centurione's bank, Peripatetic branch. Eyes only, Director Pighi-Zampini. Her life could depend on it.'

Here the legend I had become, and which now reclaimed me after my months stolen from it, went temporarily askew. For as the anchor was winched aboard the flagship the next morning before dawn, I grasped no shroud nor did I stare with that look of eagles in my eyes seaward in the manner by then expected of me. No, like some lovesick youth I faced landward as docks, Sanlúcar and all Spain seemed to slide away, and peered into the dusky pre-dawn hoping absurdly to catch a glimpse of my love rushing to join the ship, calling my name in that voice like silver, gold and precious stones.

Only when land was a smudge on the horizon of the new day did I go below the sterncastle to my quarters. And there on my hammock in a ray of sunlight I found, droplets of dew still clinging to the five perfect tiny petals of each, two blue pimpernels lying on a sealed letter. I tore it open with less than steady fingers to read these cool words:

Sorry, but I just don't see myself as a frontierswoman. Seek your destiny as you must across the Ocean Sea. Mine awaits me here.

Your

Pet

A second time I read the brief message, so dismissive of all we had meant to each other, and I thought: how foolish to dream that I could have the far Indies and Petenera too. Then I crumpled the letter around the two pimpernels and threw it out the porthole.

I felt empty of everything, even sadness.

Needless to say, I had no tears.

⚜ XVII ⚜

How Yego Recovers from Smallpox
But Has No Time
to Enjoy His Good Fortune

B OTH the official-religious and the familiar name of my *Maria-galante*-sized flagship are lost to history. Further, my biographers are no more forthcoming about this third and southernmost of my Ocean Sea crossings than about the second – for all of them draw their material from what I have written, and within hours of our departure I came down with a relapse of the Whole Sick Syndrome and hardly wrote a word until I was on my feet (shakily) and able to see (blurrily) in the Gulf of Paria off the coast of what Alonzo Ojeda would later name Venezuela – roughly, funny little Venice – for the houses built on stilts over its many picturesque waterways.

Don't expect me to supply the name of the flagship now. No, if my aim is to be judged on equal terms with my biographers, this would be taking unfair advantage. As for the voyage, there were no emergencies to call me from my cabin; I had virtually no contact with the crew of that nameless flagship, and neither will the reader.

I do remember poking my head out once or twice while we lay at anchor in Las Palmas harbor or off Gomera, taking on good Canary Island produce to make up the many deficiencies of Juan Fonseca's pork-barreling cousins. I also remember calling a captains' meeting before we weighed anchor at Gomera, to order *Niña* (Pedro Terreros commanding), *India* (Harana II commanding) and a third caravel to make straight for Hispaniola with the bulk of our supplies and most of our male colonists, including all convicts, while I led the remaining three vessels on the new route south. Presiding at that meeting wasn't easy. What if my stigmata made a sudden reappearance? What if I had a neuropsychiatric attack of some kind? Both were possible, as you'll remember, though the Admiral In His Own Right and the Hon. Fellow would continue to dismiss my malady as arthritis (or gout) and attribute my 'tired' eyes to lack of sleep. Talk about shoddy research. My eyes *bled*.

I remember nothing from the morning we dropped the Canary Islands astern until we reached the coordinates on time's map where 13 July is located. This put us, on geography's map (one of Barto's charts after Pozzo Toscanelli, actually), at latitude 9°30′N, longitude 29°W – smack in the doldrums. If there is a hotter place anywhere on the Ocean Sea, I don't know where. I emerged sweat-drenched from the oven below decks like some white-haired, red-eyed phantasm to pace the quarterdeck, glare at the windless sky and, despite that baleful sun, shake with chills. In the holds, the heat made barrels burst, snapping their hoops like twigs; wheat smouldered, scorched, and once, or so I'm told, even ignited; salted beef and bacon sizzled in their own fat and putrefied.

And there we stayed, three of S. T. Coleridge's painted ships on his one painted (flat, oily) ocean, until an unseasonable east-southeast wind brought that oily sea alive with whitecaps, bellied our long-slack sails, and sent me to my quarters, where I was seen dropping to my knees and ... Seen? By whom? But this is how the Admiral In His Own Right, who always pictures me as a conventionally religious man, would have it. The Hon. Fellow gets us to our destination with rather less piety.

It is the last day of July, a hot but not incendiary noon, when from the roundtop comes the cry 'land!' – and barely in time too. On the flagship we are down to our final water cask and precious little biscuit, all of it maggoty. So this nameless, faceless crew of my nameless flagship drops to its collective knees and sings the *Salve Regina*. Can I do any less? I at once name the island Trinidad for the Holy Trinity – or is it only for the three hills first espied from the roundtop? For it's no secret I'm undecided on the subject of religion, a Jewish Christian or a Christian Jew, on the verge of concluding, thanks to Brother Buil and the Suprema, that religion is a kind of spiritual syphilis, when along comes a Fray Juan Pérez, simple and good and full of doubts himself, and once again I don't know where I stand. Give me time to sort all this out. I'll get back to it.

Meanwhile, as these faceless grommets fish, gather oysters by the bushel, and fill our water casks, I'm back on my feet, more or less, and can see, mostly less, and am looking after the welfare of our thirty-three women colonists (choicest quarters in the crowded forecastle, sailcloth-enclosed deck space near the horses, separate garden – strict segregation and ninety per cent effective).

Their well-being assured, we go discovering.

'What's he got there?' I ask my nameless pilot as we beach the flagship's boat on an uncharted shore west of Trinidad.

It's an Indian I see, a kind of bronzy blur, carrying a basket along a beach. Behind him are great heaps of putrescent oyster shells which have been left God knows how long to rot in the tropical sun. The fact that the peaceful natives here are not Aristotle's predicted blacks but just Indians is surprising. Either we haven't sailed far enough south or the great Aristotle was wrong. But no matter, for my nameless pilot replies:

'Pearls, Admiral. A basket full of pearls. And he's wearing ropes of 'em round his neck like so many glass beads.'

And he's willing to give them away like so many glass beads too. But hear the Admiral In His Own Right: 'Columbus as yet knew naught of the pearl fisheries.' And the Hon. Fellow: 'It is not to be wondered at that, when Colón found pearls so rich and abundant in Paria, he should have been tempted to keep the discovery to himself.'

Not for the first time, they're both wrong.

It's true that the famous letter I wrote to Their Majesties from this Earthly Paradise (as I called these marshy lowlands, with some hype) made no specific mention of pearls, but I did write that treasures were to be found there aplenty. Perhaps I should have been more specific, and perhaps the mariners' chart I included with the letter should have been of more professional quality, but my vision was still far from normal. Besides, by the time I sent the letter from Hispaniola, convinced that I had found there on the southern shore of the Caribbean not just one more island but an Other World, I had little interest in piddling details. Then too, my would-be assassin –

But wait. As usual, the Whole Sick Syndrome has left me with a tendency to get ahead of myself.

On that southern shore I manage to convey by sign language to the Indians that I'll be back for pearls, willing as I am to trade hawk bells and such for them. But instead of me, late in '99 they get Alonzo Ojeda and his crass, eponymous, opportunistic passenger who receive a few bushels of pearls meant for me, and late in '00 they get Peralonso Niño, and Peralonso gets rich, and it couldn't happen to a nicer fellow.

But I'm getting ahead again. I meant to explain this Other World concept. Through the Gulf of Paria flows a mighty current, emptying into the sea at the Dragon's Mouth between the Paria peninsula and the island of Trinidad, and into this current we dip buckets and bring up *water so sweet it is drinkable*. Not the Guadalquivir, not the Tagus or Tiber or Thames, not even the great Nile or Euphrates, carries quantities of fresh water miles out to sea. Can such a current flow from the streams of a mere island? It cannot. There in the current surging past our hulls is the outflow of the great Orinoco river system, and there, finally, stretching south to the horizon and for all I know a thousand miles beyond, are the alluvial plains and great hardwood forests of the unknown continent that will be so egregiously misnamed. So I write the royals in high excitement and in almost a prophetic vein, predicting that they and their heirs will rule this land mass, this vast arcanum, this Other World that I have discovered, forever.

A word here about the so-called New World. I know that locution is preferred to my 'an Other World' – but why should it be? This world I discovered wasn't new; it was exactly, to the microsecond, as old as the one I came from, both having existed since God or whatever created them. I mean, we're dealing with two hemispheres of a single spherical planet, after all. My detractors, led by the champions of the Florentine Vespucci, claim I never realized I'd found the New World. This is a malicious semantic quibble, and my letter to Their Majesties is refutation enough.

But I'm getting ahead again. The pearls; I don't hang around for them because I have a premonition. Why the Whole Sick Syndrome leaves me open to mystical experiences I'm not prepared to say. And not just premonitions either. Dreams too, the kind fraught with significance.

Like my first St Christopher dream. In it I'm big, I mean really big, some kind of a giant almost, and I'm standing on the bank of this stream (a tributary of the Orinoco?) when along comes this little kid begging me to carry him across. Which I agree to do. But even though I'm a giant and it's not a very wide stream and the kid is small, by the time we're in midstream, me chin-deep on tiptoe with the kid perched on my shoulders, my knees are about ready to give out and I complain, 'Jesus, kid, you weigh a ton.' At which he pipes, 'Does that surprise you, giant? You're carrying the whole world, and all the world's sins, right here on your shoulders.' If you know the hagiography, this is where I'm supposed to sink under my burden (and underwater), then rise vowing to serve only this heavyweight kid for the rest of my life – all three days of it – before death and speedy sanctification. But the dream doesn't end as it should, with me very saintly and Him very Christlike. Because instead of sinking underwater as we near the far bank, I fling the kid from my shoulders and, while he's floundering and trying to swim the last few yards, I taunt him, 'Get a move on, stow that stuff about the weight of the world,' and then in the blink of an eye the kid looks like a grown man and he is awkwardly carrying something heavy that I can't quite see as he staggers out of the water. And just to be mean, I holler again, 'Go on, get a move on,' and he turns to look back at me and says, 'I'll get a move on, wise guy, but you'll stay right here until I come back.' Which he doesn't. Come back, I mean. He just clambers up the bank carrying whatever he's carrying and disappears into a sudden fog, and I'm stuck there in the stream unable to move a muscle.

I wish we had a Freud or somebody in those days to explain that one.

All right, I know. The pearls. I don't wait around for them because I have this premonition – and it's strong – that there's trouble in Hispaniola. So on 15 August, with me firmly gripping a shroud and peering straight ahead, we pass through the Dragon's Mouth and race north.

On the last day of August 1498 we sail into the harbor of the first permanent city established in the New or an Other World, our little fleet casting anchor in the Ozama River two years and five months after I sailed from Isabela for Spain. This is my first look at the new colonial capital of Santo Domingo – the inevitable fort surrounded by a cluster of wooden buildings, one of them two stories high with what looks like my coat-of-arms flying from a flagstaff.

The expected crowds line the dock, too far away at first for them to differentiate male from female heads over our bulwarks, which is why there isn't a waterborne stampede for the flagship. For there at our waist staring eagerly shoreward for a first look at their new home are our thirty-three women colonists (only three of them pregnant). Waves are waved, shouts are shouted, a lombard booms from the fort. A single sailboat tacks across the water toward us. As it approaches, I recognize no-nonsense Dr Chanca first, and then hulking, deceptively ferocious-looking Juan Niño of Moguer. There are two other men in the boat. One, I realize with a start, is my brother Barto. I have forgotten how handsome he became after his affair with Anne de Beaujeu. But his smile, once endearingly crooked-toothed, is now hard. The fourth man I don't know. This is a young sun-bronzed fellow in a modish canary-yellow doublet (but no jerkin, for the day is hot). They wave, he most enthusiastically of all. Big D and I, on the poop, wave back. The unknown young fellow hails us: 'Welcome back, Viceroy! Welcome, welcome!' Then suddenly he dives into the water and swims hard for the flagship. I can see him grin every time his head breaks the surface. I can also see his canary-yellow wake, for his homespun doublet isn't colorfast. The boat is now closing on us, but the swimmer arrives first, scrambles up the ladder, races aft, and mounts the quarterdeck and the poop in a few prodigious bounds. While I'm still wondering who he can be, he wraps his wet arms around me in a strong embrace, making snorting sounds thanks to all the water he's swallowed on his mad swim to the flagship. And of course my Admiral's uniform, especially saved for this occasion, is soon sopping and stained a canary yellow. At this point there comes a great cry from shore as our women colonists are identified as such, and soon fully 300 men are swimming out to meet us, churning the harbor to foam. By this time my effusive greeter has stepped back and is smiling up at me. He is a well-built lad of twenty or so, a few inches shorter than I, and he shakes his head, a grin on his handsome sun-bronzed face as he says, 'You don't recognize me, you really don't.' His voice is deep, his Spanish fluent and melodious. Meanwhile Barto's boat is nudging our hull, the best swimmers are outdistancing the pack, the women are waving and laughing, the horses nearby – certain now that they smell land – are neighing and stamping with excitement, our three sows grunt indifferently, Big D has gone forward to greet Barto as he comes aboard, and this drenched young fellow who has ruined my dress uniform continues to stare at me with a challenging display of dazzling white teeth. He shouts over the animal and human racket, but all I can catch is ' . . . Yego.'

'What about him?' I demand, uneasy. I haven't let myself think about Yego, not since his icy correctness at our parting in Isabela.

Before the young stranger can answer, Barto comes running up to embrace me, wet canary-yellow-stained uniform and all, then stands back, grips my upper arms and says, his unique vocabulary intact, 'Oh wow, am I glad to see you.' Then Juan Niño is on the quarterdeck, pounding my back and grinning his ferocious grin. While doing this he still manages to steal glances behind him to the waist of the ship, where thirty-three women are appraising him, this deceptively ferocious-looking Juan Niño of Moguer, with mixed emotions. Next comes no-nonsense Dr Chanca, that consummate professional. 'Hello, Viceroy, I'll want the women isolated until I examine every man in the colony, because we still have a thirty-per-cent syphilis rate.'

Then they're all speaking at once.

Barto says, 'How come you sent the advance fleet under Pedro Terreros straight into Roldán's hands?'

Dr Chanca says, 'Keep those swimmers away from your female passengers.'

Juan Niño says, 'Who's the pretty little lady in the white cap with that fluffy stuff on top instead of feathers?'

I answer, respectively:

'What do you mean, straight into Roldán's hands?

'Yes, doctor, I'll keep them isolated.

'Her name is Inocencia Premiada, and she's a widow.' I happen to know this because Inocencia Premiada has become the women's official spokesperson.

They begin again.

Barto: 'I mean, they landed west of here where Roldán and his rebels are holing up and Roldán sweet-talked seventy of your new colonists – convicts, according to this Harana fellow – into joining him, not to mention making off with most of the supplies you sent. Jeepers, Cristóbal, it's bad news.'

Dr Chanca: 'Keep all your people away from the Indians a few days too. Back in '96 Peralonso Niño arrived with a couple of cases of smallpox aboard and our Arawak friends had no resistance at all. Mortality rate's almost a hundred per cent. The island population's been decimated since you left, and the epidemic's not over.'

Juan Niño: 'A widow? Why, that pretty little thing couldn't hardly be more than seventeen or – '

At which point the young stranger interrupts with an exasperated: 'Will all of you please shut up a minute and give him a chance to talk to his own son?'

'Yego!' I cry. 'Good God, you're Yego!'

He just smiles.

'But you look like a Spaniard.'

He keeps on smiling.

'And you talk like a Spaniard.'

Really grinning now, he brushes awkwardly at the dilute canary-yellow stains on my dress uniform and says, 'Two and a half years is a long time, Admiral Father.'

The sovereign remedy for the fatigue of a long journey is a good night's sleep. Which I don't get. Instead, I get the picture of what's going on in the colony, and that's enough to give anyone a sleepless night.

'Here's the picture,' Barto says as Yego tosses a line to a dockhand and we step ashore, but at that moment four big men, whose faces make Juan Niño's look cherubic, shoulder Barto and Big D and me into a tight little group, rather like sheepdogs herding sheep, so I don't get the picture then.

I gesture wordlessly at our escort, which Barto seems to take for granted.

'Bodyguards,' he tells me.

'You need bodyguards?'

'So do you, bro. Believe me.'

So escorted, or herded, with Dr Chanca and Juan Niño and Yego following behind, we move in a body up the unpaved street toward Santo Domingo's not very imposing plaza.

The crowd lining our way isn't exactly ugly, but it isn't pretty either.

'Bunch of damn pharaohs!' someone shouts.

To my amazement, Barto takes this in his stride.

Pharaoh is an epithet of contempt, worse than Marrano, once used by low-class Spaniards to describe affluent Jews – and now New Christians. But how do they know? Even Barto doesn't, not unless he got it from Santangel.

He smiles that new hard smile of his. 'That's their latest name for me, pharaoh. But I don't let it bother me. In Rome they call Borgia the Marrano Pope, and you know he's not. It's just envy. You'll get used to it.'

Big D, while walking, thumbs through the *Handbook of Regulations and Right Conduct for Colonial Administrators*, like a priest through his breviary, but apparently can find no entry for 'pharaoh'.

We reach the plaza. Shy Brother Ramón Pane is standing at the door of his prefab church, which must have been taken apart and shipped around the island from Isabela. As we cross the plaza he disappears inside.

'What's the matter with him?' I ask. I've usually got along well with Brother Pane.

Instead of answering, Barto gestures at the façade of the now undeniable Viceregal Palace. This is the relatively large two-story building from whose flagstaff my coat-of-arms is flying. The shutters are shut, the doors are multilocked, and musket-bearing sentries patrol back and forth.

'Your new home, Viceroy,' Barto says with a smile. 'How do you like it?'

But I won't be sidetracked. 'What's with Brother Pane?'

'He disapproves of the gallows.'

Then I see that horrible structure. At this hour of the afternoon its elongated shadow falls across Brother Pane's prefab church. You can even see the huge black shadow of the noose above the portal, swinging gently in a light breeze.

Big D drops his *Handbook*. He picks it up, looking embarrassed.

'You better believe it keeps them in line,' Barto says, only a shade defensively.

'Who?'

'Would-be defectors. I'm thinking of building a wall around the entire town.'

'But you can't hold your own people prisoner.'

'Sometimes I think it's the only way. Roldán's populism really turns the masses on.'

Big D is thumbing furiously through the *Handbook*.

I ask Barto, 'Did you ever, uh, use that gallows there?'

'No. I told you, a threat like that hanging over their heads keeps them in line. Sometimes,' Barto adds.

When I give him a wordless look of disapproval, he gets defensive again. 'Well, wasn't it Cardinal Borgia who said if you can't be both feared and loved, let the love go?'

Big D says, excited, 'Here it is, right here in the *Handbook*. Populism is a crime against the colonial administration, it says. See rebellion.'

Barto glances at him, older-brother-condescending. 'Sure, kid. You go and tell that to Francisco Roldán.'

We wait while the many locks are removed from the front door of my Viceregal Palace.

'Now here's the picture. A lot's been going on while you were taking things easy in Spain,' Barto tries again, but just then along the street come Pedro Terreros and Harana II.

'We let you down, Admiral,' says Pedro forthrightly.

'Viceroy,' Barto snaps at him. 'Ashore the title is Viceroy.'

Harana II is raging at himself. 'How stupid can I get? Letting this Roldán walk off with our supplies and the convicts. God!'

'Letting him?' says Pedro. 'He took them at musket-point.'

'Not the convicts. They went willingly when he promised them land, and Indians to work it.'

'Good riddance,' says Pedro, 'to the convicts.'

But, 'Seventy able-bodied convicts will double the size of Roldán's renegade army,' Barto warns us as we all go inside.

Indian servants scurry around opening shutters, but my Viceregal Palace still has a gloomy look, a musty smell. Large splotches of bluish-green mold cover every wall.

Does reality ever live up to the dream?

The conference room is large and airy – with a view, unfortunately, of that gallows. But the mold is minimal, and the long mahogany table impressive with a wine cup and cigar alongside each rush mat. The chairs look comfortable. There's also lots of scratch paper.

'Hey now, this is okay,' says Big D.

'Now let me give you the picture,' Barto begins. But as soon as we all sit down, everybody starts talking at once again and not one word is comprehensible until Barto pushes back from the table and roars: 'Out! Everybody out!'

He yanks the door open. 'Beat it, you clods.'

This behavior seems to surprise no one but me. Well, maybe Big D. The rest of them sigh, get up and file out the door. That leaves three Colón brothers in the conference room.

'You too,' Barto tells Big D.

'Me?'

'Yeah, beat it. I want to talk to Cristóbal.'

Big D, large, soft, pale, his long nose buried in his *Handbook*, slouches out.

'Now here's the picture of what's been going on while you were sitting on your duff back in Spain,' says Barto, but I tell him: 'Barto, I already got more of the picture than you think and if you don't mind I'd like to see the rest of it for myself.'

Which I do in the weeks that follow. It is less than encouraging. The only almost contented colonist I encounter is Juan Niño of Moguer, and even he is lonely for his brothers back in Spain, where Peralonso is seeking another royal charter. 'But I like it here,' Juan Niño says. 'My people were farmers in Moguer, you know. Brought sugarcane to Spain from the Canaries and – ' a proud smile ' – I brought it here. Put it in with my own hands. Look at that brake over there. This is real

430

sugarcane country, Viceroy. No, my sailing days are over.' And then – if his usual audience of one, Inocencia Premiada, is near – Juan Niño's ferocious face creases into an almost sunny smile.

But this old sailor of Moguer is hardly our typical colonist. When most of them aren't busy complaining, they grumble, grouse, crab, beef, bellyache, whine or just plain disapprove. Heard often is this meteorological grievance: 'Ain't even any seasons here, just your eternal spring all year long.' Or this vinous one: 'How do they expect a man to get through life on a wine ration of one little quart per diem every day?' The libidos aroused by willing and lubricious indigenous ladies are dampened by the ever-present danger of syphilis. This leads to what Big D assures me the *Handbook* calls an approach-avoidance conflict. On the matter of work, there's no conflict. It's all avoidance and no approach. Our colonists are adventurers who came here believing they could get rich without working – should I be surprised that they complain?

Occasional defectors slip out of Santo Domingo, despite the perimeter guards and the dogs, to join Roldán. The blunt-spoken soldier who saved my life when I was wandering off time's map through the jungle is now a demagogue. He holds his listeners with those palest blue, opaque, conquistador eyes while his deep, sincere voice weaves a spell, promising all things to all people:

Spaniards, listen! Will you let the pharaohs of Santo Domingo work you like peons the rest of your lives? Join me, and there's land for you, and Indians to work the land ...

Indians, listen! Are you sick to death of the tribute? Obey your headman and we'll get along fine – without any tribute ...

Headmen, listen! Keep your workers in line and for every head that does a proper month's work I'll pay you some beeootiful red glass beads, blue if you want, and if we get a trouble-free quarter out of your people you earn yourself a genuine knife of good Toledo steel ...

'How'd it happen, anyway?' I ask Barto one day. 'This rebellion of his?'

'Listen, bro, you were back in Spain more than two years, and even though I'm your brother don't you think the thought crossed my mind that just possibly you weren't ever coming back? Well, it crossed Francisco Roldán's mind too, and he's not your brother. Remember, that royal charter of yours authorizes you to appoint a chief magistrate, but show me where it says anything about an executive officer. So Roldán claimed that as chief magistrate he was Number One on the island, not me, and he was damned if

431

he'd take my orders. Besides, I'm a foreigner.'

This change of tack gets a 'so am I' from me.

Barto gives me an odd sort of questioning glance. 'Cristóbal, is there something about our background that you know and I don't? I mean, all this pharaoh business.'

'You said it yourself, it's just envy. It goes with holding power,' I dissimulate. We have enough trouble without my brother undergoing an identity crisis like mine.

'Well, Roldán got the envy, and he's working on the power.' Barto's eyes get hard. 'I'll tell you straight, bro. With those convicts in his renegade army, he can put more men into the field than we can. So if you're going to move first, you'd better move fast.'

'What do you mean, move?'

'March on Xaragua, capture Roldán, and hang him right here in the plaza.'

'I can't do that.'

'Why not?'

'Because even if I didn't want to avoid civil war, which I do, I owe Francisco Roldán. He saved my life.'

Barto turns away. 'Sentimental weakling,' he mutters.

'What did you say?'

But he backs off. 'I didn't mean that. I don't know what makes me say things like that.' Barto stares out the conference room window at the gallows. Then he says: 'Listen, you know what kind of world this is? Dog eat dog, that's what kind. You need to show your teeth or they'll chew on you. Come with me, come on. Right now. I want you to meet someone.'

Barto strides off in the direction of the stables. I expect a couple of Mosén Pedro's nags, but the grooms lead out a pair of mettlesome warhorses brought over by Peralonso Niño in '96. I can't help remembering how Barto, the kind and gentle Barto I used to know, was so inept around animals, especially horses. But not anymore. While the grooms help me board my impatient dapple-gray, my brother just saunters over to his roan stallion, gives it an affectionate whack on the muzzle, leaps astride, digs in his spurs and gallops off. I'm aware of mounted bodyguards hard on my heels, and then not much else, except that we ford the Jaina River in mid-afternoon. For someone more at ease on a mule than a horse, this is one hell of a headlong ride up into the central highlands.

At sunset Barto shouts a password at an Indian sentry who pops out of nowhere and soon we trot into the Indian village of Bonao.

The place could almost be the siege city of Santa Fé. Hundreds of warriors are camped outside, and the air is hazy with cookfires. There are half a dozen horses in a well-guarded corral. These are like no Indians I ever saw; they're not even afraid of horses.

But they're afraid of Barto.

He vaults off his roan and snaps his fingers with studied arrogance to bring a couple of Indians scurrying. While I am doing my bone-weary, saddle-sore best to dismount with dignity, Barto's already striding past cookfires, two bodyguards in his wake, into the village proper.

'Where the hell is she?' he shouts, kicking a lounging Indian or two out of his way. Soon we're in the presence of the most powerful chieftain of them all, now that Guacanagarí's in the mysticism business and Caonabó is dead. This is the latter's still-young widow, the cacica Anacaoná. Built along lines that later will be called Wagnerian, she swaggers toward us smoking a cigar, hugely naked in the twilight except for her *nagua*, a minimalist breechclout of regal gold cloth. She towers over Barto as most men and a lot of women do.

'Why you no come up see me sometimes no more?' she demands in passable Spanish.

And whammo! Barto lets her have it, a solid clout that knocks the cigar from her nose.

'I'll see you when I have time to see you.'

'Yes, Lord.' She bows her head, but then looks up at Barto sidelong and says:

'Fuck now, Lord?'

And whammo! he lets her have it again. But then he sighs and tells me, 'Make yourself comfortable for half an hour, bro. I've got to go attend to Indian relations.'

Later, over a dinner of some kind of roast rodent that tastes like rabbit, he says, 'Get the picture? They're on *our* side now.'

Which seems indisputable. These warriors with their painted faces and poisoned arrows, the most feared on the island, are respectful, even groveling, to us. Or to Barto.

'Of course, the cacica's only got eight or nine hundred men left out of an original three or four thou. Smallpox. But it's hit Guarionex just as hard.'

'Guarionex?' I ask. 'Where does he fit in?'

'Over in Xaragua's where. When Guacanagarí went on his mystic kick, Guarionex took over his brother's people – took them right over to Roldán. And he's the biggest power on the island after Anacaoná.'

433

But with her we'll breeze right through Xaragua when we march on Roldán.'

'We're not marching on Roldán.'

Barto argues, but can't budge me. 'Where's Higueymota?' he asks the Wagnerian cacica.

A sleeker, scaled-down version of her mother joins us. She is maybe fourteen, and gorgeous.

'Want her?' Barto asks me.

Who wouldn't? But I shake my head.

Barto urges, 'You just might feel more warlike after a good f – '

'No,' I say. Firmly. 'She's only a kid.' This isn't exactly true. By Spanish, let alone Indian, convention, at fourteen Higueymota's a grown woman, very much into nubility and sex.

Barto reaches out a finger to trace the contour of Higueymota's firm young breast. 'You sure? She does whatever I tell her.' His finger sculpts the curve of Higueymota's hip. It traces her rump. 'And she's getting pretty good in the hammock.'

Jealousy meanwhile is crackling from the Wagnerian cacica like electricity in a cat's fur.

With his free hand Barto pats Anacaoná's knee reassuringly, but when he turns to me what he says is, 'If the kid's age really bothers you that much, you can have the mother and I'll take Higuey myself.'

Anacaoná glowers.

Whammo!

The cacica worries a fat lip with her big thumb and eyes my brother adoringly.

I give Barto a look myself. Is it surprise? Contempt? Admiration? I'm not sure.

Whatever, I spend the night alone. Barto spends it however he spends it.

We're already mounted for the long ride back when Anacaoná joins us. The cacica's eyes are puffy with lack of sleep, but she looks content. I expect Barto to say goodbye, kiss her maybe. But he just sits there. Imperious, waiting. The cacica approaches. She kisses his stirruped boot.

He demands, 'Hey, what about those three hundred P.O.W.s?'

'Tomorrow. Start south tomorrow, Lord.'

Barto gives her an exasperated frown. 'She learned tomorrow from the Spaniards,' he tells me.

I ask, 'What P.O.W.s?'

'Indians. Anacaoná and Guarionex are at war. I thought you knew.

434

And since she's my ally, her prisoners are my prisoners.' He shouts at Anacaoná: 'Tomorrow for sure.'

'For damn sure, Lord.'

'She'd work those prisoners to death if I let her,' Barto tells me.

'What will you do with them?'

After a pause he says, 'Big D wants to send them to Spain.'

'As slaves? That's out.'

'Slavery's okay for prisoners of war, Cristóbal. Even your precious royals know that.'

'I said slavery's out.'

'What makes you so moral?'

I never thought of myself as particularly moral. So why does Barto's question make me feel so defensive?

He doesn't wait for an answer. As we gallop from the village he rides down three or four Indians who are slow getting out of his way.

Back in the Viceregal Palace late that night, Barto's sitting on the edge of my bed. Sobbing.

'How come?' he cries. 'How come I act that way? Inside me, Cristóbal, there's the brother you used to know, somewhere way down inside trapped in there and he can't get out.'

What can I tell him?

Except for me, my brother Barto would be a prosperous mapmaker in Portugal, a respected publisher of fine books maybe, the acknowledged inventor of the terrestrial globe certainly, an Academician and a consequential figure in Lisbon society instead of a hated pharaoh in Hispaniola. Possibly, I think, and this is the darkest, most awful might-have-been of all, he'd be married to Felipa, a happy Felipa with a houseful of growing children and a gentle husband like the Barto I used to know – a *living* Felipa.

No, how can I blame Barto for what he's become?

So I hold him, and rock him in my arms, and I stroke his grizzled hair until finally he falls asleep. Then I go into the empty conference room and open the shutters to see the new dawn backlighting Barto's gallows.

One of the servants finds me there. 'You better come, Viceroy. Yego very bad sick.'

At the door of the sickroom, no-nonsense Dr Chanca greets me with, 'Did you ever have smallpox, Viceroy?'

'Not that I remember.'

He studies my face. 'No pits and scars, that I can see. I wouldn't go

435

in there if I were you. We've got known survivors of smallpox, plenty of them, and they're immune. They can nurse that son of yours, make dying easier for him.' That's what Chanca always calls Yego, with a slight sarcastic emphasis on the word son, as if the relationship is somehow my idea of a joke.

'Admiral Father?' a faint voice calls, and I brush past Chanca and inside.

Wrestling with a twisted, sweat-stained counterpane, Yego looks up at me with glassy eyes. I touch his feverish head. He stops tossing and turning, and his cracked, dry lips part. This is almost a smile. He raises one hand weakly, and I squeeze it. 'Water,' he says. I lift his head and bring the jug to those parched lips.

Later, when he's fitfully sleeping, Dr Chanca tells me: 'Assuming it isn't the fulminant hemorrhagic variant of smallpox that kills before the appearance of the characteristic eruptions, here's what you can expect. Forty-eight hours of this prodromal period with extreme prostration and high fever. Then on the third day, except for the appearance of the eruptions, the patient will seem much better. Fever drops, he's stronger, he's lucid. The macules spread typically from the forehead and temples to the mouth, then rapidly to the neck, arms, scalp, finally the whole body. On palpation they feel hard and deeply implanted. By the fifth day, fever returns suddenly along with that severe prostration, and the macules become pustules that sometimes converge and hemorrhage. That's when the Indians invariably die.'

'Invariably? You mean there's no hope?'

'I do know of an Indian in Concepción de la Vega who survived smallpox, but it was a mild case, almost subclinical. Assuming the disease runs its course and the patient does survive, you can expect two weeks of slow recovery, cutaneous desquamation and, probably, the loss of hair, eyebrows, nails – where are you going?'

'Inside.'

He calls after me, 'It's your funeral.'

The morning of the third day Yego is alert and cheerful. He has no fever. He wants a big breakfast, and when I come back from ordering it, he's standing unsteadily beside the bed.

'I'm getting better,' he says with a weak smile. 'I feel almost better already.'

'You're still sicker than you think,' I tell him. 'You know what the calm before a storm can be like, at sea?'

He nods earnestly, sways, sits on the edge of his bed.

'So why don't you conserve your strength?'

Trustingly, he lets me ease him back down. Soon he's sleeping.

If you're into clinical details, the deep lesions that Yego now develops all over his body are what Dr Chanca on his next visit coolly calls 'umbilicated and multilocular, and surrounded by pink areolae. And notice,' he says just before I chase him from the room, 'how they are all chronologically in the same stage of development, like fruit maturing on a healthy tree.'

When Yego wakes, he's thirsty and he hurts all over. But he wants to talk. It's as if he knows there isn't much time left and he has to crowd everything in. Sentiment, metaphysics. Absolution, even.

'Remember that day you came ashore on the island of Guanahaní?' he asks. 'And you said, "There's someone in the woods over there," just before I came out.'

'How do you know that's what I said?'

'That's what you looked like you were saying,' smiles dying Yego a bit mysteriously as, for a fleeting instant and despite the lesions all over his poor face, he reminds me a lot of Guacanagarí. Suddenly I wonder –

'I thought you were a god that day,' says Yego with amused filial affection, 'but I soon learned better.'

'Yego,' I ask, pursuing the riddle of his birth, 'were you born on that island of Guanahaní?'

'When I was an infant some women found me in a basket in the rushes on the shore there. Or so I've been told,' he says with a shrug of his pox-covered shoulders.

And on he talks, and day gives way to evening, and memory to metaphysics. Or religion. Is there a difference?

'But if you are not God, and God is not anyone I can see, then *is* He? Have you ever seen God, Admiral Father?'

'No, Yego. I simply hope He's there. Because the world needs God, believe me.'

And I'm thinking inside myself as hard as I can: *Whoever You are, whatever You are, make him get well.*

'Is there an end of time?' Yego asks me. 'I mean, if God turned time on like turning a sandclock, what happens when all the sand runs out?'

I recognize a death thought when I hear one.

Listen, You. He's too young for all the sand to run out yet, I'm thinking as hard as I can. When I realize this is praying, I add a hasty *please*.

437

'Well,' I say, 'if all the sand in the world is in that clock, it's an awful lot of time you're talking about.'

'I guess,' says Yego, and then he drifts off.

The next day, the last lucid one he'll have, according to Dr Chanca, Yego is one horrible mass of confluent sores, but his eyes are bright.

'Remember the day you sailed away from Isabela? I hated you. I kept thinking, why'd he come here, if all he was going to bring was death and destruction? Who needs his civilization? Who needs him? I wanted to kill you, Admiral Father.' That brightness in his eyes is tears. 'For two years I hated you. I swore I was going to kill you when you came back and every time I swore it I cried.'

There's something that feels like a big colón bean in my throat. When did that happen before?

'Finally I went up into the mountains to find Guacanagarí. I thought he could make me understand if anyone could. Two ancient ladies led me to him and his eyes blazed a scary red.'

'I know.'

'Have you seen it too?' When I just nod, Yego continues: 'He doesn't talk anymore, not even our native language. Just signs. Is it because signs are more universal? Without me asking anything, his eyes blazing, he signs, "First contact between alien cultures is always tragic for the more primitive." But I'm angry enough to say, "Well, we didn't ask for that first contact, it was all their idea," and he signs sadly, despite those blazing eyes, "People don't often get what they ask for, my son. No one is to blame for what had to happen. No man and no god. A thing happens because a thing happens. Seek no deep mysteries where none are hiding. Free will is a myth, predestination the same. Blind chance spins the world. No one is to blame." I didn't understand all that. "I don't understand," I say, and he signs, "No one is to blame. This time."

'That was his message, Admiral Father. *No one is to blame.* So I came back over the mountains to Santo Domingo and I didn't have to kill you after all.'

He looks up at me. A chill shakes him.

'I love you, Admiral Father,' he says. 'I am happy I can say that now.'

In a few hours he's burning with fever, he's no longer conscious, and Brother Ramón Pane comes to give him the last rites of the Church. And if I know anything I know that Guacanagarí's message was not, *No one is to blame*, though poor Yego had to believe it was. No, the great mystic's message was, No one is to blame *this time*.

438

Will there be a *next time*?

I smell the incense, I hear Brother Pane intoning, and a deep, soft voice crying. It is Big D standing at my side, tears flowing down his face, and it's as if I'm lying there in bed dying, not Yego. Except that I didn't die, did I, all those years ago in Rome? Suddenly I'm filled with an irrational conviction – and never mind what Dr Chanca says – that Yego won't die either.

Dr Chanca says, 'Not long now.'

Big D pats my shoulder awkwardly.

'Listen, God,' I pray. 'I know I'm not much of a Viceroy, but I'm really not a bad discoverer, am I? No hubris intended. I know all about this business of hubris and gods. But I wander a lot, you know, and when you wander you're bound to discover and maybe even understand a few things.

'Let him get better, God, and I'll keep on wandering and discovering for the rest of my life – *ad majorem gloriam Dei.*'

Darkness comes and goes.

I'm aware of Dr Chanca at my side again.

'That's it. You don't need me here anymore,' he says.

'You mean he's dead?' I cry in disbelief, so sure was I that he'd live.

'No. I mean the crisis is over. It looks like that son of yours is going to live.'

What with Yego recovering and one thing and another, I am in pretty high spirits this sixth Columbus Day. And I am not the only one.

'Peralonso will never believe it,' Juan Niño of Moguer keeps telling me.

'That you're getting married? He did.'

'That such a pretty little thing like Inocencia would have me.'

At noon, our day-long celebrations already well underway, I escort her to the altar of the prefab church where Brother Pane performs the first wedding of Europeans in the New or an Other World. Then the wedding party, Inocencia looking like a not-quite-life-size doll next to hulking Juan Niño, makes its way across the crowded plaza to inaugurate the marriage register in the Viceregal Palace.

Miners have come in from the outlying camps for the historic occasion, and many of Anacaoná's Indians have wandered down from the highlands to see the Spanish fiesta. Wine flows unrationed, a feast is in the offing, the din in the plaza is terrific, and it is a relief to see a smile on every face.

Every face but Yego's.

439

I find him in the dimness of his former sickroom. He has pulled the shutters closed.

'We missed you at the wedding.'

'Leave me alone.'

'At least come out and drink to the bride.'

'Come out?' He unbars the shutters and throws them open. 'Look at my face.'

The deep pock-marks are still red and raw. His hair has started coming out in tufts, giving his head a mangy look.

'It's a face to scare children with!' he cries.

'It's not that bad and it will get better.'

'I look like some kind of monster.'

'Yego, in Europe lots of people who had smallpox lead normal lives.'

'I'll never leave this room as long as I live.' He turns his back. 'Why didn't you let me die?'

The Columbus Day ceremonies won't be the same without Yego. The first Indian ever to communicate with white men and the first to be baptized, he is supposed to make a short speech, after mine, from the balcony of the Viceregal Palace.

My speech isn't all it might be. I keep thinking of Yego, in his dark room, in the knowledge of his disfiguration, in the gloom of his soul, as I look down from the second-story balcony at the jammed plaza and across to Barto's gallows and the prefab church.

Sharing the little balcony with me are Juan Niño, my shipmate on that historic October day six years ago, and his bride. Not that they're paying any attention to my attempt at rhetoric, which concludes like this:

'All of you here today must know that without your faith and your fearlessness ... without your dreams of a new Spain across the Ocean Sea ... without your sacrifices and your toil ... nothing that we have accomplished thus far or, God willing, will yet accomplish ... would have been possible.'

As I'm shouting these words across the plaza, I hear the balcony doors open behind me, and a fourth figure comes out to the balustrade. It is Yego, wearing a broad-brimmed hat to shade his pitted face.

I resume happily: 'Standing here beside me is a young man ... who should be honored above all others today ... for it was he who ... alone but for his handful of equally young followers ... stepped boldly out that day six years ago ... to greet the first Spaniards, the first Europeans, ever seen by any of his people ... So it is with special pride ...'

Below in the mobbed plaza there is a glint, a flash like sunlight reflected off a mirror. Then I hear a cry and see movement at my side, so swift that by the time I realize it is Yego, thrusting himself between me and the balustrade, he staggers back against me, then shudders and teeters forward, and I have to grab his suddenly unresisting weight to stop him from tumbling off the balcony. Then up from the plaza rises that Valencia sound as people mill about, confused by what they haven't quite seen. Some surge forward toward the Palace, others back toward the prefab church. A few are trampled. Still others are forced from the plaza into the narrow, converging streets, under the gaily fluttering flags and pennants strung overhead. Individual shouts and cries rise to the balcony. 'It's the Viceroy! They got the Viceroy!' Then Inocencia starts to scream and I see Juan Niño's look of horror as Yego's broad-brimmed hat falls off to reveal his tufted, mangy hair, his pitted face and his wide-staring sightless eyes.

❧ XVIII ❧

Happy New Century

I SIT for hours at the window of the empty conference room of the Viceregal Palace, watching the shadow of the gallows move with each wasted, meaningless day across the façade of the prefab church. Sometimes the room fills with voices: Barto's, commanding, despite his unique vocabulary; Big D's, soft and deep, sonorous with jargon from the *Handbook*; Brother Pane's, shy with an artless humility; Dr Chanca's, no-nonsense as ever, reporting to the Governing Council of poor diet, rotten teeth, disease; Harana II's, suspicious – but hear him speak in one of those rare reports meant for my ears only. This is a while – some days or weeks, two or three months – after I send my nameless flagship and the caravel *Correo* back to Spain, their holds full of tobacco, bales of cotton and valuable hardwoods, my Other World letter to the royals with the chart showing the course of my westbound voyage (drawn when such things still mattered to me) in the safe-keeping of *Correo*'s captain. That the letter and chart will pass through crass, opportunistic hands before reaching the Peripatetic Royal Court I have no way of knowing. Not that I would care now if I did.

But I started to tell you about Harana II's report on the events of that Columbus Day.

'You know what's the best place to commit a murder, Admiral?' he begins. Like Pedro Terreros, he always calls me Admiral unless Barto's there to remind him of my *terra firma* titles. This is one of the things I like about him. Though I haven't said it in so many words, if the royals read between the lines of my letter that I'm thinking of going out of the Viceroy business, it's all right with me. In fact, shortly after they receive it (as Little D will later tell me) they are heard to say: 'He is a good enough Admiral but does he have the right stuff to be Viceroy?'

'No,' I ask Harana II, 'what's the best place to commit a murder?'

'In the middle of a crowd,' he says, 'at a public event in broad daylight.'

This surprises me. 'Why?'

'Because, first, the event's got everybody's attention and the perpetrator or perpetrators will have that vital second to act unnoticed. How long does it take to throw a knife? Second, the confusion of the crowd affords the perpetrator or perpetrators ideal cover for their escape. Third, a hundred witnesses invariably come forward, each with his own definitive description of the perpetrator or perpetrators – '

'Will you stop calling them that? They killed him. They're killers.'

'Sorry. The killers then. A hundred descriptions, all different. Some witnesses even name names, but these are always of people they owe money or someone they suspect has been moving in on the Indian girl they're sleeping with. You can't trust an eye-witness in a crowd to recognize his own brother. Oh, you can follow every lead, and believe me I have, but it gets you nowhere. I'm sorry, Admiral. It looks like we'll never find them.'

There is something monstrous about his objective finality. Not that I blame Harana II. It's the knowledge that's monstrous, the knowledge that my son is dead and whoever killed him will live.

Sometimes I think that the rhythm of the seasons, where there are seasons, helps put an end to grief. For each year the cycle of birth, life and death is repeated, spring through winter and back again, and each individual life and its death are seen as part of all living and all dying. Even Christ dies eternally for the sins of mankind – last and greatest in a long line of gods whose death and resurrection each spring cause the winter-bare earth to turn green and fruitful again. And before these earlier reborn gods, before Osiris and Adonis, before the Dionysus of the Greek Mysteries, and even the demigoddess Persephone who spent four months each year in Hades to bring the cycle of life around – before them there were scapegoats and sacrificial lambs and, yes, back far enough, human sacrifice. In whatever form, the message is the same: in life there is death, and in death life.

But we have no seasons in the Indies, and my grief persists.

I mope around the Viceregal Palace under Barto's censorious gaze, and finally he says, 'Jeepers, Cristóbal, you've got to pull yourself together and start making with the old charisma again, or one of these days Roldán will march right into Santo Domingo and nobody will lift a finger to stop him.'

How can I make Barto understand that I just don't care?

'Viceroy's all washed up,' they say in Santo Domingo.

'A regular burnt-out case.'

'Well hell, he's forty-nine years old. A man his age don't spring back so good.'

'They say he has some Jewish blood, and those pharaohs they *like* to suffer. They got this big stone wall in Jerusalem or someplace where they just sway back and forth in front of it and wail all day long.'

'You been on top as long as he has and you fall, you're gonna fall hard.'

'What I said,' they say. 'Viceroy's all washed up.'

And maybe I am.

On 12 October 1499, exactly one year from that Columbus Day, Brother Ramón Pane makes the infant Cristóbal Yego Niño de Moguer y Premiada, at his baptism, the subject of a sermon. He is, after all, the first child born in wedlock in the colony. Even the boy's name, says Brother Pane, more mindful of symbolism than sanctity, signifies God's will and His intention — a name that speaks with the tongue of Spaniard and Indian, a name that surely must remind us of the Indian lad, first among his people to leave the spiritual wilderness for the haven of Holy Faith, who with selfless devotion made the final sacrifice for our . . .

Here the infant's godfather, seeing not the simple whitewashed interior of our little prefab church but the Gothic extravagance of the Barcelona cathedral, and not the bawling infant Cristóbal Yego in his mother's arms but the grinning teenaged Yego resplendent in his baptismal attire, walks swiftly up the aisle and out.

'I've got to get away,' I tell Barto.

He seems, if anything, relieved. Doesn't object, just asks me where.

'I want to get out among the people, see what they're thinking.'

A dubious look, a cocked eyebrow from Barto, but he must think out-of-sight, out-of-mind is the best answer to Viceregal melancholia,

444

for he says: 'I'll give you a crack team of bodyguards. How soon can you leave?'

I leave the next morning. At first the trip only makes me feel worse. People in the back country often don't even recognize me. This is understandable if hardly uplifting. Plenty of settlers in places like Esperanza or Santiago de los Caballeros, Concepción de la Vega or Spanish Bonao, came over with Peralonso Niño and have no idea what I look like.

'Who's the old boy with the white hair?'

'It's some kind of government commission, I hear. So he must be the commissioner.'

'Waste of good tribute gold, if you ask me. But what can you expect, with the Viceroy dead?'

'The Viceroy's dead?' I ask.

'You come from there. So how come you don't know?'

'I've been on the road a long time.'

'Yeah, wasting our tribute.'

As I look back on my journey around the entire island (except for the southwest, Roldán's turf), I find I did learn something: Hispaniola is no longer a dot on the map of the world. It has towns and villages, each with its own mayor, its own priest, its own few frontierswomen, even children, and before long children will mean schools, and probably soon we'll have a regular police force, and tax farmers, clerks, accountants, innkeepers, salesmen, prostitutes, all those providers and parasites that come under the general heading of service industries once you get above bare subsistence, even writers (my biographer Bartolomé de las Casas will be the first), to prove that Hispaniola is a real, bona fide, growing, sophisticated *place*. And the *place* that Hispaniola is becoming (and that the rest of the Indies inevitably will become) will need more than a foreign-born explorer and his brothers to govern it. I mean, what do I know about zoning ordinances, building permits, legal codes? What do I care about the nitpicking of notaries or the pettifoggery of lawyers? Am I a bureaucrat or a discoverer? In short, that junket (to call it what some of our settlers do) has served its purpose. If the island is becoming a *place*, I realize it needs a professional administration to run it.

But I'd better tell you about my bodyguards almost getting sacked for returning to Santo Domingo without me.

I get part of the story from Barto, who gets part of it from yet another Cristóbal, one Cristóbal Rodríguez, called the Tongue, a third-generation New Christian shipped out to the Indies by the Blue

445

Pimpernel network because of a loquacity that promised to get him into trouble with the Holy Office, and sooner rather than later. This Cristóbal Rodríguez was chief of the bodyguard detail on my junket, and here is pleading with Barto:

'Give us a break, Exec. You hardly expected us to put your brother the Viceroy in irons, did you? Believe me, from the time we left Bonao we did everything but. Even so, one night up in the northwest mountains maybe two, three hours before dawn, he – '

'We'll get to that,' snaps Barto. 'Tell me about Bonao.'

'Bonao, Bonao is a whole different bunch of bananas altogether, believe me,' says Cristóbal Rodríguez the Tongue. 'Completely.'

Barto says he is waiting.

'Well,' says the Tongue uneasily, 'it was in Bonao we lost Hernando de Guevara, as you know. Believe me, these things happen.'

'I'm listening,' says Barto ominously.

Cristóbal Rodríguez's version of the events goes on. And on. Since I was there in Bonao, I'll give you mine.

All my bodyguards have been to Bonao before except the youngest, Hernando de Guevara. At seventeen, this handsome son of a noble Castilian family with estates near Avila is definitely a sex object to women.

The cacica Anacaoná, for example.

'I want to fuck this one,' she says.

If Hernando de Guevara responds with a straightforward 'Now, lady?' or something like that, things might turn out differently. But he doesn't, because he can't take his eyes off strapping Anacaoná's daughter, the sultry young Higueymota – and she can't take her eyes off him.

Anacaoná gives her daughter a baleful Wagnerian glare. This makes Higueymota pout. And Higueymota looks even more sultry when she pouts.

Barto, I'd better point out, has by this time completely switched his sexual attentions from mother to daughter, and Anacaoná is still steaming from both ears.

Well, that night in Bonao, Higueymota makes it with Hernando de Guevara, and in the morning Wagnerian Anacaoná wallops her serpent's tooth of a child and gets in return a Barto-style swipe across the chops from Guevara, which brings her warriors running. At this point I pull rank on Anacaoná, giving a head start to Guevara and Higueymota who take off in a generally southwesterly direction, the direction of Xaragua province and the renegade Roldán.

Barto, hearing Cristóbal Rodríguez the Tongue tell all this in far greater detail, and clenching his fists at each mention of Guevara with Higueymota, then asks almost calmly: 'All right, now how did you lose my brother?'

'We did not lose him, he lost us. Like I was saying, we are up in the northwest mountains somewhere – '

'What were you doing in that Godforsaken area? We've got no settlements there.'

'Your brother the Viceroy wanted to go, how can we stop him, he is the Viceroy, am I right? So there we are in the northwest mountains somewhere, and it is maybe two, three hours before dawn, when something wakes me. I start to get up and your brother the Viceroy conks me one with a rock or something, and the next thing I know there is sun in my eyes and they are spilling water on my face, and your brother the Viceroy is gone and he can be headed anywhere on the island, and the island is not small.'

The island is not small but I can have only one destination. For I need a sign, a portent, a marvel of some kind, an interruption in the natural flow of things, a crossing of the line between history and myth, reality and magic, of the sort that's not disparaged in my day but would indicate mental derangement in yours. Looking back on it, I think that in my grief I was waiting for such a sign of cosmic interest – not in me, no; but to explain why my son had lived and died. For he was no ordinary son. He had chosen his father through what you would call free will, and his choice led to his untimely death. Which, apparently, Guacanagarí had not been able to foresee. Hadn't he told (or signed) Yego that blind chance spins the world? Yet earlier hadn't he told (or signed) me that certain things were preordained? Or at least foreseeable? Was Guacanagarí telling each of us what he needed to hear? Or can the world be blind chance for one and inexorable fate for another? If there was a truth to learn, I wanted to learn it.

So, in that first month of the New Year and the New Century, fifteen hundred years since the birth of the Saviour, some fifty generations of humanity delivered from Original Sin, including my son but also Brother Buil and Torquemada (what is God up to, anyway?), I slip away from my bodyguards and go to the one place I might find an answer.

The squalid little village is abandoned. The jungle has sent creepers to infiltrate its silent streets and vines to occupy its thatched huts. At my approach, something slithers away through a thorny thicket.

The two withered crones appear from nowhere.

When I tell them I have come to see Guacanagarí, they exchange meaningful looks.

'You don't know?' they ask.

Obviously, I don't.

'He climbed the highest mountain where the coldest winds blow to seek the loneliest truths. But these truths claimed him and he perished. Guacanagarí is dead.'

Then the crones are gone.

And the squalid little village is gone.

And Hispaniola and the Indies and the world are gone, and I am deep inside my second St Christopher dream, more askew than the first. There I am, gigantic, my legs rooted like tree trunks in the stream bed, wondering when or if the kid I flung into the water (and who clambered ashore full-grown taunting me that I'd have to wait there until he got back) will ever return to free me.

'Hey, kid, where the hell are you?' I shout. 'It's late, it's cold, I want to get out of the water. Kid? Hey!'

No answer. The temperature drops, the stars come out. Shivering, I doze off with my chin just touching the surface of the water. And like one of those clever boxes that open to reveal another box inside, I dream a dream within a dream.

The room is ancient, its ceiling blackened with smoke. Books line the walls and, to judge by the one open on the table, they antedate the Gutenberg-Schöffer printing press. For these pages being studied by a middle-aged man in monastic habit are manifestly handwritten. The monk looks up. I stamp snow off my boots. There is snow on my cowl and on the shoulders of my robe.

'Come in, Herne,' the monk says. 'Warm yourself by the fire.'

Herne, that's me in the dream inside the dream. Herne the Hunter. Bearded (frost in my beard), young, big-framed, with red, powerful hands. Winters I do odd jobs at the monastery. This is St Albans in England. When? I can't tell, not yet. But it is long ago. I (that is, Herne the Hunter) go gratefully to the fire and lift the skirts of my robe. And the monk reads on in his book until he hears footsteps on the stairs. He is joined by a heavyset man wearing a huge pectoral cross over black robes.

'And how is the much-traveled Archbishop of Armenia?' the monk asks in one of those handy phrases that crop up in dreams so the dreamer will know who he's dreaming about.

'Rested, my dear Roger Wendover, and eager to converse with the learned historian and chronicler of St Albans,' the Archbishop of Armenia says, completing the introductions.

While they discuss ecclesiastical matters, I warm myself at the hearth and admire the library's opulent tapestries. St Albans is famous for such things, I know, as the churches of all England are famous for the artistry of their woven altar cloths and the silk-soft tissues used to wrap relics and sacred vessels and particularly – this I learn as the conversation shifts – for the gold-embroidered vestments worn by high prelates. In fact, the real reason for the Archbishop of Armenia's visit is to obtain copes and chasubles heavy with gold thread, with jewels, with tiny enamel plaques.

The Archbishop of Armenia is a world-class storyteller and, in those early days before printing, he's expected, as it's said, to sing for his supper – or his Sunday-best. This becomes apparent when the historian Roger Wendover asks eagerly, 'And have you a new tale to tell me, my friend?'

'A true one?'

'I leave that to you,' says Wendover, and pours his guest more wine. At the fire I, Herne the Hunter, am as eager as the cloistered historian.

'Shortly before I left Armenia, I dined with a stranger who claimed he was the doorkeeper of Pontius Pilate during the tribunal in which the Son of God was condemned.'

Here Roger Wendover laughs a worldly laugh. 'Ah, it's *not* true then! You'd hardly have dined with a fellow twelve hundred years old!'

So now I can work out that my dream is taking place around the year 1230.

'I dined with him. As for the truth of what he told me, you must decide for yourself. He called himself Cartaphilus.'

'Map lover,' muses Roger Wendover.

'And a good thing,' smiles the Armenian. 'For he is condemned to wander forever – or at least until Christ returns.'

'But whatever for?' asks Wendover.

At the fire, Herne the Hunter feels his heart pounding. He has the eerie conviction that, in some way he will never be able to explain, he was the stranger who dined with the Archbishop of Armenia.

'For want of humanity, I suppose you might say. Because, you see, Cartaphilus told me that as the Condemned left the tribunal of Pontius Pilate he struck Him, and knocked Him off balance, and shouted after Him, "Move along there, you're blocking the

449

doorway!" at which Christ turned and replied, "I'll go, but you will tarry until I return." And Cartaphilus has done so ever since.'

'Has – tarried?' says Wendover. 'Not rooted to one spot, surely. Not if you met him in Armenia.'

'Tarry on this earth, I think he meant. He must wander all his days, Cartaphilus said, off the map of time. For just when his days and his wanderings have brought him to the threshold of death, he finds himself recreated a young man with all the world's map to wander again, and all the world's wisdom to seek. Forever – until the Son of God returns.'

Herne the Hunter at the fireplace is now trembling violently. Until this night he has not known the legend. But now, with the knowing, he has just experienced a glimpse through the interface between the mundane and the miraculous, common in his time and by no means rare in mine, and he sees himself not just as the stranger of the tale but as Pontius Pilate's doorkeeper.

He holds his breath, waiting to hear more, but the monk and the archbishop leave the library then, still talking.

Later he sees Roger Wendover writing an account of the wondrous tale. When he finishes, Wendover pauses, gazes up at the thick beams supporting the smoke-blackened ceiling, and as if inspired he swiftly draws a symbol:

Herne the Hunter cries out.

'Whatever is it, Herne?'

Herne knows the symbol. It is the very one employed for his own signature by Cartaphilus. But how could Roger Wendover know it?

And how, come to think of it, could Herne?

Or I, for that matter?

In terror Herne the Hunter flees the monastery and the grounds and St Albans.

Whether he's been frightened away forever I don't know, at least not yet, for by then I'm back in the outer box of the dream, coming awake with much stretching and creaking of shoulder muscles, still stuck fast in the stream, and then I'm back in the abandoned village of Guacanagarí, wondering about that weird symbol and the whole weird dream.

What can I make of it? Remember, I come before Freud and Jung and the elucidation or invention of archetypal myths. In my day it's generally believed dreams foretell the future, period. Or is it question mark? Because what kind of future is there in dreaming someone else's dreams? It's all pretty disturbing.

But that symbol, that signature, is another matter. I find it enormously impressive. More, I feel at home with it, almost as if it belongs to me. So in a way this second instalment of my St Christopher dream has served its purpose – for it is somehow the sign I have been waiting for, the crossing of the threshold, the slipping through the interface (and fortunately back again), the cosmic interest, mythic, enigmatic, yet implying a world not spun by blind chance, which makes it possible for me to return to Santo Domingo and, even, a normal life.

Or as normal as my brothers, governing in my absence, permit.

If the great poet Dante (1265–1321) had written his *Divine Comedy* a couple of centuries later, after the invention of the Gutenberg-Schöffer printing press, I'm convinced he would have reserved a special place in Hell for the publishers of how-to and self-help books. After all, he lost no sleep over placing seven Popes in his *Inferno*, not to mention various Roman emperors and personal enemies. But unlike me, Dante had a thing against anachronism, and about such publishers he never said a word.

It's hard to know which are worse – how-to books with their incomprehensible instructions smothered in jargon, or self-help books offering abysmal advice wreathed in lofty platitudes – but the champion offenders are those that manage to include how-to and self-help between one set of covers. Such a volume, so deadly in the hands of the credulous, is the *Handbook of Regulations and Right Conduct for Colonial Administrators* (Waldseemüller Press, Córdoba, 1497).

My well-meaning brother Big D never lets his copy out of sight. He even sleeps with it at his bedside.

'Be reasonable, Cristóbal,' he says the day of my return, waving the *Handbook* in my face. 'I know how you used to feel about slavery, but that was before we ever heard of the House of Trade and Fonseca and the *Handbook*. Did you know that Fonseca owns a forty per cent interest in the Sevilla slave market? Would he – if slavery was against the regulations or right conduct? Not on your life.' Big D thumbs through the *Handbook*. 'Here it is, right here on page ninety-seven. "*Slavery*. Maximization of adversary captive potential for proprietary labor-intensive capability." What's wrong with that?'

From the window, looking past Barto's gallows to the harbor, I can see the four caravels that sailed with the morning tide, still beating against the wind a mile or so offshore.

'I don't understand a word of it,' I say, 'so I can't tell you what's wrong with it.'

'I would have hoped,' says Big D in his *Handbook*-inspired style, 'you'd allow the true facts to impact on you.'

I point out, 'All facts are true or they wouldn't be facts.'

'Otherwise,' warns my brother, 'you risk obsoleting yourself. Speaking of which, it used to be okay to go off into the wilderness to get your head back on straight, but all that's out now. In the present time-frame a leader enhances his position by staying where the action is.'

'Big D,' I say, 'I want you to recall those caravels and pull those Indians off them.'

'Be reasonable, Cristóbal. I've monitored this historywise. When Granada was besieged in 1492 it didn't really resist. So, no slaves. But Málaga put up a really tough battle. And Their Majesties' contingent reciprocal option, implemented at that point in time, was to acquisition 12,000 prisoners and gift favored courtiers and foreign dignitaries. Twelve *thousand*, and we're only talking about 300.'

It's futile to argue with a true believer in how-to and self-help. I order the signal fire lit myself.

Vaqueños, first of the four caravels to return to dockside, is, according to her manifest, carrying ninety-five slaves. I board with a reluctant Big D, who clutches the *Handbook* to his breast while I detail a party of crewmen to strike the Indians' irons. ('It's the Viceroy! Jesus! I thought he died out in the boonies somewhere.') In the hold a section has been fitted with shelving on which the slaves, manacled and fettered, lie as tightly packed as bolts of fabric in a draper's shop. The air is stifling and the stench awful, for *Vaqueños*, beating all day into the wind, has been pitching and rolling, and the seasick Indians have vomited on themselves and each other. As I enter the narrow aisle with the crewmen, Big D hangs back, his normally pale face now a pasty gray-white like unbaked manioc flour.

'Give him your tools,' I tell the last grommet in line, but my brother says, 'I can't go in there, Cristóbal.'

'You know how to use a hammer and chisel, don't you?'

Big D looks at the simple tools in perplexity, and at me in horror.

But I won't let him off. 'Did you ever consider what it's like crossing the entire Ocean Sea on a narrow shelf in irons wedged in with the living and the dead? Because they do die, you know, a good half of them, and sometimes the bodies aren't taken away for days. And for those unlucky enough to survive the eight or nine weeks lying in their own filth – '

'That's enough, Cristóbal. I don't want to go in there,' Big D pleads.

'Do you think they did?'

I want him to see the captives up close, to see flesh already rubbed raw by manacles and fetters, to see urine dripping from higher to lower planks, to see baby slaves smeared with feces. None of this is to be found in the *Handbook*.

Cries of fear roll like a wave through that fetid hold, cresting when I strike the first irons myself. Then the freed slave recognizes me and the shout of 'Admiral! Admiral!' is taken up on all sides and the fear gives way to a relief so profound (and, I think, a trust so unearned) that tears almost spring to my tearless eyes.

We work methodically with hammer and chisel, all except Big D. Now that he is off the pages of the *Handbook* and facing the results of the ideas he and Fonseca bounced off each other, he starts wielding hammer and chisel in such a frenzy I have to restrain him, afraid he'll injure someone.

It is later. The slaves from all four caravels sprawl on the dock. There are buckets of water, and food for those who can eat. One man who survived eighteen months of hard labor ashore has died on his first and only day at sea, and his body lies a little way apart, as if contamination is feared. Brother Pane kneels beside him in prayer.

Big D stares about in a daze. 'I never knew,' he says. 'I never knew.' Then he walks among the slaves and in his heavily accented Arawak shouts that they are free. But they just look up at him dully. He pinwheels his arms and bellows, 'Free! Free!' But they lie unmoving except for one tall fellow who drags himself slowly to his feet and faces me. 'Is it true, Admiral, that we are free?' I tell him it is true. 'Then,' he says, 'if the Admiral says it, it is so.' And again 'Admiral! Admiral!' is chanted like a litany. I turn away, embarrassed, and see that Big D has turned away too. He is staring down at the *Handbook*.

Then he looks at me. Then back at the *Handbook*. Then he walks to the edge of the dock and hurls the *Handbook* as far as he can into the water.

'We can't do anything right without you,' he says, 'not me, not Barto, not any of us,' and hurries off so I won't see him crying.

His sentiments are not echoed in the letter I write the next night to be carried to the royals when the fleet sails again, its slave shelving ripped out and replaced by balks of mahogany and brazilwood.

' ... and since I feel I cannot be entirely objective in this factional strife that threatens the colony, I respectfully ask that Your Majesties send an experienced magistrate, a man of probity, to administer justice on the island with the full authority of the Crown.'

On impulse I sign this letter with the signature from my dream, as I will all documents from now on, adding 'Admiral & Viceroy' below so they will know whose signature it is.

As I finish, admiring the curiously cabbalistic arrangement of letters, there is a knock at the door of the conference room. 'Come!' I call, and my erstwhile bodyguard Cristóbal Rodríguez enters.

'No hard feelings, Viceroy,' he says.

'That's very kind of you, Rodríguez,' I say.

'I am really glad to see you made it back on your own, believe me.'

I assure him his sentiments are appreciated.

He hems and haws a while. Cristóbal Rodríguez can hem and haw with the best.

Then he says, 'Especially since your brother the Exec is up there in Indian Bonao right now.'

This isn't much by way of news. Just more hemming and hawing, probably. Barto's often in Bonao.

'What's he doing there?' I ask.

'I am glad you asked, Viceroy,' says Cristóbal Rodríguez. After a while he adds, 'Believe me I am.'

'Well then, suppose you tell me what he's doing there.'

Rodríguez can be an extremely uninformative person. 'What is the penalty for desertion, Viceroy?' he now wants to know.

I assume he's worried about his friend Hernando de Guevara. 'Death. You ought to know that.'

He looks out the window at the gallows, silhouetted by a full moon, then back at me. He clearly wants to talk but doesn't seem to know what conversation he'd like to have.

'Did you ever see the *areitos*, Viceroy?' he inquires.

The *areitos* is a Haitian dance. There are two stages, first the sex dance, which can go on without interruption for two or three days to fire the Indians up, then the war dance.

'The sexy part,' says Rodríguez when I shake my head, 'if you are into sex, is really something. Believe me. Every maiden in the village. The Indian village,' he adds quickly. 'There was no Spanish lady present during this time.'

The trading post of Bonao, north of Santo Domingo on the Jaina River, is two villages in one. The Spanish village on the right bank is, after the capital, our largest settlement on the island. On the left bank is the Indian village from which Anacaoná rules her people.

'I must,' says Rodríguez, 'have got laid seven times in two days. Begging the Viceroy's pardon.'

I wave a man-of-the-world hand, then realize the import of his words. They have already danced the *areitos* for two days. More, if you count the time it took Rodríguez to return to Santo Domingo.

And sex dance is always followed by war dance.

And war dance by war.

'If you were into sex with all those maidens, why did you leave Bonao?'

'Because stage one turned into stage two this morning, and your brother the Exec volunteered me for the war dance. Also Pedro Valdivieso and Diego de Escobar, in case you are interested.'

I'm interested. Rodríguez, Valdivieso, Escobar and Higueymota-abducting Hernando de Guevara were my four bodyguards.

'Which is why your brother the Exec did not sack us after we lost you up there in the northwest,' says the Tongue bitterly. 'He was saving us for the war dance.'

The *areitos* is a most realistic dance. Sex, as you've heard the Tongue relate, is hardly symbolic. Neither is war. Though the number of participants is wisely limited, the casualty rate in the war dance is uncomfortably high – or so they say. Few Spaniards have seen, and none have participated in, the *areitos*.

Somehow I don't see this as anthropological research on Barto's part.

Cristóbal Rodríguez the Tongue confirms my fears: 'Your brother the Exec will be marching on Roldán's base in Xaragua as soon as the *areitos* ends to get back that Arawak Helen of Troy, Higueymota.'

The night is clear. The full moon has risen above the gallows. 'Saddle two horses,' I tell Cristóbal Rodríguez.

'Now? It is the middle of the night.'

455

But I'm already heading for the door.

Shortly after dawn, with Rodríguez hanging back a few lengths, I ride my lathered horse into Spanish Bonao. The throb of drums carries across the river, the rhythm no longer libidinous but ominously martial.

Bonao's mayor and a knot of frightened citizens are in the church plaza after a night-long vigil.

'It's the Viceroy!' someone shouts.

'Thank God!' shouts someone else.

Now that I've decided to go out of the Viceroy business, notice how everybody seems to appreciate me more. But this has to be coincidence; I've told no one.

When they see no cavalry behind me, just Rodríguez, some of their enthusiasm fades.

'Are the Indians going to attack?' the mayor asks.

I shake my head. 'But they may be fording the river and marching through here. Keep your women indoors.'

'Women, hell,' says the mayor.

'Maybe,' says Cristóbal Rodríguez the Tongue as I turn my horse toward the river, 'I ought to stay here and help them lock doors and windows and things.'

But I give him a look more eloquent than his loquacity and he rides into the shallow river after me.

When we're in midstream I hear the crackle of musket fire. 'How many men's my brother got?' I ask the Tongue.

'More than eight hundred and as you can hear they are on the warpath.'

'I mean Spaniards.'

'Just Escobar and Valdivieso. But they have probably been killed by now.'

More musket fire crackles as we near the left bank.

'Oh,' says Rodriguez, 'if you mean the muskets, your brother the Exec took fifty to Indian Bonao.'

So it's happened. In his jealous rage my brother Barto has introduced firearms to the Indians.

The first Indian we encounter is streaming sweat, gulping air. His eyes are glazed, blood wells from an ugly gash in his shoulder that shows white bone, and his face and torso are decorated with the customary martial charcoal slashes, as if someone has tried to cross him out.

I rein up and ask him, 'Where's my brother?'

He bows low. 'Whore Higueymota not worth war,' he says in pidgin Spanish. 'Thank Great *Cemis* Viceroy here.'

This puritanical and pacifistic Indian is, alas, unique. But still, observe the continued pattern of appreciation, even adulation, since I decided to quit. There is definitely a philosophical point here, if I could find time to make it.

Barto and Wagnerian Anacaoná stand together outside the cacica's large hut. She, naked except for her *nagua*, is decorated with those charcoal cross-out slashes. He, in sweat-stained jerkin, is holding the bridle of his great roan warhorse. The animal paws the ground, nostrils aquiver at the smell of gunpowder and blood.

I dismount, aware of Indians drifting slowly into a circle around us.

Up close, Barto's eyes, like Anacaoná's, are glazed after three days of *areitos*. He is snapping his fingers in a jerky rhythm. Walking in a quick pointless little circle. Bobbing his head up and down.

'Well, well,' he says. 'The prodigal brother returns.'

'I want every musket stacked right here in front of this hut right now.'

But, looking past me with those glazed eyes, 'Would you believe a twelve-casualty *areitos*,' Barto asks dreamily, 'not even counting the wounded? Anacaoná says it's a record. Of course,' he admits with a hyped-up grin, 'muskets helped.'

Anacaoná beams at my brother. Maybe, after this record-making *areitos*, she's even willing to share the Exec with her sultry daughter, if they get her back.

Weighed against a *ménage à trois* like that, what's one war more or less?

Barto recognizes Cristóbal Rodríguez and says calmly, 'Kill that deserter.'

Rodríguez dives through the door of the cacica's hut.

Two Indians as hyped-up as my brother and gripping knives of finest Toledo steel stalk the hut as if expecting it to flee.

I block the doorway and try to reason with Barto. 'You want to kill him because he wouldn't dance the *areitos*?'

'I warned him. It's the same as deserting under fire.'

By now the Indians are so close I can see the glaze of their eyes.

'Kill him,' Barto says, and in his hyped-up state who knows if he means Rodríguez cowering inside or me?

'Give me those knives.' Trying for Viceregal disdain, I stand my ground – thinking of the eschatological difference of opinion between Petenera and her poor brother Luís, killed by Indians.

457

But here it comes again. Not just appreciation and adulation now that I've decided to quit, but even obedience from *areitos*-crazed warriors.

For both knives are meekly surrendered.

Not that I'm out of the woods yet.

'The muskets,' I remind Barto.

'Oh wow, you have got to be nuts if you think I − '

And whammo! Anacaoná lets him have it, a solid clout to the mouth.

'Nobody call Viceroy nuts,' she says, while Barto in astonishment fingers a fat lip.

One by one, and then in twos and threes, Indians emerge from the shadows with the muskets and drop them at my feet.

Anacaoná bows submissively before me. It looks as if I am finally making it in the Viceroy department even with the strong-willed cacica.

Unless she's just grateful that I'm leaving her sultry daughter in Xaragua, far from Barto's hammock.

When the muskets are loaded on a string of mules, Barto, Rodríguez and I board our horses. Anacaoná, waiting until the last possible moment, timidly approaches my brother, expecting rebuff. But he allows her to cling to, then kiss, his stirruped boot. Tears pour from her eyes. 'Lord Barto, please forgive! Please! I had to whammo. He is Viceroy.'

I'm Viceroy, and late that night back in the Palace in Santo Domingo, sitting in my accustomed place at the open window of the conference room, the gallows sharply etched in the moonlight, I make the toughest Viceregal decision of all. Which is, not to destroy my letter of resignation − for all intents and purposes, that's what it is − before the fleet sails. The uneasy knowledge that history is looking over my shoulder (along with those gallows) decides the issue for me. I recognize my recent triumphs for what they are. I'm on a roll of classic dimensions, but it won't last forever. They never do.

'Viceroy? *Psst!*'

I whirl, Golden Stag (or Hind) knife in hand, and peer into the moonlight, telling myself that something will definitely have to be done to tighten up Barto's security arrangements.

'It's me. Hernando de Guevara.'

And in through the window comes this young scion of a noble family of Avila, Higueymota's abductor.

He collapses into a chair. His jerkin is minus its sleeves, his tights are in tatters, his handsome face is a topographical map of scratches. He explains that he has come through the jungle on foot from Xaragua.

'Alone,' he says, and his youthful voice breaks on the word. 'Without Higuey,' he amplifies.

I bring him wine. 'Easy does it, boy.'

Young Guevara drains the cup. 'How could my own cousin do this to me?'

At this point Barto comes in. No longer hyped up, he begins, 'Cristóbal, it occurs to me that — Guevara!'

'Hiya, Exec,' says this simple, overmuscled youth, not detecting the murderous rage in Barto's voice.

I invite my brother to sit down and listen to Guevara's story — with pointed emphasis on the 'listen'. Never mind his jealousy. We need any intelligence we can gather about Xaragua and Roldán's rebels.

Barto flings himself into a chair. 'You're looking lousy, Hernando,' he says enthusiastically.

'It's a long way back through the jungle,' says Guevara. 'Alone. Without my darling Higueymota.'

Barto half-rises. I wave him back.

'That poor sweet kid,' says Guevara, pouring himself another cup of wine. 'What a tragic life! First her father dies in a Spanish jail, and the next thing she knows, some old guy, one of our sea captains — ' apparently Guevara doesn't know it's Barto he's talking about ' — starts playing around with her mother. Then he includes Higuey in on his perverted fun and games. And then he includes the mother out. Pretty soon he's teaching this innocent fourteen-year-old child the kind of sexual gymnastics you just *know* have to come from France or someplace decadent like that.'

This lucky shot is dead on target. A gnashing of teeth comes from Barto's chair. I give him a warning look.

'I mean, you wouldn't believe how kinky,' Guevara goes on. 'God! If I could just get my hands on that dirty old man!'

Fortunately, Barto's growl is barely audible.

'Hernando,' I suggest, 'why don't you get to the part about your stay in Xaragua?'

But he can't talk about anything but Higueymota.

'It was love at first sight for me and my lovely Higuey,' he says and heaves a forlorn sigh. 'The first time we made love, I'll never forget what she said. "I never dreamed, oh Hernando darling, I never dreamed sex could be beautiful like this." God! After all she'd been through, can you blame her?' Here young Guevara's eyes gleam with suppressed tears. 'Every time I touched her, she'd moan with ecstasy. And, and when she, you know, when she's ready to – uh, her whole body sort of *ripples* and she...'

Barto springs to his feet and rushes for the wine jar. He spills as much as he pours.

There are about ten more minutes of this. Luckily, in the wistful memory of his young love, heart-broken Guevara becomes increasingly incoherent. Finally, wiping his eyes, he cries vehemently:

'I saved her! Me! From a fate worse than death with that depraved sea captain. Everything was going to be beautiful, even if it meant living in Xaragua, as long as we were together.'

'Yes,' I urge quickly, 'tell us about Xaragua.'

'My cousin Adrian Múxica came out in '96 with Peralonso Niño and he was one of Roldán's earliest followers, so I figured we'd be safe there, my darling Higuey and me. But I should have known better, my cousin's an older man, twenty-six if he's a day. And he feeds Higuey this smooth line. A more innocent girl never walked the cloisters of any convent. The next thing I know, she goes to live with my cousin. Doesn't even pack her spare *nagua*, just leaves me and moves right in with him.' I expect young Guevara to be devastated by this, but instead he snorts derisively: 'Hah! Not that it lasts long. Because pretty soon Francisco Roldán himself catches a glimpse of Higuey, minus her one *nagua*, and he *is* the Maximum Leader there in Xaragua.'

'Is that his official title?' I ask. This is our first real bit of hard intelligence on Xaragua.

'Yes, sir. Maximum Leader.'

This is a title that will prove durable in the Caribbean.

'What are the living conditions over there in Xaragua?'

'The living *arrangements*,' says one-track-minded Hernando de Guevara, 'are that the Maximum Leader snaps his fingers and Higuey sends someone to my place for her spare *nagua* and moves out of Múxica's wattled hut into Roldán's bigger one.'

Guevara manfully holds back a sob.

'You said wattled hut? Even the Maximum Leader over there in Xaragua lives in a wattled hut?' I inquire.

'Right. And that's the awful part of it. I mean those wattled walls. You can hear right through them. You see, because I was a bodyguard here, Roldán puts me in his security unit. In fact I pull guard duty right outside his hut. Night shift. And every night, all night long, I hear my poor mixed-up Higuey telling the Maximum Leader, "Oh, Francisco darling, I never dreamed sex could be beautiful like this," and I – I can tell when she's beginning to *ripple* like that because she makes this sort of a trilling sound that...'

Here, finally, he sobs. But Barto's white-faced composure is impressive. I pour another cup of wine and hold it to Guevara's lips.

He pulls himself together.

'Every night, and not just once a night. Roldán! This is an old man, at least thirty-five. I couldn't take it anymore, I had to get away.' Then, plaintively: 'Can I live here in Santo Domingo again?'

'I don't see why,' says Barto unfeelingly.

'I'm begging you, Exec. Because it's either stay here or go back to Spain, and at least if I stay here I'm on the same side of the Ocean Sea as my darling mixed-up Higuey.'

'She's unhappy with Roldán?' Barto smiles.

'Sure she is. Oh, maybe she thinks she isn't but I know better. And it isn't Roldán I blame either. Maximum Leaders have perks, after all. No, I blame my cousin Adrian Múxica. Well, he's getting what he deserves – his whole career right down the tube. He may still be liaison to Xaragua's Indian allies, but that's as high as he'll go, and they used to say he was in line for bigger things. But not after the argument they had. You should have heard them fighting over poor Higuey. The old goats! I never want to get that old, it's...'

While he's discoursing on the pitfalls of age, Barto insists that we deny him asylum in Santo Domingo.

'Every time I see him I'll want to wring his neck.'

'You'll get over it.'

'The hell I will.'

We're going round on this when I hear young Guevara saying: '...broke up that anniversary celebration...'

In a split second I'm looming over him.

'What anniversary celebration would that be?' I ask.

White-faced he looks up at me. I've frightened him.

'Try to reconstruct the conversation, Hernando. You were saying, "broke up that anniversary celebration." What did you mean?'

Guevara still doesn't say anything, just stares at me bug-eyed.

'Let go of his throat,' Barto suggests.

And, after Guevara downs another cup of wine:

'It's the night my cousin Adrian Múxica sees Roldán to try and get Higuey back. He goes, "Where will you find another experienced military man who's fluent in Arawak? Because unless you give me Higueymota, I just might re-defect to the Viceroy."'

461

'We could use Múxica all right,' says Barto thoughtfully.

I tell him to shut up.

'And the Max,' continues Guevara, 'he just laughs in my cousin's face and goes, "That's very funny." Or maybe, "Don't make me laugh." One of those contemptuous little set phrases, you know? "Because," Roldán goes, "if you defect to the Viceroy, I'll make sure he finds out who broke up that anniversary celebration of his."'

A red haze swims before my eyes.

'Was that the end of it?' I hear myself saying, as if from a great distance.

'No, sir. My cousin Múxica goes, "Well, who do you think I did it for?" and the Max goes, "Not on my orders you didn't, sonny, not on my orders." Sonny, to a man the age of my cousin Adrian Múxica. I swear, if I live to be thirty I'll never understand – '

Barto takes a quick reading of my face and hurriedly tells Guevara, 'You better skip the frills, boy.'

Which he finally does. 'Well, then the Max goes, "If I wanted to make a martyr out of the Viceroy, don't you think he'd be dead by now? But I'd have sent someone who could do the job. Where'd you ever learn to throw a knife?"'

What's the purpose of history?

According to the father of all historians, Herodotus of Halicarnassus (c.480–425 B.C.), it's to perpetuate the memory of 'great and wonderful deeds.' I guess history's become a lot more sophisticated since then, because its practitioners are equally inclined to perpetuate the memory of mean and awful deeds. Not that they seem to get any closer to the truth, whatever truth is.

Historians all say I negotiated with Roldán for fear he was getting too strong in Xaragua and too popular in Santo Domingo. That I negotiated with him is true. The reasons given are not.

Some say I was the most craven negotiator this side of Neville Chamberlain at Munich. The rest say I was merely unpardonably inept. The first claim hardly merits refutation. The second you must judge for yourself.

Let's start with a bird's eye view of the promontory known in those days as Point Escondido, midway along the coast between Santo Domingo and Roldán's encampment – why dignify it by calling it a village? – in Xaragua. Point Escondido rises seaward to an elevation of 500 feet, curving to shelter a small bay and a beach of white coral sand. Anchored in the bay is *Niña*, which has brought my negotiating team to Point Escondido. *Niña*'s boat rides the surf toward the beach but does not land. Instead, four men wade ashore and the boat returns to the caravel. Meanwhile, four other men are making their slow, careful way along the trail zigzagging down the face of the cliff to the beach. They are vulnerable, but no more so than those waiting on the hard-packed sand at the water's edge. Mutual vulnerability assures the survival of both groups. At least that's the theory, not well tested in my time.

A broad-shouldered man in the seaside group, peering suspiciously at the negotiating team descending to the beach, tips his hat back. As if this is some pre-arranged signal (it is not) the two parties advance toward each other across the sand. Their steps are measured, as if they are aware of marching to the distant drumbeat of perfidious history. A seabird soaring overhead on motionless wings utters a piercing cry. Or laugh. Who can say? None of the eight men has made a sound as yet. When a scant hundred yards separate the two groups, their leaders stride forward so that they meet alone. Both are tall, both slender. A faint breeze ruffles the white hair of one. The sun momentarily dazzles the other and he shades those palest blue, opaque, conquistador eyes. The seabird soars away.

The white-haired man speaks first. 'Roldán.'

'Colón,' responds the man with the opaque eyes.

Instinctively they raise hands in that immemorial peace sign. Meanwhile, *Niña*'s lombards are trained on the clifftop to cover whatever ordnance may be deployed there. Why take chances?

'Usually reliable sources,' Roldán accuses me, 'reported an *areitos* in Bonao. If this is true, what's the point of these negotiations?'

'War games,' I assure him. 'A training exercise. Nothing more, Max.'

There are, in all, six negotiating sessions on three successive days. My team returns to *Niña* every night and Roldán's to its facilities atop the seacliff. This seems to give us an advantage. Climbing up and down the cliff each day is strenuous. But the Xaraguan advantage, according to history, is greater. I am the Xaraguan advantage.

Not on the first day. At the first day's sessions we hammer out agreement on weapons systems, e.g. the permissible payload of manioc poison per arrowhead; how many Indian bowmen (40) equal one Spanish musketeer, how many (70) equal one Irish wolfhound, how many (208) equal one cavalryman; how many war canoes equal one lombard- and falconet-equipped caravel. This third point is a sticky one. Roldán has no ships.

Historians please note this part of the transcript:

MAX: Parity is unattainable as long as you have a navy.
VICEROY: The existence and size of our fleet are non-negotiable.

Does this sound craven? inept?

In fact, I'm congratulated on all sides that first night back aboard *Niña*. Even by congenitally suspicious Constable Harana II. 'You gave better than you got, Admiral,' he tells me. These being negotiations, I assume he means that the other way around. Or perhaps he's anticipating what's to come.

The balance shifts on the second and third days, and I have to admit a certain embarrassment as I set this account down on paper.

Morning session, day two, is the last bright spot.

MAX: The Woman Gap.
VICEROY: The what?
MAX: The Woman Gap gives you a decided psychological edge. You have thirty-three Spanish women in the colony, and in Xaragua we have none.
VICEROY: But you have Higueymota.

Our experts huddle to see how many Spanish women equal one Higueymota, but no consensus is reached because Barto holds out for an unrealistically high figure.

MAX: We want you to cede fifteen Spanish women to Xaragua.
VICEROY: Our women are not chattel but, like all citizens of Santo Domingo, are free to come and go as they please. We believe in open borders, openly arrived at.

I remain firm, historians please note, on the Woman Gap.

Afternoon session, day two, Roldán demands a pardon, in writing, for all past treasonable activities and retroactively for any that might come to light in the future.

I agree to this.

Big D pens the document, looking uneasy.

Barto mutters that we should not surrender a bargaining chip and get nothing in return.

Harana II gives me a searching stare somewhere between suspicion and disbelief.

464

Roldán isn't satisfied with what Big D's written.

MAX: This won't do. There's no signature but Colón's. I can't accept this document unless it's signed by twenty leading citizens of Santo Domingo.

To demand those additional signatures is, of course, a scurrilous attack on my honor. But:

VICEROY: No objection.

Barto calls a brief recess to ask me, gloves off, 'Oh wow, why are you letting him walk all over you?'

'You are kind of knuckling under, Cristóbal,' Big D points out in his gentle way. Big D has stopped speaking jargon since he threw away the *Handbook*.

'What the hell is this anyway, a goddamn sell-out?' protests Harana II in a voice loud enough to carry to Roldán's negotiating team huddled fifty yards away across the sand.

'He once saved my life,' I point out.

As soon as day three's morning session gets underway, Roldán demands his reappointment as chief magistrate of the island while still keeping his independent base in Xaragua.

Barto and Big D laugh in his face.

Harana II, forewarned by the previous afternoon's negotiations, awaits my answer warily.

'Done,' I say.

During lunch break, much laughter can be heard from the opposing team picnicking fifty yards away across the sand.

'You're caving in to every demand he makes, no matter how outrageous,' Barto reproaches me.

'Without him we couldn't have saved *Niña* back in that hurricane in '95,' I remind my brother.

'I swear to God I don't *believe* this!' roars Harana II.

Herewith, transcript and gloss, the final session:

MAX: I want the right to maintain my own security forces to be paid out of Crown or Viceregal funds.

'Now he has gone too far,' says Barto hopefully.

'Here's where Cristóbal really reams him,' predicts the usually mild-mannered Big D.

465

Harana II keeps his suspicious counsel.

VICEROY: Granted.

'I would never,' shouts Harana II in total disgust, 'have believed this if I hadn't heard it with my own ears.'
Next come's Roldán's bombshell.

MAX: I have one final demand.
VICEROY: Granted.

Harana II's eyes track from me to Roldán and stop there. The Maximum Leader arches an eloquent eyebrow.

MAX: Don't you even want to hear it?
VICEROY: (*indifferent*) If you insist.
MAX: I want the express right to raise a citizens' army to put down the government if the Viceroy fails to honor any or all of these commitments.
VICEROY: Approved.

'Well, that wraps it up,' I say offhandedly, and tell Big D, 'Put that final demand in writing for my signature.'
'To be countersigned,' insists Roldán, insolent to the end, 'by those same twenty leading citizens of Santo Domingo.'
We are about to return to *Niña* when Harana II makes his move. Hailing the other foursome across the sand, he calls:
'Now that you'll be having an official, salaried security force, you wouldn't happen to need a good constable in Xaragua, would you? I'm suspiciously thorough and thoroughly suspicious – it runs in the family.'
Following this traitorous speech Harana II turns to me with a woeful countenance, youthfully Quixotic, and says, 'I'm awfully sorry, Admiral, but these three days have been a real eye-opener. Now that we're all on the same side, sort of, I think I'll be happier where there's more potential for advancement.' And after an enthusiastic affirmative to his job application from the Max, he marches off selfconsciously to throw in his lot with the Xaraguan delegation preparing to climb the zigzag trail up the cliff.
I look sadly after my friend, my protégé, the uncle of my son.
Then I turn back to my brothers.

466

Once more we start toward *Niña*'s boat – when suddenly one of Roldán's base-camp contingent comes hurrying down the cliff path.

'Enemy sail, Max! Two caravels running hard for the point. They'll be in the bay in half an hour.'

The Roldán team whirls to face us, unanimous in suspicion – except Harana II who for once just looks surprised.

'It's a trick!' cries a Roldán man. 'A dirty foreign trick!'

'That's why he caved in on everything,' cries another. 'To keep us off guard until his fleet arrived.'

'They're going to kill us all!'

Roldán himself casts an imputing eye at my team, now reduced to the three Colón brothers, but before I can protest innocence, Harana II, in an unexpected shift, speaks in my defense:

'They're not the Admiral's ships, or I'd know it. He was always up-front with me.' This carries the ring of truth. Quite possibly because it's true.

I know no more than anyone else does. When the two caravels loom off Point Escondido and cast anchor near *Niña*, I don't recognize them. But as a boat pulls for shore, the figure standing in its prow looks familiar.

Alonzo Ojeda, that swashbuckling neurotic, that carefree *condottiere*, that bedizened bantam rooster, springs from the boat even before it scrapes bottom. Waving both arms (slash-sleeved *and* particolored in red, purple and gold) as he splashes toward shore, he shouts:

'Viceroy! By God, didn't I tell you we'd meet again in these Indies when you least expected? By God!'

As he comes swaggering up from the water's edge, two grommets leap from the boat and steady it. A third sets in place a long plank, a makeshift gangway. Onto this plank, careful that his velvet-booted feet stay dry, steps a tallish fellow with the fastidious air of a pure-bred Egyptian cat grooming itself after a misadventure among the scruffy felines of some Levantine back alley. Only slightly less bedizened than Ojeda in jerkin of pink velvet, tights of green silk, and those velvet boots that exactly match his scarlet velvet cloak (far too warm for Hispaniola), he steps ashore gingerly, as if testing the sand, and says in the stagy voice gentlemen-adventurers often affect, 'Terra firma! Terra firma at last!'

Alonzo Ojeda turns to this dilettante-explorer (for by now I have seen enough of the breed to recognize a specimen) and says, 'Didn't I tell you, Amerigo my friend? The minute I spotted *Niña* in the bay I

467

knew you'd soon be meeting the discoverer of an Other World, Don Cristóbal Colón, Admiral of the Ocean Sea and Viceroy and Governor of the Indies, whose very own map led us to Paria the Earthly Paradise and those sacks full of pearls you hid in your sea chest. Admiral, may I present – '

But his friend introduces himself with a sweeping, stylized bow: 'Vespucci, a Florentine.'

And, all unwitting, I welcome to Hispaniola the crass eponymous opportunist who will displace me on all the maps of the world.

'To think,' he says (limp moist hand, deceptively steady eye contact), 'that here I stand on the far side of the Ocean Sea, and all because of the difficulties of a bank in Sevilla.'

'Centurione's,' I guess.

'Been cooking the books for years,' explains Amerigo Vespucci, 'and Genoa sent me to straighten out the mess. Which took some time and entailed an eventual encounter with the shadiest financial wheeler-dealer it has ever been my misfortune to meet.'

'Pighi-Zampini,' I say. This is hardly a guess.

'That is the superannuated scoundrel's name, yes. Runs the Peripatetic branch these days and has so many friends at Court I wasn't able to touch him. But the Sevilla branch of Centurione's, I can assure you, is now under sounder management. Well, in the course of my investigations I met Captain Ojeda here, and he introduced me to that organizational marvel Juan Fonseca, and then, to make a long story short, Ojeda and I sailed, in command of those two caravels, to a land I call Venezuela after that most picturesque of Italian city-states.'

'*You* call?' says Ojeda. 'You didn't even know what Venezuela meant until I told you.'

'Well, actually, now that I think back upon it, Captain Ojeda did more or less imply informally that it might possibly be an appropriate name,' Vespucci admits in his fluent north-Italian-accented Spanish. 'But *paisan*'! Tell me! Tell me everything! How are things in this New World of ours?'

Note the first person plural possessive pronoun. I should have known right then. Ojeda did. But then, he'd spent weeks with that preening Florentine fop.

'My *passenger*,' explains Ojeda, dismissing Vespucci's claim that he commanded a caravel, 'fancies himself a travel writer.'

'A sixteenth-century Marco Polo,' says modest Amerigo Vespucci.

'Oh?' I contribute.

'And you must be Don Diego Colón, and you Don Bartolomeo!'

cries the Florentine. 'Tell me, I want to know everything! What's new in the New World?'

This, as you'll have figured, is a poor time to ask my brothers how things are going in the New or an Other World. So Roldán fills the conversational gap.

'Actually, it's a historic occasion you've walked in on, gentlemen. In return for open borders, openly arrived at, the Viceroy has named me chief magistrate – '

'Didn't he do that before he left in '96?' Ojeda asks.

'*Re*named me chief magistrate, exonerated me from slanderous charges brought by malicious enemies, and given me the right not only to maintain my own security forces but, in the event of a conflict of interest with the brothers Colón, to raise my own citizens' army.'

Is this when the crass eponymous opportunist begins to suspect that, whatever else it is called, the New or an Other World will never be Colónia? Or Colónica or Colonzuela. For today it seems obvious that, though a legend in my own lifetime, I lack the single-minded self-promotion of an eponymous hero. In fact, a couple of weeks like the last couple of days and I will be lucky to get Colombia named for me.

As soon as we are back in Santo Domingo – except it isn't soon, it is a whole weary week of beating into an east wind – it is clear my roll has rolled to a dead stop.

The colonists conduct uncharitable post-mortems on the Roldán negotiations. They comment acidly on the defection of Harana II. They even make invidious comparisons of my sartorial standards with Captain Ojeda's.

Still, though Ojeda is monopolizing my limelight and, worse, has served as carrier for my personal plague Vespucci, I am almost glad he has come, for he brings my Viceregal subjects what they are most avid for – news. Our own inbred world generates so little, at least of the welcome variety. And we have left the world of our birth so unthinkably far behind that it sometimes seems as if by coming to these Indies we have erased the very civilization which made their discovery possible.

Ojeda's cargo of news begins with the completion after only a hundred years of the largest Gothic building in Christendom, Sevilla Cathedral (sixty-seven architects, 200 feet of vaulting above the transept, etc., etc.). It goes on to Court bulletins (Crazy Joan, now Crown Princess, is going further round the bend while her husband Philip the Handsome philanders in Flanders; there are rumors Crazy

Joan is pregnant). It includes gossip, and scandal, and the latest in feminine fashions (scented leather fans, gimp and galloon, the daring new color black).

For a time the colonists play with the news, batting items back and forth rather like Juan Fonseca and Big D bouncing ideas off each other at the House of Trade, and when the newness has worn off they settle down, each with a favorite item, and imagine themselves back in Spain receiving communion in that vast statistic of a cathedral, or attending this bullfight or that Auto-de-Fé, or being fitted for a black gown adorned all over with gimp and galloon (whatever they are). Thus inevitably novelty gives way to nostalgia. But this time it turns sour.

'If I *had* a gown like that, where would I wear it?'

'Sounds like one helluva bullfight. I can't hardly even picture a fighting bull anymore, just sick, spindly cows.'

'Built by an army of stonemasons right up to the sky, and what have we got here that's even made of brick?'

'Why are we wasting our lives on the wrong side of the Ocean Sea in this Godforsaken hole?'

'Now that Torquemada's dead, I'd go home like a shot.'

'Home ... '

'Sure, but the pharaohs decide who stays and who goes, and nobody goes except seamen – who just come back with more victims.'

'Who,' asks Amerigo Vespucci, 'are these, uh, pharaohs?'

Answered by a ringing chorus of eager informants, Vespucci moves several paces away from me and wonders aloud, 'Surely my *paisan*' the legendary Admiral Colón is no member of that unfortunate Nation.' But he studies my physiognomy with renewed interest.

So perhaps it is at this point that Vespucci begins to suspect that whatever else it is called, the New or an Other World will never be named after me.

Still, for one item of news I'm Vespucci's obvious audience:

On Midsummer Day 1497 a certain John Cabot of Bristol Town, England, commanding the forty-ton ship *Matthew* under royal charter from King Henry VII, made landfall on what he convinced himself was part of Asia (how naive, I can't help thinking) but in reality was an other, more northern, mainland than the one I recently discovered.

'He's a *paisan*'!' cries Amerigo Vespucci. 'He's a *paisan*' named Gaboto!'

'From Genoa, not Florence,' I'm quick to differentiate, eager for once to be thought Genoese if this will distance me in the eyes of history from Vespucci.

In the days that follow, while that swashbuckling neurotic Alonzo Ojeda is up to his usual tricks – cutting hardwood without royal license, using conscript Indian labor to drag the felled trees to the beach, leading armed marauders inland to resupply his caravels by pillaging Indian crops – Vespucci is busily telling anyone who will listen what an important person he is. Pighi-Zampini has been transmogrified from a superannuated scoundrel to 'the unofficial state treasurer of Genoa, Florence, Venice and Milan, with close Vatican ties,' and Vespucci, of course, is his confidant. Furthermore, says he, 'I'm as tight as a tick with old Ludovico Centurione himself, who's not only founder of the House of Centurione but governor-in-chief of St George's Bank, and *they* rule Genoa as much as the Borgia Pope rules Rome. Why, between us, Pighi-Zampini and Centurione and I – if we had a mind to – could put together a consortium of Italian city-states that could buy these Indies three times over.'

Ojeda's behavior in the hinterland brings me a rare visit from that Wagnerian cacica Anacaoná. 'Small captain take too much. Small captain no pay nothings. Either he go quick back to Heaven or we dance *areitos*, that for damn sure.'

I call in Ojeda. 'How soon were you thinking of leaving?'

He takes this question philosophically. 'Indian trouble?' And, when I nod: 'It always happens. I'm just not your born colonial. I'm at my best with a sword in my hand.' I get a twinge of recognition here. Substitute a quarterdeck underfoot for a sword in hand and he could be talking about me.

A few minutes before they sail, Vespucci takes me aside. '*Paisan*,' he comes right to the point, 'you aren't exactly the most popular man in Hispaniola.' I say something Biblical about a prophet not without honor, etc. He waves that aside. 'I *am* close to Ludovico Centurione, you know, and I could learn to do business with that superannuated scoundrel Pighi-Zampini. And St George's Bank really is the *de facto* government of Genoa.'

'What are you trying to say?'

'That you owe these ungrateful Spaniards nothing. Our Italian merchant banks all took a bath when Constantinople fell to the Turks. They've been looking for an investment on the grand scale ever since. Such as these Indies of ours.'

'Listen,' I say, beginning to get his drift, 'if it weren't for the King and Queen of Spain, I'd be sitting in a little shop somewhere selling maps.'

'You've paid them back a hundredfold already, *paisan*'. So why not

471

try this scenario?' He gazes seaward. 'One day out there you see the combined warfleets of Genoa and Venice, a hundred ships and more. You know resisting is suicidal, so you open Santo Domingo to their functionaries and let their armies march upcountry to pacify the natives. You know what you'd be? The richest man in Christendom. And I could arrange it. Just say the word, *paisan*'.'

'I didn't hear you,' I tell him.

'Didn't hear − ?'

'Get aboard that ship. And get out of my Indies.'

I wonder how that crass eponymous opportunist ever thought I'd swallow anything so far-fetched. Not the part about Genoese banks and Venetian warships − that's not impossible − but the idea of Amerigo Vespucci masterminding the whole grandiose scheme.

Still, to how many disaffected colonists did he mention his 'scenario'? And what part did he imply I'd play in it?

No matter, I think. He's gone.

Gone from these pages, too. A walk-on part is all he gets here, and he deserves no more from history − or geography. He does sail in New or Other World waters on three more occasions, captain-general of a fleet according to his chatty travel writings, a passenger according to Peralonso Niño and others who ought to know, for it is their voyages he describes. But first, he describes Ojeda's. Not that Ojeda has any role in it by the time Vespucci's finished. No, that swashbuckling neurotic disappears from the Florentine's account, which is predated more than two years to make Vespucci arrive off the South American (*sic*) coast a full year before me. When, later, he gets wind of a prominent publisher who is teaching cosmography at St Dié in France and who will soon bring out, in partnership with a famous cartographer, a new edition of Ptolemy featuring an updated map of the world, Vespucci deluges them with letters. Possibly he even visits them. The evidence is inconclusive. But this much seems certain: the publisher, one Martinus Waldseemüller, and the cartographer, one Martin Behaim, faced with the alternative of an eponymous me, are only too happy to give Amerigo Vespucci the place I have earned in geography.

Not that I'm miffed. What's in a name?

One day in August when Juan Niño of Moguer is showing me around his new farm a few miles inland ('Salt air's lousy for the plantation, Viceroy') a horseman gallops into view. Or into earshot, actually, for standing in the high canebrake we can't see him until he enters the row where Juan Niño and I are companionably munching two lengths of cane.

The horseman is Cristóbal Rodríguez the Tongue, and he is breathless.

'. . . banana!' he seems to gasp.

Juan Niño says, 'Sorry, we don't grow them here. Have a nice piece of sugarcane.'

Cristóbal Rodríguez, trying to catch his breath, gets out an almost clear:

'Harana – '

'Don't mention that traitor's name in front of me,' growls Juan Niño with one of his truly ferocious frowns.

' – is back!' elaborates the Tongue.

Interpreting this correctly, Juan Niño has a swift change of heart. 'You mean good old Harana's redefected?'

I feel a tightness in my chest and realize I'm not breathing. Has Harana managed to pull it off?

'He got in this morning with the prisoner you sent him to Xaragua for, Viceroy,' says the Tongue.

How Harana II entered Xaragua a hero, supposedly the highest-level defector ever to go over to Roldán's rebels; how he soon saw that Adrian Múxica, liaison to Xaragua's native scouts, treated the Haitians no better than animals; how he plotted with these Indians to capture Múxica; how the Max got wind of the plot in time to pursue Harana II and his prisoner to the very gates of Santo Domingo – all these events, though interesting in themselves, lie outside the modest scope of this volume.

Roldán is waiting for me with an armed escort at the Juzgado when I return from the Niño farm.

'I want the prisoner.'

I tell him, no way.

'He was taken from Xaragua by force, and besides I didn't issue a warrant for his arrest and I'm chief magistrate.'

I send inside for Harana II. 'Did Múxica confess?'

'I'm working on it, Viceroy. But now that he's here, you'd be amazed how the eye-witnesses' memories have improved. You see, once they – '

'You've had positive identifications?'

'Yes, sir. Eight of them. As for his confession, give me a few more minutes.' Harana II returns inside the Juzgado.

Actually, it takes another hour before the constable appears at the door once more, waving a sheet of paper.

With Múxica's confession in hand, Roldán can hardly object any further, so he just turns with the rest of us to stare at Barto's gallows.

At dawn of that fateful Saturday, 27 August 1500, the gallows are cordoned off by Barto's security forces (Cristóbal Rodríguez commanding), and so is the street leading to the Juzgado, but the rest of Santo Domingo surges with people. Everyone in the colony wants to see the hanging, Hispaniola's first — even the bedridden carried on litters to the plaza, even our growing population of halfbreed children perched on accommodating shoulders, even our usually reserved Spanish ladies (except Inocencia, who has remained up at the farm). Their combined voices, when the condemned man is finally slow-marched up Juzgado Street to the plaza, is so like that remembered Valencia sound that for one panic-stricken, guilt-laden moment I shut my eyes and see again the Burning Place and that whole horrible day, and I wonder, am I any more (or less) than a transplanted Tomás de Torquemada or Brother Buil? Though I don't dwell on it, I know how Harana II extracted that confession. But no, no; pangs of conscience have no place here. This condemned man is guilty of more than hair-splitting heresies. He has killed for personal advantage and in cold blood, and he has killed my son.

Manacled, Adrian Múxica still manages the short journey up Juzgado Street, his final one anywhere, with a swagger. This gains the mercurial crowd's sympathy. But when he reaches the gallows, Múxica's bravado (it is not bravery) gives way to a terror so profound that, to a mob weaned on the spectacle of public death (execution is, after all, a well-known deterrent) it even has its gruesomely comic aspect. For in his terror Múxica, despite Brother Pane's gentle urging, is unable to confess.

'Come on, Adrian old fellow,' shouts someone. 'Surely you can dredge up an appropriate sin or two!'

'Hangman steal your sins, Múxica?'

'Give the poor man a few sins, somebody, it seems murder ain't enough.'

Múxica falls to the ground and, contorting himself, manages to grasp behind his back with his manacled hands the bottom rung of the ladder that climbs to the scaffold. When his fingers are pried loose, he hooks a leg over the ladder rung, clinging there with superhuman strength.

'I can't, I tell you. I want to but I can't!' he cries in a paroxysm of terror while Brother Pane continues to exhort him to save his soul.

474

'How can I confess? How? If I can't remember a single sin, not one, not even a small one, then I can't confess, and you wouldn't let them kill me when I'm not in a state of grace, so we'll have to postpone things, won't we?' shrieks Adrian Múxica with an ultimate, or at least a penultimate, logic.

Finally he is prodded and pulled up the ladder to the scaffold of Barto's gallows.

When he is standing over the trap, his eyes seek out mine (no hoods were used in those days), his bravado returns, and he says, 'I only wish it was you I got, you dirty pharaoh!' And right after that if you shut your eyes (I must have, for a moment), you'd think that surf is giving that rockbound coast an awful pounding, but whether the sound is judgment for or against Múxica, for or against me, I cannot say. And when you open your eyes you can see Adrian Múxica's abrupt descent checked by the definitive jerk of the noose, and you can see him swinging and turning, swinging and turning, his head cocked far to one side by the knot.

But I have already turned away. The crowd parts for me like the Red Sea for Moses, and except for an occasional muttered 'pharaoh' it is quiet then, and quieter still when I leave behind in the plaza my execution of justice and my exaction of vengeance. Walking, then running, through the deserted streets, I feel nothing of all the things I thought I might have felt. At the stables I sling a saddle on the nearest horse, jump aboard and gallop inland to the farm where my friends Juan and Inocencia raise livestock and sugarcane. And a ten-month-old son they call Yego.

The next day (as Big D will tell me) the citizens of Santo Domingo heading for Sunday Mass suddenly veer in a body toward the waterfront. For just off the harbor stand two ships waiting for the morning offshore breeze to slacken so they can make port.

This is almost too much for our colonists – Ojeda's caravels with their quota of news, the boastful Vespucci with his high connections, then the hanging, now two more strange caravels. The little colony almost seems a crossroads of the world. The dock is crowded, the prefab church empty, the plaza deserted, and the body swinging gently in that offshore breeze ignored, belying the supposed deterrent value of leaving a corpse dangling until it is ripe as any well-hung partridge.

Though ignored in town, the hanged man is the object of considerable speculation on the quarterdeck of the caravel *Gorda*. Recent

475

arrivals take hangings seriously; recent arrivals carrying royal letters of credence proclaiming them new magistrate and governor, with powers of arrest and sequestration, even more so. Thus Don Francisco de Bobadilla, fifty-year-old knight commander of the military Order of Calatrava, member of the King's Own Household, former lord mayor of half a dozen cities, the very sort of man laden with probity and honors I would have chosen myself.

While everyone on shore wonders who's aboard, Big D – alone in command of the capital with me at the Niño farm and Barto looking into some minor unrest upcountry – sends Cristóbal Rodríguez in a canoe to find out.

Ushered to the quarterdeck of *Gorda*, Cristóbal Rodríguez introduces himself as chief of security. Don Francisco de Bobadilla nods brusquely, his flinty eyes never leaving the tiny corpse dangling from the toy gallows.

'Does that sort of thing happen often?' he demands.

'First one ever,' says the Tongue.

'Ahh,' sighs Bobadilla.

'But believe me, from now on things will be different. The Exec is upcountry right now checking out the trouble in Concepción de la Vega and he has less forbearance than his brother the Viceroy, so you may soon see more rebels swinging in the wind.'

'Was the executed man a rebel then?'

'Yes and he murdered an Indian.'

'A Spaniard was hanged for killing an Indian?'

Cristóbal Rodríguez starts to explain the special circumstances of the case, but just then the wind at last shifts, orders are bellowed on all sides, tackle thunders through the blocks, sails fill, and *Gorda* and her sister caravel *Antigua* make for shore.

Rodríguez, no seaman, finds it hard to keep his footing. He resumes his explanation.

'The Viceroy's son?' repeats Don Francisco de Bobadilla with distaste. 'Was he sired on an Indian woman?'

'Well, yes, but the Viceroy was not the father.'

'Explain!' barks Bobadilla, even though Rodríguez is doing his best.

Where Bobadilla was when Yego Clone was baptized in Barcelona Cathedral, I can't say.

'The boy never knew his father,' tries Cristóbal Rodríguez.

'Then the so-called murder victim was not only an Indian but a bastard?'

Cristóbal Rodríguez's last clear words are, 'He never knew his mother either,' for by the time *Gorda* enters the placid waters of the harbor he is seasick. This may explain why he fails to clarify Yego's status not only as my son but as the King and Queen's godson. And by the time Bobadilla learns these things, it is too late. He may be a man of probity but he closes his mind in a hurry.

Ashore, he immediately asks for me.

Big D in his monkish robes identifies himself. Pale, soft, uncertain, he is hardly a commanding figure. Bobadilla is. When he produces his letter of credence, Big D reads it and blurts, 'It says here chief magistrate *and* governor. What's going on?'

Ignoring the question, Bobadilla asks, 'You said your brother is visiting inland somewhere?'

'He needed to get away after the execution.'

Just then someone in the crowd calls out, 'Dirty pharaoh, you bet your ass he did!'

Variations on this theme are heard.

'And your other brother, the one they call the Exec?'

Big D confirms that he too is inland, attending to some troublesome colonists.

'Is this a frequent occurrence, Don Diego?'

Big D, no thinker on his feet, cannot decide whether a positive or a negative answer will serve us better. So he tries an offhand, 'Oh, minor insurrections are no big deal around here.'

Don Francisco de Bobadilla's eyes widen.

Here Roldán enters the conversation, introducing himself as chief magistrate.

'You are relieved of that post,' Bobadilla informs him curtly.

Roldán, instead of objecting, says a fervent, 'Thank God.'

Bobadilla gives him a contemptuous look. 'More trouble than you can handle?'

'It isn't that. Rebellion is one thing, I can handle rebellion. But what can any one man do about a foreign plot to seize the Indies – a plot that can be traced right to the Viceroy himself?'

The scaffold of circumstantial evidence is skilfully built. The recent visit of Amerigo Vespucci, Vespucci's known (*sic*) closeness to both the notorious Pighi-Zampini and old Ludovico Centurione himself, the fact that yet another Genoese (even if sailing under British colors) has recently claimed lands to the north ...

'Is the Viceroy a pharaoh, as these settlers call him, or is he then Genoese?' demands Bobadilla testily.

Roldán shrugs. 'I suppose he could be both.'

Before long Francisco de Bobadilla's three secretaries will take depositions on subjects ranging from the imaginary Italian consortium of Amerigo Vespucci to the miscegenous amorous entanglements of Barto. But first the new chief magistrate and governor needs a place to stay. He asks Big D: 'Where is the governor's mansion?'

'We don't just have a governor's mansion, we have a real Viceregal Palace — that imposing two-story building over there flying the Viceroy's coat-of-arms.'

'Take it down. I shall be moving in directly with my retinue.'

Big D is a gentle fellow who will give in rather than cause a ruckus. But when, finally, he has had enough, he surprises people.

'The hell you will,' he tells Bobadilla.

The new governor says two things in response.

'Arrest that man,' is the first. Pointing at Big D in case there is any doubt.

And the second: 'Find out exactly where his brother is.'

I'm at the Niño farmstead bouncing little Cristóbal Yego on my knee and convinced he is repeating 'horsy, horsy' like any middle-aged man with a favorite nephew or grandson. And I'm listening to Inocencia explain her idea — to which obviously she's given considerable thought — for an Indian school.

'I know about all those plans for sending them to Spain, the grown-ups, that is, but the only way they seem to go is as slaves,' she points out. 'So why don't we educate the children here instead? I've already spoken to Brother Pane, and he approves. Naturally, he'll want to supervise the course of study. Some of us women would be only too happy to act as teachers, and if you start them young there'd be a whole new generation of Indians who speak fluent Spanish and have good Christian educations.'

Little Inocencia, with a bit between her teeth, is anything but shy. But when I ask her, 'Can you read and write?' she blushes prettily — not because she can't but because she can. 'I wanted to learn, when I was young. Some girls are like that.'

I want to buy a book, I can almost hear Beatriz say.

Just your regular kind of usual book.

Is it a good book to learn to read from?

You mean I have to know how to read before I can buy a book? It isn't fair. How can I learn to read unless I buy a book?

'Yes,' I say, 'some girls are like that.'

Did you ever notice how dandling nephews or grandchildren and reminiscing often go together?

I was dandling and reminiscing, and telling Inocencia, 'No need to wait for an official schoolhouse. There's more than enough room in the Viceregal Palace,' when we hear horses galloping up. Soon Juan Niño appears at the door, his face a ferocious shade of purple.

'There's a squad of soldiers here, Viceroy,' he says. 'They claim they've come to arrest you.'

Two hours later Harana II bursts into the Juzgado, opens the cell at the back, takes one look at me and Big D seated on either side of a small table, manacled and fettered, and shouts: 'I just heard, Admiral. I'll strike those irons right away. Of all the crazy, ridiculous – '

He is too enraged to say any more. Big D gives him a hopeful look.

But, 'If Their Majesties sent that man with authority to put us in irons,' I say, 'why then, in irons we'll stay until Their Majesties give someone else authority to remove them.'

Big D sighs.

'Go up to Concepción and bring back the Exec,' I tell Harana II.

He smiles. 'I get it. With his Indian allies from Bonao?'

'No. A warrant's been issued for his arrest too. I want him to give himself up.'

'Peaceable?' gasps Harana II. 'But why, Admiral?'

It's simple. If I resisted, if I sent word to Barto to have the *areitos* danced in Indian Bonao, I'd divide the island into two warring camps.

No one is to blame. This time. Thus the prophet Guacanagarí.

I want there to be no next time.

So the following day Barto joins us in the Juzgado, submitting with silent fury to his irons. And we wait. Don Francisco de Bobadilla is a very thorough taker of depositions. By the time we board *Gorda* for the return to Spain in irons, weeks have passed and a 500-page report is entrusted to her captain, one Andrés Martín.

Bobadilla remains in Santo Domingo as governor.

The sad thought crosses my mind that Inocencia will probably never have the chance to start her school.

As soon as we are well out of the harbor an embarrassed Captain Martín comes with a lantern into the gloomy portholeless cabin where we are incarcerated.

'I'm terribly sorry about this, Admiral,' he says. 'I'll have those irons struck at once.'

But I shake my head.

Why do I refuse, now that we're at sea?

To ask this question is to miss the whole point of me. Are these manacles and fetters my humiliation? No, they are the badge of my honor, the cold forged iron of my glory. For I have served and been ill-used by people in high places. The shame is theirs, not mine. If I could, I would take these irons to the grave with me.

'Stubborn mule,' says Barto, but in his hard voice there is fondness.

Not that he really understands, nor does Big D. My serenity on the long voyage back to Spain baffles them. Poor Big D is terrified of the future; Barto nurtures his outrage. But I wear my new-found serenity like a suit of armor. Nothing can touch me. For I have given my best. A man can do no more.

The weather is fair, the food good, the wine plentiful. At night sometimes I dream of Petenera. What was it she wrote, the day I sailed, so long ago? *My destiny awaits me here.* Two years and more it has been: a lot can happen in two years. This also is part of my new serenity. Perhaps she and I, once I find her ...

'What's that idiot grin for?' asks Barto.

'Nothing. Just wool-gathering.'

The attentive reader will observe that no slops are tossed to me in the deepest hold of the ship right down in the bilges by some foul-mouthed lout with a peasanty voice, as happened in that dream I had when I was sixteen and lay dying in Rome. I don't deny the discrepancy, but I still think that for a teenager's first prophetic dream it was a pretty impressive performance.

A lot has been made of my return to Spain in irons, and more written about it than anything but my First Voyage. How are the mighty fallen: it's too tempting a subject to resist. I resent none of this excessive recounting of the low ebb — at least professionally — of my life.

With one exception.

Why did a latter-day novelist in John Cabot's part of the New or an Other World, a Nobel prizewinner, have to end his longest and most famous novel like this?

'Columbus too thought he was a flop, probably, when they sent him back in chains. Which didn't prove there was no America.'

Sure I thought I was a flop. Who wouldn't? But using the Vespucci eponym is really rubbing it in.

⚜ XIX ⚜

The Almost Unexpected Return of the Blue Pimpernel

Here's an ill-starred royal family for you.

Isabel and her cousin Fernando, marrying to unite all Spain, could easily have founded a dynasty to eclipse the Habsburgs and Hohenzollerns, the Bourbons and Romanovs. After all, they had ten children.

But half died at birth or in infancy.

And then Crown Prince Juan, as you've seen, died of love on his honeymoon.

And Princess Isabel, the King's beloved Isa, died in childbirth, to be replaced as Portugal's queen by her younger sister Maria.

And Isa's son, the heir who could have forged Iberia into Europe's greatest power, died of a fever. (A fever was often a euphemism. For poison.)

And Philip the Handsome, that flamboyantly unfaithful Burgundian husband of Crazy Joan, would reign in Spain only two years before dying of a chill after a game of handball. (A chill, like a fever, was often a euphemism.)

And Crazy Joan lived up to her name.

By 17 December 1500, all these tragedies except Philip's had come to pass, which should have been enough to make Fernando and

Isabel the sourest royal couple in Christendom.

'They're not that bad, though,' Juana de Torres assured me. The Queen's confidante, sister of my old friend Captain Antonio Torres, stood chatting with me in the small anteroom to that audience chamber in the Alhambra in Granada where once blind musicians had played for the sultan. 'Because the youngest daughter Princess Catalina is a real sweetheart and they're pinning all their dynastic hopes on her. They're arranging a marriage with that nice Arthur, Prince of Wales. So actually you'll find their spirits up.'

Arthur, as history buffs should know, would die (of a chill or a fever or a euphemism) three months after the wedding, and Catalina — Catherine of Aragon, as the British called her — would, soon after he succeeded to the crown, marry that nice Arthur's younger brother, that nice King Henry the Eighth.

The House of Atreus in spades.

'How are my boys?' I asked Juana de Torres. I should have been miffed that I hadn't seen them yet, but in my new-found serenity I reminded myself how busy everyone at Court had been.

After concluding a treaty with France's new king, and organizing a war against several Italian city-states (my new serenity wavered when I heard that, wondering if it had anything to do with the improbable Vespucci plot), Their Majesties had finally sent for me and my brothers. And sent *to* us — a very good sign — 2,000 gold ducats so we could make the trip from La Rábida in style. We'd cooled our heels there long enough, at my insistence still in irons. By the time a royal order to strike them arrived, I felt naked without them.

'Your boys,' said Juana de Torres, 'are keeping a pretty low profile these days. A lot of disgruntled ex-colonials hang around Court, you know, screaming for back pay among other things. Oh, their insults seem to roll right off Fat Ferdy, but that Diego — what a hunk of a man he is! — he takes them more to heart. Once he lost his temper and knocked down and kicked some cavalry officer, a former favorite of the Queen's, whose name skips my mind.'

'By "Fat Ferdy" did you mean my son?'

'Well, that's what he's called. Sorry.'

At that moment roly-poly eleven-year-old Fernando in his gold and purple royal livery came to escort us into the blind musicians' chamber. He was too old to call it baby fat; right then I made up my mind that he needed toughening.

As there were eight or ten other people hanging around the anteroom, Fernando did not greet his father and uncles effusively.

'Papa. Nice to see you. Uncle Barto, Uncle Diego. Well, they're ready for you.' He did add, 'No time limit that I know of.'

'Where's your brother?'

'Eating iron. He spends more time eating iron than any fellow I ever met,' said the fattest of the royal pages.

We were ushered in under that gallery where blind musicians had played. No shadows flickered in a torchlit dream at once timeless and insubstantial like the arabesques circling the wall which, I saw now, were after all only cheap stucco. As a wise old Greek named Heraclitus once wrote, time is a river and you can't step into it twice at the same place.

I dropped to my knees before the twin thrones, eyes downcast, feeling injured and self-righteous until I reminded myself of my new-found serenity. Behind me Big D prostrated himself, I think. I'm not absolutely certain, because I was shocked to see Barto still standing tall (for a shortish man) and speaking up in defiance of protocol.

'Oh wow, Your Majesties, just what kind of a number are you trying to do on me anyway? I left a pretty soft life up there in Fontainebleau seven years ago to come and help my brother, and Your Majesties were only too willing to send me out with a rescue fleet, and you better believe the Admiral needed all the help I could give him. I spent the best years of my life out there in your Indies and a lot of the time upcountry. I can count on the fingers of both hands the nights I slept in a comfortable bed. With or without company. Jeepers! Whose service was I in, my own? I was in yours. And how do you show your gratitude? By arresting me, and shipping me back three thousand miles weighed down with irons – even in the middle of the Ocean Sea, for crying out loud – and then leaving me shut up in a monastery.' Barto added, 'My brothers too,' and paused for breath.

Too flabbergasted to do anything but lean forward in their thrones and listen, the King and Queen leaned forward in their thrones and listened.

'Well, thanks for nothing,' said Barto. 'Thanks whole heaps. My brother Cristóbal may still think he owes you something, for reasons best known to himself, and my brother Diego never did like to make waves, but I'm not them. So don't expect me to answer to a bunch of insulting charges. If you have something to offer by way of interesting and lucrative employment, I'll consider it. Otherwise I'll be on my way. Gosh, there are other kings and queens on the map of Europe, and most of them are easier to catch up with than you and a whole lot easier to pin down when it comes to loyalty. Because they recognize that loyalty is a two-way street. Got all that?'

They got all that. It was a speech of perhaps 300 words, mostly shouted, and every phrase an act of lese-majesty. I was sure my brother Barto would be dragged to his own garotting at the flick of a royal finger, but he got away with it. Maybe he had learned something about royalty up there in Fontainebleau that I never understood.

The King said, 'There is perhaps some slight truth to your – interpretation of events, Don Bartolomé.'

The Queen said, 'Dear me, did we do all that? Surely not. At least, I hope not.'

Then I looked up at them, mostly at her, for the first time. I got another shock. Woe had pulled down the corners of her mouth; wretchedness and misery (or was it merely ill-fortune?) had covered her face with a tracery of fine wrinkles; adversity had turned the former dark-red glory of her hair a sparse white now tucked haphazardly into her travelling crown. In short, she was an old woman. Yet she was almost exactly my age, and my fiftieth birthday still lay some months in the future.

Was I an old man in her eyes?

'We have,' the King said, 'looked into the matter of those Italian city-states poised to strike with their war fleets at our realm across the Ocean Sea.'

'Only to learn,' said the Queen, 'that it was a baseless rumor.'

'Nevertheless,' pursued the King, 'and you may make of this what you will, we are at war with the Italian city-states.'

'A little dispute over Naples,' the Queen reminded him deprecatingly, 'unrelated altogether to any alleged plot against our Indies.'

'Perhaps,' said the King grudgingly, and even more grudgingly told me: 'And perhaps you did not exceed your Viceregal authority when you executed that assassin, Don Cristóbal, but even so we can't help wondering . . .' Here his voice trailed off and he turned to the Queen. 'What was it we couldn't help wondering?'

'Why in the world Knight Commander Francisco de Bobadilla exceeded *his* authority by clamping the Colón brothers in irons. But you can't expect the Admiral of the Ocean Sea to answer *that*.'

'No,' agreed the King, 'I suppose I can't. But we did give Bobadilla the authority to *send* anyone back to Spain who menaced the peace and security of the colony, didn't we?'

'I believe that we did,' admitted the Queen.

'Well then, you see?' the King said doubtfully.

In my new serenity I listened to their usual Through-the-Looking-Glass approach to statecraft and knew that Barto's opening sally, lese-majesty or no, had been inspired. For it had set them to bickering, and with the royals that was half the battle.

Even Big D must have realized this as, confidently, he spoke up. 'We menaced the peace and security of the colony?'

'Watch that!' lashed out the King. 'We'll tolerate no lese-majesty here.'

This was Big D's last attempt at court diplomacy.

I asked in my new, serene voice, 'But my various offices, Sires? They were to be lifetime appointments. In fact, hereditary.'

'You remain', said the Queen, 'our very own Admiral of the Ocean Sea.'

Did 'very own' sound patronizing?

'The title is still yours, Don Cristóbal, and it is still hereditary,' said the King, with a definite emphasis on 'title'. 'And you may continue to bear the honorific "Viceroy".'

'Honorific, hell,' Barto said. 'Give him his twelve and a half per cent.'

The King suggested: 'How about a nice duchy here in the province of Granada instead, Don Cristóbal?'

I shook my stubborn white head. 'I'm too young to settle down. And I'm an Admiral and Viceroy, not a duke.'

'You must realize,' said the Queen, 'that no man, however deserving, can expect to receive indefinitely one-eighth of the revenues from our overseas realm.'

'It won't do to be grasping, Don Cristóbal,' said the King. Still Don Cristóbal, I noticed. Not Viceroy. Not even Admiral or Governor.

'Because,' went on the Queen, 'what with the discoveries of Vicente Yáñez Pinzón and that dashing Captain Ojeda and your good friend Peralonso Niño and Bastidas of Sevilla and Lepe of Palos and – I forget the names of the others – that realm, that New or Other World, is far bigger than Old Spain.'

'You can no more rule it as Viceroy and expect your heirs to do the same than you can go on collecting your inordinate percentage,' chimed in the King in one of those occasional displays of royal unanimity.

They were right, of course. While I had been putting down insurrections and averting wars in Hispaniola, not to mention languishing in irons, history had been passing me by. But in my new serenity I wasn't going to let a little thing like that trouble me.

'I'm sure,' the Queen eased the blow, 'that we can work out an acceptable settlement with your agent Luís de Santangel.'

'He's back, My Lady?' I cried.

'Not that you'll know him,' predicted the King.

'I never did fancy obesity,' said the Queen. Then her newly old face smiled at Barto. 'Well, Don Bartolomé, will you be remaining in our service?'

'The Portuguese,' suggested the King pointedly, 'are accepting Spanish captains on the African trade these days. Or, if you prefer, our own Spanish navy needs experienced officers in the war against that consortium of Italian city-states.'

'None of which is Genoa,' said the Queen hastily.

Barto's cold eyes held the King's. 'I'm no Spaniard, no more than the Admiral, and thank God for that. Portugal suits me.'

So Barto would sail as captain-general of a fleet setting up forts between Fernando Po and the Cape of Good Hope, and leave this narrative for a couple of years.

'And you, Don Diego?' asked the Queen.

'Why don't you join your brother in Portugal,' said the King. This was no question.

But, 'I got to like La Rábida,' said Big D with his shy smile. 'It's peaceful there.'

So he'd spend a good part of the rest of his life at that isolated monastery and, for all I know, be happier than either of his brothers.

'And you, Admiral?' asked the Queen. 'What will you do?'

But I didn't know.

I could only think: the work of a lifetime born of a grieving Julian decade on the far northern rim of the world, the Great Venture so long in the making, so swift to pass, those Indies of mine in other hands, other hearts, other men's dreams...

But no. In my new serenity regrets were foreign to me.

As soon as the fattest of the royal pages escorted us from the now prosaic chamber of the blind musicians with its cheap stucco arabesques, I went alone to the Household section of the Alhambra to find Luís de Santangel.

Except for the perfectly rolled cigar that lived in one side of his face I wouldn't have recognized him. The Keeper of the Royal Household Budget was slender, and with his vanished avoirdupois had also vanished his persona. While he paced back and forth dictating a letter to his executive secretary Espina de Chopito, he no longer projected an air of power but only of nervous energy, as if, now that his fat was gone, his neurons and ganglia and things were too close to the surface.

But at least the cocksure voice was intact.

' ... trouble and lighting candles in every church in Christendom won't help if you don't believe me go ahead and bet the only ass you got but don't say I didn't warn you. Well, that's it, Chopito. The usual periods, commas and semi-colons. Three copies.'

'What, no exclamation points?' I said.

A puff of smoke screened blank eyes at first, then: 'Kid! I knew you'd got back but you've kind of accrued in the age department. Jesus, I never thought I'd lay eyes on you again. Espina, get lost somewhere, willya?'

Espina de Chopito did that.

'Where is she?' I asked.

'You want me to lie? If I do, the answer is I don't know. If I give it to you straight, the answer is I can't tell you. I'm sorry, kid. Now how'd it go with the royals?'

While talking, Santangel, this new bundle of nervous energy, was puffing on his superb cigar, pacing between the desk and the window (view toward Sacromonte), cracking his knuckles, elevating and lowering his left eyebrow sporadically. This last definitely came under the heading of a tic.

'You've got to tell me,' I said.

He seemed to change the subject. 'I wasn't ruthless enough. How's that for a sock in the old ego, a fellow who starts out nine years old blowing the whistle on his whole family and fifty years later it turns out he's not ruthless enough.'

'For what?'

'To find out where the Suprema greenlanded my son Santí. Not that I didn't try, back in '97–8. But when it was obvious I wasn't ruthless enough to get anywhere, we had us a Movers and Shakers meeting – stormy? don't ask! – and found someone that was.'

He'd lost me. 'Was what?'

'Capable of getting to Santí before he started talking. Because sooner or later the Suprema can break anybody. But so far that kid of mine, Jesus! You got to hand it to him. Five years in a dungeon and still holding out. Not word one, according to our moles inside the Holy Office. Anyway, there was just one person ruthless enough, so I delegated myself to go down to La Rábida to tell her, and ever since, she has been in charge of the operation to find where they greenlanded my boy Santí.'

'Petenera?' I gasped, almost forgetting my new-found serenity.

Santangel shook his head in mute, urgent warning, then did his usual paranoid production with doors and windows, locks and bolts. 'Don't even mention her name out loud,' he said.

'She's looking for Santí?'

He just nodded. I knew I would have to sort out this 'ruthless' business later.

Santangel looked at the butt of his cigar, decided it had outlived its usefulness and ground it under his heel.

While he went through the ritual of lighting a new one, his mood swung. Expansively he asked, 'So what do you think of the great new colonial fleet they're sending out next year?'

'They didn't mention anything about it.'

'No? This will be a whole new game of pelota in the Indies trade, the big push to make it a real New Spain over there, the colonial equivalent of total war. Twenty-five, maybe thirty ships. Three or four thousand colonists. It's history, kid. We're lucky to be living in times like this, despite everything.'

'When do they expect me to take command?' I asked. Never mind serenity. My heart was racing, my mouth was dry. I could see that fleet already, stretching from horizon to horizon.

Santangel saw the tile floor, because that's where he was looking. 'I hate to be the one to tell you, kid. But they've included you out. Antonio Torres already got the nod as captain-general.'

Now it was my turn to stare at the floor. I don't know what I was looking for. My serenity, maybe.

'It's tough, kid, but you've had a good run. So don't let the nostalgia trap get you,' Santangel advised.

But he didn't understand. Sometimes I was even nostalgic for places I'd never seen. This was hardly your ordinary variety of nostalgia.

Not that nostalgia was the issue here. The issue was being passed over, learning what it meant to be a has-been.

Santangel apparently didn't think so. Or he wanted me to think he didn't. 'This doesn't mean you're all washed up. You are definitely not in that category. At all. Don't tell me you think the commander of that fleet's got more clout than the Admiral of the Ocean Sea?'

'That's only an honorific now. Same as Viceroy.'

'My ass it is. How do you think they're going to fill those colonial rosters?'

I didn't follow.

'I don't follow,' I said.

'That Margarit everybody keeps knocking down, and that Bernal de

Pisa and them, they've been bad-mouthing the Indies for years. What's needed is somebody to drum up enthusiasm for the colonial life. And who better than the Admiral of the Ocean Sea himself? You're going on the leather chicken circuit, kid.' (Rubber hadn't been discovered yet.) 'Expect riches. I'll get the legendary Colón the fattest lecture fees ever, plus a percentage of the gate. I'll make you a wealthy man yet.'

He lit a third cigar and with it went through another mood swing. Now his eyes were as bleak as northern seas on a gray winter day, Thorshaven eyes. 'That boy of mine, how long can he hold out? It's superhuman, what he's doing. This is the greatest unsung hero in the history of Spain. Well, she'll find him.' He studied the glowing end of his new cigar. 'They burned her whole family at the stake, not counting the kid brother you lost at Christmas Town, and they gave her a sample of their torture mill in Toledo. She's ruthless enough. Oh, she'll find him,' Santangel said confidently – but I saw tears in his eyes.

I asked, 'What happens when she does?'

A gloomy cloud of smoke. A long silence. And: 'I thought you understood. The whole point of finding Santí is to kill him.'

Downriver from Sevilla at Sanlúcar the great fleet assembled – five huge carracks, twenty-four caravels, three *barcos*, upwards of 1,000 men to crew them, 3,000 colonists including several hundred women and twelve Franciscan friars (nominated by Brother Buil, alas) to help Brother Ramón Pane, horses, cattle, swine, goats, even luxuries for the ladies like bolts of real silk, lace mantillas, ostrich plumes, leather fans, ivory fans, scented fans. There were three large sea chests crammed with books (including several copies of *La Celestina*, the first novel ever written, very much in demand, as good novels always would be). This was no mere fleet; it was a whole world afloat.

Sailing day found me on the quarterdeck of the flagship *Bonanza* as Captain-General Antonio Torres's guest.

For one awkward moment I took my accustomed stance and reached for a shroud as I squinted eagle-eyed out to sea, but I checked myself in time, withdrawing my hand the instant before Antonio Torres took *his* stance and grasped the same shroud.

Just then another man, red-faced and corpulent, wearing an astonishing uniform of black (it had caught on as the New Century's fashionable color for both sexes) with white facings and enough gold braid for an entire navy, appeared on the quarterdeck.

Antonio Torres beamed at us both. 'Governor,' he said, 'it's my honor to present you to the man who, as everyone knows, made all this possible.' Here Antonio Torres let go the shroud to sweep his arm slowly in the general direction of everywhere. 'Admiral Colón, Governor Ovando.'

This Ovando, during the introductions, was looking at the binnacle as if he had never seen a binnacle before. He was also smoothing out a few score loops of gold braid. Here was a fellow very much into self-esteem.

'In fact,' went on Torres, 'it would be no overstatement to say the Admiral taught me all I know about the Ocean Sea.'

The governor turned with one of those self-absorbed smiles that make people look near-sighted. 'A pleasure, Captain Pinzón,' he said, confusing me for some reason with Vicente Yáñez Pinzón, original captain of *Niña* and now Number One of the new crop of explorers, the man who would shortly discover the Amazon River, not that the governor seemed the sort who could figure that out in advance.

Torres looked at me uncomfortably but, wrapped in my new serenity, I just smiled. 'Governor Ovando,' the captain-general explained, 'is replacing Governor Bobadilla, who is being recalled for malfeasance.'

My smile, I have to admit, broadened.

'The pleasure is mine, Viceroy,' I said, throwing in the exalted title to prove to myself I felt no resentment.

'Not Viceroy,' Ovando corrected me in a severe tone. 'Governor. The honorific of Viceroy's been retired with that has-been Colón fellow, my dear Captain Pinzón.'

I shrugged this off serenely. Ovando smoothed his gold braid. Torres said, 'You know, Admiral, I got every top officer I wanted except one. The captain I wanted most turned me down.'

'Oh? Who was that?'

'That brilliant youngster Terreros. Said he wouldn't cross the Ocean Sea except under your command. Also said – ' here Antonio Torres gave me a quizzical look ' – he expected to be crossing before the year was out.'

'Not with me. My sailing days are over,' I said, and it hardly hurt at all.

'Well, you are carrying a bit of spare blubber amidships – '

'The leather chicken circuit,' I explained, embarrassed.

' – but otherwise you look shipshape to me. Who knows? Terreros could be right.'

We both smiled. Antonio Torres was pleased with his own tact, and I with Pedro Terreros's faith in me. But it gave me, despite my new serenity, the suggestion of a colón bean in my throat. So I quickly took my leave of Torres and his officers, wished the new, glitteringly gold-braided governor luck, and left the flagship.

Ten minutes later I was astride a sorrel mare and galloping hard for Dog Point, the landspit at the mouth of the Guadalquivir where, thinking nostalgic thoughts, I could get a final look at the great fleet as it put to sea. Low clouds were scudding in and I could see squall lines to the south. At the tip of Dog Point a horse was browsing on the salt-marsh grass and a lone figure, black cape ballooning in the wind, stood gazing upriver where the vanguard of the fleet could just be seen.

I set my mare to browse, a bit concerned about the stranger's stallion. But it only looked up, gave a single loud whinny, and resumed browsing.

At the sound, the stranger with whom I shared the lonely landspit turned.

The wind blew her cowl back to expose the vivid comet streak of white in that hair black as the space between the stars on a clear night at sea.

She cried, 'But – but you're with the fleet there! So how can you be here? Watching yourself leave.'

She came running into my arms. We clung and kissed. She was crying. Tears sprang to my tearless eyes.

After rather a lot of this it was raining very hard and the first squadron of ships went by, all but unseen.

She said breathlessly, 'I knew you were going around recruiting for the biggest colonial fleet in history – in fact I know how marvelously many of our New Christians you managed to get included, darling, and barely in time too – so naturally I assumed you'd be in command and I just had to see you off even if you wouldn't know except for – '

For the second time in as many hours I heard myself say, 'No, my sailing days are over.' And then I kissed her again, gently. The rain pelted us. Fog rolled in from the sea and there was no Torres fleet.

We clung and stroked and squeezed and hugged and kissed less gently and then not gently at all and somewhere in there I said, 'I love you, Petenera,' and she said, 'I love you too, Cristóbal, I never stopped,' in a voice made flat and disembodied by the fog.

After a while she began to laugh. 'Who *is* the admiral of the fleet?' she asked.

'He's a captain-general — Antonio Torres.'

'I wonder — ' more laughter ' — what he'll think when he finds three perfect — ' more kisses ' — blue pimpernels on his bunk? God, what a day! What an unbelievable, glorious, magnificent day!'

It was, of course, pouring. Which I pointed out.

'What a wonderful rain. I've never seen a rain quite exactly like it before, have you, darling?'

This, obviously, was a woman in love.

We found an inn near the center of Sanlúcar, low, rambling, whitewashed, and by the time we stabled our horses the clouds were breaking, the sun had emerged, and a perfect rainbow spanned the sky. Brilliant purple bougainvillaea should have been cascading down those whitewashed walls, but bougainvillaea still waited undiscovered on the islands of an unknown sea. An *allée* of stately eucalyptus trees would have been nice too, but they were also undiscovered on the other side of the world, sheltering in their branches undiscovered koala bears. You can't have everything.

We had each other, and that should have been enough.

Our second evening together, wandering hand in hand through Sanlúcar's narrow streets, we heard gypsy music and, following it to its source, found a mean little bodega near the waterfront.

'Let's,' she said.

'You'll be the only woman in there.'

'So?'

As we entered, a guitarist struck a mournful chord and we heard from a leathery-skinned old gypsy the abrupt but prolonged wail of despair that precedes true deep song. Another mournful chord on the guitar, while every pair of eyes in that den of thieves fastened on Petenera. Then suddenly my love and the music fused into one, for the gypsy sang:

> Who called you Petenera?
>   Your lovely name's a lie.
> You should be called Perdition —
>   Men love you but to die.

'Take me out of here.'

I looked at her haunted eyes and hurried outside with her.

Later she stood pensively at the window of our room gazing out at the rising moon. The bed was still warm, still fragrant with the scent of her. I got up and stood behind her and slid my hands around her to cup those flawless breasts like chalices of ivory. Then she turned into my arms and I carried her back to bed. She made love this time with all the shy wonder of a virgin, as if by some secret alchemy she had eradicated ten years and all the men from her life, as if now not her name but the song was a lie, and yet as if she knew this would be the last time, and presenting me with her born-again virginity was her way of saying goodbye. In the moonlight streaming through the open shutters I saw tears in those incredible emerald-green eyes. I kissed the saltiness on her cheeks. She pulled me close and for a long moment wouldn't let go. Then she said, 'I have to leave now,' and her voice was so cool, so remote, it could have belonged to the moonlight.

In disbelief I watched her calmly start to dress.

'Petenera, what in God's name – '

'I'm no good for you, Cristóbal. Can't you understand? You're better off without me.'

'Without you? This is the first day I've felt whole since we were together at La Rábida. I'm in love with you, Petenera.'

'I don't deserve your love. And even if I did, love is something I can't allow myself now.'

'Petenera, it's just a song. Surely you don't believe – '

'It won't do any good to talk about it.'

But she agreed finally to share a last jug of wine with me. We crossed the moonlit courtyard to the inn's wine room. A sleepy barman brought a jug of rough red to our table.

We raised our cups.

For a long time neither of us spoke.

Then I said, 'It's young Santangel, isn't it?'

'Yes, but not in the way you think.'

'His father told me what you – have to do.'

I touched her hand on the table. It was ice. She seemed to stare past me into another place, another time. 'That song,' she said. 'Santí used to sing it to me. Said it *was* me.'

'Santí and you were – '

'He idolized my brother Luís, and then Luís had to go away and he idolized me. I was the big sister. And then inevitably Santí had to see me as the Older Woman.' She tried a smile that almost worked. 'He wanted me to be a *femme fatale* so he could be a tragic young lover. He wanted to believe that song. And, in a way, that's how it turned out for him, isn't it? Because, except for me, he'd be a rising young courtier now, wouldn't he? But instead I got him involved ... And now the

Inquisition...' Her voice faltered. This time her hand sought mine on the table. 'His father and the others – they wanted to send the most ruthless person in Spain. And they sent me.'

'Petenera,' I began gently, 'it's not because you're ruthless but because you're the one who – '

But my words were like an improvised melody plucked from a guitar and they stopped in mid-thought, going nowhere.

The one who what? Loved him like a sister? Let him love her? So she could kill him more easily, because after his years in a Suprema dungeon it would be an act of mercy?

'You were always going away,' she said suddenly. 'Your life was there, and mine was here. Should I have gone on just being a big sister to Santí? Should I have refused Medinaceli? Or the others – ? You weren't here. You *weren't here*.'

'All that's going to change. I told you, my sailing days are over.'

We were alone except for the sleepy barman and a black cat that rubbed against Petenera's leg, arching its back and purring.

'Yes, everything's going to change,' she said softly. 'You won't be sailing – and I won't be looking for Santí any longer.'

For an instant my heart sang. 'Because you can't bring yourself to do it?'

'Because they've got him hidden too well. And because he's already told the Suprema enough to blow half our networks in Spain.'

The song in my heart died a sudden, dissonant death. 'You mean they've broken him?'

'Five years. Five years in solitary confinement it took, and God knows how many days of torture.' In her bleak voice I could discern a stubborn note of pride.

I drained my wine and poured another cup.

'But if they did break him,' I asked, 'then where are you going? What can you possibly hope to accomplish now?'

Her head came up. Her eyes narrowed to green fire. 'Everything,' she said. 'Because Santí's not going to suffer anymore, and neither is anybody else. They've agreed to wait.'

'The Suprema? But if Santí talked, why would they – '

She leaned across the table toward me, her sleeve brushing my wine cup.

'Because our old friend Brother Buil is eager to make an exchange.'

I just looked at her.

'And so am I.'

I drank my second cup of wine down to the bitter dregs of what I refused to understand. 'An exchange?' I asked.

I think I would have guessed before she spoke but suddenly I saw two Peteneras, both insubstantial, blurry-edged. Everywhere else I looked was blackness. The cat jumped on my lap. Clumsily I knocked over my empty wine cup. I tried to reach out to touch her, but I could not move my arm.

'Because Buil says we have unfinished business, he and I. They'll trade Santí – for me.'

She got up. I tried to. She came around the table like a refraction of herself, eerie in the darkness, the double image coalescing. Her fingers touched my cheek lingeringly. I could not move. She kissed my lips. I could not move. The black cat leaped to her shoulder. I could not move. She turned, and looked back once at me, and turned again. My head hit the table.

The next afternoon in Sevilla, where the Peripatetic Royal Court was currently in residence, Espina de Chopito told me, 'You'll have to wait. He's convened an emergency session of the Movers and Shakers.'

I was doing some shaking myself. Whatever Petenera had put in my wine still hadn't entirely worn off. I had to concentrate to see a single solid Espina de Chopito. After a while I gave that up and slumped in my chair and let my head spin.

A hand shook me. I could smell the cigar smoke. Luís de Santangel looked beside himself. But then so did Chopito. I blinked hard. Santangel still looked like that.

'We had a meeting,' he said in a voice so matter-of-fact you had to know something was terribly wrong. His left eyebrow was going up and down, up and down. 'The Movers and Shakers.'

'I know. Chopito told me.'

'"The Blue Pimpernel," I informed them, "is willing to make a trade. Herself in exchange for Santí."'

'I know. She told me.'

He accepted this with a shrug and continued his story:

'"What?" they cried. "How can this be?"

'It couldn't be, I told them. "It was Brother Buil who suggested the exchange," I explained, "so I don't trust it. I don't trust anything about it." You can bet this was torturing me, kid. Here was a chance to get the son and heir out alive. But why would they do this? What was in it for the Suprema if they already had my boy's confession? Or

495

worse, if she agreed to the exchange, what was to stop them from keeping the confession *and* my boy Santí *and* the Blue Pimpernel? So I said, destroying myself in the process, "We have to let them kill him." Santí – flesh of my flesh!

'Well, the most cold-blooded Mover and Shaker agreed with me. He was also the dumbest, and they immediately told him to shut up.

'"Shut up and let us figure this out," they told him,' Santangel told me.

'This was not at all the usual procedure, and I objected. Not on behalf of the dope but on behalf of me. "I've got more to say," I told them.

'They said, "Shut up and let us figure this out."

'They! Said that to me! And for the first time ever, I did.'

Santangel looked haggard. His eyebrow was jumping furiously.

'What happened?' I asked.

'"Buil's willing to trade Santí," they asked me, "for the Blue Pimpernel? You're sure?"

'"That's the message he sent her," I said, "but like I told you, it's a trick."

'"But they already have Santí and his confession, naming names, blowing everything wide open. The Blue Pimpernel's got to have something up her sleeve. So if they want to make a trade – what have we got to lose?" they asked me.

'"The Blue Pimpernel," I said, "is what we have to lose. So the answer is no."

'"The answer," said the dumbbell, "is definitely no," but they hooted him down.

'They were sad when they looked at me. Believe me, kid, I was sadder. "You want to let your own son die instead of making a trade for him?" they asked me.

'"That's the way it has to be," I explained.

'They went into a huddle. And in this gentle kind of a chorus, not meeting my eyes, as you can believe, they said, "Chinillo is wrong."

'I couldn't believe my ears. I just looked from face to face and saw the same verdict on all but the dope's.

'Then they said, "Chinillo's absolutely wrong."

'This is their new formula to adjourn a meeting.'

His cigar had gone dead in his face. A long shuddering sigh issued from his mouth. 'What can I tell you, kid?'

'You can tell me how to find her.'

'But I can't. From now on our liaison with her won't report to me

496

but to them. The Movers and Shakers have been easing me out ever since Santí was greenlanded. Today was the end. My moving and shaking days are over.'

My old friend looked at his dead cigar. Then he stared into his own future, seeing nothing.

'Be gentle with him,' I told Espina de Chopito, but he was already cleaning out his desk when I left to find Pighi-Zampini.

The old banker had set up his makeshift benches, his scales and packing crates in the back room of the public scribes' open shop near the Tower of Gold on the riverside promenade that would one day be called Paseo Cristóbal Colón – in retrospect a good sign.

But he wasn't there.

'Who are you?' I asked the rabbity-faced boy of nineteen or twenty seated at one of the benches.

'Pighi-Zampini the international financial wheeler-dealer,' he said.

'The hell you are.'

'You must be looking for Grandfather. He's breaking me in. Can't go on forever, you know.'

'Where is he?'

'He won't be back from Córdoba till Thursday at the earliest.'

It was Friday before he came bustling in past the six scribes busily writing letters for illiterates. He glanced at his gold portable clock. His eyes sparkled and all his bristles were bristling.

'Young man!' he cried. 'What a pleasure!' Less pleased, he asked, 'The little snot-nose been telling you I can't go on forever? Not that he isn't right. I am slowing down a bit. All this peripatting around, a man my age. Which is eighty-seven. And a half. You're looking a little along in years yourself, young man – that must have been some drug she put in your wine.'

This latest example of his omniscience was decidedly encouraging.

'What happened to her?' I asked. 'Did she do it – go ahead with the exchange?'

'She most certainly did,' said Pighi-Zampini. He looked at his rabbity-faced grandson. 'Go eat lunch,' he said, and the boy left. 'The reason I happen to know, I brokered it.'

'You were working for Buil?' I asked coldly.

'Please! Young man, make some sense. You know where my sympathies lie, or you wouldn't have sent me that S.O.S. when you sailed from Sanlúcar. But I work for nobody. I just know everything about everybody and sooner or later they all have to come to me. Now I have transcripts of Santí Santangel's confession *and* Buil's confession

– the only copy except the Blue Pimpernel's. Quite a nice addition to my archives.'

'Buil's confession?' I almost asked, 'How can this be?' But then the import of his words really hit me. 'The Blue Pimpernel's copy, you said – she's all right?'

'That girl,' said Pighi-Zampini, 'is going to take a lot of killing,' and I could have cried with relief.

'Where is she?'

'All I know, she left the rendezvous with Santí Santangel in a Hungarian coach – they're all over the roads these days, you know – hell-bent for somewhere.'

'If you know everything about everybody, how come you don't know where they went?'

'Young man – ' testily ' – I am who I am but I am definitely not God. But I can tell you this: she is definitely all right. He is definitely not all right.'

'But ... what ... happened?'

'What happened,' said Pighi-Zampini, 'was the sweetest trap ever sprung. Right here in Sevilla – on the wrong side of the river in Triana where gypsies are beginning to settle. Buil brought a dozen body-guards, all heavily armed.'

'God!'

'Relax, young man. She had a hit team of twenty. Young New Christian hotheads, half of them, the other half gypsies. Even more heavily armed. They took Buil over there in Triana to a location, the name of which I would rather not recall, and – are you sure you want to hear all this?'

I grabbed two frail shoulders and shook them as I fervently assured him I wanted to.

My new serenity, so carefully nurtured, had finally deserted me. Just as well. What's so great about being serene?

'To begin with,' Pighi-Zampini began, 'Brother Buil was serenity itself. He was, from his viewpoint, wearing the white hat. But then ...'

Then two blank-faced gypsies shoved the plump, brown-robed Brother Buil down the cellar stairs. He descended precipitately, bumping alternate sides of the stairwell. Torches spaced around its rough stone walls lighted the cellar. What Buil might at first have taken for a hangman's noose dangled from the ceiling.

'When you have to improvise,' Petenera explained, 'the easiest Inquisition device to approximate is the strappado.'

'I can see that, yes,' Brother Buil smiled reasonably.

No one had hurt him yet. He probably could not believe anyone would. What purpose could it possibly serve?

The strappado was hardly more than a rope and a pulley, but the rope was stout enough to support stout Brother Buil when dangling by his wrists. With his arms behind his back. With or without weights suspended from his feet.

Petenera invited him to confess.

'My dear woman, I have my own confessor who shrives me regularly.' Brother Buil's smile was now condescending.

It is interesting to note that the hotheaded New Christian members of Petenera's hit team waited outside on sentry duty. Her torture attendants were all gypsies. One theory is that the New Christians would have been loath to hurt a man in clerical robes, but this cannot be substantiated.

'Strip him,' said Petenera to her gypsies.

Soon Buil was standing pinkly, doughily naked and trying to cover his private parts with plump, dimpled hands.

'Raise the object,' Petenera told her gypsies.

Buil was beginning to shiver with cold. Or perhaps the word 'object', so common in any Inquisition dungeon, triggered the first stage of his fear.

'Did you say "object"?' he inquired.

By then his wrists were bound behind his back, and up he went with a creaking of the pulley as the gypsies tugged on the free end of the rope.

Whether the sound Buil made was a laugh or a scream is difficult to say.

'Here are the terms we're prepared to offer you,' Petenera said.

Buil laughed and laughed or screamed and screamed.

'You go free. Santiago Santangel goes free. You keep his confession provided – '

'That is already,' laughed or screamed Brother Buil, 'out of my hands.'

'But what use is made of it, is that out of your hands too?'

No answer. A smug, if pained, smile.

'Drop the object.'

The pulley screamed (or laughed) and down plunged Buil, his feet almost reaching the floor as the rope paid out all the way and stopped his fall with a jerk that dislocated both his shoulders. Without any weights on his feet. Whatsoever.

His laughter, if it was that, was really something then.

'Raise the object.'

When an object with already dislocated shoulders is raised on the strappado, even a jury-rigged strappado, the effect is enhanced.

'Object, listen to me. You keep the Santangel confession. And we keep yours.'

'I have confessed to nothing.'

'Drop him.'

This sequence was repeated several more times. With increasingly heavy weights suspended from the object's feet.

Eventually, Brother Bernardo Buil signed a confession incorporating the following points:

(1) That Bernardo Buil did at various times and in various Inquisition dungeons commit acts of aggravated fornication upon various female detainees. (*Why Buil considered 'aggravated fornication' a term of lesser opprobrium than 'rape' is not recorded.*)

(2) That Bernardo Buil did at various times and in various villages on the island of Hispaniola commit acts of bestiality with various Indian maidens, many under the age of ten.

Q: Why bestiality? Do you mean you buggered them?

A: I mean *beast*iality, since these sexual acts were not performed with humans.

(3) That Bernardo Buil answered unsatisfactorily the two standard questions asked by Inquisitors at each initial interview (*although in the case of Bernardo Buil it was the only interview, and already well advanced*):

(a) Q: (*when revived by the attending physician, not for the first time*) Do you believe in God?

A: Good God, what a question!

Q: We are talking about the conventional model – Father, Son, Holy Ghost.

A: (*Here Buil may well have spoken from his deepest conviction because he assumed, despite assurances, that he would shortly be killed.*) Oh, that God. If the truth be known, I have always considered Him somewhat simplistic and, well, common. Not so vulgar as the Devil, perhaps, especially the conventional Devil, but if less vulgar then also less interesting and decidedly less powerful. Altogether an inferior figure to worship. It would be extremely difficult, however, to convert the masses to Devil-worship, and even if we could, a whole new complex of heresies would have to be codified. It simply isn't worth the bother.

(b) Q: We live in an age when secular humanists are demanding that our nation divest itself of religion. A cacophony of voices — the printing press, the universities, scientists snooping into God's secrets, explorers going where God never meant them to go — undermine the very moral and spiritual bedrock from which Spain became a great nation. True or false?

A: What a very devil of a question.

Q: Answer.

A: I think I already have. For if it would be difficult to convert from the worship of a simplistic triune deity to a sophisticated Devil, think how much more difficult it would be to start from scratch with a nation divested of both God and the Devil. As to the second part of your question, if it is a question, they unquestionably do.

Q: True, then?

A: No, false. (*There is considerable uncertainty regarding Buil's meaning at this point in the interrogation.*)

He signed his confession twenty-four hours after arriving in Triana. An exchange of prisoners was effected at midnight the following (foggy) night at the exact middle of the (temporarily closed) Triana bridge. It was agreed that if any Suprema activities indicated use of material from the Santiago Santangel confession, an equivalent amount of material would be released from the Bernardo Buil confession.

The limping, wraithlike figure of Santiago Santangel was helped into a waiting Hungarian coach — Petenera was already inside — and off it went.

'But where,' Pighi-Zampini said, 'I don't have the faintest idea. Spain's a big country.'

'Surely with your connections you can find out.'

Here Pighi-Zampini impatiently consulted his gold portable clock. He had never been impatient with me before. 'I told you all I know.'

'I've got to find her.'

'I wouldn't. If I were you.'

His advice was irrelevant. I didn't know where to start.

I took rooms on San Fernando Street off the Alcázar Gardens not far from the world's biggest Gothic cathedral. Once I went in and lit a candle in the royal chapel behind the high altar. At first I didn't know why. And then I did. With my candle I hoped to call God's attention to the fact (if God attended to mundane facts these days) that Brother Bernardo Buil was no worshipper of his. I thought God would have liked knowing that. I know I did. Of such bits of information can faith be rekindled, and who could say what the state of God's faith in mankind was?

That was the only act of consequence I performed between February and April.

If you ever hear someone forced into retirement utter the words, 'I'm keeping busy,' be kind to that person. For there are no words more self-denigrating, more hopeless, no words more obviously one ghastly grin this side of terminal despair.

But that's what I told people when I met them in the street. A variation was, 'Oh, I try to keep my hand in.'

I learned to play chess and let Luís de Santangel beat me at it. I saw Fat Ferdy occasionally and Little D often.

Fat Ferdy began asking me about my youth, as if he knew he would some day write that biography I don't recommend. 'Well,' I would say, in answer to some question, 'I was even younger than you, son, when I first went to sea.' This wasn't strictly true. In fact, it was strictly false. I also said, 'But I interrupted my seafaring to study classics and cosmology at the University of Pavia.' This wasn't any more accurate. But when all a person can do, most days, is try to keep busy, a person will often embellish past exploits. It is possible I gave Fat Ferdy some wrong notions, but he asked at a bad time.

Little D, twenty-one and an officer in the Queen's Guard, became (now that Luís de Santangel was also keeping busy) my man at Court. And a good one. Lower-key than Santangel but firm in standing up for my rights. Not to mention his own. Admiral of the Ocean Sea was a hereditary title, after all, and would be his after I died. I thought of death a lot. That's an indication you're not trying hard enough to keep busy.

Little D was, as Antonio Torres's sister had observed the year before, quite a hunk of man – tall, with that thatch of red hair, those steely blue eyes, and that saddle of freckles across his proud prow of a nose. Who did he remind me of?

He had lots of girls, all of them artistic. I never could remember their names, but I remember the artists'. One girl, seventeen or so, was a sultry brunette who could have stepped right out of Goya's 'Maja Vestida', had Goya been alive and painting in my day. Another of his artistic beauties, a little younger, had red-gold hair and a fuller figure, of the sort already romping across the canvases of Titian. There was also a peaches-and-cream blonde, *zaftig*, who might have been a premature Rubens.

He was with the Goya when he told me, 'You know, Papa, the royals are willing to charter another voyage of discovery – as long as you steer clear of Hispaniola.'

My heart rattled the bars of my ribcage at the thought of being bound away once more. But, 'No,' I said with my keeping-busy smile, 'my sailing days are over.'

He was with the Titian when, seeing how well I was keeping busy, he suggested, 'Why don't you write your memoirs, Papa?'

It was a brilliant idea and I went right out and bought a lot of paper and many quill pens and a large jar of ink. I began to write, 'I was born here in Sevilla fifty-one years ago of New Christian parents. My father's name was Domingo, my mother's Susanna. My father was a weaver by trade. I had an older brother, Bartolomé, who would be called Bartolomeo and eventually Barto. The family left Spain on a roundship bound for Genoa the year I was born and – '

And I stopped writing. Just like that. Never touched it after my initial effort. It lacked pizazz. I wasn't ready or something.

I told Little D (he was with a Botticelli, all ethereal curves): 'A man shouldn't write the story of his life until it's all over. And then of course it's too late.'

'Well, why don't you take up a hobby then? It will give you something to do.'

I walked a lot, especially in the former Judería, trying to find where my parents might have lived, but it was now a fashionable neighborhood, with upwardly mobile young couples moving in and changing things. I slept a lot. Sleeping is a good way of keeping busy if you can't think of anything else to do.

One night I had another of those Chinese box dreams. At first I tried to call it off, saying, 'I'll keep busy in my own way, thanks,' but that rarely works with dreams.

So there I was – or there he was, the giant mired in the streambed of my original St Christopher dream – shouting just one forlorn protest in the direction the kid had disappeared, then dozing with his chin resting on the surface of the water and dreaming his box-in-a-box dream about Herne the Hunter. At this point I got interested.

Some years after fleeing the sight of what I now regard as my signature, Herne (that is, I) returns to the monastery of St Albans. He's got to talk to the monk Roger Wendover, got to find out more about Pontius Pilate's doorkeeper, doomed to wander — was there something about off time's map? — forever.

Herne enters the monastery grounds just in time to join the funeral procession of poor Roger Wendover. He stands sadly over the grave marker, confirming the date estimate for my previous St Albans dream.

Roger Wendover

1187–1236

R.I.P.

Herne crosses himself and goes inside.

The new chronicler of St Albans, one Matthew Paris, remembers him, and Herne is given his old job as handyman.

And also the opportunity to watch the new historian Matthew Paris at work. This is a much more rational sort of fellow, both feet planted firmly on the ground, than his predecessor. Deficient in imagination but not in energy, he reads through all of Roger Wendover's chronicles, shaking his head often in exasperation.

He is, Herne thinks with dismay, going to bowdlerize them. Bowdlerize, of course, is not the word in Herne's mind, since six centuries would pass before Bowdler eviscerated Shakespeare. But still Herne understands the spirit in which Matthew Paris is going to expurgate the inexplicable from Roger Wendover's chronicles.

First thing excised is my — or, that is, Cartaphilus's — signature. 'Wonder where he got that henscratch?' mutters Matthew Paris. 'Embarrassingly childish.'

Second is the phrase 'off the map of time.'

Paris shakes his head. 'Not even a good paradox. Just a silly word play.'

Third is a short list of names at which Herne hears Matthew Paris complain, 'Surely the old fool didn't mean to suggest the Armenian actually knew the names of those to come who ... poor Wendover! Definitely round the bend.'

The legend of Cartaphilus is otherwise left pretty much intact.

Over the years, Herne observes, the St Albans copyists have made six copies. All are consigned to the fire. Matthew Paris is writing his censored version from the original, and the night he finishes — the morning, actually, almost sunrise — he blows out the candles and falls asleep at the table. Herne stands watching a long time. A pale dawn

504

creeps in at the window. Herne ponders. I know what he's thinking. *Take it*, I urge him in the dream. *Go on, take it.* He picks up the original chronicle. Puts it down again. *Take it!* I urge him. And he does.

Takes it, tucks it under his arm and leaves St Albans heading in the general direction of Oxford.

And the dreaming giant stirs.

And so do I, thinking: except for the original stolen by Herne, there'd be no signature of Cartaphilus that I've long since co-opted as my own, and no suggestion that one can escape time's map, as I did in my Julian decade — and no list of names. Which I didn't get to see anyway. And as I think of those dream-things, I lose them. They just slip right out of my mind, and if anyone were to ask me about that signature I could look him straight in the eye and say it was all my own idea. But a dream doesn't slip *out* of the mind, does it? It just burrows down deep.

Whatever, Herne is gone and maybe I won't have to fret anymore about somebody else taking over my dreams. This is not the way these things are supposed to be run. How about a little personal integrity here?

Well, it was only a dream.

Early in April a letter from La Rábida came. I recognized Big D's childlike handwriting at once, and even though my kid brother never wrote the world's most stimulating letter, I opened it right away because I hadn't planned anything special to keep me busy that afternoon.

Dear Cristóbal,

I'm still trying to make up my mind — should I take Holy Orders or shouldn't I? I like it here at La Rábida and your old friend Fray Juan Pérez is all for it, but it's a pretty big decision to make, and I guess there's no hurry. Maybe in another year or two, when I've seen a bit more of the monastic life and all, I'll be ready to think about making a decision.

A funny thing happened last week. I accidentally disturbed the monastic tranquility around here. At the back of the monastery's property, hidden in a thick stand of pine trees, is this little stone cottage. Well, I wandered back there, I think it was Wednesday last. Just when I was coming within sight of the cottage, I saw this lady in the pine woods, and then a few big monks, tough-looking fellows, which is unusual for La Rábida, came running at me and hustled me back to the monastery. Fray Juan Pérez tells me I must forget what I saw and tell no one. But I guess writing to you about it is okay because you're not no one, you're my brother and his old friend. Anyway, here's the funny part. Remember that time you and that old man in the Hungarian coach I was driving rescued that beautiful lady from that place in Toledo? Well, at first I thought it was the same lady I saw in the woods there. But it wasn't. The way I could tell was, this beautiful lady outside the stone cottage in the pine woods at the back of La Rábida had a white streak in her hair, otherwise as black as the underside of a raven's wing, and the one that time in Toledo didn't have the white streak. So it was a different lady after all.

I dropped Big D's letter and ran outside and across the Alcázar Gardens to the royal stables.

Fray Juan Pérez asked hopefully, 'Is it your brother you've come to visit?'

'I've come for Petenera.'

'I was afraid of that.' The prior of La Rábida sighed. 'She is not the first we have given sanctuary from the Suprema and she will not be the last. Which makes us guilty of the worst heresy of all – impeding the work of the Holy Office. But things have come to such a pass, I truly believe that by impeding their work we are doing God's.'

He joined me at the window. There was no wind and the mouth of the Río Tinto far below was glassy calm under a blue sky.

I said, unable to hide my impatience, 'Is she all right?'

'*She*'s fine.' He added thoughtfully, 'But she's changed. It was a long time she spent searching for him, knowing if she found him she must kill him. And when she devised a better plan, it seemed so unlikely that even the boy's own father opposed it. But she did it, and his life was like a gift from God. Not to him, to her. Because she didn't have to kill after all.' He stared out to sea. 'They were wrong about her, you know. She is capable of ruthless acts, yes. But also of great selflessness. Well, you'll see, my friend.'

I saw.

As I hurried alone through the pine woods I heard La Rábida's monks singing the great Canticle to the Sun, composed by St Francis himself. The words followed me toward the cottage where I would find her.

> Be Thou praised, my Lord, with all Thy creatures,
>   above all Brother Sun, who gives the day ...
> Be Thou praised, my Lord, of Sister Moon and the stars ...
>   of Brother Wind ...

And finally, faint behind me as I plunged deep into the woods, a single clear tenor voice brought back a ruined fortress high on a rocky island in a cold northern sea:

> Be praised, Lord, for our Sister Death
>   from whom no man can escape.

Three hooded figures watching from the deep shadows of the pines disappeared with scarcely a sound as I approached the cottage. Except for the blue haze of hearth smoke, it could have been deserted. I knocked, and knocked again when there was no answer. I went to the windows, but they were shuttered. The stable was empty. When I returned to the front of the cottage she was just coming out, saying reassuringly, 'There's nothing to be afraid of, dear. He's a friend.' Then the door shut and she was facing me. She wore black. That vivid comet streak in her hair looked silver in the sunlight. When I tried to kiss her she turned her face away.

Her green eyes were furious. 'Why'd you have to come here? Why? Do you think I liked leaving you, that night in Sanlúcar? Do you think it was easy for me?' she cried. 'Why do you have to make me live it all over again?'

'Petenera, this is no place for you. I want you to come away with me.'

'*You* want. And does it matter what *I* want, or that poor boy in there? Who'll take care of him if I go away with you?'

'His father will. Luís de Santangel's a rich man, and he's on the beach these days so he has a lot of time on his hands, and he loves his son. He'll see that he gets the best of care.'

'Santí doesn't need the father who wanted him killed, he needs me. Besides, he'll never feel safe as long as he's in Spain. They're making arrangements to send us to Italy.'

Her anger had faded while she spoke, but it was no sanctuary in Italy she saw with those now-wistful emerald-green eyes.

'You don't have to take him,' I said. 'His father would. So there's nothing to stop us from – '

'Don't. Please don't say any more. You'll only make it harder.'

But I told her, 'Their Majesties will let me make one last voyage across the Ocean Sea, my son Diego is sure of it. This time you'll go with me. There's a land I've found, an Earthly Paradise, an other Eden. Who says we ever have to come back?'

She shut her eyes as if to make the impossible dream vanish. Or perhaps to keep it forever. I kissed the sad smile on her lovely mouth. For a long and, I sensed, final moment, she pressed me against the beautiful length of her body, and then she drew back, her hands on my shoulders, those eyes almost on a level with my own. 'I can't. I can't do it, Cristóbal,' she said.

'You can. If you want to you can.'

'Remember, when we were here together, I needed you so desperately that every time you went away I thought I'd die? I hated being dependent like that, no matter how I loved you.'

'Loved?'

'Oh, I still love you. That's not changed. But ... don't you see? What you were to me, that's what I am now to Santí ten times over. You picked me up when I was hurt, but Santí was more than hurt, he was shattered. You put me back together, but Santí can never be whole. You let me lean on you until I could stand, but there will never be a time when Santí can stand alone. He depends on me for everything. I have to take care of him. Have to and — and want to.'

'I can't let you throw your life away.'

'No? And if I went with you, would you take him with us? Because I can't leave him. I know what it feels like, that desperate panic when you think the one person who's your anchor has abandoned you. I'll never do that to Santí.'

'My God, Petenera, you don't owe him your whole life.'

'Don't I? I cost him his. But I don't think of it as an obligation, taking care of him. Truly. I never knew how much ... joy ... there could be in helping someone. One other human being. In being needed. Santí, he needs me in a way you never did. Really, I'm the lucky ... the luckiest ...'

Her eyes squeezed shut and she turned toward the cottage.

'Come,' she said, 'I want you to see him.' She called, 'It's all right, dear. You don't have to be afraid. He's an old friend. He's almost the best friend I have.'

The door opened a few suspicious inches and I could see him in profile, a man in his middle twenties, tall, with his father's strong features. But there was a look of childlike bewilderment in the one eye I could see.

'Have they come for me?' he asked. 'I never want to go back to that place. You promised.'

'It's all right, Santí. Admiral Colón's an old friend of your father's too.'

'The Admiral of the Ocean Sea, is that who you are, sir? Oh, sure, I heard of you.' Santí smiled at us both, impartially. The cadence of his speech was like a small child's. 'Did you really sail to the other side of the world?'

'Yes.'

'And bring back Indians and everything?'

'Yes.'

'I saw an Indian once,' he said. 'In Barcelona in the cathedral where he was baptized. He was the adopted son of the Admiral of the Ocean Sea. I remember it all so clearly.'

'But I'm – '

Petenera gave me a swift warning glance.

' – sure that you do,' I finished.

Santí by then must have been convinced that I meant him no harm, for he opened the door wider. The entire right side of his face was one terrible burn scar. The eye was gone. Even the socket was covered by scar tissue. He held out his hand and Petenera took it. Then he leaned toward her, trustingly, and with an overwhelming tenderness she kissed the mutilated side of his face.

I went from there without even stopping to see my brother.

That pure tenor voice had been singing of no man's death, nor any woman's, nor even of the death of love, not this time, but only of my *faege*, a fate that was of my own making after all, though I had not known it when I was young.

❧ XX ❧

The Whole Sick Syndrome
Takes On God

You could call this Ferdy's voyage and his chapter, but it would be misleading.

Not that the youngest of *Santa Maria*'s grommets wasn't a good sailor who stood his watches and spliced his lines, who sluiced and scrubbed his share of deck, who pumped out the bilges, turned the sandclock, wiped the slate clean for the pilot after the master's watch, helped set and strike sail, trimmed sheets, made chafing gear from old rope, doused pot island at night. Oh, he was a sailor all right, and never mind that he was the son of the Admiral of the Ocean Sea and captain-general of the fleet of four caravels that sailed from Cádiz on 9 May 1502, bound away for Cipango, Cathay and India via the Indies, if there was a passage through the islands and if we could find it.

Still, though this isn't his chapter, it begins with the youngest of *Santa Maria*'s grommets coming aft with his fat boy's waddle, well suited to a pitching deck, and munching on a slab of flat bread he has baked himself, Arab fashion, in the ashes of the firebox. It is 29 June and the fleet lies outside the mouth of the Ozama River waiting for the tide to turn so we can enter Santo Domingo harbor. I don't like the look of that oily swell rolling in from the southeast, nor of the cirrus clouds, insubstantial as spiderweb, coming high and fast from the same direction. Nor do I like the oppressive heaviness in the air that makes everyone's fuse short — and maybe explains the fatal pig-headedness of Governor Ovando. Least of all do I like that warning meteorological twinge in every joint in my body. So I've sent Captain Terreros of *Gallega* (yet another caravel of that name, as the flagship is another *Santa Maria*, but it's the same loyal Pedro Terreros who has made every voyage with me) — I've sent him in *Gallega*'s boat to get Governor Ovando's authorization to bring our four caravels in before the hurricane strikes. And also to urge Ovando, whose thirty ships are now gathered in Ozama mouth ready for the return voyage to Spain, to get his people ashore until the coming storm passes.

What Terreros won't mention is that I have strict orders from the royals to avoid Hispaniola on my outward voyage, except in case of emergency. Which means now.

There is, I think as Fat Ferdy approaches the quarterdeck with a 'good morning, Papa — I mean Admiral,' something both flattering and insulting about the royal injunction. Flattering because it accords me the stature almost of a deposed monarch who still might have followers in the Indies. But insulting because it implies I might exploit the situation. Don't they know me at all? I've had it with colonies — and colonists. Still, I can't help picturing Juan Niño of Moguer walking his canebrakes, that ferocious smile on his face. And Inocencia and little Yego — and a new baby sister maybe? And Dr Chanca bullying his patients as ever.

But all that's just nostalgia. It has nothing to do with colonies. If you get right down to it, these aren't colonists anyway, they're people. And even they pale beside the prospect of a voyage of discovery, four sleek caravels, 135 eager men and boys, most of them recruited for me in Palos and Huelva and Moguer by Pedro Terreros, to explore the unknown lands beyond Cuba and find, maybe, that passage west, all the way west this time, until west becomes East.

'You feel it?' I ask Captain Diego Tristán, who follows Fat Ferdy up the ladder to the quarterdeck. (Another Diego; sorry about that. I don't make these people up. They're real, and this one — *Santa Maria*'s captain — is named Diego Tristán.)

'Something's coming,' he says tersely, and casts his weather eye to the southeast. On the voyage over Tristán has struck me as a competent mariner who sails too much by the book, a sort of sea-going Juan Fonseca.

From *Bermuda*, lying perhaps a cable's length inshore, Barto hails us. Back from Africa just in time to join the fleet as second-in-command, my brother is no more captain of *Bermuda* than I am of *Santa María*. Now that we're both over fifty we're expected to let younger men command our ships. These captains – Terreros and Tristán, Porras of *Bermuda* and *Vizcaína*'s ebullient Genoese captain Fieschi – know we'll take over when the actual discovering begins. But meanwhile Barto, who devotes most of his attention to the three Irish wolfhounds kenneled aboard *Bermuda*, calls himself with a straight face the dog-handler. And I, who call myself Viceroy and Admiral of the Ocean Sea and Captain-General, am no busier.

Well, Barto hails us: 'Here comes Pedro, and it's not good news.'

How bad is evident when *Gallega*'s boat reaches *Santa María* and Pedro's head appears at the top of the ladder.

Have you ever known Pedro Terreros to lose his temper, this loyal steward turned ship's captain? Not in these pages. But now he's as red-faced as Governor Ovando. He shouts:

'Two months in Santo Domingo and already he knows more than God Almighty in holy Heaven standing there dripping loops of gold braid from that whore's costume of his and saying – I swear, Admiral, this is a direct quote – "Storm? What storm? Couldn't have asked for a more beautiful day to start the fleet on its way home." Which is what the murderous fool intends, as soon as the tide lets them clear the bar. Not that he'll be aboard. No, *he'll* be sitting snug and secure in what rightfully is *your* Viceregal Palace while he sends Antonio Torres and how many hundreds of seamen out to – '

'Did you get to speak to Captain Torres?'

'For all of two minutes. If you mean is he worried, sure he is. He doesn't like the look of that sky any better than we do. But he has orders to put to sea.'

'And so have we, I take it.'

Pedro confirms this. 'The harbor's off limits to the likes of us. Here's another direct quote, if you can believe it: "Terribly sorry, Captain Terreros, but you see the problem – the last thing we'd want is to stir up the old factional strife between our good people here and the pharaoh's, that is, the former Viceroy's, partisans." Shit, piss and corruption! Is Ovando out to kill everybody today?'

Pedro Terreros, who ordinarily uses expletives about as often as the Guadalquivir freezes over, now notices Fat Ferdy seated near the steerage hatch. 'Sorry, kid. I didn't know you were here.' Pedro still treats Fat Ferdy like the Admiral's son instead of the youngest of *Santa María*'s grommets.

This of course makes Fat Ferdy say, around his last mouthful of flat bread, 'I hear worse in the fucking forecastle fifty times a fucking day, Captain.' Which I'm sure he does.

'What are we supposed to do now?' asks that sailor-by-the-book Diego Tristán.

But Pedro Terreros hasn't finished. 'And as if that's not enough, refusing us shelter and rejecting your advice, he has to ridicule you. Joking with Francisco Roldán and ex-Governor Bobadilla, even the cacique Guarionex. They're all there waiting to board ship, and Ovando turns to them and laughs. "Does the Admiral of the Ocean Sea fancy himself a soothsayer these days? Does the old boy slit open gulls and divine the weather from their entrails to keep busy?" Balls! If it weren't for your seamanship, Admiral, none of them would even know there was an Indies. Why don't you just sail on in there and *order* them to stay at anchor?' Here Pedro turns away and stares mutely out to sea.

All I can say is a lame 'Steady, boy,' because we both know the answer and it's more hurtful to this loyal captain than to me. I'm Viceroy in name only. As for the Ocean Sea, I'm Admiral of as much of it as our four small caravels displace at any given moment.

And I can't let it bother me, can't allow myself the luxury of anger. This is the last chance to follow the glory route west, to seek what has only been dreamed of until now, the Magellanic dream before Magellan, the discoverer's Holy Grail.

This is the High Voyage. Nothing must go wrong, this time.

'We'd better find ourselves some good holding ground,' I say, in answer to Diego Tristán.

I'd rather sit out the hurricane ashore, of course. But it's not to be. Next best is at good anchorage with protection from the wind and plenty of sea room. The mouth of the Jaina River, a few miles west, is wide and sheltered by headlands. The anchor flukes will bite deep into the sandy bottom and there's no coral to foul and sever holding tackle. So, with the right kind of luck, we can ride out the storm there.

We'll be better off, anyway, than Antonio Torres.

Give it one more try? I ask myself. Maybe sending a known loyalist like Pedro Terreros was a mistake. I could ask Diego Tristán to try talking some sense into — but a shout from the roundtop interrupts these thoughts.

'They're making sail!'

And they are — too much sail for the fitful gusts already beginning to blow. Antonio Torres will trim here outside the harbor as soon as they leave the mouth of the river. But then what?

Even thinking about it is an exercise in futility. They're committed; Antonio Torres, as his flagship crosses the bar, knows that as well as I do. I fire a single lombard shot in salute, and Torres replies. Then, with *Gallega* towing her boat, our four caravels head for the Jaina.

By Sunday we are together again at our post-storm rendezvous in Escondido Bay. *Santa Maria* has arrived first, bare-masted before the stiff winds still blowing in the wake of *huracán*, a most subdued Captain Diego Tristán at my side on the quarterdeck. Two nights earlier with lightning dancing on all three masts and the seas so high that cresting a wave was like being hurled from a cliff, when we were winching up from the hold the great anchor of salvation, our last hope because we were dragging all four bowers, he turned to me and said, 'She's your ship, Admiral.' Not through fear – that would never be one of Diego Tristán's shortcomings – but because he was out of his depth and knew it. Barto wasn't. When *Bermuda* lost her anchors my brother let her run wild out to sea with the monster winds then blowing off the hills, and gave her room for her ordeal. By the time *Bermuda* arrived at Escondido Bay, wreckage was starting to float in – planks and spars and timbers, crates and barrels, the taffrail from a four-master with bonaventure mizzen still attached – and we could guess that the worst had happened. Later, much later, when we learned the extent of the disaster, it was already history. Antonio Torres's great fleet was strung out along the hurricane's track when it struck. Some ships foundered in seconds, others were pounded to pieces on the rocky coast near Monkey Passage. Twenty went down with all hands, the flagship among them. Five hundred lives were lost – my friend Antonio Torres, Francisco Roldán and the disgraced governor Bobadilla, Guarionex on his way to Spain or Heaven. A few ships were blown back into the safety of Santo Domingo harbor. One – one single ship, *Needle*, the meanest, smallest, oldest, crankiest of the lot – got through. To her hold Ovando had consigned a cargo of gold belonging to me, 4,000 pesos that Bobadilla had finally relinquished, if not a king's ransom then a duke's. (God's justice? If so, He hands down complex verdicts, for we have not heard the last of *Needle* and that gold.)

At first light Sunday, twelve hours after *Gallega*'s arrival at Escondido Bay minus her boat, *Vizcaína* scuds in past the headland. Captain Fieschi calls from her prow, 'Hey, Colombo! Now we go discovering, hey?' Then as dawn turns the sea gold, Fieschi sees the flotsam. And this ebullient man drops to his knees and bows his head.

Two weeks later, repaired and rested, me gripping a shroud and gazing west from *Santa Maria*'s quarterdeck, Captain Tristán at my side, Fat Ferdy taking his turn in the roundtop, we sail from Escondido Bay, where once I used guile to catch a murderer, and into the unknown western sea to look for that passage to Cathay and India which, I tell myself, has to be there and, if it is, then by God we will find it.

This is the High Voyage. Nothing must go wrong, this time.

I'm still telling myself that, and we are still looking, when the New Year rolls around.

Barto is less sanguine.

'It's a mainland. How much of it do you have to see before you'll admit it?'

'According to the Indians, there's a great land to the north and another to the south. This is sort of the waist of the sandclock, an isthmus. According to the Indians, there's a great sea on the other side, and it's only a nine-day march across the mountains.'

'Or fifteen, or twenty, depending on which Indians you listen to. And that jungle looks impenetrable to me. And the mountains look worse.'

'Sure, but if the isthmus is so narrow, why can't there be a strait through it?'

'The Indians are sure there isn't.'

'Well, the Indians,' I say, since it suits me now to disparage their geographical acumen.

There has to be a strait.

We're lying at anchor, as we've been for forty-eight hours. The men are fishing, swimming, washing their clothes in a stream. I am in my doghouse, knocked together on the poop a few months back by *Santa Maria*'s carpenter so I don't have to drag myself out of the stern-castle fifty times a day.

Barto, on hands and knees, backs out. Then he pokes his grizzled head back in. 'How're you feeling today anyway?'

'I'm feeling absolutely fine,' I say, raising my voice.

It's really quite pleasant with the sun filtering through the palm-thatch roof. Hot in here, in fact, so the chills aren't so bad. But my eyes are murder (jar of water at my side, refilled often) and the fever comes and goes. I've already been through a period of extreme biliousness (which I didn't need Dr Chanca to predict). No neuropsychiatric manifestations that I'm aware of. But you never know. And, thank God, no stigmata.

'Do you need anything?'

'No!'

'Take it easy, bro. I only – '

'I'm perfectly fine, damn it.'

Some of the biliousness might still, just possibly, remain. But I've got it under control.

Later, while I'm sketching a map of the isthmus, Fearless Ferdy knocks at the doghouse door. 'Papa?'

'Come in, son.'

And this lean dark boy, not an ounce of spare flesh on him, crawls into my poopdeck cabin.

Ferdy got his new name way back in the summer, and I didn't give it to him, the other grommets did.

The first thing that happened when we reached the isthmus was four straight weeks of storm. As if the hurricane hadn't been enough! We lost anchors, we lost rigging and sails so recently repaired, we lost cables and a second boat, *Vizcaína*'s. It got so bad the men started hearing one another's confessions. The first chills hit me then, and the fever, and the stiffness in my joints so I could barely hobble around. But I could watch Ferdy, and he was something to see, patching gear together, and climbing the ratlines, and casting the lead, and somehow finding time to cheer his shipmates. My son Fernando, a born seaman, who would have thought it? And when they carried me below to the cramped captain-general's cabin, the bulkheads creaking and shuddering so you almost expected they'd fly apart, there was Ferdy trying to cheer me up. At least, he was laughing.

'What the hell's so funny?' I was very bilious at the time.

'You know how people say, "They're all against me?" I never really understood what it meant before.'

'What the hell are you talking about?'

Ferdy smiled his new undaunted nautical smile. 'This damn weather. It's all the elements of the ancients – earth, air, fire, water – ganging up on us. The earth's reefs and rocky lee shores, the air's a howling gale, the fire's lightning, and as for water – ' He flung his arms up. 'But we'll get through. I know we will.'

And he ran topside to see that we did.

'Fear,' I once heard him explain in words of one syllable to a grommet five years his senior, 'is a waste of time.'

Now he sits cross-legged in my doghouse on the poopdeck. The map I'm sketching seems to inspire him.

'Tell me what's on the other side,' he says.

And I begin to. Half-way through my discourse – I'm speculating that, for all we know, the mouth of the Ganges is but a ten-day sail from the far side of the isthmus – I pull up short. Fearless Ferdy has started this conversation before.

'Ferdy,' I ask him, 'are you trying to humor me?'

In the sunlight filtering through the palm fronds I can see Fearless Ferdy blushing. 'Well, you don't have much to do, cooped up in here. So I thought – '

'I'm in here because they don't need me out on deck right this minute!' I shout.

Ferdy nods immediate agreement.

'I'm right here if they need me any hour of the day or night.'

'I know, Papa.' Ferdy uncrosses his legs and, with some difficulty in my not very commodious poopdeck cabin, crosses them the other way. After an extended silence he asks, 'How come the Indians speak so many different languages?'

I warm to this question – so much that for a while I don't realize Ferdy's doing it again.

We've passed through several language zones, acquiring an interpreter in each. This volunteer is kept aboard to the end of his language zone, then traded in. To be accurate, he is not a volunteer. He is an impressed seaman, to be accurate. But we do send him on his way with gifts, hawk bells usually. And he's no interpreter in the ordinary sense, because he can't speak Spanish any more than we can speak his language. But he gets used to us, and he can tell the new Indians we encounter – this isthmus is a pretty crowded place compared to Hispaniola – that our inclinations are peaceful.

Going through the language zones we have to enter every bay, every cove, every inlet. For hidden somewhere in the tangled mangrove swamps may be the entrance to the strait, the passage west, the discoverer's Grail.

The first month we beat ironically *east* – that's the lay of the isthmus along the section my men are already calling Honduras. It's hard to blame them. It rained the whole time and nothing could be seen but those dripping mangrove swamps. And sometimes great lizards like Nile crocodiles, only bigger. And slovenly-looking, slow-swimming, brownish and decidedly homely creatures that the Indians call manatees. These disappointed Ferdy and the other grommets. They expected certain minimal standards in their mermaids. (But note that Ferdy, identifying manatees with the legendary creatures, recognized a sea-dwelling mammal when he saw one; Ferdy had a pretty scientific turn of mind.) Each night when we cast anchor off those mangrove swamps some smart-ass grommet would say, 'I swear to Christ that's the same goddamn rock we anchored off this morning,' and it was hard to argue with him. All this by way of explaining how Honduras got its name. Spaniards call places as they see them. I know a river named Ugly River south of Granada, and it is. Honduras means the lower depths, the pits. Well, that's how we saw it.

But Ferdy was asking about the Indians and their Babel of languages. Always a subject of great fascination, even if he's brought it up before.

These isthmus Indians are various. The first ones we encountered would have been at home, except for the language barrier, in any great Continental port. Their dugout canoes, as long as caravels and eight feet wide, carried twenty paddlers, twice that many passengers, and enough cargo to fill *Santa Maria*'s forward hold. Amidships stood palm-thatched cabins (a lot like my doghouse on the poopdeck, built not long after), and the women wore long robes of cotton and covered their faces to the eyes like Arabs, and some of the men wore quilted cotton jerkins that would stop any Indian arrow I ever saw, and they had swords and copper hatchets. They called themselves Maya, but their kingdom lay some distance to the north and we never got to see it, though they invited us. We wouldn't like it there, they apologized. The isthmus was wider, the mangrove swamps more tangled, the jungle thicker, the mountains inconceivably high, the mosquitoes bigger and hungrier. It even rained more. There was, they assured us, no strait through the isthmus. But come if you want. By all means.

The Jicaque Indians, otherwise unmemorable, had this in common with the Maya: they assured us there was no strait through the isthmus.

Further south lived the Talamanca, crude naked savages after the Maya, but friendly enough. Too friendly. In trade they offered two naked virgins – one fourteen, one eight in case we were into pre-puberty. Just sent them right up the ladder after we anchored in an inlet. This country later would be called Costa Rica, and I mean to cast no aspersions on future *Costarriqueños* by reporting the trading habits of the indigenes. The girls showed no fear; they were poised and proud. When they boarded – I had just come down with the Whole

Sick Syndrome and was in my newly-built doghouse – I heard the shouts of the crew, almost that Valencia sound, followed by a sudden, even more ominous silence. So I hurried out – as much as one can hurry on hands and knees – not knowing what to expect. What I saw was disbelief on every face as, calmly and with courtly manners, Fearless Ferdy the royal page draped both girls in cloaks and in sign language explained that they must leave. And they did. And the crew didn't resent Ferdy, they admired him. He's a strange boy in some ways, but there are times when I like his instincts.

These virgin-offering Talamanca had this in common with the Maya and Jicaque Indians: they assured us there was no strait through the isthmus.

The Cuna Cuna Indians wore necklaces heavy with polished disks of pure gold. They lived in stilt-houses on islands off the coast of what would be Panama. My interest in the gold was minimal, since we had a strait to find, but out of curiosity I asked where they got it. They got it from the Guaymi people, who lived on the isthmus – back that way. And how had we missed them? Their villages lay a few miles inland, in the jungle, on some nameless rivers. So, impelled by nothing more than curiosity, we doubled back to find the Guaymi.

The otherwise naked, gold-necklace-wearing Cuna Cuna had this in common with the Maya, the Jicaque and the Talamanca: they assured us there was no strait through the isthmus.

Here this brief catalogue of isthmian Indians ends, and here is Ferdy in my doghouse asking, 'But how can the Maya and the Talamanca be so different, when they live so near each other?'

'Spanish and French,' I say with a shrug, and wonder what is keeping his Uncle Barto, who took *Bermuda*'s boat over the bar of a still nameless river early that morning to find the Guaymi. I don't point out to Ferdy that he's asked me this question before too – his way of showing solicitude for his sick old father.

He is definitely growing up.

Barto returns toward dusk. I'm out on deck then. All things considered, I don't feel too bad. Sometimes the Whole Sick Syndrome gives me a breather, though it's inside me somewhere, lurking.

'I visited three villages,' Barto says. 'There's no strait, not here and not anywhere south of here.'

Barto on this subject is beginning to sound like an Indian himself.

'The Guaymi told you that?'

'No. But every other Indian on this isthmus did.' Barto is holding something back. 'Glad to see you up and around,' he says.

'I'm feeling fine,' I assure him. 'Did you get to communicate with these Guaymi at all?'

'Well, in a manner of speaking.'

'What does that mean?' I demand, with a trace of biliousness.

'They're not as cultured as the Maya and not as generous as the Talamanca. We couldn't impress ourselves an interpreter. This is going to take time.'

All the while he's talking, Barto's tossing a drawstring pouch in the air. It looks heavy.

'That bar there,' he says. He means the sandbar at the river's mouth. 'It might not be easy, but at high tide we ought to be able to tow the ships across. There's a basin on the other side of the bar, and good anchorage.'

'What for? It's a river. We're looking for a strait.'

Barto keeps tossing the pouch and catching it.

Finally he hands it to me. 'Happy Three Kings, bro.'

Three Kings is Epiphany, January the sixth, and it is when Spaniards give each other Christmas gifts.

'Good God,' I say, 'is it Three Kings already?'

'Aren't you going to open it?'

I reach into the pouch and withdraw a gold nugget the size of a walnut.

We spend some time looking at it.

'There's more where that came from,' Barto tells me. 'A lot more.' He draws his poniard. 'And all I needed to dig it out of the ground was this.'

The crew is listening to every word. Gold has a way of focusing attention.

'It's time to face it,' Barto tells me. 'There's no strait.'

The gold nugget gleams with that special golden gleam and is heavy with that special golden weight. I try reminding myself: this is the High Voyage. Nothing must go wrong, this time.

Yet I know as well as Barto that there is no strait.

Ever since the Maya, I've been deluding myself.

Barto sees my hesitation. 'I'm sure we'd have room to clear the bar at high tide.'

We only have two boats left, I find myself thinking. It would take both to tow each caravel. Probably couldn't get all four across with one flowing tide.

'What have you got in mind?' I ask my brother.

He looks at the gold in my hand. 'A couple of weeks, maybe three.

The men need a rest anyway.'

'I never knew a Spaniard to rest when he was looking for gold.'

'This is different. It's just lying there.'

'That's not what I mean,' I say.

Barto shrugs.

'What are the Guaymí like?'

'I told you we couldn't get an interpreter.'

'Why not?'

'The usual,' says Barto. 'They're suspicious of foreigners, pale skins, muskets – '

'Was there any fighting?'

'No. Absolutely not,' says Barto devoutly. 'None at all. They just made some noise and we made some back.' He answers my next question before I ask it. 'With horns and drums. And they beat the river with clubs.'

'They're hostile then?'

'I didn't say that. They were frightened. We must have frightened them.'

Captain Diego Tristán says, 'The Exec's right, the men do need a rest.' His eyes are moored to the gold.

The sky is clear, the sun setting. Every man aboard *Santa María* stands absolutely still. Someone clears his throat thunderously in the silence.

'We could,' says Barto, 'pick up more gold here in a few weeks than a whole year's tribute on Hispaniola.'

There is a fleeting instant when the gold in my hand, reflecting the last rays of the sun, is the color of blood.

Fearless Ferdy is holding his breath.

So, I realize, am I.

There is no strait. This is the one undeniable fact we have learned about the isthmus. And if a dream dies on you, how often do you find another waiting to take its place?

I mean, this is almost too good to be true.

Or so I tell myself.

I tell Captain Diego Tristán, 'Take soundings. When we've got more than a fathom, we'll try going in.'

There is a roar of voices and a stamping of feet on deck. Barto is smiling.

'We'll give it two weeks,' I tell him.

But it rains for forty days and forty nights. By actual count. The rain is excessive, indecent, biblical. It beats like the hooves of stampeding horses on the deck and turns the air into a slaty gray wall. Below, the mud-brown flood of the Bethlehem River – so named because we first stood off its mouth on Three Kings – rushes turbulently by. Ironically, the sandbar is now under almost three fathoms of water. Not even a groundswell marks its location. We spent two days towing the ships in – slow, back-breaking work with just two boats – and a few days later, if we wanted, we could sail right out. The thought is tempting.

If for as little as ten minutes the rain stops, mosquitoes come from wherever they have taken refuge, tormenting us so much we wish for rain. And soon enough get our wish. And wish for mosquitoes.

Fearless Ferdy slaps at his bare arm and leaves a smear of blood. 'Got the bastard.' A whine homes in on my ear.

'One dry anything, anywhere,' pleads Captain Tristán. 'One dry plank of wood, one dry biscuit, one dry piece of clothing or a dry firebox to start a fire in – if we had any dry kindling.' He sighs. 'Even a dry cough,' he says, and doubles over in an explosive sneeze.

Most of the men are coughing and sneezing. Many have fever, so the insidious return of my own chills and fever goes unnoticed in the general state of poor health. As for a certain undeniable biliousness, who isn't? I don't tell Captain Tristán about my dry, burning eyes. Why make him envious?

The men not only have colds but cabin fever. It's bad enough to be cooped up on a long voyage. But being shipbound a stone's throw from shore is far worse. Sometimes when the sky lifts briefly there are tantalizing glimpses of great hardwood trees along the riverbank, and verdant hills beyond. Sometimes the start of an Indian trail (a freshet now) can be seen at the edge of the jungle, as inaccessible as the moon. The men of Palos and Moguer, of Lepe and Huelva, are fine swimmers, but no one could last more than a few seconds in that raging brown flood. These men are explorers by temperament or they wouldn't be here. And they're young, most of them, with a youthful excess of energy. Yet it rains so inordinately we can't even occupy them with make-work.

Two grommets, heads down, naked – what's the point in wearing clothes wetter than you are? – go slouching past.

'Look at them,' says Captain Tristán darkly. 'Too quiet. They're planning something.' He slaps at a mosquito. No blood.

'How can you tell?' The men look bedraggled to me, not mutinous.

'I can't tell,' Tristán admits. He grunts a laugh. 'But I can hope, can't I? Even a good old-fashioned mutiny would be welcome.' He slaps at his ear and glares triumphantly at the blood on his hand.

The rain starts again. We stand there letting it sluice down our bare bodies. Going below is no better; the bilges are foul. A chill makes me shudder. Captain Diego Tristán sneezes. I turn my eyes, ironically dry, up to the downpour.

The next morning birds are calling in the jungle. Dawn comes up lambent gold in a crystalline blue sky. Only the rushing floodwater and the leathery gleam of drenched foliage recall the rain.

Fearless Ferdy succeeds in lighting the firebox. Spirits rise with the flickering flames. Drenched clothes are spread on deck and draped over rails to dry. A piper plays a melody across the water on *Gallega*, and there's singing. Ferdy is superintending the creation of a stew of salt beef, garlic and red wine. The aroma drifts aft over the stench of the bilges. I'm sitting outside my doghouse in the sun. There is just enough breeze to discourage the mosquitoes. A bird with plumage of flame and green flashes by, squawking a question at me. Grommets swarm over *Santa Maria* swabbing, scouring, airing out. Grommets descend to *Santa Maria*'s and *Bermuda*'s boats to bail them. There are even grommet-volunteers for that most odious of jobs, the cleaning of the bilges. This takes three full days, and that stench gets unbearable before it gets better. Crates and barrels are hoisted on deck and sluiced down with seawater, the bilges themselves scraped clean and scrubbed with vinegar. All this activity drives the bilge rats and cockroaches on deck, providing lively sport.

Late on the third day Captain Tristán goes below. He comes up smiling. 'Like all the perfumes of Araby,' he says.

Fearless Ferdy, one of the bilge cleaners, approaches. He doesn't exactly smell like all the perfumes of Araby.

'Stand downwind,' I suggest.

Instead he turns, springs to the quarterdeck rail and executes a graceful dive. The river has dropped but it's still flowing an angry brown. I go anxiously to the rail. Ferdy's head surfaces. He's grinning. He spouts a fountain, submerges, and reappears elsewhere in that brown flood. Soon the rest of the bilge party is splashing in the water.

Captain Fieschi calls from *Vizcaína*, 'Hey, Colombo! Hey, this place is all right!'

We're getting our first real look at it. Inside the bar, the Bethlehem River forms a basin big enough to accommodate two dozen caravels. To the southeast the river disappears inland under the green canopy of jungle. Beyond, freshets and falls plunging down the hillsides gleam silver in the sun. I see movement to starboard. A dark brown log detaches itself from the bank, drifts in our direction and opens its great jaws. Ferdy shepherds the other swimmers to the ladder. One by one they scramble up. He's the last one. 'Fellow can lose a toe that way,' he tells me, very macho. But his sun-darkened face is pale. After that we deploy climbing ropes along the hull. Lookouts are posted.

A few days after the end of the rainy season, Barto takes *Bermuda*'s boat upstream with a dozen men. They're gone overnight and return towing four small canoes.

'We're going to need them,' he tells me. 'You can navigate upstream only a couple of miles in a boat. *And* we must have passed thirty tributaries.'

'Indians friendly?'

Barto has a way of slipping past a question. It must be a family trait. 'Twelve hawk bells for the four of them,' he says.

Captain Tristán asks in a tight voice, 'You didn't happen to find any more gold, did you, Exec?'

This is the question everyone's been waiting for. There's a general movement toward the mainmast, where we're standing.

'Place is still under a couple of feet of water,' Barto says. 'But it'll drop. Meanwhile we can do some exploring with the canoes.'

'What are the villages like?' I ask.

'Only saw one. These are pretty primitive people, compared to the Maya.'

'Everybody is pretty primitive compared to the Maya,' I tell him. Because Barto is slipping past a question again.

He gives me a rueful smile. 'Well,' he says, 'they're not cannibals anyway.'

'Warlike?'

'Let's say wary.'

I do my lurching hobble over to the bulwark and stare across at the jungle. No one dares comment on my new method of locomotion, the best I can manage these days. My eyes aren't so bad, though. I glance quickly at my hands as I have a habit of doing now. No stigmata. I look pensively at that green wall of foliage.

Barto grips my shoulder. 'Gosh,' he says softly, 'it must be tough, bro.'

'What,' I demand, my back up at once, 'must be tough?'

He looks at my face and changes tack. 'I just meant having to stay here to direct the whole operation, that's all.'

'You think I couldn't go if I wanted to?'

'Jeepers! You don't have to bite my head off. Sure you could. Did anybody say you couldn't?'

I lurch back to the group at the mainmast. Is it safe to stay? What exactly does Barto mean when he says these Guaymi Indians are wary? Sure, he's slipping past my question. But how much past?

Half-crippled the way I am, I will have to let others be my eyes and ears. Go upriver without me. *Discover* without me. And whatever decision I make will have to be based on second-hand knowledge.

This is what it's like to feel old. An invalid. Dependent. I hate it.

'Take Fieschi with you tomorrow,' I suggest.

Barto, who has more experience with Indians than anyone but me. And Fieschi, who has almost none. Maybe between them they'll arrive at something close to the truth.

Fieschi springs aboard *Santa Maria* forty-eight hours later, the conquering hero. Barto holds back, letting him have center stage. Fieschi's normal ebullience is soaring now. A grin splits his bearded face and he prances back and forth, pulling from a good-sized pouch like a conjurer golden marvels – a dozen disks polished like mirrors, two masks, a tangled skein of fillets. 'They wear them around their heads,' he explains, and uses Diego Tristán for a model.

'He's a second Ovando, I swear,' smiles Pedro Terreros who has just come over from *Gallega*.

Fieschi's ebullience is uncontainable. Around the deck the Genoese goes, giving away golden fillets as if they grow on trees. And maybe they do.

'We can do business with them,' he says with a broad grin. 'Hey, Exec? Hey?'

'What are they like?' I ask.

Fieschi and Barto exchange a quick glance. 'Noisy,' says Fieschi.

'Weapons?' I ask.

Barto has his list ready and recites it swiftly: 'Spears, bows and arrows, slingshots, clubs.'

'What's this about "noisy"?' I ask Fieschi.

'They drink a lot,' he admits.

We have yet to encounter alcohol among the Indians.

'Called *chicha*,' Barto explains. 'Fermented from maize, and it's strong. Like strong beer.'

'They drink a lot,' repeats Fieschi, and grimaces. 'Terrible stuff.'

'And get violent?' I pursue.

'Noisy,' says Fieschi.

'Nothing to worry about,' says Barto.

They go back upriver towing two canoes and return in a few days – Barto almost blasé – with an assortment of gold nuggets. Fieschi drops one as big as an olive and it rolls across the cambered deck toward the scuppers, causing a mad scramble of grommets. One extricates himself from the pile-up triumphantly with the gleam of gold in his hand.

'It's like the Exec says,' exults Fieschi. 'You just pick them out of the ground with your knife. Once we really start digging – ' he rolls his eyes ' – I just might buy myself a half interest in Centurione's.'

And he laughs at his little joke.

No one else does. In his enthusiasm Fieschi has broken the unwritten rule. No adventurer who ever went anywhere to seek gold in whatever company under whatever auspices failed to secrete some away for himself. This is a fact of life. But you don't talk about it, you just do it. This is especially true of officers. Officers are supposed to behave in an exemplary manner. And Fieschi's not just an officer, he's a foreigner. From my putative hometown. Which, it was rumored, wanted to move in on the whole Spanish Indies operation.

'Captain Fieschi was joking,' Barto says coldly.

On cue Fieschi laughs again, less convincingly.

The men look on in silence.

Next morning I send Pedro Terreros and Captain Porras of *Bermuda* upriver with fifteen men. They're back in a couple of days with the familiar disks, masks and fillets of gold.

'Noisy,' says Captain Porras. 'They drink a lot.'

By now the words are familiar too.

I wait for Pedro Terreros to speak. I count on this straight arrow, even more than Barto, to tell me the truth.

'I never saw any Indians like them,' he says. 'They're utterly unpredictable. One minute you can swear they're friendly, the next they're blowing those horns and beating those drums and banging on trees and they won't even look at you.'

Porras holds his head. 'Could be that beer of theirs,' he hazards.

'It's like they're doing their best to pretend you don't exist,' Pedro says. 'But you'd have to see it for yourself.'

I get the chance when Barto returns from his next journey upriver with visitors, five good-sized canoes carrying the local chieftain, called El Quibián, and his entourage. Four canoes pull up on shore and soon the Indians are blowing horns and banging drums and whacking trees with staves and the river itself with their paddles, ignoring us completely while the fifth canoe bumps against *Santa Maria*'s hull.

Indians swarm up the ladder, naked except for cotton breechclouts. Barto, in *Santa Maria*'s boat, is smiling and nodding up at me. Maybe he's talking, but with the din from shore I can't hear. Last Indian aboard is this El Quibián, who waits seated astride the bulwark while his associates search the deck, managing with neither hauteur nor hostility not to see us. Soon they return to El Quibián, palms up and scowling. He shouts. They make another circuit of the deck, poking into coils of rope, stomping on hatch covers. Meanwhile El Quibián astride the bulwark hasn't budged. The Indians trot back to him, smiling now. Whatever they want, they've found it. El Quibián, scrawny and wrinkled, vaults from bulwark to deck. His arms are powerful. One of his legs, I notice now, is withered. He walks with a bad limp. I hobble toward him in greeting, but he turns away. Literally turns his back. This is a new one on me. I've met a lot of Africans and a lot of Indians, but these Guaymi and their El Quibián are originals. Two members of his entourage lift him suddenly and it looks like they're going to hurl him overboard. Instead they deposit him in the garden where he sits isolated in his regality during our conference, if that's what it is. The noise from shore has if anything increased, the tooters and drummers and bangers warming to their task, hitting their stride, finding their rhythm. El Quibián points at me and makes a walking motion with his fingers. I approach the bulwark and his garden seat. Three Indians block my way. Again El Quibián indicates I'm to move. Again my way is blocked. Apparently it's forbidden to approach El Quibián too closely. Then I realize what he wants. He wants to see me walk. Or hobble. Lameness is a bond between us. I hobble aft and return. When he's satisfied with this demonstration of our kinship, one of his people hands him a gourd. He drinks, then passes it to me. The *chicha* is sharply sour, and bitter too. It tastes awful, leaves chaff in my mouth. The gourd, unfortunately large, is passed back and forth, and whenever he gets his hand on it, El Quibián seems to weigh it to make sure I'm drinking my share. To vary this routine I have paper brought and draw a map showing the coast, the Bethlehem River. Or, I start to. As soon as those Indians looking over my shoulder see the black lines appear on the paper, they turn their backs and cry out. This is new magic. El Quibián on the garden seat grows pale. A big bronzy-skinned fellow swiftly produces an animal horn from which he strews orange powder which leaves a sickly sweet smell. Writing thirty years after the events, my son Fernando mentions the turning of backs without reflecting on its significance. He does observe that the Guaymi seem to fear drawing. But is it necessarily fear? Perhaps there's a totally different reason for Guaymi back-turning and powder-casting, a reason that fits their alien view of the world but won't pass the scrutiny of our self-limiting logic. Are these Guaymi and their El Quibián, then, crazy? Or does insanity, like beauty, lie in the eye of the beholder? Fernando doesn't speculate on these matters thirty years later, possibly because Fearless Ferdy now, like all the other young grommets, is gawking at the garden-ensconced El Quibián as if waiting for him to do something really *outré* – defecate in some spectacularly original fashion, maybe. But what El Quibián does, using those strong arms, is turn around in the garden so that he is seated backwards. This seems to puzzle Ferdy so much that the writer Fernando will fail to mention the rapport my hobble has established with the limping El Quibián. Who now drops the gourd into the water and holds a hand over his shoulder for another while the din on the riverbank intensifies. El Quibián drinks and I drink. This *chicha* is worse than English ale, but I'm doing what is expected of me. El Quibián raises one hand about three inches, not much of a peremptory gesture, but the noise on the riverbank stops dead. El Quibián speaks. On a sound anthropological impulse I turn my back. El Quibián's voice is so loud that my ears are ringing when finally he falls silent. I turn to face him, and see that he is, once again, sitting the right way around in the garden. Does this indicate a new level of trust? His mouth parts in a smile revealing a few tooth-stumps. He nods his head up and down, up and down. This may signify nothing more than a surfeit of *chicha*. I try my map again and the orange powder is strewn as before. El Quibián squirms uneasily in the garden seat but this time doesn't turn his back. Instead he signals in some subtle manner, and his people help him back to the deck. Let me remark here that the garden where El Quibián has been ensconced is not the afterguard garden for officers but forward off the forecastle, the other ranks' garden. No one is tempted to point this out to him. Any seat at such a remove is still regal. On deck El Quibián ranges himself at my side. I haven't realized how small he is. Comes barely to my shoulder. He takes a step and turns to wait for me. I take a step, he another. He wants to synchronize our mutual infirmity and for once I don't try to minimize my hobble. We reach the ladder. El Quibián raises a hand in that three-inch casual signal and the din on the riverbank recommences. Then El Quibián tries some complicated sign language. He makes it understood that we are permitted to paddle upriver, and to dig (for gold, I assume), and he has begun to explain that he strongly prefers our peoples to keep their distance when, encouraged by all the signing, a young grommet raises his hands palms outwards in a peace sign and, smiling broadly, approaches an equally young member of El Quibián's entourage. The young Guaymi freezes in horror. But apparently he is too slow. Or perhaps he should have turned his back. Whatever, El Quibián speaks briefly and the luckless young Guaymi is clubbed to the deck with a stave. Two of his companions lift his inert form over the bulwark and hurl it into the river. It surfaces, rolls over, floats a while, then swims slowly for shore. By this time El Quibián is following his entourage down the ladder. His noise-makers are already getting into their canoes. Soon even their sound effects have faded into the jungle.

'Oh wow, what was all that about?' Barto says, shaking his head.

My own head is throbbing from too much *chicha*. But I'm thinking half-formed anthropological thoughts about the meaning of this encounter. My son Fernando is not. Fearless Ferdy is now cheering on a fellow-grommet who has leaped astride the garden backwards, just managing not to overshoot it and plunge into the river.

There is no real answer to Barto's question. I rub my forehead with the heel of my hand, as if trying to erase that *chicha* headache. 'If we don't understand them, and I for one don't,' I tell him, 'then we ought to keep contact to a minimum. Which El Quibián obviously wants.'

'But they don't object to us digging for gold.'

No argument there. 'How long would it take you to fill our coffers?' I ask.

Barto smiles.

'Provided,' I say, 'there's gold enough to fill them.'

'Are you kidding? Now that the floodwater's dropping you can see it glinting in every streambed. Jeepers, Cristóbal – it'd take fifty years to get all the gold in there. A hundred. But just give me a month, and we'll bring back twice as much as they ever dreamed of on Hispaniola.'

I spend a sleepless night thinking about it, and the thinking is complicated.

This is the High Voyage, I remind myself. Nothing must go wrong, this time.

Except that something already has. About as wrong as can be. There is no strait, no passage west, no discoverer's Grail.

So that's it for the High Voyage. You can't fight geography.

During that long hot sleepless night in my doghouse on *Santa Maria*'s poopdeck I see myself back in Spain, see myself as others might, and I don't like it – an old man on the beach, another Vásquez de la Frontera with no sargassum seaweed, just a lot of memories.

Discovered all the islands of the Indies. Discovered Hispaniola, crown of the Caribbean, made it a *place*, but he's not allowed to go there. Discovered the New or an Other World. Sad old guy, nothing to do nowadays. Would read a lot, maybe, all those books he never had time for, but his eyes'll never hold up.

But my eyes can see this. They can see, in Sanlúcar and Sevilla, in Cádiz and in Palos, younger men dreaming big dreams and making them happen. Or even failing but at least *trying*.

Not that I'm old. Who's old? I ask myself. Not me. I'll know it when I'm old.

Sometime in that long hot sleepless doghouse night I see myself in the latest temporary throne room of the Peripatetic Royal Court telling the royals: gold – real gold, not like in Hispaniola. Pick it right out of the ground with a knife, in the isthmus. No need for slaves, no tribute. I learned my lesson. Listen, My Lady, we'll get us a good chief of mission, someone like Fray Juan Pérez ... what? Well, all right, a younger man if you want ... and we'll bring the caciques back to get a good Spanish education, and before you know it your new subjects will be as loyal as any in the realm. Wear clothes even. The Queen smiles. The King, reaching with his toes for the dais, smiles.

I know what to do. I learned in Hispaniola.

But Hispaniola's too big a place, I tell myself in that long hot sleepless doghouse night. Bound to be unruly. Keep the new colony small, hardly more than a village, find exactly the right people, not colonists, not adventurers, just *people* like Juan Niño and Inocencia Premiada. I know the pitfalls now. I'm wiser, but still young enough to have a dream. A sort of elder statesman except *I am* NOT *old*.

In the morning Barto asks, 'Well?'

We're leaning on the taffrail. The air is sweet. White water breaks over the sandbar. Birds call in the jungle. That hill above the left bank of the Bethlehem River is flat on top, almost as if God put it there to build a settlement on.

'Do we prospect or don't we?' Barto asks. A touch truculently.

I turn my back. Almost like a Guaymi. 'Barto,' I say softly, 'I want you to stay.'

He misunderstands. 'You mean you'll go upriver? Gosh, Cristóbal, the trouble you're having with your legs and your eyes, I don't think that's such a hot idea.'

My old serenity has been reborn. Allusions to my infirmity mean nothing to me now.

'We're going to build a settlement,' I tell Barto. 'I want you to stay here with half the men while I return to Spain for a royal charter and colonists. Only, they won't exactly be colonists, because what I have in mind – '

Barto tries a small laugh while I flounder for a word that doesn't yet exist. 'Very funny,' he manages. But gently he takes hold of my elbow and turns me to face him. My formerly ugly, now handsome, brother looks ugly again, almost as if the warts and all have returned. 'Tell me you're joking,' he pleads.

How to explain? I can't say Utopia, for Thomas More won't coin the word for another thirteen years (Fernando will correspond with his fellow-humanist not long before the latter's execution at the hands of that nice King Henry the Eighth). But Utopia is what I'm trying to express. Barto forestalls me with:

'I never knew a Spaniard yet who didn't lose his head over gold, not to mention Indian women, and there are thousands of Indians out there and a hundred and thirty of us, with four ships that can use a good careening, by the way, if *Bermuda*'s any indication, because I've got some sections of hull that look like honeycomb, so this bay must be full of woodworm – and you want to start all *that* over again?'

'Barto, we've learned a lot since the early days. We could – '

'Why don't you have done with it and call this new settlement of yours Christmas Town?'

This shakes my serenity. And worse is coming.

'Don't you think I know what you're going through?' my brother says. 'Trying to prove you're as young as you used to be? I went through all that with Higueymota.'

'It's not the same thing.'

'I almost started a war before you brought me to my senses. How can I bring you to yours?'

'I can sail back with less than half the men,' I tell him. 'So never mind Christmas Town with its forty greenhorns. There's no comparison. You can have seventy volunteers and I'll leave you a ship. *Gallega*. She has the most fire-power and, if push comes to shove, you can always leave. Not that you'll have to. You know the ropes.'

'I know that you're a disappointed man trying to live his life over again.'

Barto goes on in this vein for a while. But I'm not listening. Because, chronologically at least, I can't argue with him. A Pighi-Zampini's an anomaly. In our day most men are dead before fifty. So this is no tardy midlife crisis Barto's talking about. This is definitely old age staring us in the face.

' ... some fountain of youth,' Barto is saying. His face all knotted. Warts too, I swear I can see them.

Behind the barrier of my new-old serenity, I say nothing.

'To prove you haven't lost your edge, you're going to leave seventy men here to die.'

'Nobody's going to die. You've even got Irish wolfhounds aboard *Bermuda*, and you know how terrified Indians are of Irish wolf-hounds.'

'Three,' Barto says. 'Three hounds and seventy men. And no guarantee you'll ever get back. You're a sick man, Cristóbal. You could die back there in Spain. Then what happens to us? Don't you realize how sick you are?'

My hand is stinging. I realize I've struck my brother.

Just below us a few grommets are at the quarterdeck rail, their backs turned. Diego Tristán stands at the binnacle, studiously looking out toward the sandbar. Maybe the Guaymi know what they're doing, maybe it's better to pretend some things *aren't*.

'I'm sorry,' I tell Barto, a colón bean in my throat. 'I didn't mean to do that.'

'Sure. It's all right.'

'But I'm going to start that settlement — with or without you.'

Now Barto goes Guaymi on me, for a long time staring across the water at that low flat-topped hill so evidently put there by God for my purpose. 'Cristóbal, you're probably the greatest instinctive navigator who ever took out a ship, anywhere, anytime,' Barto says slowly, groping for words. 'And, and it makes me proud, just being your brother. But if a man doesn't know when to stop — '

Very softly, so softly that I'm not even sure I've spoken, I say, 'I can't. I can't stop, Barto.'

Maybe he hasn't heard me, for he says, 'But what if you go back to Spain and for some reason, some reason that's got nothing to do with health or anything, you can't get back here? You don't think anyone but you would ever be able to find this place, do you?'

'Barto,' I say, again softly, 'one way or another I'm going ahead with this.'

And he turns, and looking younger than he has in years, he says, 'Oh, I'll do it. I'll stay. Sooner or later I always wind up doing everything you want. Only this time, this time it's going to get me killed.'

I wake. It's just before dawn. There's the blare of horns, the throb of drums somewhere off in the jungle, but that isn't what woke me. We're used to that. It's been going on for several nights now, all night long. Ever since we began building the settlement? Yes. Ever since the water level dropped, exposing the bar at low tide and effectively trapping us in the basin at the mouth of the Bethlehem River? That too. El Quibián can't be reached for comment. In fact, we haven't seen an Indian in days.

I hear again what woke me, a soft thumping sound, very close. A log bumping the hull? A canoe?

Then footfalls on deck, and a sudden shouted:

'Right there! Stop right there and identify yourselves.'

This is Fearless Ferdy's voice.

I scramble on hands and knees out of my doghouse. Two grommets carrying muskets – not primed, fortunately – are backed against the bulwark, Fearless Ferdy confronting them with a lance. 'Officer of the watch!' he shouts, and directly below me suddenly looms *Santa Maria*'s pilot, popping up out of the steerage hatch where he must have been catching forty winks.

'Canoe,' says Fearless Ferdy to the pilot. 'They just came on deck from a canoe.'

'Right,' says the pilot, not happy.

'I'd search them if I were you.' Fearless Ferdy sounds very officious for a boy not yet fourteen.

But searching is hardly necessary. The dim light is enough to show the sack slung over one grommet's shoulder.

'Fink,' says the sack's owner.

It will be a while before my son is referred to as anything but Ferdy the Fink. These frequent name-changes say something about his personality. My younger son, as you'll have noticed, is a pretty complex character.

The sack contains the usual gold disks, masks and fillets.

The culprits are resentful.

'Why us?' one of them says. 'It ain't fair. Why us when everyone's doing it?'

And the other one says, 'Everyone but the *Ad*miral's son. Ferdy the Fink. That's why.'

A search of the ships turns up gold artifacts in every time-honored hiding place and in some that show real imagination.

A typical interrogation:

Q: You took a canoe out the night before last?

533

A: Me and Manolo Méndez, yeah.

Q: Where'd you go?

A: Who knows? Upriver in the moonlight. Then we find a trail into the bush and pretty soon we reach a village.

Q: The Indians welcomed you?

A: They made noise. We made noise.

Q: How?

A: With a musket.

Q: Then what happened?

A: They gave us some gold masks and things.

Q: In exchange for what?

A: (*silence*)

Q: What did *you* give *them*?

A: They didn't want nothing. Well, they wanted us to leave.

Q: Did you?

A: We're here, ain't we?

Q: But you didn't leave immediately, did you?

A: Well, no. We had a little fun with a couple of girls out in the bush — they were willing! I swear, they were willing!

Barto said it already: *Why don't you call this new settlement of yours Christmas Town?*

How could I expect anything different? The word Utopia is a coinage from the Greek and it means 'no place.'

But I'm not ready to give up yet.

I'm standing outside my doghouse staring moodily off into space when Ferdy the Fink asks me, 'What'd I do wrong?' From his tone it's clear the very thought of his having erred is inconceivable to him.

'Sometimes a man's backed into a position where whatever he does is the wrong thing,' I tell him, but this sounds sententious. I try, 'You were damned if you did and damned if you didn't.' This sounds banal. I try, 'You were caught in the middle.' Worse all the time. Finally I shout, 'Goddamnit, Ferdy, why didn't you let someone else rat on them?'

'They're nothing but illiterate peasants,' Ferdy shouts right back. 'What do I care if they hate my guts?' And he stalks off.

Later Barto and Pedro Terreros visit my doghouse. I join them outside. I know what's coming.

'Listen to those drums,' Barto tells me. 'There goes the settlement.'

'Why? What's a little Indian trouble? We can handle it.'

Barto just shakes his head.

There's a pained look on Pedro Terreros's face. He clears his throat. 'Admiral,' he says, and you can see he's agonizing over every word, 'Admiral, I've sailed with you since the First Voyage. 1492. Everything I know you taught me. And I ...' Up and down bobs Pedro's Adam's apple. 'Admiral, I think the Exec's right. We ought to forget the settlement and get the ships ready to pull out as soon as we can.'

'I'll think about it,' I growl, and turn my back Guaymi-fashion to hide the real tears stinging my eyes.

The next night Ferdy the Fink disappears.

No canoe is missing, but he's not aboard *Santa Maria* or any of the other ships. I try the settlement – a cluster of wattled huts around a central storehouse, no palisade. There's protection on one side from a steep gully, on two from the river itself. But inland, higher wooded hills command the position. (Details like this you're liable to miss when you're thinking Utopian thoughts.) A few minutes are enough to show Ferdy's not there either.

Barto and twenty volunteers (and those three Irish wolfhounds) have been garrisoning the settlement since construction got underway. No problem finding volunteers, or the fifty more who will join them. Everybody wants a crack at that gold before I bring back reinforcements from Spain. I know, I know; Barto already told me: Christmas Town revisited. But I'm not thinking of that now.

'He can't just disappear.'

I have to repeat that because the horns and drums are particularly loud today. Then I feel the blood draining from my face. 'What if they kidnapped him? What if they hold him hostage to make us leave? And kill him if we don't?'

'They don't know he's your son,' Barto points out.

I take a heavily armed search party inland. Pick a jungle trail at random. But what's the use? A dozen other trails branch off it. When we're on our way back there's a quick rustling sound in the undergrowth and an arrow thuds into a tree trunk half a foot from my face. A discharge of muskets discourages the unseen bowman from trying again, and we hurry back with horns and drums pursuing us.

Barto has begun building a palisade after all. While we watch the palings being driven into the ground he urges me, 'Call it off. Before it's too late.'

'What's a little noise? You know Indians. The more racket they make, the less they're looking for a fight.'

'Yeah? Forgetting the *areitos*, aren't you? If we don't get out of here soon – '

'And leave Ferdy?'

'I meant after he comes back.'

'You think he just went off somewhere?'

'Maybe. He's a funny kid. If he gets back safely, will you at least think about pulling out?'

'We can't. Look at the sandbar.' The groundswell is breaking and foaming over it. 'We're not going anywhere even if we want to, not until it rains.'

It rains all the next day, and the day after that. Diego Tristán takes *Santa Maria*'s boat out to sound the bar and comes back drenched but happy. 'Water's up a foot already, Admiral.' A jagged bolt of lightning splits the sky. Thunder booms. Tristán smiles. But there's still a long way to go. And still no sign of Ferdy.

The fourth morning after his disappearance, I wake in my doghouse shaking with chills, drenched in sweat, eyes on fire. Even getting to hands and knees is painful. My back is killing me. I lurch outside. Men are shouting and laughing, crowding around the mainmast. Something so rivets their attention that no one sees my painful progress down from the poopdeck. As I approach I hear:

' ... done it again!'

' ... right into their camp ...'

' ... doesn't know the meaning of fear.'

'Fearless Ferdy strikes again!'

And there he is, borne aloft on shoulders.

'It was nothing,' he grins.

When they put him down he comes over to me. His face is puffed with insect bites, he has a black eye, his jerkin is in tatters.

'What happened to you?'

'I figured someone ought to find out what the Indians were up to. So I just sort of homed in on those horns and drums and spent a couple of days prowling around the perimeter of their camp.'

'Camp?' I ask. I don't like the sound of that word.

'Oh, I didn't walk in there, never mind what the boys said. But I know a military encampment when I see one. There have to be two thousand Guaymi there. Maybe more. Armed to the teeth.'

Someone asks, 'Are they going to attack us, Ferdy?'

And my son nods a very grown-up sort of nod.

Someone else – me, to be specific – asks, 'What makes you so sure?'

'Because I stumbled on a sentry, and we had a little tussle at the side of a stream, and I sort of held his head underwater until he told me what I went there to find out.'

536

'*Told* you?'

'Sign language,' explains Fearless Ferdy, 'becomes more coherent in direct proportion to the severity of the threat.'

Note the lecturing tone. Fearless Ferdy is beginning to sound like the writer Fernando Colón he will one day become.

'They're going to attack,' he says. 'That much he was sure of.'

'When?'

'He didn't know.' Here this complex son of mine shows a reckless dazzle of teeth like Alonzo Ojeda. 'And I guarantee you he'd've told me if he had known.'

That night I'm sweating and shaking under a heavy cloak in my doghouse. I hear a roll of thunder far out to sea, which Captain Diego Tristán uses as an excuse to pay me a visit.

'Storm wake you, Admiral?'

'What is it?' Decidedly bilious.

'I can come back later.'

'I said, what is it?'

'Exec's been aboard, Admiral. He saw no reason to disturb you, but now that the storm's got you up – '

It isn't raining, not yet, but thunder rumbles far off again. 'What's been going on?' I ask, less bilious.

'Morale's so low at the garrison, the Exec doesn't think he can count on them in a fight.'

Barto's twenty men have been holed up in the unfinished settlement for days, keeping guard around the clock in anticipation of the attack that hasn't materialized.

'We could send some reinforcements in.'

This suggestion is ignored. 'The river's rising, Admiral. I been out to the bar.' This isn't exactly news; he sounds it twice a day. But, 'Six feet of water at high tide,' says Tristán, 'and I figure there'll be seven or eight by morning even without more rain. And it's going to rain.'

I don't say anything. The first raindrops patter on the palm-frond roof of my doghouse.

Diego Tristán says, 'The Exec thinks we ought to call it quits while we still can. Admiral?'

'I heard you.'

'So if the Admiral wanted, I could take one more sounding before dawn and maybe we could start towing the ships out tomorrow. Be lucky to do the job in one day with just two boats.'

'I know how many boats we have.'

For a long time after that we're both silent, Tristán thinking whatever thoughts he's thinking, me lying in my sweat with my teeth chattering and trying to think of nothing.

'Admiral? You asleep?'

Utopia. No place.

'Tell my brother to get the settlement's essential supplies back aboard *Gallega.* Sound the bar at first light. If she's deep enough, we'll move out.'

I cover my head and try to sleep. All night it rains hard.

At first light I see the stigmata. They hardly surprise me. The way I've been feeling, I'm surprised they were so long in coming. I study them. Raw sores on both hands. No bleeding. Just your ordinary miraculous stigmata. The ultimate manifestation of the Whole Sick Syndrome? Not quite. Because a really acute attack, as you know, exposes me to the supernatural. Which it would be a mistake to explain away as delirium. When Socrates suffered from the 'falling sickness' he saw visions and he heard voices, and nobody said he was delirious. No, if humanism has any drawback it's a compulsion to explain away the inexplicable.

Of course the humanists could be right.

Also at first light I hear shouting. Captain Tristán's voice. 'Both away! Pull!' And moments later, almost imperceptibly at first, *Santa Maria* begins to move.

Tristán again, close now, not shouting: 'Admiral? I thought you'd want to know we're going out.'

I grunt an answer but just then there's a peal of thunder. I think I hear a dog whimpering. This has to be my imagination.

'Admiral?'

'Right. I heard you.'

'There's five hundred Guaymi screaming and tooting and banging on that hill over the settlement. Threw a few spears. But the Exec thinks it'll be a while before they work themselves up,' says Diego Tristán. 'I took in a boatload of reinforcements and put a gunner aboard *Gallega.* Brought out most of the carpentry tools and one of the wolfhounds that got nicked in the shoulder.'

My fever's high and my head spinning. The wolfhound whimpers somewhere close outside.

'Get you anything, Admiral?'

'No.'

'You want to come and watch the operation, I'll give you a — '

'No!' I look at my stigmata. My burning eyes remind me to ask,

538

'Have we enough water for the voyage?'

He almost cracks then. How can I blame him? 'Jesus! Two boats're all we've got to tow four ships over the bar plus evacuating the garrison, except the Guaymi could come screaming down off that hill if we go back in there and anyway what's the point getting them out till *we* get out? And you remind me we've got empty water butts on top of everything and the river running brown with mud. Jesus!'

'Steady as you go, Captain. See to the water when you can. One of those thieving grommets might be able to locate a spring for you.'

'Yes, sir. Anything else?'

'Steady as you go, Captain.'

Santa Maria's forward motion stops as she scrapes bottom on the bar and lists to starboard. 'Port boat! Port boat!' cries Captain Tristán on the run.

I try to sit up. But it proves difficult. Impossible, in fact. All the movement's in my head, going round and round. I roll over on one side and try to keep going, get onto my hands and knees. Same impossible. Chills follow one after another, deep inside me. There's a scraping sound forward. *Santa Maria* shudders. Then I can feel the scraping directly beneath me and suddenly *Santa Maria* surges ahead buoyantly, clear of the bar. This is the last thing I remember for some time.

The next thing I know, it's dark again. Not full dark but getting there. At least that's what I think. Must have slept the whole day. But it's not getting darker, it's getting *lighter*. Have I slept all day and all night? I look at my hands. Same old stigmata. Worse if anything.

Except for the creak of timbers, the ship is silent. Too silent. Absolutely silent.

'Hey!' I call, sounding rather like the unsaintly St Christopher of my dream.

I hear the scurry of footsteps.

'Who's out there?'

A whimper. A large dog's head pokes in. I sit up and stroke his sopping muzzle and scratch his sopping ears. Shoulder wound, as Captain Tristán said, but hardly serious enough to ... I sit up. *I sit up.* How about that? Experimentally I arrange myself on hands and knees, the wolfhound retreating but licking my face as I crawl slowly from the doghouse. Not raining at the moment. Lightning far off. No one on deck. I climb to my feet. Not rock-steady but in no immediate danger of falling. I try a few footsteps. The wolfhound wags his tail.

'Hey! Anybody on here?'

But the ship's deserted. I'm on the quarterdeck now, wobbly, doing a quick 360° scan. Vision not too bad, even if my eyes are on fire. Nothing out to sea. *Vizcaína* and *Bermuda* riding at anchor just outside the sandbar, a good half-mile away. How come? as Barto might ask. I wonder if anything's left of Barto and the garrison. At first I can't figure out what those dots are there in the water, a long way off, passing abeam of *Vizcaína*. Then the caravel's falconets let go, flame and smoke blossoming all along her starboard bulwark. The dots in the water are canoes and they are filled with Guaymi, and most of them are past *Vizcaína* now, heading straight for *Santa Maria*.

There's a roll of thunder, not far off.

The wolfhound whimpers.

'Easy, fellow. It's only thunder.'

Far off inside the sandbar I see blossoming red. Then, some time later, hear a boom. *Gallega* firing. Someone's alive in there. Whatever's happened, at least they're still holding out.

I'm on maindeck when the lead canoe passes under the bowsprit. I go in a lurching run to the Jacob's ladder, unhook it and send it clattering down the hull into the water. I shout triumphantly, and then my heart jolts as I remember all those ropes trailing from the bulwarks for swimmers. The Guaymi are hollering now, right below me. With a snarl the formerly whimpering Irish wolfhound is at the bulwark, great forepaws up, jaws snapping. Inshore, *Vizcaína*'s main course unfurls. They see the problem. They see I'm a dead man, or shortly will be. That's the problem. Because even with a brisk wind they'd never get here in time, and all we have is a fitful breeze But then it rises. Hope, futile hope for the as-good-as-dead man. *Vizcaína*'s mainsail fills. I wave an arm, trying to show them I'm still alive. She's moving now. Not fast but beginning to come.

I find myself looking up the mainmast. Then I start climbing the ratlines. I'm not sure why. So they'll see me from *Vizcaína*? Perhaps. Left hand. Right foot. Right hand. Left foot. Up the ratlines I go, shaking with chills one second and burning with fever the next, and when I feel secure enough, half-way up the steep climbing-net, I wave again. I intend to call but only a weak sound escapes my lips. Looking down I see the wolfhound leap and a spear-carrying Guaymi hurtle over the side. Two more aboard now. I keep climbing. Haven't done this since – when? Not since I was a grommet. Captain Catastrophe and that run from Genoa to a shipwreck off Cape St Vincent? Or on the northern rim of the Ocean Sea, when I was off time's map?

Whichever, I was a *healthy* grommet. Up I go. That's an arrow thudding into the mast over my head. I look down. But this is a mistake, because I am high now, and at this level the mast has a noticeable sway, I am swaying with it, and it's a long drop to the deck. I cling to the ratlines. Labored breathing. Another arrow thuds home. And a third into the mainsail, tightly furled on the yard. I climb, not exactly swarming up like a fifteen-year-old. Finally I am at the roundtop. *Vizcaína* is closer. But not close enough. Still, faintly across the water I hear them calling encouragement.

Have they seen me, clinging to the ratlines? Now huddled in the roundtop lookout post? Maybe not. And I want them to know I'm here, I'm alive. So I draw a deep breath to shout.

At that moment Fieschi fires two lombards, flame and smoke spouting from *Vizcaína*. To frighten the Guaymi, give me a few more seconds?

I yell.

An urgent call for help? Desperate, even? That wouldn't be inappropriate.

But no, in the loudest voice I can muster, laden with a lifetime of frustration and anger, I shout:

'God!'

And over my head, just above the topsail spar, lightning strikes, rolls, hangs – a ball of St Elmo's fire glowing down at me in my swaying perch high above the deck now overrun with Guaymi. From the brightness of that lightning flash I avert my eyes and look down to see twenty, thirty of them aboard, running forward and –

Not running, no.

In an attitude of running, leaning well forward, one foot pushing off perhaps, and one leg kicking high, but all of them frozen in place like statues. The Irish wolfhound likewise, suspended in midair as he leaps for a Guaymi throat, his lightning-cast shadow dark on the deck, his jaws open. And *Vizcaína*, half a lombard shot away now, cresting a sea – just holding there, prow out of the water, bow wave unmoving, frozen white froth painted on motionless blue. Against the sullen gray sky – here's the weirdest one of all – a small black object. Round. Like a nailhead. This has to be a lombard ball. Just hanging in air, not moving.

Dizziness washes over me, and I cling to the low side of the roundtop. Delirium. It has to be. The Whole Sick Syndrome finally hitting me with its biggest gun. I cry out:

'God!' and tighten my grip on the flimsy rail of my little perch, hardly more than an oversized basket a hundred feet above *Santa Maria*'s deck.

– Who is it this time?

A voice. On the impatient side, harassed. You might even say bilious.

I look up.

The ball of lightning glows at the masthead. That's normal, I tell myself, St Elmo's fire will do that.

But is hearing voices normal? Socrates, sure, but –

It's a normal enough voice, anyway. I can't say it reminds me of anyone special. Again it says:

– Who is it this time? Oh, I see. Colón. Well, what do you want?

And all the pent-up disappointment of the High Voyage bursts from me:

'What do I want? You tell me. What am I doing clinging here to the roundtop of an abandoned ship anchored off an impassable isthmus with a hundred Guaymi howling for my blood and me already half dead from a disease that won't even be identified for God knows how many centuries? Why? What did I do?'

I'm so worked up it takes me a while to realize the voice is answering.

– Never mind those centuries. Never mind your befores and afters, your pasts and your futures. All that there is, is already identified, here.

'Where?'

– Here.

'Who are you?'

This question is not answered. But the ball of lightning pulses brighter. I soon learn it does this when it's angry.

I look away. But I'm calm enough now. Compared to what awaits me below, what's a ball of St Elmo's fire? Even if it talks.

I try to rephrase my original question. This takes me way back, to the day Luís de Santangel told me about my origins.

'Who am I?' I ask. '*Why* am I?'

The ball of lightning pulses brighter yet. Wrong question.

'Am I a Christian or a Jew or what?' He ought to know the answer to that one.

– Or what, says the voice as the lightning shimmers at the edges, to show amusement possibly. I remember once giving a similar answer. It's one you can't really argue with.

But the voice has more to say on the subject.

542

– They're different models of the same thing. What's in a name? Don't you think the Holy Spirit is big enough to work in all people – Christians and Jews and Moslems, the learned and the ignorant? Women too. Now tell me what you want, I'm busy. This isn't the only world I have to spin.

And I remember Yego's visit to the mystic Guacanagarí: *Blind chance spins the world.* I'm disappointed, but I have to ask:

'Are you Blind Chance?'

– Some men call me that. I've been called worse.

'Did the mystic Guacanagarí ever speak for you?'

– Guacanagarí the mystic never spoke. Now, what is it?

Bilious. No doubt about it.

So I ask the ur-question, the question I figure will cover the most territory. I ask:

'Why?'

– Why what?

'Just why.'

I cast a quick glance down. The Guaymi are still frozen in the attitude of running, the wolfhound in a leap. I see the lombard ball hanging in the air. *Vizcaína* is still cresting a sea.

The lightning pales, flickers, almost goes out. From the corner of my eye I see movement. The lombard ball jerks closer, then stops, suspended again. I hear a strangled sort of a partial growl from the Irish wolfhound, then silence. This is not your ordinary silence. Preternatural. Then:

– Try to restrict your question. Do you mean why certain things went wrong in your life?

'Certain things? *Certain* things? Is this some kind of a cosmic mockery? God's idea of a joke?'

– No names, please.

'Then tell me. Why did Yego die so young? Why did Tristram? Why? Why did Pozzo Toscanelli have to send Martin Behaim of all people to Lisbon? And why did Felipa ... never mind. Why couldn't my first *Santa Maria* have slid right over the reef that Christmas Eve of 1492? Why couldn't You have put a strait through the isthmus? Or let Petenera and me go off into the sunset together? Why, God? Why? Why did the truth have to kill Guacanagarí? Why did the first missionary in the Other World have to be Brother Buil? Why do You let a Buil or a Torquemada act in Your name?'

– No names, I warned you. But they didn't act for me, as you ought to know. And skip the capital letters when you address me.

'Or why, tell me why, after I discovered this Other World, they sent me home in irons? Or why my brother Barto, or my brother Big D for that matter, always – '

– Don't ask me if you're your brother's keeper. Please! I get enough chaff about that one. Let's stick to why you're dissatisfied with your life.

'I never said that.'

– Foolish man! What have I done for anyone, what have I done even for Moses or David, that I haven't done for you? Didn't I take care of you from birth? Send you to learn from Borgia? Didn't I save your life when you were poisoned? Save you from a shipwreck too? Not to mention an iceberg? And a hurricane? Two, in fact. Didn't I give you the Indies to do with as you wished? I opened the Ocean Sea for you. Did I do more for the children of Israel when I led them out of Egypt? Or for the shepherd David, when I made him King of Judea? Didn't I give you fame in all Christendom? Didn't I let you wander, to fulfill this part of your destiny?

'This part? Then there's more? You mean those weird – '

– You're going to ask me about your dreams of the ill-mannered St Christopher, and of Herne the Hunter rescuing from St Albans the chronicle telling the tale of the Wandering Jew, aren't you?

He knows, I think. He knows. He can tell me.

'Yes!' I cry.

– You mustn't. It's foolish to believe everything you dream.

'You *don't* know,' I say. Almost an accusation.

The ball of lightning pulses extremely bright. I turn away and shield my eyes.

– All is known, where I am.

'Where are you?'

No answer.

'*What* are you?'

The lightning flickers pale. With doubt?

– I am that I am.

Who said that once? Or almost that? I remember: Pighi-Zampini. *I am who I am but I am definitely not God.*

'Does Pighi-Zampini, who knows everything about everybody, speak for You?'

– I told you (bilious again) no capital letters. And I told you the Holy Spirit dwells in everyone. But I'll tell you now, it's stronger in some people. I don't know why.

Very pale and faint. I hear a half-howl below. *Vizcaína*'s prow edges

544

over the crest, then stops.

'*You* don't know *why*?'

– From your point of view I'm omniscient, omnipotent. (This is said with surprising diffidence.) But sometimes I have to go elsewhere, spin those other worlds – some, I can tell you, larger and more important than Earth. Besides . . .

The lightning is tinged with palest pink. Embarrassed?

– Besides, if you must know, and being you I suppose you must, it is decidedly possible I am not truly omnipotent. Speaking from a higher vantage point.

'I don't understand, God.'

– No names! How many times must I tell you?

'Sorry. Sir.'

– Once the Indians thought you men from Spain were gods. Were you?

I laugh, nervously, man-to-God.

– So it's just a question of viewpoint, isn't it? If you hadn't made all those mistakes, if you hadn't brought violence to their pristine world, you might have remained deities to them. Can't you see the possibility of worlds within worlds of this?

'I don't understand,' I say again.

He pulses impatiently.

– Chinese boxes, my dear Colón. Couldn't your Heaven be my Spain? On one level you were gods to the aborigines (their mistake, ha-ha). On a vastly higher one I am that I am to you. Don't you think I wonder about the next, bigger box? I mean, what's out there? Does . . . something watch over my world, and perhaps other worlds I can't even comprehend? Is that why, sometimes, He isn't there when most desperately needed? You can hardly say this about me, not at the moment anyway. I'm here.

'Yes, but – '

I cast an uneasy glance at the deck below.

– Don't vex me with buts. I have my own problems, and you'd be unwise to read anything into your stigmata.

'No, I understand. They're just part of the Whole Sick Syndrome.' I almost ask: 'Are *You* just part of it too?'

But I hold my tongue.

– I heard that.

Now I hold my breath.

– Believe what you want. Anything is possible. Here, I'll show you.

Suddenly the lightning transforms itself. I see letters of fire. I almost fall from the roundtop.

– Is that your signature?

'God! Yes.'

He says nothing about no names. I wonder what blasphemous transgression I've committed, using that symbol.

The letters coruscate, become multicolored. Is this divine laughter?

– What do the letters mean?

'I don't know. I only borrowed them from a dream.'

– I know.

'What *do* they mean?'

But, instead of answering:

– The Admiral In His Own Right will make something very pious and Christian of them, the Hon. Fellow something very cabbalistic and Jewish.

He knows! He knows about my future biographers. How can He? How can I?

'Which one's right?' I ask.

– Neither. Or both.

'There's so much I don't know. My own signature ... '

– You knew enough to discover your Other World.

Note that He calls it that. Not New. Other. *My* Other.

Embarrassed, I say, 'For a long time I thought it was Asia.'

– And if you knew exactly what you were doing, you for whom I parted the Ocean Sea, wouldn't you have been a danger to all those who knew less? Those who built their Gothic spires reaching up to their Heaven (and possibly, my Spain), when the time had come for them to stretch their reach instead across the face of their own world? You didn't know! What had you to know – to explore, to discover? To wander? From what you came? To what you are going? Why must you know those things? The time had come for people to cross the seas and live on the lands of all of their world. The time had come for them to explore this Earth and, exploring it, explore inside themselves. Do you think a Don Quijote or a Hamlet, an Abraham Lincoln or an Einstein, would have been possible without your Other World?

'I suffered the slings and arrows of – '

– Please! That comes later. You suffered because you gave yourself an importance you never had. What you did was important, not you. Would the rights of man have been heralded, without this Other World? Would people have found a new continent of wonders inside themselves, without this Other World? Would the wellspring of creativity have overflowed, without this Other World? And it was given to you, you with your faulty vision and confused ideas of geography, to find it. You *suffered*? You didn't *know*? Fool! *To how many men is it given to discover an Other World?*

The lightning vibrates, the mast shakes, thunder rips the air.

I hear a final word through the interface between the miraculous and the mundane.

– *Wandering* ...

And the lombard ball whistles harmlessly past, and *Vizcaína* once more is scudding over the living sea toward the flagship, and below on deck for an instant I swear I see not one but twenty wolfhounds and soon all the Guaymi that can have dived overboard, but three lie dead, their throats ripped out, and the dog is dead too, just one dog now, impaled on a spear.

A face, a Guaymi face, peers over the edge of the roundtop. A Guaymi hand raises a knife. It looks a lot like my own Golden Stag (or Hind) knife. Who knows? Does it matter? After all this, despite God or whoever doing His best, I'll be dead in seconds.

Then the air itself vibrates, the mast shakes, the lightning blazes. I'm thrown from side to side of the roundtop. The Guaymi screams, hangs on a moment, then plunges from that shaking mast to his death.

And the lightning is gone. There's even an opening of blue in the overcast.

Possibly all this was no more than a neuropsychiatric aspect of the Whole Sick Syndrome. Possibly that's all *He* was. Did I ask Him that? No, but I thought it, and He heard the thought. And said what? – Anything is possible. Is that an answer? Not where I come from. But it's all the answer He gave me.

I report here only what I experienced, and it ends with me climbing unsteadily out of the roundtop and seeking a foothold on the ratlines. I slip, get tangled for an instant, start to fall. Wildly I reach out. My hand closes on a shroud. I slide down, both hands around the rope, so fast I can smell the burning of flesh.

I land on deck hard, roll over, sit up and stare at my friction-burned hands.

The stigmata are gone.

First aboard is the ebullient Captain Fieschi. 'Thank God you're in one piece. Never figured the Guaymi would come this far out, or we wouldn't have left you alone on here.' He grins. 'But you don't kill easy, Colombo.' He looks down at the wolfhound corpse. 'That was some hound. From *Vizcaína* for a while there he looked like ten dogs, a dozen. He was everywhere at once.'

'Yes,' I say. In the air there is still the acrid lightning smell.

'And if the Guaymi didn't get you, then that lightning should have. What were you doing way up the mast anyhow?'

'Calling. Calling for help.'

'Most spectacular bolt of lightning I ever saw. Came out of nowhere and gone just as fast. You are one lucky man.'

'What did you say?'

'That you're lucky to be alive.'

'No. About the lightning.'

'Tremendous clap of thunder and it rips right into the mainmast. Thought she'd split, or burn like a torch.'

'No St Elmo's fire hanging on the masthead or anything?'

He gives me an odd look. 'Single lightning bolt. Blink and you'd've missed it. But you were right here so . . . ' He shrugs.

'Where do we stand?' I ask. I'm not. Standing, I mean. I might be able to, if my life depended on it.

'Well, *Bermuda*'s safe too, as you can see. So it looks like we'll only lose *Gallega*.'

This usually ebullient man studies the deck planking. He knows what's coming next.

'What about my brother and the garrison?'

'We'll never get *Gallega* out of there with just one boat to tow her. Be foolhardy to try.'

'One – '

Fieschi doesn't raise his head. His voice is a monotone. 'Tristán took the flagship's boat in with additional reinforcements and a load of empty water butts just before the real fighting began. He said you'd told him to get water. The reinforcements were my idea. Sorry if I did the wrong thing, Admiral.'

'No. I'd have done the same.'

Fieschi is really studying that deck like he never saw pine planking before.

'As near as I can figure, Tristán must have been right off the settlement when the real fighting started. So he had two choices, am I right? Either go in to help the Exec, or come back to the safety of the ships to wait out the battle. But he didn't do either. He apparently just kept on going upriver to find some spring your boy knew about.'

'Right in the middle of the battle?'

'That's the way I make it.'

'But it would have been suicide to go inland when – '

'I know,' says Fieschi.

We're both silent. Then I remember something he said. 'One boat left. You said one boat.'

'Wreckage started drifting downriver an hour or so ago. *Santa Maria*'s boat, no doubt about it. The Guaymi must have broken her up.' He says, 'But some full casks came down too. We'll have drinking water.'

'What about Tristán's boat crew?'

Fieschi shakes his head.

There's another silence, bleak as the way to Calvary.

'You said Ferdy knew where to find that spring?'

'Yes sir.'

'Was he aboard the boat?'

'Yes sir.'

Fieschi looks at me then. His voice catches. 'He was the bravest boy I ever knew.'

We sail back slowly, a skeleton crew aboard *Santa Maria*, me on *Vizcaína*. We cast anchor under a bright midday sun. Flotsam from *Santa Maria*'s boat still swirls in the eddies near the sandbar.

I'm on the quarterdeck with Fieschi, watching *Bermuda*'s boat crew fishing a water cask off the bar. The last boat left, and for three ships to sail without a single one between them would be courting disaster. There's no way I can send that boat to shore. So Barto and the garrison, if anything is left of Barto and the garrison, are on their own.

'There's a body in the water!' comes the cry from *Vizcaína*'s roundtop, and soon we can see one, and then two, and then half a dozen corpses floating face-down in the muddy brown current. Large black crows perch on their backs, pecking.

Ferdy, I think. My knees give. I grasp the rail for support with my bandaged hands.

Thirteen years old. I brought him along to make a man of him.

Some of the bodies are hung up on the sandbar. One finds a channel and floats through, no crows pecking at his flesh.

He raises a hand.

'That man down there's alive!'

Fieschi and three grommets dive overboard.

Ten minutes later the grommet Manolo Méndez is stretched out on deck. Spewing water, gagging, writhing. Captain Fieschi blows air into his mouth. He vomits. They sit him upright so he doesn't choke.

He gasps, 'All ... dead. Captain took a spear ... through the eye. Others never...' Manolo Méndez slumps unconscious in Fieschi's arms.

And we wait. This is a useless vigil. At the settlement there are no signs of life. Nor on *Gallega*. Still we wait. The afternoon darkens. The air is hazy. The sun sinks in the west, a great crimson ball. Someone brings food but I leave it untouched. Fieschi tries to get me to lie down. If not in his tiny cabin then on deck. Can string a hammock...

'No.'

I grip the quarterdeck rail and stare across the sandbar into the Bethlehem River, willing there to be even one survivor clinging to even one piece of flotsam. They can't all be dead. They can't.

Beside me at the rail there are suddenly voices, people pointing.

'What's that down there?'

'More wreckage. Looks like a section of palisade.'

'It's not in the water.'

'You being funny? Not in the water. Of course not. As anyone can see, it's in the sky.'

'I mean it's riding way up on top of the water.'

Fieschi's voice brings me wide awake. 'That's a raft out there!'

And it is — palings roped together and lashed across two dugout canoes. A dog barks. Men call across the water. Soon they're coming up the ladder. I can't see too well. Vision going, finally. I blame it on the dusk. There are glad cries all around me.

I hear laughter, not quite hysterical.

It's Barto.

'Brought out some gold,' he says. And the laughter bubbles. 'Not a whole lot of gold, but enough maybe to pay for a sixty-ton caravel. So that makes us even — because we'll never get *Gallega* out.'

'Rotten with woodworm anyway, Uncle Barto.'

FERDY!!!

A most subdued Ferdy who says, 'By rights I shouldn't be here. I should be dead like the rest of them. Because Captain Tristán refused me permission to go.'

'Go where?'

'To Uncle Barto. Because he needed me to lead them to that spring. But I had to help Uncle Barto, didn't I? So I drew a map for the captain and before anybody could stop me I jumped out of the boat and swam like hell for the settlement. Was that wrong? Uncle Barto needed me.'

'It was,' Barto points out dryly, 'Ferdy's idea to build the raft that got us out.'

The next morning we sail for Spain.

Not that *Santa Maria* or *Bermuda* or *Vizcaína* ever get there.

❧ XXI ᵊᵂ

In Which a Single Loose End Is Left Untied

I T took three days by express courier for the news to come to
Sevilla and to my large rented house in the barrio of Santa Maria.
Queen Isabel was dead.

She died on 26 November 1504 at her castle of Medina del Campo in
her native Castile and lay in state in her royal city of Segovia.

'Almost her last words,' said Fray Juan Pérez, who had come up
from La Rábida to see me, 'were that her subjects, whether Old, New,
or Very New Christians, should be afforded equal protection under
the law.'

'Very New?' I asked.

'Indians, my friend. How are you today?'

'Better,' I said.

I was almost able to sit up and look out into the courtyard.

'Your Dr Chanca said I could only stay ten minutes.'

'Well, Chanca, what can you expect?'

So she's dead, I thought and, shutting my eyes, I tried to see her as I
had that day in the Alhambra in the chamber where blind musicians
once had played for the sultan, with her red hair glinting gold and the
passion of the Reconquest making her beautiful.

'Sleeping?' Juan Pérez asked softly.

I shook my head, lost in a dream of arabesques.

He said, 'I've brought you a book.'

I thought I knew what to expect. Religious, inspirational, *The Little Flowers* of St Francis perhaps.

But the book was ancient, handwritten.

I sat bolt upright. Sat up for the first time since I was carried here. 'Where did you get this, Prior?'

'Get it? I got it from you, of course.'

'This book?'

He nodded. 'It was after your Second Voyage, when you stayed for a while in sackcloth and ashes at La Rábida – sicker than you are now. You'll get well, if God wills it.'

'Of course I'll get well. I have too much to do to die.' I opened the book and said, 'I couldn't have given this to you.'

'Sometimes,' said the good prior gently, 'a man as busy as you can forget a trivial detail or two. You even told me where you'd got it.'

'Where, then?'

'It was a book Petenera Torres gave you to take to her poor brother Luís at Christmas Town.'

I remembered. 'She gave me a whole chest full of books and I never opened it. It got lost somewhere.'

Fray Juan Pérez shrugged. 'Well, obviously this volume didn't. Because you had it with you when you returned. You even told me you'd been intending to read it, which is why, when I found it in my library, I was so pleased that I could bring it to you now.'

The book was the *Chronicles* of Brother Roger Wendover of St Albans. I opened it. Though I could read the title, my vision was so impaired that the handwriting on the flyleaf was a blur. I brought it close to my eyes.

I could make out Petenera's name. Nothing else.

'I could read it to you if you wish,' said Fray Juan.

Just then Dr Chanca came in. He'd been back in Spain, practicing here in Sevilla, for two years. He'd aged – who hadn't? – and he now wore, sometimes, a pair of spectacles perched on his nose. But he still had the same no-nonsense attitude.

'That's it for now,' he told the prior.

Fray Juan said he'd be back.

'Are those things any good?' I asked as Chanca put on his spectacles – round lenses in a wire frame that attached to his ears – to look at the Wendover book.

'For reading. Of course they are.'

He put the book on the side table and poked here and there on my body. 'Feeling lousy?' he asked.

I denied this strenuously.

'Thought so. I'd like to see you out of bed, moving about some. But then, it's only delaying the inevitable, so if it's too much trouble...'

His no-nonsense attitude angered me. Since I was already sitting up, I swung my legs over the side of the bed. Chanca helped me to the window that looked out on the courtyard where half a dozen sailors were taking the wan November sun.

'You a millionaire?' Chanca grunted. 'Just how many of those freeloaders have you, anyway?'

'I never counted. And they're not freeloaders.'

There were four dozen, crewmen of the High Voyage, on which everything had gone wrong.

'Whatever you call them, they'll bankrupt you,' said Dr Chanca.

What was I supposed to do, let them starve? Beg in the streets? Scrounge for odd jobs? The economy was depressed these days, work was scarce, and my men had received six months' advance pay and no more.

Six months! For a voyage that began in May 1502 and ended with our return – on a ship I'd chartered in Hispaniola with my own money – to Sevilla on 7 November 1504.

Some thirty months, and when last seen we were leaving the Bethlehem River in April 1503?

This is embarrassing but it's easily explained.

We were marooned on the coast of Jamaica. Barto had been right about the plague of woodworm in the Bethlehem River, our bottoms were like honeycomb, the pumps couldn't keep ahead of the water and we were lucky to reach Jamaica at all, where we beached the caravels and waited. Captain Fieschi bravely volunteered to take a canoe across the Windward Passage to Hispaniola, which he did with just four Indians, and *he* waited. Because Governor Ovando was busy pacifying the island, and all the Indians danced the *areitos*, but Ovando had 1,000 well-armed soldiers and the slaughter was terrible. Eighty caciques and headmen were executed – hanged or burned, Fieschi told me – including the Wagnerian Anacaoná. Only then did Ovando send a caravel for us – and only if I paid for its hire. It was a crankier ship even than *Needle* and it almost went down. Ovando probably hoped it would. He had a good thing going for him in Hispaniola and he was a rich man, really rich – something I'd never been able to manage. He was afraid I'd spark a popular rising. But I wasn't interested. More than half my men left for Puerto Rico, to become its first settlers. The rest returned to Spain with Barto, Ferdy and me in a large caravel — also chartered at an extortionate price.

About being marooned all those months, it's not really part of the story of my life. The High Voyage, what there was of it, ended the day we left the Bethlehem River. And being marooned is a bore. Being marooned for over a year is a terrible bore. Why should I subject you to the tedious details? Fernando does, in his book, and the rest take their cue from him. But at the time Ferdy was fourteen-going-on-fifteen, and for him playing Robinson Crusoe must have had its moments.

Back in Spain, Ferdy went straight to Medina del Campo to resume his duties as a page. I insisted — no hanging around an old man's sickbed.

Barto did, though. Wouldn't go anywhere till I was on my feet, he said. Captain Fieschi stayed too. Barto was glad of his sunny company, and I even more so. Ebullient Fieschi was all Genoese. More and more, we spoke in Italian. It was nice to feel the musical language of my youth slipping off my tongue. It almost made me forget I was a foreigner everywhere.

When word came from Little D, now at twenty-five an officer in the King's Own Guard, that my High Voyage crews would be paid not a maravedí beyond their six months' advance, I hit the roof — as much as someone lying flat on his back could.

I wrote asking Little D to get me an audience with the King.

'You can't go,' Chanca told me.

'If he grants the audience, I've got to go.'

'It's your funeral.'

As months passed and no audience was granted, I often picked up that strange, that unlikely, that impossible book at my bedside. But always I put it down again. Unopened.

'Want me to read it to you? My Spanish isn't so hot but I could manage.' This was Fieschi. He'd just come in, flung open the shutters, let in the light, *brought* the light in with him.

'It's in Latin,' I told him.

That book disquieted me. I was so sure I had never seen it. And Fray Juan Pérez was as sure I had.

Was it the book Herne the Hunter, in my dream, had taken from St Albans?

Somehow I knew it was.

Why then did I avoid having it read to me?

By March I was up and around. At least, around that courtyard in the big house in Sevilla. I had rented the houses on either side too. A couple of dozen of my seamen lived there, and the board was always laden and the wine good.

Barto said, 'You're going into debt.'

This was no admonishment. Just a statement of fact. Barto almost seemed his old sweet self again. Homely even, in a nice way. How had I ever thought him handsome? I liked him better homely, and I think he liked himself better too.

'I can borrow from Centurione's against gold of mine that's still impounded in Santo Domingo.'

'Jeepers, Cristóbal, you'll never get it.'

'Pighi-Zampini's willing to take the chance.'

'You've seen him?' An odd sideways look from Barto.

'No. He's too busy for an old sailor's little problems. But I got a nice letter from the grandson. Listen, Barto, if the King refuses to pay the crew, do you think writing to Rome will help? I mean, the Pope – '

Barto turned away and spoke softly. 'I thought you knew. He died while we were in Jamaica.'

So had Luís de Santangel – just died one day while trying to keep busy.

After Barto left, I spent the rest of the afternoon in bed. Everybody was dying these days.

Late in April a letter came from Segovia. King Fernando had at last granted me an audience.

'We'll hire a Hungarian coach,' Barto said.

But I shook my head. 'Travel in luxury while they won't even pay my men? I can't do it.'

'Horseback would be too much for you.'

'I'll ride a mule.'

We reached Segovia in May and climbed the steep trail to the Alcázar looming like a ship's figurehead over the city and the green valley.

They provided apartments for us. I rested three days before I was ready for the King.

The most-traveled of the royal pages escorted me as far as the anteroom. I walked with the aid of a stick. Ferdy looked very much the royal page again in his purple and gold livery, but he'd kept his nautical terminology. 'Don't expect smooth sailing, Papa. His first response is usually no. Doesn't matter what the petitioner wants. So be ready to change your tack.'

Lieutenant Diego Colón was waiting in the anteroom, a tall, red-headed, spectacularly handsome courtier.

'The King said,' he informed me, 'that you can have anything you want as long as it isn't money, power, or position.'

'That doesn't leave much.'

'I'm sorry, Papa. If it doesn't work out today, we'll keep at it. I see him all the time and he doesn't dislike me.'

The sight of King Fernando seated alone on a single throne with no Queen at his side was somehow wrong.

'No long tales of woe, Colón. I've got more work than I can handle without My Lady, God rest her. So let's get right at it.'

I told him I wanted to be Viceroy of the Indies again.

He glowered. His regally slippered feet had no trouble reaching the dais. I wondered if he'd adjusted the throne, now that he sat up there all alone.

'Out of the question. You're too old. You're also too sick, from what I hear. And you look it.'

I told him I hadn't received my twelve and a half per cent of the Indies profits for some years now.

He shouted, 'No man can expect one-eighth of the Crown's revenues from our vast Other World' (*sic*) 'across the Ocean Sea.'

He was right, of course, and I didn't — no more than I expected reappointment as a doddering old Viceroy.

But they were good bargaining chips.

'I would like it in writing, Sire, that my Admiralcy will pass down through the male line of my descendants, beginning with Lieutenant Diego Colón of Your Majesty's Own Guard.'

'It isn't done. Admiralcies are not inherited.'

'The Queen — '

'Is dead,' he said. Rather harshly, I thought.

'Sire,' I said, 'my men haven't been paid. If not for a certain source of charity, they'd be starving.'

'They were paid for six months, and after six months they did nothing that qualifies as serving the Crown. This has been broken down by the royal comptroller, if you're interested. From the beginning of 1503 to mid-April, stirring up the natives of the isthmus and stealing gold. That is hardly serving the Crown. Sixteenth of April '03 to 25 June, at sea trying not to sink. That is hardly serving the Crown. Twenty-fifth of June '03 to 7 March '04, marooned on an inhospitable island. That is hardly serving the Crown. Seventh of March '04 to 7 November, lounging on chartered caravels, one en route to Hispaniola, the other to Spain, with God knows how many months sitting on the beach in between. That is hardly serving the Crown.'

In short, I got nowhere.

I went back to bed. I had brought the Wendover book along in my saddlebag, but even if I wanted to read it now, every word except Petenera's name at the bottom of the flyleaf was a blur.

The Peripatetic Royal Court moved bag and baggage to Salamanca, and I dragged myself after it on muleback, Barto and Captain Fieschi my total entourage.

Months passed in Salamanca, but the House of Shells where the Court resided was closed to me. We rented a small house.

One evening Barto came into my room. 'How you feeling?'

I was feeling lousy. 'Restless,' I said.

'We've got a small problem. I saw Little D and – '

'Why doesn't he come around?'

'He just got back from Toledo. King's business. The problem is this – in Toledo he heard some talk that the Inquisition's interested in you.'

'Interested' covered a lot of territory.

'What for?'

'Well, you know how Buil's been running wild since the Queen died, accusing anybody who ever crossed him. Apparently the Holy Office has a dossier on you.'

'What am I supposed to have done?' I was more curious, excited almost, than frightened. Lying in bed is tiresome.

'A couple of things. One goes back to '02, the other to '98. They're both pretty weird.' Barto looked at me uneasily, as if he was sorry he'd brought it up.

Fieschi came in. 'Go ahead, tell him. He needs a good laugh.'

'Well, remember, in '02 there was that hurricane in Hispaniola when Ovando wouldn't let us into the harbor. We came through okay anyway, thank God. But twenty ships were lost and hundreds of lives – including your enemies Roldán and Bobadilla. And the only ship that did make it to Spain – the only one – was that cranky little *Needle* carrying a cargo of *your* gold. So some people from Hispaniola are saying you caused that hurricane by sorcery.'

'Colón the warlock!' shouted Fieschi. 'Colón the worker of black magic!' He hooted.

Barto didn't even smile.

'Second,' my brother said, 'an accusation has been made against

Petenera Torres for the murder in 1498 of the Grand Inquisitor Tomás de Torquemada.'

'Murder? Didn't he die in his sleep?'

'They say poison. They say Petenera Torres poisoned him. And they say you helped.'

'But all of '98 I was in the Indies.'

'They say you sent her a special slow-acting Indies poison to use on Torquemada.'

'Jesus Christ!' shouted Fieschi.

'I told you, Buil is settling scores,' Barto said. 'But Big D says they probably wouldn't bother a sick man, a famous sick man.'

'If you think I'm going to lie low, you're crazy. The King owes my men two years' back pay.'

Barto sighed. Fieschi smiled.

'Then we'd better pack,' he said. 'The Peripatetic Royal Court's leaving for Valladolid, and I've never seen the place.'

First thing into my saddlebag was Petenera's book.

I was still keeping three large houses in Sevilla for my beached seamen, so all we could afford for ourselves in Valladolid was two rooms on a back street near the cathedral where Fernando and Isabel had been married almost forty years ago.

The King wouldn't grant me an audience. But I still had some irons in the fire.

Little D saw him almost every day.

And Crazy Joan was due back in Spain that spring with her husband Handsome Philip of Burgundy. How crazy Crazy Joan was nobody knew. But Philip was anything but. And championing the legendary Admiral of the Ocean Sea and his destitute crewmen might be a popular move. There was talk in Spain about a royal power struggle – Fernando against Handsome Philip.

'I'll be waiting in La Coruña when they first set foot on Spanish soil,' Barto told me.

'Wait a few days and I'll be strong enough to go with you,' I said.

'You're staying here. You don't want the Inquisition catching you up and around.'

We said goodbye. Just a routine see-you-soon. But, bedridden and more depressed than I wanted to admit, I was afraid I'd never see him again.

One morning a few days later I got out of bed and shouted for Fieschi. 'Where the hell are my clothes?'

I sounded like a peevish old man. Must have been something I ate.

'Right where they — '

'I mean my Admiral's uniform.'

Fieschi found it and helped me dress. I wobbled around a while.

'You're splendiferous,' he said.

'Shut up,' I said. 'Where's my stick?'

Fieschi found that too. I opened the door. It was raining.

'Where do you think you're going?'

'To see the King.'

'I'll come with you.'

'No you won't. I don't want to be seen with you.'

'*What?*'

'You're Italian. Someone at Court might be reminded of Vespucci and his alleged consortium to take over the Indies.'

Mollified, Fieschi said, 'It's seven miles to the castle.'

'Hire me a coach.'

'You can't go alone. I better get one of your sons.'

Fieschi was gone most of the day and returned with Ferdy in a royal coach.

'The King paid *me*,' Ferdy said. 'Since I wasn't on your fleet roster he said it was only fair that I receive all my back wages as a royal page. Are you really coming to the castle with me?'

'Damn straight I am.'

'Ship's never been built that can sail directly into the wind, Papa.'

But we left early the next morning.

Just getting as far as the coach was hard work. I leaned on Ferdy's arm and my stick. Fieschi helped me climb in. He wished me luck. It was the only time I ever heard that ebullient Genoese sound doubtful.

We drove right into the castle keep, Ferdy just showing his face at the window of the coach.

I alighted with some difficulty. The keep was crowded.

'That's Admiral Colón with the page.'

'Thought he died years ago.'

'No, but he's living in abject poverty.'

This was not true. I was keeping my men in the style they deserved and living a bit carefully myself as a consequence. I ignored everybody. It was just my uniform that attracted attention. Gold braid and all, it was too big on me.

We walked through a lot of halls. Ferdy knew all the shortcuts.

'I can get you in between the Venetian ambassador and Handsome Philip's liaison officer, but keep a weather eye peeled for Little D.'

'Why?'

'He's a courtier. He's never been out in the real world. You'd embarrass him.'

I must have looked shocked.

'*I* do,' Ferdy said.

Had my sons exchanged personalities?

Little D, handsome in his uniform, was in the anteroom when we got there. My heart was beating hard. I leaned on my stick.

'Good God,' he said when he saw me. But then he said, 'You ought to be in bed, you know,' and it was almost all right.

Ferdy asked, 'The Venetian ambassador still inside with the Big Cassava Bread?'

'Ferdy,' said Little D severely.

'Is he?'

'He just left.'

Ferdy took me right inside. Again it seemed odd – especially since this castle throne room was full-sized – to see the King alone. I advanced and bowed after Ferdy announced me.

The King said what Little D had. 'Good God,' he said.

'Sire,' I implored, 'grant the boy my title when I die.'

He just stared at me.

'And let my men have their back pay.'

I was beginning to wobble.

'Hold onto him!' the King shouted at Ferdy.

But Ferdy had already grabbed my arm.

'Was this charade your idea?' the King asked him.

'No, My Lord. It's my older brother who gets the title, and you already gave me my pay.'

The King coughed and muttered something that sounded like, 'Title could be going to the wrong Colón boy.' Then, louder, 'Very well, Admiral. Your title's hereditary. But Diego will have to prove himself.'

To take a quick glance into the future, Little D did. He acquitted himself well as governor of Hispaniola for a few years beginning in 1509. But then he got the glory bug and came back to Spain to petition to be Viceroy of All the Indies. The dream wore him down and he died young.

'My crew,' I said, 'has two years' pay coming.'

The King said nothing. Then he told Ferdy, 'If you ever bring him in here again without an appointment I'll have to dismiss you, Colón. You know that, don't you?'

'Yes, My Lord. But if he asks me to bring him I will.'

The King mulled this over. He looked at me, then at Ferdy. 'You're the best page I've got,' he grumbled.

Ferdy didn't react.

'So I guess I'd better pay your men,' the King told me.

The clan was gathering.

And not just the clan. Fieschi was with me every day, and Dr Chanca came (I detested the bloodletter sent by the Court), and so did Fray Juan Pérez all the way from La Rábida, with Big D.

I was glad to see them but less than wild about all this visiting.

I mean, I wasn't dying or anything.

I had plans.

The best one was, I'd go to Genoa with Fieschi when I got better.

When I mentioned it he thought it was a wonderful idea.

Little D and Ferdy were all for it too.

Big D said, 'I brought someone to see you.'

I wasn't seeing so good that morning. She leaned over my bed. An ample woman in black.

'Cristóbal,' she said tremulously. She kissed my cheek. 'This is the first time I've ever been north of Córdoba in my whole life.'

'Beatriz! What a wonderful surprise.' It was, but still –

Worst of all was Barto's coming back.

'It's all arranged,' he said brightly.

Barto is a very bad liar, same as me. You can tell by his voice.

'As soon as you're well enough to travel, Handsome Philip will see you. Not that he promised anything definite about your twelve and a half per cent. And you'll have to be careful.'

'Of what?'

'The Holy Office. If you weren't bedridden I really think they'd move against you right now.'

A few days later he said, 'They're going to anyway.'

'Who? What?'

That feeble voice was mine, I think.

'The Inquisition. Unless we pretend you're dying. These days they'll move against anyone but a man on his deathbed.'

I wished he weren't such a bad liar.

But maybe he wasn't lying. I was – lying in bed. Staring at the ceiling all day you can get too suspicious.

'So if – so don't be surprised if one of these days Fray Juan Pérez just appears to be giving you the last rites.'

Was I that afraid of death? Did it show?

But I wasn't afraid of death. I just liked living. Doing things. Going places. Wandering.

'Because it'll all be part of the plan,' Barto said. 'We pretend you're dying until you're strong enough to get going.'

'To see Crazy Joan and Handsome Philip?'

'No. Your own plan – you're going to Genoa with Fieschi.'

Fieschi told me this was true.

I thought there was a pretty good chance it all boiled down to them wanting me to die with hope. I wouldn't be going to Genoa or anywhere with Fieschi or anybody.

Dr Chanca came.

'How am I doing?' I asked when he finished examining me.

'Write your will,' he said.

This, paradoxically, was the one visit that cheered me. Chanca had always been an alarmist. Still, I called in a notary and dictated a short will, leaving everything to Little D and asking him to take care of the family, Beatriz included. (Which, to take another glance into the future, he did – as soon as he got my gold in Hispaniola unimpounded.) The notary started to leave.

'Wait!' I called.

He came back and reopened his portable desk.

'Lisbon, there's a fellow in Lisbon named Isaac Levi. The owner of what passes for a shop in one of those new – well, not so new – northern suburbs. I want to leave him a gold escudo.'

I signed the will

and the notary left. In the will I also instructed Little D to use that signature if he became Admiral, but I didn't think he would. (He didn't.)

Dr Chanca came back in. 'Can I get you anything?'

I steeled myself. 'Those spectacles you wear – do you suppose you could lend them to me?'

Chanca did and I fitted them over my ears. They made Chanca and the doorway he was disappearing through blurrier than ever.

But when I picked up Petenera's book and opened it, the words she had written on the flyleaf came into focus.

Luís dear,

If there was one book I knew you had to have, it's this one. Because I know how fascinated you've always been by the legend of the Wandering Jew (called Cartaphilus here), and this Wendover version may be the very first written account. Now that you've undertaken far travels of your own (which won't, I trust, last until Judgment Day!) and now that you too embody something of both Christian and Jew, no doubt you'll be even more drawn to the story. I can finally see what appeals to you so — the cyclical re-creation of the mythic figure, doomed to wander, who spreads his acquired wisdom to all mankind. It would be nice to believe it. Perhaps you'll persuade me when we're together again.

But now, my brother, please say a thank-you loud enough so I can hear it across the Ocean Sea. Because if you knew the trouble I had getting this for you . . . ! It was Abraham of Lucena (remember him?) who found it, years ago, on his travels around Europe. Apparently the book was gathering dust for generations on a shelf until some student at Oxford ran across it. The student was a sort of acolyte to an alchemist Abraham knew; he remembered particularly because he had the odd idea the student was a girl masquerading as a boy. (I'm smiling, reminded of the time you took me to the yeshiva as your visiting cousin Pedrín.) Anyway, you know Abraham and rare books. He didn't want to part with it. But I got it for you, never mind how. He's a pretty lively old man. And that's the story behind this book.

Your loving sister
Petenera

I found the right place in the book and started to read. How Roger Wendover was visited by the Archbishop of Armenia, who told him a tale of dining with a stranger, Cartaphilus by name, who had been Pontius Pilate's doorkeeper and who, when Christ came out of the tribunal —

Then it hit me.

Tristram! With one intermediate step, Petenera got the book from Tristram.

Impossible, you say?

That's the way it happened.

The first and last loves of my life, the only two real loves of my life, conspiring to tell me ... what?

Someone takes the book out of my hands. I try to object but I seem to have no voice left. The glasses are removed. I hear Fray Juan Pérez's voice.

And of course this is no ordinary bread and wine I'm tasting, it's the viaticum.

For the dying.

They're all really into Barto's elaborate plot to foil the Inquisition, even good old Fray Juan Pérez.

I hear unworldly Big D say something like, 'Dying's such a weird way to go.'

This weird remark only Big D could have made.

He's crying now and Fray Juan Pérez, unlike Salutati the Youngest, waits politely for him to finish.

So, I'm lying here. A man who once roamed the Ocean Sea, and now my whole world's reduced to one bed.

But even if this is real, even if it isn't part of Barto's clever plan – I'm aware of Little D and Ferdy standing vigil on either side of me – they could all be wrong. I wouldn't be the first man to fool his doctor by getting off his deathbed, would I?

I mean, I can't just die without finding out what Tristram and Petenera were trying to tell me.

Can I?

I have to get up from this bed.

Tell you what. When I do get up, when I do get better, I'll write my memoirs. That's how *you'll* know. No memoirs and it means I died right here. But when you see what I've written, then you'll know for sure –

Or will you? Because some opportunist even crasser than Amerigo Vespucci could exploit this situation, couldn't he? Write a book in my name, and 'prove' I wrote it by writing what I'm writing right here this minute.

Maybe there's a better way to do this.

All of them are gathered around the bed. Blurs. I wish I could see just one of them alone. Fieschi would be my man. I try to say, 'Would you all please clear out for a few minutes except Fieschi?'

Apparently I succeed, because that's what happens.

'Fieschi,' I say, 'I want to see Pighi-Zampini. Bring him here.'

'I'll go right away,' he says.

The night passes. They're all around the bed again in the morning.

565

That's 20 May 1506, Thursday, the sixth Thursday after Easter, if anyone's interested, which happens to be Ascension.

Then they all leave and there's just one blurry face at the bedside.

'Who's that?'

'Pighi-Zampini, the international financial wheeler-dealer.'

I remember a rabbity boy. 'The hell you are.'

'Oh, you must mean poor Grampa. He died last year.'

I turn my face to the wall.

The rabbity boy is still there. I can hear him breathing.

'Is it about all those files he had?' he asks in a worried voice.

I nod.

'I'm not anything like my grandfather. I was terrified of them. I destroyed them.'

Well, there goes my last hope. I won't be able to prove anything.

But for some reason the boy stays right there, hovering over the bed.

'Except one,' he says, sounding less rabbity. 'Because Grampa felt so sentimental about you, he made me promise that when he died I'd save the copy of the Buil confession. Grampa thought you might one day need it. Such as now.'

I wish I could see the boy better. I'm willing to bet he's grown springy ear and nose bristles.

'You have the confession with you?' I ask.

He gives it to me and I put it under my pillow.

All right. Here's the thing. The Inquisition has this dossier on me – wild-eyed stuff, but you know Brother Buil. A lot of people have gone to the Burning Place for witchcraft. I could too.

If Barto was right, they're only lenient with the dying. But I plan to get better.

So this is what we'll do. As soon as I'm strong enough, I'll take a copy of the copy of that confession over to the local Inquisition Palace. I'll find Buil in residence because he tends to peripat around with the Royal Court, that being where the power is.

And I'll show him what I have.

And unless he quashes the Inquisition's case against me, I'll go public with his confession.

And that will tell the tale.

If I remain the first undeniable hero to generations of school-children, unsullied by Inquisitional accusations however outrageous, you the reader will know I got up out of my so-called deathbed and confronted Buil.

If my reputation's tarnished by the Suprema, you'll know I didn't make it.

Pighi-Zampini the Younger seems right with me, because I don't even have to make a copy of Buil's confession.

'I brought a duplicate, young man,' he says.

Young man!

Bristles, I'm sure of it.

A while later, I'm equally sure I can get out of bed.

So I give it a try.

Nobody's around and that's a bit odd, but it's lucky too. They're not about to let me go anywhere.

I put on my dress uniform. This takes some doing. I find my stick. I fold one of the copies of the confession under my arm. Anything else? Well, you never know. It might be a while before I get back. So I take that book – Tristram's book and Petenera's – and tuck it under my arm too. Then I go to the door.

Outside it's darkest night.

Walking isn't easy. Like sailing close to the wind without luffing.

But my vision clears.

I was wrong. It isn't night, it's day. A perfect blue-sky deep-water day – if there were a sea anywhere near Valladolid. A dream day for a sailor on the quarterdeck of a caravel racing before a fresh wind bound away for a far land where men are noble, women are beautiful, the air is fragrant with spices, and the rivers run with gold.

The street is unfamiliar, alien. But I keep walking anyway. This is only a little less difficult than climbing those ratlines that day I woke to find myself alone aboard *Santa Maria*. Left leg, right. Then I rest a moment against a wall, stand unmoving while doubts churn inside me. Will Buil cooperate? It's a lot to expect. Will he even be there?

Or is this a kind of deathbed delirium after all?

Maybe. But weak as I am, when I'm in doubt like this I have to get moving. You know me.

So I do. I go ...

... hurrying through the narrow alleyway toward the bazaar, trailing my hand along the stone wall. Have I just paused to rest against this wall? Funny. Who needs rest? I'm bursting with enthusiasm, energy. What ever was I thinking of? Yes, that's it, I *was* thinking of something – some kind of rope ladder going up a ship's mast? Me and my daydreams.

Father's always telling me, get your head out of the clouds. Wait till he sees what I'm going to spend my confirmation gold on. He'll throw a fit.

But I have to. A map like that, how can I live without it?

Just as I reach the tiny shop of the chartseller Abu'l Qurra I hear a muezzin's ululating wail and all along the alley men are dropping to their knees, prostrating themselves. I wait politely. Old Abu'l Qurra is just rising from his prayer rug when I go in.

'The chart's expensive,' he reminds me. Old sourpuss.

I show him my little pouch of confirmation gold. 'This is all I have.'

He counts the coins, muttering. He scowls. 'A chart of the entire world drawn by the famous Piri Re'is of Constantinople,' he tells me, 'is worth a lot of money.'

He finishes counting.

I'm holding my breath.

'It's hardly enough,' he says. 'I've already told you this chart is from the hand of Piri Re'is – the greatest living chartmaker – but even more important, a part representing the islands of the Antilles is copied from an older chart bought by Piri Re'is some years ago from an infidel sailor, pox-ridden and penniless, one Q'intero. And that other chart was drawn by the hand, may Allah strike me dead if I lie, of the renowned infidel discoverer Christophorus Columbus on his first journey across the Ocean Sea. You can see a genuine facsimile of his signature right here.'

I look, and there in the Antilles part of the map is this strange sign:

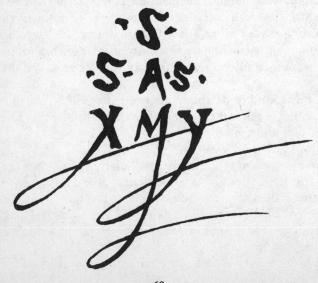

'That says Columbus?'
But I didn't use that signature, not then, so how ...
I jump back. Where did that thought come from?
... just another of my strange St Christopher dreams ...
'What is it, boy?' Abu'l Qurra asks. 'What perplexes you so?'
I don't answer.
'I assure you that signature is Columbus's.'
'God!' I whisper, awed.
'To explorers and cartaphiles, perhaps,' the old man concedes. With feigned reluctance he accepts my bag of coins.

I run home carrying the chart and dreaming of far places. Not Columbus's places, not the Indies. But my own. Inside my head is a litany of their names – Venice, Jerusalem the Golden, Trebizond, Babylon of the Hundred Gates, Samarkand, Kara Korum – and I know I will see them all as surely as my name is ...

STEPHEN MARLOWE studied philosophy at the College of William and Mary in Virginia. He served in the Korean War and became the first writer in residence at William and Mary. *The Memoirs of Christopher Columbus* is his eleventh novel.